Short Stories
for Students

National Advisory Board

Short Stories
for Students

**Presenting Analysis, Context, and Criticism on
Commonly Studied Short Stories**

Volume 21

*Ira Mark Milne and Timothy Sisler,
Project Editors*

THOMSON

GALE

Detroit • New York • San Francisco • San Diego • New Haven, Conn. • Waterville, Maine • London • Munich

Short Stories for Students, Volume 21

Project Editor
Ira Mark Milne

Editorial
Anne Marie Hacht, Timothy Sisler

Rights Acquisition and Management
Denise Buckley, Shalice Caldwell-Shah, Jessica Schultz, Kim Smilay, Ann Taylor

Manufacturing
Drew Kalasky

Imaging and Multimedia
Lezlie Light, Mike Logusz, Kelly A. Quin

Product Design
Pamela A. E. Galbreath

Product Manager
Meggin Condino

ISBN 0-7876-7029-4
ISSN 1092-7735

Printed in the United States of America
10 9 8 7 6 5 4 3 2 1

Table of Contents

Why Study Literature At All?

Short Stories for Students is designed to provide readers with information and discussion about a wide range of important contemporary and historical works of short fiction, and it does that job very well. However, I want to use this guest foreword to address a question that it does *not* take up. It is a fundamental question that is often ignored in high school and college English classes as well as research texts, and one that causes frustration among students at all levels, namely—why study literature at all? Isn't it enough to read a story, enjoy it, and go about one's business? My answer (to be expected from a literary professional, I suppose) is no. It is not enough. It is a start; but it is not enough. Here's why.

First, literature is the only part of the educational curriculum that deals directly with the actual world of lived experience. The philosopher Edmund Husserl used the apt German term *die Lebenswelt*, "the living world," to denote this realm. All the other content areas of the modern American educational system avoid the subjective, present reality of everyday life. Science (both the natural and the social varieties) objectifies, the fine arts create and/or perform, history reconstructs. Only literary study persists in posing those questions we all asked before our schooling taught us to give up on them. Only literature gives credibility to personal perceptions, feelings, dreams, and the "stream of consciousness" that is our inner voice. Literature wonders about infinity, wonders why God permits evil, wonders what will happen to us after we die. Literature admits that we get our hearts broken, that people sometimes cheat and get away with it, that the world is a strange and probably incomprehensible place. Literature, in other words, takes on all the big and small issues of what it means to be human. So my first answer is that of the humanist—we should read literature and study it and take it seriously because it enriches us as human beings. We develop our moral imagination, our capacity to sympathize with other people, and our ability to understand our existence through the experience of fiction.

My second answer is more practical. By studying literature we can learn how to explore and analyze texts. Fiction may be about *die Lebenswelt*, but it is a construct of words put together in a certain order by an artist using the medium of language. By examining and studying those constructions, we can learn about language as a medium. We can become more sophisticated about word associations and connotations, about the manipulation of symbols, and about style and atmosphere. We can grasp how ambiguous language is and how important context and texture is to meaning. In our first encounter with a work of literature, of course, we are not supposed to catch all of these things. We are spellbound, just as the writer wanted us to be. It is as serious students of the writer's art that we begin to see how the tricks are done.

Seeing the tricks, which is another way of saying "developing analytical and close reading skills," is important above and beyond its intrinsic literary educational value. These skills transfer to other fields and enhance critical thinking of any kind. Understanding how language is used to construct texts is powerful knowledge. It makes engineers better problem solvers, lawyers better advocates and courtroom practitioners, politicians better rhetoricians, marketing and advertising agents better sellers, and citizens more aware consumers as well as better participants in democracy. This last point is especially important, because rhetorical skill works both ways—when we learn how language is manipulated in the making of texts the result is that we become less susceptible when language is used to manipulate us.

My third reason is related to the second. When we begin to see literature as created artifacts of language, we become more sensitive to good writing in general. We get a stronger sense of the importance of individual words, even the sounds of words and word combinations. We begin to understand Mark Twain's delicious proverb—"The difference between the right word and the almost right word is the difference between lightning and a lightning bug." Getting beyond the "enjoyment only" stage of literature gets us closer to becoming makers of word art ourselves. I am not saying that studying fiction will turn every student into a Faulkner or a Shakespeare. But it will make us more adaptable and effective writers, even if our art form ends up being the office memo or the corporate annual report.

Studying short stories, then, can help students become better readers, better writers, and even better human beings. But I want to close with a warning. If your study and exploration of the craft, history, context, symbolism, or anything else about a story starts to rob it of the magic you felt when you first read it, it is time to stop. Take a break, study another subject, shoot some hoops, or go for a run. Love of reading is too important to be ruined by school. The early twentieth century writer Willa Cather, in her novel *My Antonia*, has her narrator Jack Burden tell a story that he and Antonia heard from two old Russian immigrants when they were teenagers. These immigrants, Pavel and Peter, told about an incident from their youth back in Russia that the narrator could recall in vivid detail thirty years later. It was a harrowing story of a wedding party starting home in sleds and being chased by starving wolves. Hundreds of wolves attacked the group's sleds one by one as they sped across the snow trying to reach their village. In a horrible revelation, the old Russians revealed that the groom eventually threw his own bride to the wolves to save himself. There was even a hint that one of the old immigrants might have been the groom mentioned in the story. Cather has her narrator conclude with his feelings about the story. "We did not tell Pavel's secret to anyone, but guarded it jealously—as if the wolves of the Ukraine had gathered that night long ago, and the wedding party had been sacrificed, just to give us a painful and peculiar pleasure." That feeling, that painful and peculiar pleasure, is the most important thing about literature. Study and research should enhance that feeling and never be allowed to overwhelm it.

Thomas E. Barden
Professor of English and
Director of Graduate English Studies
The University of Toledo

Introduction

Purpose of the Book

The purpose of *Short Stories for Students* (*SSfS*) is to provide readers with a guide to understanding, enjoying, and studying short stories by giving them easy access to information about the work. Part of Gale's "For Students" Literature line, *SSfS* is specifically designed to meet the curricular needs of high school and undergraduate college students and their teachers, as well as the interests of general readers and researchers considering specific short fiction. While each volume contains entries on "classic" stories frequently studied in classrooms, there are also entries containing hard-to-find information on contemporary stories, including works by multicultural, international, and women writers.

The information covered in each entry includes an introduction to the story and the story's author; a plot summary, to help readers unravel and understand the events in the work; descriptions of important characters, including explanation of a given character's role in the narrative as well as discussion about that character's relationship to other characters in the story; analysis of important themes in the story; and an explanation of important literary techniques and movements as they are demonstrated in the work.

In addition to this material, which helps the readers analyze the story itself, students are also provided with important information on the literary and historical background informing each work. This includes a historical context essay, a box comparing the time or place the story was written to modern Western culture, a critical essay, and excerpts from critical essays on the story or author. A unique feature of *SSfS* is a specially commissioned critical essay on each story, targeted toward the student reader.

To further aid the student in studying and enjoying each story, information on media adaptations is provided (if available), as well as reading suggestions for works of fiction and nonfiction on similar themes and topics. Classroom aids include ideas for research papers and lists of critical sources that provide additional material on the work.

Selection Criteria

The titles for each volume of *SSfS* were selected by surveying numerous sources on teaching literature and analyzing course curricula for various school districts. Some of the sources surveyed include: literature anthologies, *Reading Lists for College-Bound Students: The Books Most Recommended by America's Top Colleges*; *Teaching the Short Story: A Guide to Using Stories from around the World*, by the National Council of Teachers of English (NCTE); and "A Study of High School Literature Anthologies," conducted by Arthur Applebee at the Center for the Learning and Teaching of Literature and sponsored by the National Endowment for the Arts and the Office of Educational Research and Improvement.

Input was also solicited from our advisory board, as well as from educators from various areas. From these discussions, it was determined that each volume should have a mix of ''classic'' stories (those works commonly taught in literature classes) and contemporary stories for which information is often hard to find. Because of the interest in expanding the canon of literature, an emphasis was also placed on including works by international, multicultural, and women authors. Our advisory board members—educational professionals—helped pare down the list for each volume. Works not selected for the present volume were noted as possibilities for future volumes. As always, the editor welcomes suggestions for titles to be included in future volumes.

How Each Entry Is Organized

Each entry, or chapter, in *SSfS* focuses on one story. Each entry heading lists the title of the story, the author's name, and the date of the story's publication. The following elements are contained in each entry:

- **Introduction:** a brief overview of the story which provides information about its first appearance, its literary standing, any controversies surrounding the work, and major conflicts or themes within the work.

- **Author Biography:** this section includes basic facts about the author's life, and focuses on events and times in the author's life that may have inspired the story in question.

- **Plot Summary:** a description of the events in the story. Lengthy summaries are broken down with subheads.

- **Characters:** an alphabetical listing of the characters who appear in the story. Each character name is followed by a brief to an extensive description of the character's role in the story, as well as discussion of the character's actions, relationships, and possible motivation.

  Characters are listed alphabetically by last name. If a character is unnamed—for instance, the narrator in ''The Eatonville Anthology''—the character is listed as ''The Narrator'' and alphabetized as ''Narrator.'' If a character's first name is the only one given, the name will appear alphabetically by that name.

- **Themes:** a thorough overview of how the topics, themes, and issues are addressed within the story. Each theme discussed appears in a separate subhead, and is easily accessed through the boldface entries in the Subject/Theme Index.

- **Style:** this section addresses important style elements of the story, such as setting, point of view, and narration; important literary devices used, such as imagery, foreshadowing, symbolism; and, if applicable, genres to which the work might have belonged, such as Gothicism or Romanticism. Literary terms are explained within the entry, but can also be found in the Glossary.

- **Historical Context:** this section outlines the social, political, and cultural climate *in which the author lived and the work was created.* This section may include descriptions of related historical events, pertinent aspects of daily life in the culture, and the artistic and literary sensibilities of the time in which the work was written. If the story is historical in nature, information regarding the time in which the story is set is also included. Long sections are broken down with helpful subheads.

- **Critical Overview:** this section provides background on the critical reputation of the author and the story, including bannings or any other public controversies surrounding the work. For older works, this section may include a history of how the story was first received and how perceptions of it may have changed over the years; for more recent works, direct quotes from early reviews may also be included.

- **Criticism:** an essay commissioned by *SSfS* which specifically deals with the story and is written specifically for the student audience, as well as excerpts from previously published criticism on the work (if available).

- **Sources:** an alphabetical list of critical material used in compiling the entry, with bibliographical information.

- **Further Reading:** an alphabetical list of other critical sources which may prove useful for the student. It includes bibliographical information and a brief annotation.

In addition, each entry contains the following highlighted sections, set apart from the main text as sidebars:

- **Media Adaptations:** if available, a list of film and television adaptations of the story, including source information. The list also includes stage adaptations, audio recordings, musical adaptations, etc.

- **Topics for Further Study:** a list of potential study questions or research topics dealing with the story. This section includes questions related to other disciplines the student may be studying, such as American history, world history, science, math, government, business, geography, economics, psychology, etc.

- **Compare and Contrast:** an "at-a-glance" comparison of the cultural and historical differences between the author's time and culture and late twentieth century or early twenty-first century Western culture. This box includes pertinent parallels between the major scientific, political, and cultural movements of the time or place the story was written, the time or place the story was set (if a historical work), and modern Western culture. Works written after 1990 may not have this box.

- **What Do I Read Next?:** a list of works that might complement the featured story or serve as a contrast to it. This includes works by the same author and others, works of fiction and nonfiction, and works from various genres, cultures, and eras.

Other Features

SSfS includes "Why Study Literature At All?," a foreword by Thomas E. Barden, Professor of English and Director of Graduate English Studies at the University of Toledo. This essay provides a number of very fundamental reasons for studying literature and, therefore, reasons why a book such as *SSfS*, designed to facilitate the study of litererture, is useful.

A Cumulative Author/Title Index lists the authors and titles covered in each volume of the *SSfS* series.

A Cumulative Nationality/Ethnicity Index breaks down the authors and titles covered in each volume of the *SSfS* series by nationality and ethnicity.

A Subject/Theme Index, specific to each volume, provides easy reference for users who may be studying a particular subject or theme rather than a single work. Significant subjects from events to broad themes are included, and the entries pointing to the specific theme discussions in each entry are indicated in **boldface**.

Each entry may include illustrations, including photo of the author, stills from film adaptations (if available), maps, and/or photos of key historical events.

Citing Short Stories for Students

When writing papers, students who quote directly from any volume of *SSfS* may use the following general forms to document their source. These examples are based on MLA style; teachers may request that students adhere to a different style, thus, the following examples may be adapted as needed.

When citing text from *SSfS* that is not attributed to a particular author (for example, the Themes, Style, Historical Context sections, etc.), the following format may be used:

> "The Celebrated Jumping Frog of Calavaras County." *Short Stories for Students*. Ed. Kathleen Wilson. Vol. 1. Detroit: Gale, 1997. 19–20.

When quoting the specially commissioned essay from *SSfS* (usually the first essay under the Criticism subhead), the following format may be used:

> Korb, Rena. Critical Essay on "Children of the Sea." *Short Stories for Students*. Ed. Kathleen Wilson. Vol. 1. Detroit: Gale, 1997. 42.

When quoting a journal or newspaper essay that is reprinted in a volume of *Short Stories for Students*, the following form may be used:

> Schmidt, Paul. "The Deadpan on Simon Wheeler." *Southwest Review* Vol. XLI, No. 3 (Summer, 1956), 270–77; excerpted and reprinted in *Short Stories for Students*, Vol. 1, ed. Kathleen Wilson (Detroit: Gale, 1997), pp. 29–31.

When quoting material from a book that is reprinted in a volume of *SSfS*, the following form may be used:

> Bell-Villada, Gene H. "The Master of Short Forms," in *Garcia Marquez: The Man and His Work*. University of North Carolina Press, 1990, pp. 119–36; excerpted and reprinted in *Short Stories for Students*, Vol. 1, ed. Kathleen Wilson (Detroit: Gale, 1997), pp. 89–90.

We Welcome Your Suggestions

The editor of *Short Stories for Students* welcomes your comments and ideas. Readers who wish to suggest short stories to appear in future volumes, or who have other suggestions, are cordially invited to contact the editor. You may contact the editor via E-mail at: **ForStudentsEditors@thomson.com.** Or write to the editor at:

Editor, *Short Stories for Students*
The Gale Group
27500 Drake Road
Farmington Hills, MI 48331–3535

Literary Chronology

1821: Sir Richard Burton (Richard Francis Burton) is born in Torquay, Devonshire, England.

1835: Mark Twain (Samuel Langhorne Clemens) is born on November 30 in Florida, Missouri.

1850: Guy de Maupassant is born. It is believed that Maupassant was born at Château de Miromesniel on August 5, 1850, although it is speculated that his parents moved him from their humble house in Fécamp to the imposing Miromesniel mansion to give their first-born child a high-sounding birthplace.

1865: Rudyard Kipling is born on December 30 in Bombay, India.

1880: Guy de Maupassant's "Boule de Suif" is published.

1885: Sir Richard Burton's *The Arabian Nights* is published.

1890: Sir Richard Burton dies.

1891: Zora Neale Hurston is born. Although census reports indicate that Zora Neale Hurston was born on January 7, 1891, she claims to be born in 1901 or 1903. The actual date remains a mystery, as does her exact burial site.

1893: Guy de Maupassant dies in an asylum in Paris.

1895: Rudyard Kipling's "Rikki-Tikki-Tavi" is published.

1896: F. Scott Fitzgerald (Francis Scott Key Fitzgerald) is born on September 24 in St. Paul, Minnesota.

1907: Rudyard Kipling receives the Nobel Prize in Literature "in consideration of the power of observation, originality of imagination, virility of ideas and remarkable talent for narration which characterize the creations of this world-famous author."

1910: Mark Twain dies on April 21 in Connecticut.

1915: Jean Stafford is born in Covina, California.

1926: Alice Adams is born on August 14 in Fredericksburg, Virginia.

1928: Gabriel García Márquez is born on March 6 in Aracataca, Colombia.

1932: F. Scott Fitzgerald's "Crazy Sunday" is published.

1934: Harlan Ellison is born on May 27 in Cleveland, Ohio.

1935: Woody Allen (Allen Stewart Konigsberg) is born in Brooklyn, New York.

1936: Rudyard Kipling dies on January 18 and is buried in Poets' Corner in Westminster Abbey.

1939: Toni Cade Bambara (Miltona Mirkin Cade) is born on March 25 in New York City.

1940: F. Scott Fitzgerald dies of a heart attack on December 21 in Hollywood at the age of forty four.

1950: Zora Neale Hurston's "Conscience of the Court" is published.

1950: Gabriel García Márquez's "Eyes of a Blue Dog" is published.

1953: Jean Stafford's "In the Zoo" is published.

1960: Zora Neale Hurston dies on January 28 in a welfare home in Fort Pierce, Florida, after suffering a stroke in 1959.

1965: Harlan Ellison's "'Repent, Harlequin!' Said the Ticktockman" is published.

1966: Peter Ho Davies is born on August 30 in Coventry, England, to a Chinese mother, Sook Ying Ho, and a Welsh father, Thomas Enion Davies.

1969: Mark Twain's "No. 44, The Mysterious Stranger" is published.

1970: Jean Stafford receives the Pulitzer Prize for Fiction for her *Collected Stories*.

1971: Toni Cade Bambara's "Gorilla, My Love" is published.

1972: Akhil Sharma is born in New Delhi, India. Subsequently, he moved with his family to Edison, New Jersey, USA, where he grew up.

1977: Woody Allen's "The Kugelmass Episode" is published.

1979: Jean Stafford dies of complications following a stroke in 1979, leaving her estate to her housekeeper.

1981: Alice Adams's "Greyhound People" is published.

1982: Gabriel García Márquez receives the Nobel Prize in Literature "for his novels and short stories, in which the fantastic and the realistic are combined in a richly composed world of imagination, reflecting a continent's life and conflicts."

1995: Toni Cade Bambara dies of colon cancer on December 9.

1995: Akhil Sharma's "If You Sing like That for Me" is published.

1999: Alice Adams dies in her sleep on May 27 in San Francisco.

2000: Peter Ho Davies's "Think of England" is published.

Acknowledgments

The editors wish to thank the copyright holders of the excerpted criticism included in this volume and the permissions managers of many book and magazine publishing companies for assisting us in securing reproduction rights. We are also grateful to the staffs of the Detroit Public Library, the Library of Congress, the University of Detroit Mercy Library, Wayne State University Purdy/Kresge Library Complex, and the University of Michigan Libraries for making their resources available to us. Following is a list of the copyright holders who have granted us permission to reproduce material in this volume of *Short Stories for Students (SSfS)*. Every effort has been made to trace copyright, but if omissions have been made, please let us know.

COPYRIGHTED MATERIALS IN *SSfS*, VOLUME 21, WERE REPRODUCED FROM THE FOLLOWING PERIODICALS:

American Notes & Queries, v. 20, November/ December, 1981. Copyright © 1981 by Erasmus Press. Reproduced by permission of The University Press of Kentucky.—*Australian Journal of French Studies*, v. 18, January–April, 1981 for "The Decline and Fall of Elisabeth Rousset: Text and Context in Maupassant's 'Boule de suif,'" by Mary Donaldson-Evans. Copyright © 1981 by *Australian Journal of French Studies*. Reproduced by permission of the publisher and the author.—*Explicator,* v. 46, spring, 1988; v. 51, fall, 1992; v. 59, spring, 2001. All reproduced with permission of the Helen Dwight Reid Educational Foundation, published by Heldref Publications, 1319 18th Street, NW, Washington, DC 20036–1802.—*Extrapolation*, v. 40, 1999. Copyright © 1999 by Kent State University Press. Reproduced by permission.—*Journal of Arabic Literature*, v. 5, 1974. Copyright © 1974 by Leiden/E. J. Brill. Reproduced by permission.—*Literature & History,* v. 3, spring, 1994. Copyright © 1994 by Manchester University Press. Reproduced by permission of Manchester University Press, Manchester, UK.—*Midwest Quarterly*, v. 41, autumn, 1999. Copyright © 1999 by *The Midwest Quarterly*, Pittsburg State University. Reproduced by permission.—*Southern Quarterly,* v. 22, fall, 1983. Copyright © by The University of Southern Mississippi. Reproduced by permission.—*Studies in American Humor*, v. 3, 1998. Copyright © 1998 American Humor Studies Association. Reproduced by permission.—*Studies in the Novel*, v. 31, spring, 1999. Copyright © 1999 by North Texas State University. Reproduced by permission.—*Twentieth Century Literature*, v. 20, April, 1974. Copyright © 1974 by Hofstra University Press. Reproduced by permission.—*Virginia Quarterly Review,* summer, 2004. Copyright © 2004, by *The Virginia Quarterly Review*, The University of Virginia. Reproduced by permission of the publisher.

COPYRIGHTED MATERIALS IN *SSfS*, VOLUME 21, WERE REPRODUCED FROM THE FOLLOWING BOOKS:

Ellison, Harlan. From "A Time for Daring," in *The Book of Ellison.* Edited by Andrew Porter. ALGOL Press, 1978. Copyright © 1978 by ALGOL Press and Andrew Porter. Reproduced by permission.—Ensslen, Klaus. From "Toni Cade Bambara: *Gorilla, My Love* (1971)," in *The African American Short Story: 1970 to 1990.* Edited by Wolfgang Karrer and Barbara Puschmann-Nalenz. Wissenschaftlicher Verlag Trier, 1993. Copyright © by WVT Wissenschaftlicher Verlag Trier. Reproduced by permission of the author.—Ferguson, Christine. From "Alice Adams," in *Dictionary of Literary Biography*, Vol. 234, *American Short-Story Writers Since World War II. Third Series.* Edited by Patrick Meanor and Richard E. Lee. The Gale Group, 2001. Copyright © 2001 by the Gale Group. All rights reserved. Reproduced by permission of the Gale Group.—Gale. From "Akhil Sharma," in *Contemporary Authors Online.* Gale, 2002. Reproduced by permission of the Gale Group.—Grebstein, Sheldon. From "The Sane Method of 'Crazy Sunday,'" in *The Short Stories of F. Scott Fitzgerald: New Approaches in Criticism.* Edited by Jackson R. Bryer. University of Wisconsin Press, 1982. Copyright © 1982 by the Board of Regents of the University of Wisconsin System. All rights reserved. Reproduced by permission.—Kahn, Sholom J. From *Mark Twain's 'Mysterious Stranger': A Study of the Manuscript Texts.* University of Missouri Press, 1978. Copyright © 1978 by the Curators of the University of Missouri. All rights reserved. Reprinted with permission.—Martin, Robert A. From "Hollywood in Fitzgerald: After Paradise," in *The Short Stories of F. Scott Fitzgerald: New Approaches in Criticism.* Edited by Jackson R. Bryer. University of Wisconsin Press, 1982. Copyright © 1982 by the Board of Regents of the University of Wisconsin System. All rights reserved. Reproduced by permission.—Wallace, Albert. From *Guy de Maupassant.* Twayne Publishers, 1973. Reproduced by permission of the Gale Group.—Wilson, Mary. From *Jean Stafford: A Study of the Short Fiction.* Twayne Publishers, 1996. Copyright © by Twayne Publishers. All rights reserved. Reproduced by permission of the Gale Group.—Zaidman, Laura M. From "Zora Neale Hurston," in *Dictionary of Literary Biography*, Vol. 86, *American Short-Story Writers, 1910–1945. First Series*. Edited by Bobby Ellen Kimbel. Gale Research, 1989. Copyright © 1989 Gale Research, Inc. Reproduced by permission of the Gale Group.

PHOTOGRAPHS AND ILLUSTRATIONS APPEARING IN SS*f*S, VOLUME 21, WERE RECEIVED FROM THE FOLLOWING SOURCES:

Actor performing the role of King Arthur's Merlin, photograph. © Richard T. Nowitz/Corbis. Reproduced by permission.—Adams, Alice, photograph. © Jerry Bauer. Reproduced by permission.—Allen, Woody, photograph. The Library of Congress.—Bambara, Toni Cade, photograph by Nikky Finney. Reproduced by permission of Nikky Finney.—Burton, Sir Richard, photograph. The Library of Congress.—Businessman looking at a clock, 2004, photograph by Kelly A. Quin. Copyright © Kelly A. Quin. Reproduced by permission.—Davies, Peter Ho, photograph. © Jerry Bauer. Reproduced by permission.—"Diego and I," painting by Frida Kahlo, photograph. AP/Wide World Photos. Reproduced by permission.—Ellison, Harlan, photograph by Chris Cuffaro. Reproduced by permission of Chris Cuffaro.—Fitzgerald, F. Scott, photograph. The Library of Congress.—García Márquez, Gabriel, 1982, photograph. AP/Wide World Photos. Reproduced by permission.—Greyhound "Highway Traveler," March, 1948, photograph. © Bettmann/Corbis. Reproduced by permission.—Hands of a pecan farmer, photograph. © John B. Boykin/Corbis. Reproduced by permission.—"Harlequin," painting by Paul Cezanne, photograph. © Corbis Sygma. Reproduced by permission.—Hindu bride at wedding, photograph. © Earl and Nazima Kowall/Corbis. Reproduced by permission.—Hurston, Zora Neale, at the "New York Times" book fair, photograph. The Library of Congress.—Kipling, Rudyard, photograph.—Maupassant, Guy de, photograph.—Men standing next to gun carriages loaded at the end of the Franco-Prussian War, probably Paris, France, photograph. © Hulton-Deutsch Collection/Corbis. Reproduced by permission.—Offterdinger, Carl, illustrator. From *Arabian Nights*, by Sir Richard Burton. ca. 1900. © Bettmann/Corbis. Reproduced by permission.—Orleans Parish Criminal District Courtroom, where Judge Edward A. Haggerty, Jr., will hear the "Clay Shaw Conspiracy" trial, commencing on January 21, 1969, photograph. © Bettmann/Corbis. Reproduced by permission.—Polar Bear, ca. 1993, photograph by Kennan Ward. © Corbis. Reproduced by permission.—Sabu, with Maria Montez, in a scene from the film *Tales from the 1001 Nights*, photograph. Universal/The Kobal Collection. Reproduced by permission.—Sappers from the Royal Engineers at work constructing the Bailey Bridge, June, 1950, photograph. © Hulton-Deutsch Collection/Corbis. Reproduced by permission.—Sharma, Akhil, photograph. © Jerry Bauer. Reproduced by permission.—Silver dinnerware set, drawing. © Elio Ciol/Corbis. Reproduced by permission.—Sixteenth-century printing shop showing engravers and hand-operated printing presses, illustration. © Hulton-Deutsch Collection/Corbis. Reproduced by permission.—Sony movie theater lobby, photograph. © Gail Mooney/Corbis. Reproduced by permission.—Stafford, Jean, photograph. © Corbis/Bettmann. Reproduced by permission.—Taddei, Richard, illustrator. From a cover of *Gorilla, My Love,* by Toni Cade Bambara. Copyright © 1960, 1963, 1964, 1965, 1968, 1970, 1971, 1972 by Toni Cade Bambara. Used by permission of Random House, Inc.—Thalberg, Irving, photograph. AP/Wide World Photos. Reproduced by permission.—Twain, Mark, photograph. The Library of Congress.—Victorian homes and San Francisco skyline, photograph. © Charles O'Rear/Corbis. Reproduced by permission.—Yellow mongoose biting a snake, photograph. © Gallo Images/Corbis.

Contributors

Bryan Aubrey: Aubrey holds a Ph.D. in English and has published many articles on contemporary literature. Original essay on *Think of England*.

Cynthia Bily: Bily teaches English at Adrian College in Adrian, Michigan. Entry on *Gorilla, My Love*. Original essay on *Gorilla, My Love*.

Liz Brent: Brent holds a Ph.D. in American culture from the University of Michigan. Entry on *No. 44, The Mysterious Stranger*. Original essay on *No. 44, The Mysterious Stranger*.

Jennifer Bussey: Bussey holds a master's degree in interdisciplinary studies and a bachelor's degree in English literature. She is an independent writer specializing in literature. Entries on *Conscience of the Court* and *Crazy Sunday*. Original essays on *Conscience of the Court* and *Crazy Sunday*.

Laura Carter: Carter is currently employed as a freelance writer. Original essays on *Boule de Suif* and *Conscience of the Court*.

Tamara Fernando: Fernando is a freelance writer and editor based in Seattle, Washington. Entries on *If You Sing like That for Me* and *Rikki-Tikki-Tavi*. Original essays on *If You Sing like That for Me* and *Rikki-Tikki-Tavi*.

Joyce Hart: Hart is a freelance writer and author of several books. Entry on *Greyhound People*.

Original essays on *Greyhound People* and *If You Sing like That for Me*.

Diane Andrews Henningfeld: Henningfeld is a professor of English literature at Adrian College who writes widely on literary topics for academic and educational publications. Entry on *"Repent, Harlequin!" Said the Ticktockman*. Original essay on *"Repent, Harlequin!" Said the Ticktockman*.

Catherine Dybiec Holm: Holm is a short story and novel author, as well as a freelance writer. Original essay on *Eyes of a Blue Dog*.

Lois Kerschen: Kerschen is a freelance writer and adjunct college English instructor. Original essay on *Eyes of a Blue Dog*.

Uma Kukathas: Kukathas is a freelance editor and writer. Entry on *The Kugelmass Episode*. Original essay on *The Kugelmass Episode*.

Anthony Martinelli: Martinelli is a Seattle-based freelance writer and editor. Entry on *Boule de Suif*. Original essays on *Boule de Suif* and *Crazy Sunday*.

David Remy: Remy is a freelance writer in Pensacola, Florida. Entry on *Think of England*. Original essays on *Greyhound People* and *Think of England*.

Scott Trudell: Trudell is an independent scholar with a bachelor's degree in English literature.

Entries on *Eyes of a Blue Dog* and *In the Zoo*. Original essays on *Eyes of a Blue Dog* and *In the Zoo*.

Carol Ullmann: Ullmann is a freelance writer and editor. Original essay on *"Repent, Harlequin!" Said the Ticktockman.*

Mark White: White is the publisher at the Seattle-based press Scala House Press. Entry on *The Arabian Nights*. Original essay on *The Arabian Nights*.

The Arabian Nights

The Arabian Nights, also known as *The Thousand and One Nights* and known in Arabic as *Alf Layla wa Layla,* is a collection of fables, fairy tales, romances, and historical anecdotes of varying ethnic sources, including Indian, Persian, and Arabic oral traditions. While their specific origins are unknown, it is certain that the stories were circulating orally for centuries before they were written down in the fourteenth century in a Syrian manuscript, housed at the Bibliotèque Nationale in Paris as of 2004.

The first printed edition of the tales, which was based on the Syrian version, was published by Fort Williams College in Calcutta and edited by Shaikh Ahmad ibn-Mahmud Shirawani, an instructor of Arabic at the college. The first European translation was by the French statesman Antoine Galland, whose editions appeared in twelve small volumes between 1703 and 1713.

The public response to Galland's work was positive and immediate: translations and versions of the tales spread throughout Europe. The first English translation was made by Edward Lane in 1841, followed by John Payne in 1881 and, most famously, by Sir Richard Burton in 1885. Burton, who relied heavily on Payne's earlier work (and is even said to have plagiarized much of it), published his version in ten volumes as a private edition of one thousand under his imprint of Kama Shastra Society. He later added an additional six volumes of supplemental material, which he called *Supplemen-*

Richard Burton

1885

tal Nights. Burton's edition quickly sold out, providing him with his first profit ever as a writer, and he was in the early 2000s credited as the popularizer of the tales among English-language readers.

Historically considered by Arabic scholars as a form of ''low brow'' literature and rarely regarded for its literary merits, *The Arabian Nights,* in its many incarnations, was in the twenty-first century considered nonetheless a classic of Western literature and continued to be one of its most influential works.

The Plot Summary, Characters, Themes, and Style sections below discuss the stories from Book 1 of the *The Arabian Nights.*

Author Biography

Sir Richard F. Burton (1821–1890) was considered one of the most famous nineteenth-century Western adventurers and travel writers. His accounts of his journeys to India, Arabia, Africa, and North America gave him widespread fame in his lifetime, and his sixteen translations, including that of *The Arabian Nights* in 1885, brought him continued fame long after his death in Trieste, Italy.

Burton was born in Torquay, Devonshire to Joseph Netterville Burton, a British army officer, and Martha Baker. As a youth, Burton was exposed to many cultures, and upon entering Trinity College at Oxford at the age of nineteen, he had already mastered several languages and dialects.

After his expulsion from Oxford in 1842 for going to horse races, Burton took a commission in the army of the East India Company and moved to India; by the time he left India in 1849, he had already mastered several of the region's languages. A study he was commissioned to undertake on the homosexual brothels of Karachi got Burton into some trouble with his authorities which, together with his having been ill with cholera, severely hindered his army career upon his return to England. He was, however, quickly able to turn his travels into his first published book: *Goa, and the Blue Mountains; or, Six Months of Sick Leave,* an account of the native population of Goa, of the Malabar Hindus, and of the mountain-dwelling Todas, who practiced polyandry.

In 1852 Burton became the first Westerner to visit the holy cities of Mecca and Medina—an act that was forbidden to non-Muslims under penalty of

death and therefore required Burton to assume an elaborate disguise. News of his travels enhanced Burton's reputation in England, and the resulting book of that adventure, *Personal Narrative of a Pilgrimage to El-Medinah and Meccah,* enjoyed considerable success and was considered in the early 2000s to be one of his finest works.

In 1861 Burton married Isabel Arundell, a woman of some means and a devout Catholic. After his marriage he continued his cultural studies, receiving appointments in such locales as West Africa, Brazil, and Damascus. He eventually settled in Trieste, where he completed his best-known works: the ten-volume *A Plain and Literal Translation of the Arabian Nights' Entertainments,* an additional six volumes called *Supplemental Nights,* and the translation of the Eastern erotic masterpiece, *The Kama Sutra of Vatsyayana,* which he was forced to publish anonymously because of obscenity laws.

Although Burton, who was committed to the exploration of other cultures, found many cultural practices in his travels that he considered superior to Great Britain's, he nevertheless remained a staunch imperialist throughout his life, believing ultimately that the African and Middle Eastern races were inferior to white Europeans.

Burton was knighted in 1886. Upon his death four years later, Isabel, who was alarmed at her husband's interest in erotica, burned several of his manuscripts. Nevertheless, several cartons of Burton's writings survived: posthumously published works included *The Jew, the Gypsy, and El Islam* and *Wanderings in Three Continents.*

Plot Summary

The Porter and the Three Ladies of Baghdad

Three wealthy and beautiful sisters invite, over the course of an evening, a porter, three one-eyed Kalandars, and three merchants—who turn out to be the Caliph and his companions in disguise—into their home for shelter, food, and drink. Upon entering each guest must take the following oath: ''Whoso speaketh of what concerneth him not shall hear what pleaseth him not!''

The eldest lady interrupts the festivities to attend to her duty. Two black bitches (female dogs) are brought out to her; she proceeds to beat them with a whip; then, tearfully kissing them both, she sends them away.

The cateress then sings a sad song, causing the portress to penitently rend her garments, revealing to the guests the marks of a terrible beating.

The men, unable to contain their curiosity, break their oaths and demand an explanation of the women. The eldest lady grows angry at their presumption and commands her slaves to bind them. The lady demands each of their stories in exchange for their lives.

The First Kalandar's Tale

The first Kalandar reveals that he is actually a Prince. His adventure begins with a visit to his cousin, who is also a Prince of another kingdom: sworn to an oath of secrecy, he agrees to conceal his cousin in an underground dwelling with his cousin's lover. He then returns to his father's kingdom, where he discovers that the King's Wazir has slain his father and taken over the kingdom. The Wazir puts out the Prince's left eye and condemns him to execution in the wilderness, but he manages to escape and immediately makes his way back to his uncle's kingdom, where his uncle is grieving over the disappearance of his son. The Prince breaks his oath and shows his uncle the entrance to the secret dwelling, which they enter only to find the burnt bodies of the cousin and his lover. The uncle spits upon the face of his son and then explains that the lady is the cousin's own sister whom he was forbidden from seeing. They return to the palace to find it taken over by the same evil Wazir. The uncle is killed and the Prince, disguised as a Kalandar, heads to Baghdad to seek the aid of the Caliph.

The Second Kalandar's Tale

The Second Kalandar also reveals that he is a Prince. Attacked by a band of robbers while journeying to Hind, he flees to a foreign city where he is taken in by a friendly tailor, who aids him in his finding work as a woodcutter.

While in the forest, he discovers an underground dwelling, where he finds a beautiful Princess who is held prisoner by an Ifrit. After spending the night with her, he foolishly summons the Ifrit, who appears and captures him; he kills the Princess for her infidelity and punishes the Prince by transforming him into an ape.

After a time of wandering, the Prince, still in the form of an ape, comes upon another kingdom

Sir Richard Burton

where he manages to use his intelligence to impress the King.

The King's daughter Sitt al-Husn, who has magical abilities, realizes that the ape is really an enchanted Prince; she defeats the Ifrit in a terrible battle in order to set the Prince free, only to be killed herself. The Prince is returned to his former shape, but he has lost his left eye during the battle. He takes on the garb of a Kalandar and makes his way to Baghdad.

The Third Kalandar's Tale

The third Kalandar, Ajib son of Khazib, is also a Prince. He is marooned on the island of the Magnet Mountain after his ship sinks. Guided by a voice, he kills the island's horseman, after which a man appears on a skiff to rescue him; however, before arriving at dry land the skiff overturns, and Ajib ends up on another deserted island.

Ajib meets a boy hidden in an underground dwelling. It has been prophesied that the boy would be killed by the killer of the horseman of the Magnet Mountain, and so his father has hidden him there to avert death. In fulfillment of the prophesy Ajib accidentally falls with a knife on the boy and kills him.

The tide recedes enough for Ajib to wade to the mainland, where he meets ten men, each with a missing eye; they take him in under the condition that he asks no questions. Every night the men perform a penance by covering themselves with ash; Ajib's curiosity finally overcomes him, and he asks their story.

The men then have a bird carry Ajib to a palace of beautiful women, where he remains in luxury for a year. One day the women leave him alone in the palace, and he opens a forbidden door behind which he finds a black stallion. He mounts the horse, which then flies away and, upon landing, knocks Ajib's eye out with his tail. Ajib penitently takes on the garb of a Kalandar and eventually makes his way to Baghdad.

Amazed by the men's stories, the eldest lady lets them go free. The next morning, the Caliph summons the ladies to reveal their tales.

The Eldest Lady's Tale
The two black female dogs are the enchanted elder sisters of the mistress of the house, also known as the eldest lady, who are under her care after having been left destitute by their husbands. One day the lady and her sisters, while on a sailing trip, end up in a mysterious city where everyone has been turned to stone. The lady meets a handsome youth reciting verses from the Koran. He is the Prince of that city, preserved from being turned to stone because he was the city's only worshipper of Allah.

The lady and the Prince return to the ship with plans to marry. The sisters, envious of their sister's happiness, throw the lady and the Prince into the sea. The Prince drowns, but the lady floats to shore and survives. On her way back to Baghdad, she comes upon a serpent being chased by a dragon, which the lady slays. The serpent turns out to be a Jinniyah, who, in gratitude to the lady for saving her life, turns her two envious sisters into black dogs. The Jinniyah warns the lady that if she does not whip the black bitches three hundred times a night, she will be imprisoned under the earth forever.

Tale of the Portress
An old woman, under false pretense, leads the portress to the home of her master, who is secretly in love with the portress and wishes to marry her. Seeing that he is handsome, the portress falls in love with him, and they are married immediately; however, he makes her take an oath to never look at another man. They live happily together for a month.

On a trip to the market with the old woman, the portress makes a purchase from a young man who asks for a kiss as payment. Pressured by the old woman, the portress reluctantly allows the young man to kiss her on the cheek. He bites her instead. When her husband sees her wound, he discovers her unfaithfulness and intends to kill her. He is deterred by the old woman, however, and instead beats her and sends her away. She returns to the home of her eldest sister, where she mourns her misdeed and the banishment from her beloved's home.

The Caliph, having heard the entire story, puts everything back to order: he orders the Jinniyah to change the two dogs back to human form; he then marries the three oldest sisters to the three Kalandars. He returns the Portress to her husband and takes the cateress as a wife.

Characters

Ajib
See The Third Kalandar

The Black Bitches
These two dogs appear to belong to eldest lady, the mistress of the house, who for mysterious reasons beats them severely every night. The eldest lady's story reveals that the bitches are the enchanted sisters of the eldest lady, who were transformed into dogs as a punishment for their envy by the Jinniyah and are then ordered by the Jinniyah to receive three hundred lashes every night.

Caliph Harun al-Rashid
The Caliph represents compassionate justice. Having entered the home of the three ladies under the disguise of a merchant, he witnesses the women's strange rituals and hears the fantastic tales of the three Kalandars. The next day he orders the eldest lady and the portress to come before him and relate their stories. Having heard everyone's fantastic tales, he orders that all be put right: he has the two dogs changed back into their human form, and he reunites the portress with her husband; he then gives the three older ladies in marriage to the three Kalandars and takes for his own wife the cateress. Order is restored in that the women are no longer alone, and the men are able to stop their wandering.

Media Adaptations

- *The Arabian Nights* has been the inspiration of several film productions: the 1940s produced a handful of *Nights*-inspired films including: *Ali Baba and the Forty Thieves* (1944), starring Arthur Lubin and Maria Montez and released by Universal Studios; *Sinbad the Sailor* (1947), starring Douglas Fairbanks Jr. and released by RKO Pictures; and *Arabian Nights* (1942), directed by John Rawlins, which is only loosely based on the story of Scheherazade. The Italian director Pier Paolo Pasolini released his *Il Fiore delle mille e una notte* (*The Tales of One Thousand and One Nights*) in 1974, which was met with much controversy due to its explicitly erotic nature. All are available in VHS.

- The following film adaptations appeared later: Disney's animated feature, *Aladdin,* released in 1992 and starring Robin Williams (VHS); Dreamworks Entertainment's animated feature *Sinbad: Legend of the Seven Seas,* released in 2003 and starring Brad Pitt and Catherine Zeta-Jones (VHS and DVD); and the TV miniseries *Arabian Nights,* which aired September 18, 2001, and was subsequently available on DVD and VHS.

- An audio recording of Burton's *Arabian Nights* is available from Blackstone Audiobooks as an eight-hundred-minute set of audiocassettes. It is narrated by Johanna Ward.

The Cateress

The cateress, also called the procuratrix, lives with her two sisters, the eldest lady and the portress, in a mansion. She assists the portress in her penance by singing the song of penitence while the portress mourns and rends her garments in sorrow. The Caliph takes the cateress as his wife at the end of the story.

The Eldest Lady

The eldest lady is the mistress of the mansion and the eldest sister of the cateress and the portress. While sailing with her older sisters she comes upon a city of stone and falls in love with the Prince. Her older sisters, out of jealousy, throw her and her lover, the Prince, off the ship. She survives and, while making her way back home, saves a serpent from a dragon. The serpent, which turns out to be a magical Jinniyah, shows her thanks by changing the envious sisters into two black dogs. The Jinniyah orders the lady to beat them both every night or be imprisoned under the earth forever. The eldest lady is very wealthy and, therefore, independent. Her wealth has been amassed from the treasures of her Prince as well as her inheritance. However, the lady

previously worked as a weaver and sold her goods, which indicates that she was independent. That she is married off to one of the Kalandars at the end of the story—at which point the Caliph compassionately reestablishes order and justice—implies that it is unfortunate for a woman, even a woman of independent means, to be without a male guardian.

The First Kalandar

One of three one-eyed Kalandars who arrive on the ladies' doorstep looking for shelter, the First Kalandar reveals that he is actually a Prince in disguise. He has come to Baghdad in search of the Caliph, in flight from an evil Wazir who slew his uncle and father and took over their kingdoms.

(A Kalandar, more commonly known as a dervish, is an ascetic Muslim monk, known for an austere lifestyle.)

The First Kalandar's Cousin

The First Kalandar's cousin is also a Prince and the Kalandar's best friend. He exhorts the Kalandar to help him escape into a secret underground dwelling with his lover, who is actually his sister with whom he is forbidden to have a sexual relationship.

He and his lover are burned to death in their underground dwelling by a fire, which his father attributes to Heaven as a punishment for their sin of incest.

The First Kalandar's Uncle

The brother of the First Kalandar's father, he is also the father of the First Kalandar's cousin. He finds his son's body, together with that of his sister and lover, burned to death in their secret dwelling. Displaying righteous anger, he spits upon his son's face and condemns him for committing the sin of incest. The uncle is later slain by the evil Wazir, who takes over both his kingdom and his brother's kingdom.

The Ifrit

The Ifrit (*afreet* in English) is a type of powerful demon that figures in many of the *Arabian Nights*. The Ifrit of the Second Kalandar's story, whose name is Jirjis bin Rajmus, holds the Princess of Abnus in a secret underground dwelling and does not allow her to see any other human beings. When he discovers that she has been unfaithful to him with the Second Kalandar, he executes her and turns the Second Kalandar into an ape. He is later slain by the sorceress-like Princess Sitt al-Husn, who kills him to transform the Second Kalandar back into a human.

The Ifritah

See The Jinniyah

Ja'far

Ja'far is the Wazir to the Caliph of Baghdad. He accompanies the Caliph on his nighttime strolls around Baghdad in the guise of a merchant, serving as the Caliph's protector and mouthpiece.

The Jinniyah

In the form of a serpent when the eldest lady comes upon her outside of Baghdad, the Jinniyah is being overtaken by a dragon. The eldest lady slays the dragon, and in return, the Jinniyah exacts revenge upon her sisters who had betrayed her and her lover, the Prince, by turning them into the black bitches.

Jirjis bin Rajmus

See The Ifrit

The King

This King in the Second Kalandar's tale meets the Kalandar when he is still in the form of an ape. However, he is impressed by the Kalandar's knowledge and talents and makes him his new minister. Out of his sense of justice, he asks his daughter Sitt al-Husn, a woman with sorceress-like powers, to rid the Kalandar of his enchantment, only to lose her in her battle with the Ifrit. Realizing the Kalandar is bad luck he sends him back to his wanderings.

Magians

In the eldest lady's tale, the Magians are the people of the city where the lady's ship docks. The Magians are fire worshippers who do not believe in Allah despite warnings of judgment. On judgment day, they are all turned to stone.

The Old Lady

The old lady is characterized as conniving and untrustworthy. She is sent to the home of the portress by her master to trick her into coming to his home, which results in their happy union. However, she later undoes their happiness by goading the portress into breaking her oath and taking a kiss from a stranger. Although it seems that she is setting up the portress for death at the hands of her husband, the old lady begs for her life at the last minute, invoking Allah, and convinces the husband to scourge and banish her in lieu of execution.

The Porter

The porter is an unmarried man who hires himself out to transport goods from the market. The cateress hires him to assist her in her shopping and accompany her back to her mansion. The porter is smitten by the beauty of the three ladies and, impressing them with his improvisational skills, is invited to stay in their company. The ladies, who are all unmarried, are quite free with him, and the porter feels as if he has been transported to Paradise. His ecstasy in the fine and luxurious company of the ladies, however, is quickly overturned when the ladies proceed to horrify him, and the other guests, with their nightly penitence.

The Portress

The Portress is the second lady of the story. She evokes the curiosity and concern of her guests when, during a love song performed by her sister, the cateress, she rends her garments and faints, exposing scars of a beating on her body. She later, at the order of the Caliph, reveals the story behind her beating. Upon her marriage, her husband made her take an oath never to look at another man. However, one day at the market while she is shopping with the old lady, they stop at a stand. The shopkeeper asks for a kiss; she refuses, but being goaded by the old lady she finally relents and allows the man to kiss her cheek. He, however, bites her and leaves a wound, which she cannot hide from her husband. He beats her for her infidelity and turns her out of the house, for which she laments every night by listening to her sister's song and rending her clothes. She is reunited with her husband by the Caliph.

The Prince

The Prince in the eldest lady's story is the son of the King of the Magians. He was raised to worship Allah by a devout Muslim woman and is therefore spared when the city people are turned to black stone. He is drowned when the jealous sisters of the eldest lady throw him overboard.

The Princess of Abnus

The Princess of Abnus was kidnapped by the Ifrit Jirus bin Rajmus and hidden in an underground hall. She had not seen another human being in twenty-five years until the Second Kalandar chanced upon her hideaway. She and the Second Kalandar fall in love, only to be discovered by the Ifrit. The Princess withstands the Ifrit's tortures to protect the Second Kalandar and is eventually murdered.

The Procuratrix

See The Cateress

The Second Kalandar

The Second Kalandar is a Prince and a re-nowned scholar whose story explores the power-lessness of the individual against chance and fate: on his way to visit the King of Hind, he is attacked by a band of robbers and flees to a foreign city, where he is taken in by a tailor. While working as a woodcutter, the Prince comes upon the Princess of Abnus. She is the prisoner of the Ifrit Jirjis bin Rajmus, who turns him into an ape as a punishment for having a sexual relationship with the Princess.

While still under the guise of an ape, the Prince manages to become an advisor to a King and is freed of his curse when the daughter of the King summons and kills the Ifrit. He loses his left eye during the battle between the Ifrit and the Princess. After being banished from the King's court, he takes on the guise of a Kalandar and makes his way to Baghdad.

His story, however, ends with fate treating him kindly: the Caliph of Baghdad marries him to one of the three older sisters.

Sitt al-Husn

A sorceress-like Princess, Sitt al-Husn recognizes that the ape in her father's court is really an enchanted Prince: the Second Kalandar. At her father's request, she summons the Ifrit Jirjis bin Rajmus and, in a powerful battle, slays him, freeing the Second Kalandar from his enchanted ape form. She, however, is also killed in the battle.

The Tailor

The tailor takes in the Second Kalandar after he arrives in his city, having escaped from a band of robbers. The tailor takes care of the Second Kalandar, puts him up and keeps him under disguise for his safety. He aids the Second Kalandar by purchasing for him a woodcutter's tools. He is kind and hospitable.

The Third Kalandar

The Third Kalandar, whose name is Ajib (son of Khazib), is the son of a King who, while sailing one day, is stranded on the island of the Magnet Mountain. A voice in a dream instructs him to slay the mounted horseman on Magnet Mountain, which he does. Meanwhile, astrologers have prophesized that the son of a man of great wealth will die at Ajib's hands fifty days after the horseman has been slain. Ajib makes his way to an island where the young man is living, and he befriends him, but on the forty-ninth night, he accidentally kills the young man when his knife falls from its sheath, thus fulfilling the prophecy of the astrologers. He leaves the island, only to meet the ten men with missing eyes. After a series of further adventures, Ajib ends up losing his eye, and in great sadness he becomes a Kalandar.

The Wazir

The term *wazir,* another form of the English word *vizier,* is the title held by the King's advisor in medieval Islamic states. The Wazir of the First Kalandar's story slays both his father and his uncle and takes over their kingdoms. He holds a grudge against the First Kalandar, who as a child accidentally put out his left eye while throwing a stone. In retribution, he puts out the First Kalandar's left eye with his own finger and condemns him to execution in the wasteland.

Topics for Further Study

- In his preface to his translation, Burton promotes the study of the *Arabian Nights* among the British as a means of understanding the cultures and customs of the Muslim world, which made up a large part of the British Empire at the time. The popularity of Burton's *Arabian Nights* translation was due in part to British interest in their "Oriental" colonies. Compare the British attitudes towards the Middle East in the nineteenth century with the policies of the United States and Britain towards that region today. Do you see any similarities? Differences?

- A. S. Byatt writes, "Collections of tales talk to each other and borrow from each other, motifs glide from culture to culture, century to century." *The Arabian Nights,* itself a compilation, bears much resemblance to stories and folktales found in cultures around the world. It is also cited as one of the most influential works in English literature. Bearing both these points in mind, can you think of any authors, works of literature, or other folktales that bear a resemblance to *The Arabian Nights*? Describe these similarities.

- As a nineteenth-century British explorer and anthropologist, Burton showed in his work, life, and philosophies that he was very much a part of the British imperialist system. Much in his writings reveals that he shared the imperial attitude of racial and cultural superiority particularly over non-white and non-Christian races and cultures. Discuss how the British ideology of superiority and progressive empire-building contributed to different forms of racism throughout the world and history.

- The violent treatment of women in *The Arabian Nights* is a major theme. The killing of women for acts of infidelity is treated as common and seems to be accepted widely. Yet, many female characters in the tales hold positions of authority and rule over the men around them. Research the role of women in fourteenth-century Iraq and Persia. Limit your research, if possible to a particular country. What were some of the positions of authority that women held? Were there women political leaders? Was the violent treatment of women widespread, or was it relegated to particular economic classes?

- In *The Arabian Nights* social classes of all kinds interact with one another. Prostitutes and thieves socialize with Princes and Kings, and porters party with ladies-in-waiting. Historically, how were Persian economic and social classes structured? Did classes come into contact with one another, or was there greater class separation than the tales indicate? How is Iranian society structured today? Is there a great class distinction, or are classes more democratically structured?

Themes

Infinity and Immortality

The passing on of stories is a universal means of preservation. It is a way to circumvent mortality. That *The Arabian Nights* is a story about storytelling conveys this idea of immortality: Scheherazade's telling stories is literally a means by which she preserves her own life, and the structure of her stories—stories within stories whose endings interweave with the next story's beginning, night after night—seem never-ending and, therefore, are a symbol of infinity.

Sexuality

The original *Arabian Nights* are full of sexuality, which the nineteenth-century translations previous to Burton's, in keeping with the stringent Victorian sexual mores of the time, largely left out. However, Burton's translation, in his effort to present a more complete version of the tales, preserves the sexual references, allusions, scenes, and themes.

Moreover, his long annotations include extensive notes on Arabic sexual practices and the meanings of allusions, a feature that causes his translation to be much more sexualized than even the original tales.

Misogyny

The mistreatment, beating, and outright killing of women is regarded as lawful and just, especially as punishment for a woman's infidelity to her husband. This value recurs in the outermost frame, in which the King kills one maiden after another in retribution for his first wife's infidelity. In the story of the portress in "The Porter and the Three Ladies of Baghdad," the portress breaks her oath to her husband by allowing another man to kiss her, for which her husband severely beats her. The portress must then perform nightly penance for wronging her husband. The Jinniyah herself, who represents a form of justice in this tale, excuses the husband's action as just and even would excuse him for killing her: "He is not to be blamed for beating her, for he laid a condition on her and swore her by a solemn oath . . . she was false to her vow and he was minded to put her to death . . . but contented himself with scourging her." At the end of the story, the Caliph puts the portress's situation aright not by punishing her husband for his violence against her but by reuniting them.

Chance and Fate

Chance and fate are inescapable forces in the tales; many of the tales begin with a character setting out on a journey to a specific place, only to be waylaid by circumstances beyond his control. In the story of the Third Kalandar in "The Porter and the Three Ladies," for example, the Kalandar never reaches his intended destination and instead is stranded on two separate islands, kept in a castle for over a year, and has his eye knocked out by a horse. He decides to become a Kalandar and ends up in Baghdad. However, he ends up happily marrying one of the beautiful sisters of the story, which seems to suggest that in the end he meets the happy fate he is intended to have. In this way the stories seems to illustrate the reality of human powerlessness over outcomes: The Second Kalandar sums it up thus: "I resigned my soul to the tyranny of Time and Circumstance, well weeting that Fortune is fair and constant to no man."

Fidelity

Fidelity is one of the most important aspects of the relationships between the characters: this factor includes faithfulness of a wife to her husband and obedience of any person to his or her oath. Just as the breaking of a marriage oath results, on numerous occasions throughout the tales, in the injury or death of the woman, so too does the breaking of an oath lead to punishment for other characters. For example, in the "Tale of the Porter and the Three Ladies of Baghdad," the men break their oaths of silence to the women, only to be threatened with death. The Third Kalandar breaks his oath of silence to the ten one-eyed mendicants, only to meet with their same fate and eventually lose one of his own eyes.

Style

Frames

The Arabian Nights is a collection of stories within stories, also known as "frames." One narrator's story contains or frames another narrator's story. The outer or first frame is the story of the King who, in revenge for the infidelity of his first wife, marries a new maiden every night, takes her virginity, and slays her in the morning. This frame contains the second frame of Scheherazade's story. In order to preserve her life, Scheherazade tells a seemingly endless story, and in her story, characters begin to tell their stories (additional frames). The convention of having a narrator tell the story of other narrators telling stories is seen in such works as Dante's *Divine Comedy,* Boccaccio's *Decameron,* and Chaucer's *The Canterbury Tales.*

Medieval or Archaic Language

Burton's translation is especially characterized by an ornate, archaic language style that he developed in order to imitate the medieval Arabic in which the original stories were written. Burton looked to earlier sources of English literature for his inspiration, such as Chaucer's works and Elizabethan poetry and drama. Burton's intentional use of archaic terms such as "blee" and "wight" contribute to the medievalization, as do the cadence and structure of his sentences. While Burton's attempt at inventing a medieval English style was sharply criticized for its convoluted structure and weightiness, his work was admired for its Shakespearean-like wordplay.

Internal Rhyme

Burton's prose translation features alliteration and internal rhyming in imitation of the Arabic style known as ''seja,'' a convention earlier translators rejected as being foreign to British ears. A description of a lady in the story ''The Porter and the Three Ladies of Baghdad'' offers an example:

> Thereupon sat a lady bright of blee, with brow beaming brilliancy, the dream of philosophy, whose eyes were fraught with Babel's gramarye and her eyebrows were arched as for archery.

Verse

Poetry is used by many characters as a mode of communication, including arguing, praising, entertaining, and grieving. Couplets, quatrains, and extended verses are scattered throughout the text and give the tales a sense of literary playfulness.

Magical Realism

Most of the tales in *The Arabian Nights* contain an element of magic or the fantastic: jinns, ifrits, flying horses, and talking fish figure as characters; people are turned into dogs and apes; ships are regularly tossed upon magical islands. That the reader is asked to suspend disbelief and accept the magical components of the story constitutes both a distraction from reality and entertainment for the imagination.

Historical Context

Translation of The Arabian Nights

Sir Richard Burton's *The Arabian Nights* was an immediate hit upon its publication in 1885. Based on the 1881 translation by John Payne, Burton's work not only fed the growing demand of English readers for tales and images from the Oriental reaches of their empire, but its comparatively frank sexual references, its bawdiness, and its wild adventures also spoke to, as much as it shocked, the repressed prurient interests of its Victorian readership.

While Burton's translation of the actual tales was nothing more than a slightly revised version of Payne's, his ten-volume collection included copious notes on the histories of the stories, etymologies of Arabic phrases, and explanations of various Arabic customs and conventions. Of particular interest to his readers were his extensive notes on sexual allusions and references, a subject in which Burton

had acquired a great deal of interest and expertise from his years of travel and study in the region.

Sexual practices had long been a part of Burton's cultural and anthropological studies. While he was on military commission in India for the East India Company before his career as an explorer or writer began, he undertook a study, on the request of his superior Sir Charles Napier, of the homosexual brothels in Karachi. Burton's clinical and graphic work fell into unsympathetic hands after Napier's retirement, and as a result Burton's military career was permanently damaged. Nevertheless, the experience set the tone for nearly all of Burton's future expeditions and writings. Sexual practices continued to be the focal point of much of his career, so much so that upon his death, his wife burned several of his translation manuscripts because of their explicit erotic content.

Burton was well aware of the impact the sexual content of his work would have, and out of fear of prosecution under British obscenity laws, he published *The Arabian Nights* anonymously under his private imprint, the Kama Shastra Society, which he founded with F. F. Arbuthnot in order to produce joint, but anonymous, translations of several Indian sexual manuals, including the famous *Kama Sutra of Vatsyayana*.

In his preface to that work, Burton wrote, in anticipation of the furor that would arise surrounding the sexual explicitness, that his mission was to publish a ''full, complete, unvarnished, uncastrated copy of the great original.'' The success of Burton's endeavors only proved the hypocrisy of Victorian society. While the society exuded an air of prudish indifference, nineteenth-century readers had in truth a keen interest in the subject, a point certainly proven by the first printing's immediately selling out and making Burton his first profit as a writer.

The popularity of Burton's tales can also be attributed to Britain's growing interest in Islamic and Middle Eastern culture. At the time of Burton's publication, Great Britain ruled the entire Indian subcontinent, including Afghanistan, and held sovereignty over Egypt and much of northern Africa—all areas containing large Muslim populations.

The Arabian Nights, like many of Burton's travelogues, effectively became a window to the Islamic and Arabic culture, providing understanding of which the British, as an imperial presence, were otherwise seriously lacking. Burton stressed

Compare
&
Contrast

- **Middle Ages:** As portrayed in *The Arabian Nights*, women are regarded largely as property: a woman who is unfaithful to her husband can lawfully be executed. Single women who exercise sexual freedom are designated to a separate, lower class from married women.

  Today: In many parts of the world, the inequality and mistreatment of women is still a major problem. However, due to women's rights movements working from the late nineteenth century onward, in Western society in the early 2000s women have the same legal rights as men and can exercise both economic and sexual freedom and independence.

- **Late Nineteenth Century:** Burton's translation of *The Arabian Nights* includes copious anthropological notes that, in many cases, reveal an attitude of cultural and racial superiority, reflecting an institutionalized racism that is an inherent part of the British Empire.

  Today: Prejudice between races is still a problem; however, by and large the governments of Western society have removed institutionalized racism from their laws and have created domestic policies such as affirmative action in an attempt to reverse the damages of racist policy.

- **Late Nineteenth Century:** Victorian society is scandalized by the frank sexual content of Burton's translation and annotations of *The Arabian Nights*.

  Today: Looser sexual mores allow for frank discussion of sexuality to figure as a significant theme of twenty-first-century modes of entertainment, including television shows, movies, popular music, and books.

- **Late Nineteenth Century:** Although Oriental studies programs have become a part of most major European universities, there is widespread general ignorance of Arabic literature and culture. Aside from the few major works, most Arabic writing is untranslated and therefore not known to the Western world, and little is known about other Arabic art forms.

  Today: Although cultural ignorance of the Arabic world is still a problem in the West, many major Arabic works are translated, and many contemporary Arabic writers are also translated and published in the West. Additionally, Middle Eastern films are distributed widely and help spread Arabic culture into the west.

---

the need for British education in the Oriental culture in his introduction: "England . . . is at present the greatest Mohammedan empire in the world. . . . her crass ignorance concerning the Oriental people which should most interest her, exposes her to the contempt of Europe as well as of the Eastern world." His concern, however, with teaching the English the ways of the Orient was strictly for the success of British imperialism. He continues: "He who would deal with [Muslims] successfully must be . . . favourably inclined to their manners and customs if not to their law and religion." This statement reveals that Burton, although committed to the examination of other cultures, was at heart, like most of

his countrymen, an imperialist, believing that, although there was worth in other cultures, British rule and conquest was completely justified by British cultural and racial superiority.

However, while modern scholarship criticized the many inaccuracies and cultural and racial prejudices in Burton's studies and beliefs, it must be remembered that his work was groundbreaking for its time, both for its treatment of sexual content and for its anthropological and linguistic notations. While his *Arabian Nights* was not the first European or even the first English translation of the tales, it was without a doubt the translation that put the collection on the literary map in the west and opened

European doors to the vast influences of Arabic culture.

Arabic History

Most of the tales of *The Arabian Nights* are obviously fictional; however, several historical figures appear throughout, which may indicate a historical basis for some of the tales. For example, the name Abbaside khalif Haroun er Reshid, also known as ''Aaron the Orthodox,'' appears frequently in the text, leading some scholars to believe that the tales may have originated in his courts.

Arabic Social Classes

The characters of the *Arabian Nights* are defined by their social classes and include slaves, prostitutes, mendicants, merchants, the upper class, Princes, Kings. The clear definition and delineation of the characters' classes is indicative of the social structure of the medieval Arabic society in which the tales originated.

Critical Overview

The *Arabian Nights,* known as *Alf Layla wa Layla* in Arabic, although one of the most famous and influential works in English literature, was never regarded by Arabic scholars as a work of literary worth. The tenth-century historian Ali Aboulhusn el Mesoudi, as cited by Joseph Campbell in his introduction to *The Portable Arabian Nights,* condemned the stories, saying ''I have seen the complete work more than once, and it is indeed a vulgar, insipid book.'' The tales were regarded as lowbrow literature both for their frank and comedic dealings with sexuality and for their form; they were not intricately composed works of literary craftsmanship, but stories passed down orally through the generations; in other words, they were folktales. They were considered vulgar especially in comparison to what was considered high literature in medieval Arabic culture: the *adab* and the *maqama,* both of which were highly stylized forms of composition.

Despite their disfavor in the eyes of the Arabian literary establishment, when the *Arabian Nights* was first introduced to Europe in the early 1700s in a French translation by Antoine Galland, the stories were met with instant enthusiasm, not only for their highly entertaining subject matter but for their use as a window into the otherwise mysterious Islamic world.

The tales were cited by many writers over the centuries as having a profound influence: A. S. Byatt, in her introduction to the Modern Library edition of Burton's translation, states that for the Romantic poets of the late eighteenth century, such as Samuel Taylor Coleridge and William Wordsworth, ''the *Arabian Nights* stood for the wonderful against the mundane, the imaginative against the prosaically and reductively rational.'' Edgar Allan Poe went so far as to try to write the story that might follow the one-thousand-and-one tales, and the tales influenced the works of twentieth-century writers such as Salman Rushdie and Jorge Luis Borges.

The English translations of the stories that predated Burton's censored the more sexually graphic parts that exist in the original *Arabian Nights,* either by glossing them or leaving them out altogether. Burton's translation, however, left none of the sexual content out; it even included copious notes annotating the sexual practices of the Arabic culture. This extreme focus on sexuality shocked the Victorian establishment; in fact, there was an immediate call for censoring the work.

The clamor for censorship, however, engendered spirited defense of the work and discussion of Victorian hypocrisy. Byatt's ''Introduction'' includes the following quotation from John Addington Symonds: ''When we invite our youth to read an unexpurgated Bible . . . an unexpurgated collection of Elizabethan dramatists, including Shakespeare . . . it is surely inconsistent to exclude the unexpurgated Arabian Nights, . . . from the studies of a nation who rule India and administer Egypt.''

Criticism of Burton's translation was not limited to the explicit content, however. Many critics took issue with his ornate style and use of archaic language, with which he attempted to imitate the cadence of the original medieval Arabic.

Symonds offered this criticism in his same defense: ''Commanding a vast and miscellaneous vocabulary, [Burton] takes such pleasure in the use of it that sometimes he transgresses the unwritten laws of artistic harmony.'' Byatt included an excerpt from an 1890 review in *The Nation* that also sharply criticized Burton's overwrought style, calling it ''unreadable for its own sake,'' declaring his annotations ''a perpetual menace'' and his archaisms and phrasings ''barbarisms,'' and concluding that ''the book was a flat failure.'' However, Burton's translation received a great reception from the general reading public; the first printing of one thousand sold out, turning Burton his very first profit as a writer.

Criticism

Mark White

White is the publisher at the Seattle-based press Scala House Press. In this essay, White argues that Burton's reputation as a preeminent translator of The Arabian Nights *is not deserved.*

In 1885, Richard Burton assured himself of a longstanding place in the literary world with the publication of his ten-volume translation of *Alf Layla wa Layla,* variously known in English translation as *A Thousand and One Nights,* or *The Arabian Nights.* Burton's work, which he originally titled *A Plain and Literal Translation of the Arabian Nights' Entertainments,* sold out quickly of its initial print run and gave the British-born explorer, Orientalist, and writer recognition as the tales' preeminent translator—a reputation that would last well into the twentieth-century. Burton, however, was never deserving of that reputation. His version was essentially plagiarized, with some modifications, from an existing translation by John Payne. While some of his revisions improved Payne's work, many of them gave the text an archaic and formal feel that bears little relationship to the original. The real "value" that Burton gave to the work was to be found in his salesmanship, and for that he relied on his potential readership's age-old desire, despite the veneer of Victorian prudishness, for sex. Burton knew, long before the advent of Madison Avenue marketing campaigns, that sex, particularly exotic sex, sells, and he made certain that his version of *The Arabian Nights* had plenty of it.

That Burton's translation was, at a minimum, a revision of the existing work by John Payne was widely accepted as fact as of 2004. Writing in her book-length study of *The Arabian Nights, The Art of Story-Telling,* Mia I. Gerhardt states emphatically: "There is no other way of putting it: Burton plagiarized Payne." Echoing Gerhardt, Joseph Campbell, writing in the "Introduction" to *The Portable Arabian Nights,* is slightly more diplomatic, but no less emphatic, when he states that "Payne's superb translation . . . was appropriated straightaway by his

Movie still from the 1942 film version of Tales from the 1001 Nights, *starring Sabu and Maria Montez*

colourful friend, Captain Richard F. Burton, who immediately reissued it, slightly modified and garnished with a plethora of 'anthropological' notes, under his own name.''

In the ''Preface'' to the first volume of his translation, Burton describes how after years engaging himself in ''a labour of love'' (referring, of course, to the translation), sometime in 1881 or 1882 he came across a notice in literary journals that a ''Mr. John Payne, well known to scholars for his prowess of English verse,'' was also working on a translation of the tales. (According to Gerhardt, who cites several sources, Burton had not yet translated a single word of the tales when he first met Payne). Payne's work, which took him six years to complete, appeared between 1882 and 1884 in a private subscription. Although he had a subscriber base of two thousand, for inexplicable reasons he limited his original edition to only five hundred copies.

Payne's distinction is that his work was the first, unexpurgated English translation of the tales. Although a previous English translation had been published by Edward Lane, Lane had translated fewer than a third of the original stories, omitting ones that he considered ''comparatively uninterest-

What Do I Read Next?

- Husain Haddawy's translation of *The Arabian Nights* is based directly on the fourteenth-century Syrian manuscript and is considered, as of 2004, the best English translation of the tales. A version of this translation was issued by W. W. Norton in 1995.

- *The City of the Saints: Among the Mormons and across the Rocky Mountains to California,* originally published in 1861, is Burton's account of his travels in western North America, including his encounter with Brigham Young, the founder of the Mormon religion.

- Burton's first published work, *Goa, and the Blue Mountains: Or, Six Months of Sick Leave,* was released in 1851 shortly after his stint as part of the East India Company. The work is a study of the indigenous peoples of the Goa region of India.

- Burton's *Personal Narrative of a Pilgrimage to Al Madinah and Mecca* (1855–1866), which first appeared in three volumes, is Burton's first-hand account of his dangerous visit to the sacred cities of Medina and Mecca. Burton, who as a non-Muslim disguised himself as an East Indian to preserve his life, was the first non-Muslim Westerner ever to visit these cities.

- *The Lake Regions of Central Africa* is Burton's account of his three-year expedition to find the source of the Nile River. It was first published in 1860.

- In *Wanderings in West Africa: From Liverpool to Fernando Po* (1863), Burton describes his travels across the northern half of Africa. His account includes descriptions and analysis of the cultures he encounters which, to the modern reader, can be shocking in their racist nature.

---

ing or on any account objectionable.'' In other words, in addition to general stylistic editing, Lane took it upon himself to censor his translation of explicit sexual subject matter, a point that Burton goes at length to point out in his own notes and supplemental material.

One might question why Burton would undertake the arduous task of translating the more than two hundred tales so closely on the heels of Payne's publication. To begin with, he knew that Payne had fifteen hundred subscribers who had yet to receive their copies of Payne's translation, a potential business that was not insignificant to Burton. Furthermore, as he writes in the ''Preface'' to his edition, ''These volumes . . . afford me a long-sought opportunity of noticing practices and customs which interest all mankind and which 'Society' will not hear mentioned.'' Essentially, a new translation would give Burton the opportunity to address his Victorian counterparts on matters of a sexual nature—matters that Lane omitted entirely and Payne did not emphasize.

But Burton does not mention that Payne had already done the bulk of the work. Gerhardt, who backs her argument with textual comparisons and citations from Payne's translation and from Burton's biographers, writes:

> Burton set to work on his translation in April 1884 and finished it in April 1886. He was always a fast worker, and his notes were mostly ready for use. But this extraordinary speed . . . finds its real explanation in the fact that Burton borrowed extensively from Payne. Whole sentences and paragraphs are copied almost word for word, whole pages (especially in the later volumes) taken over with only the slightest of modifications. Burton's translation really is Payne's, with a certain amount of stylistic changes, and the poetry translated anew.

While it is widely acknowledged that Burton's revisions of the more than ten thousand lines of verse contained in *The Arabian Nights* generally improved upon Payne's translation, other revisions made by Burton to the text had the opposite effect. One issue that is most obvious to the eye and ear of the English reader unfamiliar with Arabic is the ornamentation in Burton's translation that gives it a more formal and archaic tone than Payne's already had. In addition to obsolete verb forms—replacing "quoth" for "said," for instance—Burton adds more "thou's" and "thee's" and "-eths" that take the translation further away from the original. In the story, "The Porter and the Three Ladies of Baghdad," for example, what Payne translates as, "He who speaks of what concerns him not, shall hear what will not please him," is rendered by Burton as "WHOSO SPEAKETH OF WHAT CONCERNETH HIM NOT SHALL HEAR WHAT PLEASETH HIM NOT!" While such a difference is only a matter of degree, its effect on the reading experience over the course of four hundred pages should not be understated.

A major characteristic of *Alf Layla wa Layla*, what Campbell calls its most "salient characteristic," is, in Campbell's words, its "extreme simplicity." In their original forms, the diction of the stories is straightforward and simple, and the tales themselves, over one thousand years after they were originally conceived, can still be understood by modern readers of Arabic. Burton's versions, not much more than a century old, are virtually unreadable to the early 2000s' reader due to the archaic phrasings added to the text. His ornamentations created an elevated diction, awkward even to the Victorian reader, which bears no relationship to the original. Burton clearly had the ability to write in a less formal, archaic tone; one need only compare the prose Burton chose for his translation with the prose of his "Preface" and "Terminal Essay" to see the difference. C. Knipp, writing in "The Arabian Nights in England: Galland's Translation and Its Successors," an article published in the *Journal of Arabic Literature,* goes so far as to say that as a result of these and other related issues with the translation, that "Burton's only real distinctions are that his version of John Payne's version of the *Nights* is the lengthiest and most unreadable."

If Burton's "version of John Payne's version" differed only in degrees to Payne's, then why did it so quickly and irreversibly supplant Payne's as the standard English translation of *The Arabian Nights*? The answer is, simply, sex.

Aside from his extensive experiences as a translator, explorer, linguist and scholar, Burton was a noted sexologist. He not only firmly believed that the study of sexual practices in a region could provide invaluable insights into the psychology of the people, he was also, at heart, a rebel, and there

> If Burton's 'version of John Payne's version' differed only in degrees to Payne's, then why did it so quickly and irreversibly supplant Payne's as the standard English translation of The Arabian Nights? The answer is, simply, sex."

were few practices more contrary to Victorian society than engaging in explicit studies and discussions of sexuality.

There can be no denying that Burton set out to translate *The Arabian Nights* largely as a result of the tales' erotically charged content. In the preface to his translation he writes that it was his mission to publish a "full, complete, unvarnished, *uncastrated* copy of the great original" [emphasis added]. Additionally, Burton's first edition of the translation was published by the Kama Shastra Society, an imprint that he and a partner had set up for the explicit purpose of publishing joint, but anonymous translations of several Indian sexual manuals.

The Arabian Nights is replete with descriptions of sexual activity and behavior, including orgies, homosexuality, sadomasochistic practices, and incest. However, not only did Burton effectively take Payne's work several steps further than Payne was even comfortable with, he took them several steps beyond which the tales themselves warranted. A combination of Burton's vast knowledge of Arabic customs, his personal obsession with sexuality, and his profound belief in the hypocrisy of Victorian society when it came to matters of sex combined to create a formula that led to his translation's tremendous success.

Burton effectively emphasized and exaggerated the sexual themes of *The Arabian Nights* in two ways: first, by enhancing Payne's with some creative rewording, and second, through his supplemental notes and "Terminal Essay."

With respect to the first, Knipp describes how Burton sexually charged Payne's work through some judicious editing. In Burton's hand, for instance, Payne's "rascal" became "pimp," "impudent woman" became "strumpet," and "vile woman" became "whore." Gerhardt also shows that on occasion Burton tampered with the text to allow him additional opportunities for sexual annotation. In a passage from the story, "The Moslem Hero and the Christian Maid," Burton adds a reference to the maid being "circumcised" after converting to Islam, despite there being no reference to circumcision in either Payne's version or the original. The revision, however, allowed Burton to provide an extensive annotation on that particular practice.

Although notable, these matters are of minor importance compared to the issues with respect to his notes and, especially, his "Terminal Essay," a piece of writing that Knipp calls "an interesting piece of Victorian pornography."

While most of the notes related to sexuality that Burton includes in his work are relevant, even if exaggerated, on occasion Burton goes far beyond what the original calls for. By example, Gerhardt points to a note in the story of "Ali Zaibak" in which Burton, in reference to a trick that Ali does with lamb's gut, offers an entirely irrelevant note on contraceptives. But most remarkable of all is Burton's "Terminal Essay," a 220-page essay of which over fifty pages are devoted to pederasty and sodomy. While there are stories that contain male homosexual acts, there are certainly not nearly enough to warrant a fifty-page explanation. Ironically, toward the conclusion of this section of his essay, Burton defends *The Arabian Nights* against its moral critics by saying as much. "Those who have read through these ten volumes will agree with me," he writes, "that the proportion of offensive matter bears a very small ratio to the mass of the work."

The late Palestinian post-colonial theorist Edward Said, writing in *Orientalism,* points out that for nineteenth-century Europe, sex "entailed a web of legal, moral, even political and economic obligations of a detailed and certainly encumbering sort." In other words, according to Said, there was no such thing as "free" sex for Europeans. But with Europe's imperial expansion in the Orient, the Orient became "a place where one could look for sexual experience unobtainable in Europe." Over time, as more and more writers ventured into the area, and as they each returned with tales of their own sexual "quests,"

as they invariably did, according to Said, Europeans could have "Oriental sex" without ever having to leave their homes. By the time Burton's edition hit the market, Oriental sex had effectively been commodified. With the publication of his "version of John Payne's version" of these magnificent tales, Richard Burton instantly became the greatest salesman of Oriental sex that the English world had yet seen. It is unfortunate the same could not be said of his translation abilities.

Source: Mark White, Critical Essay on *The Arabian Nights,* in *Short Stories for Students,* Thomson Gale, 2005.

C. Knipp

In the following essay, Knipp examines various translations of The Arabian Nights, *including that of Antoine Galland, whom he calls "the discoverer and source of" the work.*

The story of the translations of the *Arabian Nights* is a colorful and even lurid one. In this story's English segment, very close to center stage, gesticulating wildly, is Sir Richard Burton—explorer, adventurer, polemicist, orientalist, scribbler, and enemy of Victorian morality. We might as well begin with him, since the curtain will not go down anyway until he has done his turn. Here is how Burton, already waving both sock and buskin, begins the *Foreword* of his edition of the *Arabian Nights*: "This work," he says,

laborious as it may appear, has been to me a labour of love, an unfailing source of solace and satisfaction. During my long years of official banishment to the luxuriant and deadly deserts of Western Africa, and to the dull and dreary half-clearings of South America, it proved itself a charm, a talisman against ennui and despondency. Impossible even to open the pages without a vision starting into view; without drawing a picture from the pinacothek of the brain; without reviving a host of memories and reminiscences which are not the common property of travellers, however widely they may have travelled. From my dull and commonplace and "respectable" surroundings, the Jinn bore me at once to the land of my predilection, Arabia, a region so familiar to my mind that even at first sight, it seemed a reminiscence of some by-gone metempsychic life in the distant Past. Again I stood under the diaphanous skies, in air glorious as aether, whose every breath raises men's spirits like sparkling wine. Once more I saw the evening star hanging like a solitaire from the pure front of the western firmament; and the after-glow transfiguring and transforming, as by magic, the homely and rugged features of the scene into a fairy-land lit with a light that never shines on other soils or seas . . .

And so on, and so on: Burton continues in this vein for some time, becoming purpler and purpler, rising to the bathetic pinnacle of the English pseudo-oriental style.

And English and pseudo-oriental it certainly is, for Burton was laying the groundwork of a deception. The ''long years of official banishment'', as he self-pityingly calls them, spent in such ''dull and commonplace and 'respectable' surroundings'' as South America and the deserts of West Africa, were never spent laboring on a translation of the *Arabian Nights*. Burton did not work on this text for twenty-five years, as his mendacious dedication to Steinhauser implies, and he did not graciously hold back its publication for four years merely to give John Payne ''precedence and possession of the field'', as his *Foreword* rather disingenuously asserts. He waited in order to crib. He based his translation, which is therefore hardly a translation at all, on John Payne's version (1882–84); he did it in only two years, toward the end copying Payne verbatim for whole pages at a stretch; he did it to make money, and he sold it as he had planned in advance to the 1,500 subscribers left over from Payne's limited edition of 500.

This story was told by Thomas Wright in 1906 and 1919 and repeated by the two eminent authorities on the *Alf Layla,* Duncan B. Macdonald (1929; 1938) and Enno Littmann (1956). But Burton's most recent biographers, as Mia Gerhardt points out, have not been aware of the extent of Burton's debt to Payne. Burton did his publicizing well, and its boom drowns out the quiet voice of scholarship. As Jorge Luis Borges (himself characteristically unaware of Payne) has written, the romantic legend of Burton the explorer gives him a prestige that no other English Arabist can compete with. He was a far more colorful figure than Payne. The Burton legend gives his version the attraction of the forbidden, an attraction on which the fame of Burton's *Arabian Nights* still rests. The result is another confusion: just as westerners mistakenly consider the *Arabian Nights* a ''classic'' of Arabic literature, whereas it is obscure to, and largely despised by, the Arabs themselves, so English readers for the most part erroneously think that Sir Richard Burton is the pre-eminent translator of the *Arabian Nights,* whereas the chief distinction his version can claim is to be the most recent lengthy one in English, and, despite its undeniable interest as an element in the Burton legend, the most nearly unreadable one in our language. Burton's edition is certainly fascinating as a personal document; but a translation that is to this

> To begin with, we need to be told (or reminded) that any acquaintance with the Arabian Nights, whether limited or extensive, is due to Galland."

extent a personal document is at cross-purposes with itself. The famous sexological *Terminal Essay* (the title itself borrowed from Payne) is an interesting piece of Victorian pornography; I myself doubted the authenticity of the strange and supposedly first-hand observations of eastern sexual practices when I first read them some ten years ago, and subsequent studies strengthen the suspicion that many of them are Burton's own fantasies and extrapolations. This feeling is shared by Mia Gerhardt, whose excellent chapter on the major European versions, wider in scope than this paper, should be read by anyone who wants an informed, thorough, and critical discussion of the subject.

The East as seen by westerners has always contained a strong element of legend. Burton deserves credit for recognizing this fact and capitalizing upon it to increase English sympathies toward the Islamic world, and thus help to change ignorance and suspicion to curiosity and sympathetic interest. In this cause, Sir Richard performed an invaluable service. But it must be admitted that his methods were not highly scrupulous. Just as many minor and half-forgotten works have a secondary, parasitical kind of existence, so Burton's famous translation depends for its existence on the much-neglected John Payne. It was Payne, not Burton, who gave the English-speaking world its first lengthy and unbowdlerized version of the *Arabian Nights* translated directly from the original; and yet this parasite has survived to engulf its host.

So, too, have the subsequent versions engulfed Antoine Galland's original one. The scene has greatly expanded since 1703–1713, when Galland's twelve handy duodecimo volumes first appeared and were brought across the Channel, where they were immediately both read in French and translated into English by a ''Grub-street'' unknown. In England

and America, there are two basic kinds of *Arabian Nights* to contend with in the nineteenth and twenti- eth centuries: the children's, which exists in many forms, always short and always derivative, though sometimes very different from the base translation; and the adults', usually long and heavily annotated, putatively scholarly, and "unexpurgated"—though the latter claim is mainly post-Victorian advertising and perhaps designed to counteract the tedium pro- duced by the repetitious length. There is not so much to "expurgate" unless one possesses the Victorians' inexhaustible ability to create prurience where there is none; there is merely more repetitious length than any children and most adults have time for—so that it is now the children's versions that chiefly matter to our culture. Galland, from the beginning, was both: suitable for young listeners, worthy of adult readers. The division and diffusion of interest and scope came later.

My purpose now is to re-evaluate Galland's translation of the Arabic *Alf Layla wa-Layla* and present it in just relation to other versions available in English since. So many pretentious new transla- tions, so many popular editions, so many children's condensations have come along since Galland, that even students of Arabic literature find the scene confusing. Translators, though not all by any means as unscrupulous as Sir Richard Burton, must be good publicists: to sell their version, they are obliged to provide a strong hint for the critic by including a preface debunking or undercutting the work of their predecessors. The inevitable result is that though still nodded to respectfully by all—he is, by now, at a safe distance—Galland has lost his place of pre- eminence. He deserves to have it back.

To begin with, we need to be told (or reminded) that any acquaintance with the *Arabian Nights,* whether limited or extensive, is due to Galland. The book was *discovered* by him in a larger sense than is generally known. Arabists perhaps need not be told, but western readers at large are almost wholly unaware, that Galland discovered the *Arabian Nights* for the literate Arab of today, and for us, as well as for the eighteenth-century European readers who first encountered his *Mille et une Nuit.* Only re- cently, with Suhayr al-Qalamawi's book-length study in Arabic (1966), has there been solid evidence that the medieval collection of tales is beginning to be taken seriously in the Arab World as well as in the West. As Suhayr al-Qalamāwī makes clear, it is the *Alf Layla's* familiarity in the West that has led to this belated interest on the part of Arab scholars and men of letters such as Ṭaha Ḥusayn. Thus the obscurity

and humble status of the work are such, that if Galland had not come upon the story manuscripts he acquired and translated, the *Arabian Nights* not only might never have become well known to western- ers, but also would remain despised, little known, and unread in the Arab countries. Galland's moment was special. The European public was eager for just the sort of stories he supplied in just the form in which he was able to supply them. There is no certainty that translated oriental tales would have caught on, and hence ultimately become the "clas- sic" they are now said to be, had they made their first appearance at some time and place other than France in the early eighteenth century. Burton would certainly never have discovered them; and no fame would have echoed back from the West to the point of origin. For all of us, then, for orientalists and common readers, for easterners and westerners alike, Galland is the discoverer and source of the *Ara- bian Nights.*

All this might be true, of course, and yet Galland's translation might remain dated and inade- quate. In fact this is not the case: Burton's is far more dated, and the question of what is "adequate" is a complicated one with many special but no universal answers. Naturally Galland was "handi- capped" by the lack of all the paraphernalia of modern scholarship, and by the lack of all that specialized knowledge of the *Alf Layla wa-Layla* which he could not have, because his pioneering work alone was to lead to its acquisition. But Galland's knowledge was the most advanced possi- ble in his time, and it enabled him to produce that rare thing among scholars, an entertaining, read- able, gracefully written book which at the same time only a man of very special learning could have done.

No; speaking as one who has compared various Arabic texts of the *Arabian Nights* with as many English and European versions as were available to me, and speaking also as one who, though biased a little in favor of the literature of the eighteenth century, at least has no new translation to sell, I am compelled to say that I prefer Galland's French, and the Grub-street Englishing of Galland, to any other version and even to the original, which, in its more authentic written forms—after all, it is essentially an oral work—is poor and uninteresting Arabic. In its chief printed manuscript versions, as distin- guished from the bowdlerized and grammatically "corrected" modern Arabic editions, the Arabic *Alf Layla wa-Layla* is a bastardized mixture of literary language and colloquial dialect which in the context of Arabic literature as a whole must seem ungraceful.

Mia Gerhardt rather begs the question in her interesting book on the *Arabian Nights* when she argues that her ignorance of Arabic need not hamper her from judging the translations reliably, because in the case of stories the precise wording is not important. Words do matter. "Style" is not easily separated from "content." Each translation ought to be judged finally on its own merits as a collection of stories, but can be judged *as a translation* only by comparison with the principal manuscripts. Ideally a translation will pass both tests, and it competes successfully with all other translations of the work only if it does. The question of the special requirements of particular readers apart, Galland is most successful in achieving the delicate compromises translation requires. His free-flowing version captures the simplicity of the original, but the genius of the French language allowed him to do this without being (as the Arabic tales are) inelegant.

I have said that Burton's translation is "far more dated" than Galland's, and that Burton's only real distinctions are that his version of John Payne's version of the *Nights* is the lengthiest and the most unreadable. Perhaps the most telling remark on this subject is that of the distinguished Italian Arabist and the editor of the Italian *Arabian Nights* translation, Francesco Gabrieli, to the effect that to understand Burton's translation he often has to refer to the Arabic text: this is very nearly true even for a native English speaker. The other "adult" versions of the *Nights* in English suffer from similar stylistic defects, which have been best described by the late A. J. Arberry in the *Introduction* to his *Scheherezade* (a pleasant, but fragmentary and, like some of its predecessors, subtly prudish entry into the field of *Alf Layla* translation). "Earlier translators of the *Arabian Nights*", Arberry remarks, referring to his own countrymen,

> have almost without exception been so mesmerized by the stylistic peculiarities of Arabic that they have not hesitated to imitate them slavishly in their versions, a thing they would probably have scorned to do, and been soundly schooled to avoid, were their task Homer or Herodotus or Horace or Livy. Not content with inventing a strange Eurasian sort of English, that was the more readily accepted because it seemed profanely to echo the Old Testament in the Authorized Version—and for a good reason, the Semitic original of those Scriptures—they went farther than they needed to have done and, being caught up in the eddies of the Gothic Revival, imported into their diction all the bogus flummery of Ye Olde Englysshe.

As Arberry says later on in his discussion, the Arabic of the *Alf Layla wa-Layla* is "colloquial or half-colloquial", is consequently close to the conversational in its flavor, and in fact "differs surprisingly little from the Arabic of conversation today." In substance surely Arberry is speaking with wisdom here. Certain Arabic works, the *Maqāmāt* for example, could perhaps best be translated into some kind of *Kunstprose*; but the simplicity and naturalness of the *Alf Layla* unmistakably call for more direct language. Yet the "adult" English versions of the *Arabian Nights* are not at all conversational or contemporary. Lane's is overly literal: instead of finding equivalents of idioms, we get things like "he almost flew with delight" (taking the verb *ṭāra* literally and in the wrong sense); but Lane's biblical style is not the *mere* result of this literalness: a phrase like "rejoiced with exceeding joy" is not *merely* "literal", but reflects its author's conscious efforts to echo biblical style. Lane's translation is further marred by excessive prudery and is incomplete. For the seeker of an "adult" *Arabian Nights,* it is of no use; contrarily, Lane has been frequently used as the basis of modern "children's" versions. Payne's translation suffers from a greater degree of overwroughtness (a pity, since his is the only complete and genuine translation from Arabic into English): he adds archaic verb and pronoun forms, a more recherché vocabulary than Lane's, and a more involuted sentence structure. To Payne's style, which Burton had found not "plain"—that is, vulgar—enough, the latter adds stronger words ("rascal" becoming "pimp", "impudent woman" "strumpet", "vile woman" "whore", and so on); odd hyphenated words, often of his own coinage and occasionally barbarous; still more archaisms, usually with an added pseudo-Elizabethan flavor; and still greater misplaced faithfulness to "literal" meaning. "Literal" seems to be one of those words—like "reality"—which should rarely be used without quotation marks; it is obvious that one man's "literalness" is another's grotesque and artificial clumsiness. The pseudo-medieval approach to the *Arabian Nights,* culminating in Burton's cribbed and crabbed Elizabethan-Gothic style, is seriously inappropriate, since the language of the original is as simple as it could be, and Arabic has changed relatively much less than English since the Middle Ages; it is probably best, at any rate, for a translator to stay close to the idiom he is most familiar with and therefore most able to handle with ease—the idiom of his own time and country. Arberry's clear, lively, accurate translations of Arabic prose (his sparkling version of the *Tawq al-Ḥamama* of Ibn Ḥazm is an outstanding example) show that, in most respects at least, he was a man for the job; it is a pity that the lengthier project he evidently had in mind was never continued beyond the "Aladdin" and "Judar" stories published in 1960.

Although he meant his bowdlerized selection of the *Nights* for a general audience, Lane made the accompanying notes so lengthy and elaborate that his nephew (and champion against the inroads of Payne and Burton) was later able to publish them as a separate volume complete unto itself. As Mia Gerhardt concludes, this imbalance suggests a certain confusion in the overall planning of the project; and the failure to meet more than *some* of the demands of such a project is characteristic of English translations of the *Arabian Nights*. The producers of the many English and American children's editions have chiefly, perforce, used Scott (1811) or Lane as their basis. Since Scott's edition is a translation of Galland (with a few dubious additions at the end), and since the children's editions far outnumber the adults', and Lane's version did not come along until the 1880's, it is still true that the Grub-street Galland, or some abridged, amended version of it, is the form in which most English-speaking readers have been encountering the *Arabian Nights* over the past two hundred and fifty years. Macdonald (1932) was not able to identify the author of the original English translation, whose exact date of first publication (no complete set being extant) is unknown (1706? 1708?), but certainly close to that of the French. Retranslators of Galland (e.g., Frederick Gilbert: London, 1868), predictably enough, have remarked on the Grub-street version's "errors" and "inelegancies." In fact, as befits a piece of hack work far less pretentious than Burton's, the Grub-street Galland departs little from its source; one finds few actual cuts or alterations. . . .

In the larger context such comparisons as these provide, we can see Galland's virtues and limitations fairly clearly. One of course notices the seventeenth-century Frenchman's decorum, the restraint and poise of his tone, and comparing that with the grotesqueries of Payne-Burton or even the relatively simple style but still heavy movement of Lane, at first one is inclined to feel that Galland may have watered down his source. After consulting the Arabic texts, however, one realizes that simplicity, even spareness of diction to the point of crudeness, is quite appropriate here. Mardrus and Khawan aim at capturing this crudeness in repetitions that are probably deliberately somewhat awkward ("palais . . . palais"; "endormis . . . dormaient"). Galland's chief unfaithfulness consists in adding polish. But he adds nothing else irrelevant. As Muhammed

Abdel-Halim shows in his authoritative *Antoine Galland: sa vie, son œuvre* (1970), Galland was so imbued with the spirit and schooled in the method of Arabic story-telling that, faithful though he was, he was capable of creating an Arabic story himself out of a slender outline, had in effect himself become an Arabic story-teller—a feat not, in practical terms, ever duplicated by translators of the *Alf Layla wa-Layla* since the French scholar's historic discovery.

Galland's story-telling skill is not only unusual in a scholar but perhaps also represents a deeper affinity with the Arabic tales than other redactors have shown, the kind of affinity without which any translation is likely to be cold and mechanical, no matter how well-meaning the translator may be. The reader who goes back to Antoine Galland's *Les Mille et une Nuit* is truly returning to the source. It is difficult to find a more happy, creative, and successful translation in the West. One could only wish that this good fortune had befallen some greater work of the literature of the Islamic and Arabic worlds, which contains so many treasures still unknown among us.

Source: C. Knipp, "*The Arabian Nights* in England: Galland's Translation and Its Successors," in *Journal of Arabic Literature*, Vol. V, 1974, pp. 44–54.

Sources

Burton, Richard F., "Preface," in *The Arabian Nights, Tales from A Thousand and One Nights,* translated by Richard F. Burton, Modern Library, 2001.

———, "Terminal Essay," in *A Plain and Literal Translation of the Arabian Nights' Entertainments,* translated by Richard F. Burton, Vol. 10, Burton Club "Baghdad Edition," 1885–1886, pp. 63–302.

Burton, Richard F., trans., *The Arabian Nights, Tales from A Thousand and One Nights,* Modern Library, 2001.

Byatt, A. S., "Introduction," in *The Arabian Nights, Tales from A Thousand and One Nights,* translated by Richard F. Burton, Modern Library, 2001, pp. xiii–xx.

Campbell, Joseph, "Editor's Introduction," in *The Portable Arabian Nights,* translated by John Payne, edited by Joseph Campbell, Viking Press, 1952, pp. 1–35.

Gerhardt, Mia J., *The Art of Story-Telling,* E. J. Brill, 1963.

Knipp, C, "*The Arabian Nights* in England: Galland's Translation and Its Successors," in *Journal of Arabic Literature,* Vol. 5, 1974, pp. 44–54.

"On Translating the *Arabian Nights*," in the *Nation,* 1890, quoted in "Introduction," by A. S. Byatt, in *The Arabian*

Nights, Tales from A Thousand and One Nights, translated by Richard F. Burton, Modern Library, 2001, pp. 868–69.

Said, Edward, *Orientalism,* Vintage, 1979.

Symonds, John Addington, *The Academy,* 1855, quoted in "Introduction," by A. S. Byatt, in *The Arabian Nights, Tales from A Thousand and One Nights,* translated by Richard F. Burton, Modern Library, 2001, pp. 867–68.

Further Reading

Irwin, Robert, *"The Arabian Nights": A Companion,* I. B. Tauris, 2004.
   Irwin, an authority on Middle Eastern history and culture, provides an academic history of the origins of the *Arabian Nights,* including examination of its origins and translations, as well as the sociological insights the tales give to Islamic culture and history.

Lovell, Mary S., *A Rage to Live: A Biography of Richard and Isabel Burton,* Norton, 2000.
   Lowell's biography of Richard and Isabel Burton is especially noteworthy for the fresh look it takes at Isabel. Lowell argues that Isabel did not, as is commonly held, destroy Burton's manuscripts out of prudery, but out of concern for the quality of her husband's writing and to protect not his moral reputation but his scholarly reputation.

Rice, Edward, *Captain Sir Richard Francis Burton: A Biography,* DeCapo Press, 2001.
   Rice, a renowned biographer, provides an account of Burton's travels and adventures around the world. This reprint was originally published as *Captain Sir Richard Francis Burton: The Secret Agent Who Made the Pilgrimage to Mecca, Discovered the "Kama Sutra," and Brought the "Arabian Nights" to the West,* Scribner, 1990.

Zipes, Jack, *When Dreams Came True: Classical Fairy Tales and Their Tradition,* Routledge, 1999.
   Through a discussion of many of the great, familiar fairy tales, including *The Arabian Nights,* Zipes provides an examination of the fairy tale genre and the roles it plays on a literary and sociological level.

Illustration from The Arabian Nights *circa 1900 by Carl Offterdinger*

Boule de Suif

Guy de Maupassant

1880

''Boule de Suif'' was first published in 1880 in the anthology *Les Soirées de Medan*. Often considered his greatest work, ''Boule de Suif'' was published the same year that Guy de Maupassant made his poetic debut with *Des Vers*. The theme of the anthology of short stories was the Franco–Prussian War from a decade earlier. Other writers contributed, including Émile Zola and J. K. Huysmans, but it was Maupassant's short story, often considered the best example of naturalism, that has reigned as the most famous.

Maupassant is known for his insightful descriptions of characters and their actions and dialogues. His ability to capture a scene and recreate it in literary form has earned him a notable place in the history of naturalists. Maupassant's ''Boule de Suif'' is not only a sound reflection of retreating France during the Franco–Prussian War, but a resounding exploration of morality and ethics in a divided society. The title character is caught in a repetitious cycle of self-examination that has forced her into a circular ethical conundrum. All the while, her position is created not on her own accord, but through the manipulation of spiteful members of the *respectable* social order. The complexity that lies beneath Maupassant's imagery, his representation of humanity, and his ability to convey vibrant humor separates him from his contemporaries, placing him in a class only matched by Gustave Flaubert.

Author Biography

Guy de Maupassant, a nineteenth-century naturalist author, is one of France's most distinguished and celebrated writers of short stories. An incredibly productive writer, Maupassant achieved recognition quickly in France, and the amazing bulk and quality of his work left an impressive and permanent mark on the literary world of short fiction.

It is believed that Maupassant was born at Château de Miromesniel on August 5, 1850, although it is speculated that his parents moved him from their humble house in Fécamp to the imposing Miromesniel mansion to give their first-born child a high-sounding birthplace. Château de Miromesniel is located in a small village outside of Dieppe, called Tourville-sur-Arques. His parents separated when he was eleven years old, and he lived all of his early years in his native Normandy. Maupassant was born with the gift of a photographic memory, and this innate talent helped him to remember the nuances of Norman people that later made his stories so descriptive.

In 1869, Maupassant moved to Paris to study law, but by the age of twenty he volunteered to serve in the army during the Franco–Prussian War. After the war he joined the literary circle headed by Gustave Flaubert. The famous writer was a friend of Maupassant's mother. Flaubert introduced his new protégé to other writers, including Émile Zola, Ivan Turgenev, and Henry James. Flaubert was wholly impressed with Maupassant and became obsessed with teaching the young Maupassant the art of seeing. Although the young author was grateful for Flaubert's instruction and doting, he was much more lighthearted and cynical than his mentor.

During the years between 1872 and 1880, Maupassant spent much of his time hating his work as a civil servant and all of his free time writing and chasing women. He made his literary mark in 1880 with the publication of his greatest masterpiece, ''Boule de Suif.'' The title translates as ''Ball of Fat,'' but in most English translations the title is left in Maupassant's native tongue. During the 1880s, Maupassant penned over three hundred short stories, six novels, three travelogues, and one volume of verse. From this incredible body of work, Maupassant created many remarkable stories, including the novels *Une Vie* in 1883, and *Pierre et Jean* in 1888.

Although many of his stories were considered immoral—his subject matter was frequently cen-

Guy de Maupassant

tered on sex, adultery, prostitutes, and food and drink—a small portion of his corpus was dedicated to short horror stories. From this smaller, later, body of his work, no story was more terrifying than his harrowing tale of madness, ''Le Horla,'' published in 1887. Many of his horror stories spawned from the impact of a syphilitic infection he contracted during his raucous twenties. From the course of the infection, Maupassant began to lose his sanity. The infection and madness eventually took permanent hold of Maupassant's mind, and on January 2, 1892, he attempted to slit his own throat. Following his attempted suicide, Maupassant was committed to an asylum in Paris, where he died a year later. Due to his ''immoral'' subject matter, Maupassant did not receive adequate praise from English-speaking literary circles until the latter half of the twentieth century, yet it cannot be denied that his work influenced, and has been imitated by, countless authors across the globe.

Plot Summary

''Boule de Suif'' opens with a description of French soldiers retreating from the advancing Prussian army. They are fleeing through Rouen as the Prussians begin to take hold of the city. Many Prussians are boarding up with townspeople and, in general, acting quite respectable in the townspeople's homes. Outside in the streets, they are gruffer and carry themselves with a stronger, more ostentatious air. Many who attempt to flee the city are held captive or turned back. However, some individuals are given permits to leave Rouen. Ten such individuals have gathered together in the courtyard of a hotel to ready themselves for their trip out of Rouen to Le Havre. From Le Havre the travelers will cross to England if the Prussian army continues to advance. Gathered together at the coach are the driver and ten passengers: Comte and Comtesse Hubert de Bréville, Monsieur and Madame Loiseau, Monsieur and Madame Carré-Lamadon, Cornudet, Boule de Suif, and two nuns. The first six are of a higher social class, either extremely wealthy or members of the government or both. The man traveling alone, Cornudet, is a democrat and a political leftist opposed to the aristocratic government. The woman traveling alone, Boule de Suif, is a fat, appealing prostitute. The two nuns are simple and spend most of the time praying.

The passengers board a chilly train, the floor of which is covered with straw, and begin their long journey through the night and cold to Tôtes. Everyone begins to reach a point of breaking, as the trip is painstakingly slow and they are filled with discomfort from hunger and thirst. Unfortunately, no one but Boule de Suif has brought provisions for the trip, and since the wealthy, respectable travelers have deemed her immoral and cast insults at her, they are hesitant to ask for food or wine. Eventually, Monsieur Loiseau breaks the silence and asks for some food. Boule de Suif swiftly and happily complies, eventually feeding everyone in the coach. The respectable individuals have a change of heart in regard to Boule de Suif. Now, after being fed, the higher social class is happy to pay respect to the plump prostitute.

Eventually the coach arrives in Tôtes. In Tôtes, Prussian soldiers greet the passengers at their coach, an event that makes everyone quite nervous. Luckily, their documents appear to be sufficient to allow them to continue their travels. The passengers and the driver intend to stay in Tôtes one night and depart for Le Havre in the morning. While having dinner at the inn, Boule de Suif is called up to talk to the Prussian commandant. He propositions her, which she angrily and gallantly refuses. All of the other passengers are outraged by the commandant's indecent proposal. The next day, the passengers rise to see that their coach has not been harnessed. It

soon becomes apparent that they will not be able to depart Tôtes until Boule de Suif has sex with the Prussian commandant. At first, all of the other passengers support her decision, as it would be morally unjust and unethical to support forcing a woman into such a painful sacrifice. However, as the days go by, her fellow passengers begin to scheme a way to coerce Boule de Suif into sleeping with the commandant. The only person still opposed is the democrat, Cornudet.

After keenly manipulative speeches at dinner and final monologues from Comte Hubert and the Old Nun, Boule de Suif caves to the Prussian commandant's proposal and the other passengers' coercion, and on the fifth night in Tôtes she sleeps with the enemy. The following morning, nine passengers rise early to pack and collect provisions. Yet given her long evening of pleasing the Prussian commandant and saving her fellow passengers, Boule de Suif has been left with no time to pack food or drink. She is forced to hurriedly board the coach. With the coach safely back on the road heading toward Le Havre, no one has the decency to thank Boule de Suif for her sacrifice. In fact, they scorn her and call her shameful. No one extends the courtesy she offered to the other passengers on the road to Tôtes. Boule de Suif is left to cry in hunger and thirst, while the others feast and insult her. Pained from the previous night's events and the cruelty of her fellow passengers, Boule de Suif is reduced to tears, sobbing into the night as the coach creeps along to Le Havre.

Characters

Boule de Suif

Boule de Suif is the title character of Maupassant's short story. She is one of ten passengers in a coach, bound for Le Havre, which is leaving Rouen to flee from the advancing German army. She is traveling alone. Her birth name is Mademoiselle Élisabeth Rousset; however, it is her appearance that has earned her the nickname, Boule de Suif, or in English "Ball of Fat." Boule de Suif is a short, perfectly round, fat little woman with plump, sausage-like fingers, shiny skin, and enormous breasts. Her face is reddish and round with black eyes and large lashes, a small mouth with nice lips, and tiny teeth. Boule de Suif carries herself with dignity and a freshness that makes her attractive and desirable. It is well known that she is a prostitute, and although she is sought after, her seemingly honorable travel companions deem her an immoral woman, even though she helps them on several occasions. Without Boule de Suif as their companion, the entourage would have suffered greatly, as they all forgot to bring provisions for the long trip. During the first leg of the journey, the sophisticated prostitute provided her condescending companions with food and drink when the group was near fainting from hunger. Next, in Tôtes, which was already occupied by Germans, Boule de Suif compromised her own categorical imperative—not to have sex with a man against her own wishes—and slept with the Prussian commandant to free herself and her companions. If she had not made such a utilitarian sacrifice or, even worse, if she had not been on the coach at all, then there was a chance that the German officers would have kept them indefinitely in Tôtes or possibly even raped the female travelers. Boule de Suif is emotionally damaged from the event that saved her companions, but she is even more deeply hurt when they turn against her, once again regarding her and her actions as immoral: On the trip out of Tôtes, Boule de Suif is hurried and does not have time to pack provisions, but none of the other passengers will share food with her, speak with her, or thank her in any way.

Madame Carré-Lamadon

Madame Carré-Lamadon is one of the ten travelers aboard the coach bound for Le Havre. Her husband and companion is Monsieur Carré-Lamadon. Madame Carré-Lamadon is a small, dainty, pretty woman who is much younger than her husband. The officers in Rouen were comforted by her beauty and presence. In the coach, dressed in furs, the young wife faints from hunger, only to be rescued by the two nuns and a glass of Boule de Suif's claret.

Monsieur Carré-Lamadon

Monsieur Carré-Lamadon is one of the ten travelers in the coach bound for Le Havre. He is traveling with his wife, Madame Carré-Lamadon. He, like the Comte, is a member of the superior social class. Monsieur Carré-Lamadon holds a substantial position in the cotton business, owning three spinning-mills. In addition, he is a member of the Legion of Honour and the General Council, where he serves with Comte Hubert.

The Coachman

The coachman is the driver of the coach containing the ten passengers leaving from Rouen for

Media Adaptations

- "Boule de Suif" was adapted as a film by Christian-Jacque in 1945, starring Micheline Presle, Berthe Bovy, and Louis Salou. It was released in the United States as *Angel and Sinner* and *Grease Ball.*

- *The Short Stories of Guy de Maupassant, Volume I* was published as an audio-book recording through Audio Connoisseur in 1999. The recording includes "Boule de Suif" and four other short stories.

Le Havre. The driver does little besides navigate the coach to Tôtes. After they spend one night in Tôtes, the Prussian commandant tells the coachman that the travelers are not allowed to leave. The travelers are disturbed by this news and the coachman tells them that he has been instructed to stay in Tôtes until the commandant says otherwise. After this, the coachman is nonexistent until the travelers are granted leave from Tôtes four days later.

Cornudet

Cornudet is one of the ten travelers aboard the coach bound for Le Havre. He is traveling alone. He is a well-known democrat, and thus his liberal and social beliefs are a threat to all *respectable* people, such as the Carré-Lamadons, Hubert de Brévilles, and the Loiseaus. He has a long red beard and loves to drink beer. Cornudet has spent a good portion of his fortune inherited from his father, a retired confectioner. Although he is a democrat who professes to be eagerly awaiting the coming republic, Cornudet is quite lazy, politically active only in that he frequents democratic bars. For some unknown reason, he believed that he had been recently appointed prefect. Yet when he tried to take up duties, no one recognized his position, and he was forced out of the office. Cornudet is generally quite harmless and accommodating and is a thoroughly kindhearted man. In Rouen he worked to organize the fortification of the town, and upon leaving he hopes his skills can be used in Le Havre. Throughout the story, Cornudet is in verbal opposition with the respectable men and women with whom he is traveling. He disagrees with their politics and their social views. During the first night in Tôtes, Cornudet tries to persuade Boule de Suif to sleep with him. She refuses his advances because she believes it would be shameful with all the Prussians about. Given this patriotic spin, Cornudet complies, kisses Boule de Suif on the cheek, and returns to his room. Cornudet is the only one of all the travelers that is unflinchingly outspoken about the shameful act of coercion the travelers impose on Boule de Suif in forcing her to have sex with the commandant to benefit their own desires. Yet, in the end, even Cornudet, like the others, denies Boule de Suif food, sympathy, and appreciation as they leave Tôtes.

Madame Follenvie

Madame Follenvie is the innkeeper in Tôtes. She and her husband, Monsieur Follenvie, run the inn, which has been taken over by Prussians. The ten travelers stay at their inn with the German soldiers. Madame Follenvie does not appreciate the German soldiers, first of all because they have cost her so much money and second because she has two sons in the army. She is a pacifist at heart, not appreciating any killing whatsoever. However, Cornudet challenges her, stating that killing in defense is sacred. Madame Follenvie responds stating that it would be much easier to kill all the kings, as she believes that would end all war. Cornudet is impressed with the peasant innkeeper's comment, as he, too, is opposed to the aristocracy.

Monsieur Follenvie

Monsieur Follenvie is the innkeeper in Tôtes who hosts the ten travelers. He runs the inn with his wife, Madame Follenvie. He is the only direct link between the Prussian commandant and the ten travelers. No other civilians are allowed contact with the officer, unless otherwise specified by the commandant. Monsieur Follenvie is a fat, wheezy man who has asthma. He has so much trouble breathing that he cannot talk while he eats. Also, when he sleeps, he snores at a tremendous volume and rises no earlier than ten o'clock. He is kind but sluggish and oaf-like.

Comte Hubert de Bréville

Comte Hubert de Bréville bears one of the oldest names in all of Normandy. Comte, as he is referred to in the story, is one of the ten travelers

aboard the coach bound for Le Havre. He is traveling with his wife, the Comtesse. He dresses like Henry IV, hoping to accentuate a resemblance to the king, because it is a family legend that King Henry IV impregnated a de Bréville and gave her husband a governmental position, accelerating their family's standing in the social classes. Comte Hubert serves with Monsier Carré-Lamadon on the General Council, representing the Orleanist party. His fortune, all in landed property, produces an annual income of over half a million francs. The Comte Hubert is the most distinguished and gentlemanly of all the men. When Boule de Suif first tells her companions of the commandant's offensive, immoral proposition, Comte Hubert is the most disturbed and outspoken— even as the others begin to wish Boule de Suif would sleep with the commandant—stating that no woman should be called upon to make such a painful sacrifice. Oddly enough, it is his final prodding that convinces Boule de Suif that she should, for the good of the others, sleep with the Prussian commandant. Although he carries himself with an air of chivalry, Comte Hubert is just as self-centered and self-righteous as the other, despicable, passengers.

Comtesse Hubert de Bréville

Comtesse Hubert de Bréville is one of the ten travelers bound for Le Havre. Her husband and companion is Comte Hubert. The Comtesse is the daughter of a small Nantes ship-owner. She has very distinguished manners, is an impressive hostess and entertainer, and is believed to have been a mistress to one of Louis-Philippe's sons. Thus, she was familiar with the local aristocracy, and they often frequented her salon.

Madame Loiseau

Madame Loiseau is one of the ten travelers aboard the coach bound for Le Havre. She is traveling with her husband and business partner, Monsieur Loiseau. Madame Loiseau is a wine merchant in the Rue Grand-Pont. She is a tall, thick, bull-headed woman. Her voice is annoyingly shrill, and she makes quick decisions. She is determined and runs the firm, doing all the bookkeeping. Her attitude and voice make her an ill representative of the company, as she often makes insulting or coarse comments. Her husband is the jovial front man of the winery and has little interest in the day-to-day management; thus they make an excellent team. Madame Loiseau is never courteous to Boule de Suif, even after the prostitute feeds her and her husband. She is also the first to call the prostitute shameful after she sleeps with the commandant and saves the travelers from captivity in Tôtes.

Monsieur Loiseau

Monsieur Loiseau is one of the ten passengers on the coach headed for Le Havre. He is traveling with his wife, Madame Loiseau. Monsieur Loiseau is a wine merchant from Rue Grand-Pont. He is a fat hedonist, with a red face and graying beard. Originally, he was a clerk at the winery. Eventually, when the former owners had driven the winery into bankruptcy, Monsieur Loiseau purchased the floundering company, turned it around, and made a fortune. He makes terrible wine and sells it at a very inexpensive price. He is considered a jovial scoundrel, almost a crook, because of his low-quality wine. He is widely recognized throughout the region surrounding Rouen as a practical joker, and most everyone knows that he is full of duplicity, yet no one seems to mind because he is so merry. Monsieur Loiseau's attitude is noted throughout the story. In the coach, he looks hungrily upon Boule de Suif, both for her body and her food. Later, when Boule de Suif finally complies and sleeps with the commandant, Monsieur Loiseau is so excited that he buys everyone champagne and makes jokes about what is going on upstairs in the commandant's chamber.

The Old Nun

The Old Nun is one of the ten passengers on the coach bound for Le Havre. She is traveling with her companion, the Puny Nun. The Old Nun has red, pitted skin from smallpox. She says very little during the entire story, spending most of her time praying over her beads. Near the end, it is the Old Nun that gives the religious approval to Boule de Suif regarding her indecision as to whether or not to sleep with the commandant. The Old Nun states that the church has no trouble granting forgiveness when the act committed is for the glory of God or the benefit of others. The Old Nun's words may have been crucial in Boule de Suif's decision to go against her categorical imperative and commit the difficult, but utilitarian act of sleeping with the enemy.

The Prussian Commandant

The Prussian commandant is staying in the best room at the Follenvie's inn. Although he is scarcely seen, the commandant is obviously egotistical and self-centered, as he does not allow the travelers to leave even though they have documents from his superior authorizing their safe passage. He sends comments down to the travelers through Monsieur Follenvie. Most frequently, he inquires as to whether or not Boule de Suif is yet willing to sleep with him. At one point, the Prussian commandant allows for a meeting with the *respectable* men—Monsieur Loiseau, Monsieur Carré-Lamadon, and Comte Hubert—to discuss their departure, but he quickly turns the men away. All the commandant desires is to conquer Boule de Suif and then let the travelers go ahead with their journey.

The Puny Nun

The Puny Nun is one of the ten passengers bound for Le Havre. She is traveling aboard the coach with her companion, the Old Nun. The Puny Nun is very slight, with a pretty, but sickly face. She has a narrow body that appears to be devouring itself. She is so petite that she appears to be caving in. The Puny Nun spends most of her time praying over her beads and has little impact on the course of the story.

Themes

Naturalism

Maupassant is a French author from the naturalist school of thought. Naturalism in literature describes a type of work that tries to apply analytic principles of objectivity and separation to the literary study of the human being. In opposition to realism, which focuses on technique, the naturalist author takes a philosophic position. The objects of study, human beings, are creatures that can be studied through their relationships to their surroundings. Maupassant's characters are no exception. Boule de Suif is understood not through her inner thoughts and feelings, but through her actual words and actions. She is revealed through Maupassant's ability to report details that create an insightful depiction of the prostitute. Her inner thoughts are unneeded because all of her being is available through her relationship to others and her environment. Through this type of objective study, naturalist authors believe that the underlying forces that reign over human beings may be unearthed. Maupassant was incredibly adept at this type of revelation because of his photographic memory and keen ability to express and depict scenes and dialogue with exceptional clarity.

Topics for Further Study

- The title character, Boule de Suif, is unwilling to do something that is against her own understanding of right and wrong—sleeping with the Prussian commandant—to appease her companions. However, she is pressured to do so by her companions, who push utilitarian principles upon her, stressing that sometimes one is forced to do wrong to produce a good end. Explore this situation, and try to come up with at least three examples, either personal, historical, or literary, in which you may or may not believe that the ends justify the means.

- Morality is at stake in Maupassant's tale. The prostitute seems to be the noblest character in that she has a code of ethics and makes the greatest sacrifice for others. But after they get her to do what they want, her companions shun her and draw back to their supposedly more respectable morality. Choose a historical event, such as a presidential election or a modern war, and evaluate how morality is applied, abused, or assessed in these historical events as compared to "Boule de Suif." Present a comparison to the

class of the morality invoked by these historical events alongside the morality of the characters in the short story. Defend your own ethical position in light of your research.

- Other authors writing in Maupassant's era were also exploring unscrupulous characters. Take, for example, Gustave Flaubert or Emile Zola. Look into the publishing history of these authors. Were they ever banned? Did they have any trouble with the law because of their works? What impact, if any, did the translation of these works into English have on the puritanical societies in the United States and Britain?

- Maupassant met a bitter demise at the hands of syphilitic infection. Although it is likely that he contracted the disease from a prostitute, Maupassant did not transfer any anger to his characters, often making prostitutes his heroines. Yet the madness brought on by his infection helped to create his most horrific work "Le Horla." Read this short story and compare and contrast the style to "Boule de Suif."

Social Order and Scandal

Maupassant uses the social order to create a hierarchy inside the coach. The entourage is composed of differing social orders: two nuns, a prostitute, a democrat, and respectable, socially elite individuals. The nuns are dedicated to God. Appropriately, they engage in very little regarding scandal or squabble in the social order. The prostitute is a fringe element of the social order, dedicated to hedonism and immoral earnings. The democrat, a political leftist, is available to voice opinion against the aristocratic government and the respectable, socially elite travelers. Finally, the respectable individuals are in the vast majority, as it is expensive to flee to Tôtes. The respectable travelers look down upon the lower social classes. However, Maupassant, with a keen naturalist eye, unfolds several scandals. First of all, the respectable individuals damage their

reputation when they give in to their carnal desires and feed upon the prostitute's wealth of food and drink. Later, they are again dependant upon Boule de Suif to rescue them from the Prussians. Their greed and selfish desires propel them into another damaging scandal. The *respectable* passengers manipulate and coerce Boule de Suif to commit an immoral act. They do not take the respectable, moral high ground—standing behind the prostitute's categorical imperative not to sleep with the Prussian Commandant—instead, the respectable characters push her over the precipice of immorality only to commit their last and final scandal. In the end, with Boule de Suif flustered and emotionally damaged by her actions, Maupassant unfolds the final scandal as the respectable individuals not only grant her no appreciation for her act, but they actually shun her and show her great disrespect, calling her shameful and immoral. Maupassant uses the social order and scandal to unearth the heart of his characters through their interactions with each other.

Promiscuity and Moral Confusion

Although Boule de Suif is an antihero, her promiscuity does lead to her own moral confusion. Oddly enough, the prostitute possesses the most exemplary code of ethics. She has set for herself rules and maxims that she holds with categorically imperative conviction. She desires to stand up for what she believes. However, as is often the case with someone who truly stands on a higher moral ground, she also wants to bring happiness to others. Her work as a prostitute is an example of bringing pleasure to someone else, in a sense increasing the collective happiness. However, this type of utilitarian behavior is a troubled spouse to an ethic composed of axioms and imperatives. Boule de Suif runs herself into this debacle when she is morally troubled by the prospect of sleeping with the enemy to free herself and her companions. On one hand, Boule de Suif has lived her life bringing utilitarian pleasure to a vast number of people. On the other hand, she has trouble using the same skills to bring to a life a different kind of utilitarianism, namely freeing her companions from the Prussians. Maupassant effectively uses promiscuity to unleash a cornucopia of moral confusion.

Style

The Prostitute as an Antihero

The antihero is a central character who lacks traditional heroic qualities. Antiheros are not strong or physically powerful. Rarely do they muster up great courage to defeat a monster. Antiheros are usually outside the social norm, and they appreciate their position. Antiheros are usually distrustful of conventional values and are plagued with an inability to commit to any one set of ideals. The title character in Maupassant's "Boule de Suif" is no different. She is an exceptional antihero. She is not physically powerful. In fact, she is quite short, fat, and soft. She is certainly outside the social norm, as she is a prostitute—a profession not only considered fringe, but immoral. She is incredibly distrustful of the aristocratic government and often makes her opinions on such matters heard. On a final and most potent note, Maupassant's Boule de Suif cannot

commit to one set of ethics. She waffles between categorical imperatives and a flexibility that is loosely bound to utilitarian principles. Boule de Suif holds to her moral rules only to be convinced that there is a better set of ideals. Nonetheless, her actions are heroic because she does them for the benefit of others. In the end, Boule de Suif saves her companions, entitling her to her antihero status.

Historical Context

The Franco–Prussian War

The Franco–Prussian War raged between 1870 and 1871. The war was essentially fought between France and Germany, although Germany was unified under Prussian control. France eventually lost the war to Germany. The underlying cause of the conflict was Prussian statesman Otto Edward Leopold von Bismarck's desire to unify Germany under Prussian control and eliminate France's power over Germany. On the other side, Napoleon III, emperor of France from 1852 to 1870, wanted to regain national and international status lost as a result of various diplomatic setbacks, most notably those suffered at the hands of the Prussians during the Austro–Prussian War of 1866. Lastly, the military strength of Prussia, as was revealed in Austria, added to France's desire to dominate the European continent.

The war was precipitated by a series of feather-ruffling events that would eventually lead to Germany unifying itself under Prussian leadership to wage war against the French. The prince of Hohenzollern-Sigmaringen, Leopold, was pressured by Bismarck to accept candidacy for the vacant Spanish throne. This move alarmed the French, as they were wary of a Prusso–Spanish alliance. The French sent an ambassador to speak with William I, the king of Prussia, demanding that Leopold withdraw his candidacy. Although angered, William I agreed to their demands.

Unfortunately for the French, Napoleon III was not content and was determined to further humiliate Prussia. A French foreign minister was dispatched to William I, demanding that the king issue a written apology to Napoleon III. This was the final straw. The king rejected the French emperor's demands and immediately gave Bismarck permission to publish the French demands. Bismarck edited the document so as to inflame both the Frenchman and

Compare & Contrast

- **1870–1880:** In 1870, Germany invades France after France declares war on Germany, which starts the Franco–Prussian War and signals a rise in German military power and imperialism.

  Today: Following many decades of war and upheaval, Germany and France have made amends and have united under peace as two of the strongest and most prosperous European nations.

- **1870–1880:** In 1877, Queen Victoria is named the empress of India, illustrating a rise in European and, most notably, British imperialism.

  Today: India is a free country and, although overpopulated and struggling, it has become a powerful nation through its contributions to progressive politics and technology.

- **1870–1880:** In 1876, Alexander Graham Bell invents the telephone, sparking a new dawn in communication.

  Today: A large percentage of the developed nations' populations carry a cellular telephone with them at all times. Communication has been established via satellite, cable, digital, and wireless networks, linking the world together.

- **1870–1880:** In 1871, Charles Darwin publishes *The Descent of Man,* challenging creationism and putting into use the term *evolution* for the first time.

  Today: The battle over creationism and evolution rages on, with one side defending evolution on the basis of scientific knowledge and the other side defending creationism on the basis of faith.

the Germans. France's egotism not only instigated war, but it had a dramatic psychological effect on the Germans, rallying them to unify under Prussia's cause.

The French were quickly and soundly defeated in multiple battles, due exclusively to the military superiority of the Prussian forces. Most notable was the battle at Sedan, when Napoleon III was captured along with 100,000 troops. Another significant defeat was at Metz, where an additional 180,000 soldiers were surrendered. However, the workers of Paris refused to accept defeat, and revolutionaries seized control of the capital. Unfortunately, the French army did not embrace the rebellion and, under the tacit support of the Prussians, the French soldiers took Paris from the revolutionaries and executed tens of thousands in what was known as *Bloody Week.*

From the earliest moments of the Prussian invasion, it was apparent that their forces were far too powerful for the French forces. During this time, most French troops and many citizens began a steady retreat toward the coast of the English Chan-

nel. Anyone with the means to leave planned to escape to England. Maupassant witnessed this mass exodus and his keen eye and photographic memory enabled him to absorb and store a vast collection of imagery and emotions from his fellow Frenchman. Eventually this collection of images and memories spawned his masterpiece ''Boule de Suif.'' As a soldier in the retreating French forces, he had a front row seat for the emotional responses to war and the results of aristocratic narcissism, both of which played key roles in his character development and plot construction.

Critical Overview

The literature of Guy de Maupassant, while widely read, has received little in the form of critical study. It may be that Maupassant's large readership has made it of little interest to critics, in that much of what is considered popular is often considered unworthy of analysis. It may also be that Maupassant has received little attention from critics and academics because his subject matter was considered immoral for so many decades. Regardless of the reason, his lack of attention is seemingly unmerited, considering the scope and clarity of his writing. However, Maupassant's own talent may be the reason so many critics have turned their backs on his work. Roger Colet, a rare Maupassant scholar and translator, states in his "Introduction" in *Selected Short Stories,* "[Maupassant] is the victim, in a sense, of his own perfect art."

Although much of his work was banned or condemned for being immoral, this did not slow his popularity. However, it did slow his publication in the United States. It took many decades before anyone was willing to publish his stories of sex, prostitutes, and madness on the other side of the Atlantic Ocean. Eventually, it became apparent that, at the bare minimum, Maupassant possessed an amazing ability to create characters of great depth and stories of immense clarity, even if the paradoxical protagonist were an immoral, heroic prostitute.

Criticism

Anthony Martinelli

Martinelli is a Seattle-based freelance writer and editor. In this essay, Martinelli examines how the main character's dialogue and actions create a confused ethic of both ontologism and utilitarianism, the two major schools of philosophical thought of the nineteenth century.

In "Boule de Suif," Guy de Maupassant tells the tale of Boule de Suif, a short, plump, inviting French prostitute, who is fleeing the advancing Germans during the Franco–Prussian War. Although seemingly immoral by profession, Boule de Suif actually adheres to a code of ethics. By the very nature of her profession, Boule de Suif feels as though she is spreading happiness through her service: Her clientele leaves with a greater level of satisfaction, thus adding to the greater good. In addition, Boule de Suif has several imperatives that she makes her best attempt to stand behind. Boule de Suif believes that these axioms should never be broken, namely that there should always be a different means to achieve the same end that would not require doing acts in opposition to her imperatives. Unfortunately, Boule de Suif, by following two codes of ethics—one utilitarian, the other onto-

logical—lands herself in the ethically uncertain apex between these two opposed moral philosophies.

Utilitarianism is probably the most famous normative ethical dogma in the English-speaking history of moral philosophy. The doctrine's purpose is to explain why some actions are right and others are wrong. Although it had roots in philosophical history and although it is still widely appealed to by many modern philosophers, utilitarianism reached its peak in the late eighteenth century and the first twenty-five years of the nineteenth century. The leading philosophers in this school of thought were Jeremy Bentham and John Stuart Mill. In its earliest formulation, utilitarianism was simplistic. It was hinged to an idea called *The Greatest Happiness Principle.* This basic tenet of utilitarianism purports that the ultimate good is simply the greatest happiness of the greatest number of people. Happiness is seen as the maximization of pleasure and the minimization of pain. Thus, utilitarianism judges all consequences by the amount of pleasure derived from each consequence. This, of course, leaves no concern for the means to the end of the consequence: No examination is given to duty or to what is right or good; the aim is purely targeted on the greatest happiness for the greatest number.

Utilitarianism, if strictly followed, leaves little room for any sort of law, let alone ethical categorical imperatives. Bertrand Russell writes in *A History of Western Philosophy,* "In its absolute form, the doctrine that an individual has certain inalienable rights is incompatible with utilitarianism, i.e., with the doctrine that right acts are those that do most to promote the general happiness." Russell is summarizing one of the greatest difficulties with utilitarianism, not only in relation to governmental law but also to any law in general. Utilitarianism has a democratic feel, in that a majority of people feeling happiness is similar to a majority of people approving of initiative, thus making it a law. However, as this statement implies, and with the definition of utilitarianism, a law would be considered inconsequential if breaking the law—something wholly undemocratic—created greater happiness than not. Herein lies the paradoxical problem inherit in both utilitarianism and Maupassant's character, Boule de Suif.

Yet neither Boule de Suif nor utilitarianism can be wholly scrutinized without a keen examination of the ontological code of ethics described by Immanuel Kant. Kant is a nineteenth-century philosophical giant. Kant cannot be contained by any one

Men and weapons during the time of Paris Commune, an insurrectionary government formed at the end of the Franco-Prussian War, the setting for ''Boule de Suif''

distinct *ism* because his philosophy is incredibly profound and complex. His theories arose out of the stagnating doctrines of two of the most important philosophic theories: rationalism and empiricism. Kantian ethics were grounded in his definition of pure practical reason. For Kant, pure practical reason is concerned with the a priori grounds for action and, most important to his ethics, moral action. For Kant, this implies that there is an a priori moral law—a dogma that is already grounded and indisputable—with which all people should act in accordance. From this law springs moral maxims. Kant calls these laws *categorical imperatives,* which define morality through objective requirements, independent of individual desires. Kant states in *Grounding for the Metaphysics of Morals:*

> The practical [application of the categorical] imperative will therefore be the following: Act in such a way that you treat humanity, whether in your own person or in the person of another, always at the same time as an end and never simply as a means.

Herein lies the second calamity of Boule de Suif. Not only has she treated herself as a means to an end, but so also have her passengers. Through the passengers' act of coercion, Boule de Suif is placed in opposition to Kantian moral law. In addition, the passengers commit the greatest immoral act in that they are using Boule de Suif's physical body to achieve their own desired end.

With a clearer understanding of both utilitarianism and a Kantian ontological ethic, Boule de Suif's plight begins to take shape. Boule de Suif lives through a moral code drenched in utilitarianism. Through her profession alone, Boule de Suif is married to a utilitarian code of ethics. It is her job to deliver happiness in the form of sex to her clientele. If she is adequately doing her job, the people whom Boule de Suif services should leave her, reentering society with a greater happiness and thus contributing to the pool of greater happiness for the greatest number. This alone upsets Kantian ethics in that Boule de Suif is using her physical body as a means to an end, that is, the physical happiness of another individual.

However, this trouble goes even deeper because Boule de Suif also acts in accordance with her own set of a priori imperatives. Most prominent are her axioms established in relation to patriotism. For example, when the Prussian officer orders the passengers to exit the coach, Boule de Suif and Cornudet

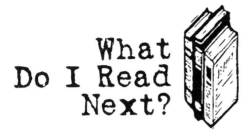

What Do I Read Next?

- *A Life: The Humble Truth,* by Guy de Maupassant, was originally published in 1883. The book chronicles the life of a Norman woman whose kindliness is both a virtue and a vice.

- *Bel-Ami* (1885), by Guy de Maupassant, depicts the life of a journalist lacking moral scruples, whose success is built upon hypocrisy, lecherousness, and corruption.

- *Pierre et Jean,* by Guy de Maupassant, was originally published in 1888. The book is crafted around the psychological study of adultery involving a young wife and two brothers.

- *Guy de Maupassant, Mademoiselle Fifi, and Other Short Stories,* by Guy de Maupassant, was published as a collection in 1999. This collection contains many short stories that are not available in the Penguin Books collection, *Selected Short Stories.*

- *Madame Bovary,* by Gustave Flaubert, was originally published in two volumes in 1857. In a depressing, but rich, tale of adultery and love gone amiss, Flaubert has created what is often considered one of the greatest books ever written.

- *Nana,* by Emile Zola, was originally published in 1880. It is a risqué novel that tells the story of a ruthless prostitute's rise from poverty to the height of Parisian society.

- *First Love and Other Stories,* by Ivan Turgenev, was published as a collection in 1999. This book contains the famous title story, plus five other well-known tales from this exceptional Russian writer of the nineteenth century.

---

stay inside. Maupassant writes, "They [Boule de Suif and Cornudet] were anxious to preserve their dignity, conscious that in encounters of this kind everybody is to some extent the representative of his country, and both were disgusted at their companions' obsequiousness." Boule de Suif is enraged that her companions are so subservient to the occupying Prussians. She sees their weakness as an immoral action. Yet, on the other hand, Boule de Suif is easily swayed. Although Boule de Suif is opposed to bending under the oppression of Prussian demands, she is more flexible when it comes to the demands of her countrymen. In an early encounter with the Prussian commandant, her companions plead with her to comply with the commandant's first demands to simply speak with the prostitute. Boule de Suif is initially stubborn, but eventually she takes the utilitarian route, saving her companions from a possible backlash. She even states, "All right . . . but I'm only doing it for your sakes." This decision is in step with a utilitarian code of ethics.

However, there seems to be a limit to Boule de Suif's flexibility. Although it is apparent that she is a jumbled mess of utilitarianism and Kantian ontologism, the prostitute takes an incredibly firm stand against the Prussian commandant's sexual advances. When the officer states that he will hold the passengers captive until Boule de Suif has sex with him, the prostitute exclaims, "Tell that blackguard, that scoundrel, that swine of a Prussian that I'll never do it. Have you got that clear? Never, never, never!" Boule de Suif's conviction, at first, carries over to her passengers. In fact one character, Comte Hubert de Breville, even outlines Kantian morality stating, "no woman could be called upon to make such a painful sacrifice, and that the offer must come from herself." Essentially, the Comte's comment is that no one individual should use another person as a means to a desired end. Unfortunately, it soon becomes apparent that all of the people aboard the coach are more concerned with their own individual well-being than with any type of moral or ethical code.

Soon, the other passengers' support of Boule de Suif's moral imperative begins to waffle. They want her to sleep with the enemy so they can get back on

> " So herein lies the ethical calamity of Boule de Suif: the impossible decision to follow one moral code in opposition to another. No matter which tenet she selects, her actions will be viewed as immoral by someone."

the road to Le Havre. The passengers even begin to resort to insults. Madame Loiseau proclaims, "Seeing that it's that slut's job to go with any man who wants her, I don't think she's any right to refuse one man rather than another." Oddly enough, and as crass as Madame Loiseau's comment may be, this statement is at the crux of Boule de Suif's moral confusion. As a prostitute, Boule de Suif is a master of the art of pleasure, committing utilitarian acts that return a greater happiness to a greater number of people. However, as a patriot, Boule de Suif desires to follow a stricter code of imperatives that she allows to override her utilitarian principles. While in Tôtes, Boule de Suif could employ her occupation and give back to the world a greater happiness for the greatest number. Not only would the Prussian commandant be sexually satisfied and thus happier, but also nine of her fellow travelers would be happier in that they would be allowed freedom from their Prussian captives. So herein lies the ethical calamity of Boule de Suif: the impossible decision to follow one moral code in opposition to another. No matter which tenet she selects, her actions will be viewed as immoral by someone.

In the end, Boule de Suif selects the utilitarian dogma and breaks her own personal moral code for the greater good. She caves under the weight of her utilitarian principles, coupled with the manipulation of her fellow passengers, and sleeps with the Prussian commandant. Her actions free her and her traveling companions, but Boule de Suif, crushed under guilt and self-disgust, is reduced to tears. Not only has she broken her own moral tenet, but she also realizes that her companions used her as a means to their own end. Plus, her companions are thankless; they even scorn their liberator, stating

that Boule de Suif is "crying because she's ashamed of herself."

Ironically, Maupassant was frequently banned for his immoral stories and subject matter, and Boule de Suif's predicament is spawned from her own promiscuity. In an odd twist, Maupassant's naturalistic dissection of the dueling moral philosophic trends of the eighteenth and nineteenth centuries proved not only to question ethical codes but also, sardonically, to support a more puritanical society. Although it may not have been wholly intended, Boule de Suif's occupation is the catalyst that allows the other passengers to rationalize their coercion. None of them would have felt entitled to manipulate another woman, even a peasant, to commit an immoral act for his or her own benefit. It would have been unthinkable. Yet since in the eyes of her fellow travelers Boule de Suif was already muddied with impurities and immorality, the passengers—even the nuns—were less inclined to stand behind the prostitute's moral convictions. This left Boule de Suif destroyed and embarrassed, wallowing in a state of moral peril.

Source: Anthony Martinelli, Critical Essay on "Boule de Suif," in *Short Stories for Students,* Thomson Gale, 2005.

Laura Carter

Carter is currently employed as a freelance writer. In this essay, Carter examines Immanuel Kant's moral argument for God in relation to Maupassant's story.

The protagonist of Guy de Maupassant's "Boule de Suif" learns that virtuous acts do not always reap rewards. In fact, her altruism or self-sacrifice jeopardizes, rather than improves, her own life. Boule de Suif is a victim of her own good nature. In her acts of charity she refuses to see how others have treated her. Such acts only win her even more disdain or hatred from the group.

Much of the interaction among the group of travelers in Maupassant's story revolves around the character nicknamed Boule de Suif. Throughout the narrative, she is put in a self-sacrificing position by a group of strangers who barely recognize or appreciate her generosity. First, because she is a prostitute, Boule de Suif receives the group's disdain. However, when she is the only traveler to produce a basket of food, it is the hungry travelers who eventually dine with her, albeit reluctantly. And, when captured by German and Prussian officers, these same travelers turn to Boule de Suif, insisting she respond to the Prussian soldier's demands to see her despite her resistance to the idea. Ultimately she does accept, exclaiming, "All right . . . but I'm only doing it for your sakes." Finally, when Boule de Suif learns that the enemy wants to sleep with her, she is appalled, as is the group; yet the group thinks nothing of exploiting her to that end, pressuring her to comply for their sakes.

Generosity in the narrative is not a two-way street. The ladies in the coach react with a ferocious contempt at the sight of Boule de Suif's basket of food, for instance, misinterpreting her generosity as an affront to their pride. This reaction to their traveling companion is one of many indications that the group, with the exception of Boule de Suif, is driven largely by selfish motivations rather than self-sacrifice. After their capture, several members of the party could have easily negotiated their release. Yet they respond not out of generosity, but of greed. Says the narrator: "The richer members of the party were the most terrified, already seeing themselves forced to pour out sackfuls of gold in the hands of the insolent soldiers in order to save their lives." However, rather than resorting to bribery to put an end to the group's captivity, they spend considerable time concocting or thinking of ways "to conceal their wealth and enable them to pass themselves off as the poorest of poor."

Interestingly, these same group members think nothing of sacrificing Boule de Suif to their own advantage. They put a considerable amount of energy in winning the prostitute over, of convincing her that she comply with the Prussian's demands for sex for the sake of the group. They feel "almost annoyed" with Boule de Suif "for not having gone to the Prussian on the sly so as to provide her fellow travelers with a pleasant surprise in the morning," despite the fact that her self-sacrifice in this situation is fraught or filled with dangerous implications. In surrendering herself physically to the Prussian, she could subject herself to violence, even death at the hands of the enemy—indicated when the travelers themselves engage in moments of worried silence for the prostitute. Expecting Boule de Suif to sacrifice her person in the name of the group is hardly given a second thought. When it comes to reaching down into their pockets, however, the group is reluctant to part with even a handful of coins to quickly resolve their situation, nor do they feel obligated to do so.

Ironic too is the method that Boule de Suif's companions use to persuade her to sacrifice herself

> **"Expecting Boule de Suif to sacrifice her person in the name of the group is hardly given a second thought."**

to the Prussian. The group engages in a general theological or religious argument, based on their interpretation of the will of God, to manipulate her, an activity one could hardly regard as being the least bit noble or pious. Beginning with a vague conversation on self-sacrifice, the discussion emphasizes the idea that "a woman's only duty on earth was perpetual sacrifice of her person." When Boule de Suif is not convinced, the group engages the elder nuns in a conversation about the nature of one's deeds in life, and the ability of the church to grant absolution for those deeds "committed for the glory of God or the benefit of one's neighbor." The Comtesse makes the most of this argument, asserting that no action "could be displeasing to the Lord if the intention was praiseworthy." So persuasive is the Comtesse, she "eggs on" the old nun of the group to speak to the moral axiom "The end justifies the means." Says the nun: "An action which is blameworthy in itself often becomes meritorious by virtue of the idea which inspires it."

Like de Maupassant, Immanuel Kant's interest in the dynamics of human social interaction shaped much of his work. Kant, an important German philosopher who died at the turn of the eighteenth century, makes a "moral argument for God" that closely parallels the Comtesse's argument. In his early writings or pre-critical discussions of God, according to Philip Rossi, in his entry in the *Stanford Encyclopedia of Philosophy,* Kant's moral argument for God rests on the relationship between a person's ability to lead a virtuous, moral life and the satisfaction of that person's desire for happiness. Kant believed that a moral or practical use of human reason constituted the "highest good." Essentially, within the context of his moral argument, our ability to exercise our will to choose actions solely in view of their moral rightness constitutes the practical use of reason. Exercising such choice, according to Kant, means that we will our actions on the basis of a "categorical imperative" or highest good. The highest good, therefore, consists in proper proportioning of happiness to match the measure of the virtue each person acquires in willing right moral actions. The highest good thus includes a harmonious balance or proportioning of happiness to virtue for all moral agents. Essentially, actions that one wills to be moral actions, those chosen on the basis of the categorical imperative, must be actions that will effect a proper proportion of happiness to virtue, not only for the person directly involved, but for everyone.

In the case of Boule de Suif's sacrifice, for example, the group justifies putting her in harm's way for the sake of the highest good. In light of Kant's beliefs, revisiting the old nun's version of the moral axiom "the end justifies the means" reveals an argument riddled with complexities. The group consensus as to the prostitute's fate seems to be that she should be willing to comply for the sake of their freedom, that sleeping with the enemy, because of her line of work, "was such a trivial thing for her." Publicly, all of the women lavish "intense and affectionate sympathy" to win over their reluctant companion. Privately, they justify her sacrifice by pointing out that "it's that slut's job to go with any man who wants her," believing she has "no right to refuse one man rather than another." For the group, the end does truly justify the means. For their own sakes, all group members believe, or at least have convinced themselves that Boule de Suif's act of self-sacrifice is for the highest good—to preserve their own wealth as well as their safety, and to ultimately affect their release. In the end, it is their ability to make use of Kant's strong philosophical argument that wins Boule de Suif over.

At the end of the story, however, the prostitute does not emerge triumphantly in the eyes of her traveling companions. After a night with the Prussian, Boule de Suif returns to the carriage only to meet rejection, her companions turning away, "as if they had not seen her." The group, rather than praising her for her sacrifice, engages in open displays of contempt, even disgust. The result of this rejection, states the narrator, is that Boule de Suif "felt angry with her neighbors, ashamed of having given way to their pleas, and defiled by the kisses of the Prussian into whose arms they had hypocritically thrown her." Clearly, the group's rejection of Boule de Suif was not the response she was looking for, or had even anticipated, for that matter. After all, she had agreed to sleep with the Prussian with the idea that somehow her actions would transcend the unpleasant, distasteful sacrifice she had to make, and that her fellow companions

would be pleased, even grateful for her efforts. In light of the group's response, her sacrifice goes unrewarded; the whole exercise becomes, to some degree, a lesson in futility for Boule de Suif.

According to Rossi, despite his hypothesis, Kant himself offered evidence to suggest that such willing of the highest good may be an exercise in futility. First, simply willing one's actions to be moral is not sufficient to insure they will effect the happiness appropriate to their virtue, chiefly because of one's tendency to choose morally right actions without consideration of the happiness they might reap as a result of these actions. In some cases, Kant feels that at least some of these choices may have the opposite effect on one's own life. In other words, on the basis of the categorical imperative, these choices, by their very nature, forbid individuals to consider any effects they may have on their own happiness. Consistently, Boule de Suif makes choices that satisfy Kant's moral imperative for the highest possible good, without much regard for consequences. She generously and willing shares her provisions for the trip with the ill-prepared group. She speaks with the Prussian and even sleeps with him to appease her fellow travelers. Yet she fails to recognize or even predict the possible outcome of these actions—that she may go hungry, have to live with the shame of sleeping with the enemy and, in turn, earn the disdain or contempt of the group for doing so.

Immanuel Kant's moral argument forms the basis for Guy de Maupassant's *Boule de Suif.* The story's protagonist, Boule de Suif, discovers that despite her heroic acts of self-sacrifice, she cannot rise above her circumstances to win the admiration of the group. Her story mirrors the failings of Kant's categorical imperative, that it is difficult to make choices for the highest good while realizing happiness proportional to those choices. In this way de Maupassant masterfully weaves his instructional tale, using this philosophical approach to expose the follies of mankind, in its infinite greed, selfish motives and unfounded justifications.

Source: Laura Carter, Critical Essay on "Boule de Suif," in *Short Stories for Students,* Thomson Gale, 2005.

Mary Donaldson-Evans

In the following essay excerpt, Donaldson-Evans discusses the main sexual theme and subthemes of nutrition, socioeconomics, and the military in "Boule de suif," while placing the story within the context of Maupassant's "war" and "whore" stories.

As can be discerned from this outline, "Boule de suif" is constructed upon the interplay of three thematic "sub-codes"—the nutritional, the politico-economic and the military—with the main code which is sexual. To understand the way in which these codes function, it is necessary to consider the text in both its diachronic and synchronic dimensions. It is also useful, although not essential, to place "Boule de suif" in the context of Maupassant's war stories, on the one hand, and his "whore" stories, on the other. It is not by chance that the two themes frequently collide, and that his most unforgettable prostitutes are war heroes as well.

Let us begin, then, with the sexual code. As a prostitute, Boule de suif is the incarnation of sexuality. She is a "marchande d'amour", her *marchandise* being her body. Aggression is the *sine qua non* of her trade. In the eyes of society, she is immoral, ignoble; yet, as Forestier has pointed out, Boule de suif, like many of Maupassant's prostitutes, has managed to retain her self-respect by transferring her moral sensibility to a domain other than the sexual. She thus possesses a sense of dignity despite public opinion, and when the whispered insults reach her ears at the outset of the journey, she is not intimidated; rather, she looks directly at her insulters with "un regard tellement provocant et hardi qu'un grand silence aussitôt régna." That they let themselves be silenced by her is not an indication of respect, however, and the epithets used to describe the prostitute as seen through their eyes ("honte publique", "vendue sans vergogne") make it quite obvious that at this point in the story she is held in low esteem indeed. In fact, a study of the terms used for the prostitute throughout the story reveals that they follow a curve, corresponding closely to the rise and fall of her "value" in their eyes. Her proper name, Elisabeth Rousset, is used only four times, in each case by the innkeeper Follenvie in transmitting the Prussian's message. To the others, and to the narrator, she is Boule de suif, an *objet de consommation* in the eyes of all. Moreover, as Sullivan has suggested, the evocation of the bourgeois origins of the French military officers, "ex-marchands de suif ou de savon" is not gratuitous; rather, it establishes a symbolic link between these ill-qualified leaders "nommés officiers pour leurs écus ou la longueur de leurs moustaches" and the travelling bourgeois who use Boule de suif as their merchandise, who reify her and look upon her as a

> " Seen as a mirror-perfect image of France herself, la belle, la douce France, humiliated and betrayed by her very own people, those whom she had succoured and nourished, Boule de suif acquires a tragic grandeur."

means to their dual end, escape from the Prussians (hence freedom) and financial gain.

If the women are, or pretend to be, shocked by the presence of a harlot in the carriage, the men are clearly aroused. The vulgar Loiseau is the only one not to lower his eyes under the prostitute's provocative gaze; rather, he continues to look at her "d'un air émoustillé." Cornudet, the only male traveller unaccompanied by a woman, can afford to be bolder. The first night in Tôtes, he openly propositions her in the hotel corridor and only reluctantly returns to his own room after her adamant refusal, somewhat impressed despite himself by "cette pudeur patriotique de catin qui ne se laissait point caresser près de l'ennemi." Maupassant cleverly presents us this scene through the eyes of Loiseau who, peeking through the keyhole from his hotel room, is sufficiently titillated to return to his bed and the "dure carcasse de sa compagne" to whom he transfers his sexual interests (one is reminded here of the French adage, "Faute de mieux on couche avec sa femme"). The other two male characters, prevented by their class consciousness from any overt reaction to the prostitute's sexuality, effect a similar transfer the last night when, during the "celebration" dinner, they engage in a seemingly innocent flirtation with one another's partners: "Le comte parut s'apercevoir que Madame Carré-Lamadon était charmante, le manufacturier fit des compliments à la comtesse." The evening, filled with laughter and bawdy jokes made at the prostitute's expense, is not without orgiastic overtones. Loiseau's tasteless and vulgar farces shock no one "car l'indignation dépend des milieux comme le reste" and even the women and the count make a few discreet allusions to what is taking place upstairs. Only Cornudet does not participate, and his departing words ("Je vous dis à tous que vous venez de faire une infamie [. . .] une infamie!") threaten to end the evening on a sour note until Loiseau, doubling over with laughter, reveals to the others "les mystères du corridor." Indeed, it must be said that Cornudet *is* somewhat tainted by his attempted seduction of the prostitute, and his refusal to collaborate with the others cannot be unequivocally attributed to purely Republican patriotic sentiments. Moreover, he is himself identified with the Prussian, not only by his relationship to the prostitute, but also by his pipe and his favorite beverage, beer. The first two syllables of his name clearly suggest his role at the sexual level of the text: he is indeed the cuckold, betrayed by Boule de suif herself and above all by the others who have served as *proxénètes,* forcing her into the arms of the Prussian officer for their own monetary benefit (for they have "de gros intérêts engagés au Havre").

The sexual activity of the first night in the hotel had been limited to Cornudet's fruitless attempt to overcome the resistance of Boule de suif and Loiseau's supposed seduction of his wife. The only sound disturbing the silence of the night had been Follenvie's heavy breathing, "un ronflement puissant, monotone, régulier, un bruit sourd et prolongé avec des tremblements de chaudière sous pression" In contrast, the last night in the hotel is a restless one:

> Et toute la nuit, dans l'obscurité du corridor coururent comme des frémissements, des bruits légers, à peine sensibles, pareils à des souffles, des effleurements de pieds nus, d'imperceptibles craquements. Et l'on ne dormit que très tard, assurément, car des filets de lumière glissèrent longtemps sous les portes. Le champagne a de ces effets-là; il trouble, dit-on, le sommeil.

Follenvie exits from the story once his role as go-between has ended, but the emotion evoked by his patronym has remained and once again it is *folle-envie* which troubles the stillness of the night. Whether the sexual activity of the last night is legitimate is not made explicit by the text, but the fact remains that the travellers' prurient appetites have been aroused—and satisfied—by the presence of Boule de suif.

Nor do the other women play a completely passive role. Even the nuns, whose position places them beyond sexuality, are involved. Maupassant's ingenuity in using a nun to weaken the prostitute's resistance must not be forgotten, and the elder nun's *emportement* is not unlike Boule de suif's own. In fact, a study of Maupassant's lexicon reveals the presence of a contiguous relationship between Boule

de suif and the nuns. For example, the prostitute's chubby fingers, "pareils à des chapelets de courtes saucisses" evoke both the literal *chapelets* of the two nuns and the *saucisson* upon which they lunch during the final stage of the journey. Moreover, the nuns are characterized as "de saintes filles habituées à toutes les soumissions", and are the first to obey the Prussian officer when he asks the voyagers to exit from the carriage upon their arrival in Tôtes. Only the epithet "saintes" apparently subverts the equation nuns = prostitutes, and one senses that, in the case of the elder nun at least, it is merely an accident of nature (the disfiguring smallpox) which made of her a "sainte fille en cornette" rather than a "fille" *tout court.* Her virtue is only habit-deep and when she surprises everyone by her unhoped-for complicity in the plot, Maupassant cleverly shifts from indirect dialogue to direct, thereby enabling his countess to address the nun as "ma sœur." More than a mere formula, these words strongly suggest that the nun has been accepted into the sisterhood of all women. Seen in this light, the "forbidden pleasure" represented by the nuns' first-ever taste of champagne during the celebration dinner must be accorded its full symbolic value.

Among the other women, it is clearly Madame Carré-Lamadon who bears the closest resemblance to Boule de suif, despite physical dissimilarities mirrored in the geometric connotations of the names by which they are most often known in the text (*Boule* de suif and *Carré*-Lamadon). Pretty and delicate, Madame Carré-Lamadon is much younger than her husband; the statement that she was "la consolation des officiers de bonne famille envoyés à Rouen en garnison" is deliberately suggestive, and the frequent references to her sexual fascination with the Prussian officer are not gratuitous. Once again, it is the jealous termagant Madame Loiseau to whom is given the role of making specific what is merely suggested elsewhere in the text. Speaking of "cette chipie", Madame Carré-Lamadon, she laments to her husband, "Tu sais, les femmes, quand ça en tient pour l'uniforme, qu'il soit Français ou bien Prussien, ça leur est, ma foi, bien égal. Si ce n'est pas une pitié, Seigneur Dieu!" In fact, even Madame Loiseau is not beyond imagining herself in the prostitute's place, and her statement that the Prussian officer would doubtless have preferred one of the three married women can only be regarded as wishful thinking.

The countess' virtue is equally questionable. She is not of noble birth and it is above all her sexuality ("elle [. . .] passait même pour avoir été aimée d'un des fils de Louis-Philippe'') which has won for her the respect of her adoptive class. Her duplicity is underlined often and her own role in the seduction of the prostitute is a major one, since it is she who brings the elder nun into the plot.

Only the younger nun does not participate actively in the alliance against Boule de suif, although her silence must be understood as compliance with the efforts of the other women. Among the male travellers, the prostitute's ostracization on sexual grounds is mirrored by Cornudet's politico-economic isolation, as Sullivan has suggested. Just as the women are sisters in their supposed ''virtue'', the men draw together against Cornudet, ''frères par l'argent.'' In actual fact, however, the distance which separates the moneyed males from Cornudet is travelled as quickly as that separating the ''virtuous'' women from the prostitute. Cornudet has inherited a large sum of money from his bourgeois father. Unlike the other bourgeois, however, he was not imbued with the bourgeois ethic. Rather than invest his money to increase his wealth, he had spent it; rather than work, he had played. Now a ''have not'', he is associated with the prostitute who is by definition *déclassée*. Unlike her, however, he is untrue to himself, and his passive role in the collaboration (he does nothing to alert Boule de suif to the plot and only expresses his dismay after it has succeeded) makes a mockery of the ideals embodied in his loudly proclaimed Republicanism. In his case, too, liberty, equality and fraternity have sold out to egotism. As eager as the others to reach Le Havre, he has sacrificed Boule de suif just as surely as they have. For him, too, the prostitute has a *valeur marchande*. That her value in his eyes is sexual rather than material is of little importance, for the result is the same: not only does he fail to defend her against the collaborators, but he shows no pity for her when the voyage resumes, his sense of fraternity for this unfortunate war victim being too weak to persuade him to share his lunch with her. Equally absent from Cornudet's moral makeup are sentiments of equality. The social superiority displayed by the Carré-Lamadons and the Brévilles is matched by Cornudet's intellectually superior attitude. Apart from singing the Marseillaise, smoking his pipe and drinking beer, his activity in the story is very nearly confined to approving or disapproving the opinions of others. Furthermore, although his flight from Rouen, like Boule de suif's, can be justified (having had trees felled, traps set, holes dug around Rouen in order to retard the Enemy's invasion of that city, he is now going to organize similar defensive activi-

ties around Le Havre), Cornudet is above all characterized by his refusal to confront the Enemy. When the news of the Prussians' approach reached Rouen, ''il s'était vivement replié vers la ville''; when the other male travellers ask him to accompany them to the Prussian's chambers where they hope to learn the cause of their detention (hardly a compromising mission), he refuses, proudly declaring that ''il entendait n'avoir jamais aucun rapport avec les Allemands.'' This fear of confrontation masquerading as pride is in stark opposition to Boule de suif's humility and courage. Cornudet, with his knowing smiles and political aphorisms, is a man of words, not of action, and his Republican reputation has been established largely in cafés. It is hardly surprising, then, that his pipe enjoys among his followers ''d'une considération presque égale à la sienne'' or that he himself has difficulty in distinguishing between his two passions, ''le Pale-Ale et la Révolution.''

The thinly veiled sensuality with which Cornudet contemplates his beer, his extreme physical enjoyment of his pipe which is ''admirablement culottée [. . .] parfumée, recourbée, luisante, familière à sa main'' are but variants upon what one might refer to as the nutritional code, a lexical and metaphoric network which threads its way into every corner of the text and which, as Bourneau has pointed out, is closely affiliated with the sexual.

The nutritional code is present at all levels of the text. The alimentary uses of animal fat are well-known, and Boule de suif is the first to be assimilated to the nutritive, both literally and metaphorically:

> Petite, ronde de partout, *grasse à lard*, avec des doigts bouffis, étranglés aux phalanges, pareils à des chapelets de courtes *saucisses* [. . .] elle restait cependant *appétissante* et courue, tant sa *fraîcheur* faisait plaisir à voir. [. . .] Sa figure était *une pomme rouge* [. . .] (italics mine)

If the metaphorical alliance of the sexual and culinary can be considered a literary commonplace, as James Brown has shown, Maupassant's exploitation of the theme is far from hackneyed, thanks to the constant *va-et-vient* between the literal and the figurative. As a prostitute Boule de suif is to be bought and consumed, much as one would buy a cutlet from a butcher shop. Moreover, it is clear that her bourgeois travelling companions are voracious consumers, and Maupassant's description of the contagious yawning which is transmitted from one to another places the emphasis, not upon the various ''styles'' of yawns dictated by etiquette and social class, but rather upon the common ''trou béant d'où sortait une vapeur.'' The intensity of their hunger darkening their moods, the travellers react with shock when Loiseau jestingly proposes to do as the popular song says and to eat ''le plus gras des voyageurs.'' The allusion to Boule de suif is direct and is followed almost immediately in the text by the harlot's sudden resolution to take out her basket of provisions. That it had been hidden under the bench, ''sous ses jupons'' establishes a blatant link with the sexual and Loiseau's earlier stares at the prostitute are matched now by his lascivious ogling of the chicken. The first to accept Boule de suif's offer of food, he is followed by the two nuns, then by Cornudet, finally by the more ''distinguished'' company, but only after Madame Carré-Lamadon has fainted from hunger. The rapidity with which the travellers empty the strumpet's basket, and the savagery of their appetites are suggestive of a cannibalistic carnage, the victim of which is Boule de suif herself: ''Les bouches s'ouvraient et se fermaient sans cesse, avalaient, mastiquaient, engloutissaient férocement.'' While part of the savagery of this scene may be explained by Maupassant's desire to remain faithful to the tenets of Naturalism, we can also see in it a scarcely veiled Darwinism which is verbalized later in the tale by the count himself: ''Il ne faut jamais résister aux gens qui sont les plus forts.'' Indeed, the sacrificial nature of Boule de suif's generosity and the humility with which she offers to share her food are thrown into relief by the hubristic condescension of the others whose reluctance to sully themselves by accepting the harlot's food is finally overcome by the anguish of their hunger.

In Tôtes (which suggests ''tôt'' and ''toast'', both derivatives of the Latin *tostus,* meaning ''grilled'' or ''cooked'') the metaphorical union of the sexual with the nutritional is again underlined by the fact that each of the Prussian officer's three ''invitations'' to the prostitute is extended, through the intermediary of the aptly named Follenvie, at dinnertime. The fifth dinner, which we have characterized as a celebration dinner, is, as we have seen, consumed in the absence of Boule de suif who is otherwise engaged upstairs, this time quite literally sacrificing herself for the good of her compatriots. But unlike the previous nutritional sacrifice, this giving of herself had not been spontaneous; rather it had been wrenched from her through a carefully planned and skilfully executed verbal aggression. The scenario of the conspiracy had been sketched the previous day while Boule de suif attended a baptism. Thus, while the prostitute, ostensibly the

symbol of vice, prayed, the married couples, apparent bastions of all that is proper and ''moral'', plotted against her, the women in particular deriving vicarious pleasure from their planning. Maupassant's choice of a culinary metaphor to describe their activity is not unexpected:

> Un étranger n'aurait rien compris tant les précautions du langage étaient observées. Mais la légre tranche de pudeur dont est bardée route femme du monde ne recouvrant que la surface, elles s'épanouissaient dans cette aventure polissonne, s'amusaient follement au fond, se sentant dans leur élément, tripotant de l'amour avec la sensualité d'un cuisinier gourmand qui prépare le souper d'un autre.

Assimilated at once to the food itself and to the gluttonous cook, it is these women who, beneath their veneer of sophistication and righteousness, are the true *marchandes d'amour.*

The attack is mounted at lunchtime and, given renewed vigour by the nun's timely intervention, the attempts at persuasion continue through the evening meal as well. Here too, the concomitance of these two activities is quite deliberate, and such temporal indications as ''Aussitôt à table, on commença les approches'' or ''Aussitôt le repas terminé on remonta bien vite dens les chambres [. . .]'' are more than merely referential. The warmth, the sense of community and *bien-être* afforded by a meal are guarantors of vulnerability as well as being evocative, throughout Maupassant's work, of that other physical pleasure which is the prostitute's special fare. Boule de suif's hypocritical travelling companions choose their moments as carefully as they choose their words.

The final betrayal of Boule de suif, the arrogance which the bourgeois display as they continue their journey, and their insensitivity and egoism in eating in her presence and without offering her even their leftovers (the nuns wrap up their remaining sausage after having eaten their fill) once again evoke the culinary. The fact that the prostitute is identified with animal fat by her nickname, and that all but one of the travellers lunch on meats (suggestive of Boule de suif's role by the nouns used to characterize them: *morceau, gibier,* etc.) reinforces the notion of self-sacrifice. Cornudet, whose meatless repast consists of eggs and bread, is the only one who has not enjoyed a ''forbidden pleasure'' at Boule de suif's expense.

This discussion of the nutritional code would be incomplete were we to fail to evoke the most arresting metaphor of all, that of the pigeons pecking at the horses' steaming excrement in the final scene at Tôtes. The passage deserves to be quoted in its entirety:

> La diligence, attelée enfin, attendait devant la porte, tandis qu'une armée de pigeons blancs, rengorgés dans leurs plumes épaisses, avec un œil rose, taché, au milieu, d'un point noir, se promenaient gravement entre les jambes des six chevaux, et cherchaient leur vie dans le crottin fumant qu'ils éparpillaient.

The solemnity and decorum with which the coprophagic pigeons feed upon the horses' dung is clearly symbolic of the arrogance and outward "dignity" with which the travellers had committed the most shameful and undignified of betrayals. The double evocation of the digestive in this passage (the pigeons ingesting what is in fact the residue—one is tempted to say "end-product"—of the alimentary process) in addition to suggesting the repulsive nature of the bourgeois' treason and collaboration with the Enemy, mirrors the circular movement of the narrative itself and subverts the notion of a plot built upon the horizontal line of a journey. Many critics have remarked upon the symmetry of the last carriage scene and the first: it does indeed close the circle, and such oxymoronic expressions as "voyageurs immobiles", "gredins honnêtes" suggest the paradox implicit in the text itself. Despite the geographic distance covered, these bourgeois have not budged from their stance of hypocritical complacency. With the exception of their physical mobility (which had been effected by the horses and, not coincidentally, by Boule de suif who might be likened to the "pauvre cheval qui ne venait pas volontiers"), the only movement they had ever known had been the vertical movement of their climb through society. It is not by chance that this movement, too, had been made possible by the sacrifice of the humble.

Finally, the almost obsessive identification, in Maupassant's work, of the sexual with the excretory, finds its echo in this passage, and the repulsion which the travellers display towards Boule de suif on the last lap of the journey indicates clearly that they no longer see in her a saviour, a *mère nourricière,* but rather a whore who, like the horses' excretions, represents "[un] contact impur" from which they must keep their distance, "comme si elle eût apporté une infection dans ses jupes."

In addition to its frequent intersections with the sexual, the nutritional code is closely associated with the military. The first and most obvious meeting takes place at the semantic level of the plot. The Rouen bourgeois lodge and nourish the occupying army, affecting alienation and animosity in the street while displaying an obliging hospitality and even a certain affection for the soldiers in the privacy of their own homes:

> On se disait enfin, raison suprême tirée de l'urbanité française, qu'il demeurait bien permis d'être poli dans son intérieur pourvu qu'on ne se montrât pas familier en public, avec le soldat étranger.

The bourgeois' hypocrisy (represented by the interior-exterior opposition) stems both from their materialism (they would perhaps be given fewer soldiers to feed if they caused no trouble) and from their cowardice ("pourquoi blesser quelqu'un dont on dépendait tout à fait?"). Such egotistical logic brought to the defence of what is in fact collaboration with the Enemy stands in direct contrast to the passionate patriotism of the lower classes, farmers, prostitutes, *petites gens* of all sorts whose silent nocturnal murders of Prussian soldiers endanger their lives without bringing them fame or glory: "Car la haine de l'Etranger arme toujours quelques Intrépides prêts à mourir pour une Idée." It is not these fearless idealists, true heroes of the war, who are responsible for France's defeat, but rather the bourgeois whose economic clout has placed them in positions of military as well as social leadership. And what about this formidable enemy, the Prussian? The modest citizens of Tôtes, who, unlike the wealthy *Rouennais,* are not versed in the art of hypocrisy, make no secret of their relationship with the Enemy, and the latter can be seen scrubbing floors, peeling potatoes, caring for babies, splitting wood:

> [. . .] et les grosses paysannes dont les hommes étaient à "l'armée de la guerre", indiquaient par signes à leurs *vainqueurs obéissants* [italics mine] le travail qu'il fallait entreprendre [. . .] un d'eux même lavait le linge de son hôtesse, une aïeule toute impotente.

That these plump provincial women have succeeded in domesticating the occupying soldiers can only be seen as a further indictment of the "bourgeois émasculés." Throughout Maupassant's war stories, Prussian officers are portrayed as barbaric, destructive, insensitive and sadistic ("Mademoiselle Fifi", "Deux Amis", "Un Duel") but the foot soldiers are more often than not described as merely naïve, even stupid, *l'air bon enfant* ("Saint Antoine", "L'Aventure de Walter Schnaffs", "La mère Sauvage"). France's ignominious defeat by these unworthy opponents becomes thus all the more difficult to accept and, notwithstanding the truism advanced by the old sexton of "Boule de suif" ("c'est les grands qui font la guerre"), the outcome of this war was made possible by complicity at all levels. The exemplary value of Boule de suif's resistance is lost upon her bourgeois travelling companions who are incapable of any action which would jeopardize their own material welfare. In their betrayal of the prostitute, they are comparable to the bourgeois who quietly nourish the occupying soldiers: indeed, they "feed" Boule de suif to the Prussian in exchange for their own freedom. With their help, he realizes a sexual invasion of the unwilling prostitute which is but a metaphor for his army's military invasion of France. Little wonder, then, that the vocabulary of their conspiracy is borrowed from the arsenal of military terminology:

> On prépara longuement le blocus, comme pour une forteresse investie. Chacun convint du rôle qu'il jouerait, des arguments dont il s'appuierait, des manoeuvres qu'il devrait exécuter. On régla le plan des attaques, les ruses à employer, et les surprises de l'assaut, pour forcer cette citadelle vivante à recevoir l'ennemi dans la place.

Seen as a mirror-perfect image of France herself, *la belle, la douce France,* humiliated and betrayed by her very own people, those whom she had succoured and nourished, Boule de suif acquires a tragic grandeur. In the story's final scene, it is not a mere prostitute who sobs; rather, in the words of Armand Lanoux, "c'est la France qui est humiliée, qui pleure et se révolte." In the wake of the Franco-Prussian war, Frenchmen could find no justification for their ignominious losses. It was France itself which had so confidently declared war, convinced of the invincibility of its army, the French bourgeois who had made the occupation so effortless for the Enemy, the French Republicans who had needlessly prolonged the war after the defeat of the Empire, when Prussia's final victory seemed to all but a reckless few a foregone conclusion, the French who, in the end, turned against their own compatriots in one of the bloodiest Civil wars in French history, the war against the Paris Communards. The disarray and unpreparedness of the French army is attested to by historians as is the disgraceful ease of the invasion and occupation of Rouen. Maupassant's version of the retreat is further corroborated by an eye witness account of the events which took place in Rouen on 4 and 5 December 1870, as described in a letter written by a well-known Rouen citizen, Dr Hellis. Besides confirming the precision of detail which characterizes Maupassant's narrative, Hellis' letter sheds a new light on the story as political allegory in its revelation of the occurrences which preceded the army's retreat:

> Dimanche 4 décembre MM. de la Rouge firent une démonstration contre l'hôtel de ville; tout étant en désarroi, ils trouvèrent des armes et saccagèrent l'intérieur, Ils se promirent [. . .] de proclamer la république rouge avec l'établissement de la commune comme à Lyon. [. . .] Le lendemain, les frères et amis se rendent à la place Saint-Ouen pour achever leur ouvrage quand tout à coup la panique s'empare de tous. Les Prussiens, les Prussiens! A ce mot nos braves s'enfuient jusqu'au dernier et la place fut entièrement vide. J'étais là [. . .] j'ai vu arriver nos vainqueurs. Sans tambours ni musique, au pas, graves, silencieux, comme stupéfaits d'un succès aussi inespéré [. . .].

Hellis' legitimistic prejudices are obvious here; they even lead him, later in the letter, to write almost affectionately of the Prussians whom he credits with having saved Rouen from the revolutionaries! One would be hard put to find a more apt illustration of the bourgeois attitude which Maupassant so mercilessly ridiculed in "Boule de suif." But the real interest of this letter lies in the documentary proof which it offers of the Revolutionaries' attempted takeover of Rouen prior to the Enemy's invasion. Seen in the perspective of these occurrences, Cornudet's attempted seduction of Boule de suif acquires symbolic value, clearly evocative of the Revolutionaries' interrupted looting of the town hall. For Cornudet, Boule de suif was *la gueuse Marianne,* and his desire for her was as great as his desire for the establishment of the Republic, identified in his mind (and in the minds of all of Gambetta's followers) with a French victory over the Prussians. The Prussian officer's triumph over Boule de suif thus comes to symbolize the humiliating Prussian victory over France. It should be remembered too that Boule de suif, as a *bonapartiste,* represents the Empire; by not allowing Cornudet to possess her, she was resisting the Republic. As for the other characters, all had prospered under the reign of Napoleon III, and the Second Empire saw, for a time at least, the alliance of two conservative forces, the bourgeoisie and the Church. Seen in this light, the nun's collaboration is not unexpected. It is, finally, with a stroke of malicious irony that Maupassant paints even his supposed aristocrats the same colour as the bourgeois, not only because of their mercenary attitudes, but also by specifying that their nobility had been purchased. The historical *justesse* of this phenomenon is well-known, but Maupassant cannot resist adding a sexual dimension to his account of the Brévilles' aristocratic origins. The count Bréville has Henri IV to thank for conferring upon his ancestors their nobility: "Henri IV [. . .] suivant une légende glorieuse pour la famille, avait rendu grosse une dame de Bréville, dont le mari, pour ce fait, était devenu comte et gouverneur de province.'' The count's nobility thus results directly from a royal indemnity to a cuckold! To further mock this ignoble pair, Maupassant asserts that the countess' ''nobility'' is acquired at least partly through her sexual activities.

As morally dissolute as the more distinguished company, but without their overlay of elegance, Loiseau and his wife become the *porte-parole* of the group, verbalizing what the others dare not express. The wine merchant who, not surprisingly, lives on the Rue du *Pont,* is thus the first to bridge the social gap and to open the dialogue with the prostitute, and the first to accept her offering of food. It is he, moreover, who makes it possible for the others to accept her food without suffering a loss of dignity in the process. (''Et, parbleu, duns dcs cas pareils tout le monde est frère et doit s'aider. Allons, mesdames, pas de cérémonie: acceptez, que diable!'') The count, finally, is persuaded to speak for the foursome (the Brévilles and the Carré-Lamadons) and his acceptance, executed with a curious mixture of condescension and genteel humility, unseals the mouths of his starving companions. The historical event to which Maupassant alludes in describing the difficulty and sudden resolve of the count's decision to accept is highly significant: ''Le premier pus seul coûtait. Une lois le Rubicon passé on s'en donna carrément.'' Our appreciation of Maupassant's punning (''carrément'') should not blind us to the *sérieux* of the classical allusion. Caesar's crossing from ancient Gaul back into Rome despite the order of the Roman Senate carried with it the notion of betrayal. In a similar way, this sharing of Boule de suif's abundant provisions is the first step in the bourgeois' betrayal of the prostitute and, by metaphorical extension, of France.

Source: Mary Donaldson-Evans, ''The Decline and Fall of Elisabeth Rousset: Text and Context in Maupassant's 'Boule de suife,''' in *Australian Journal of French Studies,* Vol. XVIII, No. 1, January–April 1981, pp. 16–34.

Albert H. Wallace

In the following essay excerpt, Wallace argues that Maupassant's admiration and love for women and disdain for men is a common theme in Maupassant's works.

I The Growth of a Favoring Prejudice

Maupassant was not showing us a Romantic ''femme fatale'' when he repeatedly told tales in which the woman gained ascendancy over the man.

His admiration for woman grew out of personal contact and observation, not from fear inspired by a superstitious cult. Among the strangely few men who enjoyed Maupassant's unstinting admiration, most had chosen celibacy and so were relatively safe from acts of weakness that so often characterize a husband's behavior and which would have lowered them in his esteem. Flaubert, of course, was so far in the vanguard of this select few as to be the god of the microcosm.

To Maupassant, marriage was a form of servitude which the female refused to accept because she recognized it as such, and to which the male submitted while deluding himself with the notion that he was free, the master. The calm demeanor and unflinching resolve of Maupassant's mother inspired early his admiration for woman and caused him to question the myth of male superiority. Madame de Maupassant's influence upon her son can never be accurately evaluated, for the more one ponders his work the more one is struck with her presence in the character of heroine after heroine. Far more accurate assessments can be made of the influence of Maupassant's father in shaping the son's prejudicial view of husbands as self-centered weaklings who deserved cuckolding, and of the role his disappointment in his father had in determining him to seek in Flaubert a father who was not weak or unworthy of the charge.

Paradoxically, we find Maupassant writing, near the end of his days, in favor of marriage. The cruel spark of loneliness ignited this twilight mania in a man who had spent most of his career satirizing or openly denouncing the institution. Celibacy confirmed the strange and haunting terror that was typical of Maupassant's bouts with insanity. He speaks of his terror of loneliness in a letter to his mother: ''I fear the arriving wintcr, I fccl alone, and my long, solitary evenings are sometimes terrible. Often when I'm alone seated at my desk with my lamp burning sadly before me, I experience such complete moments of distress that I no longer know where to turn'' IV, cxxvii.

It should be stated that Maupassant did not always write with the aim of inciting sympathy for the married woman's plight or of excusing her extramarital affairs. *Une Famille* typifies a number of stories whose aim is clearly to decry how marriage destroys friendship between old male cronies and to express his repugnance at how the wife is always certain to drag her husband down to her

> "Philogyny is not merely a tone in Maupassant, it is the basic trait of his attitude concerning the human species."

level. However, these stories, with their strange male prejudice, lack the power of those which speak with admiration of woman. What vitality they have results from a sudden and ephemeral anger, and not from the slowly nurtured conviction that lends the moving power and lasting vitality to his writings which praise woman.

II War Demonstrates Woman's Superior Courage

The magnificent courage and nobility of woman in time of war and defeat inspired what many consider to be his greatest story, *Boule de Suif.* War was a fact of Maupassant's life. This makes his praise of woman's behavior as contrasted to the less admirable, often even cowardly behavior, of her counterpart the more striking. But it does not seem out of character to the one who has opened his eyes to the apparent philogyny in his other works. Philogyny is not merely a tone in Maupassant, it is the basic trait of his attitude concerning the human species.

The prostitute Rachel, in *Mademoiselle Fifi,* behaves in the way that epitomized for Maupassant the *effective* disdain of the conquered. Women can deal with a derisive effectiveness above man's capacities, Maupassant believes, because their long-suffering experience as prisoners of male conventions has taught them the mastery of derision. "You think you're raping the women of France," sneers the proud Rachel to the sadistic Mlle Fifi (Wilhelm d'Eyrik), "As for me! Me! I'm not a woman, *I* am a whore, that's indeed all the Prussians need or deserve" X, 23. Her stabbing of him and the ringing of the bells which had remained silent in the face of his ironic threats to have the townsmen's blood or be the cause of their ringing again are almost anticlimatic, following as they do in the wake of her success in making the Prussian feel the littleness ascribed to him and his kind by those he had conquered but could not break.

The Comtesse de Bremontal's sensitivity, in the unfinished *L'Angelus,* her love of poetry and her melancholy surroundings are all reminiscent of Laure de Maupassant. Abandoned too by a husband whose seignorial, Norman bravado presents to his whimsical mind the going off to serve as a higher calling than remaining with his pregnant, defenseless wife, the Countess behaves with disdainful composure in the face of threats by the Prussian officer who has taken over her house. So effective is her contempt that the Prussian suffers the ignominy fatal to all conquerors' pride. Maupassant had great plans for this novel to be entitled *L'Angelus.* It was to be his masterpiece in the genre. His dedication to the project and the magnitude of the idea he had in mind can be guessed at from notes sketching what was to follow the events described above: the Countess' boy child would be born on Christmas a cripple in one of the chateau's outbuildings, his disfiguration the result of his mother's having been brutalized by the Prussian. The religious sources are perhaps a little too obvious, but it must be kept in mind that the story came to him as something that had to be written only when he was already hopelessly in the grip of his tragic malady. No one can say what turn he might have given the theme had he been in good health.

The tragic fate of the lovely Irma of *Le Lit 29* has none of the mawkish sentimentality of so many stories of its kind. While showing us how war so tragically truncates those seemingly perfect love affairs, Maupassant demonstrates how it is the male's weakness and imperfections that are really responsible for their failure. The lady killer, Captain Epivent, was happy to rattle his medals truculently against an enemy who had had the gall to rape his woman and then take her life, and to hurl threats toward Germany in case of any future incursion. But when he found that his beautiful former mistress was alive and had syphilis, it was another matter; for in order to protect the noble image of himself he sought to foster he would have to go through the troublesome formality of paying her a solicitous visit. The visit began on an ironic note which demonstrated clearly the selfless contrast of her love for him: she expressed pride in his medals and avoided complaining about her own wretched condition. Only when he pressed her did she reveal the patriotism that had prompted her to refuse treatments for the infection a Prussian had brought her: she had taken it upon herself to spread the infection amongst the hated army of occupation, using her beauty as a lure. It was what she could do to avenge her country's lost pride. She had known she would end up here, but it had been worth it. "And I also infected all of them, all, every single one, the most I was able" XXIX, 82. The Captain left with the intention of never returning. But he could not play the hero before the people. Though he ignored her letter of entreaty, he had to go to save face when the hospital chaplain came after him.

Maupassant's description of her contempt for her former lover removes any doubts as to his dedication to emphasizing the sharp contrast between the pusillanimity of the male with his illusory strength, and the strong courage of the female with her alleged frailties. Irma's choice of a name for the man she was dismissing was forged in the mind of a creator burning with a sense of outrage at men blinded to the truth by their stubborn, ego-inspired antifeminism. "get away from me, *capon*! More than you, yes, I killed more of them than you, more than you" (italics mine) XXIX, 88. She died the following day.

Berthine of *Les Prisonniers* is a healthy peasant girl whose vengeance against the invaders is blunt, unsophisticated, and as final as a wily Norman peasant's business transactions. She allows them in her house, tricks them into her basement from which escape is impossible, and then convinces them that surrendering to the local constabulary, ignominious though it may be, is the wisest choice for them. Evidence that Maupassant did not deem a male capable of this sort of clear design and execution is the fact that he presents an exceedingly satirical and damaging picture of the ostentatious, bungling militia commander who joyfully accepts total credit for the capture.

One sees the same admiration for the concise manner in which women exact their vengeance against the enemy in the story about the madwoman— insane with grief because she had befriended the Prussians, being an innocent in politics, until she had learned their army had killed her son—and how she beguiled her Prussian "guests" into affixing their signatures to a document before incinerating them in her house as they slept soundly, sure of her friendship. She wanted their signatures as proof to their loved ones that they were dead and that *she* and *she alone* had been responsible for their deaths. Her steady dedication to her purpose is the quality with which Maupassant often endowed his women: it is consistent with his depiction of woman as uniquely capable of the kind of discipline necessary to overcome the greatest obstacles.

III Boule de Suif

The high place *Boule de Suif* occupies in French literature is merited, for it presents with almost unparalleled power woman's courage and resolve to survive defeat and personal degradation. This story provides the clearest and most moving presentation of Maupassant's admiration for female strength in times of dire disillusionment. Defeat breaks the souls of most of the men it tries. And even those strong survivors of the initial shock, upon viewing the tragic shambles of their fellow beings' broken spirit, often knuckle under to despair. The very few who can look upon defeat and its waste and still remain whole are the real heroes who cause others to pick up their pride and begin again. A person familiar with Maupassant's life and work will know why he chose a prostitute for this almost superhuman accomplishment. But one must see his treatment of woman in the proper light and must be familiar with every line he wrote about her to reconcile his ambivalence regarding woman as a general class, for the question continually arises as to how he could have set a course in his own life which seemed oriented upon degrading her. We must conclude that the women he met in the bordello he found to be the consummation of all the qualities he considered important and admirable: we have Boule de Suif as evidence. It is also quite evident that choosing a prostitute was the best way for Maupassant to continue his effective needling of society's pride in its conventions, in particular the ones that tended to assign a priori the virtues of acting heroically to the male and faintheartedness and ineffectual sentimentality to the female. And even more pointedly he could mock the conventional stigmatizing of prostitutes as socially destructive and morally inferior. The lovely figure we see emerging from the wretched world that spawned, abused, and reviled her, even giving her the derisive name, Boule de Suif, to mock her, is the brainchild of a loving and admiring creator, whose philogyny is evident.

Maupassant knew that the best milieu in which to test individual greatness was a world disillusioned with itself—a world of defeat where wound-licking is often the last vestige of struggle. Boule de Suif comes upon a scene where people are more concerned with adapting to defeat and calling it by another name than with refusing to be servile. It is a world where her refusal to accept the defeat the others took for granted both sets her apart from the common herd and brings her into conflict with it. She would not have been able to utter their eloquent idealistic cliches, but she possessed idealism and the courage to pursue it. Maupassant wastes no time in stamping her with the mark of superiority. The coach has scarcely begun its journey before his concise artistry has revealed to us that the other passengers, and especially the women with their conventional morality leading at best to the delusion of the rectitude of their ambitions for peace and material prosperity, are indeed impoverished human spirits with whom this brave, engaging prostitute contrasts sharply. The author thus wins our esteem early and causes us to be more wary of the others.

Loiseau, the wine merchant, spouts the kind of cliches typical of the articulate among the society with which Maupassant found himself at loggerheads. His pronouncement which removes the other women's hypocritical compunction against accepting food from a prostitute is the type of thing one finds in Flaubert's *Dictionnaire des idees recues.* And Boule de Suif's ignorance of their absurd cliches sets her above them in our minds. Her fellow passengers are shown from the beginning to be people with nothing for the desperate times but talk. Boule de Suif would never articulate the accepted idea that ''in such cases all men are brothers and should aid one another,'' but she would so act. Maupassant with this brief incident has shown us the larger meaning of his story, and how the meaning of his story transcends the boundaries in which he had given it light. He could not have been more effective in drawing the line between the others and Boule de Suif. The latter returns what she takes from life and more, and in so doing she is neither a conventional prostitute nor a conventional human being; she is a woman and a superior human being.

Later, at the inn, in the scene in which the other traveling companions quarrel over what they think would be the right thing for Boule de Suif to do, the latter herself has figuratively ascended to an empyrean where the pettiness of her erstwhile companions is not permitted to trouble her deliberations upon her course. Maupassant shows considerable artistry in the symbology of having Boule de Suif upstairs in the inn, separated from the others physically by some *small* distance, while the distance of her spiritual separation is so vast, as vast as the distance between positive and negative. With the use of this symbol the author is able to reemphasize what he is saying with the whole story. The terrible pettiness of rationalizing to which we all resort brands itself upon our minds as they deliberate: ''Since that's what the slut's trade is, to do that with

any man, I find she has no right to refuse one anymore than another'' IV, 56–57.

Maupassant makes us see the real question that we all must face with such startling clarity that we know we are in the presence of a master. Through Boule de Suif's unerring understanding of what it means to give herself to the enemy, we come to understand what it means for us to give ourselves to the enemy. And, moreover, we learn that most people in giving themselves to everything give themselves to nothing and that the enemy will settle for nothing but the greatest individual as his price. Maupassant, like us all, mourned in the face of the realization that so often the sacrifice of the greatest only causes those who benefit from the selfless act to respond by a show of their utter unworthiness. He chose a woman to show us his admiration for the unique strength of the great. And as if to dismiss the male race from consideration for such a role, he depicts the self-anointed revolutionary and the only one of the other travelers who hesitates to throw Boule de Suif to the wolves, as incapable of action when it counted. He talks: ''I'm telling you all, you've just done an infamous thing!'' IV, 69. And the next day Cornudet, the revolutionary, eats with the others from whom only inefficacious words had ever separated him and continues deluding himself by singing the ''Marseillaise.'' Maupassant thereby is able to register again bitter disappointment and cynicism regarding the behavior in general of his countrymen. If *Boule de Suif* is truly Maupassant's masterpiece, it owes the honor to an insistent admiration for woman which receives its finest artistic expression and compression in the story. The theme is not new, nor does it end here. Philogyny is omnipresent in his writing.

IV The Image of Laure de Maupassant

Madame de Maupassant's fear that the very genius of which she was so proud would be the cause of an ever-widening gulf between her and her son, though it might have proven well founded, need not have tormented her. In Maupassant's creative output alone, her influence is apparent, more apparent than it was to either mother or son. She perhaps could not see her success for the troubling fantasies her mind served up to her as she watched him move restlessly about Europe and Africa and as she watched him become more and more a recluse because of his art and his illness. The novels especially provide us with portraits of women who closely resemble Laure de Maupassant. The problems they face and their superiority in dealing with them seem to have been inspired by his observations of his mother's life.

In *Notre Coeur* we see a bitter rendering of a situation which Maupassant must have viewed as but a slightly exaggerated version of one his mother had faced. He speaks of the heroine, Michele de Burne: "Married to a well-mannered but worthless man, one of those domestic tyrants, before whom everything had to give, to bend, she at first had been wretched" XII, 7. Like Laure de Maupassant, Madame de Burne was not the kind of woman who would permit herself to become a slave to the shallow ambitions and vanity of an inferior husband. The difference in the way Maupassant causes Madame de Burne to work out her problem is the fictional aspect; the forces that aggravate the problem, a complacent and indifferent husband and a social milieu bent upon justifying rules to make the superior accept what the mediocrity takes for good remain the same. The story is told with varying emphasis in the other Maupassant novels. Each time the solution is different. We see Maupassant following in the footsteps of his teacher, Flaubert, in undertaking a study of the series of environmental forces that encircle a kind of woman who, rather than surrender her own ideas of her happiness and destiny, will struggle dramatically if inefficaciously. Maupassant's heroines resemble Emma Bovary because they are placed in identical situations, not because of the way they deal with them. That they do deal with them, either through a stoic acceptance of fact or by establishing themselves as mistresses of their social fate, shows how they are different from Flaubert's heroine.

When death removed Madame de Burne's primary problem, she vowed never again to compromise herself in marriage. But she needed men. She needed to dominate them and succeeded in doing so. Then Andre Mariolle (whose determination not to be compromised by love was quite as strong as hers) came into her life. A paltry investment of her emotions shattered his resolve to remain independent. This easy conquest resulted from the Maupassantian conviction that the male is the weaker of the sexes when it comes to achieving the destiny he has set for himself. Mariolle was a nonwriting talker about writing. Maupassant's male characters were more frequently talkers than doers. But his females were more likely to be doers, despite the fact that the author had his character, the novelist Gaston de Lamarthe (whom some have seen as Maupassant himself), tell the weak Mariolle: "Look, my dear fellow, woman was created and came into

the world for two things, which alone can cause her true, her great, her excellent qualities to bloom: love and childbearing" XII, 144. Maupassant was fond of dropping this line with acquaintances who took it as evidence of a misogynism which does not appear justified considering all of the evidence to the contrary. Lamarthe is probably closer to expressing his creator's conviction when he argues that the Realist-Naturalist novelist in suppressing the poetic quality of existence and dealing only with life's grim realities is to blame for woman's turning upon her weaker counterpart: "Nowadays, my dear sir, there's no longer any love in books, nor any love in life. You were the ones who invented the ideal, they [the women] believed in your inventions. Now you're only exponents of precise realities, and following you they have begun to believe in the vulgarity of everything" XII, 146. How strongly this suggests Maupassant's great depth of understanding of both *Madame Bovary* and of the Realist-Naturalist movement in literature! Mariolle's failure to reach any of the admirable goals he had set for himself is a presaging of his surrendering of all of his male prerogatives. Maupassant's hatred for inadequacies in the male flows into the book with as much force as his admiration for the female's ability to turn the tables on an environment fostering the conventions that threaten her individuality. This dual emphasis is one of the book's weaknesses. The latter half of the book is crowded with analyses of Mariolle which make it more and more apparent that such a weak prize is hardly worthy of Madame de Burne's efforts and that any dramatic reversal in his conduct is unlikely. Maupassant gives us a bit of autobiography in reverse in the character of Mariolle. Speaking of his hurt he says: "The arts having tempted him, he did not discover sufficient courage to give himself entirely to any one of them, nor the persevering obstinacy necessary to triumph in it" XII, 205. Are we to assume, then, that the author's success in the arts being the opposite to his hero's failure, his success with women was just as clearly the opposite? Probably so. But that scarcely is sufficient to justify our admiration for the novel. Mariolle's algolagnic relationship with a serving girl whom he called upon to read to him every night from *Manon Lescaut* evidences the strange, almost maniacal proclivity Maupassant developed in later years for debasing the male. He exaggerates to the boring degree. He had already done an excellent job of reducing man to a low state in his treatments of cuckoldry. Perhaps in so doing he had spent his artistic capacities to deal with the subject.

Source: Albert H. Wallace, ''Chapter 3: Maupassant's Women: His Mother and His Heroines,'' in *Guy de Maupassant,* Twayne's World Authors Series, Twayne Publishers, 1973.

Anonymous

In the following essay, the critic argues that de Maupassant's writing is dazzling but lacks imagination.

De Maupassant was, of course, a born writer. Observe, *writer.* No one ever said what he wanted to say with a nicer exactitude or a more certain effectiveness than did de Maupassant. The sentence was a marvellous tool in his hands. But, having admitted that, one has the right to inquire: what did he want to say? What of importance had he seen? We cannot believe, for ourselves, that de Maupassant's imagination and insight were of the first order, or even of the second order. His philosophy was a Parisian cynicism. His spirit was happy in that world of sense which the greatest writers have either ignored or assumed. Animalism is good, but it is not the best. There are writers who might have taken a story of de Maupassant's and, using it for a mere concrete foundation, might have built upon it the more delicate fabric of the essential story—the intimate spiritual drama which he had either missed or, in the ruthlessness of his animalism, disdained.

The main secret of de Maupassant's mere vogue is that he dazzles. As a cyclist at night, he rides down the highway with Dexterity flashing ahead of him like an acetylene lamp. In that illumination you can perceive no defects: you can only wonder. De Maupassant will not survive translation. Although translation may retain every ingenuity of construction, the last finish, the ultimate polish, is lost in it. The magic dazzle fades. You wake as if from enchantment. *Boule de Suif* in English (good English, too) is a shock. The superficiality, the trickery of it, stand forth ashamed and convicted. . . .

Boule de Suif is deficient, not only in fine observation, but in imagination. To us, in this English version, it positively lacks fire. It seems to be a little smug even in its elaborate cynicism. Regarding it technically, the opening is somewhat fumbled and shapeless; and surely no one will deny that the conclusion is forced, against probabilities, into a conventional shape. (Get a climax; get it honestly if you can, but get it.) Let us not be accused of belittling de Maupassant. We assert our intense admiration for much of his work. He wrote the last fifty pages of *Une Vie*, and, by a fortunate concate-nation of circumstances, therein produced an effect of pathos which, crude though it is, has scarcely been surpassed in all fiction.

Source: Anonymous, ''The Finest Short Story?'' in *Academy,* n.s. Vol. 57, No. 1421, July 29, 1899, p. 107.

William Barry

In the following essay, Barry argues that Maupassant's stories contain the ''suffocating atmosphere and cold analysis'' of Zola's school of writing but also ''humour, pathos, strong character-drawing, and the most deceptive air, not merely of Realism but of real life.''

All that is revolting in [Zola's 'physiological school']—its suffocating atmosphere and cold analysis, —might be illustrated from 'Boule de Suif.' But there was something more in it than Zolaesque brutality, or the tedious yet impressive collocation of details with which Flaubert's name is inseparably associated. There was humour, pathos, strong character-drawing, and the most deceptive air, not merely of Realism but of real life. . . . 'Boule de Suif,' who gives her name, or rather her nickname, to the story, —how can we praise her sufficiently? Describe her, indeed, we cannot, except by a circumlocution, yet in her degraded but still womanly nature, the oddest notions lurk of the base and the honourable, making her, —poor bedraggled creature, —a sort of heroine, in the 'General Overturn.' It is the absurdest, yet most touching situation.

And it is in the spirit of Flaubert. If there is in it a throbbing vein of compassion, there is also unconquerable cynicism. . . . Never, from the day he began to write until the pen dropped from his convulsed fingers, did Maupassant grow weary of enlarging on 'the infamy of the human heart.' With the insolent gaiety of youth he paints it in the faces, actions, gestures, . . . of Frenchmen and Frenchwomen. . . . This we may call satire, if we will, but it has risen to a great height, and is in a key untouched, we are sure, by Juvenal.

But the root of bitterness remains. Our feeling, as we read the last words of 'Boule de Suif,' is not so much pity for the victim, as a loathing like that which overcame Gulliver on returning from his last voyage, and falling in with the Yahoos who were his own kith and kin. It provokes an indictment of human nature. That anarchic moral returns in Maupassant's stories like a refrain. The disgust of his own species never quits him. For dogs and horses he can feel; nor is he without a thrill of compassion when he comes across suffering or tormented children. He pities the miserable, too; outcasts, vagabonds, cripples, of whom he knows many sad and melting stories, appeal, not, he would say, to his humanity (for the human is vile and selfish), but to that quality of tenderness in the modern, highly civilized man, which is artificial, and not in any sense due to nature. He is eloquent on the struggle maintained by choice spirits against the something that made the world, and made it so brutal and ugly. That Promethean strain, so marked in a stage of Goethe's life and poetry, which Shelley also has harped upon in exquisite golden verse, inflicts on us a sense of surprise, when we hear it in Maupassant. But the antique symbol of a rebellious, suffering spirit which defies the god of nature, whether he is to be styled Zeus or Satan, has never perhaps died out of men's minds; and in 'L'Inutile Beauté' it finds vehement expression, though in language too gross and violent to be quoted. (pp. 483–84)

[Maupassant felt,] in his own language, 'a violent passion' for the sea and the river. In all his books the clear and astonishingly precise description of the quick changing forms, and dancing or slumbering beauty of the waters, would satisfy at once a scientific observer like Mr. Tyndall, and a dreamy artist like Turner in his best period. The resources of French prose since Victor Hugo have been strikingly enlarged; and a new and refined colour-sense betokens its presence by the added suppleness, the continual gleaming of words which fill the eye with a vision as distinct as a photograph, while adding to it the tints of the landscape. With Maupassant there is no affectation of artistic phrase. He writes a limpid French, bright and unembarrassed wherever it has no reminiscence of Flaubert, as in most of his later stories. In the conversations which he so admirably fits to the personages brought on his mimic stage, there is no sign of mannerism. They are quite unaffected and true to nature. . . . By and by, Maupassant, when his mental tone was enfeebled, did lapse occasionally into the morbid style of the symbolists. At no time, however, was it truly his own. The rude Norman vigour, the good sense, not quite unencumbered with a certain—shall we say stupidity?—which he inherited from his forefathers, and which ought to have kept him sound and healthy, would have sent him away laughing from lackadaisical poetasters, in whom there is no genius, but only a serious cultivation of aesthetic follies. He had no wish to be a prose Verlaine.

From nature he had received the endowment somewhat rare, among Parisian novelists, of hearty laughter. As a born Frenchman we might expect him to be witty and amusing; but humour we should not have looked for. . . . Maupassant, however, was not a scented popinjay, like those to whom Paris means all the world they have travelled in, or those others who have come up from the provinces young, and are glad to forget the miseries of their peasant childhood. In his acquaintance with fields and hedgerows, with the life of the farm, with its sounds at morning and eventide, with wild birds and wild flowers, he resembles George Sand, though he lacks her untiring good-nature, and is not in the least a Utopian or a Socialist.

Suggestive, indeed, as well as saddening, is the descent from lightsome and touching romance, in 'La Petite Fadette' and 'Les Maitres Sonneurs,' to the naked reality, though we grant its flashes of the ludicrous, which fills Maupassant's country scenes. They leave a feeling on the mind not unlike a medieval Dance of Death, painted among cornfields and vineyards. Everywhere we are sensible of a fixed and ingrained hardness which strikes home like a breeze from an iceberg, deadly cold and pitiless. . . . [We] may compare 'L'Histoire d'une Fille de Ferme' with 'Adam Bede,' or 'Le Père Amable' with 'Silas Marner.' Upon the English stories, for all their tragic burden, a mild radiance seems to be shed; the great sky, with its stars and sunsets, hangs above us while we move among these men and women, whose thoughts are not invariably bent earthwards, nor their spirit become a tired and fretful beast, dragging the plough with unwilling muscles. There is sunshine on the land, which yet we know is not simply a painted operatic scene, but, in some measure at all events, taken from life. And, from life, too, Maupassant draws, but in what ashen colours! . . . The painting is always, — we fear, because the facts warrant it, —a depressing 'grey in grey;' true doubtless, but spectral as the mists in Ossian, with ghosts murmuring hollow on the wind, and unspeakably desolate.

And still, bursts of laughter are not wanting; genuine, unforced hilarity, to which the dialect adds a keen flavour, as in 'Une Vente,' and 'Tribunaux Rustiques.' There is even at times (would it came oftener!) a vivid touch of the old world, something quaint, and lovable, or perhaps affecting: witness 'La Ficelle,' with its Teniers-like drawing of market-day in Goderville; or the exceedingly piteous tale of 'Le Gueux,' the starved cripple, in whose hunger none will believe until he dies of it. . . . Like these

> **It provokes an indictment of human nature. That anarchic moral returns in Maupassant's stories like a refrain. The disgust of his own species never quits him."**

are the most taking of the country stories, which almost persuade us to unsay the charge we have brought against their author, of hatred of the human race. That he loves a joke is much in his favour; and we allow that his laugh has an infectious ring about it which ought to scatter some of our dislike for the self-conscious misanthrope. Moments there are when we acknowledge that Maupassant, like all who have mixed with high and low sympathetically, can be genial and even kind-hearted. When he talks his native patois, with its delightful yet unconscious touches of the comic, its rude repartee, quaint farce, and explosive jollity, one cannot help laughing all down the page, and the air clears in a surprising manner.... When Maupassant's peasantry laugh their best, they seem to stand back from their grim and sordid existence, like men looking at a picture; and the strings of their heart, nay, of their purse, are loosened. The fine Celtic gaiety, of which traces yet live in these stories, though less frequent as we move on with them, may love pleasure and excitement; but it is too eager, too delicate, to dwell, in the icy mood of the Epicurean, upon its own sensations. It is warm and tender, somewhat given to change perhaps, but as unlike as possible to the nature of the voluptuary, whose fancy swings to and for between Tiberius and the neo-pagans, and whose weary dreams Maupassant chose to delineate with ever-growing earnestness during his brief career. (pp. 485–88)

[*Bel-Ami*] is an edifying romance, not marred, be sure of it, in the telling. The style is crisp, high-strung, and exceedingly photographic, —the perfection of that which impressionists aim at but seldom achieve. From its descriptions, an archaeologist of the twenty-first century might reproduce, with most admired exactness, the form and habit of Parisian life as it goes on in the many-storied houses and outside them. We are here shown, with singular clearness, the Paris of [Daudet's] 'Les Rois en Exil.' ... Yet in the multitude of human beings we distinguish an amazingly small variety of types. Huge Paris, with its two million mortals living inside the barriers, seems no larger, no more opulent in character and circumstance, than one of Terence's comedies. The scene has grown to vast proportions; it is an immense spectacle; but the players, and even the masks they wear, disappoint us with their eternal monotony. (p. 492)

['Notre Coeur' has] its brilliant pages; but in subtlety of colour and high-wrought passion it will not compare for an instant with George Sand's 'Elle et Lui,' to say nothing of 'Lélia' or 'Indiana.' Neither is the self-conscious, half-poetic mood which Bourget is fond of dissecting and of adorning with his passionate melancholy, quite in the vein of our sturdy Norman. Where sentiment is concerned, Maupassant does little more than make believe. He prefers a drinking scene, in which his comrades laugh over barrack-room stories, and make the glasses on the table ring again. ...

In 'Notre Coeur' there is a sort of murderous enchantment, which takes prisoner soul and sense, though certainly not those of an Englishman, who despises what to his Gallic neighbour might seem to be luxuries of feeling. It is a dream, hanging clear above our heads—detached from duties and moralities—where instinct may do as it will and no fault found. (p. 494)

[In] the painfully vivid sketch called 'Un Fils,' the fathers of all the criminal vagrants, of the diseased, forsaken, and dangerous members of society, are neither the poor nor the hardworking, but the bourgeois intent on enjoyment, the academician, the artist, the deputy, the senator. Note, of course, the exaggeration; but mark also how much truth lurks in the gibe. ... Our guide to these heartrending sights is only too competent. He paints and he speaks, not as a religious man, —he is no Frà Angelico, —but calmly, like a citizen of the world. Yet his voice trembles a little; and, in the midst of his shameful narrative there will break out, as it were, a sob from the depths of his heart, —as in the piteous story of 'L'Armoire.' The tale itself is slight, is nothing. But the picture of the child, turned out of its poor little bed and sent to sleep all night as well as it can, on a chair in the cupboard, —and the child of such a mother, engaged in such a trade, —who can express the things of which it is an evidence? They are as touching as they are horrible. (pp. 496–97)

When Maupassant tells a story like this, which goes to the heart, we bear with his coarseness, much as it offends a healthy nostril; we are almost willing to forgive and to like the man. But he is a creature of instinct; the pity which fills his eyes one moment is forgotten the next. He cares only for excitement, nor does he reck of what species, tender, morose, or even cruel. Not that he gloats over cruelty as done by himself; but he has a mania for studying its phases. The world of detestable, though still human vice, seems to undergo a transformation as we pass with him along his dark galleries. Our step falters where he gains assurance. Why explore these Bedlams, whether of life or literature? 'Why?' he replies, 'because they are the truth, the only solid ground beneath the world's illusion.' Thus he indulges, in a mood of mocking complicity, all the bizarre fancies which haunt the last agonies of reason. (p. 497)

[In the supernatural sketches of Maupassant] there comes the delineation of maniacal fury, bent on gratifying its cravings in a series of heightened atrocities. The coarse and illbred humour which disfigured Maupassant's Norman tales was harmless in comparison. It could only disgust. But the miasma of insanity exhaling from narratives such as 'Un Fou,' 'Moiron,' 'Chevelure,' and 'Le Horla' betokens, if we may venture on the expression, a decaying brain. We turn with unconquerable dread from the like phenomena in those high-coloured and plague-stricken artists Edgar Poe, Baudelaire, and William Blake. In this weird region of nightmare and hallucination nature seems dead. (p. 499)

Source: William Barry, "The French Decadence," in *Quarterly Review*, Vol. 174, No. 348, April, 1892, pp. 479–504.

Sources

Colet, Roger, "Introduction," in *Selected Short Stories,* by Guy de Maupassant, edited and translated by Roger Colet, Penguin Books, 1987, p. 7.

De Maupassant, Guy, "Boule de Suif," in *Selected Short Stories,* edited and translated by Roger Colet, 1971, Pengiun Books, pp. 19–68.

Kant, Immanuel, *Grounding for the Metaphysics of Morals,* translated by James W. Ellington, Hackett Publishing, 1993, p. 36.

Rossi, Philip, "Kant's Philosophy of Religion," in *The Stanford Encyclopedia of Philosophy,* Fall 2004 ed., edited by Edward N. Zalta, http://plato.stanford.edu/archives/fall2004/entries/kant-religion/ (accessed December 3, 2004).

Russell, Bertrand, *A History of Western Philosophy,* Simon & Schuster, 1972, p. 628.

Further Reading

Christiansen, Rupert, *Paris Babylon: The Story of Paris Commune,* Penguin Books, 1996.
    Christiansen gives a detailed description of Parisian political and social life both before and after the Franco–Prussian War.

Hartig, Rachel M., *Struggling under the Destructive Glance: Androgyny in the Novels of Guy de Maupassant,* Peter Lang Publishing, 1991.
    Hartig's book is a challenge to the prevailing critical analysis of Maupassant's novels, purporting that his heroines do, in fact, undergo substantial change.

Howard, Michael Eliot, *The Franco–Prussian War: The German Invasion of France 1870–1871,* Routledge, 2001.
    Howard provides a definitive history of one of the most dramatic invasions and decisive conflicts in European history.

Milner, John, *Art, War and the Revolution in France, 1870–1871: Myth, Reportage and Reality,* Yale University Press, 2000.
    This collection surveys the response made by artists to the massive upheaval caused by war and revolution in France during the Franco–Prussian War.

Conscience of the Court

Zora Neale Hurston

1950

Zora Neale Hurston is best remembered as the Harlem Renaissance novelist who contributed *Their Eyes Were Watching God* to the American canon. Like so many novelists, Hurston also produced a fair amount of short fiction over the course of her career. Toward the end of her life, she continued to write but was unable to support herself doing it full time. In fact, when ''Conscience of the Court'' was published in the March 18, 1950, issue of the *Saturday Evening Post,* she was working as a maid. It would be her last original short story published.

''Conscience of the Court'' is a relatively simple story of devotion and justice. A black maid is on trial for assaulting a white man. As the details of the story come to light, the maid is exonerated and even commended for her behavior and the devotion that motivated it. The story reveals Hurston's affinity for themes of genuine love and devotion and her belief that these themes are relevant to the human experience, whether crossing racial lines or not.

Author Biography

Although census reports indicate that Zora Neale Hurston was born on January 7, 1891, she claimed to be born in 1901 or 1903. The actual date remains a mystery, as does her exact burial site. In 1973, prominent African American feminist and novelist Alice Walker was determined to find Hurston's unmarked grave and provide a suitable marker.

After much effort, she found the spot she believed to be Hurston's grave and mounted a headstone that reads, "A Genius of the South" (a phrase from one of Jean Toomer's poems).

Hurston was the fifth of John and Lucy Ann (Potts) Hurston's eight children. Lucy was a former teacher and seamstress who wanted her children to reach higher, to "jump at de sun." John was a handsome and popular Baptist minister, who also served as Eatonville's mayor for three terms. Eatonville was founded by and for African Americans, and this unique all-black community provided the context for most of Hurston's early years. She recalled her childhood as happy until her mother's death in 1904, after which her father married a woman Hurston found impossible to embrace. Entering young adulthood without a mother, Hurston became independent, outspoken, and bold.

Hurston graduated from Morgan Academy in Baltimore in 1918. She enrolled immediately in Howard University in Washington, D.C., where she studied for five years while working as a waitress and a manicurist. She also tried her hand at writing and was encouraged enough to go to New York City to pursue writing. There, she met other writers such as Langston Hughes, Claude McKay, and Jean Toomer. The collective effort of these writers is known as the Harlem Renaissance.

Hurston accepted a scholarship to Barnard College, where she studied anthropology under Franz Boas. Upon graduation, she combined her love of anthropology with her love of writing by collecting folklore. Her efforts produced 1935's *Mules and Men*. This book is historically important, as it is often regarded as the first published collection of African American folklore.

Hurston went to Florida in 1935 to work for the Works Progress Administration before conducting anthropological research in Haiti. While in Africa, she wrote *Their Eyes Were Watching God* (1937) in only seven weeks. With its regional flavor and its black female protagonist, Hurston did not expect the novel to be important in American literature. In the mid-1970s, this book was popularized by feminist writers and critics such as Walker. Unfortunately for Hurston, she never enjoyed great critical acclaim during her lifetime. In the last decade of her life, she did some freelance writing and worked variously as a maid, teacher, reporter, and librarian.

Zora Neale Hurston

Hurston suffered a stroke in 1959 and died on January 28, 1960, in a welfare home in Fort Piece, Florida. Because she had so little when she died, a collection was taken to pay for a funeral and an unmarked grave in a segregated cemetery. Today, visitors can visit the marker where Walker believes she found the gravesite.

Plot Summary

Laura Lee Kimble is Mrs. Celestine Beaufort Clairborne's maid. She is in court for assaulting a white man named Clement Beasley. Although she has been in jail for three weeks awaiting trial, she is calm and respectful, even in the face of the scorn she feels as she enters the courtroom. The judge and the onlookers all have preconceived ideas about her, but she does not know this is all working against her.

After the jury is brought in to their box, a series of witnesses testify to the brutality of the beating she gave Beasley. Then Beasley himself is helped from his cot to the witness stand to give his version of events. He tells the court that he arrived at Mrs.

Clairborne's house to collect on an overdue loan he had made to her. Although Mrs. Clairborne was not home, he found her maid packing silver and became concerned about his loan. Believing that Mrs. Clairborne had left town for good and was sending for her things, he felt he had to act. The house and its furnishing had been the collateral on the loan, so he resolved to take the furniture. He claims that even though the furniture would not cover the loan, he wanted to be kind to the widow. When he arrived for the furniture, however, the maid physically attacked him. He claims she beat him terribly, as his apparent pain indicates.

Beasley's account outrages Laura Lee, who cannot believe the lies she is hearing. The first thing that offends her is his suggestion that Mrs. Clairborne would not honor a loan and that her beautiful antiques were not worth six hundred dollars. As she reflects on her bad luck at being in this position, she thinks about Mrs. Clairborne and how she feels betrayed by her. Laura Lee sent word as soon as she was put in jail, and yet Mrs. Clairborne had neither responded nor returned to town. Her heart is so broken that she does not care what the court decides to do with her.

Laura Lee is given her chance to tell the story, and she does so without an attorney. After assuring the court that Mrs. Clairborne is an honorable woman who would never leave a loan unpaid, she proceeds with her version of the story. According to Laura Lee, she was at the house when Beasley arrived, and she told him that Mrs. Clairborne was out of town and gave him the address where she was staying. The next day, he arrived with a truck and tried to take the furniture. Laura Lee blocked him, and when he hit and kicked her, she attacked him. She beat him until he could not stand upright, so she carried him to the gate and tossed him off the property.

Laura Lee does not try to make a case for her own innocence or guilt. While she feels justified in protecting her employer's belongings, she wonders if her husband had been right about her extreme loyalty to others. She goes on to explain her loyalty to the jury. She has known Mrs. Clairborne (then Miss Beaufort) since she was an infant and loved her so much she took care of her and mothered her for years. When her father died, Laura Lee married a man who worked for the family so she could stay with the family. She saw Miss Beaufort marry and become Mrs. Clairborne, and she was there when

she lost her parents and then her husband. The widowed Mrs. Clairborne needed a fresh start and a smaller house, so she asked Laura Lee to consider moving to Florida with her. Laura Lee could not bear the thought of being separated and convinced her very reluctant husband to move. After much negotiating, they all moved to Florida. When Laura Lee's husband died, Mrs. Clairborne generously paid for his coffin to be returned to his hometown for burial, and she paid for Laura Lee and herself to go with it. As it so happens, this is why she had borrowed the money from Beasley.

When Beasley finally releases the promissory note to the court, the judge discovers that the due date is not for three more months. The judge chastises him for his attempted burglary and for trying to manipulate the court into helping him punish Laura Lee for protecting her employer's property against trespassers. The judge goes on to praise Laura Lee's loyalty to her employer.

Returning to the house, Laura Lee realizes that Mrs. Clairborne did not get her message about being in jail, and she asks God to forgive her. Inside, she polishes a silver platter to a high sheen as a symbolic act of cleansing her heart that loves Mrs. Clairborne so much.

Characters

Clement Beasley

Clement Beasley (whose name, not coincidentally, sounds like "beastly") is manipulative, untrustworthy, and opportunistic. By the end of the trial, everyone realizes that he is a liar, a thief, and a bully. He takes advantage of Mrs. Clairborne by attaching her valuable belongings as collateral to a loan that is worth far less than her possessions, and then when she is out of town, he comes to collect on his loan. In reality, he is trying to steal Mrs. Clairborne's valuables, but he underestimates Laura Lee. When she tries to prevent him from taking anything, he does not hesitate to respond with violence, punching and kicking her. Then when she beats him and throws him off the property, he seeks revenge in court. He expects his crooked lawyer and his pitiful appearance (he arrives on a cot, even though it is three weeks after the attack) will sway the jury.

Mrs. Celestine Clairborne

Although Mrs. Clairborne never appears in the story, her character is extremely important to the events. Born Miss Celestine Beaufort to wealthy landowners, she grew up with Laura Lee. She depended on her for friendship and comfort, almost like a second mother, even though Laura Lee is only five years older. Through the years, she treats Laura Lee with nothing but respect and honor, making sure her needs are met and her dignity is preserved. As loyal as Laura Lee is to Mrs. Clairborne, Mrs. Clairborne seems to be equally loyal to Laura Lee. She wanted so much for Laura Lee and her husband, Tom, to accompany her on her move from Georgia to Florida that she made the offer irresistible to them both. She made promises to them that she keeps, even at high costs, because she values friendship and loyalty above possessions. Her influence on Laura Lee is profound, and without Mrs. Clairborne, Laura Lee would have become a completely different person.

The Judge

The judge in the story is the character who undergoes the most change. At the beginning, he has practically decided that Laura Lee is a vicious would-be killer before he even hears her case. Her demeanor in the court and the innocent trust she exhibits remind him of why he loved the law as a young man. He remembers the passion he felt toward justice and how he longed to be like his hero, Justice John Marshall. These thoughts and feelings sweep over him, and his conduct and attitudes change completely. He disregards an unethical deal he had obviously made with the prosecuting attorney, and he allows Laura Lee to say as much as she wants to say, even when it goes beyond the scope of the case itself. When he discovers that Beasley had intentionally tried to hide the promissory note because it was damning to his case, he is filled with righteous indignation. He not only lectures Beasley about his offense to the court, but goes on to lecture him about the Constitution and justice itself.

Laura Lee Kimble

Forty-nine-year-old Laura Lee Kimble works as a maid in the house of Mrs. Celestine Clairborne.

She has been taking care of Mrs. Clairborne since she was born, and she loves her with a deep, motherly love, although she is only five years her senior. Laura Lee's love for Mrs. Clairborne has motivated all of her major life decisions (who to marry, where to live, and what opportunities to ignore), and now it is just the two of them.

Laura Lee's parents were servants of Mrs. Clairborne's family, and she grew up in a small servant's house on their property. She then became a maid for them, a position she never wanted to quit. She was with Mrs. Clairborne through her childhood and her marriage and is now with her in widowhood. Laura Lee is also a widow with no children.

Laura Lee is uneducated, outspoken, bold, strong, devoted, loving, and extremely determined. Although she is humble, she has a strong sense of herself and is accepting of whatever life brings her way. She is not intimidated by Beasley, the judge, or the jury but freely speaks her mind. Completely lacking in ego, she does not understand the judge's admiration after the trial and merely returns home to continue taking care of Mrs. Clairborne's house.

Themes

Loyalty

Laura Lee's devotion to Mrs. Clairborne compels her to protect her things, even if it means putting herself in the path of a violent man. She bodily defends her employer's furniture when Beasley arrives to take it, and when he hits and kicks her, she incapacitates him. She is passionate in her loyalty, and she will not let Beasley steal Mrs. Clairborne's treasured possessions without a fight.

Laura Lee's story of her history with Mrs. Clairborne is moving to the reader and to the jury. Her relationship began at Mrs. Clairborne's birth, and the affection between the two women deepened over the years. Unable to think about life away from Mrs. Clairborne, Laura Lee convinces Tom, her husband, that they should follow the family. Laura Lee's devotion seems to have a dual nature: She loves Mrs. Clairborne and wants to be with her for that reason, but she also wants to continue to play a part in taking care of her. It is a familial love she

Topics for Further Study

- Put together a character sketch of Laura Lee that includes her personality strengths and weaknesses, her motivations, her relationships, her appearance, and anything else you find interesting or relevant. Wherever there is missing information, feel free to speculate, as long as your conclusions do not conflict with what Hurston provides about Laura in the story.

- How realistic do you think the trial is, given its time and place? Why? Imagine that the trial had concluded unfavorably for Laura Lee, and write a script depicting how you think it would have gone. Recruit classmates to act out your version; then discuss the differences with the class.

- Dialect is difficult to write but generally easy to read. Choose a dialect other than the one used by Hurston in the story, and rewrite Laura Lee's testimony with a new character. In addition to dialect, be sure to incorporate sayings and vernacular as appropriate. When you are done, write a brief reflection describing the experience of writing this way. If it changes the way you think about Hurston and other writers who use dialect, include some comments about that too.

- The judge in the story is reminded of the way he once respected the law and the Constitution, and it changes the way he conducts himself for the rest of the trial. He remembers his hero, Justice John Marshall, and what an influential figure he was to the judge in his university days. Who was John Marshall, and what is his significance in American history? Why would he have been the judge's hero, and why would his example alter the way the judge performs his job?

- Hurston's depiction of the friendship between Laura Lee and Mrs. Clairborne is touching and memorable. How are friendships between women depicted today? Think of three examples of female friendships in modern literature, movies, drama, or television. Try to find three that are very different from each other. Create a visual presentation of the similarities and differences between the three you have chosen and the one in ''Conscience of the Court''; for example, you may want to make a simple table or be creative with a collage. Of the four, which do you think represents the most typical friendships between women today?

---

describes when she says, ''I love her so hard, and I reckon I can't help myself.''

In return, Mrs. Clairborne is loyal to Laura Lee. She continues to employ her and see that her needs are met, and she trusts her. When Laura Lee is widowed, Mrs. Clairborne offers to pay for Tom's body to be transported back to his hometown for burial, something Laura Lee would never have been able to afford on her own. In truth, Mrs. Clairborne cannot afford it either, and she must borrow the money until her next dividend check. She offers as collateral the most cherished and prized possessions in her home, items she has refused to sell repeatedly because she loves them so much. But to keep her promise to her friend to bury her husband in the family cemetery in Georgia, she includes them in her negotiations with Beasley. She values her friendship more highly than her finest possessions.

Justice

The title, ''Conscience of the Court,'' underscores Hurston's theme of justice as a moral and reliable force in the American judicial system. Even though the case presented in the story is one involving a lowly black maid with no attorney against a moneyed white man, the side of good wins in the end. At the beginning of the story, justice is at a disadvantage, as the people in the room and the judge himself all look on Laura Lee as guilty. Hurston writes that when Laura Lee entered the courtroom, ''The hostility in the room reached her without her seeking to find it.'' When the judge sees her struggling to understand protocol, he hesitates before helping her because "[t]his was the man-killing bear cat of a woman that he had heard so much about." Besides all of the impressions and rumors Laura Lee must overcome to attain justice, there is clearly a secret deal between the judge and the prosecutor of which she is unaware. Faced with the trusting innocence of Laura Lee, the judge remembers his early fervor for justice when he was a professor, and it awakens in him his old sense of judicial integrity. So when the issue of the promissory note is presented, he demands to see it, which is clearly in violation of an agreement made with the prosecutor. Hurston describes the lawyer's response: "The tall, lean, black-haired prosecutor hurled a surprised and betrayed look at the bench."

Despite so much weight against her case, Laura Lee manages to win. The judge and jury set aside any prejudices that initially impede good judgment, and they are able to see clearly that Laura Lee was justified in her attack on Beasley and that he is petty and has violent tendencies.

Style

Flashback

Because the story involves a court case in which the parties testify, Hurston uses flashback to relate the story of the fight between Laura Lee and Beasley. Of course, the two versions do not match, and when evidence is introduced, Beasley loses his credibility. This is an interesting use of flashback because Hurston in effect uses it with two different narrators, one reliable and one not. It demonstrates the flexibility of flashback as a narrative technique, and it reminds the reader to approach flashbacks with the same critical eye as any other style of storytelling.

Laura Lee's explanation of why she loves Mrs. Clairborne so much is another use of flashback, as she recounts her long and emotional history with her friend and employer. In this case, Hurston uses flashback for emotional effect, taking the reader (and the jury) to the origins of the love and the long-standing closeness between the two women.

Dialect and Vernacular

Hurston is famous for her use of dialect in fiction; she loved the way it brought her characters

to life and gave her stories a streak of realism. "Conscience of the Court" is no different. Besides doing much of the work in revealing Laura Lee's personality, her dialect and vernacular serve as a reminder to the reader (who cannot see the characters, but who can hear them) of how different Laura Lee is from Beasley. Hurston introduces this element almost immediately in the story, as she reveals Laura Lee's first thoughts upon entering the courtroom: "*Lawdy me*! she mused inside herself. *Look like I done every crime excepting habeas corpus and stealing a mule.*" Her personality and self-expression is consistent, whether she is talking to herself or to the jury. A humble woman, she tells the jury, "It don't surprise me to find out I'm ignorant about a whole heap of things. I ain't never rubbed the hair off my head against no college walls and schooled out nowhere at all." Her sayings become even more colorful and amusing when she tells the story of the actual fight between herself and Beasley. She says, "He just looked at me like I was something that the buzzards laid and the sun hatched." Then later, "He flew just as hot as Tucker when the mule kicked his mammy," and in response she says, "I jumped as salty as the 'gator when the pond went dry." Laura Lee's unique expressions give a sense of her strong personality and make her real and likeable to the reader.

Historical Context

Race Relations in the 1940s

In the years following World War II, changes in race relations began to gain momentum. Racial tensions heightened in part because black soldiers returning from the war had a new perspective on segregation and other restrictive measures taken against them at home. Having risked their lives and seeing their fellow soldiers lose theirs, they found it difficult to accept second-class status.

Advocacy groups were organized, calling for more social and political equality. Areas such as housing, public accommodations, education, and the military were targeted for reform. More cases were tried before the Supreme Court, and the National Association for the Advancement of Colored People played an important role in legal battles at almost every level. Tensions were especially difficult in the South, where 75 percent of African Americans still lived in 1945. Although major changes would not sweep American society until

Compare & Contrast

- **1940s:** Major legal battles are waged to establish more equality under the law for all races. Changing attitudes are slowly making it easier for African Americans to get fair decisions handed down by courts. For example, the Supreme Court declares that whites-only deed restrictions are unenforceable (1948) and that segregated interstate travel is unconstitutional (1946).

  Today: Tremendous progress has been made in the interest of equality under the law. The law calls for equal treatment in education, travel, business, hiring, military service, and other aspects of daily life. Although court cases continue to be filed, the legal standard is for everyone to receive equal opportunity and free access to the justice system.

- **1940s:** Fully 75 percent of the African American population resides in the South. With racial tensions on the rise, this creates a great deal of social unrest in the South, and change is inevitable.

Today: The African American population is represented throughout the United States. Racial tensions have subsided dramatically, although racially motivated incidents are not yet obsolete. These incidents, however, can occur anywhere in the United States, not just in the South.

- **1940s:** Some households still have live-in servants (maids, cooks, etc.), especially in wealthy Southern families whose prior generations hired the prior generations of their servants' families to live with them. In most cases, the servants are minorities employed by white families. This is becoming less common as work opportunities become more available for minorities and racial dynamics change.

  Today: Only the wealthiest households have live-in domestic staff, and members of such staffs can be of any race. Given the history of race relations in America, most families employing such staff members would not even consider hiring only minorities.

---

the 1950s and 1960s, the seeds of the Civil Rights movement were planted in the 1940s.

The Harlem Renaissance

After World War I, many people moved to northern cities, and African Americans began creating a community in Harlem. Because Harlem became the center of African American culture in the 1920s, the artistic efforts of African Americans during this dynamic and prolific time is known as the Harlem Renaissance. A major literary and cultural movement, the Harlem Renaissance was the first to support African American voices expressing and interpreting their unique experiences and histories. One of the most influential contributors to the Harlem Renaissance was Alain Locke, a Harvard University professor and the first black Rhodes scholar. He also edited *The New Negro*, an anthology that gave a forum to fresh voices in fiction,

drama, poetry, and essay. Other prominent figures of the Harlem Renaissance were Langston Hughes, W. E. B. DuBois, Claude McKay, Zora Neale Hurston, Wallace Thurman, Duke Ellington, and Louis Armstrong. Poet and novelist Arna Bontemps was a participant in and historian of the movement, ensuring that its accomplishments would be preserved.

Although black writers were recognized and appreciated in the United States, the Harlem Renaissance generated the cultural effort required to give this body of writing the stature it deserved. Over the course of the movement, black writers were encouraged to develop their unique voices and styles. As a result, there were fewer imitative works, or works heavily reliant on dialect, and more works exploring the heart of the culture. Novels, plays, poetry, and art reflected the depth of the heritage, and they empowered their creators to express their frustration, hope, and pride in their identity. The Harlem Renaissance was inclusive, featuring not just works of African American blacks, but also writers like Claude McKay, who came from Jamaica. As a result of these creative efforts, the African American experience reached people all over the country.

When the depression hit the United States, the Harlem Renaissance waned as writers, artists, and musicians were forced to seek other work, often in other cities.

Critical Overview

Much of Hurston's writing is overshadowed by *Their Eyes Were Watching God*, especially her drama and short stories. As a result, there is little critical commentary specifically about "Conscience of the Court." It was published in 1950 in the *Saturday Evening Post* but was not published in a collection during Hurston's lifetime. In fact, it was the last work of fiction she had published, and it seems to bring to light the complex race issues she had witnessed in the 1940s.

In *The Columbia Companion to the Twentieth-Century American Short Story,* Blanche H. Gelfant and Lawrence Graver consider "Conscience of the Court" in the context of Hurston's other fiction. They observe, "If outcomes are not necessarily happy, it is important in Hurston's stories that innocence triumph over corruption," explaining that Laura is the "beleaguered innocent" in the story, who is released by the court. Ultimately, however, they find the story confusing, noting that "the story draws on conventions that may make the reader queasy. Is Hurston assuring whites of black loyalty? Blacks of white protection?" In their "Introduction" to *Zora Neale Hurston: The Complete Stories,* Henry Louis Gates Jr. and Sieglinde Lemke comment, "This story is about altruism. . . . It is also about an idea of justice and the fact that the court was on the side of a simple black woman." As if considering the historical context of the story they add, "Good is being rewarded—even in black skin— and those who mean well will be rewarded in the end."

Gates and Lemke view "Conscience of the Court" as thematically representative of Hurston's short fiction. They observe that "morality is the issue in most of her stories, which usually end happily for the disenfranchised and powerless. The moral values that Hurston cherishes are loyalty, justice, and love." Commenting on her narrative style, they note that her pace is never rushed, instead allowing the reader to enjoy and absorb "the nuances of speech or the timbre of voice that give a storyteller her or his distinctiveness." Speaking in general terms about Hurston's short fiction and the place it deserves in American literature, Gelfant and Graver write:

> Hurston's stories are playful and provocative but somehow they never quite conform, never seem to play by any rules. Which is hardly to say that these stories are not valuable, both for students of Hurston and for students of the short story. . . . [T]he best of them can stand on their own alongside any of the short fiction of her contemporaries and should be included in anthologies of classic American short stories as fine examples of the genre. Zora Neale Hurston was deeply interested in the form of the short story, particularly its adaptability to oral traditions, folklore, and the vernacular, and she returned to it again and again throughout her life, experimenting with its possibilities and bringing to bear on it all of her varied and complex interests.

Criticism

Jennifer Bussey

Bussey holds a master's degree in interdisciplinary studies and a bachelor's degree in English literature. She is an independent writer specializing in literature. In the following essay, Bussey compares Zora Neale Hurston's short story "Conscience of the Court" with Harper Lee's novel To Kill a Mockingbird.

Zora Neale Hurston's "Conscience of the Court" is about an outspoken black woman whose fierce loyalty to her friend and employer lands her in jail. While defending herself and her employer's belongings from an unethical moneylender, Laura Lee attacks a white man and is sent to jail to await trial. Her trial goes favorably, and she is exonerated when the prosecutor's deception is revealed. Harper Lee's *To Kill a Mockingbird* also concerns a court case that happens to involve interracial conflict. Tom Robinson is falsely accused of attacking and raping Mayella Ewell. Although the very capable and honorable white attorney Atticus Finch represents Tom, the jury in his trial finds him guilty. These two stories have some common ground and also draw some sharp contrasts. There is enough common ground to warrant a closer look, but it may be

Silver dinnerware set like the silverware that Clement Beasley accuses Laura Lee Kimble of stealing in "Conscience of the Court"

necessary to look at the texts hand in hand with their social contexts to find meaning in the comparison.

The authors themselves bear some interesting similarities and differences. Hurston was a well-educated black woman who is now strongly associated with the Harlem Renaissance. Although she is best known for *Their Eyes Were Watching God,* she wrote other novels, along with nonfiction, short stories, and plays. Her life's ambition was to be a writer, and at the end of her life she worked odd jobs to support herself, all the while clinging to the hope of completing another novel. Harper Lee is also well educated, although her career path is law. *To Kill a Mockingbird* is her only published fiction, and she seems to have no desire to follow it up with another. She is not associated with a particular literary movement. Despite the differences between the authors, these two obviously intelligent and perceptive women had something to say about justice and the legal system when they wrote the works discussed here. Examining the texts themselves will begin to reveal their motivations for writing their respective works.

In general terms, there are important similarities between "Conscience of the Court" and *To Kill a Mockingbird.* Both stories involve court cases

with interracial implications, and both cases are observed by members of the community. Although the community anticipation in *To Kill a Mockingbird* is greater than it is in "Conscience of the Court," both trials begin under the scornful eyes of onlookers. When Laura Lee is brought into the courtroom, "The hostility in the room reached her without her seeking to find it." Similarly, when Tom's trial begins, the courtroom is packed with members of the community. The seating is segregated, and the white section is noticeably hostile. Another similarity is that both defendants are black and charged with attacking a white person, yet they both receive the sympathy of other whites who help with their cases. Laura Lee wins the sympathy of the judge and the jury, and Tom is fortunate enough to have the representation of Atticus Finch. That both stories are set in the South—"Conscience of the Court" in Jacksonville, Florida, and *To Kill a Mockingbird* in Maycomb, Alabama—only heightens the racial implications of the trials.

There are also significant differences to consider in comparing these two fictional trials. While both trials involve interracial conflict, *To Kill a Mockingbird* is about charges of a black man sexually assaulting a white woman, which is a weightier

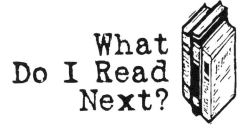

What Do I Read Next?

- Robert E. Hemenway's *Zora Neale Hurston; A Literary Biography* (1977) provides the student with information about Hurston's unique life and influences, with a particular eye toward her writing career. Much of Hurston's life story is unknown, so Hemenway focuses instead on her place in American literature.

- Hurston's *Their Eyes Were Watching God* (1937) is now considered an important contribution to the Harlem Renaissance and feminist writing in general. It is the story of Janie, who finally finds love in her third marriage, only to be widowed. Her story is one of overcoming adversity, maturing, and self-determination.

- Written by Harper Lee, *To Kill a Mockingbird* (1960) is a classic American novel about race relations, small communities, and the justice system. In this story, Atticus Finch, a white lawyer, suffers the scorn of his town when he defends a black man accused of attacking a white woman.

- *The Portable Harlem Renaissance Reader* (1994), edited by David L. Lewis, is a comprehensive sampling of the contributors and key works that defined the movement. The works of forty-five writers are included.

---

charge than the black woman's physical attack on a white man in ''Conscience of the Court.'' At a deeper, philosophical level, the two stories are divergent. Written in 1950, ''Conscience of the Court'' presents an ultimately optimistic view of the legal system. Written ten years later, however, *To Kill a Mockingbird* depicts a pessimistic view of the court system as one that is vulnerable to the flaws of the people on the jury. Atticus says this explicitly in his closing arguments when he appeals to the jury to do their job responsibly because the judicial system can really only be as honorable as the people who serve in juries. Despite Atticus's plea, Tom Robinson is deemed guilty by a prejudiced jury. His life ends tragically when he is killed trying to escape while en route to prison, his innocence relegated to irrelevance. In contrast, Laura Lee is deemed not guilty, is commended by the judge, and returns home to polish silver. These are two dramatically different results.

At the center of the differences between *To Kill a Mockingbird* and ''Conscience of the Court'' are the contrasts between the protagonists. Tom is quiet, imposing, betrayed by someone to whom he showed kindness, and courageous even in his fear. Laura Lee is more approachable-looking, outspoken, bold,

loyal, fearless, and betrayed by someone with whom she has no personal relationship. Both characters are black and living in the South, and thus have little social power or influence. And both are brought to court by white accusers who expect their privileged social status to ensure their victories. Laura Lee's accuser is wrong about that, but Tom's accuser is right.

What do all these comparisons and contrasts mean, besides the fact that two different authors with different experiences will inevitably write two different stories? Hurston and Lee are both ultimately writing about where to find justice and racial harmony in American society, and where to find hope for change. The message of *To Kill a Mockingbird* seems to be that there is little hope in a flawed legal system that relies on flawed people to determine innocence and guilt but that there is tremendous hope in personal relationships. As badly as Tom was treated by the people of Maycomb, and specifically the Ewell family, he was treated with respect as a fellow human being by Atticus and his family. In short, Lee offers a model for change— one *individual* at a time. On the other hand, the message of ''Conscience of the Court'' seems to be that there is hope in the legal system with its

> **It is easy for the reader to assume that Hurston and Lee are commenting somehow on what they have seen and experienced as reality, when in fact there may be an element of teaching or warning in their writings.**"

heritage of justice and pursuit of fairness. The courts, the Constitution, and the judicial legacy all feed into a reliable source of justice in the legal system. In short, Hurston offers a model for change—one *case* at a time. Either way, change takes time and patience, whether it comes about on an individual level or at a legal level.

It is interesting that the message of hope in the legal system comes not from the white lawyer (Lee), but from the black writer (Hurston). Speculation can be made that Lee was more jaded, having experienced firsthand the inner workings of the legal system. In all likelihood, she had witnessed how people are sometimes mistreated by it. If Lee herself had doubts about the legal system, her fictional attorney, Atticus Finch, did not. In his closing remarks to the jury, he declares:

> But there is one way in this country in which all men are created equal—there is one human institution that makes a pauper the equal of a Rockefeller, the stupid man the equal of an Einstein, and the ignorant man the equal of any college professor. That institution, gentlemen, is a court. . . . Our courts have their faults, but in this country our courts are the great levelers, and in our courts all men are created equal.

Atticus reminds the jury that the court system can only be as good as the men in the jury. He appeals to them to do the job they came to do, and to do it responsibly. Atticus knows that for all the preparation and planning, the evidence and the witness testimony, if the jury decides to make a decision based on racism or fear of community backlash, the system will fail Tom. He knows he is fighting an uphill battle, but it is one he must fight because it is for the cause of right. Lee shows that

the legal system entire is really the collective efforts of individual Americans.

There is also the issue of social and historical context to consider. Hurston's story was published in 1950 as the National Association for the Advancement of Colored People was gaining prominence in its support of the growing number of legal battles being fought for equal rights at every court level. Lee's story was published in 1960, after the tumultuous decade of the 1950s that saw racial tensions intensifying and resolution coming too slowly. It is easy for the reader to assume that Hurston and Lee are commenting somehow on what they have seen and experienced as reality, when in fact there may be an element of teaching or warning in their writings. Hurston may have hoped that her depiction of justice would serve as a model for how the courts *should* operate, and Lee may have intended her depiction as something of a cautionary tale. Without explicit instructions from the authors, readers are left to speculate on how these works are to inform their perceptions of the world around them, just as great literature almost always challenges us to do.

Source: Jennifer Bussey, Critical Essay on "Conscience of the Court," in *Short Stories for Students,* Thomson Gale, 2005.

Laura Carter

Carter is currently employed as a freelance writer. In this essay, Carter explores Hurston's notions of justice and altruism and how these values ultimately impact the outcome of the story.

In "Conscience of the Court," as in many of her stories, Zora Neale Hurston creates a narrative framework that serves to raise broader questions about the notions of justice and altruism, particularly the legitimacy of the legal system and the consequences of serving one's community. The character of Laura Lee illuminates these principles. She is, in many respects, the "conscience" of the court. Her lack of faith sparks the conscience of the judge, causing him to pause in shame over the circumstances of her arrest and renewing in him an interest in seeing justice served, despite the color of Laura Lee's skin. Ultimately, it is Laura Lee's fierce devotion to her employer that also serves her well. Her outstanding character, specifically her generous nature, is recognized and rewarded by the judge, and she is exonerated.

From the moment he sees her in the courtroom, the judge is moved by Laura Lee's presence. His assessment of her somehow runs counter to all that he has heard about Laura Lee and her supposed crime. Consequently, he sees her as "a riddle to solve" and "a challenge to him somehow or other," rather than the "man-killing bearcat of a woman" described by the prosecutor. It is Laura Lee who puts her position into perspective for the judge when she refuses the right to an attorney, suggesting that because of her race and social standing, her prosecution is inevitable. And the judge's response moves from one of curiosity to one of deep shame. Laura Lee is not a mystery to be solved. The judge recognizes his folly in not seeing her as a human being deserving of the rights and protections he dedicated his life to promoting, protecting, and preserving.

In the story, the judge's "greatest hero" is John Marshall, known in history as the Great Chief Justice, "his inner resolve to follow in the great man's steps, and even to interpretations of human rights if his abilities allowed." The judge claims Laura Lee has revived his college fascination with human rights and justice and his resolve to uphold Marshall's values.

Much of what drives Hurston's story is the notion of justice. The judge does not forsake Laura Lee; rather, in the name of "two thousand years of growth of the concepts of human rights and justice," he is resolved to hear her side of the story. Despite overwhelmingly negative testimony to the contrary, Laura Lee is asked to tell her side of the story in earnest, leading to a promissory note and ultimately the discovery that, in fact, the so-called victim or plaintiff is guilty of far more than Laura Lee. Ironically, the judge in this case demonstrates what another great Justice, the first African American on the Supreme Court—Thurgood Marshall, believed, that by following the letter of the law, justice would ultimately prevail, or lead to the truth of the matter in question, the color of one's skin aside. Certainly, by allowing Laura Lee to speak, the prejudice of the court room is all but erased with a simple presentation of the facts surrounding the alleged attack against the plaintiff.

According to journalist Juan Williams, in a National Public Radio (NPR) interview concerning his work *Thurgood Marshall: American Revolutionary,* Justice Thurgood Marshall began his career in the 1930s, well after John Marshall, working as a

"Just as Thurgood Marshall won over his biggest critics with his superior intellect, charm, and grace, Laura Lee, a simple black woman, wins over the judge with a proud, erect stance and humble nature."

lawyer for the NAACP, before his appointment to the Supreme Court. It is felt by many historians that Thurgood Marshall, more than any figure, black or white, has done more to advance the rights and liberties of blacks in America. By using the Constitution to remedy the issue of segregation, he took some amazing strides to resolve social inequities: he won equal pay for white and black teachers; he opened Southern juries on primary elections; he filed several law suits that integrated school buses; and he banned discrimination in suburban neighborhoods. And, in the landmark Supreme Court case, *Brown v. Board of Education,* Marshall outlawed segregation in public schools.

Marshall's passion was fueled by a belief that integration was necessary to change the hearts and minds that made up a community. A brilliant legal mind, his success was predicated or dependent on his ability to bring a more human element to his courtroom. He was a calming force with a manner and attitude that complemented his legal skills, and attracted people from all walks of life. And unlike Dr. Martin Luther King, he did not advocate passive resistance as a means of accomplishing his objectives. Marshall had been trying to get blacks out of jail all along, and recognized the mistreatment and violence that protestors may encounter in jail for their acts of civil disobedience. An advocate for justice, Marshall believed in following the law with the belief that ultimately, through reform, justice would indeed prevail.

The "conscience" of Hurston's "court" echoes with the voices of the Supreme Court, and by extension, Laura Lee. It is Laura Lee who stirs the judge's own conscience, admitting to him that she has little faith in the court, and for obvious reasons. By virtue of her skin color, as the narrator intimates or suggests, Laura Lee has been typecast in the roles of "savage queen," and "two-legged she-devil." The judge flushes in shame at Lee's assertions and his failure to recognize her as a person worthy as any other of the protections of the law. Just as Thurgood Marshall won over his biggest critics with his superior intellect, charm, and grace, Laura Lee, a simple black woman, wins over the judge with a proud, erect stance and humble nature. She readily admits she does not know whether she is innocent or guilty, and that she is not educated in the ways of the court or much of anything, for that matter, stating, "I ain't never rubbed the hair off of my head against no college walls."

And, like Thurgood Marshall, the judge brings a human element to his court room by insisting that Laura Lee speak on her own behalf. Hearing her side of the story not only humanizes her in the eyes of the jury and all present in the courtroom, but it leads the judge to make some conclusions on his own that ultimately lead to Laura Lee's acquittal. Laura Lee's story reveals a woman genuinely respectful in the courtroom, and one so devoted to her employer that she would fight to the death to protect her. Her story also brings to light the inequities of the plaintiff, whose case is ultimately destroyed with one simple promissory note. Given a proper representation of all of the facts, justice was indeed served. As Marshall ultimately believed, so too did Hurston believe in the notion that justice would always prevail, no matter how initially daunting or discouraging the evidence may seem.

The judge rests his decision on the idea that "the protection of women and children," was "implicit in Anglo-Saxon civilization," and attributed to the English-speaking people (those of "civilized" or Anglo-Saxon descent) the honor of giving the world "its highest concepts of the rights of the individual." At the root of true justice for all, then, according to the judge, would be the white or Anglo-Saxon culture, a culture that at its core has been historically reluctant to rescind or withdraw the notion of segregation. Hence the reading of the story becomes decidedly more complex, even problematic. Justice does indeed prevail, but it does so at the whimsy of a judge whose long-buried college ideals have been suddenly revived. In support of his romantic notions, the judge responds to the prosecutor's rude interruption of Laura Lee, stating: "The object of a trial, I need not remind you, is to get at the whole truth of a case."

The judge's notions of justice, however romantic, ultimately save Laura Lee. Readers never learn the judge's name, amplifying the idea that perhaps ultimately it is the "law," rather than the judge, that prevails. As some critics have suggested, the story is to be read as one concerned with the quality of justice, and rightly so. In more than one instance the judge appears to have been "shaken out of a dream," or restored to a sense of reverence more fitting to his profession. In fact, the judge does indeed acknowledge the key role Laura Lee has played in his so-called enlightenment, at least in her case, responding to her gratitude at the story's end by stating: "That will do, Laura Lee. I am the one who should be thanking you." But this vote of confidence is no consolation; rather, it leaves the reader to speculate how many people of color the judge has overlooked in similar circumstances.

Presented hand in hand with the notion of justice is the concept of altruism in the story. Laura Lee was devoted to her employer to the degree that she was willing to suffer a jail sentence for her in order to protect her. It could be argued that leaving Laura Lee to watch over Celestine's things was a less than appropriate choice. Arguably, given the tenor of the community and its prejudice toward blacks, such a move could be seen as an open invitation for abuse, making Laura Lee an easy target. As demonstrated by the nature of her arrest, Laura Lee had been tried and convicted by the citizens of the town, most of whom had made assumptions concerning her crime without much substance. This bias demonstrates the lack of respect, and by extension, the lack of security with which black citizens of the town were accustomed to living.

Laura Lee recognizes her folly in her generous assessment of her neighbors, now surrounding her in the courtroom, filled with hostility. She herself admits "The People was a meddlesome and unfriendly passel and had no use for the truth." She also chides herself for not listening to something her husband Tom had told her repeatedly: "This world had no use for the love and friending that she was ever trying to give." And, worse than the "atmosphere that crawled all over Laura Lee like reptiles," was the notion that Celestine had failed her by not coming to her aid. Again, her generous spirit does not go forsaken. Because of her devotion, Laura Lee is not only exonerated by the judge, but is made an example of, "which no decent citizen need blush to follow."

In the introduction to Hurston's collection of short stories, *The Complete Stories,* Henry Louis Gates Jr. and Sieglinde Lemke discuss the concepts of justice and altruism in Hurston's "Conscience of the Court." They claim, that in the story, "Good is being rewarded—even in black skin—and those who mean well will be rewarded in the end." Morality, in fact, is the thematic glue that binds all of Hurston's stories. Despite the odds, "a simple black woman," as Laura Lee is lovingly referred to by the editors, realizes justice as a result of her steadfast loyalty and fierce love for her employer, all qualities Hurston deeply valued and has woven into much of her work.

Source: Laura Carter, Critical Essay on "Conscience of the Court," in *Short Stories for Students,* Thomson Gale, 2005.

Judith Musser

In the following essay, Musser examines autobiographical elements in Hurston's "Conscience of the Court."

Zora Neale Hurston's "Conscience of the Court," originally published in the *Saturday Evening Post* in March of 1950, is a little-known and rarely discussed story. Considering the recent attention to Hurston's importance in the development of African-American women's writing, it seems unusual to discover this neglect of one of her works. One cause for this neglect may be that the story was the last work Hurston published during her lifetime, a period in which her popularity as a writer was waning. And even Robert Hemenway, Hurston's biographer, suggested that the story was weak. He wrote that Hurston, once again in financial trouble and working as a maid on Rivo Island near Miami, was desperate to publish a story. Hemenway proposed that the story's faults probably stemmed from the fact that it was "heavily edited by the *Post*'s staff, and by the knowledge that [Hurston] badly needed to sell a story." Although Hemenway shifted the blame for the weaknesses of the story to the editors of the *Post,* it is still clear that he believed the story was not Hurston's most exemplary piece of writing. Other biographers and critics have expressed their lack of interest by simply ignoring the story. One exception is Lillie P. Howard who mentioned only the circumstances surrounding its publication without commentary on the text itself. These circumstances are certainly noteworthy: a *Miami Herald* reporter discovered that Hurston "was dusting bookshelves in the library while her mistress sat in the

Interior view of a courtroom, perhaps similar to the one in "Conscience of the Court" in which Laura Lee Kimble defends herself

living room reading the *Saturday Evening Post*— and discovering a story written by her 'girl.'"

This disapproving analysis of Hurston's "Conscience of the Court" is not the only instance of pessimism towards Hurston's writings, for her career is riddled with negative criticism. Her peers blacklisted her and dismissed her work on the grounds that her personality, charming and amusing as it was, was considered an expression of her need "to reach a wider audience," that is, a white one. Often, her writing was given little value. In fact, Wallace Thurman described her as "a short story writer more noted for her ribald wit and personal effervescence than for any actual literary work." Langston Hughes remembered only that "in her youth she was always getting scholarships and things from wealthy white people, some of whom simply paid her just to sit around and represent the Negro race for them." Most of the negative criticism centers on how her characters are portrayed. For example, after the publication of *Mules and Men,* Sterling Brown wrote that the characters in the book "should be more bitter; it would be nearer the total truth." Having included one of her stories in

> "Considering Hurston's anger, her anonymity as a writer in 1950, her current position as someone who also shines silver platters for a wealthy white woman, I do not accept that Hurston is catering to a white audience as Laura Lee caters to her mistress."

The New Negro, Alain Locke was nonetheless concerned with her representation of rural African Americans:

> The elder generation of Negro writers expressed itself in . . . guarded idealization. . . . ''Be representative'': put the better foot foremost, was the underlying mood. But writers like Rudolph Fisher, Zora Hurston . . . take their material objectively with detached artistic vision; they have no thought of their racy folk types as typical of anything but themselves or of their being taken or mistaken as racially representative.

Likewise, Richard Wright felt that the novel *Their Eyes Were Watching God* was counterrevolutionary in portraying simple, minstrel-show African-Americans: he complained that Hurston's characters existed in ''that safe and narrow orbit in which America likes to see the Negro live: between laughter and tears.'' Overall, Hurston was criticized because she opened up to whites too easily, practiced cultural colonialism by collecting folklore, wasn't bitter enough about the African-American condition, and used folklore too obtrusively in her fiction.

Although not explicitly stated, it would seem that a cause for the unease with ''Conscience of the Court'' most likely stems from Hurston's portrayal of stereotypical characters. The story takes place in a courtroom where Laura Lee, an African-American family servant, is accused of assault for physically preventing a loan shark from removing her mistress's belongings from the house. Laura Lee is pointedly characterized in terms of the stereotypes

of the mammy, the comedian/fool, and the savage. She appears in a courtroom wearing a head rag and a shabby housedress. Her ignorance of courtroom procedures entertains the observers while at the same time makes her appear pitifully naive. Yet the charges against her cause the judge to view her as a ''man-killing bear cat of a woman'' and a ''savage queen.'' The caricature continues as Laura Lee offers her own defence. She describes her commitment to her mistress, ''Miz Celestine,'' since birth. Celestine Beaufort Clairborne, in her infancy, was placed in Laura Lee's care when Laura Lee was but a child herself. Portraying the role of the dutiful, loyal, and lifelong servant, Laura Lee remains in the household, rejecting offers of marriage which would allow her to leave the household of her mistress. Instead, she agrees to marry Tom, another older servant in the house. Hurston's Tom, unlike Harriet Beecher Stowe's Uncle Tom, is completely against the idea of accommodation to the will of white people. He acts as Laura Lee's foil and thus intensifies her self-sacrificial embodiment of the perfect servant. Laura Lee's most recent sacrifice for her white employer was to physically defend Celestine's valuables from Clement Beasley, a sleazy loan officer. Because Mrs. Clairborne was vacationing in Miami and could not be located, Laura Lee must endure the present trial alone. Laura Lee's dramatic storytelling ability, her willingness to abide by an Uncle Tom philosophy of putting ''other folk's cares in front of [her] own,'' and her entertaining, folksy speech win the hearts of the jury and judge, and she is acquitted.

The portrayal of a woman facing a jury in a trial is certainly not new in Hurston's fiction. The courtroom drama in *Their Eyes Were Watching God* is a significant scene. The key difference between Janie's trial and Laura Lee's trial is that Laura Lee's words on the witness stand are presented directly and completely, whereas Janie's speech in *Their Eyes* is summarized by the narrator. Thus both the content and the manner in which Laura Lee presents her case factor into her acquittal. In addition, an important similarity between the two trials is how characters react to the court's decision. The white women in Janie's courtroom are as equally pleased at Janie's acquittal as those in the courtroom of Laura Lee. Despite the thirteen years between the publication of *Their Eyes Were Watching God* and ''Conscience of the Court,'' Hurston still recognizes the need to accompany an obvious act of justice with approval from the white community. Hurston, catering to the predominantly white, middle-class readers of the *Saturday Evening Post,* is reassuring them that they can feel at ease with their white middle-class values—an African-American woman prevails over a white man and therefore there is no racism in the white courts of America. Even the *Post*'s artist catches this mood of patriotic justice in his/her depiction of an American flag in the background which practically enfolds Laura Lee on the witness stand. Perhaps it is no wonder that the story is ignored by critics and blamed on intrusive editors.

I believe, however, that subtleties in the text as well as the circumstances under which the story was written suggest that Hurston's last piece of fiction was not a sell-out to the formula demands of a white readership. The most significant reading of this story stems from the fact that it is remarkably autobiographical. This is not an unusual characteristic in Hurston's writings. After the publication of her second story, "Drenched in Light," Hurston openly admitted that Isis embodied many of the characteristics of her o[w]n childhood. In another story, "Muttsy," Hurston recreates her own entrance into the mainstream of Northern life through the experiences of an innocent young woman from the South, Pinkie Jones, as she enters the bewildering city of Harlem. And Janie's relationship with Tea Cake in *Their Eyes Were Watching God* is often read in light of Hurston's own relationship with a man she met in New York in 1931. "Conscience of the Court" presents another period in Hurston's life, although the relevant difference here is that the circumstances are far from pleasant.

Like Laura Lee, Hurston was equally devoted to her own "mistress," or "godmother," the term she used to address Mrs. Rufus Osgood Mason. Hemenway describes the powerful, almost perverse control that Mason exerted over Hurston's career. Invariably, Hurston was placed in a position of constantly needing to subject her own interests to those of Mrs. Mason in order to maintain Mason's financial support. Hurston's sensitivity was not reciprocated, for Mason was careful not to involve herself in any of Hurston's controversial episodes. One such even stands out. In 1931, Langston Hughes, another dependent of Mason, accused Hurston of claiming sole authorship of the play *Mule Bone,* a production that was supposed to be a collaboration between the two writers. The argument over the authorship of *Mule Bone* is complicated, but in the end, Hurston was vindicated of the accusation. During the very public controversy, however, Mason refused to back Hurston, which caused a strain in their relationship. In her hour of need, Hurston was

left to face the accusations of plagiarism alone, much as Laura Lee was left to singly face the false accusations of Beasley.

But a closer parallel between Hurston's life and "Conscience of the Court" appears in 1948, just two years before she published the story. Hurston had to appear in a courtroom to defend herself against accusations of committing an immoral act with a ten-year-old boy. According to Hemenway, this trial should never have made it to court. Hurston's passport proved that she was in Honduras when the alleged acts of sodomy were said to have taken place. It was later revealed that the child was mentally disturbed and had previously been in Bellevue for psychiatric testing. Karla Holloway writes that Hurston "was 'prostrate and hysterical' in the courtroom, defending herself of these charges." By the time the case was dismissed, the damage had already been done. Papers all across the country printed lurid headlines about the famous writer's sexual appetites. One of the most disturbing was a paper which used a quotation from one of the characters in Hurston's recently published *Seraph on the Suwanee*—"I'm just hungry as a dog for a knowing and a doing love" and asked if Zora sought the same affection. Hurston's personal world had collapsed. In the end, what shocked Hurston more than the negative publicity was the way the judicial system took the word of a ten-year-old boy over that of an adult. "Would they have done the same to a white person? . . . It smacks of an anti-Negro violation of one's civil rights. . . . If such an injustice can happen to one who has prestige and contacts, then there can be absolutely no justice for the little people of the community."

Only a year after the trial, Hurston wrote her last piece of published fiction and it appeared in a well-known magazine which catered to an American middle-class white readership. She presents a fictional scenario of how justice is meted out to the "little people." The circumstances of Hurston's recent trial and the trial in "Conscience of the Court" are similar. As in Hurston's own situation, the case against Laura Lee should never have come to trial. There was documented evidence that Mrs. Claireborne still had three months to pay back the loan and therefore Beasley had no right to take her possessions. We learn this vital information at the end of the trial, long after Laura Lee has been required to endure the scornful glances of the spectators in the courtroom and to struggle through relating her story to the jury. Also, in both cases, the defendants—Hurston and Laura Lee—did not have support from the white community. Laura Lee didn't even have a lawyer defend her for her trial. And finally, in the end, both Hurston and Laura Lee were found innocent.

But here the list of similarities ends, for instead of recreating herself in the character of Laura Lee, Hurston carefully constructs a completely different kind of defendant. Hurston is educated, articulate, stylish in her dress, emotionally outraged during and after the the trial, and, in 1950, financially independent of white patronage. Laura Lee, however, speaks with a strong dialect, misuses the English language, wears a head rag, acts comically ignorant of the dominant society's system of justice, entertains the audience with her simplistic re-telling of her story, and fulfills perfectly the role of the dependent servant (renamed "the faithful watchdog" by the judge in the story). After she is acquitted, Laura Lee "diffidently" thanks the judge and he remarks, "I am the one who should be thanking you." Laura Lee is surrounded by "smiling, congratulating strangers, many of whom made her event so welcome if ever she needed a home. She was rubbed and polished to a high glow." On the other hand, Hurston, after her acquittal, vehemently attacked the injustices in the court system and was harassed by the news media. After the trial, Hurston wrote to Carl Van Vechten, "All that I have ever tried do has proved useless. All that I have believed in has failed me. I have resolved to die. It will take a few days for me to set my affairs in order, and then I will go . . . no acquittal will persuade some people that I am innocent. I feel hurled down a filthy privy hole." Hurston's emotional despair is a complete reversal of Laura Lee's spiritual restoration at the end of the story. Laura Lee returns to her mistress's home and performs a sacrament of devotion to the world. Before she enters the house, she, "like a pilgrim before a shrine," confesses her sin in doubting the white world. Despite her hunger, she first "made a ritual of atonement in serving. She took a finely wrought silver platter from the massive old sideboard and gleamed it to perfection. So the platter, so she wanted her love to shine."

Considering Hurston's anger, her anonymity as a writer in 1950, her current position as someone who also shines silver platters for a wealthy white woman, I do not accept that Hurston is catering to a white audience as Laura Lee caters to her mistress. Laura Lee's glaring overtures to the white world and Hurston's blatant stereotypical characterization of Laura Lee reveal Hurston's most creative and powerful work of protest. Hurston's last piece of

published fiction is an overtly dramatic and scathing critique of the social and justice system in America. An African-American woman like Laura Lee satisfies society's expectations of what she should look like and how she should behave; therefore society recognizes her rights and justice prevails. For the readers and editors of the *Post* (and perhaps critics who have chosen to ignore the story), the court was acting "conscientiously" because it sided with an African-American woman over a white man. But the reason the court can make this decision is not because the evidence clearly indicates that the African-American woman is truly innocent; it is because the woman's behavior was socially acceptable to the white audience/readership. Perhaps if Hurston had enacted the part of the passive, ignorant, and loyal African-American during her trial, her innocence would have been as easily accepted as it was for Laura Lee.

The story of a black woman in a court of law, whether it be fictional or autobiographical, is certainly familiar to us today. One cannot help but think of the Anita Hill/Clarence Thomas case. Anita Hill did not fit into the accepted stereotypes of a African-American woman in the 1980s. Nell Irvin Painter writes that Hill had the choice of adopting either the role of the mammy, the welfare cheat, or the oversexed-black Jezebel. Hill found no shelter in stereotypes of race and therefore there was no way for her to emerge a heroine of the race. Hurston, on the other hand, was immediately characterized as the oversexed-black-Jezebel stereotype because of her emotional reaction during the trial as well as her depiction of sensuality in her writing. Thus, despite the outcome of the trial, she was believed to be guilty of a sexual crime. And Laura Lee, the woman who fits the stereotypes of the mammy, the comedian/fool, and the savage, emerges as honorable because she knew her place in that society. In this one short story, Hurston has subtly revealed the power behind racial and gender stereotyping, a situation that has been and continues to be repeated throughout African-American history. And what is even more amazing is the fact that readers, both then and now, may have missed her message.

Source: Judith Musser, "Significant Stereotypes in Hurston's 'Conscience of the Court,'" in *Midwest Quarterly,* Vol. 41, No. 1, Autumn 1999, p. 79.

Laura M. Zaidman

In the following essay excerpt, Zaidman discusses "Conscience of the Court" in light of the decline in Hurston's popularity.

A departure from the Eatonville setting toward the folklore of the Bible is found in "The Fire and the Cloud," published in *Challenge* (September 1934). Edited by Dorothy West, this Harlem Renaissance magazine also published works by writers such as Langston Hughes, James Weldon Johnson, Arna Bontemps, and Frank Yerby. The first issue's lead editorial presented a challenge to young black writers to better the achievement of earlier writers who "did not altogether live up to our fine promise." "The Fire and the Cloud" fails to surpass the quality of Hurston's previous stories, yet it does briefly explore the richness of the Moses mythology, especially Moses's stature as a black folklore hero, a subject expanded in her 1939 novel, *Moses, Man of the Mountain.* In this germinal story, Moses sits on his grave on Mount Nebo and explains to a lizard how he delivered the Hebrew people from bondage in Egypt. He is not so much the great Jewish leader who gave his people the Ten Commandments; he is the great African hero who performed the greatest voodoo magic ever with his rod of power that struck terror in the Pharaoh to set the slaves free. In *Tell My Horse* (1938), a study of Caribbean voodoo practices, Hurston writes, "This worship of Moses recalls the hard-to-explain fact that wherever the Negro is found, there are traditional tales of Moses and his supernatural powers that are not in the Bible. . . ."

Hurston's devotion to anthropology disappointed those friends who wanted her to concentrate more on fiction writing. An interesting perspective is found in Wallace Thurman's satiric treatment of Sweetie May Carr, a thinly disguised portrait of Hurston, in his novel *Infants of the Spring* (1932). A short-story writer from an all-black Mississippi town, she is "too indifferent to literary creation to transfer to paper that which she told so well." Sweetie May says, "I have to eat. I also wish to finish my education. Being a Negro writer these days is a racket and I'm going to make the most of it while it lasts . . . I don't know a tinker's damn about art. . . . My ultimate ambition, as you know, is to become a gynecologist. And the only way I can live easily until I have the requisite training is to pose as a writer of potential ability." Thurman questions Hurston's commitment to writing—and in a larger context, the fate of the entire Harlem Renaissance spirit. Yet in the 1930s Hurston would produce the best fiction being written by a black woman, including the novel *Their Eyes Were Watching God* (1937), written in Haiti in seven weeks, and considered to be her best work. Despite Thurman's cynicism about

> "The sixteen years between 'The Fire and the Cloud' and Hurston's last published story, 'The Conscience of the Court' (Saturday Evening Post, 18 March 1950), created an embittered writer, frustrated by the lack of popular acclaim from both blacks and whites for her four novels and two books of folklore."

Hurston's priorities, he does offer some truths about Hurston through Sweetie May Carr's character. For example, she was "more noted for her ribald wit and personal effervescence than for any actual literary work. She was a great favorite among those whites who went in for Negro prodigies. Mainly because she lived up to their conception of what a typical Negro should be. . . . Her repertoire of tales was earthy, vulgar and funny. Her darkies always smiled through their tears, sang spirituals on the slightest provocation, and performed buck dances. . . . Sweetie May was a master of Southern dialect, and an able raconteur . . . [who] knew her white folks." Thurman's fictional portrait is confirmed by Langston Hughes's comment in his autobiography *The Big Sea* (1940) that Hurston entertained wealthy whites with her "side-splitting anecdotes, humorous tales, and tragi-comic stories of the South." Hughes concludes, "no doubt she was a perfect 'darkie' in the nice meaning whites give the term—that is a naive, childlike, sweet, humorous, and highly colored Negro. But Miss Hurston was clever too. . . . "

The sixteen years between "The Fire and the Cloud" and Hurston's last published story, "The Conscience of the Court" (*Saturday Evening Post,* 18 March 1950), created an embittered writer, frustrated by the lack of popular acclaim from both blacks and whites for her four novels and two books of folklore. In the early 1940s Hurston worked for four months as a story consultant at Paramount

Studios but failed to have her novels made into movies; then she lectured on the black-college circuit while she continued writing. Her autobiography, *Dust Tracks on a Road,* her most successful publication, gave a partially accurate, partially fictionalized account of her life. In the following years she made many attempts to receive funding for folklore research trips to Central America; finally, an advance on a new novel allowed her to travel in 1947 to British Honduras, where she completed *Seraph on the Suwanee* (1948), her first work that excluded blacks—and her last book. In September 1948 Hurston was arrested in New York City on a morals charge that devastated her personally and professionally. Although the accusation of sodomy with a ten-year-old proved to be false and she was cleared of this morals charge in March 1949, Hurston's world collapsed. A national black newspaper, the *Baltimore Afro-American,* gave the story sensationalized, inaccurate front-page coverage. Writing to Carl Van Vechten, Hurston explained how she was unjustly betrayed by her own race which "has seen fit to destroy [her] without reason" in the "so-called liberal North." She concludes, "All that I have ever tried to do has proved useless. All that I have believed in has failed me. I have resolved to die . . . no acquittal will persuade some people that I am innocent. I feel hurled down a filthy privy hole." However, after a brief period of depression, she attempted to restore her reputation. She taught drama at North Carolina College for Negroes in Durham for a short while and published several nonfiction articles in national magazines.

When "The Conscience of the Court" was published Hurston was working as a maid on affluent Rivo Island, one of Miami's fashionable neighborhoods. As she dusted bookshelves in the library, her employer sat in the living room reading a story written by her "girl." Hurston's unusual situation was inaccurately depicted in a *Miami Herald* feature article (and picked up by the wire services). "Miss Hurston," the interviewing reporter wrote, "believes that she is temporarily written out." (Hurston's agent was at this time holding her eighth book and three short stories—about a Florida religious colony, a turpentine worker at a political meeting, and myths explaining Swiss cheese's holes—none of which was ever published.) Hurston covered up her need for money by stating, "You can only use your mind so long. Then you have to use your hands. It's just the natural thing. I was born with a skillet in my hands. I like to cook and keep house. Why shouldn't I do it for someone else a

while? A writer has to stop writing every now and then and live a little." Continuing to weave her stories, she assured the reporter that she only wanted to learn about a maid's life so she could begin a magazine "for and by domestics"—as if she did not know already from her earlier experiences. She told her employer that she had bank accounts overseas where her books had been published, but she refused to be unpatriotic and spend the money abroad. The publicity about her being a maid and being arrested lends an irony to "Conscience of the Court," which is about a black maid arrested for attacking a white man.

The story focuses on Laura Lee Kimble, who is being tried for assaulting Clement Beasley. Refusing a defense lawyer, Laura justifies her actions by explaining that Beasley attempted to remove valuable property from the home of her white employer, Mrs. J. Stuart Clairborne, on the grounds that he was collecting on an unpaid debt incurred when the white woman borrowed six hundred dollars to pay for Laura's husband's funeral. As the lifelong maid of the Clairborne family, Laura is intensely devoted, despite the fact that she thinks her employer has now abandoned her. She protected the home as if it were her own, and when the man verbally and physically abused her, she stopped him. She tells the judge, "All I did was grab him by his heels and flail the pillar of the porch with him a few times." When the truth comes out that the money was not yet due, and that the man was trying to steal property in excess of six hundred dollars, the judge praises Laura's courage and loyalty and instructs the jury to free her. Laura then finds out that Mrs. Clairborne never knew she had been arrested. Having doubted the woman's friendship for not coming to her aid, Laura expiates her sin when she arrives home by performing a "ritual of atonement" in solemnly polishing the silver before she eats her meal.

Laura's extreme humility, dependence, and loyalty toward whites illustrate the formula writing Hurston knew would sell. The rejection of her last completed novel, about wealthy blacks, led her to believe that whites could not conceive of blacks beyond lower class stereotypes. However, in this story she helped perpetuate the stereotyped images of her race, allowing the *Post* staff to heavily edit the piece because she badly needed the nine hundred dollars she was paid for it.

A year after this last published story appeared, Hurston wrote her agent that she was "cold in hand" (penniless); she confessed, "God! What I have been through. . . . Just inching along like a stepped on worm." This once-famous writer, who had received honorary doctorates and had been on the cover of *Saturday Review,* spent the final decade of her life in relative obscurity. From Rivo Island, she moved around Florida—Belle Glade, Eau Gallie (for five peaceful years), Merritt Island (during which time she worked briefly as a technical librarian for the space program at Patrick Air Force Base), and Fort Pierce, where she wrote a column, "Hoodoo and Black Magic," for a black weekly, the *Fort Pierce Chronicle,* from 11 July 1958 to 7 August 1959. She also taught in a black public school. In 1959 she suffered a stroke, leaving her unable to care for herself adequately. Wracked with pain, she continued to labor at a three-hundred-page manuscript about Herod the Great. Against her will she entered the St. Lucie County Welfare Home in October 1959 and died of hypertensive heart disease on 28 January 1960. No one noticed that her middle name was misspelled (Neil) on her death certificate; moreover, her funeral was delayed a week while friends and family raised the four hundred dollars for expenses. Hoping to make some money to pay Hurston's debt, a deputy sheriff used a garden hose to save the Herod manuscript from being burned, for the welfare-home janitor had been instructed to destroy Hurston's personal effects. Hurston was buried in an unmarked grave in Fort Pierce's segregated cemetery, Garden of the Heavenly Rest.

Hurston's short stories signal the beginning of an important literary career that also produced four novels, two folklore books, an autobiography, and several nonfiction journal articles. However, "The Conscience of the Court" seems to support Darwin T. Turner's criticism of her work's "superficial and shallow" judgments because she became too "desperate for recognition" and "a blind follower of that social code which approves arrogance toward one's assumed peers and inferiors but requires total psychological commitment to a subservient position before one's supposed superiors." Yet Turner praises her early work, particularly "Sweat," for its skill in presenting the picturesque idiom of Southern blacks, its credible characterization, and its emphasis on love and hate in family relationships. Turner sums up the intensity by which Hurston herself seems to have lived: "In her fiction, men and women love each other totally, or they hate vengefully." Perhaps because she wrote against the prevailing black attitudes of protest in the 1950s, black critics often dismissed her work. Yet in 1972 Arna Bontemps (her literary executor) prophetically wrote that Hurston "still awaits the thoroughgoing critical analysis that will properly place her in the pattern of American fiction."

That comprehensive appraisal came in 1977 with Robert E. Hemenway's *Zora Neale Hurston: A Literary Biography.* Acknowledging his "white man's reconstruction of the intellectual process in a black woman's mind," he offers a favorable assessment of her literary career and tries to explain her enigmatic personality. Praising her work as a celebration of black culture, he concludes that her failure to achieve recognition in her life reflects America's poor treatment of its black artists. The critical acclaim awarded Hurston's writings in the past ten years has allowed readers to discover what Alice Walker (writing in the foreword to Hemenway's biography) finds: a "sense of black people as complete, complex, *undiminished* human beings." She honors Hurston's genius as a black woman writer and delights in her dynamic personality: "Zora was funny, irreverent (she was the first to call the Harlem Renaissance literati the 'niggerati'), good-looking and sexy."

Hurston, who produced a substantial body of literature of intense human emotions, died poor but left a rich legacy. In 1973, as a tribute to that inspiration, Walker placed a gravestone inscribed: "ZORA NEALE HURSTON / 'A GENIUS OF THE SOUTH' / 1901–1960 / NOVELIST, FOLK-LORIST / ANTHROPOLOGIST."

Source: Laura M. Zaidman, "Zora Neale Hurston," in *Dictionary of Literary Biography,* Vol. 86, *American Short-Story Writers, 1910–1945, First Series,* edited by Bobby Ellen Kimbel, Gale Research, 1989, pp. 159–71.

Sources

Gates, Henry Louis, Jr., and Sieglinde Lemke, eds., "Introduction," in *Zora Neale Hurston: The Complete Stories,* HarperPerennial, 1995, pp. ix–xxiii.

Gelfant, Blanche H., and Lawrence Graver, "Zora Neale Hurston," in *The Columbia Companion to the Twentieth-Century American Short Story,* Columbia University Press, 2000, pp. 305–08.

Harmon, William, and Hugh Holman, *A Handbook to Literature,* 9th ed., Prentice Hall, 2003.

Howard, Lillie P., "Zora Neale Hustorn," *Dictionary of Literary Biography,* Vol. 51, *Afro-American Writers from the Harlem Renaissance to 1940,* edited by Trudier Harris, Gale Research, 1987, pp. 133–45.

Hurston, Zora Neale, ''Conscience of the Court,'' in *The Complete Stories,* edited by Henry Louis Gates Jr. and Sieglinde Lemke, 1995, HarperCollins, pp. xxii–xxiii, 162–77.

''The Politics of Civil Rights: Ending Racial Segregation in America,'' in *Civil Rights in America: 1500 to the Present,* Gale, 1998.

''Race Relations,'' in *Dictionary of American History,* Charles Scribner's Sons, 1976.

Williams, Juan, Interview, in *All Things Considered,* NPR, October 31, 1998.

Further Reading

Howard, Lillie P., ed., *Alice Walker and Zora Neale Hurston: The Common Bond,* Greenwood Press, 1993.
   Hurston is an influential writer for many African American authors, and Walker has been among her most outspoken champions. Here, Howard analyzes Hurston's and Walker's writings to find similarities and areas of influence.

Klarman, Michael J., *From Jim Crow to Civil Rights: The Supreme Court and the Struggle for Racial Equality,* Oxford University Press, 2004.
   Beginning with 1896's *Plessy v. Ferguson,* Klarman summarizes landmark Supreme Court decisions as they pertain to racial issues and civil rights. In addition to the facts of the cases themselves, Klarman includes the political and social contexts and ramifications for each case.

Peters, Pearlie Mae Fisher, *The Assertive Woman in Zora Neale Hurston's Fiction, Folklore, and Drama,* Garland Publishing, 1998.
   Hurston, an independent and outspoken woman, is credited with creating assertive female characters that were in many ways ahead of their time. Peters draws from Hurston's canon of work to evaluate the importance of her bold protagonists. Unlike many studies of Hurston's work, this one considers her drama alongside her fiction.

Watson, Steven, *The Harlem Renaissance: Hub of African-American Culture, 1920–1930,* Pantheon, 1995.
   Going beyond the writings that came out of the Harlem Renaissance, Watson explores the cultural influences of the movement, along with the cultural forces that led to it. Watson enhances his exploration with photos and art from the period.

Crazy Sunday

F. Scott Fitzgerald
1932

F. Scott Fitzgerald's short story "Crazy Sunday" is the story of a young screenwriter and his personal and professional difficulties in the complex Hollywood film industry. Intent on impressing the elite in his industry, Joel instead finds himself ensnared in the personal problems of a high-profile couple. The story was originally published in a magazine called *American Mercury* in October 1932. Fitzgerald included it in his final collection of short stories, 1935's *Taps at Reveille.*

Joel Coles, the main character, is based on Fitzgerald himself, and Joel's embarrassment at Miles Calman's party is autobiographical. At a party hosted by Hollywood producer Irving Thalberg and his wife, actress Norma Shearer, Fitzgerald had too much to drink and was booed after performing a song he meant to be humorous but which was actually juvenile and in bad taste. Rather than hide this humiliating moment in the recesses of his memory, Fitzgerald turned it over to his imagination, and it became "Crazy Sunday." The story was turned down for publication from a number of magazines for various reasons, including its ending, length, characters, and sexual content, but Fitzgerald refused to revise the story just to please magazine editors. Ultimately, *American Mercury* bought it intact for two hundred dollars.

Author Biography

F. Scott Fitzgerald (Francis Scott Key Fitzgerald) was born on September 24, 1896, in St. Paul, Minnesota, to a businessman and an heiress. His desire to become a writer crystallized early and remained a driving force throughout his life. Regarded as the preeminent writer of the Jazz Age, Fitzgerald created characters and stories of youth, love, excess, eccentricity, and style. During his lifetime, his success was based on his standing as a niche writer. It was not until after his death that his writing was appreciated and placed among the American greats.

By the time Fitzgerald entered Princeton University in 1913, he had already begun to develop his writing skills. His work for school newspapers and theater groups had exposed him to various types of writing. At Princeton he wrote for a literary magazine, a humor magazine, and a performance club. He put in so much effort on such activities, however, that he could not keep up with his schoolwork, and he left Princeton in 1916. His return a year later was interrupted by enlistment in the U.S. Army during World War I.

Upon leaving the military in 1919, Fitzgerald worked briefly as an advertising copywriter while he revised his first novel, *This Side of Paradise* (1920). Things moved fast as he enjoyed acclaim for his novel and promptly married Zelda Sayre. Later that year, his first collection of short stories, *Flappers and Philosophers*, was published. Over the course of his career, more novels followed, most notably *The Great Gatsby*, in 1925. Fitzgerald also continued to produce volumes of short stories at almost the same pace as he was completing novels. ''Crazy Sunday'' appeared in his last collection, *Taps at Reveille.*

The Fitzgeralds lived the fast-paced life of the Roaring Twenties to the hilt. Much of Fitzgerald's material was drawn from his own life. Because his income was inconsistent, he accrued a great amount of debt by borrowing money from his publisher and from his agent. The 1920s were the greatest and most trying years for the Fitzgeralds. While they enjoyed a high standard of living and an exciting lifestyle, Zelda became increasingly mentally ill, Fitzgerald struggled with alcoholism, and he ultimately fell out of favor when his contemporary subject matter became passé.

The pace at which Fitzgerald wrote had slowed so that by the time *Tender Is the Night* (1934) and *Taps at Reveille* (1935) were published, American readers were enduring the Great Depression, a far cry from the carefree heydays of the 1920s. With Zelda in a mental hospital, mounting debts, and little income from his writing, Fitzgerald drank heavily, and his health suffered. He rallied in 1937, however, and returned to Hollywood (where he had worked briefly in 1927) to work on such screenplays as *Gone with the Wind.* A life of fast living with extreme highs and lows ended on December 21, 1940, when forty-four-year-old Fitzgerald died of a heart attack in Hollywood.

Plot Summary

Part I

Joel Coles is a twenty-eight-year-old screenwriter who arrived in Hollywood six months ago. Already, he has enjoyed some success and has impressed many of the right people. He is enthusiastic and optimistic, not yet jaded by the competitive industry he has chosen.

It is Sunday, and having been invited to a party at the home of a major director, Miles Calman, Joel imagines how he will impress him. He promises himself he will not drink and that he will prove his worthiness to be in the kind of company Miles keeps. Once he arrives, he is reunited with Stella Walker (now Stella Calman, Miles's wife), whom he knew as a struggling actress in New York. They are comfortable with each other, and soon Joel has finished a few cocktails. He meets up with another writer, Nat Keogh, and they join the other guests to watch a hired singer perform.

Part II

After the singer's performance, Joel asks Stella if he can entertain the guests with a short act he wrote. She agrees and even stands in as the second actor. As he performs, he realizes that the audience is not enjoying it, and he even hears someone ''boo'' him. Humiliated, he sends a note to Miles the next morning apologizing for the display. Later, he receives an invitation from Stella to her sister's house for supper the next Sunday. Delighted, he accepts.

Part III

At the supper, Joel and the other guests witness tension between Miles and Stella. Apparently, they have been fighting about Miles's lengthy affair with an actress named Eva Goebel. Stella talks with Joel about the situation, and when the discussion goes on long enough, Miles suggests that the three of them go back to their house. There, Stella, Joel, and Miles talk about the infidelity until the conversation turns to work.

The next morning, Stella invites Joel to accompany her to dinner and a theater party Saturday night while Miles is out of town. He agrees but plans to tell Miles about the invitation. Miles changes his plans because he does not want Stella going out with Joel or anyone else. Even though Joel realizes he is in love with Stella, he assures Miles that he would never make a pass at her. Miles invites Joel to join them at the party, and Joel accepts.

Part IV

Joel arrives at the theater to meet them, discovering that Miles went on his trip after all. He thinks Stella looks breathtaking, and when she suggests skipping the party and going to her house, he agrees. A telegram from Miles is there, but she is suspicious. She is not convinced that he has really gone away on business. He may be seeing his mistress, she surmises.

Joel tells Stella he is afraid that she is using him to get back at Miles. She admits that she is attracted to him but adds that she loves Miles and is uncomfortable about the evening she just shared with Joel. He prepares to leave, a little vexed but also a little relieved, when the phone rings at midnight.

Part V

Shortly after midnight, Joel has hurriedly made love to Stella. He pours himself a drink, and as Stella leans toward the telephone, Joel picks it up to hear the wired message that is replaying. It says that Miles has been killed in an airplane accident. Stella is vaguely aware of the message, but Joel insists on having her doctor or a friend present before she hears the news. As she realizes that Miles is dead and Joel is stalling, she becomes frantic and insists that he stay with her. He continually presses her for the name of a girlfriend to come to be with her.

A messenger delivers a telegram confirming the phone message, and Stella has trouble absorbing the news. Joel manages to get in touch with some of her friends to come to be with her, but she begs him not to leave. Feeling that she is only clinging to him in an effort to keep Miles's memory alive, Joel leaves once other people begin to arrive. As he

F. Scott Fitzgerald

leaves, Joel is overwhelmed by the enormous presence of Miles, even in death.

Characters

Miles Calman

Miles Calman is a Hollywood director who commands a high level of respect in the industry. The narrator explains that he ''was the only director on the lot who did not work under a supervisor and was responsible to the money men alone.'' The films he directs are those he considers worthy of his artistic vision, and he is known for being uncompromising. Still, he is depicted as having problems and frailties: He has been carrying on a lengthy affair with another woman (after cheating on his first wife with Stella); he is ''tall, nervous, with a desperate humor and the unhappiest eyes Joel ever saw,'' and ''one could not be with him long without realizing that he was not a well man.''

For all his success in his career, Miles is basically insecure. He is jealous of Stella to the point of being hypocritical. He makes excuses for his inability to stop seeing his mistress altogether, yet he cannot think of Stella going to a party with

Joel. In all likelihood, it is his insecurity that leads him to seek female attention and admiration in affairs.

Stella Calman

Stella Calman is Miles's young, beautiful wife. She knew Joel when she was a struggling actress (Stella Walker) in New York. Reunited, she finds herself attracted to Joel for reasons she does not fully understand. She seems to enjoy her ability to capture his attention, but she also seems to sense a certain kinship with him. Perhaps she feels out of her element among the Hollywood elite, and she associates Joel with her past.

When Stella discovers Miles's affair, however, she seems determined to find in Joel the intimacy and validation lacking in her marriage. Her insecurity and self-doubt are clear in her emotional shifts from Miles to Joel and back again. Her naïveté is evident in the fact that she was Miles's mistress during his first marriage, yet she is stunned when he takes a mistress during his marriage to her.

Joel Coles

Joel Coles is a twenty-eight-year-old screenwriter who has been in Hollywood for six months pursuing a career as a screenwriter. In his first six months, he has landed some ''nice assignments'' and is proud of his accomplishments and potential. The narrator tells the reader that Joel is ''not yet broken by Hollywood,'' adding that he is an enthusiastic worker. His high opinion of himself is bolstered by the invitation he receives to Miles Calman's home for a party. Imagining the Hollywood celebrities that are sure to be there, Joel pictures himself fitting right in with them and impressing Miles in the process. The embarrassment he endures at the party does not destroy his ego, however, as he is flattered by the attentions of Miles's wife, Stella.

Even as a young man, Joel is no stranger to theater life. His mother was a successful stage actress whose career took Joel back and forth between New York and London. It was during his time in New York that he first met Stella, who was a struggling actress and an admirer of Joel's mother.

Joel is immature and ill-equipped to handle the issues surrounding his relationship with Stella. This may be because his early life revolved around theater, or it may be because at such a young age he has had few meaningful personal relationships.

Regardless, he falls in love too easily and for the wrong reasons, and he has difficulty knowing how to have integrity with Miles and affection for Stella. Ultimately, he has no tools to help Stella handle the tragic loss of her husband, and his only recourse is to leave.

Nat Keogh

Nat is a screenwriter and an acquaintance of Joel's, described by the narrator as ''the good-humored, heavy-drinking, highly paid Nat Keogh.'' Although he drinks and gambles too much, he is highly successful in his career; he makes enough money to hire a manager in addition to an agent. Nat is friendly and reassuring to Joel after the embarrassment at Miles's party.

Themes

Insecurity

All three of the main characters exhibit insecurity that prompts them to reach out for external approval and reassurance. Fitzgerald shows how insecurity strikes anyone, regardless of background, career success, or personal egoism. More specifically, he seems to be revealing that insecurity is prevalent in Hollywood.

Joel possesses the antithetical combination of insecurity and arrogance that is common in youth. On the one hand, he perceives himself as a talented writer (''He referred to himself modestly as a hack but really did not think of it that way'') who is ready to move among the elite in his industry. He even considers himself somewhat superior professionally because he can refuse alcohol (so he claims), unlike many of his peers. At the same time, he desperately seeks approval from others. He seeks the approval of Miles, Stella, and the partygoers, always switching his focus according to whom he thinks he can best impress. When Stella starts paying attention to him, he finds her irresistible, despite the fact that she is married to a powerful director and personal acquaintance of his. Even when he realizes that she is using him, he does not cut her out of his life right away. He is simultaneously disappointed and relieved when she suggests that her chauffeur drive him home. His conflicted

Topics for Further Study

- Besides Fitzgerald, William Faulkner also worked in Hollywood in the 1930s. Research Faulkner's experience in Hollywood and draw comparisons and contrasts with Fitzgerald's Hollywood years. Prepare a "movie pitch" about these two literary figures in Hollywood. For fun, consider casting your movie with contemporary actors and actresses.

- In what ways did the Great Depression affect the Hollywood film industry? What kinds of films were produced during this time, and who were the prominent actors and actresses? What insights does your research give you into American culture and the American psyche?

- What do you think happens with Joel and Stella after the events of the story? Write another section for the story, trying to mimic Fitzgerald's narrative voice, letting the reader know what the nature of their relationship was, what direction Joel's career took, and any other additions you would like to make to the story.

- Imagine you are a psychologist in Hollywood at the time and one of the main characters (Joel, Stella, or Miles) is your patient. Prepare notes from your first few sessions, along with your assessment of your patient's psychological health, problems you observe, and solutions or exercises you would like to suggest. Feel free to include predictions.

---

feelings stem from his insecurity, his need to feel desirable, and his vague awareness of ethics.

Stella's insecurity is evident in her pursuit of Joel, which accelerates when she discovers Miles's affair. Initially, she enjoys the way Joel admired her and how he reminds her of her past. She knew him during a time of less social pressure, scrutiny, and judgment. His comment that she looks sixteen makes her feel youthful and carefree. When she learns that Miles has been unfaithful, Stella turns to Joel as a confidante and an admirer. She knows he is captivated by her, and in the wake of the rejection and self-doubt brought on by the affair, she needs another man to make her feel desirable. Ironically, this is exactly what Joel predicted in their first conversation.

Despite his professional success and large circle of friends, Miles is deeply insecure. He is repeating the pattern of his first marriage, in which he took a mistress to make him feel sexy. He is seeing a therapist to work out his personal problems, but there is little evidence of progress. In his career, Miles is confident and unconcerned about making everyone happy, but in his personal life he craves reassurance and validation.

Appearance

In the competitive culture of the Hollywood film industry, appearance is critical. Fitzgerald touches on this in "Crazy Sunday" through Joel. Anticipating his evening at Miles's party, Joel resolves to stay away from alcohol because he knows Miles judges writers who drink too much. Joel wants to make a good impression and show that he fits in with Miles and his friends. In reality, Joel knows he drinks too much, but he wants his appearance to conform to Miles's standards. The narrator explains, "Calman was audibly tired of rummies, and thought it was a pity the industry could not get along without them." Knowing this, Joel hopes that Miles will be in earshot when he turns down an offer of cocktails. At the party, however, Joel has some drinks and realizes too late that he is humiliating himself before his peers. He fears that the damage to his image may be irreparable, which could mean the end of his career. In his embarrassment, he struggles to maintain the appearance that he is still self-assured, and the narrator remarks that "he clung desperately to his rule of never betraying an inferior emotion until he no longer felt it." Later, Joel, self-conscious in his silk hat, reveals his awareness of appearance when he waits for Stella and Miles at the theater. He is beginning to understand that appearances in Hollywood often mask reality.

Style

Foreshadowing

Fitzgerald uses foreshadowing to hint at Joel's misfortune at Miles's party and later with Stella. In Part I, Joel is full of the anticipation of the party and promises himself he will not have anything to drink. The first indication that alcohol is a stumbling block for Joel is when the narrator comments, "Ordinarily he did not go out on Sundays but stayed sober and took work home with him." The first words spoken by Joel in the story are to himself, when he declares, "I won't take anything to drink." Joel's fears about lowering his inhibitions at such an important party foreshadow his humiliation when he breaks his promises to himself and has several cocktails. By the time the narrator reveals "He took another cocktail—not because he needed confidence but because she [Stella] had given him so much of it," the reader knows that his confidence is false.

The closer Joel gets to Stella, and the more attracted he is to her, the more he begins to realize that she lacks the self-assuredness to make her own decisions. This character weakness foreshadows the demise of their relationship when she tells Joel that she is attracted to him but loves Miles. By this time, Joel has learned that Stella is overly influenced by Miles and probably only liked Joel because Miles liked him first. He remembers a conversation in which Miles said, "I've influenced Stella in everything. Especially I've influenced her so that she likes all the men I like—it's very difficult." In retrospect, Joel realizes that the signs of her rejection were there all along.

Film Industry Setting

As the story opens, the narrator describes the day-to-day reality of working life in Hollywood. He writes:

> Behind, for all of them, lay sets and sequences, the long waits under the crane that swung the microphone, the hundred miles a day by automobiles to and fro across the county, the struggles of rival ingenuities in the conference rooms, the ceaseless compromise, the clash and strain of many personalities fighting for their lives.

Besides overt descriptions, the narrator subtly describes the setting of the story in ways that are reminiscent of the film industry itself. Room descriptions sound like settings, and physical environments are sometimes described in relation to their emotional impact. Miles's house is described as having been "built for great emotional moments—there was an air of listening, as if the far silences of its vistas hid an audience." Later, the Calmans' home is described this way: "Under the high ceilings the situation seemed more dignified and tragic." These are aspects that someone in the film industry would notice. In introducing them into the story, the narrator also supports the theme of the importance of appearances.

Historical Context

Hollywood in the 1930s

Early in the 1930s, color and sound came to Hollywood movies. This heightened public interest in American movies, which in turn catapulted the celebrity status of actors, actresses, and musicians. Not surprisingly, many studios capitalized on the new capabilities of film by producing musicals. This tendency toward light fare was ideal for moviegoers whose Depression-era lives contained enough tragedy and anxiety. Excitement and adventure was also evident in the popularity of gangster movies and westerns. But the Great Depression dragged on through the years, and while Americans sought the two-hour escapes offered by movies, their ability to afford them dwindled. By 1934, one-third of the nation's movie theaters had closed their doors. To stay afloat, Hollywood studios were forced to utilize less expensive means of production in order to pay the high salaries that popular celebrities earned. Without major names on the marquis, movies were rarely very successful. Among the big names that drew crowds were Katherine Hepburn, Spencer Tracy, Jean Harlow, Gary Cooper, Cary Grant, Mae West, W. C. Fields, Marlene Dietrich, and James Cagney. First introduced in 1934, Shirley Temple movies provided a loveable figure of innocence and hope for struggling moviegoers.

Movies in the 1930s represented everything that real life seemed to lack—romance, adventure, glamour, fantasy, and happy endings. Some historians have noted that in the 1920s, movie protagonists often cruised effortlessly into their happy endings, but in the 1930s movie producers depicted happy endings coming about as a gradual change of fortune. In *The Nickel and Dime Decade: American*

Compare & Contrast

- **1930s:** Despite the Great Depression, this decade is a memorable one for the American film industry. Shirley Temple movies, epics like *Gone with the Wind,* and feel-good films like *Mr. Smith Goes to Washington* make this an important decade in American film and culture.

  Today: In 2003, American moviegoers spent almost $9.5 billion on tickets. In decidedly more stable and prosperous years than the Depression era, Americans have more to spend on movies but do not rely as heavily on them for emotional relief and escape.

- **1930s:** In 1933, the Twenty-First Amendment is ratified, overturning the Eighteenth Amendment's prohibition on alcohol. This is the first time a constitutional amendment is repealed.

  Today: Laws regarding the sale of alcohol primarily dictate the legal age at which a person can purchase alcohol. There are still counties that are "dry," meaning that the sale of alcohol is illegal in that area.

- **1930s:** Fitzgerald's status as a popular author wanes, as most readers and critics have lost interest in his work. Because he is so strongly associated with the Jazz Age (1920s), he finds it difficult to sell his fiction in the 1930s.

  Today: Fitzgerald is considered one of the great American authors, and his works are taught in schools and universities around the world. According to Scribner, readers buy half a million copies a year of his works.

Popular Culture during the 1930s, Gary Dean Best quotes Will Hays, the Motion Picture Producers and Distributors of America president in 1934:

> No medium has contributed more greatly than the films to the maintenance of the national morale during a period featured by revolution, riot and political turmoil in other countries. . . . It has been the mission of the screen, without ignoring the serious social problems of the day, to reflect aspiration, achievement, optimism and kindly humor in its entertainment.

Irving Thalberg and Norma Shearer

The party that Fitzgerald fictionalizes in "Crazy Sunday" is based on an actual party he attended, hosted by Irving Thalberg and Norma Shearer. Thalberg was a very successful Hollywood producer whose rise to prominence was well known among his contemporaries. Having never completed high school, he got a job at a movie studio, where he worked hard and eventually became a major executive at MGM Studios. Thalberg had a special focus on screenplays and worked closely with writers. He was known, however, for protecting the integrity of some projects by having two writers work simultaneously on a script without letting them know. Born with a heart defect, Thalberg never expected a long life and often overworked himself to the point of collapse, intent on finishing his projects according to his vision. He died of pneumonia at the age of thirty-seven. The movie producer in *The Last Tycoon* is based on Thalberg, as is Miles Calman in "Crazy Sunday."

Norma Shearer was an actress in Hollywood who enjoyed success in silent and sound films. She was nominated numerous times for an Academy Award, winning once. Early in her career, she modeled while she waited for her big break. Her modeling experience helped prepare her for the facial expressions necessary for success in silent movies. Once she began making movies for MGM, her celebrity status rose quickly. Having made numerous silent movies, married Thalberg, and started a family in the 1920s, she and her husband decided to pursue bringing sound to movies. Luckily, she had a voice that allowed her to bridge her career from silence to sound. In the early 1930s, she was one of the highest paid actresses in Hollywood. After Thalberg's death, Shearer continued her acting career and stayed active in the movie business.

Although she remarried, she was buried alongside Thalberg upon her death at the age of eighty.

Critical Overview

"Crazy Sunday" was included in the last collection of Fitzgerald's short stories published in his lifetime, *Taps at Reveille*. Unfortunately, by the time the book was published in 1935, few reviewers were interested in Fitzgerald's work. Those who were interested noticed the changes taking place in Fitzgerald's maturing fiction. In *F. Scott Fitzgerald: The Man and His Work*, Alfred Kazin quotes a *New Republic* review by T. S. Mathews: "The yearning toward maturity is even more noticeable in some of these short stories than it is in his novels." Mathews adds that many of the characters grapple with the fact that life requires them to mature and behave like adults. Although "Crazy Sunday" is well liked among Fitzgerald's readers, there is little critical commentary about it beyond grouping it with Fitzgerald's better-known Hollywood stories, such as the Pat Hobby series of short stories and his unfinished novel, *The Last Tycoon*.

Much commentary on Fitzgerald's short fiction in general sheds critical light on "Crazy Sunday." In *Student Companion to F. Scott Fitzgerald*, for example, author Linda Pelzer observes that Fitzgerald's best short stories share connections with his novels. She writes, "All of his best stories are connected thematically to his novels. In fact, several seem to anticipate or repeat not only thematic concerns, but also plot elements and figurative motifs that are integral to the novels." "Crazy Sunday" is set in Hollywood, and a main character (Miles) is said to be based on Irving Thalberg. Both of these elements are repeated in *The Last Tycoon*.

Criticism

Jennifer Bussey

Bussey holds a master's degree in interdisciplinary studies and a bachelor's degree in English literature. She is an independent writer specializing in literature. In the following essay, Bussey exam-ines F. Scott Fitzgerald's "Crazy Sunday" and how its main character, Joel Coles, exhibits emotional immaturity in all of his relationships.

Based on an embarrassing incident from F. Scott Fitzgerald's own experience in Hollywood, "Crazy Sunday" is part autobiography and part pure fiction. The main character, Joel Coles, is a young screenwriter who has recently arrived in Hollywood and is enjoying a measure of success. Trying to impress all the right people, he instead humiliates himself and finds himself in the middle of a marriage on the rocks. Throughout the story, Fitzgerald portrays Joel as emotionally immature in every relationship he has. He is immature in his relationship to himself, creating a self-image that is often convenient and reassuring if not always accurate. He is immature in his relationships with others, seeking approval and validation from whoever is most likely to give it. And he is immature in his relationship to his career and his industry, setting professionalism aside in favor of soothing his ego. As the story progresses from beginning to end, Joel experiences no personal growth and misses opportunities to gain wisdom because he is too immature to seize them.

First, Joel lacks the maturity to be honest with himself and exercise discipline or self-control. He knows that he drinks too much, and he promises himself not to have any drinks at Miles Calman's party. Within the first hour, he has broken this promise, accepting a cocktail because Stella, Miles's beautiful wife, gives it to him. Rather than exhibit the self-assuredness to refuse the drink politely, he feels that he has no choice but to take it and drink it. He makes excuses that he believes are legitimate reasons to make poor decisions. Once he begins drinking, he is unable to moderate his behavior at all. To him, the first drink is never the last, and he paves his own road to ruin.

Fitzgerald shows how Joel's mind-set changes with the effects of the alcohol. He feels warm and friendly toward the others at the party, and he feels overconfident in his ability to conduct himself appropriately. This reveals his immaturity because he has been drunk enough times to know better; he should know that drinking lowers important inhibitions and alters the good judgment he needs in the company of his industry peers. However, living in the moment, he leaves such wisdom behind and once again falls prey to the deceptive powers of alcohol.

Joel also fails to be completely honest with himself about his own talent and importance in the Hollywood studio scene. He has only been working for six months, yet he exhibits admittedly false humility about his talent, feels completely entitled to be among the Hollywood elite at Miles's party, and sees himself as superior to other writers such as Nat Keogh. He initially looks down on Nat because of his reputation for being a heavy drinker, which is not only hypocritical but also ignores the fact that Nat is extremely successful and very well paid for his work in their competitive industry.

Second, Joel is immature in his relationships with other people. He is insecure and tends to shift his focus away from those who might reject him, moving toward those who are likely to accept and even admire him. When he feels vulnerable, he is less honest with others than he is with himself. Trying to shrug off the bad reception of his performance, Joel keeps his disgust to himself and clings "desperately to his rule of never betraying an inferior emotion until he no longer felt it." He craves external validation, especially from people he considers impressive. When he receives the invitation to Miles's party, he imagines all the ways he will impress the important director, but after one cocktail, he practically forgets about Miles and focuses entirely on Stella. Similarly, when he feels accepted by the group at the party, he feels warm toward them. The narrator comments that Joel "felt happy and friendly toward all the people gathered there.... He liked them—he loved them. Great waves of good feeling flowed through him." But when he senses their rejection during his performance ("the thumbs down of the clan"), he puts on emotional blinders and concentrates on Stella. In the morning, his first order of business is to send an apologetic note to Miles, but when he receives an ego-boosting message from Stella, he forgets about Miles again.

Joel's relationship with Miles is somewhat complicated. On the one hand, he wants to stay in his good graces for personal and professional reasons, but on the other hand, he continues to see Stella. He likes being on the "inside" with Miles, and at some level, he wants to be honorable. His integrity, however, is too shallow to motivate his decision with and about Stella. When she asks him to accompany her to a party while Miles is away, Joel makes sure to let Miles know. Yet when Joel finds himself unexpectedly alone with Stella, he does not leave. In the story, the purpose of Joel's relationship with Miles is to force him to make adult

Irving Thalberg, one of the hosts of the real-life party that Fitzgerald fictionalizes in "Crazy Sunday"

decisions. Joel struggles—and fails—to be mature, but this relationship seems to be the first one that has ever forced him to face such issues.

In his relationship with Stella, Joel exhibits the most immaturity. He knows her from their years in New York, but now things are different in the Hollywood scene. Their familiarity is what brings them together, and Joel feels a little awkward at first. The narrator writes, "He felt he should say something more, something confident and easy—he had first met her when she was struggling for bits in New York." Perhaps this is why when they first talk at the party, Joel makes inappropriate remarks to her about possible insecurities. Because he is insecure, he assumes she is, too. He says:

> So you have a baby? That's the time to look out. After a pretty woman has had her first child, she's very vulnerable, because she wants to be reassured about her own charm. She's got to have some new man's unqualified devotion to prove to herself she hasn't lost anything.

Despite these remarks, Stella still feels comfortable with Joel. Although he actually knows very little about her emotional reality, she probably thinks that he understands her intuitively and may even be

What Do I Read Next?

- Considered by most critics to be the definitive biography of Fitzgerald, *Some Sort of Epic Grandeur: The Life of F. Scott Fitzgerald* (1981), by Matthew Bruccoli, provides a unique depth of understanding of the author and his work.

- Fitzgerald's last and unfinished novel, *The Last Tycoon* (1941), was inspired by his experiences and acquaintances in Hollywood. Set in the 1930s film industry, it explores themes of true love, power, and greed.

- Aaron Latham's *Crazy Sundays: F. Scott Fitz-gerald in Hollywood* (1975) provides a context for Fitzgerald's fiction and screenwriting produced during his years in Hollywood. Latham recreates Fitzgerald's day-to-day life in Hollywood, drawing from original interviews, anecdotes, and existing research.

- *The Great Depression: America, 1929–1941* (1985), by Robert S. McElvaine, provides a comprehensive look at America's Depression years. McElvaine covers economics, politics, entertainment, family, culture, and more.

---

inviting her to consider him as her "new man." While Stella talks to Joel about her feelings, her marital problems, her own insecurities, and other personal matters, Joel all but tunes out her words and ponders her beauty. He allows himself to be distracted by her appearance, her clothes, and her mannerisms, with no real interest in getting to know her as a person. At her sister's house, she begins venting her emotions to him about Miles's affair:

> She sat down vehemently on the arm of Joel's chair. Her riding breeches were the color of the chair and Joel saw that the mass of her hair was made up of some strands of red gold and some of pale gold, so that it could not be dyed, and that she had on no make-up. She was that good-looking—

Only a few paragraphs later, the narrator explicitly tells the reader that Joel often ignores Stella's words in favor of taking in the details of her clothing and appearance: "Sometimes he pretended to listen and instead thought how well she was got up." Stella believes that Joel is paying her the attention she wants, when really he is only admiring her beauty. Particularly revealing is that Joel realizes he is in love with her when she suddenly switches from indignation about Miles's affair to protectiveness of him in his career. Perhaps he sees in her a lack of emotional maturity and a short emotional attention span. For Joel, of course, being in love with her only means that he wants to be around her to admire her,

feel admired by her, and perhaps pursue a physical relationship.

In the end, when Stella receives the news that Miles is dead, she needs Joel the most, and his response is to call her friends so he can leave. Here is his opportunity to undergo personal growth and be in a supportive adult relationship, but he is too insecure. Not only is he intimidated by the presence of Miles, even in death, but he realizes he does not love Stella because he believes she only likes him because Miles liked him first. Neither of these factors is good for his ego, so he cannot stay. If he had possessed more maturity earlier, he would never have let the situation with Stella go as far as it did anyway.

Third, Joel is immature in his handling of his career. He is fortunate that his arrival in Hollywood is met with opportunity equal to his talent. This initial success, however, leads him to believe he is a seasoned writer ready for great things in his industry. While it is important to be confident in his work, he allows himself to become overconfident, which will stunt his growth as a writer. Not believing he needs to improve much will prevent him from working on perfecting his craft. The other reason he does not take his career seriously enough is that when he is faced with a conflict between professionalism and ego, he chooses ego. At Miles's party, he should never have asked to perform. In the moment, however, he believed he had the chance to impress his peers and enjoy their applause. By allowing his judgment to be clouded, he humiliated himself professionally and retreated to Stella's (and, the next day, Nat's) reassurance. He is incapable of managing his own career in a mature and responsible way.

Although Joel experiences no growth over the course of the story, there is hope for him. Amidst his inappropriate remarks, drinking, self-centeredness, and insecurity, he makes occasional comments that reveal substantial insight. When Stella learns that Miles has died in the plane crash, she begs Joel to stay with her. A moment of insight actually overcomes him despite the effect her attention must have had on him:

> He stared at her, at first incredulously, and then with shocked understanding. In her dark groping Stella was trying to keep Miles alive by sustaining a situation in which he had figured—as if Miles' mind could not die so long as the possibilities that had worried him still existed. It was a distraught and tortured effort to stave off the realization that he was dead.

To be successful as a writer and as a man, Joel will have to mature and grow as a person and overcome his own self-consciousness and need for validation. He will have to allow more moments of insight to reveal themselves so that he can write believable, moving, and compelling screenplays. Only by developing sensitivity to the human condition will his talent be able to make him the writer he already believes himself to be.

Source: Jennifer Bussey, Critical Essay on "Crazy Sunday," in *Short Stories for Students,* Thomson Gale, 2005.

Anthony Martinelli

Martinelli is a Seattle-based freelance writer and editor. In this essay, Martinelli examines how the public exposure of private relationships inhibits the characters' ability to develop a meaningful love for one another.

In "Crazy Sunday" F. Scott Fitzgerald tells the tale of Hollywood citizens Joel Coles, a young, up-and-coming screenwriter; Miles Calman, a powerful movie director; and Stella Walker (Calman), a beautiful, famous actress and Miles's wife. As to be expected, the lives of famous, Hollywood inhabitants receive much more exposure and attention than an ordinary, everyday citizen. Calman and Walker are no exception. Their public actions are scrutinized, watched and reported. Yet beyond what

> To be successful as a writer and as a man, Joel will have to mature and grow as a person and overcome his own self-consciousness and need for validation."

they do in public, Calman and Walker are under a constant, inquisitive eye that desires to see past their public actions, deep into their private lives. Coles, on the other hand, experiences no overt analysis from the public realm. He lives his life publicly in a way that is similar to most individuals. He moves through life as an active participant and contributor, but when he returns to his private realm, he feels removed from the public realm. Also, because of his ordinary stature, his private life is of no interest to the public. Thus, his private life is truly his own, in that he can decide to share it or to keep it completely isolated. However, as his life overlaps with Calman and Walker's life and relationship, the destructive, invasive power that public scrutiny holds over the private realm becomes unwaveringly apparent.

To better examine the concept of a public realm overpowering the private in "Crazy Sunday," it is best to turn to German-born philosopher, Hannah Arendt. For Arendt, the public realm is common. This means that everything that is seen or heard in this realm is intended to have the widest possible publicity. There is no expectation that what occurs in the public realm would be, in any sense, unavailable to any other person. The public realm is used to communicate and validate reality. To bring ideas, stories or art into the view of the public realm brings them into reality. The existences of things in the private realm, e.g., thoughts, feelings or passions, are inherently shadowy. This means, of course, that anything completely internalized lacks any alternative perspective and, thus, an individual has no way to verify the validity of such a thing without the analysis of another person. Arendt writes in *The Human Condition,* "Each time we talk about things that can be experienced only in privacy or intimacy, we bring them out into a sphere where they will assume a kind of reality which, their intensity not

> Essentially, Calman and Walker's overexposed private life never gives them a true sense of privacy and, thus, they are damned to never develop a truly human concept of love for one another."

withstanding, they never could have had before." With the new reality of private things in the public realm, the privacy of the things inherently dissolves; Meaning that when an individual discusses feelings or thoughts, these thoughts necessarily lose their shadowy reality.

Of course, Arendt does not only delve into the nature of the public realm. However, it is with respect to the public realm that she derives the meaning of "private." For Arendt, the extreme definition of private is to live outside of reality. Arendt states that the denial of this movement from private to public "means above all to be deprived of things essential to a truly human life." However, Arendt also does not believe that a wholly public life is worthwhile. The private realm holds as much importance in the definition of the human condition as the public realm. The private realm is removed from the scrutiny of the prying and inquisitive eyes of the public. For Arendt, "the four walls of one's private property offer the only reliable hiding place from the common public world, not only from everything that goes on in it but from its very publicity, from being seen and being heard." The thoughts, feelings and passions that exist only in the shadowy sphere outside of the public realm remain outside of reality. They are perfectly and completely intimate. Therefore, just as it is necessary to be seen and heard in the common realm, to be empowered with the ability to retreat from it is also essential to a truly human life. Roughly, what Arendt proposes as a truly human life is an individual's ability to facilitate the ebb and flow between the public, common realm and the private, personal realm. To live exclusively within the public or the private realm is not simply the denial of the other, it is the denial of what it means to be human.

With this Arendtian framework in mind, Fitzgerald's "Crazy Sunday" explodes with deeper meaning. In the story, Coles is a young screenwriter with a bright future in Hollywood. When he is invited to a Sunday night party at the home of powerful director, Calman, and his famous actress wife, Walker, he has his future in mind. Coles is aware of his position in the public realm at the Calman's home. He intends to keep himself sober, as he knows that his actions will be under a great amount of scrutiny at such a high-profile party. Fitzgerald writes, "Miles Calman's house was built for great emotional moments—there was an air of listening, as if the far silences of its vistas hid an audience." Here, in Calman's house, Fitzgerald describes the Calman's private realm as a deeply inadequate separation from publicity and it would appear that the stage was set for the performance of Miles's and Stella's private affairs. Oddly, the first blunder of the story is at the hands of Coles.

The night of the party, Coles meets the beautiful and alluring Walker. Against his better judgment, her actions result in a drink finding its way into his hand. As the party and socializing continues, Coles becomes slightly intoxicated and, with the persuasion of Walker, decides to perform in front of Calman's guests. Unfortunately, Coles's skit pokes fun at Hollywood's shallowness. His performance reveals his personal disgust with Hollywood, which is not only the industry he courts, it is also the industry that supports his audience. Needless to say, his performance is ill received and he is booed off stage. It would appear, from Fitzgerald's descriptions of the house, that only Calman and Walker would suffer because it is their home and privacy that is overexposed to the public. However, Coles's actions the night of the party foreshadow the power of the public realm and how the exposure of thoughts, feelings or passions to publicity changes their reality. Coles feelings are no longer his own: he has now opened himself and his ideas to the interpretation and scrutiny of all other individuals within the public sphere.

The next Sunday, to Coles's surprise, the Calman's invite him to another party. This time, however, the stage is set for Calman's own private destruction at the hands of prying publicity. Coles enters the party and discovers the Calman's marriage in disarray because of the director's infidelity. Walker is distraught and upset as she expounds on her husband's affairs. However, the performance of her feelings is almost too theatrical. Fitzgerald writes, "She hovered somewhere between the realest of realities and the most blatant of impersonations.'' In this moment of crushing despair, Walker finds herself unable to shed the feeling of being viewed and continues to perform. Even in emotional pain, she does not allow herself a complete retreat into privacy—possibly because she lacks any truly private realm. With the actions of both Calman and Walker, inviting and exposing Coles to their innermost privacies, Arendt's statement that ''love is killed, or rather extinguished, the moment it is displayed in public'' is substantiated. The necessity of a private realm to retreat to, especially under the emotionally heavy circumstance of an exposed, extramarital affair, is revealed as a clear and obvious need in order for an individual to love and to lead a truly human life. If such a need is not met, then it is obvious that Arendt's statement about love and the public realm is resoundingly true. Essentially, Calman and Walker's overexposed private life never gives them a true sense of privacy and, thus, they are damned to never develop a truly human concept of love for one another.

Through these two *crazy Sundays,* Coles becomes more and more physically attracted to Walker. Even though he knows that the powerful director could crush his career, Coles is eager to seduce Walker. Maybe he is so drawn to her because he can see that their relationship is almost completely theatrical. Maybe he is simply so physically attracted to her that he cannot resist the temptation of her flesh. Whatever the impetus, Coles is persistent and Walker is only slightly resistant to his advances. On the third Saturday, Coles sets out to seduce Walker since Calman plans to be out of town watching a Notre Dame football game. Oddly, Calman originally intended to cancel his trip on account of Coles. In a conversation with Calman, Coles states:

''I hear you're flying to the Notre Dame game.''

Miles looked beyond him [Coles] and shook his head.

''I've given up on the idea.''

''Why?''

''On account of you.'' Still he did not look at Joel.

''What the hell, Miles?''

''That's why I've given it up.'' He broke into a perfunctory laugh at himself. ''I can't tell what Stella might do just out of spite—she's invited you to take her to the Perrys,' hasn't she? I wouldn't enjoy the game.''

Coles lies and convinces Calman that his intentions are only to accompany her as a friend. How-

ever, Calman still insists that he cannot attend the Notre Dame game, because if Coles does not go with his wife, someone else will. Regardless, Calman asks Coles to attend the party because he would enjoy his company. Coles agrees, but when he arrives at the party, it turns out that Calman changed his mind and decided to leave town. Again, Coles is motivated to seduce Walker. Calman's account of his worry that Coles would seduce his wife, then his decision to leave nonetheless is a tell-tale sign of his listless attempt to separate his private feelings from the public realm. In *The Short Stories of F. Scott Fitzgerald: New Approaches in Criticism,* Sheldon Grebstein writes, ''[Calman's] spontaneous revelation of private matters hint that despite his show of regret and anguish at his tangled emotional condition, he secretly relishes its complications as 'good material.''' Again, Calman's relationship with his wife not only suffers; it lacks any foundation in love because of his persistence to continually create heartache and then expose these private intimacies. Nothing is sacred between Calman and Walker, thus their marriage is meaningless.

After the dinner, Coles and Walker return to the stage that is the Calman's home. Coles wants to sleep with Walker. She resists, but only meekly, seeming almost inviting in her rejections of his advances. Coles continues, telling Walker, ''I'm in love with you anyhow'' and ''come sit beside me.'' With his attempts falling short, Coles decides to leave the Calman's house, yet as the clock begins to toll midnight—opening the door to the third Sunday—Walker's decision to resist falters and the two make love. After their affair, Walker receives a phone call informing her of Calman's death and ''Crazy Sunday'' concludes with a crescendo, dashing the façade of love of the Calman's marriage against the steps of their staged, publicly exposed, and completely inadequate private lives.

Although ''Crazy Sunday'' was written nearly two decades before *The Human Condition,* it is apparent that Fitzgerald witnessed the destruction of the private realm at the hands of the public. Strangely, just as Coles mocked the industry that he courted (Hollywood), so did Fitzgerald. The author Fitzgerald worked diligently and made money as a screenwriter, but it was apparent through his short stories and novels—especially ''Crazy Sunday''— that Hollywood writ large was both a simile for failed love and the conflict that Arendt aptly called the human condition.

Source: Anthony Martinelli, Critical Essay on ''Crazy Sunday,'' in *Short Stories for Students,* Thomson Gale, 2005.

Sheldon Grebstein

In the following essay, Grebstein discusses the psychological traits of the main characters.

Precise factual information which aids the reader to place an artist's work securely into a biographical-historical context is always welcome. Such information establishes a sound foundation for critical analysis and enhances our appreciation of the artist's achievements. Fortunately, any student of Fitzgerald's brilliant story "Crazy Sunday" (1932) finds an abundance of data already provided by Arthur Mizener, Dwight Taylor, Andrew Turnbull, Kenneth Eble, Henry Dan Piper, and Aaron Latham, among others. Accordingly, no further evidence is needed to prove that in writing "Crazy Sunday," Fitzgerald chose a phase of recent experience in which he suffered disappointment and disgrace, then deliberately exploited it as the basis for the story's locale, major characters, and precipitating episode. Few examples of Fitzgerald's work better illustrate the intimate yet complex relationship between his life and his art. In this instance, an unsuccessful screenwriting stint in California during the fall of 1931 and a drunken episode at a party given by the Thalbergs were soon after transformed into a work of fiction that still endures, after almost half a century, as perhaps the best American short story about Hollywood.

But if the biographical basis is manifest, what of the art? Here one can perhaps offer a contribution, for to this point there has been surprisingly little aesthetic discussion of the story. The treatments that do exist pay insufficient attention to the work's subtle and controlled method. My essay will attempt just that.

As its most obvious theme or subject, "Crazy Sunday" contrasts the physical beauty, charisma, or talent of its major characters—Joel, Stella, Miles—with the element of instability, weakness, or tendency toward self-destruction which seems to coincide, even be necessary, to their beauty and talent. Joel drinks to excess. Miles is exhausted, marked for death. The alluring Stella is emotionally fragile, subject to hysteria. What Joel first says to Stella as a conversational gambit—"'Everybody's afraid, aren't they?'"—becomes a portentous cue to this dimension of character.

The story's atmosphere and action are thus intensely psychological, not only in the specifically psychiatric sense conveyed in Miles's talk of his psychoanalysis and personal troubles, but more important in that the narrative emphasizes states of feeling and the impressions people make upon one another from moment to moment. In this, Fitzgerald expresses his vision of one aspect of the Hollywood milieu which differentiates it from the run of common life: there the most private matters—marital infidelity, sexual problems—are discussed as though they were public knowledge. Relationships that would take months, even years, to develop in "real" or "normal" life are accelerated, foreshortened, developed in one or two brief encounters. In this concentration and distillation of experience, Fitzgerald both exercises the economy of the short story form and evokes the method of a film scenario.

The story's title alerts us to its psychological focus, although it is also deliberately ambiguous. "Crazy" applies less obviously to the day than to the characters. Sunday is celebrated because it represents a release from the confines of work, but as Fitzgerald suggests throughout the story, work is really the basis of sanity for everyone in the film industry.

Among the reasons we come to believe most in Joel's probity, the truth and reliability of his perspective, is that we actually witness him at work. We may accept that Stella is a movie star and Miles a famous producer; we view the result of their success in their impressive house. Miles's achievement and ability as producer are asserted repeatedly. But unlike Joel, their professional skills are not *demonstrated* to us. Even in the one encounter between Joel and Miles at the studio (on Wednesday, not Sunday), Miles is depicted as confused, jealous, wavering—a creature wholly concerned with his personal afflictions and in the grip of his fluctuating moods, rather than as a keen, tough, decisive film executive. Although Sunday is defined in the story's opening paragraph as a time for relaxation, pleasure—"individual life starting up again"—it functions most tellingly as the time for self-disgrace, self-revelation, breakdown.

Appropriately, the emphasis on the psychological dimension is reinforced by the story's dramatic stucture. This structure basically depends not upon the five formal sections into which Fitzgerald has overtly divided it, although these are important as phases in the action, but upon three crazy Sundays. In turn, each of these Sundays serves as the occasion for the exposure and humiliation of each of the main characters.

Joel, of course, is the first to crash when, pumped up by drink and the silly desire to impress the glittering array at the Calman party, he foolishly performs a skit which inherently mocks the business they all depend on. This performance, ''Building It Up,'' betrays the worst side of him; the hired writer who professes to despise the crass elements of the film industry yet courts its favor. Despite the cruelty of his audience of celebrities, he deserves their rebuff. If he is ''not yet broken by Hollywood,'' he certainly has been infected by it. The one saving element in the occasion is the attraction that arises between Joel and Stella.

But on the next Sunday, as the guest had humiliated himself before the host, the host now takes a tumble before the guest. Joel enters another party, only to find himself immediately embroiled in the chaos of the Calmans' marriage and made confidant to Stella's bitter recounting of her husband's just-exposed adultery. In this scene the reader actually meets Miles for the first time. On the first Sunday he had been a remote, offstage but nevertheless awesome, presence; here he is precipitously lowered, immediately introduced to us as ''not a well man'': an involuntary philanderer, a helpless public target of his wife's rage, and in general deeply troubled. For Joel the effect of the second Sunday is to banish his awe of Miles and confirm his desire for Stella.

On the third Sunday, Stella falls. While it is still Saturday, she can set up a seduction scene for her own purposes, lead Joel on but still keep control and hold back at the crucial moment. Joel cannot break through her composure or allegiance to her husband. However, when the first minute of Sunday tolls and with it arrives the message of Miles's death, she collapses and pleads for the consummation she had only minutes earlier resisted. And as the story concludes, with Joel's realization that he will indeed return to take advantage of Stella's vulnerability and participate in her emotional attempt to resurrect Miles, there is the promise of yet other crazy Sundays to come.

Inextricably intertwined with the ''crazy'' motif, and equally important as a thematic and structural element, is the story's emphasis upon the artificiality and theatricality of this microcosm and the conduct of its inhabitants. This motif of frenetic make-believe is rendered both metaphorically and as direct exposition. It begins at once in the simile of the characters as enchanted puppets infused temporarily with life. It is soon reinforced by the description of the producer's home as a vast-theater or auditorium: ''Miles Calman's house was built for

> This structure basically depends not upon the five formal sections into which Fitzgerald has overtly divided it, although these are important as phases in the action, but upon three crazy Sundays. In turn, each of these Sundays serves as the occasion for the exposure and humiliation of each of the main characters.''

great emotional moments—there was an air of listening, as if the far silences of its vistas bid an audience.'' With this image the stage is prepared, not only for Joel's catastrophic performance at the Calman party but also for the significant action of the other ''Crazy Sunday'' scenes I have just summarized. The theatricality of the house is perfectly congruent with the intrinsic melodrama of the characters' behavior. Their extravagance and self-consciousness require a large arena: ''Under the high ceilings the situation seemed more dignified and tragic.'' Even nature seems sensitive to the histrionic conduct of these Hollywood people, for in each of the major scenes the condition of sea or sky collaborates with the Calman house or some other extreme feature of the California setting to supply a fittingly cinematic backdrop for the plot. In the first Sunday scene, ''the Pacific, colorless under its sluggish sunset,'' conveys an ominous mood which presages the nasty reception the unwitting Joel is about to elicit. As background for Stella's irresistible beauty and outpouring of emotion on the second Sunday, nature offers ''an eerie bright night with the dark very clear outside,'' which highlights both the bizarre nature of the Calman marriage, as it is now revealed to Joel, and Joel's sharp realization of his attraction to Stella. Finally, preparatory to the invitation-seduction involving Joel and Stella on the third Sunday, there is Fitzgerald's most openly stated California make-believe metaphor: ''the full moon over the boulevard was only a prop, as scenic as the giant boudoir lamps of the corners.'' The pseudo-romantic moon and the sexy streetlights combine to anticipate the action and, in retrospect, to offer an ironic commentary upon it.

Within this prevailing context of theatricality, each of the main characters appears both genuine and artificial. Stella seems especially at home in the melodramatic mode and glows as the story's most vivid incarnation of the enchanted puppet motif. A creation of Miles Calman—perhaps Miles's most successful production, '''a sort of masterpiece'''—it is almost impossible to tell what is hers and what his. Despite the depth of the feelings she exhibits as the narrative progresses, including pain, anger, and grief, Joel persists in thinking of her as an actress: ''She hovered somewhere between the realest of realities and most blatant of impersonations.'' In accordance both with the norms of her Hollywood status and to enhance further our sense of the theatrical, Fitzgerald usually presents Stella to us in vibrant color and exquisite clothing or, said otherwise, in the suitable make-up and costume for her role.

As actor in his own life story, Miles Calman creates almost as much fantasy and melodrama in his career and marriage as in the films he produces. Miles's spontaneous public revelations of private matters hint that despite his show of regret and anguish at his tangled emotional condition, he secretly relishes its complications as ''good material.'' The series of telegrams he sends Stella, culminated by a message from others announcing his death, would work splendidly in a film script as a kind of *montage*. Because Fitzgerald is pursuing personality above all, the story presents Miles with a minimum of detail about his appearance. Unlike Stella, Miles is depicted almost wholly in black and white. However, upon our first direct encounter with him there is a brief but striking passage emphasizing Miles's eyes and the incongruous juxtaposition of ''curiously shaped head'' and ''niggerish feet.'' This peculiar description does not, I believe, suggest only a heaven-earth or brain-body dichotomy as intrinsic to the artistic personality, but also transmits Fitzgerald's reliance upon the racial stereotypes of Negro and Jew and their supposedly inborn traits and talents as exhibited in show business. In this he was imitating a technique prevalent in Hollywood films until very recently.

Joel as performer is rendered most indirectly and tacitly of all. His overtly histrionic behavior diminishes as the story proceeds. Even so, in his carefully selected wardrobe for the second Sunday and in the calculation of his moves during the attempted seduction, he remains something of an actor almost to the very end.

I venture one final observation on the theme of theatricality and its relationship to the story's dramatic structure. Although Joel, Stella, and Miles all participate as players in the story's three big scenes, the size and nature of their roles shift significantly. Each, as it were, has the opportunity to lead, yet each in turn takes a subordinate or minor part. In the first scene, Joel plays the lead, Stella a highly visible but nevertheless supporting role, and Miles the smallest part. His presence is important; we know he stands in the background as one of the crowd, but we do not observe him directly or hear him speak. He really serves as audience or witness. In the second scene, however, Miles and Stella are co-featured, with Joel relegated to the role of audience or witness. The final scene casts Joel and Stella together again, this time as co-stars but with Stella's lines and action paramount. As in the first scene, Miles again functions as distant onlooker; indeed, even though he is physically absent, he exists more than ever as a dominant presence in the minds of the others. Note also that the varying interplay of the three characters, staged primarily in the Calman house in each of the three ''Crazy Sunday'' scenes, occurs at equivalent intervals in the story's formal divisions, Sections I, III, and V, and provides an unobtrusive but pleasing structural symmetry. Moreover, the placement of the Joel-Stella scenes at the beginning and end of the story works as a form of closure. Interspersed with these major scenes and temporarily to relieve their focus on the leading characters, there are a number of quick, sharp glimpses at others: Nat Keogh, a group of bit players at the studio, the passing crowd outside a theater. Such sidelights help to create a fullness of vision, an entire ethos.

Fitzgerald's treatment of character in ''Crazy Sunday,'' provokes some of the same tantalizing questions we ask of *The Great Gatsby*. Although the story seems to be *about* Miles Calman, is he truly its hero or protagonist? I think not. Essential as Miles is to the situation, the significant change happens to Joel. Admittedly, if Joel is too much the opportunist to win our full approval or admiration, nevertheless in comparison to Miles and Stella he does emerge as the story's most credible and thoroughly developed character. Despite his participation in all the crazy Sundays, he overcomes his initial lapse and gains authority as the story progresses. Certainly his emotional status at the end of the story is markedly improved over his condition at the beginning. We recall his unwittingly significant remark: "'Everybody's afraid, aren't they?'" I agree with Robert Sklar that Joel belongs to that class of Fitzgerald protagonists who illustrate that fate (or history) rather than free will controls man's destiny, yet I would also insist that by the third crazy Sunday he is clearly far saner, more aware, more in command than on the first. Initially an insecure and obsequious outsider, self-consciously flattering his hostess and straining to make conversation, he moves quickly into the deepest lives of Hollywood's great. In contrast, the concluding scene reveals him speaking and behaving with considerable poise and acuity: protecting Stella from the consequences of her hysteria and himself from an impossibly awkward entanglement. Still susceptible to her beauty, he at least has the presence of mind to realize her motives and to choose a more advantageous time—in short, to operate by some of his own terms. After all, what Fitzgerald hero can permanently resist a beautiful woman? In short, Joel is neither lovable nor virtuous, but we do get to know him, understand him and most important, to trust his perceptions to a considerable degree. This evolution in Joel's character from weakness toward strength is clearly evident by a simple comparison of his conduct and speech in Section I with that of Section V. As soon as he learns about Miles's death, his speech becomes terse, direct, functional. It employs the syntax of command: "'I want the name of your doctor,' he said sternly." Likewise, his actions exhibit the same assurance: "Resolutely Joel went to the phone and called a doctor." Joel's self-control in this final scene is emphasized all the more by Stella's hysteria.

The development of Joel's sanity, as overtly demonstrated by action, exposition, and dialogue, is subtly corroborated throughout by the story's narrative perspective. The choice of narrative viewpoint or voice could, as we know, pose problems for Fitzgerald, but in this case both the selection and execution are wholly felicitous. Almost instantaneously the authorial perspective merges with that of the protagonist, producing a single unified voice and consciousness.

Although the first page conveys the quality or mood of editorial omniscience, with a detached author making statements about who the characters are and what they think, the mode quickly becomes selective omniscience—the limited focus upon the sensibility of a single character. (One key phrase in

the story's second sentence cues the selective mode and distinguishes it from the editorial: "for all of them." The "them" really functions as would "us" in an I-narrative.) Indeed, after Joel is introduced in the story's second paragraph, nothing that happens from that point is, or would be, beyond his knowledge or witness—including the analysis of the thoughts and motives of Miles and Stella. What occurs, then, as intrinsic to the selective-omniscient mode when properly rendered, is a merging of the writer's voice and vision with those of his central character. The story is told in the third person, but it assumes the impact and the immediacy of a first-person narrative. The third person voice also retains the author's flexibility to provide appropriate stage directions and to probe into his characters' psyches. This merger of external and internal perspectives is further enhanced by the story's increasing emphasis on dramatic scene and dialogue as it proceeds. Virtually all of Sections IV and V are dialogue, interrupted only by brief passages of exposition. The natural impact of dialogue, the "dramatic" effect, even carries over into the exposition so that it registers as internal monologue. Note this passage as an example:

> Joel thought of Miles, his sad and desperate face in the office two days before. In the awful silence of his death all was clear about him. He was the only American-born director with both an interesting temperament and an artistic conscience. Meshed in an industry, he had paid with his ruined nerves for having no resilience, no healthy cynicism, no refuge—only a pitiful and precarious escape.

With only minimal editorial revision—merely change Joel to "I"—the passage could easily be transmuted into an I-narrative.

Concomitant with the story's portrayal of film people and its dramatic structure, much of its aesthetic method depends upon the *visual,* both as the reader's attention is focused upon the characters' eyes and in the visual exchanges among the characters. With the exception of a few bright splashes of color—especially the red-gold and ice-blue associated with Stella—the story's most vivid imagery is reserved for eyes. I count about forty direct references in the story either to eyes or to actions of sight: seeing, looking, watching, staring, etc. Whatever the clothing, manners, physical structure, or presence of the characters, their *eyes* betray the deepest truth about them.

Joel is initially described as "a handsome man with . . . pleasant cow-brown eyes," but these are soon to be shadowed by "dark circles of fatigue."

This indication of stress belies the cheerful and dashing clothes Joel has donned for the occasion. Only one small imperfection mars Stella's beauty, "the tired eye-lid that always drooped a little over one eye," but this functions subliminally as the physical blemish which foreshadows her later psychic collapse. Similarly, the reader's first sight of Miles Calman shows him with "the unhappiest eyes Joel ever saw." In the next look at Miles, a few pages later, the extent of his weariness—a premonition of his death—is defined as "life-tired, with his lids sagging." Most vivid of all are the two images used to describe the hostility of Joel's audience at his disastrous parlor game. As he begins, "the Great Lover of the screen glared at him with an eye as keen as the eye of a potato," and as he concludes in failure, "the Great Lover, his eye hard and empty as the eye of a needle, shouted 'Boo! Boo!'" Another, more sympathetic, evocation of movie people is conveyed by the depiction of bit-players, "the yellow-stained faces of pretty women, their eyes all melancholy and startling with mascara." Compositely, what Fitzgerald saw in the eyes of these Hollywood folk was indeed depressing.

As one aspect of its style that I find reminiscent of Hemingway in such stories as "Hills Like White Elephants," some passages of "Crazy Sunday" also take such words and phrases as "look," "look out," "see," and "eyes" and build them into unobtrusive little runs of incremental repetition, playing off on the varying usages and shadings of meaning inherent in the colloquial language. The first party scene is one such. It happens again early in the attempted seduction scene, as Joel is initially encouraged to approach Stella by a visual transaction in the theater: "Once he turned and looked at her and she looked back at him, smiling and meeting his eyes for as long as he wanted." As the scene progresses, it continues to utilize the visual dimension with unusual emphasis:

> On into the dark foliage of Beverly Hills that flamed as eucalyptus by day, Joel saw only the flash of a white face under his own, the arc of her shoulder. She pulled away suddenly and looked up at him.
>
> "Your eyes are like your mother's," she said. "I used to have a scrap book full of pictures of her."
>
> "Your eyes are like your own and not a bit like any other eyes," he answered.
>
> Something made Joel look out into the grounds as they went into the house, as if Miles were lurking in the shrubbery.

Clearly, Joel's attraction to Stella depends not on what she is but upon what he sees, a combination of visual appeal and sexual desire, epitomized in this: "Still as he looked at her, the warmth and softness of her body thawing her cold blue costume, he knew she was one of the things he would always regret."

I find another Hemingwayesque touch in the deliberate omission of action which is then cued by the dialogue. The first example is visual, capitalizing on a look in Joel's eyes and a facial expression that Stella sees but we do not:

> There she was, in a dress like ice-water, made in a thousand pale-blue pieces, with icicles trickling at the throat. He started forward.
>
> "So you like my dress?"

The second delicately omits certain physical details and gestures of the failed seduction:

> "Come sit beside me." Joel urged her.
>
> It was early. And it was still a few minutes short of midnight a half-hour later, when Joel walked to the cold hearth, and said tersely:
>
> "Meaning that you haven't any curiosity about me?"
>
> "Not at all. You attract me a lot and you know it. The point is that I suppose I really do love Miles."
>
> "Obviously."
>
> "And tonight I feel uneasy about everything."

Between "early" and "And," thirty minutes' worth of important but undescribed activity and conversation occur yet are not communicated explicitly to the reader. Fitzgerald trusted our imaginations. Reinforcing the dialogue and its conspicuous omission, there is the striking objective correlative "cold hearth," should anyone have missed the point. Apparently there is neither a fire in the fireplace of the Calman mansion at this precise moment during the California Christmas season nor for Joel a sufficiently warm response from his ravishing hostess.

The story's demands upon our sensitivity and capacity for attention characterize Fitzgerald's most serious and accomplished work. However, as an artistic performance, "Crazy Sunday" does not immediately impress us as a spectacular or dazzling work of fiction. Stylistically, even its most eloquent passages fall well short of the bravura effects of *The Great Gatsby* or *Tender Is the Night*. It lacks the complex symbolism and intricate stucture of "Absolution" (1924), the poignancy of "Winter Dreams" (1922), the elegant grace of "The Rich Boy" (1926). Its language is unlyrical, taut, compressed, sometimes harsh; its imagery is spare. Because of its unobtrusive method and its apparent dependence upon the verisimilitude of time, place, and character, only with difficulty does one break free of the temptation to read ''Crazy Sunday'' as disguised autobiography or embellished case history—and all the more when so full a dossier is available on the story's genesis and real-life prototypes. For example, Dwight Taylor's generally affectionate reminiscence of Fitzgerald in Hollywood concludes with a brusque but temptingly persuasive summary of the story which derives from his knowledge of Fitzgerald's personal tragedy and how the writer had manipulated actual events. Taylor says: ''The truth is turned topsy-turvy, as in *Alice Through the Looking-Glass*. . . . Just as Jupiter is said to have taken on a variety of disguises . . . in order to gain access to a woman, so did Scott project himself into the skin of others in an attempt to enjoy himself without the concomitant of guilt.'' Psychologically, this analogy may be true in part about Fitzgerald the man. It may even apply to some phases of the mysterious process by which life is ''projected'' into art. But it assumes insanity or illness or atavistic impulse as the motivating force.

I would argue to the contrary. Whatever its primal or subconscious sources, Fitzgerald's best fiction demonstrates not his illnesses and failures but the manner in which he overcame them. Certainly for the reader the triumph of ''Crazy Sunday'' finally does not consist of its success in exorcising particular demons of bad behavior or memory but rather in its sanity as art: the craft, economy, and symmetry of the whole. Finally, the story reminds us that perhaps of all American writers F. Scott Fitzgerald best exemplifies Heine's dictum, ''*Aus meinen grossen Schmerzen/Mach ich die kleinen Lieder.*''

Source: Sheldon Grebstein, ''The Sane Method of 'Crazy Sunday,''' in *The Short Stories of F. Scott Fitzgerald: New Approaches in Criticism,* edited by Jackson R. Bryer, University of Wisconsin Press, 1982.

Robert A. Martin

In the following essay excerpt, Martin discusses the place of ''Crazy Sunday'' in relation to Fitzerald's other works of the same period.

As Arthur Mizener has remarked in *The Far Side of Paradise*, the movies fascinated Fitzgerald, ''as they must fascinate any artist, because, as a visual art, they have such exciting possibilities of greatness, for all their actual shoddiness, and because they offered Fitzgerald what always drew him, a Diamond-as-Big-as-the-Ritz scale of operation, a world 'bigger and grander' than the ordinary world.''

According to Henry Dan Piper, scriptwriting offered little challenge to Fitzgerald, but ''he had always been fascinated by the motion-picture industry as literary subject matter.'' This would have been especially true for Fitzgerald around 1924 since movies were not only becoming established as the popular medium of the day, they were also becoming an art form. Fitzgerald, says Piper, had foreseen the movies as art and at one time had suggested a film about the craft of moviemaking:

> As far back as 1920, so he said, he had tried unsuccessfully to persuade D. W. Griffith that the craft of movie making itself was a wonderful subject for a picture. According to Fitzgerald, Griffith had laughed at him, but the success of *Merton of the Movies* not long afterwards proved Fitzgerald right.

With the publication of *The Great Gatsby* on April 10, 1925, followed by its disappointing sales record, Fitzgerald would have had every reason to look toward Hollywood if his next novel would not support him. Although *The Great Gatsby* contains relatively few references to Hollywood and the movies, enough remain to suggest that Fitzgerald—even after three extensive revisions—was using the medium as a background reference for the novel. Gatsby's dream of Daisy is one that must be created out of myth and metaphor, and sustained, assembled, and directed much like a silent movie in which events and emotion are symbolized through mimicry. In one such scene, Gatsby uses a movie actress and her director to impress Daisy with his ability to collect the famous and the celebrated at his parties.

> ''Perhaps you know that lady,'' Gatsby indicated a gorgeous, scarcely human orchid of a woman who sat in state under a white-plum tree. Tom and Daisy stared, with that particularly unreal feeling that accompanies the recognition of a hitherto ghostly celebrity of the movies.
>
> ''She's lovely,'' said Daisy.
>
> ''The man bending over her is her director.''

From Fitzgerald's correspondence with Harold Ober, it is clear that he was anticipating the movie sale of *Gatsby* as early as May 2, 1925. It is even possible that he wrote *Gatsby* with the intention of making it a filmable novel. On May 2, he wrote to Ober: ''By this time next week . . . it'll be obvious both whether I was a fool not to sell it serially and also whether the movies are interested. The minimum price would be $5000.00. If it goes to say fifty thousand copies I should want at least $10,000, and for anything over that, in the best-seller class I think I should get $25,000. . . .'' Before the film rights were finally sold to Famous-Lasky-Paramount in

> " Fitzgerald's criticism of Hollywood is not of an industry but of an attitude, a veneer of sophistication and acquired appearance that is fundamentally a fake."

late 1926, Fitzgerald received a telegram from Ober on April 16, 1920, concerning a possible offer:

GATSBY PICTURE POSSIBLE OFFER FORTY FIVE THOUSAND ADVISE ACCEPTANCE CABLE QUICK OBER

On the same day Fitzgerald cabled his reply:

ACCEPT OFFER FITZGERALD

The $45,000 offer for film rights to *Gatsby* did not materialize, however; out of a total income for 1926 of $25,686.05, slightly more than half ($13,500) came from the film rights to his most-praised novel. By comparison, Fitzgerald's income from book sales for 1926 amounted to $2,033.20.

As Matthew J. Bruccoli has detailed in his meticulous study, *The Composition of "Tender Is the Night,"* Fitzgerald had been working unsuccessfully on his fourth novel since the late summer of 1925. In an early version, dealing with matricide as a theme, Fitzgerald had attempted to portray a young motion picture filmcutter, Francis Melarky, who later evolved into Lew Kelly, a motion picture director. It was not until sometime in 1930 that the novel's final version emerged with Dick and Nicole Diver as the main characters and only Rosemary Hoyt faintly reminiscent of the earlier versions and the Hollywood connection. When the Fitzgeralds returned from Europe in December, 1926, Fitzgerald was offered a contract by United Artists to work on a Constance Talmadge film titled *Lipstick.* Fitzgerald surprisingly accepted the offer, which involved rather minimal terms ($3,500 in advance and an additional $8,500 if the film was made).

Fitzgerald's sudden decision to go to Hollywood in January, 1927, very likely served three purposes simultaneously. It provided an immediate addition to his dwindling finances; it would possibly help to solve the writing problems of the Melarky-Kelly version of *Tender* by adding authenticity

through direct observation of the Hollywood scene that Fitzgerald lacked; and it allowed him to take that first step after he came home from Europe—to "go to Hollywood and learn the movie business." Fitzgerald's script was rejected, and the movie was never made. Nevertheless, his first trip to Hollywood brought him into the studios through his acquaintances with a seventeen-year-old actress, Lois Moran, with whom he fell in love, and Irving Thalberg, head of MGM. Both of them were to influence his future work, and both helped Fitzgerald to experience Hollywood firsthand. As a more immediate result of the trip, two short stories, "Jacob's Ladder" and "Magnetism," both written in 1927, are the first indications that Fitzgerald began to take Hollywood seriously as theme and subject. The 1927 trip was as much symbolic as substantive, and if not quite paradise, it did at least place Fitzgerald on the inside of the studio gates.

"Jacob's Ladder" and "Magnetism" deserve a higher place among Fitzgerald's short stories than has generally been accorded them by critics and scholars. "Jacob's Ladder" in particular is an important transitional story that remained uncollected until 1973, at which time it appeared in *Bits of Paradise.* To Robert Sklar, who saw the story's merit as early as 1967, it marked "Fitzgerald's new career as a professional writer of short stories . . . but it also squandered, by its very quality and breadth, nearly all of his newly acquired material." Sklar is impressed with "Jacob's Ladder" not only as a Fitzgerald story in itself but as representing through its main character, Jacob Booth, both an advance and an extension of Fitzgerald's previous protagonists. Jacob, Sklar notes, "is Fitzgerald's old hero in a new form; in a remarkable way he sets a *leitmotif* for the next seven years of Fitzgerald's fiction, culminating in *Tender Is the Night.*"

In his biography of Fitzgerald, Andrew Turnbull describes the brief romance that took place in Hollywood in 1927 between Fitzgerald and Lois Moran as "very pure and idealistic—never anything more than a delicate flirtation." At the time, Fitzgerald was thirty-one and Lois Moran was seventeen. Turnbull was apparently unaware of "Jacob's Ladder" and says that as a result of their flirtation, "Fitzgerald put his first emotion for her into a story called 'Magnetism,' where Lois is Helen Avery, the young movie star who causes the happily married George Hannaford to waver." Although Sklar does not mention Lois Moran in his discussion of "Magnetism" and Turnbull does not mention "Jacob's Ladder" at all, the two stories actually derive from the same incident and emotion and should be viewed as early fictional harvests from Fitzgerald's first trip to Hollywood.

Both "Jacob's Ladder" and "Magnetism" were entered as "Stripped and Permanently Buried" in Fitzgerald's *Ledger* following their initial magazine publications, and passages from both appear in his later work, particularly in *Tender* during the Rosemary-Dick Diver scenes. Turnbull notwithstanding, it was not "Magnetism" wherein Fitzgerald put his first emotion for Lois Moran but in "Jacob's Ladder," where Jacob Booth, a wealthy but bored New Yorker, meets Jenny Delahanty and decides to transform her into a movie star. After changing her name to Jenny Prince and introducing her to a movie director, he falls in love with her in a passive, romantically apathetic way, and when she becomes successful as an actress, she rejects him for an actor. Jacob is left with only her image on a movie screen. In one sense, the story is a modified version of *Pygmalion,* stripped down from Bernard Shaw's play and transferred to a new circumstance and Hollywood setting. In quite another sense, it is Fitzgerald using Hollywood as a metaphor for his own romantic attraction to Lois Moran (Jenny is sixteen when Jacob first meets her) and as a fictional equivalent for his own sublimated passion.

The first time Jacob kisses her, he hesitates tentatively and is "chilled by the innocence of her kiss, the eyes that at the moment of contact looked beyond him into the darkness of the night, the darkness of the world." Later, after her transformation into a professional actress, Jacob, who is now thirty-three, visits Jenny in Hollywood; she is now seventeen:

> But at seventeen, months are years and Jacob perceived a change in her; in no sense was she a child any longer. There were fixed things in her mind—not distractions, for she was instinctively too polite for that, but simply things there. No longer was the studio a lark and a divine accident; no longer "for a nickel I wouldn't turn up tomorrow." It was part of her life. Circumstances were stiffening into a career which went on independently of her casual hours.

That Jenny Prince is modeled on Lois Moran is less important critically than her obvious reincarnation in Fitzgerald's later work as Helen Avery in "Magnetism," Rosemary Hoyt in *Tender*, and Cecilia in *The Last Tycoon*. On Sunday in "Jacob's Ladder," Jacob and Jenny go to three Hollywood parties because, as Jenny tells him, "that's what everybody does on a Sunday afternoon," thereby anticipating the theme and setting of "Crazy Sun-

day," which Fitzgerald would write in January, 1932, following his second trip to Hollywood as a screenwriter for MGM.

Among several other minor complications that Fitzgerald arranges for Jacob and Jenny, a shyster lawyer named Scharnhorst attempts to blackmail Jenny for $20,000 but is successfully disposed of through Jacob's intervention. This is the same plot device that Fitzgerald uses in "Magnetism" and that he had outlined for a projected episode in *The Last Tycoon*, in which Cecilia's father and Monroe Stahr are struggling for control of the studio. In this unwritten scene, Brady was to use his knowledge of Stahr's affair with Kathleen, while Stahr was to retaliate by threatening to reveal that Brady had arranged for the murder of his mistress's husband. Matthew J. Bruccoli, in his recent work, "*The Last of the Novelists*": F. Scott Fitzgerald and "The Last Tycoon," comments perceptively on the implications of Fitzgerald's numerous drafts and revisions but sees only "Crazy Sunday" as forming immediate background material for *The Last Tycoon*. It is my belief that "Jacob's Ladder" and "Magnetism" form the nucleus of Fitzgerald's entire Hollywood theme and, along with "Crazy Sunday" and the early Melarky-Kelly versions of *Tender*, account for nearly all of the material, characters, and plot of *The Last Tycoon*.

In "Magnetism," for example, Fitzgerald made his story more integral to his theme by moving the setting to Hollywood entirely (as opposed to New York and Hollywood in "Jacob's Ladder") and by concentrating on the portrayal of George Hannaford, an actor who attracts women without effort or design. Many of Fitzgerald's first impressions of Hollywood appear in this story, and as George struggles to keep his marriage intact by fending off the unwanted attentions of several women, we see what Fitzgerald as novelist would have seen through intensely detailed scenes describing Hollywood and the movie studios. In the two passages below, Fitzgerald follows George Hannaford as he drives from his home to the studio. These passages are not only stylistically graceful, they reflect a detailed observation based on a strong sensory impression of atmosphere and place. They are as cinematically visual as anything Fitzgerald ever wrote.

> George left and drove out an interminable boulevard which narrowed into a long, winding concrete road and rose into the hilly country behind. Somewhere in the vast emptiness a group of buildings appeared, a barnlike structure, a row of offices, a large but quick restaurant and half a dozen small bungalows. The

chauffeur dropped Hannaford at the main entrance. He went in and passed through various enclosures, each marked off by swinging gates and inhabited by a stenographer.

The studio is seen from without and within to form a complementary perspective of Hannaford in his life and work. Following his arrival at the office, he and Schroeder (a producer) walk to the studio to watch a movie in production. As they enter ''a little door in the big blank wall of the studio building,'' they are absorbed ''into its half darkness.'' Fitzgerald liked this passage so much that he incorporated it virtually intact into Chapter I of *Tender Is the Night*:

> Here and there figures spotted the dim twilight, figures that turned up white faces to George Hannaford, like souls in purgatory watching the passage of a half-god through. Here and there were whispers and soft voices, and, apparently from afar, the gentle tremolo of a small organ. Turning the corner made by some flats, they came upon the white crackling glow of a stage with two people motionless upon it.

> An actor in evening clothes, his shirt front, collar and cuffs tinted a brilliant pink, made as though to get chairs for them, but they shook their heads and stood watching. For a long while nothing happened on the stage—no one moved. A row of lights went off with a savage hiss, went on again. The plaintive tap of a hammer begged admission to nowhere in the distance; a blue face appeared among the blinding lights above and called something unintelligible into the upper blackness.

Edwin T. Arnold has noted that Fitzgerald gave Dick Diver ''some of Jacob's more unfortunate characteristics'' and that the title of ''Jacob's Ladder'' suggests a reexamination of Gatsby's ladder, which ''foreshadows the theme's further development in *Tender Is the Night*.'' In addition, Aaron Latham observes that when Rosemary Hoyt tells Dick Diver, ''Oh, we're such *actors*—you and I,'' she is repeating precisely what Helen Avery tells George Hannaford in ''Magnetism.'' Hannaford and Helen Avery are so totally within the movie industry that the story and plot have no other significance. In placing ''Magnetism'' and ''Crazy Sunday'' entirely in Hollywood, Fitzgerald was writing not only about a profession and popular entertainment but about an entire way of life that could not possibly be overstated—one that both defined and created in its life and work the myths and illusions of American middle-class society, which in Fitzgerald's vision of America equals the American Dream itself.

By 1931, Fitzgerald's ''next novel'' was still unrealized, Zelda was in the midst of a serious mental breakdown, and America was in the midst of the Depression. His short story price had risen to $4,000, while his total income in 1930 had climbed to $33,090. Though his expenses were high, Fitzgerald's second trip to Hollywood, in November, 1931, cannot be said to have resulted from financial necessity. In 1929, his income had totalled $32,448, of which $27,000 came from writing short stories, $900 from ''Talkie Rights'' to *The Beautiful and Damned* and $31.77 from all his books. In 1930, his short story sales accounted for $25,200, while his income from all books was $99. In brief, it is necessary to look elsewhere for Fitzgerald's reason for returning to Hollywood in 1931 to work on a script for MGM for six weeks on a $1,200-a-week contract.

During the four years since Fitzgerald had been there in 1927, the movies had changed from silents to sound. Given his 1936 statement in ''Handle with Care'' that ''As long past as 1930, I had a hunch that the talkies would make even the best selling novelist as archaic as silent pictures,'' his trouble in writing the Melarky-Kelly version of *Tender* between 1926 and 1930, and his statement to Perkins that if his next novel would not support him he would ''go to Hollywood and learn the movie business,'' his decision to return for a second try appears in a different perspective. In 1931, Fitzgerald would hardly have considered himself a ''best selling novelist''; indeed, it is surprising that he could think of himself as a novelist at all, since the major source of his income after *Paradise* came from writing short stories for the ''slicks'' and from the sale of film rights and scripts to Hollywood. In that year, Hollywood needed writers who could write dialogue as well as continuity, and Fitzgerald's reputation as a popular writer was very high among producers and directors.

''Crazy Sunday'' (written in January, 1932) is one of the finest stories Fitzgerald ever wrote and, like the earlier stories ''Jacob's Ladder'' and ''Magnetism,'' was derived from his experiences during the six weeks he spent working for MGM and Irving Thalberg. The theme of the story derives from Fitzgerald's observation of the tragic potential that he saw existing beneath the glamor and publicity of the studios. His alter-ego, Joel Coles, is both observer and participant (as was Fitzgerald) in the story of Miles Calman, who is based on Thalberg. Joel Coles, again like Fitzgerald, is a recently arrived New York import to Hollywood and is writing continuity at Calman's studio: ''He was twenty-eight and not yet broken by Hollywood. He had had what were considered nice assignments since his arrival six months before and he submitted his scenes and sequences with enthusiasm. He referred to himself modestly as a hack but really did not think of it that way.''

Like the Sunday afternoon parties in ''Jacob's Ladder,'' which Hollywood people attend because ''it's sort of the thing to do. . . . Otherwise you don't see anybody except the people on your own lot, and that's narrow,'' Joel Coles attends a party given by Miles and Stella Calman at which he makes a fool of himself, and is later drawn into the Calmans' social orbit and personal lives almost inadvertently. Fitzgerald's insight into the social and political undercurrents of Hollywood allowed him to merge the perceptions of a detached observer like Colts with the insider's view of Hollywood as an industry. In the two passages below, these dual perspectives flow in and out of the story to create not merely a point-of-view but a total effect, one in which Hollywood becomes not just a place but a microcosm of American society, morals, and manners. At the Calmans' party, Joel tells Stella:

> ''Everybody's afraid, aren't they?'' he said. . . . ''Everybody watches for everybody else's blunders, or tries to make sure they're with people that'll do them credit. Of course that's not true in your house,'' he covered himself hastily. ''I just meant generally in Hollywood.''

Between Sundays, however, which Fitzgerald says was ''not a day but rather a gap between two other days,'' work in the studio continues in sharp contrast to the craziness of Sunday afternoon digressions into the ''gossip and scandal'' of Hollywood:

> With Monday the week resumed its workaday rhythm, in sharp contrast to the theoretical discussions, the gossip and scandal of Sunday; there was the endless detail of script revision—''Instead of a lousy dissolve, we can leave her voice on the sound track and cut to a medium shot of the taxi from Bell's angle or we can simply pull the camera back to include the station, hold it a minute and then pan to the row of taxis''—by Monday afternoon Joel had again forgotten that people whose business was to provide entertainment were ever privileged to be entertained.

Thus the two Hollywoods, one composed of Sunday afternoons at Miles Calman's house—built, as Fitzgerald says, for ''great emotional moments''— and the other of the Hollywood bourgeoisie of film technicians, craftsmen, and extras, are portrayed as mutually exclusive elements of the film industry. The ''other'' Hollywood of the story congregates

for its emotional moments at the studio commissary during the week. Following his disgrace at the Calmans' party on Sunday, Joel enters the studio restaurant the following day:

> . . . he found a gloomy consolation in staring at the group at the next table, the sad, lovely Siamese twins, the mean dwarfs, the proud giant from the circus picture. But looking beyond at the yellow-stained faces of pretty women, their eyes all melancholy and startling with mascara, their ball gowns garish in full day, he saw a group who had been at Calman's and winced.

As intentionally grotesque as the group in this passage might appear, they are no less ''sad'' or ''melancholy'' than Stella Calman herself. Though Stella and Miles live in a Beverly Hills mansion looking ''out toward the Pacific . . . the American Riviera and all that,'' Fitzgerald's criticism of Hollywood is not of an industry but of an attitude, a veneer of sophistication and acquired appearance that is fundamentally a fake. As Stella gradually reveals some embarrassing details of her life with Miles, Joel begins to see her insecurity and superficiality emerging during a conversation in her home:

> Under the high ceilings the situation seemed more dignified and tragic. It was an eerie bright night with the dark very clear outside of all the windows and Stella all rose-gold raging and crying around the room. Joel did not quite believe in picture actresses' grief. They have other preoccupations—they are beautiful rose-gold figures blown full of life by writers and directors, and after hours they sit around and talk in whispers and giggle innuendoes, and the ends of many adventures flow through them.

> Sometimes he pretended to listen and instead thought how well she was got up—sleek breeches with a matched set of legs in them, an Italian-colored sweater with a little high neck, and a short brown chamois coat. He couldn't decide whether she was an imitation of an English lady or an English lady was an imitation of her. She hovered somewhere between the realest of realities and the most blatant of impersonations.

''Crazy Sunday'' is important not only for its realistic view of Hollywood life but also because it anticipates *The Last Tycoon* through the character of Miles Calman, to reappear in altered form as Monroe Stahr in *Tycoon,* both of whom are variations on Irving Thalberg. Like Calman, Stahr was to be killed in a plane crash and similarly possesses ''both an interesting temperament and an artistic conscience.'' Like Joel Coles in ''Crazy Sunday,'' Cecilia Brady in *Tycoon* is ''of the movies but not *in* them,'' which echoes close Fitzgerald's description of Rosemary Hoyt in *Tender* when he says, ''she was In the movies but not at all At them.''

Fitzgerald received only $200 for "Crazy Sunday," as opposed to his usual price of $4,000. The story was turned down by *Redbook, Cosmopolitan,* and *Saturday Evening Post* "on the grounds that its publication might anger the movie studios and jeopardize these magazines' lucrative movie-advertising accounts." After the story appeared, Fitzgerald received a letter from Edmund Wilson, who told him: "I thought your story in *The Mercury* was swell—wish you would do something more about Hollywood, which everybody who knows anything about it is either scared or bribed not to tell about or have convinced themselves is all right."

"Crazy Sunday" was the last, certainly one of the best, Hollywood stories that Fitzgerald wrote until he began *The Last Tycoon* in 1939. As Matthew J. Bruccoli has written in his introduction to *As Ever, Scott Fitz—*, "It is impossible to understand Fitzgerald's career without understanding his feelings about money." Numerous Fitzgerald critics have consistently overlooked this constant element in Fitzgerald's life and have attributed his final sojourn in Hollywood to a simple need for more money, an artistic retreat, or a depletion of the talent that had sustained him as a writer of popular fiction between 1920 and 1936. While there may be some validity in all of these views, Fitzgerald's own ledger is perhaps the most revealing source, together with his correspondence with Harold Ober, his literary agent. Between 1931 and 1936, Fitzgerald's income declined from an all-time high in 1931 of $37,599 to an all-time low in 1930 of $10,180.91. In 1931 he earned $31,500 from the sale of nine short stories and $5,400 (after commissions) from his work for MGM; his total income from book sales in the same year amounted to $100. By 1936, however, magazines such as *Saturday Evening Post* and *Collier's* were returning his short stories with the comment that they needed a different kind of story or that they were "too crazy . . . weak . . . and improbable." One editor suggested that a rejected story was not a typical "Fitzgerald piece," while another commented on a revision: "The new version of Scott Fitzgerald's story is a vast improvement over the first one. The writing has all the old Fitzgerald quality, but the plot values and the psychology are a bit hazy. For that reason, we must regretfully return the story." One month later, in July, 1937, Fitzgerald left for Hollywood and $1,000 a week as a scriptwriter for MGM.

As I have suggested throughout this article, Fitzgerald always was a commercial writer and yet chose to think of himself as primarily a novelist. If his novels and short story collections did not meet his extravagant style of living, there was always another short story to write for the popular magazines or a quick movie script for Hollywood to make up the difference. After 1931, however, partly due to the Depression, partly due to his own inability to write stories the magazines wanted, and partly due to his own emotional depression, Fitzgerald's short story market simply disappeared. If he had become too closely identified with the Jazz Age or the persona of "The Crack-Up" articles (which he later disowned), the ultimate cause for his move to Hollywood was that as a writer he had no place else to go that would provide him with the income he thought he needed and deserved. The only place left was Hollywood, his third and final source of substantial earnings. By the time Fitzgerald settled in at the Garden of Allah hotel in Hollywood in July, 1937, his 1925 projection to Maxwell Perkins had come full circle. He had, indeed, discovered that not only would his "next novel" not support him, but that what he had earlier considered as "trash" in his short stories was no longer wanted either. He had at last gone to Hollywood "to learn the movie business."

Of the fiction written during his last years in Hollywood, *The Last Tycoon* and "The Last Kiss" (written in 1940, published in 1940, published in 1949—probably a rejected fragment from the novel), taken together with a handful of the Pat Hobby stories, clearly indicate that Fitzgerald *was* primarily a novelist and short story writer who had the misfortune to run out of money and material at the same time. Because of its recurring presence in Fitzgerald's work as myth and metaphor, Hollywood is of primary importance in any critical assessment of his work. If Fitzgerald's life ended there on the far side of paradise, it is nevertheless Hollywood-in-Fitzgerald that helps to place his best fiction into perspective as contemporary chronicles of a particular time and place. As Henry Dan Piper has observed, "In Hollywood Fitzgerald, at any rate, had found his greatest theme." This is quite possibly what Fitzgerald meant when he wrote in a letter to his daughter during the winter of 1939: "Sorry you got the impression that I'm quitting the movies—they are always there."

Source: Robert A. Martin, "Hollywood in Fitzgerald: After Paradise," in *The Short Stories of F. Scott Fitzgerald: New Approaches in Criticism,* edited by Jackson R. Bryer, University of Wisconsin Press, 1982.

Ruth Prigozy

In the following essay excerpt, Prigozy examines the development of Fitzgerald's short fiction and the evolution of his style.

A writer's failures may tell us more about his art than his successes. Certainly, unpublished works may better reveal unfinished struggles than the whole or partial successes that manage to find their way into print. This observation is particularly applicable to F. Scott Fitzgerald, who during his lifetime devoted inordinate energy to getting as much of his work widely published as he could, who always wrote with a steady eye on remunerative, large-circulation magazines. Unlike his contemporary, Ernest Hemingway, whose large body of unpublished efforts his widow is now gradually and with much fanfare allowing into print, Fitzgerald left relatively little: some movie scripts, early drafts of some novels, and a handful of short stories and short-story fragments.

Fitzgerald's unpublished stories are particularly illuminating on several counts: through their glaring weaknesses they illustrate more clearly perhaps than anything he ever wrote, the technical problems that plagued him throughout his career, in the novels as well as in the shorter works. They reflect too the acute emotional difficulties he faced in the years following a serious physical collapse. Their chief value, however, is the light they throw on his developing style in the last years of his life. For the unpublished stories are truly transitional pieces in Fitzgerald's struggle to find new forms of expression for his most mature vision of American life and society. He was forced to recognize that many of his old fictional practices were moribund. The romantic rhetoric that had for fifteen years hauntingly underscored the tragic dissolution of his heroes no longer came easily. But while his interests never flagged and his perceptions never dulled, his formidable artistic task in the late thirties was to express them in a manner consonant with the sobriety of the Depression era and the recognition of his own senescence. These unpublished stories—all of them from his middle to late period—reveal Fitzgerald in the midst of a struggle with the right hold of the past, the dead weight of facile plot tricks, now stale and unresilient. Although failures, they tell us more than his commercial successes, for they indicate that his unfinished novel, *The Last Tycoon,* was not simply a final, inexplicable resurgence of creative energy, but the product of five years of effort that came to a tragically abortive end just as success

> "In his middle period (1929-35), the plots revert to the apprentice level, but the subjects are more serious and wide-ranging than they were in his most productive years...."

was within reach. This study of the following eight unpublished stories offers a concentrated critical view of Fitzgerald's least productive years and a new appreciation of the troubled exertions that led to his final triumph.

First we should survey briefly the development of Fitzgerald's short fiction. The apprentice stories are amateur expressions of subjects and themes Fitzgerald would treat with far greater virtuosity five or ten years later. Several were, in fact, revised and published in commerical magazines or interpolated in whole or in part, usually without revision, into *This Side of Paradise* (1920). Despite youthful romanticism and multi-episodic clumsiness, they illustrate the author's facility in plotting, his professional approach to problems of scene construction and point of view, his lifelong concern for nuance of expression. Like most of his major fiction, they rely more heavily on setting and social fabric than on complexity of incident.

Fitzgerald's best stories date from his early years as a successful writer, from 1920 through 1928. ("Babylon Revisited," 1931, and "Crazy Sunday," 1932, are the only really first-rate stories written after this period.) They rarely depart from the traditional nineteenth-century popular form with its rich social milieu, leisurely narrative, gradual character development, and, notably in Fitzgerald's work, evocative romantic rhetoric. (Fitzgerald's greatest story, "Babylon Revisited," combines a multi-episodic plot and unhurried characterization with economy of language, narrative simplicity, and rich sensory impressions. Fitzgerald would return to elements of this style years later.) In too many of his partial successes of this period, as he describes the antics of golden flappers and idealistic young philosophers, the idea seems subservient to the style as love-conquers-all, sometimes with verbal precision and elegance, sometimes with extravagant (and banal) flights of romantic rhetoric.

In his middle period (1929–35), the plots revert to the apprentice level, but the subjects are more serious and wide-ranging than they were in his most productive years: problems of marriage in middle age, unfulfilled lives, the generation gap, erosion of old values, the new morality, responsibility for others, the meaning of the past—both for the individual and for America—and the drift toward death. This is a transition time for Fitzgerald; with his mind on the social upheavals accompanying the Depression and on his own private misery, he rarely experiments with form. His best work during the mid-thirties is confessional prose, e.g., ''The Crack-Up'' (1936). His late stories, perhaps in imitation of these essays, are frequently undistinguishable from the prose sketches he began turning out for *Esquire* from 1936 on, when the big commercial magazines were rejecting his short stories. Fitzgerald's major fictional problem in this period, as both unpublished and published stories reveal, is the organization of plot: how to cast new subjects into tried, familiar forms. Thus, typical stories of these years are strangely discordant—serious statements forced out of trivial situations, overly complex yet predictable plots, trite and mechanical resolutions. More than any others, they earned for Fitzgerald the reputation as ''hack,'' but viewed in the context of his whole career, they display not so much his diminished talent as his failure to adapt new techniques to new interests. The unpublished stories, with the exceptions of ''Dearly Beloved'' and ''Thank You for the Light,'' are characteristic of the middle rather than the late stories.

Fitzgerald did not solve his technical problems until the year preceding his death, and then only fitfully in the stories. Arthur Mizener's commentary accompanying the previously unpublished ''Dearly Beloved'' in the *New York Times* on August 20, 1969, points up the ''special'' quality of Fitzgerald's late stories, ''News of Paris . . .'' (1939–40, published 1947) and ''The Lost Decade'' (1939): they ''evoke a judgment, not a world.'' The vivid scene rather than the whole story lingers in our memory; with a few selected details, usually in atmosphere or decor, Fitzgerald creates a mood against which the dramatic situation stands out in relief. In ''News of Paris,'' merely two lines, ''It was quiet in the room. The peacocks in the draperies stirred in the April wind,'' provide the ideal background for a brief but haunting retrospective ac-

count of dissolution, apathy, and tired sexuality in the pre-Depression boom. Published in *Esquire* from 1936 to his death, the late stories are typically elliptical, unadorned, curiously enervated, often relying exclusively on dialogue rather than on the expansive, adjectival narrative so prominent in his earlier efforts. They are, in fact, barely stories at all—rather, brief sketches or vignettes, anecdotal, dramatized, minimally plotted, and, for Fitzgerald, unmistakably experimental. *The Last Tycoon* combines the compression of the late stories with the spare yet evocative prose that frequently marks Nick Carraway's narrative in *The Great Gatsby.*

The length of Fitzgerald's stories parallels their chronological development. Apprentice stories are anywhere from 800 to 8,000 words; during the next ten to fifteen years, stories of 10,000 words are not uncommon. Late stories are, as noted above, brief, usually 500 to 2,000 words, the result partly of *Esquire's* stringent space limitations, partly of Fitzgerald's experimental techniques. His stories are complicated as a rule, with three to ten parts, plus epilogue, and three or more episodes subdivided according to shifts in scene, chronology, setting, and dialogue. From first to last, they are distinguished by delicate nuances of language, manners, and milieu that are often better than the stories as a whole. Although the unpublished stories fail even on the level of ''slick'' entertainment, they too offer, if only occasionally, glimpses of those delicate details that reveal the author at his best.

Source: Ruth Prigozy, ''The Unpublished Stories: Fitzgerald in His Final Stage,'' in *Twentieth Century Literature,* Vol. 20, No. 2, April 1974, pp. 69–90.

Sources

Arendt, Hannah, *The Human Condition,* University of Chicago Press, 1998, pp. 50, 51, 58, 71.

Best, Gary Dean, *The Nickel and Dime Decade: American Popular Culture during the 1930s,* Praeger Publishers, 1993, pp. 73–83.

Diorio, Carl, ''Valenti Valedictory View an Eye-Opener,'' in *Variety,* March 29, 2004 .

Eble, Kenneth, ''F. Scott Fitzgerald: Chapter 7: Stories and Articles, 1926–34,'' in *Twayne's United States Authors Series Online,* G. K. Hall, 1999; originally published as ''Chapter 7: Stories and Articles, 1926–34,'' in *F. Scott Fitzgerald,* rev. ed., Twayne's United States Authors Series, No. 36, Twayne, 1977.

''F. Scott Fitzgerald,'' in *Contemporary Authors Online,* Thomson Gale, 2004.

Fitzgerald, F. Scott, ''Crazy Sunday,'' in *The Stories of F. Scott Fitzgerald,* Collier Books, 1986, pp. 404, 410, 412, 415.

Grebstein, Sheldon, ''The Sane Method of 'Crazy Sunday,''' in *The Short Stories of F. Scott Fitzgerald: New Approaches in Criticism,* edited by Jackson R. Bryer, University of Wisconsin Press, 1982, p. 283.

''Irving G. Thalberg,'' in *International Dictionary of Films and Filmmakers,* Vol. 4, *Writers and Production Artists,* St. James Press, 2000.

Kazin, Alfred, *F. Scott Fitzgerald: The Man and His Work,* World Publishing, 1951, p. 108.

Pelzer, Linda C., *Student Companion to F. Scott Fitzgerald,* Greenwood Press, 2000, p. 26.

Prigozy, Ruth, ''F. Scott Fitzgerald,'' in *Dictionary of Literary Biography,* Vol. 86, *American Short-Story Writers, 1910–1945, First Series,* edited by Bobby Ellen Kimbel, Gale Research, 1989, pp. 99–123.

Sapienza, Madeline, *The Scribner Encyclopedia of American Lives,* Charles Scribner's Sons, 1998.

Vidal, Gore, ''Scott's Case,'' in *New York Review of Books,* Vol. 27, No. 7, May 1, 1980, pp. 12–20.

Further Reading

Fitzgerald, F. Scott, *Short Stories of F. Scott Fitzgerald: A New Collection,* Scribner, 1995.
    Edited by Fitzgerald expert Matthew J. Bruccoli, this collection contains forty-three of Fitzgerald's short stories. In his selections and introductions, Bruccoli makes a case for Fitzgerald's stature as an important short story writer.

French, Warren, ed., *The Thirties,* Everett/Edwards, 1967.
    Students interested in reading more about Fitzgerald's life and work in Hollywood will be interested in the chapter by Jonas Spatz titled, ''Fitzgerald, Hollywood and the Myth of Success.'' Spatz comments on such works as *The Last Tycoon* and the Pat Hobby stories, as they relate to the Hollywood phase of the author's career.

Kuehl, Richard, *F. Scott Fitzgerald: A Study of the Short Fiction,* Twayne Publishers, 1991.
    Focusing on eight of Fitzgerald's hundreds of short stories, this treatment explores the evolution of the author's themes, subjects, and structure in his short fiction.

Tate, Mary Jo, *F. Scott Fitzgerald A to Z: The Essential Reference to His Life and Work,* Facts On File, 1997.
    Ideal for students of Fitzgerald's work, this reference includes correspondence, biographical information, work summaries, and critical commentary in an accessible format.

Westbrook, Robert, *Intimate Lies: F. Scott Fitzgerald and Sheilah Graham: Her Son's Story,* HarperCollins, 1995.
    While in Hollywood, Fitzgerald had a stormy romance with a columnist named Sheilah Graham. Although she published her memoir about the relationship after Fitzgerald's death, this book (written by her son) seeks to tell the story objectively, culling information from letters, diaries, and other accounts.

Eyes of a Blue Dog

Gabriel García Márquez

1950

The most famous work by the Colombian writer Gabriel García Márquez is his 1967 novel *Cien años de soledad* (*One Hundred Years of Solitude*), one of Latin America's finest examples of magic realism, a literary style that incorporates fantastical or mythical elements into otherwise realistic fiction. After the international success of this novel, García Márquez went on to publish a prodigious amount of writing, winning the Nobel Prize for literature in 1982. As of 2004, he was one of the world's most influential living authors, whose broad innovations on the rules of fiction have inspired countless writers to incorporate epic, myth, and fantasy into their works, challenging the ways it is possible to perceive a story.

Some of García Márquez's most interesting, exciting, and daring work, however, was written in the years before he became internationally famous, when his unique style was still developing and he was one among many writers of a Latin American literary renaissance. In 1950, for example, he wrote an intriguing story entitled "Eyes of a Blue Dog," which takes place entirely within its narrator's dream, using the logic of the unconscious and the unique contradictions of the dream world to portray a frustrated relationship between a man and a woman. Despite their deep desire for each other, these characters are unable to meet in real life or even touch in the dream world, a situation that García Márquez uses to represent the loneliness of the unconscious mind and its desperate longings.

Anthologized in a collection by the same name in 1972, ''Eyes of a Blue Dog'' is now available in García Márquez's *Collected Stories*, translated from Spanish by Gregory Rabassa and published in 1984 by Harper & Row.

Author Biography

García Márquez was born in Aracataca, Colombia, on March 6, 1928, and lived the first eight years of his life with his maternal grandparents. After the death of his grandfather, a colonel, he moved to a river port town with his parents, and in 1940 he entered a high school near Bogotá on a scholarship. He entered law school at the University of Bogotá in 1947, but after the university closed in the following year due to civil war, he transferred to the University of Cartagena in northern Colombia.

By this time García Márquez had begun writing journalism and fiction, and in 1950, the same year he wrote ''Eyes of a Blue Dog,'' he dropped out of law school to work for various newspapers. He wrote for Bogotá's prominent periodical, the *Espectador,* until it was shut down by the government, and then he traveled in Europe and South America as a freelance writer before returning to Colombia to marry Mercedes Barcha. In 1959, he took a key role in launching a branch of *Prensa Latina,* the news-wire service started by Cuban President Fidel Castro, but he resigned from his post and moved with his family to Mexico City in 1960.

After he moved to New York in 1961, García Márquez published his first novella, *El coronel no tiene quien le escriba* (*No One Writes to the Colonel*), which deals with a small Colombian town during the 1940s and 1950s. The novella was successful, as was García Márquez's subsequent fiction, but it was with the publication of *Cien años de soledad* (*One Hundred Years of Solitude*) in 1967 that he met with international popularity and acclaim. A widely influential stylistic achievement, the novel combines fantasy with realism to tell a story across six generations in the mythical Colombian town of Macondo.

In the 1970s and afterward, García Márquez continued to write novels and short fiction, living for periods in Mexico, France, Spain, and the United States. In addition to his career as a writer, he has been involved in various political action groups, has worked as a teacher, and has made a number of films for Spanish television. García Márquez has

Gabriel García Márquez

received numerous literary awards including the Neustadt International Prize for literature in 1972 and the Nobel Prize for literature in 1982. In 1999, he was diagnosed with lymphatic cancer, and as of 2004 he was at work on volume II of his memoirs, which will concentrate on his life after 1955.

Plot Summary

The story begins with a narrator leaning back on a chair, looking at a woman whose hand is on an oil lamp. They look at each other for a few minutes, and then the narrator says, ''Eyes of a blue dog,'' which she repeats, saying she will never forget that and has written it everywhere. Walking to a dressing table, the woman looks at the narrator in the mirror and powders her nose before returning to the lamp and commenting that she is afraid someone is dreaming about the room, revealing her secrets. They each comment on the cold, and the woman returns to the dressing table where, despite the fact that he has turned his back to her, the narrator can tell what she is doing. He tells her that he can see her, and the woman says that this is impossible.

With the narrator facing her again, the woman asks him to do something about the cold, and she begins to undress. The narrator tells her he had always wanted to see her like that. Naked, the woman discusses how sometimes she thinks that they are both made of metal, and she tells him that if they ever find each other in real life, to put his ear on her ribs and hear her echoing. She says that her life has been dedicated to finding the narrator in reality, recognizing him with the phrase ''Eyes of a blue dog,'' and she describes all of the different places she has uttered and written the phrase in order to find him.

The narrator says that everyday he tries to remember the phrase but that he always forgets it. She tells him she wishes he could at least remember the city in which she has been writing it, and he tells her that he would like to touch her. She asks for a cigarette and says that she wonders why she cannot remember where she wrote the phrase, musing that sometimes she thinks that she may merely have dreamed that she wrote it everywhere. He walks over to give her the cigarette and says that if he could only remember the phrase tomorrow, he could find her. She tells him that the cigarette is warming her up, and he says that he is glad, because it frightens him to see her trembling.

After mentioning that they have been seeing each other this way for several years and that each meeting ends when they hear the drop of a spoon in the morning, the narrator remembers the first time he asked her who she was. She had replied that she did not remember, and they had realized that they had met in previous dreams. The narrator then repeats that he would like to touch her, and she tells him that he would ruin everything. He insists that it does not matter, but she says that when he wakes up he will have forgotten, and she stays behind the lamp.

The narrator tells the woman that it is already dawning, and he takes the doorknob in his hand. The woman tells him not to open the door because the hallway is full of difficult dreams, but the narrator opens the door halfway and smells ''vegetable earth, damp fields,'' telling her that he does not think there is a hallway there. She says this is because there is a woman outside dreaming about the country, and the narrator tells her that he has to leave in order to wake up. The wind and the smells cease, and the narrator tells the woman that he will recognize her tomorrow from their phrase. She tells him with a sad smile that he will not remember anything and puts her hands back over the lamp, saying, ''You're the only man who doesn't re-

member anything of what he's dreamed after he wakes up.''

Characters

Clerk

The drugstore clerk orders the woman to clean up the mess she has made after she writes ''Eyes of a blue dog'' on the floor with lipstick.

Narrator

The narrator of the story is both the speaker, from whose perspective the reader experiences the story, and the dreamer, whose mind is creating the environment into which the woman enters. Like the woman he desires, the narrator seems quite lonely, unable to find the object of his desire in real life or even touch her in his dream. The fact that he does not touch her despite his repeated desire to do so, his indistinct and puzzled knowledge of her and their history, and the cold that had given him ''the certainty of [his] solitude'' all emphasize this loneliness. Also, the narrator's ability to see the woman just as well when he is facing the wall and his inability to remember her outside of his dreams create doubt about whether he is able to interact with other people or develop any kind of connection with them.

Less physically distinct than the woman, the narrator's only descriptions, aside from the details that he is a smoker who leans back on one leg of his chair, come from the woman's perspective. She tells him that she has sometimes thought of him as a ''little brown statue in the corner of some museum,'' and she says that she once associated him with a smell that she notices in a drugstore. Although he turns his back to her, the narrator is earnestly attracted to the woman, repeatedly asking to touch her and watching her primping rituals very carefully. There is also a hint of violence toward her, such as when he tells her that he has always wanted to see her ''as if [she'd] been beaten.''

Since the narrator is dreaming the landscape and events of the story, his character is expressed by the properties of the dream itself. The woman could represent the object of his desire, the cold room with a lamp could represent how he sees himself, and his difficult and obscure interaction with the woman could represent how he relates to others. Or, the dream could be less specifically symbolic but nevertheless represent the narrator's unconscious world, full of loneliness, confusion, and frustration. The basic fears and desires of the narrator's unconscious are the main focus of his characterization, and the hints about the narrator's waking life, including the dropping of the spoon and the breathing of someone sleeping, simply add another dimension to the nature of the principle subject, his unconscious self.

Woman

The unnamed woman in the room with the narrator is a somewhat lonely and sad figure, associated with fire, ash, and metal. Made up with powder and crimson lipstick, she has long, "quiet," tremulous hands, which the narrator compares to the wings of a hen. Her skin is yellow like "soft, malleable copper," but it changes color and substance in the course of the story, turning red when she is sad and appearing like "plate," or laminated metal, when she is sleeping, as she says, "on my heart." She spends much of the story trembling, naked and cold, beside the lamp, while the narrator watches from his chair.

Beginning with a "slippery and oily" look, which gradually heats up until it is "burning, roasting," and finishing with features that are "darkened by a bitter cloud," the woman's description resembles the life of a flame such as that of an oil lamp. She is continually warming, even "toasting" and "consum[ing]" herself by the flame of the lamp; her pillow is "burning" her knee while she sleeps, and her eyes are consistently associated with ash and hot coals. Although this association with fire may partly suggest that she is passionate and romantic, it chiefly seems to be a way of emphasizing her capacity to consume herself and burn out. Indeed, the last paragraph's fluttering wind, which leaves her with a resigned smile, seems to blow out her flame and leave her "features darkened" as though she has been extinguished.

When the woman smiles sadly in resignation to her fate, she reveals that she is surrendering to the greater forces that keep her apart from the narrator. However, this contrasts with the side of her personality that is desperate and even obsessive about finding him; in fact, she tells the narrator that her entire life had been dedicated to finding him. These and other contradictions, such as the fact that she

has long and quiet hands and a pampered face despite the skin of her belly being "full of deep pits, as if you'd been beaten," make the woman seem quite mysterious. It is even possible that she is nothing more than a figment of the narrator's imagination, or the abstract object of his desire which he can never reach, despite the vividness of her character portrait.

Themes

Loneliness and Isolation

García Márquez portrays the narrator's dream world as a place of loneliness and isolation that will not allow an intimate connection between two people who desire each other. The narrator and the woman cannot touch each other, meet in waking life, control when they see each other in dreams, nor stay together when a noise distracts them from their sleep. The narrator cannot even remember the woman when he wakes, and the woman is unsure whether she has merely dreamed her agonizing search for him. Although the dream landscape is full of desire and longing, a place for powerful and literally burning passions, the narrator and the woman cannot consummate their relationship, and they remain forever at a distance.

This sense of isolation, which is common in García Márquez's early fiction, is particularly stark in the world of dreams, where the narrator's deepest and most insatiable desires emerge. However, unlike many of García Márquez's stories, there is a kernel of potential for a relationship between two people that desire each other and seem to share a deep understanding. Despite the loneliness that characterizes their relationship and the fact that they will never be together in a full or complete sense, the narrator and the woman are capable of feeling togetherness in their dreams. In fact, the woman does not want to touch the narrator out of fear that this contact will "ruin everything," which implies that they have a deep and meaningful connection that is more important than physical contact. Also, when the woman discusses her longing for the narrator in real life, or when the narrator states that his and the woman's friendship is subordinated to "the simplest of happenings," they imply that the things that make up their waking lives are somehow

Topics for Further Study

- García Márquez's collection *Eyes of a Blue Dog* (1972), anthologized in *Collected Stories* (1984), contains eleven short stories written between 1947 and 1955. Read the other ten of these stories, and compare them to "Eyes of a Blue Dog." How do the stories compare in style and structure? How do they differ? What makes "Eyes of a Blue Dog" unique? Choose one story and compare it in depth to "Eyes of a Blue Dog."

- Many critics would characterize "Eyes of a Blue Dog" as experimental in style and form. Discuss what, in your opinion, makes the story experimental, citing examples from the text. How does the story challenge you as a reader? How does it ask you to interpret the language and events of the story differently from other short stories you have read? How is it experimental in comparison to the other fiction of the 1950s? Describe why you think García Márquez is interested in experimentation, and discuss the results of his innovative stylistic approach.

- "Eyes of a Blue Dog" is a fantasy about the unconscious dream world, so it lends itself to examination from the standpoint of psychological theory. Familiarize yourself with the basic psychological theories of Sigmund Freud, and describe how García Márquez reflects or refutes these theories in his story. Or, do some research

into the psychological theory that was in vogue in the 1950s, such as that of the French psychoanalyst Jacques Lacan, and apply what you have learned to "Eyes of a Blue Dog." You may also choose to approach the story from the perspective of contemporary psychology, discussing the insights of the story that cohere, or do not cohere, with modern understandings of the unconscious. As you form your answer, think about the ways in which García Márquez's style inspires his reader to visualize the unconscious.

- "Eyes of a Blue Dog" does not appear to have much political subtext, but it was written during a tense and violent point in Colombian history, at which time García Márquez was working as a journalist. Read about La Violencia in Colombia and about García Márquez's life in the 1940s and 1950s. What were the effects of this social climate on artists and writers of the era? How did La Violencia affect García Márquez's other writings, and how did Colombian writers and intellectuals during this period affect the country's history? Describe the place of a story like "Eyes of a Blue Dog" in this atmosphere. How might politics have affected García Márquez's writing process? Can you see any traces of the political environment in "Eyes of a Blue Dog?" If so, describe them; if not, discuss why not.

---

less vital and important than the relationship of their dreams. Whereas the narrator's cigarette is able to warm the woman in the dream, it seems that nothing is able to warm her or relieve her solitude in real life.

"Eyes of a Blue Dog" poses provocative questions about what loneliness and isolation actually mean. It is possible that the story emphasizes the frustration and futility of all relationships, since the narrator will never remember the woman outside of the dream world. Or, it is possible that the story implies that two people, although they are unable to have a physical relationship and although they are

lonely and isolated in real life, can have vital and powerful unconscious connections. Either way, García Márquez challenges the reader's preconceptions about companionship and desire. Desperation and difficulty are revealed to be unavoidable aspects of a relationship, while distance and separation seem to be a necessary part of desire.

The Unconscious

The world of dreams is associated with the unconscious, and one of García Márquez's principle interests in "Eyes of a Blue Dog" is to capture the unique atmosphere of this phenomenon. Portraying the narrator's dream simultaneously as an intensely, physically real environment and a vast, obscure netherworld, the story allows the reader an insight into the complexities of the unconscious mind. Countless novels and short stories make reference to the unconscious, and the characterization process almost always takes into consideration the inner workings of the mind, but García Márquez is unique in setting the entire story in the unconscious. Reality is a side note, the subject of several memories outside the dream, which may refer to yet another dream or merely to another layer of the woman's or the narrator's unconscious minds.

From this perspective, within the unconscious world, the reader is able to perceive the desires and fears that underlie everyday life and motivate conscious actions. It is not necessarily clear from the story, however, to what degree and in what way the unconscious world affects waking life, nor is it clear what result conscious actions have in the unconscious mind. García Márquez poses questions throughout the story about the mysteries of this interaction, suggesting through the woman's obsessive quest to find the narrator that unconscious desires can overwhelm conscious life. However, the woman's situation also highlights the possibility of a complete separation between the conscious and unconscious worlds, since she will never find the narrator in real life.

The intriguing final line of the story, identifying the narrator as unique among men in his inability to remember what he has dreamed when he is awake, implies that it is impossible for the narrator to fulfill his unconscious desires. It seems to suggest that no other man has this problem, although the woman may be ironic in her statement, actually meaning that no one remembers his or her dreams. Indeed, the woman is also unable to remember her dreams, or at least encounters a disconnection between her conscious and unconscious memories, since she is unable to remember where she has written "Eyes of a blue dog" while she is dreaming. The conclusion of "Eyes of a Blue Dog," therefore, does not seem to resolve the question it poses about how unconscious desire manifests itself in waking life, despite the suggestion that the narrator and the woman are resigned to hopelessness and isolation. It is possible that García Márquez prefers to stress the ambiguity of the relationship between unconsciousness and consciousness, leaving its mysteries unresolved.

Style

Magic Realism

Magic realism is a technique associated with post–World War II Latin American fiction that blends elements of myth, fantasy, and the supernatural with an otherwise realistic storytelling technique. The fantastical aspects of this style can range from magical transformations and supernatural powers in humans and animals to epic struggles such as those found in the Bible or classical mythology to new realms of perception and awareness such as the point of view from a dead body or within an animal. In "Eyes of a Blue Dog," García Márquez uses magic realism to portray an extended fantasy about the experience of a dream world. Although a dream is not a supernatural idea, the manner in which the reader enters into this world uses aspects of fantasy and is foreign to everyday experience.

García Márquez employs the style of magic realism for a variety of reasons that relate to his thematic goals, and he is interested in challenging the way that readers interact with fiction. Magic realism is a stylistic innovation, an advance in technique that allows readers to understand events and themes in a unique and vivid way. For example, the phrase "when I sleep on my heart," though it is difficult to picture in exact terms, provides a stark insight into the woman's character. Similarly, although it does not seem to make sense that the narrator can see the woman when he is facing away from her, this detail allows the reader to understand the essence of their contradictory relationship, which is both extremely close and strikingly distanced. García Márquez is very much aware of the insightfulness that his technique can allow, and he is adept at using magic realism as a powerful tool to convey some of the perplexing and complex truths about how humans experience, desire, feel, and remember.

Dream Narrative

Aside from his general stylistic approach of magic realism, García Márquez uses a number of specific techniques such as an obscure time frame, ambiguous events in the narrative, and unclear "diction," or word choice, to make his reader feel that he or she is inside a dream world. These stylistic choices are crucial in establishing a compelling setting and addressing García Márquez's key themes, and they are vital in creating the memorable and unique atmosphere of the story. Perhaps the defining feature of these devices is their combination of haziness and obscurity with specific, intense details. García Márquez uses many contradictory phrases and describes a series of mysterious events, to the point that the reader can easily become disoriented, but the author balances this practice with striking and grounded details, which makes the reader feel that the events must actually be occurring.

For example, the time frame of the narrator and the woman's relationship is unclear, and basic details such as what will happen if they touch, where the outside door leads, and whether they will ever be able to meet in real life are not clarified. However, details such as the sound of someone sleeping and the anticipation of a spoon falling to wake them up ground the reader in a sense of reality and coherent progression. Indeed, there are many other moments described with specific, almost unforgettable detail, such as the woman's discussion about how she is made of metal and the narrator's description of how she says ''I'm warming up,'' as if the phrase had burned up on a scrap of paper, that make the dream world seem substantial and real at the same time that they draw attention to its surreal strangeness. The title phrase itself, which the narrator created after seeing the woman's eyes, variously described as ''hot-coal eyes'' and ''eyes of ash,'' is an excellent example of how the García Márquez combines the intensely specific with the mysteriously obscure, emphasizing the contradictions that define the experience of a dream.

Historical Context

Hispanic Avant-garde

The years following World War II saw an exciting and remarkable output of literature by Hispanic writers, principally in Latin America. Because they departed from previous styles like literary modernism, creating new and innovative genres such as magic realism, the writers of this period became known as the Hispanic avant-garde, a French term that means artistically advanced and daring. García Márquez was one of the most prominent of these writers, but he was preceded by the Argentine author Jorge Luis Borges, whom García Márquez admired greatly and frequently acknowl-

edged as a major influence on his own work. Rebelling against the symbolist tradition of literary modernism, Borges helped to create a new style of writing that referred not to elements of the real world, but instead to other texts, and he resisted a linear view of time and space.

The Hispanic avant-garde movement was global in nature, partly because influential Latin American writers like García Márquez and Julio Cortázar spent much of their lives abroad, and many of its writers were influenced by a new literary movement developing in Europe and the United States, called postmodernism. Heavily influenced by post–World War II psychoanalytical theorists such as Jacques Lacan, postmodernism is known for challenging traditional understandings of perception and representation. Other influences and techniques, however, were uniquely Latin American in nature, such as magic realism, which incorporates elements of myth, fantasy, and the supernatural into otherwise realistic writing. ''Eyes of a Blue Dog'' was written in the early stages of the Hispanic avant-garde movement, and it incorporates a variety of influences, including postmodernism and magic realism, into its experimental style.

Colombia in the 1940s and 1950s

Colombia has had a long history of violent political strife between its two main parties, the liberals and the conservatives, but the era of the 1940s and 1950s was particularly volatile. The political environment had been tense since a large strike in 1928 ended in violence, and tensions increased during World War II, which Colombia entered on the side of the allies. In the 1940s a liberal politician named Jorge Eliécer Gaitán rose to power on the platform that he would support peasants and the poor, and in 1947 Gaitán became the leader of the liberal party when they gained control of the congress. In 1948, however, Gaitán was assassinated in Bogotá, and the city erupted into riots in which thousands of people were killed.

In the series of events that followed, both parties organized guerilla armies that swept through the land and terrorized civilians. This period, called ''La Violencia,'' continued when, in 1953, a military coup placed General Gustavo Rojas Pinilla in power. A bipartisan coalition formed a provisional government in 1958, but not before over 150,000 people had died in La Violencia. ''Eyes of a Blue Dog'' was written at the height of these tensions,

Compare
&
Contrast

- **1950:** The Hispanic avant-garde movement, which will inspire Latin American writers for decades, is gathering momentum. Julio Cortázar and Jorge Luis Borges are currently writing some of their most exciting material.

  Today: Latin American literature continues to make use of fantasy and myth, but this style no longer dominates the literary scene.

- **1950:** Violence rages throughout Colombia. By 1953, more than 150,000 Colombians will have died as a result of the violent civil conflict that erupted after the assassination of Jorge Eliécer Gaitán.

  Today: Because of ruthless right-wing paramilitaries and Marxist guerillas who engage in the kidnapping and drug trades, violence remains prevalent in Colombia, particularly in rural areas.

- **1950:** Psychological theory about the workings of the unconscious mind is heavily influenced by French theorists such as Jacques Lacan, who is applying advances in modern linguistics to the field of psychology.

  Today: Behavioral and structural research into the makeup of the brain, assisted by new imaging technology, is providing a wealth of insight into psychology.

- **1950:** García Márquez has recently dropped out of law school and is working as a journalist for a prominent Colombian paper during a tense political period.

  Today: Nearing the end of his monumental career, García Márquez is battling lymphatic cancer and working on volume 2 of his memoirs, traveling between Mexico City, Los Angeles, and Cartagena, Colombia.

---

and, although it does not directly address political themes, its author was very politically active at the time. In fact, García Márquez, like other writers and intellectuals, was compelled to leave Colombia in the mid-1950s because he feared the consequences of challenging the government in his journalism and fiction.

Critical Overview

Although García Márquez's body of work has inspired an enormous amount of critical recognition and praise, the stories of his early period have not received the amount of attention that his later novels have. As Raymond L. Williams points out in his discussion of the author in *Twayne's World Author Series Online:* "The stories from the 1947–1952 period are mostly unknown beyond the Hispanic world and relatively ignored by critics, even among

Hispanists." "Eyes of a Blue Dog" is no exception to this rule; in fact, the Peruvian fiction and prose writer Mario Vargas Llosa notes in his 1971 book, *García Márquez: Historia de un deicidio (García Márquez: The Story of a Deicide)*, that in style and structure the story is the weakest of the period.

In his 1990 biography, *García Márquez: The Man and His Work,* Gene H. Bell-Villada suggests that in 1950 García Márquez was writing under the "lopsided spell" of Czech writer Franz Kafka's short stories, arguing that "Eyes of a Blue Dog" is a "strangely dark" story "depicting individuals trapped within their . . . heads." Later in his biographical study, however, Bell-Villada cites "Eyes of a Blue Dog" as one of the "sweeter and more touching" stories of a group that he finds "brooding and morose," and he characterizes the narrator's relationship with the woman as a "passionate amour." Raymond L. Williams also comments briefly on the outside influences of "Eyes of a Blue Dog," arguing that its central relationship "portrays a situation reflecting French existentialist lit-

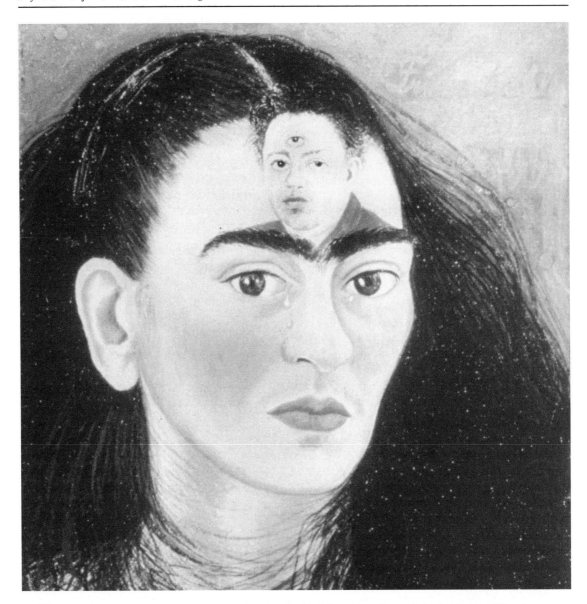

"Diego and I," surrealist painting by Frida Kahlo using fantastic imagery like that associated with dreams

erature: its point of departure is two persons isolated in a room."

Criticism

Scott Trudell

Trudell is an independent scholar with a bachelor's degree in English literature. In the following essay, Trudell discusses García Márquez's portrayal of the unconscious mind in his story, highlighting the story's commentary on erotic desire.

Perhaps the most memorable aspect of "Eyes of a Blue Dog" is the intense, frustrated passion between its narrator and the woman of his dreams. Their desire for each other is "impossible" and will never be consummated, yet they repeat their desperate meetings anyway, with incredible urgency. From the opening moment of the story, when they spend minutes simply looking at each other, to the final

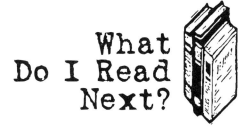

What Do I Read Next?

- *One Hundred Years of Solitude* (1967) is García Márquez's masterpiece of magic realism. Tracing the history of a family in a small Colombian town, the work incorporates elements of mythical fantasy, the supernatural, and political commentary into its compelling narrative.

- Richard Linklater's animated film *Waking Life* (2001) follows a man through a dream world in which he contemplates questions about meaning, perception, and human existence.

- *The House of the Spirits,* which first appeared in English in 1985, is Isabel Allende's first widely successful novel, and through a sophisticated use of magic realism it tells the story of four women characters that have various kinds of relationships with the passionate and violent Esteban Trueba.

- Jorge Luis Borges's short story "The Garden of Forking Paths" (1941) is an intriguing mystery tale as well as an exploration of philosophical questions about time, perception, and meaning.

- Franz Kafka's *The Metamorphosis,* written in 1915 but not published in English until 1937, is the elusive and fascinating story of a man's transformation into an insect.

---

moment, despite the woman's sad acknowledgement that the narrator will never remember her when awake, they are subject to mysterious and overpowering desires. Although they do not seem to have any coherent explanation, these erotic desires are the central forces in the narrator's unconscious mind, and it is clear that they are among his most fundamental emotions. This essay will argue that the complex, desperate, and frustrated love between the narrator and the woman is characteristic of the new ways in which writers were beginning to think about unconscious desire in the 1950s.

Unlike modernist writers, whose view of the unconscious mind tended to be influenced by the psychological theories of Sigmund Freud, García Márquez was writing during a period in which the unconscious was no longer considered to operate in a world of straightforward symbolism. Linguists such as Ferdinand de Saussure and psychoanalysts such as Jacques Lacan contributed to the view that the unconscious responded not simply to universal symbols but complex systems of meaning and representation that do not necessarily have a basis in the real world. In the late 1940s and early 1950s, therefore, as a new view of human psychology was emerging, many writers began experimenting with innovative ways of representing the unconscious in their work. Although García Márquez has always been wary of subscribing to critical theory, he and his contemporaries were inevitably influenced by this new, more complex understanding of the unconscious.

Multilayered psychological complexity is immediately apparent in "Eyes of a Blue Dog," which does not treat the dream world as a by-product of childhood trauma represented by universal symbolism. Instead, the narrator's dream world is a mysterious phenomenon that is not the source of any system of symbols or encoded meanings that can be applied to the narrator's conscious life. In fact, the story does not have much, if any, connection to reality at all; the only traces of the narrator's waking life in the narrative are the suggestion of a spoon dropping and the sound of someone sleeping. Like the woman's efforts to write "Eyes of a blue dog" everywhere she goes, however, it is possible that these are merely small traces that have escaped from another layer of dreaming. As she says when she is wondering why she cannot remember the city in which she lives: "It's just that sometimes I think that I've dreamed that too." This moment suggests that the narrator and the woman are disconnected from the real world, caught in an endless, layered system of unconscious meaning.

> " The narrator is unable to be with his lover outside of his dream world because she is an unattainable by-product of his mind's unique and untranslatable longings."

The woman's awareness that she may merely have dreamt about writing her and the narrator's phrase all over the city is one of the most striking examples of the dream world's separation from reality, but, on closer examination, it becomes clear that García Márquez makes reference to additional layers of dreaming throughout the story. One important example is the mysterious ambiguity about the history and locations of the narrator and the woman's meetings. When the woman reveals that the narrator invented their identifying phrase "on the first day," and when she remembers hazily that they must have "met in other dreams" as opposed to in real life, she implies that she is not a representation or symbol of something or someone in the real world. Also, when the narrator mentions that their relationship "was subordinated to things, to the simplest of happenings," it suggests that their relationship does not affect these actual things and happenings, but is completely separate from them. Perhaps the clearest evidence that the dream world is entirely distanced from reality, however, is the fact that the narrator cannot remember "anything of what he's dreamed after he wakes up."

Since the narrator's erotic relationship with the woman is at the center of his unconscious world, this new vision of the unconscious, which distances the narrator and the woman's relationship from real life and views their passion as locked within a labyrinth of layered memory and significance, allows García Márquez to comment on the themes of love and desire in a new and exciting manner. Erotic desire is not, here, a forbidden manifestation of childhood desires for a parent, like that of a piece of fiction influenced by Freudian theory. Instead, "Eyes of a Blue Dog" portrays desire as an internal, contained, unconscious phenomenon that is impossible to satisfy in real life. The narrator is unable to be with his lover outside of his dream world because

she is an unattainable by-product of his mind's unique and untranslatable longings.

One important piece of evidence to support this claim is the narrator's insistence on turning his chair away from the woman and his ability to see her without looking at her. The narrator describes the wall as "another blind mirror in which I couldn't see her," which is a confusing and ambiguous statement but nevertheless an apt description of how the narrator sees and feels the woman's presence without even needing to look at her, though he is still fundamentally distanced from her. This contradiction is developed further by the narrator's description of the woman seeing him "in the depths of the mirror, my face turned toward the wall." The idea of the "depths of the mirror," an image that emphasizes the many layers of dreams and worlds of meaning through which the narrator and the woman experience each other, suggests that the narrator's understanding of the woman is in fact a reflection of himself and his own distinctive desires. In other words, the object of the narrator's erotic desire is nothing more than a reflection of a reflection of himself.

García Márquez does not mean to imply that the narrator is abnormally narcissistic or self-absorbed, but that an attraction to a dream ideal of one's own creation is a central fact of unconscious desire. It is no surprise that this desire is full of unresolved frustration and confusion, because the narrator can never satisfy his desire for his own fantasy. The narrator cannot even seem to understand or remember the baffling contradictions of his unconscious life, so it is natural that García Márquez would characterize his attempt to break through all of the layers of meaning that divide him from the object of his desire as "impossible." Perhaps this is why the narrator expresses a desire to see the woman "with the skin of [her] belly full of deep pits, as if [she]'d been beaten." The violent aspect of their relationship is an expression of the desperation they feel. This may also explain why the flame of the lamp and the narrator's cigarette are recurring images. A tool both of violence and of the warmth that brings them together, fire serves as a useful emblem for the contradictory emotions of their relationship.

"Eyes of a Blue Dog" does not abandon the narrator and the woman's relationship as hopeless, and García Márquez is careful to highlight their intense connection. Descriptions of the woman's "clenched fists" and "tightened teeth" emphasize her passion, and there is a glimmer of hope that they will come together, when the narrator's cigarette seems to warm her. When the narrator is telling her he wants to touch her for the first time and when, while she is like "yellow, soft, malleable copper," the narrator seems ready actually to touch her, there is a great deal of hope for a release from the tension of their frustrated desire. The narrator has extraordinarily tender feelings for the woman, which is why he is frightened to see her trembling, and there is even the sense that, given the intensity of their desire for each other, nothing could compare to it or override it.

Because he is inspired by the period's revelations about the complex mysteries of the unconscious, however, García Márquez denies the narrator and the woman any true moment of togetherness, and he consistently renders their love "subordinated" to reality. The woman's "surrender to the impossible, the unreachable" at the end of the story reasserts the inevitable, vast distances between individuals that are characteristic of post-Freudian psychological theory. The narrator and the woman have a desperate and passionate desire for each other, stemming from the most basic of unconscious feelings, but it is ultimately impossible and unreal because it is buried in the impenetrable layers of the narrator's own mind. García Márquez recognizes advances in psychological theory and maintains that, because it is rooted in the narrator's unconscious, such a deep passion cannot be reciprocated.

Source: Scott Trudell, Critical Essay on "Eyes of a Blue Dog," in *Short Stories for Students,* Thomson Gale, 2005.

Catherine Dybiec Holm

Holm is a short story and novel author, as well as a freelance writer. In this essay, Holm looks at García Márquez's use of surrealism, magic realism, and other writing techniques that give this story its dreamlike quality.

Gabriel García Márquez is widely recognized as a writer of magic realism. Magic realism blends the fantastic with the ordinary, mundane details of everyday life. In "Eyes of a Blue Dog," García Márquez uses magic realism techniques, surrealism, and other literary crafts to give this story its dreamlike quality. This is particularly appropriate because the story occurs within the combined dream reality of the two main characters. Although one could argue that the story is not true magic realism, since it does not take place in everyday, conscious reality, many surreal and magic realism elements

are present in this example of García Márquez's storytelling.

García Márquez gives the reader immediate hints that this story will be not about the typical reality of everyday experience. In the first paragraph, the narrator refers to the woman's "slippery and oily" look. It is a strange way to describe a glance, and suggests a hint of darkness and otherworldliness, very much like a dream. When the man sees the woman's eyelids "lighted up as on every night," the reader again is given a clue that this will be a story out of the ordinary. Eyes may light up, but eyelids usually do not. Yet García Márquez has provided this information in a subtle way. Not only are eyelids lighting up, but they are lighting up every night. The author describes the woman's "great hot coal eyes," rather than using a more cliched description such as "bright eyes" or "smoldering eyes." "Hot coal eyes" also suggests otherworldliness, darkness, and night—the time of the dream. García Márquez's descriptions are packed with information, yet it is given to the reader gradually, letting the reader figure out that these characters are going through a repeated, shared dream sequence, in which extraordinary phenomena may occur. With these subtle nuances and details, García Márquez avoids insulting his reader by stating things too obviously. The reader is allowed to gradually discover the story as it unfolds.

By the second paragraph, the astute reader will probably figure out that this story is, indeed, taking place in dreamtime. The woman gives the reader a clue when she says, "I'm afraid that someone is dreaming about this room and revealing my secrets." This is the first time in the story that dreaming is explicitly mentioned. When the man says, "Maybe the sheet fell off," García Márquez is making it clear to the reader that the man (and the woman) are indeed straddling two realities—their shared dream and the ordinary reality that they occupy. And this is exciting territory for a reader to occupy; to imagine and experience being in dreamtime, even collaborating with the characters' experience of dreamtime, while maintaining a blurry awareness of the "real" world. In ordinary reality, the woman's fear that someone is dreaming about her room might seem like a paranoid delusion. But in García Márquez's surreal landscape, strange statements such as these are juxtaposed continuously with the details of everyday life (the "harsh, strong smoke" of a cigarette, a pink mother-of-pearl makeup box, the "clean, new tiles of the drugstore"). If someone else is dreaming about the room and

In the surreal world
of the dream landscape that
García Márquez has created,
much is possible."

revealing the woman's secrets, why is it that other characters never appear in the room? García Márquez seems to suggest that other people's dreams lurk right outside the door in the hallway, but perhaps these two characters are able to create boundaries around their shared dream that exclude others. In the world of magic realism, the surreal is continuously contrasted with the ordinary. People dream; people are conscious of and can sense the ordinary world around them (cold, heat, sheets coming off). But García Márquez's use of magic realism in this story makes it possible for these two characters to share a dream-world, where they will continue to meet in the dreams they intentionally create.

Above and beyond the use of magic realism, García Márquez uses many techniques to give this story a surreal, otherworldly, and dreamlike quality. Dreams often do not make sense, and do not follow the rules and conventions of ordinary life (much like magic realism). The characters' first exchange is an important clue to acclimate the reader to the surreal possibilities of the story, prompting the reader to expect more.

> It was then that I remembered the usual thing, when I said to her: "Eyes of a blue dog." Without taking her hand off the lamp she said to me: "That. We'll never forget that." She left the orbit, sighing: "Eyes of a blue dog. I've written it everywhere."

In the real world, apparent strangers do not usually greet each other this way. Gradually, the reader learns that these characters do know each other, though the woman always starts out remembering more than the man. But with the initial presentation of such strange dialog, the reader is directed to expect more surrealism. García Márquez, with this dialog presentation and the other surreal hints that have already been given (eyelids that light up, slippery and oily gazes), is directing the reader to suspend his or her disbelief and to accept that the world in this story is both ordinary and out of the ordinary.

García Márquez's use of prose also gives "Eyes of a Blue Dog" a surreal, dreamlike tone. The author's paragraphs are longer than what is often found in contemporary fiction. This has the effect of giving the paragraphs a run-on, stream-of-consciousness quality, much like the progression of a dream. García Márquez seems to ignore a modern-day writing convention that involves creating a new paragraph whenever a new character begins to speak, or when characters cease speaking and the prose returns to narrative. The author may be deliberately ignoring this writing convention. When a reader sees a paragraph break, he or she inserts a mental pause. When prose with paragraph breaks is read out loud, the reader inserts an implied pause between paragraphs. "Eyes of a Blue Dog" would read and would flow much differently if the author had used more paragraph breaks around dialog. In this example, the woman and the man talk, unimpeded by the formation of new paragraphs. It gives their words a sense of flowing into each other and unraveling; much like the fluidity of a dream. Perhaps also, since it is a shared dream, it makes sense to not separate each speaker with a paragraph break. Perhaps the author is using this technique as another subtle allusion to a shared dream experience:

> And she said: "It's like—what do you call it—laminated metal." She drew closer to the lamp. "I would have liked to hear you," I said. And she said: "If we find each other sometime, put your ear to my ribs when I sleep." I heard her breathe heavily as she talked. And she said that for years she'd done nothing different.

Imagine how differently this would read with conventional paragraph breaks:

> And she said: "It's like—what do you call it—laminated metal." She drew closer to the lamp.

> "I would have liked to hear you," I said.

These characters occupy a completely shared experience. Even when they are not using direct dialog, sentences often follow into one another. A sentence that starts "And she said . . ." is followed by a sentence starting with "I heard her . . ." It is as if the author is suggesting that these two people are almost, at least in this dream-world, one entity.

The author also uses the word "and" at the beginning of sentences to give his narrative a fluid quality. In the segment quoted below, which includes dialog, imagine how different the tone of the story would be if these sentences started without "and," and a new paragraph started each time a different character spoke. Such a conventional approach would work for a realistic, fast-paced suspense story, but it would change the tone of "Eyes of a Blue Dog" completely.

> And over the flame she held the same long and tremulous hand that she had been warming before sitting down at the mirror. And she said: "You don't feel the cold." And I said to her: "Sometimes." And she said to me: "You must feel it now." And then I understood why I couldn't have been alone in the seat.

In "Eyes of a Blue Dog" the reader never learns the names of the characters and is only given a description of the woman. This may also be a deliberate choice by the author to add to the surrealism of the story. Names carry associations for readers, and might ground the characters more firmly in readers' imaginations, making characters seem more conventionally real. Naming the characters would also bring the reader closer to the characters, as would more physical description. If the characters are not named and not fully described, the story is slightly distanced from the reader, adding to the tone of unearthliness that already permeates the story. And even though García Márquez describes the woman, her description actually enhances the surreal elements. She is, after all, the one with the eyelids that glow and the "hot coal eyes." Her otherworldly "eyes of ash" inspired the man to create the strange, signature phrase "eyes of a blue dog." The odd phrase (and the women's eyes) is simply accepted without question by both characters. In magic realism, strange happenings or odd situations (or phrases, in this case) are accepted as normal. Waiters bow reverently when the woman approaches them saying nothing more than "eyes of a blue dog." All these surreal events add to the otherworldly quality of the story.

Still more evidence of magic realism shows up throughout the story. The woman changes from "hard and cold metal" to "yellow, soft, malleable copper." The characters smell the freshness of the country outside the room, in the hallway. The man's cigarette butt seemingly dissolves into nothingness. The man says, "the butt had disappeared between my fingers. I'd forgotten that I was smoking." It is as if his forgetting that he was smoking caused the cigarette to disappear; as if his thoughts could control this version of reality. The man's other dreams also control the reality of this dream—pieces of a former dream (involving a woman who longs for the country) lurk outside the room in a hallway. Somehow the woman with the "eyes of a blue dog" understands this. Somehow both this man and woman have shared pieces of previous

dreams above and beyond their shared, repetitive dream. This makes sense in terms of conscious reality, but in this story, the reader has already been asked to suspend disbelief. In the surreal world of the dream landscape that García Márquez has created, much is possible. At the same time, the use of surrealism relates to and advances this story, and does not jar the reader out of the story.

Joseph Epstein, writing in *Commentary,* claims that García Márquez's writing improved once the author added the element of politics to his writing. Epstein calls García Márquez's earlier works, including "Eyes of a Blue Dog," "dryly abstract and bleak." While "Eyes of a Blue Dog" may not resemble the full blown magic realism of García Márquez's later work, it is easy to see the influence of surrealism and magic realism in this story.

Source: Catherine Dybiec Holm, Critical Essay on "Eyes of a Blue Dog," in *Short Stories for Students,* Thomson Gale, 2005.

Lois Kerschen

Kerschen is a freelance writer and adjunct college English instructor. In this essay, Kerschen examines an early short story of García Márquez that uses magical realism to express the fluidity between dreams and reality as well as the impossibility of crossing the border from dreams into reality.

Magical realism is a unique literary style that developed among Latin American writers. The term "magical realism" was coined in 1925 by Franz Roh, a German art critic who was trying to describe a visual response to the inexplicable aspects of reality. In the 1940s, Latin American writers took up the style. Its most notable explanation came in a 1949 essay by Cuban writer Alejo Carpentier. Eventually, Gabriel García Márquez, the 1982 Nobel laureate and native of Colombia, would popularize this branch of literature through his internationally acclaimed works, especially *One Hundred Years of Solitude,* published in English in 1970. Magical realism combines the rational with the supernatural by setting fantastic events in the normal world. It is a paradoxical literary technique that attempts a truer reality than conventional realism will allow.

Garcia Marquez first began experimenting with magical realism in his short stories. "Eyes of a Blue Dog," written in 1950, is an early example of his ability, as described by literary critic Susan de Carvalho, to create a world where, "[r]eality and fantasy are inseparable, described with no change of

> "Her makeup, a symbol of femininity, is meant to attract him, and in her waking life she is even willing to humiliate herself in her quest to find this man she sees only in her dreams."

tone, no narrative incredulity." He intricately weaves together the dream world with our perceptions of waking life, thus making "the separation between dream and reality" "as unclear as is the separation between life and death." Through this technique he explores every human being's innate need for love, for a connection to another, and the emptiness that can be consuming without love. In "Eyes of a Blue Dog," Garcia Marquez presents very real human dilemmas through the lens of a surreal dream.

"Eyes of a Blue Dog" is set in a room where a man is sitting in a chair and staring at a woman as she warms her hands over a lamp. Although readers discover later, at the end of the long second paragraph, that the man is dreaming, the story does not initially make this situation obvious. In fact, Garcia Marquez grounds his opening imagery in solid, concrete descriptions: a cigarette, the "harsh, strong smoke," the "chair, balancing on one of the rear legs," the lamp, the woman's "long and quiet hand," the dressing table, and the "mathematical light." All are familiar and tangible images that draw readers into the story and orient us to the scene. The image of the man balancing in his chair implies gravity and weight, and the possibility that these two things could work against him and tip him over. The cigarette and smoke remind us that the man is breathing and the lamp tells us that the woman can feel cold. In a dream, of course, things such as gravity, heat, and cold do not really exist, but the author is purposely trying to establish this fictive world on firm, realistic ground before he takes the readers to places they are not expecting. He locates the "realism" before he explores the "magical."

The first hints of the actual location of the characters begin to come in the second paragraph

when the man and the woman discuss the coldness of the room. The man says, "Now I feel it . . . [and] it's strange because the night is quiet. Maybe the sheet fell off." This statement is incongruous with the already given information because there has so far been no other mention of a sheet. The statement acts as a small hint of what is to come. The man is aware of something beyond what he sees and is in fact aware that he is really in bed asleep. If he feels cold, it must be because his sheet is no longer covering his body, not because there is a lack of warmth in the room in which he currently perceives himself to be. Thus the readers become cognizant that all is not what they might have originally expected.

It is at the end of the second paragraph and the beginning of the third that the readers realize that these two people are visiting each other in a dream. They have, in fact, seen each other in dreams for several years and are trying to find one another in their waking lives as well. The woman uses the phrase "Eyes of a blue dog" to help her find "the man of her dreams"—writing it on walls, saying it aloud as she walks, desperately hoping he will hear her and recognize her. However, he always forgets the phrase upon waking from the dream and, therefore, does not remember to look for her. Each is trapped in an unending attempt to merge their dreams with reality, finding that they do not have the capacity to do so.

The dream-versus-reality motif allows Garcia Marquez to explore deeper meanings and themes of the common human existence. The search that drives these two characters is representative of the universal search for connection—the search for love. Without it, the characters are left feeling listless and, as scholar Raymond Williams explains, their "stark surroundings are matched by their frigid dialogue." Indeed, even though they are in the same dream room together, and though they talk about their desire to meet each other in their waking life, the characters are unable to connect. The man reclines in his chair, facing the wall, as the woman sits in front of the dressing table mirror, yet as he stares at the wall he believes he can see her putting on her lipstick. He sees her, and yet he doesn't see her. She is there in the room with him, and yet he turns away. The man attempts to touch the woman and finds that he can't. The woman tells him, "You'll ruin everything," and slowly he realizes he is about to wake up. Just as they are about to make contact, they are forced to end the dream. The man tries to reassure himself that they will have another chance, for "all we have to do is turn the pillow over in order to meet again," but the woman knows another effort will be just as futile. She knows he is "the only man in the world who doesn't remember anything of what he's dreamed after he wakes up." These two people seek connection, and yet they have no hope of making their dreams a reality.

The female character in this story seems particularly invested in finding and making a connection with the man. She goes to great lengths, both in the dream world and in her description of reality, to find and make herself available to the male character. Her nudity throughout most of the story is a symbol of her vulnerability and of her willingness to share herself completely. In her effort to connect, she removes every boundary she can. Her makeup, a symbol of femininity, is meant to attract him, and in her waking life she is even willing to humiliate herself in her quest to find this man she sees only in her dreams. While in a drugstore one day, she becomes convinced that the man is near, so she writes "Eyes of a blue dog" in red lipstick on the floor tiles. The store clerk makes her clean it up, so she spends "the whole afternoon on all fours, washing the tiles and saying: 'Eyes of a blue dog,' until people gathered at the door and said she was crazy." Yet none of these efforts are enough to rid her of her emptiness. She feels hollow to the point that she doesn't even recognize herself as human anymore; as she says, "Sometimes I think I'm made of metal." She sees herself as no more than a cold, lifeless, impenetrable shell, and she pins her hopes on finding this man who will be able to warm her. Yet in the end, with "a smile of surrender to the impossible, the unreachable," she knows she will never see him anywhere but in her dreams.

Toni Morrison and Salmon Rushdie are just two of many world-famous authors who have used magical realism in their works. Like Garcia Marquez, they too have been able to create a world where, as Carvalho says, "characters simply adjust their lives to incorporate unforeseen and, for the reader, bizarre circumstances." A common theme that has emerged in magical realism is the use of cyclical rather than linear time. This device causes events to occur over and over again without the characters ever achieving the goals they seek. Such is the situation in "Eyes of a Blue Dog," yet this strange world addresses interesting aspects of emotion and interaction outside the bounds of standard narrative. "Eyes of a Blue Dog" breaks the boundaries between dreams and reality and thus reminds us of the

extent to which these two states of being are truly intertwined.

Source: Lois Kerschen, Critical Essay on "Eyes of a Blue Dog," in *Short Stories for Students,* Thomson Gale, 2005.

Sources

Bell-Villada, Gene H., *García Márquez: The Man and His Work,* University of North Carolina Press, 1990, pp. 72, 137–38.

De Carvalho, Susan, "Origins of Social Pessimism in García Márquez: 'The Night of the Curlews,'" in *Studies in Short Fiction,* Vol. 28, No. 3, Summer 1991, pp. 331–38.

Epstein, Joseph, "How Good is Gabriel García Márquez?" in *Commentary,* Vol. 75, No. 5, May 1983, pp. 59–65.

García Márquez, Gabriel, "Eyes of a Blue Dog," translated by Gregory Rabassa, in *Collected Stories,* Harper & Row, 1984, pp. 47–54.

Vargas Llosa, Mario, *García Márquez: Historia de un deicidio,* Barral Editores, 1971, p. 228.

Williams, Raymond L., "Gabriel García Márquez: Chapter 2: The Early Fiction," in *Twayne's World Author Series Online,* G. K. Hall, 1999; originally published as "Chapter 2: The Early Fiction," in *Gabriel García Márquez,* Twayne's World Author Series, No. 749, Twayne, 1984, p. 5.

Further Reading

García Márquez, Gabriel, *Living to Tell the Tale,* translated by Edith Grossman, Alfred A. Knopf, 2003.
    In this vivid memoir (volume 1 in a projected series of three), García Márquez deals with the time period spanning his birth through 1955.

McGuirk, Bernard, "Characterization in the Early Fiction of Gabriel García Márquez," in *Gabriel García Márquez: New Readings,* edited by Bernard McGuirk and Richard Cardwell, Cambridge University Press, 1987, pp. 5–16.
    McGuirk's book provides an interesting discussion of the characterization techniques in García Márquez's early short stories, although it does not mention "Eyes of a Blue Dog" specifically.

Pelayo, Rubén, *Gabriel García Márquez: A Critical Companion,* Greenwood Press, 2001.
    This work offers a useful blend of contextual information and criticism on the author.

Penuel, Arnold M., *Intertextuality in García Márquez,* Spanish Literature Publications Company, 1994.
    Penuel's text discusses the influence of postmodern theory on García Márquez's works.

Gorilla, My Love

Toni Cade Bambara

1971

"Gorilla, My Love" is the story of Hazel, a young girl who feels that adults do not treat children with respect and honesty. Narrating her own story, she tells of two incidents in which adults demonstrated their untrustworthiness. Hazel comes from the kind of family that the author, Toni Cade Bambara, believed was under-represented in fiction of the 1970s: she is an African American girl living in New York City, in a home with two loving parents who emphasize the values of education and of keeping one's word. Although Bambara herself was a political activist, the story is not primarily political. Hazel's feelings are nearly universal, shared by most adolescents.

"Gorilla, My Love" was first published in the November 1971 issue of *Redbook Magazine* with the title "I Ain't Playin, I'm Hurtin." A year later, it became the title story in Bambara's first short story collection. "Gorilla, My Love" is one of several in the collection that feature strong first-person narrators speaking conversationally, rather than in a standard formal English. On the strength of this story and others, Bambara was widely praised for her ability to capture the authentic sounds of adolescence and of African American voices.

Author Biography

Toni Cade Bambara was born Miltona Mirkin Cade on March 25, 1939, in New York City. She and her brother were raised by a single mother in many different homes in New York, and later in Jersey City, New Jersey. Bambara spoke and wrote often about her mother, Helen Brent Henderson Cade, as an example of strength and integrity. Helen saw to it that her children learned about their African American heritage, and encouraged them to trust their own inner voices. In 1959, Toni Cade earned a bachelor's degree in Theater Arts and English from Queen's College. She had already published her first story, "Sweet Town," in *Vendome* magazine. After graduating, she completed a master's degree while working as a social worker for several community organizations.

In the 1960s, Cade was active in both the Civil Rights movement and the feminist movement. From 1965 to 1969 she taught at City College in New York. She continued to write, but saw teaching and community work as more important. In 1970, having taken the name Bambara, she edited an important anthology called *The Black Woman*, a collection of writings by some of the most well-known African American women of the day. The anthology, intended as a corrective to the views of African American women previously offered by white feminist women and by male academics, gave black women a chance to describe and analyze their own experiences. The short story "Gorilla, My Love," narrated by a young working-class African American girl, was published the following year, as was another anthology, *Tales and Stories for Black Folks*, a collection of stories for high school and college students. In 1972 the short story collection also titled *Gorilla, My Love* was published.

In addition to writing and teaching writing at various colleges, Bambara traveled to Cuba and Vietnam to learn about the political struggles of poor women. Moving to Atlanta in 1974, Bambara founded and directed projects to help writers become effective contributors to political movements. She published relatively little fiction during her career, though several of her stories, including "Gorilla, My Love" and "The Lesson" (1972), have become standard texts for high school and college classes. Her second collection of short stories, *The Sea Birds Are Still Alive*, was published in 1977, and an experimental novel called *The Salt Eaters* was published in 1980. She had come to find a fiction writer's life too solitary, and so in her last years, she focused most of her writing energy on more collaborative projects, including television and film scripts. She also worked on a novel about the Atlanta child murders; it was published as *These*

Toni Cade Bambara

Bones Are Not My Child in 1999, four years after her death. She died of colon cancer on December 9, 1995.

Plot Summary

As "Gorilla, My Love" opens, a first-person narrator says, "That was the year Hunca Bubba changed his name." It soon becomes clear that the speaker is a young person, but not until the story is nearly over is it revealed that she is a girl, and that her name is Hazel. In the opening scene, Hazel is riding in a car with her Granddaddy Vale, her Hunca Bubba (Uncle Bubba) and her younger brother, Baby Jason. They have been on a trip South to bring pecans back home. Granddaddy Vale is driving, Hazel is navigating from the front seat and therefore is called "Scout" during the trip, and Hunca Bubba and Baby Jason are sitting in the back with the buckets of dusty pecans. Hunca Bubba, who has decided that it is time he started using his given name, Jefferson Winston Vale, is in love, and will not stop talking about the woman he loves. He has a photo of her, and the movie theater in the photo's background catches Hazel's attention because she is "a movie freak from way back."

This launches Hazel into a long digression, told in the past tense, that makes up most of the story—almost five of the story's seven and a half pages. In this story-within-the-story, Hazel, Baby Jason, and their brother Big Brood go to the movies on Easter Sunday. Apparently, they go to the movies quite frequently; they know all of the theaters within walking distance of their home in northern New York City, and what each is showing. They have already seen all of the Three Stooges films. The Washington Theater on Amsterdam Avenue is advertising a film called *Gorilla, My Love,* and they decide to see that. They buy bags of potato chips (choosing the brand that makes the loudest noise when the bag is popped) and settle in. However, when the movie starts it is not *Gorilla, My Love* but *King of Kings,* a movie about the life of Jesus.

The children go wild, "Yellin, booin, stompin and carryin on" until Thunderbuns, the sternest of the theater matrons, comes to silence them. Hazel watches quietly for a while, and realizes that the Jesus portrayed in the movie is so passive that he could never hold his own in Hazel's loud and combative family. The last straw for Hazel comes when *King of Kings* is over and a Bugs Bunny cartoon begins—one that they have already seen. Angrily, Hazel storms off to see the manager and get their money back. The manager treats her condescendingly, as adults sometimes do to children, and refuses to give a refund. Hazel leaves the office, taking the matches from the manager's desk, and sets a fire in the lobby. The theater is forced to close for a week.

When Hazel's Daddy learns what she has done, he takes off his belt to punish her. But Hazel tells her side of the story, and argues, "if you say Gorilla, My, Love, you suppose to mean it." She reminds her parents that she has been raised to trust and to be trustworthy, and Daddy puts his belt back on without using it.

Hunca Bubba's announcement about his upcoming marriage and name change seems to Hazel another example of adults being unreliable. Just as the theater did not show the movie it promised to show, Hunca Bubba has broken a promise. Hazel reminds him tearfully that when she was a very young girl he stayed with her for two days while her parents were caught in a snow storm. He told her then that she was "the cutest thing that ever walked the earth," and that when she grew up he would marry her. Now he intends to marry someone else. Granddaddy and Hunca Bubba laugh, and point out

that he had only been teasing, but Hazel will not be consoled. She cries and cries, knowing for certain that children "must stick together or be forever lost" because grown-ups cannot be trusted.

Characters

Hunca Bubba
See Jefferson Winston Vale

The Manager
The manager of the Washington cinema does not speak during the story, but hustles Hazel out of his office without giving her the refund she demands.

Thunderbuns
Thunderbuns is the nickname given to the most severe of the matrons at the Washington movie theater. Her job is to help patrons find their seats, and to help keep order in the theater. Thunderbuns comes out only "in case of emergency," that is, when the children are being particularly unruly.

Baby Jason Vale
Baby Jason is Hazel's younger brother, who likes to go wherever Hazel goes. Baby Jason is in the back seat with Hunca Bubba and the pecans on the car ride, and he goes to the movies with Hazel and Big Brood. His usual role in disrupting the theater is to kick the seats in front of him, which he does enthusiastically. When Hazel crumples into tears at the end of the story, Baby Jason cries, too. Hazel knows he is crying "Cause he is my blood brother and understands that we must stick together or be forever lost."

Big Brood Vale
Big Brood is Hazel's brother, probably a few years older than she is but not nearly as daring. At the movie theater, he enjoys the family tradition of causing trouble, but leaves it to Hazel to get it started. When they are accosted by bullies in the park, it is Hazel who fights back on Big Brood's behalf. It is Big Brood's idea that they should demand their money back from the manager, though Hazel is the one who actually does it, and it is Big

Brood who later confesses to Daddy what they did at the theater.

Daddy Vale

Daddy is Hazel's father. He has taught Hazel to expect respectful treatment, and Hazel is inspired by this lesson when she confronts the manager. But Daddy does not expect his children to set fires when they are mistreated, so his first reaction to hearing about the theater incident is to take off his belt to punish Hazel with it. When Hazel explains her side of the story, Daddy listens to her and puts his belt back on.

Granddaddy Vale

Granddaddy Vale is Hazel's grandfather on her father's side. In the beginning and ending scenes of the story, he is driving to the South to get pecans, and Hazel, Baby Jason, and Hunca Bubba have come along. Hazel enjoys these trips with Granddaddy Vale. He lets her sit in the front seat to navigate, and calls her "Scout," "Peaches," and "Precious." Granddaddy is one of the calmer members of the family, supporting the children's and grandchildren's decisions even when the other elders do not; he tries to reason with Hazel in the face of Hunca Bubba's betrayal. His calm, and focus on driving and getting proper directions, only makes Hazel more angry.

Hazel Vale

Hazel is the main character of "Gorilla, My Love," and its first-person narrator. She is an African American girl of about ten or twelve years old, and lives in Harlem, in New York City, with a close, extended family. Riding in the car with her grandfather, uncle and little brother in the story's first scene, she learns that her uncle, called Hunca Bubba, is in love and plans to be married. This angers Hazel, and reminds her of an Easter Sunday when she and her brothers went to the movies.

By her own account, half of the fun of attending movies is throwing popcorn, making noises, and leading the other children in causing disruptions. They all know how much noise they can make, how far they can push the theater matrons before they get into real trouble, and they enjoy seeing the matrons angry. On the Easter Sunday in question, although the theater was advertising a film called *Gorilla, My Love,* it actually showed a religious picture, *King of Kings,* and an old Bugs Bunny cartoon. Hazel stirs

Media Adaptations

- "Gorilla, My Love" was recorded by Listening Library and is available on at least two Listening Library short story collections. *Selected Shorts from Symphony Space,* produced in 1989, has six stories on two cassette tapes. *Selected Shorts, Volume XVI, Fictions for Our Time,* produced in 2002, has fourteen stories on three compact disks.

the children in the crowd to protest loudly, and marches into the manager's office to demand her money back. When he refuses, she steals a book of matches and lights a fire in the lobby, shutting down the theater for a week. Somehow, Hazel is so fierce in her indignation, and her voice is so strong and feisty, that she seems tough and likeable at the same time. The reader is on her side. Hazel has been raised to speak her mind, and she does. She avoids a whipping from her father by speaking up and explaining that the adults had made a promise—that they would show *Gorilla, My Love*—and broken it. Hazel's rebellion, in her eyes, was a blow for the virtue of keeping one's word. Her father, seeing Hazel's point, puts away his belt.

Now, in the car with Hunca Bubba, Hazel feels again that adults simply cannot be trusted where children are concerned. She reminds her uncle that, years before, he had promised to marry her when she was old enough. Hunca Bubba laughs and says that he had been teasing, but this only confirms for Hazel that adults, including her favorite uncle, will lie to children whenever they want to, "And don't even say they sorry."

Jefferson Winston Vale

Jefferson Winston Vale, or Hunca Bubba, is Hazel's favorite Uncle. He has been called "Hunca Bubba" by everyone in the family ever since Hazel was a toddler and unable to pronounce "Uncle," and he has been a constant and adored presence in her life. Years before the story takes place, Hunca Bubba took care of Hazel for two days while her parents were away. Affectionately, he told her she was cute, and that he would marry her one day. Although he promptly forgot this routine pleasantry, Hazel has remembered it. Now, Hunca Bubba announces that he has a girlfriend, that he is going to marry her, and that he is going to start using his real name, Jefferson Winston Vale. Throughout the car trip, he talks about the woman he is in love with, and shows off her photograph. He is surprised that Hazel is angry and sad about this; he cannot understand that she took his earlier remark as a promise.

Mama Vale

Mama, Hazel's mother, plays no direct part in the action of the story, but she is Hazel's role model. When Hazel decides to confront the manager, she pictures Mama coming into Hazel's classroom, dressed to intimidate and with her hand on her hip, telling Hazel's teachers to treat their African American students with respect. Mama has shown Hazel that an African American woman need not back down.

Themes

Betrayal

The main theme of "Gorilla, My Love," and the thread that ties the two sections of the story together, is the idea of betrayal. Specifically, Hazel comes to believe that adults, who should have children's best interests at heart, cannot in fact be trusted to tell the truth where children are concerned. In the middle section of the story, which comes first chronologically, Hazel has already learned that "Grownups figure they can treat you just anyhow. Which burns me up." She demands her money back from the theater because "I get so tired grownups messin over kids just cause they little and can't take em to court." But she does not have in mind the adult members of her own family. They have taught her to be truthful and to hold people to their word. As Granddaddy Vale puts it, "if that's what I said, then that's it."

In a world where adults routinely take advantage of children, being able to count on one's family (as gangsters can count on their partners) is important protection. But Hunca Bubba has not only changed his name to Jefferson Winston Vale but

decided to marry a woman his own age, and Hazel's family seems to be offering only double-talk in his defense. He is not changing his name, but changing it *back*, they say. The promise to marry Hazel was "just teasin," not a real promise at all. This strikes Hazel as the ultimate betrayal, because now her beloved uncle and Granddaddy show themselves to be no better than the rest of them. Completely unable to understand the adults' point of view, she is frightened and alone, with only Baby Jason on her side "Cause he is my blood brother and understands that we must stick together or be forever lost, what with grownups playin change-up and turnin you round every which way so bad. And don't even say they sorry."

Bambara and the reader, looking over Hazel's shoulder, know that Hunca Bubba and Granddaddy are not evil or unkind. They see complexities in the world that Hazel is too young to understand. But Bambara does not mock Hazel; her pain is real. In an essay called "Salvation Is the Issue," Bambara noted that the heart of "Gorilla, My Love" is a "broken child-adult contract," one of those "observed violations of the Law." Bambara takes Hazel's point of view seriously, and uses her story (and many other stories) to ask, "is it natural (sane, healthy, whole-some, in our interest) to violate the contracts/covenants we have with our ancestors, each other, our children, our selves, and God?" Although "Gorilla, My Love" is humorous, and the protagonist is limited in her understanding, the questions the story raises about betrayal and trust are important and real, especially for Bambara.

Childhood and Adulthood

At the age of ten or twelve, Hazel is a typical combination of strength and weakness, of courage and fear, of adult and child. In some ways, she is tough-minded. She is "the smartest kid P.S. 186 ever had," and takes that title seriously. Even in her daydreaming about how the extended family would react if Big Brood acted like Jesus, Hazel is working on her arithmetic while the rest of the family is shouting and swinging purses. She reasons with her parents, and sometimes avoids punishment by making good arguments. She defends her brothers on the street and in the park, even to the point of physical fighting against "bad boys." She is the leader of the renegade children, getting them all to shout, "We want our money back." And although Big Brood becomes frightened and disappears before they reach the theater manager's office, Hazel does not hesitate about going in alone. With her

Topics for Further Study

- What is the role of race in "Gorilla, My Love?" How would Hazel's story be different if she were set in another place, another time, or in a family of a different background?

- How might you film this story? Would it be difficult to capture the energy and excitement of the children disrupting the movie and still keep the audience on their side?

- What age group does "Gorilla, My Love" seem to be written for? What aspects of Bambara's writing lead you to this conclusion? How might children of Hazel's age (about ten to twelve years old) see the story differently from the way an older teen would, or from the way an adult would?

- Much of Hazel's understanding of the world

seems to come from the movies she watches. Are these movies a good guide? If people believed what they saw in today's movies, what understandings or misunderstandings might they hold about the world?

- Why does Hazel's mother come down to her school? Is she a typical mother? How involved are students' parents in the elementary schools you know about?

- Hazel lives with both of her biological parents and her two brothers; her Granddaddy and various aunts and uncles live either with them or nearby. How common are extended families like this in your neighborhood? What might account for the fact that more families today are split up by divorce and by geography than in the early 1970s?

Mama as a role model, she finds it in herself to "kick the door open wider and just walk right by him and sit down and tell the man about himself." Hazel is a tough little girl. Even though "Gorilla, My Love" does not end happily for her, the reader knows that in the long run she will be a survivor.

But Hazel the adult is not fully formed yet. Although she can be hard and cynical beyond her years, she is still a child. She is afraid that there might be rats in the buckets of pecans, so she will not sit in the back with them. She is afraid of the dark, although she tells everyone that she leaves the lights on for Baby Jason. She believes what she learns from the movies—even that gangsters tell the truth. Her behavior during the movies can only be called childish: her indignation about being shown the wrong movie aside, Hazel walks into the theater expecting the gorilla movie and buys the Havmore potato chips because they have "the best bags for blowin up and bustin real loud so the matron come trottin down the aisle with her chunky self." Clearly, much of the screaming and popcorn-tossing and seat-kicking is normal behavior, not a reaction to

being cheated. In the final scene, back in the car, Hazel cannot maintain her adult pose. She tries to deal with Hunca Bubba adult-to-adult, but she crumbles into tears, as the bewildered Hunca Bubba protests, "for cryin out loud, Hazel, you just a little girl." What makes the story so touching is the combination of childhood and adulthood that Hazel displays. Each facet of her personality is clearly and accurately developed, and the swirl of feelings that results captures perfectly what it feels like to be a pre-teen girl.

Style

Frame Structure

The structure of "Gorilla, My Love" is called a "frame" structure, because the story of Hazel, Granddaddy Vale, Hunca Bubba, and Baby Jason bringing pecans back from the South wraps around the story of the movie theater, as a frame wraps around a picture. The opening scene moves along with no hint that the story is about to move off in another direction. Readers meet the characters through the eyes of the narrator, hear the irritation in her voice, and see the photograph in Hunca Bubba's hand. A movie house in the background of the photo catches the narrator's eye, and she says, ''Cause I am a movie freak from way back, even though it do get me in trouble sometime.'' Even as that line ends, the focus is on the characters in the car.

But the next line begins, ''Like when me and Big Brood and Baby Jason was on our own,'' and the narrator abruptly changes direction to tell the story of the falsely advertised movie. Because the change is so sudden, with no explanation, the reader does not see how the stories are linked in Hazel's mind, other than the coinciding movie theaters. It seems a childish, trivial connection. When Hazel returns to the car trip near the end of the story, with another abrupt line (''So there I am in the navigator seat''), the reader still does not understand how the events are connected. Not until Hazel reminds Hunca Bubba of his earlier promise to wait and marry her is it clear why she is upset, and why the two events seem to her like two examples of the same thing. By framing the movie theater episode with the car trip episode and refusing to explain why the shifts are happening as they happen, Bambara makes the moment of realization more powerful for the reader because it is raw, unfiltered, just as Hazel experiences it.

The frame is a very old structural device, often used to tie several stories together. Examples include Geoffrey Chaucer's fourteenth-century *Canterbury Tales* and the fifteenth-century Persian and Arabian stories known as *A Thousand and One Nights.* Washington Irving's eighteenth-century tale *Rip Van Winkle,* is framed by an accounting of how the narrator found the story among the notes of a dead man. The narrator humorously casts doubt on the story by swearing that it is true.

Point of View

The term ''point of view'' describes the way an author presents a story to readers. It establishes who the narrator is—i.e., who is telling the story. In ''Gorilla, My Love'' the point of view is labeled ''first person,'' which means that the story is told by one character within the story, Hazel, who describes the events as she experiences them. Hazel uses the first-person pronoun ''I'' throughout the story, and she does not have the capacity or the desire to share other characters' feelings or reactions, except as she witnesses them herself. For example, the reader

does not overhear what is going through Daddy's mind as Hazel explains what happened at the theater. Hazels says that Daddy ''had the suspect it was me,'' and after she explains ''Daddy put his belt back on.'' But the reader has direct access only to Hazel's thoughts.

The story sounds as though Hazel were speaking it aloud, almost breathlessly, without a pause, and the listener is not identified. Shifts in direction happen abruptly, as they do happen in the human mind, and the narrator does not stop to explain connections or to censor her thoughts. The photo of Hunca Bubba's girlfriend has a theater in the background, and this reminds Hazel of how much she likes movies, which reminds her of the time she was tricked into watching *King of Kings,* which features a god who seems too weak to survive in Hazel's strong family, and this makes her more angry, which brings her back to Hunca Bubba. Presenting Hazel's raw, unfiltered speech makes the emotional weight of the story greater. Bambara does not intend for the reader to stand outside the story and analyze from an adult's viewpoint whether Hazel's feelings and actions are appropriate. And when Hazel repeats Hunca Bubba's words and says, ''I say back just how he said it so he can hear what a terrible thing it is,'' she does not explain why it is a terrible thing. From Hazel's point of view, it is obvious, and she expects the reader/listener to be on her side. The reader hears the story, not as a detached observer, but as a participant and an ally, listening to a frustrated child who is practically in tears.

Historical Context

Neo-Black Arts Movement

Bambara is often associated with the Neo-Black Arts Movement (also called simply the Black Arts Movement), a movement in art, literature, and literary criticism that grew out of the Black Power Movement and thrived during the 1960s and early 1970s. The Black Power Movement worked to establish a separate black state within the United States after many people came to believe that the mostly nonviolent Civil Rights movement was not achieving its goals. Nonviolent resistance, they believed, depended too much on the generosity of the oppressors, and loving those oppressors demanded too much of the oppressed. Further, they observed that the Civil Rights movement had focused on solving problems of segregation in the South, but

Compare & Contrast

- **1970:** Movies are primarily watched in large movie theaters, which change their offerings frequently. Still, there is relatively little choice on any given day.

  Today: With video cassettes and DVDs, a movie watcher has literally thousands of choices available for little cost. Movie theaters still show big-budget movies, but studios make most of their money from the sale and rental of videos and DVDs.

- **1970:** Most movie theaters are independently owned and operated, choosing what to show and when to show it. Managers are relatively free to show the latest big attractions from Hollywood or low-budget reruns.

  Today: Most movie theaters across the country show the same movies at the same time. Small-budget and independent movies and theaters showing movies that are not new are rare.

- **1970:** No African American has won the Pulitzer Prize for Fiction or the Nobel Prize in literature.

  Today: Excellent literature by African American writers is being recognized and celebrated. African American Pulitzer Prize–winning authors of fiction include James Alan McPherson (1979), Alice Walker (1983), Edward Jones (2004), and Bambara's editor Toni Morrison, who has won both the Pulitzer (1988) and the Nobel Prize (1993).

- **1970:** The Great Migration of African Americans that brought over two million people from the rural South to big cities in the North peaked during the 1930s. However, many families in New York and other large cities in the North still have ties to the South and make routine trips back.

  Today: The Great Migration is over, and reversing. The overall trend is for middle-class people looking for job opportunities to leave northern cities for large cities in the South. Those who remain in Harlem and other northern enclaves have been there for generations, and their familial ties to the South are weakened.

---

had not done much to improve the lives of African Americans in the northern cities. They called for direct political and economic action by the oppressed, and made it clear that they were willing to use violence if necessary to win equality for African Americans.

The Neo-Black Arts Movement created literature with a political awareness, and its critics examined literature through a political lens. Its writers believed that every work of art is political, and that every work of art featuring African Americans either helps or hurts the cause of equality. In their work, they depicted positive and powerful African Americans. They called for self-determination for African Americans, an end to global capitalism, and a new unity among African nations to fight for racial equality around the world. As Bambara explained in the essay ''What It Is I Think I'm Doing Anyhow,''

''Through writing I attempt to celebrate the tradition of resistance, attempt to tap Black potential, and try to join the chorus of voices that argues that exploitation and misery are neither inevitable nor necessary.'' Bambara took the movement's ideology one step further, and called upon African Americans to examine gender roles within the community. She believed that much of the revolutionary writing by African Americans was weakened by a male supremacist viewpoint, and looked to other countries to find models for men and women working together more equitably.

Bambara identified the writer John Oliver Killens as the ''spiritual father'' of the Neo-Black Arts Movement. Killens had founded the Harlem Writers Guild in the 1950s, and with Civil Rights leader Malcolm X, he co-founded the Organization for Afro-American Unity in 1964. Many writers associated with the Neo-Black Arts Movement, including Paule Marshal, Audrey Lorde, and Ossie Davis, had passed through the Harlem Writers Guild, and admired Killen's celebratory 1954 novel *Youngblood*. Bambara followed Killen's example as she tried in her own work to portray African Americans as strong and dignified, to take pride in black culture, and to demonstrate the evils of racism and classism.

The movement believed that black art was essentially different from art created by white people, and that only black people, using black criteria, could evaluate and appreciate black art. Of course, not all African American writers of the 1960s were part of the Neo-Black Arts Movement, or of any political movement. Not all writers agree that art is necessarily political. Influential Black Arts theorists including Amiri Baraka publicly criticized African Americans whose work was not "valid" black writing, accusing these writers of collaborating with or being deceived by their capitalist oppressors. Bambara's criticism did not challenge other African American writers to follow her lead, but in "Salvation Is the Issue," she did celebrate for herself what her "colleagues in the Neo-Black Arts Movement . . . had been teaching for years—that writing is a legitimate way, an important way, to participate in the empowerment of the community that names me."

Vernacular Black English

Most Americans who speak with whites and African Americans in informal settings can hear general differences in their speech. The label applied in the 1970s to a dialect of English widely learned at home and spoken by African Americans was "Vernacular Black English" or VBE. It is a true dialect, governed by its own set of rules for syntax, pronunciation, and grammar. Beginning in the 1970s, educators studying Vernacular Black English began to discuss and honor it as a true language, rather than rejecting it as simply "bad grammar" or "sloppy pronunciation." (The term in the 1960s had been "Nonstandard Negro English.") While they continued to believe that African American students should learn to speak what was called "Standard English" in order to succeed in a larger world that would expect it, many educators gradually came to see being able to speak both "Standard English" and VBE was as enriching as being able to speak, for example, English and French. Bambara and other writers, during the period when these issues were first reaching the general public, added to the respect given the dialect by showing its

functionality and power in such stories as "Gorilla, My Love."

Arguments about Black English have continued since the 1970s. In the 1980s, the term "African American Vernacular English" (AAVE) replaced VBE. In the 1990s, the term "Ebonics" was created to describe what some consider a separate African language, not related to English, spoken by African Americans. Although the terms have changed, and additional ethnic groups have entered the discussion, the central questions remain concerning who should speak vernacular dialects and in what contexts.

Critical Overview

"Gorilla, My Love," the title story of Bambara's first short story collection, has been universally singled out for praise since the volume, which has never been out of print, was published in 1972. Critics have appreciated Bambara's ear for the urban African American speech of her female protagonist/narrators—a voice that only infrequently had been captured so accurately. Nancy Hargrove, in an essay in *The Southern Quarterly,* writes that "one is immediately struck by . . . her faithful reproduction of black dialect. Her first-person narrators speak conversationally and authentically." A decade later, Ruth Elizabeth Burks explored the author's language in an essay called "From Baptism to Resurrection: Toni Cade Bambara and the Incongruity of Language." She heard Bambara's protagonists speaking in a "narrative voice reminiscent of the Negro spirituals with their strongly marked rhythms and highly graphic descriptions. Standard English is not so much put aside as displaced by constant repetition." For Burks, Bambara succeeds in "perpetuat[ing] the struggle of her people by literally recording it in their voices." In 1992, Klaus Ensslen described the author's ear for language as "an easy mastership with the fully embodied vernacular voice."

Critics have also admired Bambara's ability to portray authentically the feelings of the preadolescent Hazel. C. D. B. Bryan, in the *New York Times Book Review,* observed that writing about children is difficult, but that Bambara manages to avoid "sentimentality and cuteness." In 1972, a short unsigned review of the collection in the *Saturday Review* called the stories "among the best portraits of black life to have appeared in some time," and said of Bambara's stories about children

Pecans like those Hazel and her family go South to get in "Gorilla, My Love"

that they "manage to incorporate the virtues of such stories—zest and charm—yet avoid most of the sentimental pratfalls." Hargrove noted the author's "ability to portray with sensitivity and compassion the experiences of children from their point of view." Several readers have observed that there are many stories about young men—especially young white men—coming of age, but that in the early 1970s stories by women writers about young women growing up were rare.

Criticism

Cynthia Bily

Bily teaches English at Adrian College in Adrian, Michigan. In this essay, Bily looks at autobiographical elements in Bambara's "Gorilla, My Love" and the broad critical questions they raise.

Toni Cade Bambara, like all writers of important literature, wrote "Gorilla, My Love" with several purposes in mind. Bambara hoped that her work would help lift up her African American readers, by presenting a positive story of a strong African American character. She hoped her white readers would profit from seeing African American characters in that light. She hoped adults would think about their relationships with young people, and she hoped young people would find courage to stand up to whatever needed standing up to. Bambara loved laughter, and because she hoped readers would find Hazel's bravado funny, she tossed out most of her first draft to give the story a more humorous tone. Bambara did not set out to write a story that would be studied in classrooms, or picked about by literary theorists. But "Gorilla, My Love" serves well as a backdrop for considering several essential questions that succeeding waves of critical theorists have asked about literature over the last century.

In several ways, Toni Cade Bambara was an unusual fiction writer. She did not think of writing as her primary calling, as she explained in "How She Came by Her Name": "I never thought of myself as a writer. I always thought of myself as a community person who writes and does a few other things." She preferred writing short stories to novels, although novels tend to be easier to sell and promote, in part because writing short stories gave her more time for community political work. She was always reluctant to speak about her personal life, turning interviewers' questions aside to focus on political issues, or giving the same few vague

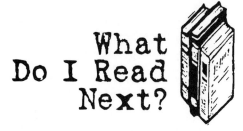

What Do I Read Next?

- In "The Lesson," another story from the collection *Gorilla, My Love,* a community worker from Harlem gives the children in her neighborhood a harsh lesson in inequality by taking them on an outing to the expensive F.A.O. Schwarz toy store in midtown Manhattan.

- Paule Marshall's novel *Brown Girl, Brownstones* (1959) is about a girl's growth into young womanhood in a Brooklyn, New York, neighborhood populated by immigrants from Barbados.

- Sherley A. Williams gives a critical analysis of heroes in African American fiction from the nineteenth century through the 1960s, focusing on what she calls "neo-black literature," in *Give Birth to Brightness: A Thematic Study in Neo-Black Literature* (1972).

- *The Adventures of Huckleberry Finn* (1884), a novel by Mark Twain, is an American classic about a white boy and a runaway slave who escape together down the Mississippi. Huck, like Hazel, narrates his own story, learns about family, friendship, trust, and human dignity.

- *Harry Potter and the Sorcerer's Stone* (1997), by J. K. Rowling, is an exciting and humorous novel about an eleven-year-old boy who learns that he is a wizard, and that he is expected to battle with forces of magic.

---

details about her mother, Speakers' Corner in Harlem, and the public library. And she is unusual in having left a rather large body of interviews and essays describing her writing practice, her philosophy of art, and her sense of how art and politics must work together to achieve social change. Bambara believed that her task was "to produce stories that save our lives," as she wrote in "Salvation Is the Issue"; the seriousness and the complexity of this responsibility led her constantly to think through and attempt to describe her intentions and her process.

In the "Sort of Preface" to her first volume of short stories, *Gorilla, My Love*, Bambara explains in a lighthearted way her attitude toward writing autobiographically: "It does no good to write autobiographical fiction because the minute the book hits the stand here comes your mama screamin [sic] how could you. . . . And it's no use using bits and snatches even of real events and real people, even if you do cover, guise, switch-around and change-up. . . . So I deal in straight-up fiction myself, cause I value my family and friends, and mostly cause I lie a lot anyway." In more serious interviews throughout her career, Bambara repeatedly insisted that she did not create her stories out of events and characters from her own life. For a writer to do so, to

exploit friends and relatives who had not given permission to be represented in fiction, would not only be simply rude. It would make a friend feel that the writer had "plundered her soul and walked off with a piece of her flesh."

Given Bambara's strong feelings, it is interesting to discover how many of the small details in "Gorilla, My Love" sprang out of her own life. In "How She Came by Her Name," an interview conducted a short time before Bambara's death and published after she died, she spoke more openly about her childhood than she had previously—at least, on the record. Although she does not refer specifically to Hazel in the interview, the parallels that emerge between young Toni's life and Hazel's are striking.

For a time, Bambara attended P.S. 186 on 145th Street and Broadway in Harlem, the same public school Hazel attends, and like Hazel she was the smartest kid in the class. Hazel comments that her teachers "don't like me cause I won't sing them Southern songs." Bambara remembers that her mother was alert for racism in her children's classrooms, and "At school we were not to sing 'Old Black Joe'" (a song by nineteenth-century American songwriter Stephen Foster, with lyrics in an exaggerated black dialect). Hazel's mother has been known to come to school to speak to the teachers when they are disrespectful to their African American students, and on these occasions she dresses to impress: "She stalk in with her hat pulled down bad and that Persian lamb coat draped back over one hip." Bambara remembers that her mother "had a turning-the-school outfit. She had a serious Joan Crawford hat and a Persian lamb coat." And, just as Hazel's mother "got pull with the Board and bad by her own self anyhow," Bambara's mother "was a substitute teacher, and she had pull with the Board of Education, she knew everybody, so 'your ass is mine.'" Hazel's mother is an inspiration to her, the one who taught her not to back down, and Bambara's mother filled the same role for the author.

Perhaps, then, it is no surprise to learn that Bambara loved the movies throughout her life. She says in the interview, "I go to movies constantly because I am a film nut," reminiscent of Hazel who is "a movie freak from way back." As a child, Bambara visited the same five movie houses that Hazel visits: the Dorset, on Broadway, for "Boston Blackie and the Three Stooges" (Hazel and her brothers reject the Dorset on that fateful Easter Sunday because they had "seen all the Three Stooges they was"); the RKO Hamilton for first-run movies and vaudeville shows;. the Sunset and the Regal (Hazel calls it the "Regun") which are, Hazel says, "too far, less we had grownups with us which we didn't," and which Bambara explains were on 125th Street, more than twenty blocks away; and the Washington Theater on Amsterdam Avenue for "sepia movies and second-string things" like the low-budget horror movie *Gorilla, My Love*. In all of these theaters, Bambara recalls,

> If you were in the movies, you were in the children's section, roped off with that lady in the white dress with the flashlight to hit you with and keep you all in check. The rest of the movie house was for the grown-ups.

But Hazel and young Toni are not the same person. Bambara never had uncles or cousins (no Hunca Bubba), though she desperately wanted one. She did not make trips South as some of the other children did, though she would have liked to. Her father did not use a belt on his children, and Bambara thinks with some horror about those parents who did. Bambara did not disrupt the movies she attended, but would "sit there and rewrite them" because she thought they were "stupid." The autobiographical details in "Gorilla, My Love" are

> " Who speaks for me? Can a man write a true and important story about women? Can white writers create 'valid' literature about people of color?"

interesting, but do they matter? Do they mean anything? The answer to that question has varied over the last one hundred years.

In the early part of the twentieth century, literary scholars were fascinated by the biographical and historical sources of a text, and their work came to be called historical criticism. They wanted to know all about an author and the times he (it was almost always "he") lived in. Given a story like "Gorilla, My Love," a historical critic would work to establish who wrote it and when and where, what Bambara's intention was in writing the story, and how she went about writing it with this information, the critic would attempt to explain to readers what meaning the story had in its own time. How would readers in 1972, at the end of the Civil Rights movement, the end of the Vietnam War, and the beginning of the feminist movement, have read the story? What about her upbringing and her time made Bambara write the story she wrote? These critics would have learned everything they could about Bambara's life to see how that life informed the writing. They would have looked carefully at the many places where Bambara explained her own theories about writing, and compared her theory against her practice.

In the middle of the century, many felt that the historical critics had lost sight of the works themselves in their hunt for context. Scholars calling themselves the New Critics questioned whether a scholar—or even an author herself—could ever know an author's intentions, and they looked for ways to bring the focus back to the literature itself. Ultimately, they rejected the significance of any information outside the text, and insisted that the only way to approach a given text was to look only at the words on the page. New critics approaching "Gorilla, My Love" would not consider Bambara's race, or gender, or politics, or the time in which she wrote. They would not consider Bambara's essays and interviews. New critics would look closely at the story only (performing an activity called "close reading") in an attempt to establish its inherent form. They would look at Hazel's diction, or at repeated motifs in the story (perhaps the mentioning of names and naming), or at relationships between the characters, or at the framing structure, and ask: How do these devices contribute to the story as a whole? Objectively speaking, what is the story's artistic value?

By the last third of the twentieth century, critical theory had swung again. Many critics now began to reject the idea of an objective evaluation of artistic merit, in part because many rejected the ability of middle-aged, middle-class white men (who had made up the largest portion of important critics) to be objective, not to mention wise, about literature by women, by African Americans and members of other ethnic groups, by gay and lesbian writers, by working-class writers, and so on. At the same time, readers began making new demands on literature, and asking new questions. Who speaks for me? Can a man write a true and important story about women? Can white writers create "valid" literature about people of color? Does it matter that Bambara is African American? Would the very same story, if it had been written by a white man, have the same value? Are the criteria for good literature the same for every body of literature? The biographies of authors became important again. For critics at the end of the century (calling themselves New Historicists, or Cultural Critics, or a variety of other names), literature was seen as an expression of a community, and it was important to uncover the social and cultural forces acting on authors—and critics—that might affect their work. A critic during the end of the century, when Bambara created her fiction, would have asked a new set of questions: How does Hazel's way of speaking bring to light a new kind of authentic narrative voice? How does Hazel's story shed light on the oppression of women, or of African Americans? How could "Gorilla, My Love" empower African American readers, or challenge white readers? How does a critic's own biases affect her reading of the story?

As the twenty-first century gets underway, critics want to know how Bambara came to understand Hazel's life; they want to know what knowledge and bias she brings to her telling of the story. They also want to know that the writer of *this* essay is white, female, middle-class, straight, educated,

liberal, from the middle of the United States, so they know what biases the essay writer might bring to her analysis. In another thirty years, the issues may be entirely different ones. What makes a story like "Gorilla, My Love" great is not that it provides an answer but that it raises so many interesting questions.

Source: Cynthia Bily, Critical Essay on "Gorilla, My Love," in *Short Stories for Students,* Thomson Gale, 2005.

Mary Comfort

In the following essay excerpt, Comfort shows how Bambara uses language in her short stories, including "Gorilla, My Love," to evoke humor and multiple meanings.

Published first in 1972, Toni Cade Bambara's *Gorilla, My Love* has been celebrated for its realistic depiction of the African American community, for its almost musical rendering of Black English, and for the resilience and energy of its first-person narrators. The only study focusing entirely on the humor in these stories is Nancy D. Hargrove's "The Comic Sense in the Short Stories of Toni Cade Bambara" (1985). Hargrove considers the humor that arises unintentionally, noting that much of it depends on the circumstances and the language of the narrators, and concluding that Bambara is "a masterful practitioner of the art of comedy." In addition to the unplanned humor identified by Hargrove, these stories contain intentional humor, much of it the result of word play. The narrators use ambiguous words, phrases, and references to multiply meanings. As an alternative reading emerges, the more accessible view of a fractured community gives way to a portrait of solidarity, affectionate pride supplants conspicuous but unlikely enmities, and, previously incongruous details become integrated into the narrative.

The subtle and varied strategies used to achieve this double vision include puns and pantomime and is a form of Signifyin(g). In his history of African American humor, Mel Watkins traces this practice to a number of sources, including "wordplay and clever verbal interchange in the oral cultures of the West African societies" and folk ballads and toasts honoring black heroes: "The expressive attributes most highly esteemed in the black folk tradition— the verbal acuity and spontaneous wit displayed in signifying, boasting, and storytelling or 'lying'— also characterize black American humor" ([*On the Real Side,* 1994], 63, 472). Double-voiced discourse, Watkins explains, was useful to slaves inscribing escape plans on a seemingly innocuous

A theater and its lobby form the setting for part of the action of ''Gorilla, My Love''

performance for vigilant masters. Until the sixties, these strategies were designedly unavailable to white audiences, but as part of an expression of racial pride, comedians during the Civil Rights movement revealed some of their strategies on stage, to all audiences. ''Not surprisingly,'' says Watkins of a parallel development in literature, ''more black authors began reflecting the comic resonance, uninhibited self-assurance, and assertively impudent tone of those stage wits and clowns'' (435). Among these authors, Bambara is one of the most passionate and consistent champions of Signifiers, and her characters employ the technique in their words and in their gestures. Indeed, the practice is not only a method but a central thematic concern in *Gorilla, My Love*.

In ''Black English,'' Bambara explains the political reasons for her interest in the language of African Americans, especially as it is used informally, on the street. ''To resist acculturation, you hang on to language, because it is the reflection of a people, of a core of ideas and beliefs and values and literature and lore.'' Activists in this resistance to acculturation are the neighborhood's young people whose ability to entertain with language is legendary. In her short stories, then, Bambara introduces

an entire population, men, women, and children, all engaged in Playing the Dozens and other forms of word play. Some use the strategy to entertain, and some use it to teach, and all enjoy themselves. In the first four stories considered in this study, male characters whose neighbors seem to fear them are shown to be popular entertainers, known for their lingistic virtuosity and applauded in figurative language. In the second part group of four stories, the relationships between female characters and their families are discussed to show that foregrounded contention masks affectionate cohesion. . . .

Another narrator who recounts her enlistment and training as a Signifier is Hazel, who narrates the title story. Early in ''Gorilla, My Love,'' Hazel explains that, for years, she has called her uncle, Jefferson Winston Vale, Hunca Bubba, ''since I couldn't manage Uncle to save my life.'' At the close of her narrative, she reminds Vale that, when she was a child, he promised to marry her. It may be that, as a child, Hazel did, indeed, have trouble pronouncing the word ''uncle.'' If, however, her continuing affection for Vale is to be appreciated, it is important to consider the phrase ''say uncle'' as a slang phrase, used to demand the cessation of some form of torment. This reading is supported by an

" Hazel in the title story complains when she finds that a film called <u>Gorilla, My Love</u> is 'clearly not about no gorilla.' When she insists on honesty--or expresses appreciation for the filmmaker's pun--Hazel sets a protestor's example for readers."

earlier incident in which Hazel could not protest effectively. When she is disappointed by the content of a film, for example, she misdirects her complaints, first to the people in the seats in front of her, then to the projectionist, and finally to the theater manager, none of whom made the film. In both her assertiveness and her powerlessness, Hazel's actions "easily call to mind a group of sixties-style demonstrators" (Willis, [*Black Women Writing the American Experience]* 147). While Hazel postures as a demonstrator and longs to join the protest movement, until she can Signify, she cannot enlist followers or "say uncle" for her community.

In a series of incidents since she was a child, Hazel has learned to Signify, an excellent way to "say uncle." And, when he recognizes her new-found talent, Vale marries her, not to himself, in the conventional sense of the word, but to the struggle for human rights, a struggle in which it is often necessary to "say uncle" and for which Hazel is now well-equipped. As defined by Bambara, who recommends the model given by Frantz Fannon during Algerian liberation struggle, "Marriages were no longer contract arrangements but freely chosen unions of individuals bound to a corporate future of freedom[.]. . . . extended kinship[s] of cellmates and neighbors linked in the business of actualizing a vision of a liberated society" ("On the Issue"). This is the kind of marriage Hazel seeks, and it is the kind Vale achieves. The transformation is marked, as it frequently is in *Gorilla, My Love*, by a name change. Prior to her "marriage," her penchant for blaming the nearest person for her problems earns

Hazel the nickname "Peaches," a name and a problem she disowns when she realizes that her uncle is a "lyin dawg," a tenacious Signifier. Then, having grown into her given name by learning to create a haze around her meaning, she announces her new identity as a "married" protestor: "'My name is Hazel.'" . . .

The title *Gorilla, My Love* is probably also figurative. And, again, a crucial clue is found in a major incongruity: Hazel in the title story complains when she finds that a film called *Gorilla, My Love* is "clearly not about no gorilla." When she insists on honesty—or expresses appreciation for the filmmaker's pun—Hazel sets a protestor's example for readers. Finding that the collection is similarly devoid of gorillas, readers might consider the rhetorical possibilities of that incongruity. Ruth Elizabeth Burks suggests a metaphorical reading if "Bambara wants us to see all males as gorillas, which the incongruousness of this volume's title does suggest" ([''From Baptism to Resurrection. . .''], 52). The title also signifies on "common European allegations of the propensity of African women to prefer the company of male apes" (Gates, [*The Signifying Monkey*], 109). It may be that Bambara recalls that allegation to dismantle the stereotype, since some women in some stories appear to be frightened by the posturing and aggressiveness of Manny and Punjab. If these men are Signifyin(g), posing as gorillas to show that they are guerrillas, however, the similarly-camouflaged women probably do, indeed, love them. Thus, it is also possible that she wants us to see both male and female characters as guerrillas, a possibility suggested by the camouflaged assertiveness of individual characters discussed in this study. Yet, to posit subversive activity in place of contention is to repeat an error identified by Watkins: "Even when the mainstream took notice, those exposed to African-American literature in which genuine humor was abundant were often predisposed toward finding angry protest tracts, thereby missing the humor" (401). Thus, it may just be that, like the notion of a black community in disarray, the idea of a militant solidarity must give way to a meta-linguistic reading in which the subject of these narratives is the emancipation of language, of the culture it represents, and of the reader. For, in the process of extricating puns, the reader joins the resistance to acculturation and becomes a [Signifyin(g)] *Gorilla, My Love*.

In "A Sort of a Preface," Bambara confesses—and boasts—of her ability to Signify. Ostensibly announcing her reason for refusing to include "bits and snatches even of real events and real people" in her fiction, she says, "I lie a lot anyway." Since her fiction contains both, allusions to real people and a whole lot of Signifyin(g), it would seem that Bambara is, alas, a liar and a truth-teller. More varied in their Signifyin(g) styles than in their commitment to racial empowerment, the characters in Toni Cade Bambara's *Gorilla, My Love* employ puns and pantomime to celebrate language as it has traditionally been used by African Americans. In creating this "hip game," Bambara finds a way to stoke the blast furnace while doing her favorite thing to be doing. Readers, too, might lean on the wall, first to enjoy the performance and then to catch their breath after the exhilirating adventure of transcending familiar perspectives.

Source: Mary Comfort, "Liberating Figures in Toni Cade Bambara's *Gorilla, My Love*," in *Studies in American Humor*, Vol. 3, No. 5, 1998, pp. 76–96.

Klaus Ensslen

In the following essay excerpt, Ensslen discusses language, naming, and Hazel's narrative in "Gorilla, My Love."

The title story "Gorilla, My Love" originally appeared in *Redbook Magazine* (November, 1971) under the title "I Ain't Playin, I'm Hurtin" which more pointedly established vernacular as the dominant linguistic and expressive of the text. The title chosen for the book derives from the title of a film which, symptomatically enough, the protagonist-narrator Hazel never gets to see—signalling a delusive promise of the media industry as part of the dominant culture, and implicitly also a gap in the language offered the child/teenager by the adult world. The book title thus assumes a kind of inconclusive, partly irritating aura, reinforced by the semantic tension between the words "gorilla" and "love," as well as by the covert stereotyping and threatening potential of the gorilla image.

The vernacular norm becomes firmly established for the volume not only through the first two stories, but even before them through the brilliantly succinct and witty adoption of black vernacular by the author in her one-page introduction ("A Sort of Preface") where "straight-up fiction" is equated with lying (in the sense in which this term has always been used in the black oral tradition, as an equivalent for storytelling) and is set up against the autobiographical impetus as detrimental to such basic social networks as family and friends. Family

TONI CADE BAMBARA

GORILLA, MY LOVE

"[Bambara] sows in her wake understanding, humanity...this book is filled with both love and respect."
— WASHINGTON POST BOOK WORLD

Book cover illustration by Richard Taddei from Gorilla, My Love, *the collection containing the title short story*

and friends, however, remain the social backdrop into which most of the stories of the volume are embedded, and the dedication of the volume "To the Johnson Girls. . ." would seem to contradict the tongue-in-cheek separation claim between experience and fiction in the preceding "A Sort of Preface" by tying the last story of the volume ("The Johnson Girls") directly back to real friends and life experience.

As all the stories in Bambara's first volume of fiction, "Gorilla, My Love" dramatizes a concrete social situation in the compact format of less than ten printed pages: While on a car trip South, for picking and taking home pecan nuts, the narrator-protagonist Hazel, in the company of grandfather, uncle and little brother, confronts her uncle (who declares he is going to marry a woman whose photo he passes around in the car) with his earlier promise to marry Hazel when she is grown up. Hazel's emotional outrage generates not only a pointed dialogue with uncle and grandfather, but also brings to her mind analogies from other conflicts and confrontations with the adult world, notably her parents, school, and one drastic and exemplary clash with a movie theater and its manager. By

> "Condescension, the verbal or communicative playing of tricks ('trickified business,' as Hazel calls it in another context) and the lack of empathy stand out as the traits of the adult world as presented by the primary dramatic situation of the story."

presenting this material as a kind of inner monologue of the child Hazel (whose age is never specified but could be placed anywhere between 8 and 12 years), the text is free to unfold as a form of improvisational speech act, starting out as a retrospective return to the situation (''That was the year Hunca Bubba changed his name''), but ending up by being completely caught up in the remembered situation as present tense action (''And don't even say they sorry'').

It is not by accident that the story's text sets in with naming as an opening motif. The title word ''gorilla'' with its reverberating inconclusive echoes has prepared the way when Hazel as narrator introduces her first protesting, or aggressive, verbal gesture by sarcastically commenting on her uncle's change of name—from the familiar Hunca Bubba (her small child approximation to the lexical term ''uncle'') to the distancing formal full version of his name, Jefferson Winston Vale. (Here ''Vale'' bespeaks the deceptive or hidden character of the person in Hazel's perspective.) ''Geographical,'' ''weatherlike,'' ''like somethin . . . in a almanac'' are the deprecating terms chosen by Hazel to characterize her disappointment with her uncle's reverting to his full name who by this act has turned from an intimate and dependable point of reference or orientation in her life into a changeable item in an anonymous listing or on a wide open map. Hazel's loss of orientation through the alleged betrayal by her uncle is vividly dramatized at the end of the text when her established role as map reader (or Scout) in the front seat of the car slips away from her because her crying prevents her from reading the map.

Hazel's emotional and rational self-perception is shaken by her uncle's changed role which spontaneously makes her switch his middle name on him (as an act of signifying, implying that his love for her is written on the wind) from Winston to Windsong. Hunca Bubba's changing role and name signal a sobering, defamiliarizing, disillusioning process for Hazel, or a forced initiation into the factual, emotionally incomprehensible values of an adult world including a first inkling of sexuality. Emotionally upset, Hazel in the course of her text recapitulates all the names attributed to herself by the familiar adult world surrounding her—names that pay tribute to different facets of her character and competence, and therefore carry the promise of potential possibilities for her unfolding life: Hazel (connoting beauty and magic power), Scout, Badbird, (a term of respect for her standing by her convictions), Miss Muffin (a term commenting her fear of physical injury), and finally Peaches and Precious (Hunca Bubba's and Granddaddy's terms of endearment for her). By rejecting her uncle's address ''Peaches'' and by reminding him of her real name Hazel, the narrator would like to request his respect for her as a full person. But instead she just invites his casual condescension on her head (''Well, for cryin out loud, Hazel, you just a little girl. And I was just teasin''), followed by a slightly contemptuous subterfuge (''That's right. That was somebody else. I'm a new somebody'') which shows Hunca Bubba and Granddaddy Vale in cahoots with each other in trying to console Hazel with an ingenuous figure of speech, talking down to her as to a mere child. The only consolation Hazel can find in this situation is the community of feeling and protest with Baby Jason, her little brother, who joins her crying in the backseat of the car:

> And Baby Jason cryin too. Cause he is my blood brother and understands that we must stick together or be forever lost, what with grownups playin change-up and turnin you round every which way so bad. And don't even say they sorry.

Condescension, the verbal or communicative playing of tricks (''trickified business,'' as Hazel calls it in another context) and the lack of empathy stand out as the traits of the adult world as presented by the primary dramatic situation of the story. (Hazel has demonstrated her fine sense for resenting manipulation by commenting on the disadvantages of sitting in the back of the car where the dust and the moving weight of the pecan sacks assume terrorizing proportions, and she has opted for the role of navigator, or Scout, next to the driver for that reason.)

If the car ride were the only situation presented by the story, Hazel's account and emotional reaction would in some ways leave her looking overly literal and childish, in so drastically misreading her uncle's earlier words and attitude. The car ride, however, serves as framing or triggering situation for other conflicts fought out by Hazel with the adult world. Her fictional character is supplemented and filled out in essential ways by these other situations which are brought in by the narrator as supporting evidence for the dishonest attitudes of adults towards children.

Central for establishing Hazel's fighting strength and non-manipulable perception of the world around her is the movie theater episode placed in the middle of the story and taking up more than half its length. Set off by the photo of Hunca Bubba's woman (who is not only never granted the privilege of a name in Hazel's narration, but is also seen as enacting a gesture that expresses fear of the camera), Hazel takes the movie house in the background of the photo as her cue for pushing out the woman altogether and for bringing her passion for movies to the fore ("Cause I am a movie freak from way back . . ."). It is at this point, when Hazel starts telling her experience with the Washington Theater on Amsterdam Avenue and the falsely announced film *Gorilla, My Love,* her vernacular text begins to unfold its full verbal, situational, comical and critical or satirical potential. The movie episode generates so much referential and visualizing energy and verve for Hazel's voice that it can casually call forth analogous illustrations from family and school situations and can in one case fuse the outlines of the crucifixion in a film on Jesus (*King of Kings*) with the imagined reaction of Hazel's family to its reenactment by Big Brood, her big brother, in an everyday setting and context, producing a virtuoso conflation of religious and domestic motifs which pours vitriolic scorn on Christian iconography while brilliantly asserting and satirizing the extended black family.

The main impetus behind Hazel's handling the movie house situation is made explicit by her text repeatedly: "Grownups figure they can treat you just anyhow. Which burns me up."—"And now I'm really furious cause I get so tired grownups messin over kids cause they little and can't take em to court."—"I mean even gangsters in the movies say My word is my bond. So don't nobody get away with nothin far as I'm concerned." In the case of the movie theater and its manager, Hazel and the group of children around her (Big Brood and Baby Jason foremost) are cheated (out of the film announced), intimidated (by the so-called "matrons," or ushers, especially the colored one called Thunderbuns) and generally victimized and exploited. This provokes at first different kinds of spontaneous protest ("Yellin, booin, stompin and carryin on") where the kids use certain guerilla tactics favored by the darkened house and well-trained by previous opposition to the power structure embodied in the theater management. When the next stage, a spontaneously organized collective verbal demand ("We want our money back" calls) is ignored, Hazel proceeds to a more formal technical step in approaching the manager personally to ask her own and her brothers' money back. When this proves fruitless, she continues her open suit by setting fire to the candy stand (with the manager's own matches!), thus putting the theater out of business for a week.

This open warfare with the white power structure is contrasted in Hazel's narration with the discussion of her actions in her own family—a much fairer handling of a case because the accused can defend herself and is declared right at the end ("So Daddy put his belt back on . . . Like my Mama say . . . Okay Badbird, you right"). The name Badbird provides the bridge to Hazel's mother who has been backing her daughter in school where she commands respect ("cause Mama got pull with the board and bad by her own self anyhow"—"bad" meaning strong and redoubtable, as used in the streets)—a backing Hazel needs against the lack of recognition for her intelligence ("When in reality I am the smartest kid P.S. 186 ever had in its whole lifetime"), the warping pressure of prejudice ("cause I won't sing them Southern songs or back off when they tell me my questions are out of order") and downright slander ("when them teachers start playin the dozens behind colored folks"). The totally antagonistic situation at the movie theater is thus contextualized by a mostly supportive, but many-voiced family situation, and by an ambivalent (because both challenging and stifling) school environment. All three vividly evoked situations partake of the same ingredients in the narrator's perspective: control over others, and the rights of others to question that control.

"Gorilla, My Love" insistently adumbrates the asymmetric relationships between adults and children and dramatizes through the voice of a child the dilemma of weaker members of a community when exposed to manipulation or breach of trust by adults. It juxtaposes the naivete (or credulity) of a non-adult perspective with the opportunism (or corruption) of the adult world. Informed by a utopia of trust, or bonding, or community, the non-adult narrator Hazel sets up resistance against the breach of trust enacted by adults (whether in the deceptive film announcement, or in the oral promise of her uncle). Hazel uses her role as narrator, her privilege of giving voice to her concerns as a weapon and countermeasure against the conventionalized speech acts of the adult world. Her spontaneously unfolding vernacular speech act probes and unmasks the formalized or ritualized speech acts of adults (both in the printed or literate form of the film title and in the oral phrase of her uncle). Hazel's vernacular speech in the process of her narration releases a vigorous unmasking force for testing the inherent values and veracity of adult verbal strategies and speech acts. Hunca Bubba's utterances thus mirror an inherent carelessness, insensibility, lack of imagination and habitual condescension towards the child Hazel and make visible a general attitude of adults towards children as immature agents with limited rights and responsibilities.

Even though Hazel's assumptions in the case of her uncle may seem naive and simplistic, her linguistic energy and storytelling verve result from, and are an expression of, her inner strength and substance. Her perspective and social norms insist on veracity, or truth, and thereby criticize and debunk the tactics and the egotism of the adult world. At the same time Hazel as narrator unswervingly insists on her rights for the pursuit of happiness, both in the dream world of the film screen (i.e. the world of imagination and storytelling, and by extension also of image control and the propagation of ethical and cultural values) and in the actual family-centered world of close personal relations. Hazel's hurt with respect to her uncle is in one sense a comedy, soon to pass—but in another sense it is a cataclysmic loss of trust and belief placed in the emotional and moral authority of her uncle. Other forms of emotional bonding (with her brothers, her family, other children) will sustain Hazel and tide her over the experienced disillusionment, the text seems to suggest; but her outlook will remain agonistic, i.e. will be inscribed with struggle, conflict, loss and suffering. If Hazel's text contains any positive promise or utopian dimension, it is to be found in her own strength of character, in

her militant intelligence and her superb command of language.

Source: Klaus Ensslen, ''Toni Cade Bambara: *Gorilla, My Love* (1971),'' in *The African American Short Story: 1970 to 1990,* edited by Wolfgang Karrer and Barbara Puschmann-Nalenz, Wissenschaftlicher Verlag Trier, 1993, pp. 41–57.

Nancy D. Hargrove

In the following essay excerpt, Hargrove discusses Hazel's narrative voice in ''Gorilla, My Love.''

In reading Toni Cade Bambara's collection of short stories, *Gorilla, My Love* (1972), one is immediately struck by her portrayal of black life and by her faithful reproduction of black dialect. Her first-person narrators speak conversationally and authentically: ''So Hunca Bubba in the back with the pecans and Baby Jason, and he in love. . . . there's a movie house . . . which I ax about. Cause I am a movie freak from way back, even though it do get me in trouble sometime.'' What Twain's narrator Huck Finn did for the dialect of middle America in the mid-nineteenth century, Bambara's narrators do for contemporary black dialect. Indeed, in the words of one reviewer, Caren Dybek, Bambara ''possesses one of the finest ears for the nuances of black English'' (''Black Literature'' 66). In portraying black life, she presents a wide range of black characters, and she uses as settings Brooklyn, Harlem, or unnamed black sections of New York City, except for three stories which take place in rural areas. Finally, the situations are typical of black urban experience: two policemen confront a black man shooting basketball in a New York park at night; young black activists gather the community members at a Black Power rally; a group of black children from the slums visit F.A.O. Schwartz and are amazed at the prices of toys. Bambara's stories communicate with shattering force and directness both the grim reality of the black world—its violence, poverty, and harshness—and its strength and beauty—strong family ties, individual determination, and a sense of cultural traditions. Lucille Clifton has said of her work, ''She has captured it all, how we really talk, how we really are,'' and the *Saturday Review* has called *Gorilla, My Love* ''among the best portraits of black life to have appeared in some time.''

Although her work teems with the life and language of black people, what is equally striking about it, and about this collection particularly, is the universality of its themes. Her fiction reveals the pain and the joy of the human experience in general, of what it means to be human, and most often of what it means to be *young* and human. One of Bambara's special gifts as a writer of fiction is her ability to portray with sensitivity and compassion the experiences of children from their point of view. In the fifteen stories that compose *Gorilla, My Love,* all the main characters are female, thirteen of them are first-person narrators, and ten of them are young, either teenagers or children. They are wonderful creations, especially the young ones, many of whom show similar traits of character; they are intelligent, imaginative, sensitive, proud and arrogant, witty, tough, but also poignantly vulnerable. Through these young central characters, Bambara expresses the fragility, the pain, and occasionally the promise of the experience of growing up, of coming to terms with a world that is hostile, chaotic, violent. Disillusionment, loss, and loneliness, as well as unselfishness, love, and endurance, are elements of that process of maturation which her young protagonists undergo....

With great sensitivity Bambara portrays through Hazel in "Gorilla, My Love" the feelings of pain and betrayal experienced by a child in a situation that adults would generally consider trivial or ridiculous. When Hazel was very young, her favorite uncle, Hunca Bubba, promised to marry her when she grew up, a promise which he gave lightly but which she took seriously. The story, centers on her discovery that he has not only dropped the affectionate name Hunca Bubba, but also intends to marry someone else. For Hazel this bitter betrayal reveals to her that even adults who are "family" cannot be trusted to keep their promises. Her disillusionment is intense and painful; as she says," I ain't playin. I'm hurtin....," speaking the words of the original title of the story.

Hazel's realization and subsequent disillusionment are skillfully prepared for from the opening lines, where the idea of unpleasant changes is introduced through her first-person narration: "That was the year Hunca Bubba changed his name. Not a change up, but a change back, since Jefferson Winston Vale was the name in the first place. Which was news to me cause he'd been my Hunca Bubba my whole lifetime, since I couldn't manage Uncle to save my life." Further foreshadowing follows. From Hazel the reader learns that she, her grandfather, Hunca Bubba, and her younger brother are in a car driving to an undisclosed destination when Hunca Bubba begins talking about the woman he loves. Hazel affects boredom with the subject and criti-

> "Hazel's realization and subsequent disillusionment are skillfully prepared for from the opening lines, where the idea of unpleasant changes is introduced through her first-person narration. . . ."

cizes a photograph of the woman, responses indicative of her true dismay, although at this point the reader has no clue as to the cause of her antagonism: "And we got to hear all this stuff about this woman he in love with and all. Which really ain't enough to keep the mind alive, though Baby Jason got no better sense than to give his undivided attention and keep grabbin at the photograph which is just a picture of some skinny woman in a countrified dress with her hand shot up to her face like she shame fore cameras."

There follow five pages (a large section in a story of only seven and a half pages) that appear at first to contain a long and puzzling digression on a memory from the previous Easter. In fact, the episode furnishes the key to our understanding of the enormous, shattering impact that Hunca Bubba's "betrayal" has on Hazel. The remembered incident seems initially to reveal only an occasion on which Hazel got into trouble as a result of her "toughness"; however, as we discover, Hazel is both sensitive and vulnerable beneath her tough exterior.

The episode concerns a movie which Hazel, Baby Jason, and Big Brood went to see. Although the marquee advertised that "Gorilla, My Love" was playing, the actual movie was about Jesus. The three were disappointed and angry: "I am ready to kill, not cause I got anything gainst Jesus. Just that when you fixed to watch a gorilla picture you don't wanna get messed around with Sunday School stuff. So I am mad." After "yellin, booin, stompin, and carrying on" to show their displeasure, they watched the feature, hoping that "Gorilla, My Love" would follow. When it did not, as Hazel so bluntly puts it, "we know we been had. No gorilla no nuthin." She daringly went to complain to the manager and to ask that their money be refunded. Getting no satisfaction from him, she took some matches from his office and set fire to the candy stand. She later explained to her father that she expected people (and marquees) to keep their word: "Cause if you say Gorilla, My Love, you suppose to mean it. Just like when you say you goin to give me a party on my birthday, you gotta mean it. . . . I mean even gangsters in the movies say My word is my bond. So don't nobody get away with nothin far as I'm concerned."

Clearly, Hunca Bubba's breaking his promise to marry her is far more devastating to Hazel than the false advertising of the movie theater. Since a person whom she has every reason to trust has betrayed her, the entire adult world becomes suspect. Indeed, throughout the story, Hazel makes numerous comments on the conflict between children and adults. When her grandfather and Hunca Bubba make a weak attempt to justify what has occurred ("'Look here, Precious, it was Hunca Bubba what told you them things. This here, Jefferson Winston Vale.' And Hunca Bubba say, 'That's right. That was somebody else. I'm a new somebody'"), Hazel is not buying and turns to her little brother for solace, bitterly condemning the perfidy of adults: "I'm crying and crumplin down in the seat. . . . And Baby Jason cryin too. Cause he is my blood brother and understands that we must stick together or be forever lost, what with grownups playin change-up and turnin you round every which way so bad. And don't even say they sorry."

Source: Nancy D. Hargrove, "Youth in Toni Cade Bambara's *Gorilla, My Love*," in *Southern Quarterly*, Vol. XXII, No. 1, Fall 1983, pp. 81–99.

Sources

Bambara, Toni Cade, "Gorilla, My Love," in *Gorilla, My Love*, Vintage, 1992, pp. 13–20.

——, "How She Came by Her Name: An Interview with Louis Massiah," in *Deep Sightings and Rescue Missions: Fiction, Essays, and Conversations*, edited by Toni Morrison, Pantheon, 1996, pp. 201–45.

——, "Salvation Is the Issue," in *Black Women Writers (1950–1980): A Critical Evaluation*, edited by Mari Evans, Anchor Books, 1984, pp. 41–47.

——, "A Sort of Preface," in *Gorilla, My Love*, Vintage, 1992.

——, "What It Is I Think I'm Doing Anyhow," in *The Writer on Her Work*, edited by Janet Sternburg, W. W. Norton, 1980, p. 154.

Bryan, C. D. B., Review of *Gorilla, My Love*, in *New York Times Book Review*, October 15, 1972, p. 31.

Burks, Ruth Elizabeth, "From Baptism to Resurrection: Toni Cade Bambara and the Incongruity of Language," in *Black Women Writers (1950–1980): A Critical Evaluation*, edited by Mari Evans, Anchor Books, 1984, pp. 48–49.

Ensslen, Klaus, "Toni Cade Bambara: *Gorilla, My Love*," in *The African American Short Story, 1970 to 1990: A Collection of Critical Essays*, edited by Wolfgang Karrer and Barbara Puschmann-Nalenz, Wissenschaftlicher Verlag Trier, 1993, pp. 41–44.

Hargrove, Nancy D., "Youth in Toni Cade Bambara's *Gorilla, My Love*," in the *Southern Quarterly*, Vol. 22, No. 1, Fall 1983, pp. 81–83.

Review of *Gorilla, My Love*, in *Saturday Review*, Vol. 55, No. 47, November 18, 1972, p. 97.

Further Reading

Bambara, Toni Cade, *Deep Sightings and Rescue Missions: Fiction, Essays, and Conversations*, edited by Toni Morrison, Pantheon, 1996.

  Toni Morrison, Bambara's editor at Random House, assembled this collection of six previously unpublished stories and six essays after Bambara's death. In "How She Came by Her Name," an interview with Louis Massiah, Bambara discusses her childhood, her early political life, and how *Gorilla, My Love* came to be published.

Butler-Evans, Elliott, *Race, Gender, and Desire: Narrative Strategies in the Fiction of Toni Cade Bambara, Toni Morrison, and Alice Walker*, Temple University Press, 1989.

  Butler-Evans examines two aesthetics in the works of these writers: an African American nationalism and African American feminism. He finds that in Bambara's fiction from the 1970s these currents are at odds with each other, but that she resolves some of the tension in her work from the 1980s.

Moraga, Cherríe, and Gloria Anzaldúa, *This Bridge Called My Back: Writings by Radical Women of Color*, Kitchen Table: Women of Color Press, 1983.

  Bambara contributed a foreword to this anthology of personal essays, criticism, and poetry by women of color in the United States. Much of the writing comes out of a desire for a unified Third World feminist movement that is not focused on the needs of men, or of white women.

Muther, Elizabeth, "Bambara's Feisty Girls: Resistance Narratives in *Gorilla, My Love*," in *African American Review*, Vol. 36, No. 3, Fall 2002, pp. 447–59.

  Muther discusses Senator Daniel P. Moynihan's 1965 report *The Negro Family: The Case for National Action* as a landmark of white liberal guilt, and "Gorilla, My Love" as a story of African American empowerment that resists Moynihan's analysis.

Greyhound People

Alice Adams

1981

"Greyhound People," which many critics refer to as one of Alice Adams's most popular stories, was inspired by the author's experiences on Greyhound buses, which she rode to get from her home to the University of California at Davis, where she taught for a brief period of time. This short story, originally published in the *New Yorker* in 1981, was recently published in the highly acclaimed *The Stories of Alice Adams* (2002), with "Greyhound People" being singled out as one of the best stories in the collection. (Note that this story may have been previously published but the exact date could not be found or confirmed.)

The long commute from home to work and the bits of conversations that the author heard during the ride must have stirred Adams's imagination. The story begins with a simple question, but one with possible complex consequences: What would happen if one day the protagonist got on the wrong bus? Where would she end up? What would she learn? And how might the experience change her? Greyhound buses, after all, are but distant cousins of city buses that rarely drive over city limit speeds, stop every two or three blocks, and never cross the somewhat barren lands that lie between two metropolitan areas. To get on the wrong Greyhound bus could have dire consequences, or, in the least, significant complications. And this is what Adams explores. In the process, the protagonist learns to loosen her grip on the stale routine that has become her life and to enjoy herself.

In a review of *The Stories of Alice Adams*, Michael Frank of the *Los Angeles Times* classified ''Greyhound People'' as falling into the category of ''snapshot'' stories—a sort of picture of life or as Frank put it, a kind of ''collage.'' This reviewer found that rather than building suspense in many of her stories, Adams tended to create sketches. In specific reference to ''Greyhound People,'' Frank wrote, ''You come away from the story feeling that you have been taken somewhere—not enlightened so much, not shaken up—merely shown.'' Then Frank adds: ''Adams is a great shower of people, of place, of social moments and moments of intimacy.'' In other words, ''Greyhound People,'' is a great vehicle for taking an enjoyable ride.

Author Biography

Alice Adams, award-wining author of hundreds of short stories and several novels, had to overcome continual challenges to her writing career until she finally published her first novel at the age of forty. Born on August 14, 1926, to southern parents, Nicholson and Agatha Adams, in the then-small town of Fredericksburg, Virginia, Adams soon discovered that in her generation, women, like children, were to be seen but not heard. Despite the fact that she managed to be accepted at the prestigious Radcliffe College at the age of sixteen, she was advised by school professionals to give up her attempts to become a writer and instead focus on getting married. Adams followed this advice rather halfheartedly and ended up unhappily wedded to Mark Linenthal Jr. one year after she graduated from Radcliffe with a bachelor of arts degree. The marriage was unsuccessful, as were Adams's attempts to get published during those years. The marriage did, however, produce the couple's only child, Peter, born in 1951. But it would not be until after her divorce in 1958 that Adams would finally achieve her dream of becoming a published writer.

After struggling through a difficult marriage and divorce, Adams's life did not get much easier. She was a single mother who had to find a way of paying the bills and putting food on the table. Although she continued to write, she could not support herself and her child without taking on menial jobs. While working as a secretary taxed her energies, the low-grade jobs she held provided her with interesting material for future stories. Adams gained first-hand knowledge about the hardships and prejudices that women faced in the years before,

and during, women's fight for equality. It was during these years that Adams almost gave up writing. She second-guessed her abilities because of the many rejections she received. At one point, she was so depressed she sought the advice of a psychiatrist who suggested that she forget about ever publishing another word. But then, in the late 1960s, Adams's long hours at her writing desk were finally compensated. The publishing world, in particular the *New Yorker,* began paying attention to her work. In the years that followed, Adams's writing, especially her short stories, began appearing everywhere.

Although she would go on to write several novels, it was Adams's short stories that drew the most attention. She would later admit that the short story form was her favorite; and this affinity of hers would shine through her work. She received so many O. Henry Awards for her short stories that in 1982 she was granted the O. Henry Special Award for Continuing Achievement, a feat only two other authors have accomplished. Her work also appeared in the publication the *Best American Short Stories* several times. In 1992, a few years before her death, Adams was presented with the Academy and Institute Award in Literature.

At the age of seventy-two, after a long history of publishing, Adams died in her sleep on May 27, 1999, in San Francisco. The posthumously published and highly acclaimed collection, *The Stories of Alice Adams* (2002), included the short story ''Greyhound People,'' which has been singled out as one of the best stories in the collection.

Plot Summary

Adams begins her story ''Greyhound People'' as she typically begins most of her stories—by immediately stating the problem or the challenge that the protagonist is facing. In the first sentence of the story, the narrator relates: ''As soon as I got on the bus, in the Greyhound station in Sacramento, I had a frightened sense of being in the wrong place.'' With this fear looming over her, she takes the closest seat to the driver that she can find. Unfortunately, as soon as she settles into it, a man angrily claims the seat as his own. The narrator relinquishes the seat to him and steps back a few paces to find a substitute.

Once settled, the narrator focuses on the people and the conversations around her. She notices that the anger of the man who made her change seats has subsided. He talks to two women across the aisle from him as if he were a friend of theirs, happy to see them. Meanwhile the narrator sits alone. She wonders, again, if she has taken the wrong bus but does not take any action to find out. Rather, she watches the bus driver enter the bus and take his seat. Instead of questioning him, she wonders why he does not collect tickets.

As the bus pulls out of the station, a child with a very loud voice begins asking a lot of nonsensical questions. ''Mom is that a river we're crossing? Mom do you see that tree?'' The questions are not only loud, they are non-stop. And eventually a black woman in the front of the bus becomes irritated by them. She tells the little boy to be quiet. The boy has a startled look on his face when he starts to add new questions to his repertoire. ''Mom does she mean me? Mom who is that?'' The narrator admits that she silently applauded the woman who told the boy to be quiet. Then a white woman walks down the aisle and confronts the black woman, telling her that her son was ''retarded'' and his constant questioning was the way ''he tests reality.'' The mother then adds: ''You mustn't make fun of him like that.'' When the mother returns to her son, his questions begin again.

The narrator, although somewhat embarrassed by her lack of sensitivity about the boy, found the taunting by the black woman to be a bit appealing. She liked the sound of defiance in the black woman's voice. This is when the narrator turns around to observe the people on the bus and notices that she, a white woman, was in a definite minority. Most of the passengers were black, which surprises her.

In the next section of the story, the narrator provides a glimpse of the scenery that is passing her by through the window. She describes the rolling hills and farmland and a view of the distant bay of water. In the middle of her description, the bus turns off the freeway, making the narrator fully realize that her fears were true. She was not on the San Francisco express bus. The bus would be making three stops: Vallejo, Oakland, and lastly San Francisco. The narrator sighs. At least the bus was going to San Francisco. The worst of her mistake was that she would be late. Her roommate, Hortense, who had volunteered to pick her up, would probably be worried about her. But that could be easily mended.

When the bus pulls into the station in Vallejo, the seat partner of the black woman who told the young boy with all the questions to be quiet stands up and turns to the back. ''And you, you just shut up!'' she tells the boy. Many people in the bus

Alice Adams

applaud her. But the narrator does not, even though she admits that she would have liked to.''

The narrator provides a small amount of information about herself: she lives in San Francisco and works in a government office there but has been temporarily assigned to duty in a Sacramento office. That is why she is commuting between the two cities. He husband has just recently told her that he was in love with a woman of Japanese descent who works as a nurse. The narrator allowed her husband to keep their apartment because she does not like to argue.

As new passengers board the bus in Vallejo, the narrator notices an extremely large woman walking down the aisle. The woman is big enough to fill two seats, the narrator states, but there are no double seats vacant. The narrator assumes that the woman heads her way because she is very thin and does not therefore take up much room. The woman apologizes for her size and the amount of room she takes up when she sits next to the narrator. They strike up a conversation, one of the few in the whole story.

The bus finally arrives in San Francisco; and as she imagined, the narrator must face her very worried roommate, Hortense. Hortense has insisted on picking up the narrator because the bus station is located in a very seamy part of the city. But she has been waiting for a long time for her late partner. Feelings amended, the two women go home to a lackluster dinner—a chef salad—because Hortense is trying to lose weight.

One morning, the narrator shares a seat with a young woman who is going to Sacramento to work. The narrator suspects that that the woman is from upstate New York, the birthplace of the narrator. When the young woman confirms that this is indeed where she is from, the narrator does not share with the girl that the narrator herself is from the same place. She also hopes that the girl does not provide any more personal information about herself. The narrator would rather keep the relationship on the surface.

Once she arrives in Sacramento, the narrator describes the bus station there. Since it is in Sacramento and many people catch buses to Reno, the narrator comments on the people waiting for the Reno bus, what she refers to as "lines of gamblers."

When she catches the wrong bus for a second time, the narrator knows that Hortense will never believe it was a mistake. The narrator starts to make up excuses to ease Hortense's potential anger but realizes how childish that was. At this moment, the narrator senses the consequences of being so dependent on Hortense. We are both "grown up," she thinks, suggesting that she is beginning to gain some confidence.

As she travels, the narrator notices a young man sleeping across the aisle from her. He stirs her memories of her husband. She then recounts how her marriage fell apart, the signs of which she is just now recognizing. When her bus finally arrives in San Francisco, Hortense is furious and does not allow the narrator to soothe her in any way. When they arrive home, the narrator refers to herself and Hortense as "the odd couple."

The narrator bumps into the young girl from upstate New York again. The girl tells the narrator about a bus pass that she can buy that would allow her not only to go from San Francisco to Sacramento but to anywhere in California. The narrator decides to buy the ticket, which according to her made California seem "limitless." Then the narrator admits that she really does understand how the Greyhound bus station worked. In other words, she knew where she had to go in order to catch the bus she intended to catch, and if she got on the wrong bus at that point, it would be on purpose. She is

tempted to go into a restaurant and order a milkshake. However, since Hortense has put both of them on a diet, the narrator feels a bit guilty about having the ice cream drink. The narrator realizes that her feelings are ridiculous, since she does not need to lose weight and can actually afford to gain some. So she orders the milkshake. While she is drinking it, the black man, who had ordered her (rather gruffly) to vacate his seat on the bus at the beginning of the story, walks up to her table and asks how she is doing. With these three events (buying the All-California bus pass, drinking the milkshake, and being recognized by a man), the narrator says "something remarkable" has happened. She is beginning to think for herself, understand her emotions, and open up to the people around her.

Characters

Handsome Black Man

The handsome black man enters the story at the very beginning. He arrives on the bus just after the narrator and demands that she get out of his seat. The narrator feels this man is rude but obeys his orders nonetheless. She had sat in that particular bus seat because she felt more secure sitting close to the bus driver, but she gives up her security in order to avoid confronting this man. The handsome black man represents all men in this story, at least from the point of view of the narrator. She gives in to men, ignoring her own needs. She later watches this man as he demonstrates his softer side; but this side is not for the narrator's benefit but rather for two other women. This man reappears at the end of the story, after the narrator has made up her mind to change her life. Having done this, the man enters the restaurant as the narrator is drinking her milkshake. He walks over to her table and asks how she is doing. With this greeting, the narrator feels flattered. This man remembered her. Not only did he recognize her, in the narrator's mind, he is also, in his own way, apologizing for having been so rude to her in the beginning of the story. He represents the narrator's revised opinion of herself and her relationship to men.

Hortense

Hortense is the narrator's roommate. When the narrator is divorced, Hortense invites the narrator to live with her. Hortense is an overweight, nurturing woman, who worries about the narrator. She insists on picking her up from the bus station because the station is located in a bad section of the city. But she has little patience when the narrator keeps coming in late. She becomes so nervous about the situation that she is short with the narrator, brushing off the narrator's attempts to soothe her. She is also overly protective of the narrator's health, confusing her own excessive eating habits with the narrator's. The narrator is very thin and yet Hortense insists that the narrator eat only a salad for dinner, for example. Although the narrator appreciates the assistance that Hortense offers her, she realizes that she can only stay with Hortense on a temporary basis.

Narrator

The narrator never gives her name, only using the pronoun "I" throughout the narrative of this short story. She works in San Francisco as a statistician in a government office that deals with unemployment; but she has been temporarily sent to Sacramento for ten weeks. This is why she commutes between the two cities and why she is on a Greyhound bus every workday. She is recently divorced and temporarily living with Hortense, a woman who fusses over her. The narrator admits that she stays with Hortense because of her "sheer dependency."

The narrator appears to be a woman who allows circumstances to navigate her through life without her making definitive choices. She questions events, such as when a bus driver appears to take two tickets from her instead of just one, but she keeps her questions to herself. She admits that she does not like confrontation. That is also why she allowed her husband to keep their apartment. She did not have it in her to fight for it. She is an observer of life. And that is the role that she plays out in this story. She observes the people around her, connecting with them almost entirely inside her head, seldom actually saying anything to anyone. When someone does open up to her, she makes a point of not asking questions that might be too personal and certainly not answering any questions with enough information to give away anything personal about herself.

By the end of the story, however, the narrator experiences the beginnings of a dramatic change. She is letting down the walls that have isolated her and opening up her horizons. Tired of her tendency to be dependent, she begins to reach out to strangers, to think for herself, to take chances, and to dream.

New York State Girl

The New York State girl is a young woman who shares a seat with the narrator on the bus. They meet accidentally a few times, sharing information with one another but not to any great extent. The young girl is from New York, as is the narrator. She also works in a similarly styled office building in Sacramento as does the narrator. They both carry valises on the bus. They are, in some ways, mirror images of one another except that the girl is a younger version of the narrator. The New York State girl also is a little more wise, more worldly. She explains things to the narrator, such as the bus pass that the narrator has almost misused. She also tells the narrator about a different kind of bus pass, one that allows a person to travel all over California. This opens a door of experience for the narrator who decides to follow the girl's suggestion. Despite her help, however, the narrator refuses to deepen their relationship in any way.

Themes

Isolation

In the beginning of "Greyhound People," the narrator isolates herself from the people around her in several different ways. First, she places her briefcase on the seat next to her. She does not do this to purposefully keep other people from sitting next to her; however, she does comment that in doing so, no one will sit next to her. On a subconscious level, her briefcase acts as a barrier. Later in the story, she consciously removes her briefcase so someone might sit next to her, signaling a slight opening in the barricade that she has built to protect herself.

The narrator also isolates herself through her silence. Although she reacts emotionally to different circumstances, she keeps her feelings to herself. For example, she emotionally applauds the woman who tells the young boy to be quiet. Even though other people express their emotions by clapping their hands and cheering, the narrator remains still. She wants to applaud, but she does not want anyone to know how she feels. She has the emotions but she is afraid of them. She does not know for sure if they are appropriate and therefore does not want to

Topics for Further Study

- Imagine that you could buy a bus pass and travel to any city or place in California. Where would you go? Choose at least four places and research the history, the cultural makeup and any annual events in your chosen place. Write a travel magazine article for each destination, trying to entice other people to visit the places you have chosen.

- Take several rides on buses that cross your town. Listen and record conversations and events that happen during your trip. Then write a story about your adventures. What new things did you learn about your town? What did you find out about the people who live in your town? What did you learn about yourself in reference to how you reacted to your fellow passengers?

- Compose a statistical report on divorce in the United States during the twentieth century. Then write a report on the changes that have occurred over the years. How have certain events, such as World Wars I and II and the Vietnam War, affected the divorce rate? What were the peak years for divorce rates? What age groups are most affected by divorce? Are there any differences in divorce rates depending on one's cultural background? Does belonging to particular religions make any difference? Compare different regions of the United States, such as the South, the West, the Northeast, and so forth.

- There are many good books that have been published on how to write an effective short story. Read some of these books and report back to your class the various components that are involved in a short story. Explain how a short story differs from a novel (more than just its length). Refer to some of the best American short story writers and provide your classmates with a list of some of these authors' best works.

expose them. In doing this, she further removes herself not only from the people around her but from her own expressions.

When she does finally have a conversation with the young girl from New York, she does not share with the girl the fact that they are both from the same region. Not only does she not open up to the girl, she is uncomfortable when the girl opens up to her. The narrator slowly opens up by the end of the story, by listening to this young girl's advice. This stimulates other reactions, ones in which the narrator begins to ease the barricades that have isolated her from her surroundings as well as from herself.

Dependency

The narrator admits that she is staying with Hortense out of a feeling of dire dependency. She has just come through a painful breakup of her marriage and a divorce from her husband and is feeling much like a child who has been forced out of her home. She leans on Hortense, not only because she needs a place to stay but because she is too emotional to make any decisions on her own. She allows her new roommate to tell her what to eat, when to come home, and how to get from the bus station to the house. Although the narrator is silently complaining of the stifling affect this is having on her, she is still struggling to stand up on her own two feet and feels she must rely on someone else to help her. In the beginning of the story, she accepts her circumstances without making any attempts to change them. She shows this through the way she reacts to the bus driver, whom she believes has taken two tickets from her instead of one. She thinks this is wrong, but does not ask for an explanation. Even when she thinks she has gotten on the wrong bus and is frightened about the circumstances of her action, she does not stand up and ask anyone, not even the bus driver, if she is indeed on the wrong bus. She just sits there and waits to be taken to wherever the bus is going. Also, when a man tells her to get out of "his" seat, she acquiesces without even a little whimper. Similarly, she has given up her apartment, not so much because she did not want to stay there but rather because she did not want to argue with her husband. She allows these things to happen to her as if she had no say in the matter.

Coming-of-Age

Although this is not a typical coming-of-age story, which usually involves a teenager moving into the ranks of adulthood, "Greyhound People" does fit into this category in many ways. The narrator is an older woman who has been married for several years, but emotionally she is still immature. Her marriage provided her with a shelter similar to the one that a young person's family home provides. Decisions were more than likely taken care of by the narrator's husband. So when the narrator is pushed out of the house, she finds that she must make all kinds of decisions on her own. At first her situation is frightening. She is fearful that she has taken the wrong bus, for instance. She is also afraid of asking anyone how to get out of the situation, and like a scared child, she sits stiffly in her seat, waiting to see what will happen next instead of standing like an adult and taking the situation into her own hands.

The narrator grows, emotionally, from the beginning of the story to the end, however. Although she is fearful in the beginning, by the end of the story she is ready to confront her overbearing roommate Hortense, for instance. Or at least, she is ready to do this obliquely. Instead of staying on the strict diet Hortense has put her on, the narrator goes into the restaurant and orders a milkshake, something Hortense would have looked down upon, if not completely forbidden. The narrator also tells Hortense that she does not have to pick her up at the bus station, thus allowing the narrator more freedom of choice as to what bus she rides and at what hour she comes home. And, whereas in the beginning of the story, the narrator took the bus only for the routine ride between Sacramento and San Francisco, by the end of the story she has bought a special pass that will allow her to travel all over California, thus opening up her horizons and eliminating at least some of the boundaries that she has set up between herself and the outside world. By the end of the story, it is as if the narrator has finally unfurled her

wings and is ready to fly. Her emotions have matured, and she has come of age on a psychological level.

Style

First-Person Point of View

This short story is told in the first-person point of view with little dialogue presented throughout. The narration comes mostly from inside the head of the protagonist, which is referred to as interior monologue. First-person narration limits the story in some ways, but also provides a more intimate relationship with the storyteller. The reader is given the opportunity to hear the thoughts of the narrator, understand the emotions the narrator is going through, and then juxtapose these elements to the actions that the narrator does or does not take in response to them. The circumstances of the story are all interpreted through the emotions of the narrator, thus giving a narrow point of view of other characters in the story. The reader can only guess at other character's reactions to the same circumstances that the narrator faces. For example, the picture of Hortense that the narrator provides is obviously one-sided. The only version of her is given through the narrator's experience. Whether Hortense is really overbearing and over-protective will never be known. All that is known is that the narrator sees Hortense in this way. It could be that the narrator is feeling overwhelmed emotionally because of her divorce and that she wants to break free of Hortense's need to nurture her. Hortense is never allowed to speak for herself because the point of view is the narrator's.

Symbolism

The story "Greyhound People" is filled with subtle symbolism. The bus the narrator travels on represents a sort of outer shell, much like the emotional shell that the narrator has built around herself to protect her emotions. She does not want to become emotionally involved with anyone around her because her emotions are still very raw from the divorce she has recently gone through. Like the bus, she travels through her day without connecting to anything around her. She moves routinely from one place to another without becoming involved.

The man on the bus who insists that the narrator is sitting in his seat represents the narrator's husband, who has insisted that she give up their apartment and their marriage. This man is very curt with her and, although she is offended, the narrator acquiesces because she does not like confrontations. This is exactly how she interacted with her husband. Then, in contrast, the narrator watches this man put on a friendly demeanor with women who sit across the aisle from him. This could represent the many affairs the narrator's husband had with other women. The narrator comments on how emotionally removed her husband had become with her, and yet he was emotionally involved with other women at the same time. At the end of the story, when this man from the bus recognizes the narrator in the restaurant and asks how she is doing, she imagines that he is actually offering her an apology for his previous behavior. This could be her wishful thinking that her husband could at some time in the future also apologize for the way he has treated her.

Hortense, the narrator's new roommate, represents the narrator's opposite self. Where the narrator is thin, Hortense is fat. Where the narrator is quiet and yielding, Hortense is aggressive and demanding. Hortense symbolizes what the narrator does not want to become. However, Hortense is also the stimulus that motivates the narrator to change. The narrator admits that she is temporarily dependent on Hortense, but she fights Hortense's attempts to dominate her life. In doing so, she learns to test her environment and her circumstances instead of giving in to the mundane daily routine of her life.

The young girl from New York might symbolize the narrator's younger self—an alternative view of herself. She and the young girl are both from the same region. They both work in Sacramento and commute from San Francisco. They both spend most of their day in similar office buildings located next door to one another. The author would not have created all these similarities if she had not intended something symbolic. It is this girl, to whom the narrator is at first afraid to open up to, who inspires the narrator to buy the bus pass that will take the her out of her routine. The young girl, although living under similar circumstances as the narrator, is more willing to talk about herself. She is also more excited about exploring new environments. She ultimately inspires the narrator to consider doing the same.

Setting

The setting of this piece is very constrictive in the beginning. The narrator sits inside a Greyhound bus for much of the action. Although she describes the countryside of California in small doses, little is said about her environment outside of the bus and the bus stations she encounters. This confining setting provides the reader with a physical example of how confined the narrator is feeling. She is closed in emotionally. She is traveling but she has little to do with her fellow companions or with the environment through which she is moving. She is moving through a land that does not touch her, nor does she touch it. She is also, for the most part, always surrounded by strangers. Although this setting does not change throughout the story, there are hints toward the end that the setting will change slightly. The narrator has bought a bus pass that will allow her to travel all over the state. She will remain inside a bus, but at least the scenery outside the bus will change. In this way, the narrator is at least expanding her experiences and seeing new things.

Historical Context

Special Education

It was not until the 1960s that groups sought federal assistance that would provide free services in the public schools for children with special needs. Under pressure from these groups, in 1966 Congress established the Bureau for Education of the Handicapped. As programs began to be developed through this bureau, the Education of the Handicapped Act was passed four years later. These actions, however, did not provide full services for all children with special needs. It would take five more years and a lot of pressure from parents of children with disabilities, as well as a few court cases that ruled in their favor, before more federal support for the education of these children would become law. Today, all children with special needs, from first grade through college, are entitled to free and appropriate public education that also provides specific services for their needs. The law ensures that these children's rights are protected and that the federal government will assist local states in providing the education that these children require.

A Brief History of Vallejo

Vallejo is a medium-sized city located in the California foothills where the Carquinez Straits meet San Pablo Bay in northern California. The city was named for Mexican general Mariano Guadalupe Vallejo in 1844. Six years later when California became a state, General Vallejo offered a large tract of land, as well as financial assistance, to help in establishing the capitol of California on his land. The state congress agreed, and the city of Vallejo was adopted as the state capitol. Although the state congress did actually convene in Vallejo in the 1850s, the buildings that General Vallejo had promised to build were nowhere to be seen. The congress met in dilapidated buildings that leaked in the rain and eventually voted to move the capitol, in 1853, to another city.

The U.S. Navy, however, found the San Pablo Bay to their liking and built the first permanent U.S. naval station on the west coast in Vallejo in 1854. When the railroad was established there, Vallejo experienced an economic and population boom. Mare Island Naval Station remained a busy installation, providing employment to many of Vallejo's population until it was closed in 1994. Although the navy is gone, Vallejo remains an ideal hub for commercial shipping, industry, oil companies, and ferry transportation in the San Francisco Bay area. Today, thousands of passengers on Vallejo's three high-speed catamaran ferries travel to and from San Francisco for work and recreation.

A Brief History of Sacramento

Sacramento, located on a major California river (the Sacramento River) was a hub of transportation too, especially during the Gold Rush. The rush began when gold was found on Captain John Augustus Sutter's land, the builder and commander of one of the first U.S. Army forts in that area. The fort was built to help ensure the bid for the control of the land that would soon become the state of California. Sutter, a man who would make a lot of money in his lifetime but would die bankrupt, is credited, along with his son, as being the founder of Sacramento.

At the height of the Gold Rush in 1849—a time during which the population of the city grew to 10,000 people in seven months—the Sacramento city government was established. Five years later, Sacramento was made the permanent capitol of the new state of California. Many historic events originated in Sacramento. One such event occurred in 1860, when the Pony Express, the first long-distance mail delivery system, began its first run from Sacramento to St. Louis, Missouri—a run that was completed in ten days.

Over time, the Sacramento Valley has become one of the most productive agricultural areas in the United States, helping to build the economy of its major city, Sacramento. Today, almost one-half million people live there. The city is located about ninety miles northeast of San Francisco and about twenty-five miles northeast of Vallejo.

A Brief History of San Francisco

San Francisco is the fourth-largest city in the United States and is located in northern California along the Pacific Coast. Although the first white settlers from Mexico and Spain began a community in this area in the eighteenth century, it was not until the Gold Rush years that a population boom occurred. In one year, from 1848 to 1849, the population of San Francisco expanded from 1,000 to 25,000 people.

The city has had at least three different names. Around 1780, Sir Francis Drake dubbed it Nova Albion; in 1846, Captain John B. Montgomery changed its name to Yerba Buena (after a wild plant of the same name); and then a year later, taking a cue from the Spanish settlers, it was finally named San Francisco, after the Roman Catholic Saint Francis of Assisi, a lover of animals.

A devastating earthquake (modern scientists estimate it must have reached 8.5 on the Richter scale) destroyed much of San Francisco in 1906. What was not destroyed by the earthquake was destroyed by subsequent fires. But by 1915, proud to show off its new face of complete restoration, San Francisco hosted the Panama-Pacific Exposition, a world's fair. Other great architectural accomplishments include the building of the San Francisco-Oakland Bay Bridge in 1936 and the Golden Gate Bridge in 1937.

Often referred to as the city of countercultural movements, many from the Beat generation, as well as those from the so-called hippie generation made San Francisco the hub of much of their activity. The Black Panthers (an African American political group in the 1960s) was headquartered just outside of San Francisco in the city of Oakland.

At the end of the twentieth century, San Francisco became the center of many of the dot.com businesses. As young computer-savvy entrepreneurs moved in, the city's rundown districts saw economic improvement as older neighborhoods became "gentrified." Today, San Francisco is the banking and financial center of the West Coast, the home of the Pacific Exchange (regional stock exchange) and a major branch of the U.S. Mint (where money is printed).

A Brief History of Oakland

Oakland was founded two years after California became a state. It is located on the east side of San Francisco Bay and to the west of San Francisco. One of Oakland's main points of interest is its port, which is one of the three most important on the West Coast.

The population of Oakland was slow to grow. After the 1906 earthquake in San Francisco, many people crossed the bay in order to make Oakland their new home. During World War II, the naval facilities in Oakland attracted large numbers of workers, who helped to build the naval force of that war. But the economic boom that occurred during the war came to a screeching halt after the war, leaving thousands of people unemployed. Those who could afford to leave moved to the suburbs. The rest struggled to make a living as they watched their city deteriorate.

In the latter part of the twentieth century, Oakland was hit with two disasters. First there was the damage caused by the 1989 earthquake that destroyed a major part of the Oakland-San Francisco Bridge; and then there was the huge wildfire in 1991 that devastated thousands of homes. Today, Oakland is enjoying a renaissance as businesses and individuals, who have grown tired of the high cost of housing in San Francisco, move in and renovate large sections of this town.

Today, Oakland's 400,000 citizens are ranked eighth in the United States in overall educational achievement, with almost one-third of its population in possession of a college degree. Major publications such as *Forbes* and the *Wall Street Journal* list Oakland as one the United States' best cities for businesses.

Critical Overview

''Greyhound People'' has been referred to as one of Adams's most popular short stories, as well as the best story in the 2002 collection, *The Stories of Alice Adams.* ''Greyhound People'' appeared in Adams's sixth collection, which speaks for itself in

terms of how many short stories she wrote in her lifetime. Most critics agree that the short story form was Adams's strong point; they often compare her style of writing to F. Scott Fitzgerald, Flannery O'Connor, and Katherine Mansfield—all great storytellers.

In his article for the *Los Angeles Times,* Michael Frank called Adams ''a writer who has a natural, almost innate gentility, an ease of being with language, character, landscape, atmosphere and emotion that is both authentic and modest.'' Another critic who highly praised Adams was Ann H. Fisher, writing for the *Library Journal,* who described Adams as a ''master fiction writer,'' one who creates ''multidimensional'' characters. Besides such critical praise, another marker of Adams's ability to write very good short prose was how often her stories appeared in the *New Yorker,* the ultimate goal of most contemporary authors. Adams's editor at the *New Yorker,* Fran Kiernan, told the *New York Times* critic Peter Applebome, that ''No one wrote better about the tangled relations of men and women or about the enduring romance of friendship.'' Kiernan then added: ''As a writer, she [Adams] was unfailingly wise.''

In her review of Adams's 1999 short story collection, Rita D. Jacobs, writing for *World Literature Today* described Adams in this way: ''There are certain writers whose short stories exemplify the kind of perfection that theorists and critics extol. Alice Adams's stories frequently achieve the deftly limned but fully realized character, the complication quickly described, and the denouement which offers insight or a catch in the throat.'' Her writing is filled with insights, Jacobs continued, an observation that other critics have also made. Furthermore, in drawing her conclusion about Adams's work, Jacobs stated that not only did she find Adams's short stories ''affecting,'' she also described them as ''models of the art.''

Another reviewer, Beth E. Andersen, writing for the *Library Journal,* was saddened by the announcement of Adams's death in 1999. Andersen, in her critique of *The Stories of Alice Adams* reflected not only on Adams's death but also on the author's ability to write. After Adams's death, Andersen wrote, ''her gift for creating the familiar landscapes of interior life with pitch-perfect diction was forever silenced.''

And finally, in a review of Adams's last short story collection, a *Publishers Weekly* writer pre-

Greyhound Bus, similar to the one the narrator rides from Sacramento to San Francisco in "Greyhound People"

dicted that *The Stories of Alice Adams*, which was published posthumously, would be well received by all—those who have read her before and those who will read her for the first time—because of "the seemingly offhand openings that carry the reader deep into the story, the swift characterizations, the effortless shifts in point of view and, of course, the almost casual but dazzling sentences."

Criticism

Joyce Hart

Hart is a freelance writer and author of several books. In the following essay, Hart searches for the source of the narrator's fear in Adams's story.

Adams's narrator in "Greyhound People" goes through some trying experiences in this tale and comes out a renewed spirit; but in the process, she exposes a lot of her fears. She tries to name them, but one has to wonder if she is being honest with herself. Her reactions to her fears do not fit the

names she attempts to put on them. Does she offer clues to what her real fears might be? And if so, are readers privilege to them? With a closer examination of the narration, can readers at least speculate what these underlying fears might be?

Adams begins her story with the narrator confessing that she "had a frightened sense of being in the wrong place." Readers assume that this means that the narrator is on the wrong bus, since she is talking about catching a Greyhound bus from Sacramento to her home in San Francisco. She asks people in the bus station (fellow riders) if she is in the right line; but then she admits that these people more than likely did not really understand what she was asking. Note that she does not ask anyone who works at the bus station for directions but rather climbs aboard a bus, which she senses is the wrong one. Because of her "anxiety and fear," she sits as closely as she can to the bus driver. Now it seems that a normal person would have asked more questions. She or he would not have gotten on a long-distance bus without knowing where it was going. If, out of awkwardness, the narrator had decided to take a chance on a particular bus, it seems reasonable to believe that she should have at least asked the passengers sitting around her on the bus, the

What Do I Read Next?

- Adams was often compared to the writer F. Scott Fitzgerald, who was more famous for his novels than his short stories, even though he was an excellent writer of both genres. A collection of his short stories called *Short Stories of F. Scott Fitzgerald: A New Collection* was published in 1995 and is a good place to find many of Fitzgerald's highly prized stories previously published in popular magazines of his time. Fitzgerald, although he wrote about a completely different generation than Adams, captured the nuances of personal relationships in a similar style.

- One collection of Katherine Mansfield's short stories (another writer to whom Adams was often compared) is the 1991 publication *Stories*. Mansfield was considered a master of the short story; she was a writer who transformed the writing style of her day. Some of her best stories include "The Fly," "At the Bay," and "The Singing Lesson."

- Critics cannot seem to say enough good things about Flannery O'Connor, a prolific writer of short stories and a woman who is often held up as the icon of the short story genre. O'Connor's *The Complete Stories* (1971) contains two of O'Connor's most popular works, "A Good Man Is Hard to Find" and "Everything that Rises Must Converge." A southern writer with a sense of humor, O'Connor is entertaining in many different ways.

- Although there is no doubt that any of Adams's collections of short stories is sure to please, she was also well received as a novelist. One of her more popular novels is *Superior Women* (1984), a story about four young women as they enter college at Radcliffe and the ensuing decades that follow as their relationships to one another develop.

---

people one could assume might be more aware of where this bus was going. But the narrator does not do this. She just sits there and hopes she has made the correct decision. Even when the bus driver enters the bus, she does not make the effort to find out the destination of this bus. So what is she really afraid of? Is she concerned the bus will not take her home? If she is, she does not mention this fact right away. Instead she makes observations about things that are happening around her. She mentions that a stranger asks her to give up her seat, and she explains her reaction to him. She also discusses the woman who insults a child with learning disabilities. Then the narrator goes through another whole range of emotions over this incident. It is not until the bus turns off the freeway and the bus driver announces that they are heading for the city of Vallejo that the narrator makes any comment at all about her destination. After the bus driver states that the next stops are Oakland and San Francisco, the narrator is relieved.

So what is the real fear in this incident. Is it a fear of getting lost? Of not being taken home? If it was, how could the narrator have gotten so casually involved in the people around her. She also has time to reflect on an incident that happened to her earlier that morning when a bus driver appeared to take two tickets from her instead of just one. During this same time, she also checks out the scenery, not necessarily looking to see where the bus is going but rather to enjoy the "very beautiful" hills, "a bright white farmhouse," and "the dark shapes of live oaks." She is describing a pleasing, relaxing pastoral scene—one of peace and tranquility. There was no mention of threatening black clouds on the horizon or gnarled, twisted branches, things that would suggest how the narrator was feeling if she was truly scared.

Rather it seems that the "frightened sense of being in the wrong place" that the narrator mentions at the beginning of the story is not a real fear—

the kind of fear one might have when one's life is threatened. What it really sounds like is excitement. She is in a ''wrong place'' in the sense that it is not the usual place that she finds herself in, day in and day out. It is a new place, one that is offering her new experiences. And one cannot help wondering if the narrator, in fact, put herself in that position on purpose. What else would explain how easily distracted she becomes with what is going on around her. Why else would she want ''to concentrate'' on the sweetness of the countryside outside her window? Maybe what she is feeling has nothing to do with being threatened but everything to do with coming alive. She gives a hint of this when she describes her ''large briefcase,'' which is taking up the seat next to her. She describes it as being ''stiff and forbidding-looking,'' blaming it for no one wanting to sit next to her. Could it be that she herself feels ''stiff and forbidding-looking?'' Does she scare people away? And does she subconsciously want to change this?

The narrator quietly applauds the woman who stands up to the noisy child at the back of the bus. The woman speaks her mind when she tells the boy: ''You the noisiest traveler I ever heard.'' The narrator shared this opinion, but would not, and probably could not, have expressed her feelings out loud. She applauds the woman not just for what she says but for the fact that she said it. The narrator obviously has trouble saying what she feels. Remember, she did not ask the right people the question she wanted answered about the bus; she did not ask the bus driver why he took two tickets instead of one; and she did not say anything in her defense when a fellow passenger insisted that she was sitting in his seat and demanded that she vacate it. She should have not only applauded the woman who told the young boy to be quiet, she should have really praised the boy himself. At least he had the guts to ask the questions that were inside of his head. And the reader should also notice that the woman whom the narrator did applaud also told the boy: ''in fact you ain't a traveler, you an observer.'' In other words, she summed up exactly what the narrator is. She too is an observer. She watches everything. In saying that the young boy is not a traveler meant that the boy was not really involved in his surroundings and circumstances but rather just someone who stands back and watches. A traveler experiences things. Events pass through them. They react and are changed by them. The narrator, in contrast, is physically present but she has placed so many

> **The narrator, in contrast, is physically present but she has placed so many barriers between herself and the world that she is not really in attendance."**

barriers between herself and the world that she is not really in attendance.

Things are made a little clearer when the narrator meets the young girl from New York. The bus is unusually crowded, so the narrator takes down her psychological walls just a bit and takes her ''stiff and forbidding-looking'' briefcase off the seat next to her so the young girl can sit down. ''We started up one of those guarded and desultory conversations that travel dictates,'' the narrator relates. The conversation conveys facts about the girl that the narrator relates to, but she does not tell the girl much about herself. As a matter of fact, what the girl did tell the narrator made her feel ill at ease. It seemed ''ominous'' to the narrator (here's the fear again) that she and the girl should share so many similarities. But why would this make her fearful? One hint comes from a statement she makes: ''Of course I did not ask the girl where she was from—too personal.'' There are those walls again. The narrator does not want anyone to get inside of her. Her fear seems not to be of talking to strangers, or getting lost, or making a mistake. Rather it seems that her greatest concern is that someone will find out exactly what she is feeling. If they knew what her emotions were they would know her better; and then what? Maybe she fears they wouldn't like her.

The narrator is scarred by these thoughts because of her recent past. She has just gone through a very emotional divorce and breakup of her marriage. Her husband has left her for another woman. And that might explain why, at the end of the story, she refers to ''something remarkable'' having happened to her. What she calls ''something remarkable'' was really just a simple act of kindness; but for the narrator, it was an outstanding event. The man who had insisted that she give up her bus seat for him notices her in the restaurant. He greets her, asking with a ''friendly smile,'' as he passes by, how she is doing. He barely pauses at her table, and yet the narrator is left ''a little out of breath.'' She wonders if he remembered her. ''Was it possible that something about me had struck him in just the right way, making him want to say hello?'' she asks. This is a woman who needs attention and yet at the same time hides from it. She is torn between her needs and her fears. She feels soft and too tender inside. Her real fear is that if she opens up, someone might hurt her again. So for the majority of the story she remains closed. She observes life from a distance. But by the end of the story, as witnessed by her reaction to this man and her anticipation of her upcoming travels throughout California, she is beginning to open up. She is starting to find hope and to recognize that the fear she is experiencing is not based on outside things, but rather it comes from inside of her; and the only way to get rid of it is to let it go.

Source: Joyce Hart, Critical Essay on ''Greyhound People,'' in *Short Stories for Students,* Thomson Gale, 2005.

David Remy

Remy is a freelance writer in Pensacola, Florida. In the following essay, Remy examines Adams's use of contrary elements to emphasize the narrator's search for self-acceptance.

The narrator in Alice Adams's story ''Greyhound People'' is a displaced person, a lonely woman caught between a world she no longer knows and another which she has yet to explore. She is a nameless character, one who embodies the yearning and doubt all humans suffer. Though she navigates quotidian complexities with a willing acceptance that borders on naïveté, she remains far from comfortable. Adams presents her narrator/protagonist in a series of situations that underscore the contrary elements in her life, opposites that seem to repel rather than attract as each event resonates with a sense of loss and displacement. Thus, by focusing on aspects of geography, personal relationships, and race that confront the narrator, Adams emphasizes her protagonist's search for balance and harmony in the world.

One of the first contrasts the narrator of ''Greyhound People'' must confront is that of geography. Transplanted from upstate New York to San Francisco, California, on the opposite coast and away from where she was raised, the narrator inhabits a region of the country that is markedly different from

the one she left behind. On the west coast of the United States, Americans are, generally speaking, much more relaxed in their attitudes and more willing to travel at a pace dictated by the individual rather than by society. Adams allows this attitude to pervade the story: each of the passengers regards the bus trip differently. For them, a bus ride can be something other than a commute. It can become an opportunity to relax and socialize. The narrator seems to have adjusted well to this philosophy, for the more than hour-long commute to and from work seems nothing more than a minor inconvenience to her—provided, of course, she boards the right bus.

However, when the narrator meets a girl from upstate New York on the bus and encounters her three times during the course of subsequent journeys, the narrator seems irritated, as though the girl's preoccupation with romance, work, and office politics serves as a grim reminder of the life she once knew. The narrator believes, perhaps erroneously, that she has put her life in New York behind her, but the girl's accent, which the narrator identifies with astonishing ease, reminds her of something ''ominous,'' as though the lives of the two women are ''heading in the same direction,'' en route to a common fate. The girl from upstate New York may reside in California, but everything about her is redolent of life back east, making her differences even more apparent. In short, she sticks out like a sore thumb. The narrator, who hails from the same part of the country, worries that she does too.

Furthermore, the narrator must travel from her temporary home in San Francisco to Sacramento five days a week because she has been assigned to study unemployment statistics in the state capital. This assignment forces the narrator out of her daily routine into yet another new environment. In Sacramento, the office she works in may be ''interchangeable'' with the one in San Francisco, but otherwise everything about the two cities is different, from the oleanders (assumed to be poisonous) that line the medians to the hordes of gamblers waiting at the bus station to board the next Reno express. This geographical displacement is compounded when the narrator takes the wrong bus. Instead of traveling directly to San Francisco, she must first stop in Vallejo and Oakland. What had at first seemed a ''straight shot'' filled with the usual highway scenery becomes a detour rich with roadside attractions. Though at first apprehensive, the narrator delights in discovering a new life onboard the bus. A mere ride becomes a journey, one she embarks upon with mounting anticipation.

Personal relationships are yet another means by which Adams highlights, through the use of opposites, her protagonist's isolation and need for change. Many of these changes come about unexpectedly, however. For example, because her husband leaves her for another woman, the narrator is forced to share an apartment with her friend Hortense. The narrator's husband, who works in advertising, drops hints about her taking a lover and their joining wife-swap parties. ''A pretty girl like you, you'd do okay,'' her husband would tell her, though he only has his best interest at heart. When he finally declares his love for another woman, the narrator is ''worse than surprised'' to learn that she has been replaced by a ''beautiful Japanese nurse,'' a woman whose exotic appeal cannot be matched, regardless of how attractive the narrator may be. Thus begins for the narrator what proves to be a ''long and painful year.''

As Adams makes clear throughout the story, all types of human relationships offer a contrasting perspective on the narrator's life, especially those that are of a personal or intimate nature. In particular, the narrator's relationship with Hortense presents a comic view of two people who are opposites in practically every way. For example, Hortense is fat whereas the narrator has kept her slim figure (though at one point in the story she wonders if adding twenty pounds to her frame would make a difference in the way the world sees her). Hortense is punctual while the narrator, alas, is not. Furthermore, she prefers drinking thick chocolate milkshakes to the fish and cold salads her roommate prepares. As the narrator observes, ''We were getting to be like some bad sitcom joke: Hortense and me, the odd couple.'' On a more somber note, the narrator deduces that Hortense is probably not poor; in contrast, the narrator, despite having a secure government position, regards herself as poor because she has known poverty, both the financial and the spiritual kind, and that badge of identity has remained with her throughout her life. These many differences between Hortense and the narrator eventually force the latter to contemplate ways in which she can garner her independence, such as taking a taxi home from the San Francisco bus station and finding an apartment of her own.

Perhaps the most obvious contrast in ''Greyhound People'' is that of the characters' racial backgrounds. The narrator, who is, the reader assumes, white, rides bus routes with a majority of patrons who are black. It is this obvious difference that makes her suspect that something is wrong.

> ''... the narrator, despite having a secure government position, regards herself as poor because she has known poverty, both the financial and the spiritual kind, and that badge of identity has remained with her throughout her life.''

''And, as I dared for a moment to look around the bus, I saw that most of the passengers were black: a puzzle.'' Indeed, the stark contrast between the racial backgrounds of the narrator and the other patrons on the bus confirms the fact that she has boarded the wrong bus. Apparently, the narrator is unaccustomed to the company of blacks because, without being quite sure why, she sits up front near the driver, filled with a ''frightened sense of being in the wrong place.'' She describes one fellow passenger as ''a big black man,'' one who is ''angry and very handsome.'' Adams has her protagonist come close to using a negative stereotype in describing her encounter; nevertheless, the narrator's description of the man emphasizes differences in race, gender, and custom (the man insists that she is sitting in his seat even though no possession of his marks the spot) that force the narrator to view herself from a fresh perspective.

Later, the narrator sits beside a large black woman who remains friendly and agreeable throughout their conversation. She is honest and self-deprecating about her size because she knows that, by sitting beside a thin woman like the narrator, she may make her emotionally and physically uncomfortable. The woman is wise enough to know that opposites, here exemplified by her size and race, more often repel than attract. She does not, however, appear excessively apologetic or obsequious. Her acceptance of herself serves as a model for the narrator to follow with regard to her own self-image, and she soon finds herself looking forward to their next encounter, for the narrator knows that, regardless of the obvious differences between them, she and the large black lady regard each other as equals. This awareness opens the narrator to the possibility of future meetings, ones that she invites with a newfound confidence. So emboldened is the narrator by these encounters with her fellow patrons that she thinks about them during the course of her subsequent journeys, and she wonders if, indeed, they are thinking about her.

This doubt is put to rest when she meets the handsome black man while she waits for the bus leaving for Vallejo and Oakland. He recognizes her and greets her with a warm hello, his demeanor contrasting sharply from their first encounter when he appeared angry and territorial. At first the narrator believes that this is the man's way of apologizing for his previous behavior, but then she realizes that such a gesture, however well intended, is simply not part of his character. "He was not at all like that, I was sure," concludes the narrator. "Even smiling he had a proud, fierce look." Nevertheless, the narrator realizes that the man's greeting was genuine, for it awakens within her an act of acceptance, an epiphany, that provides the story's climax: "Was it possible that something about me had just struck him in just the right way, making him want to say hello?" This encounter with the handsome black man, like the one she has with the black lady who sits beside her on the bus, leaves the narrator with an improved self-image, one realized as a result of confronting opposites that, by story's end, come together to form a whole, for now the narrator is ready to meet "anyone at all."

By having the protagonist of "Greyhound People" confront opposites in her everyday life, contrasts that are pronounced because of geography, interpersonal relationships, and race, Adams addresses many of the worries and fears that are common to the human condition. The narrator, though nameless, represents an individual's struggle to overcome unexpected changes and gather enough courage to venture into the unknown. As Adams makes abundantly clear by the story's end, the journey, though occasionally filled with wrong turns, can itself be its own reward.

Source: David Remy, Critical Essay on "Greyhound People," in *Short Stories for Students,* Thomson Gale, 2005.

Christine C. Ferguson

In the following essay excerpt, Ferguson discusses the characteristics of Adam's second collection of short stories entitled To See You Again: Stories.

Beautiful Girl was well reviewed and won acclaim from critics who celebrated its style and its thematic rejection of some of the more typical clichés about women and love. Susan Wood, in *The Washington Post Book World* (21 January 1979), wrote, "It is refreshing and hopeful to find a writer in this day and age who, although recognizing love's possibilities for destruction, can still write about the ways in which love, both sexual and platonic, is akin to salvation." In *The Christian Science Monitor* (12 February 1979), Janet Domowitz asserted that "Adams concentrates on emotions so poignant that they are almost beyond words of expression."

The period that followed was one of the most productive of Adams's career. In 1980 she published her fourth novel, *Rich Rewards,* the half-satirical, half-earnestly romantic first-person narrative of a divorced woman's attempt to find a place for herself through love and work. The popular reception of this novel, although manifest, was not as strong as that produced by *Superior Women* (1984), Adams's first best-seller. In the midst of this period of constant production, Adams was also able to publish her second volume of short stories. Critics generally agreed that *To See You Again: Stories* (1982) showed an expansion in Adams's narrative scope. These nineteen stories, many of which originally appeared in *The New Yorker,* range in milieu from the high society of San Francisco to the plantation life of the West Mexican coast, and in character from compulsive gamblers to teenage waitresses. Adams displays her trademark thematic concern with the durability of the human spirit and its continual desire for new stimulus and growth.

Nowhere is this focus handled more deftly than in "Greyhound People," the story that many critics have described as the finest in the collection. The story derives its premise from the dread people experience when they feel they have taken a wrong turn and lost their way, only to manipulate this sense of displacement into an opportunity for revelation. Its protagonist is a recently divorced commuter in Northern California who spends her days in transit, both literally from Sacramento to San Francisco and psychologically from the cloying dependency urged upon her by her overprotective friend Hortense to the total emotional independence she desires. One night she discovers, to her horror, that she has taken the wrong bus; instead of taking the express to San Francisco, she must take a convoluted route that stops at various small towns. Her distress quickly turns to pleasure as the trip affords her an opportunity to meet and observe people and situations

Skyline of San Francisco, the destination for the busride in ''Greyhound People''

outside her own rather banal class experience. Her exhilaration is so intense that, despite Hortense's dismay at her lateness, she is unable to refrain from repeating the experience, almost compulsively boarding the wrong bus at the end of the workday. Finally, she admits: ''Actually, the Greyhound system of departure gates to San Francisco is very simple; I had really been aware all along of how it worked.'' The wrong bus has been the right bus after all, its true destination inhabiting a psychological rather than a geographical space. At the close of the story she purchases a special pass that allows her to travel limitlessly over all of California and break the ties that have held her firmly to routine and dependency.

''Greyhound People'' is not the only story of the collection to transform a mistake or a wrong turn into an unanticipated boon. ''By the Sea'' works as a sort of modern revision of the Cinderella story. Its protagonist, Dylan Bellentyne, is an eighteen-year-old waitress working in a much-hated job at a seaside holiday resort while her former hippie mother tries to free herself from a controlling boyfriend and build a life for herself. Dylan spends her time fantasizing about being adopted by a respectable older couple or, more plausibly, of being whisked away from her mundane life by a handsome, dark, and rich stranger. With the arrival of the wealthy

and young Mr. Iverson at the lodge, the latter fantasy seems about to come true. Adams, with her usual aversion to conventional scripts, is quick to subvert romantic cliché, however. When the emphatic Mr. Iverson does woo Dylan, she views him only with mild distaste: ''Instead of being moved, as she might have been, Dylan thought he sounded a little silly . . . and she stepped back a little, away from him.'' Despite his repeated urgings, Dylan continues to resist his advances; though young, she has been freed from the myth of love as a fairy-tale solution to the banal sufferings of everyday life. Like the deliberately misdirected protagonist in ''Greyhound People,'' she is wary of those emotional paths that seem well-worn and overly familiar.

Not all of the stories in *To See You Again,* according to some of its critics, are so successful in avoiding the conventional. Benjamin DeMott, in *The New York Times Book Review* (11 April 1982), leveled the charge of repetitiveness, a criticism that continued to haunt Adams throughout her career: ''By the middle of the book I found myself in need of change, desirous of esthetic (not moral) relief.'' While DeMott laments the recurring elements of her stories, other critics condemned Adams's departure from them in the story ''Teresa.'' The first of the many collected Mexican stories spawned by Adams's

> **Adams displays her trademark thematic concern with the durability of the human spirit and its continual desire for new stimulus and growth."**

love of that country, "Teresa" details the misfortunes of a woman living in an impoverished area outside of Ixtapanejo. The narrative tone is unusually sentimental, verging on the mawkish, as it describes the murder of Teresa's husband, Ernesto, by the cruel gringo plantation owner, Senor Krupp, and the subsequent imprisonment of her son, Felipe, for his revenge killing of Krupp. In the preface to her 1990 collection of stories exclusively devoted to Mexico, *Mexico: Some Travels and Travelers There,* Adams suggests that the story was drawn from a real-life incident that she and some friends learned of while traveling through the country in the 1960s. This basis in reality perhaps prevents Adams from maintaining an ironic distance from her subject, as she does in other stories. Writes Robert Phillips in *Commonweal* (25 March 1983): "Teresa is the least convincing protagonist in the book. It is as if the author needs the trappings of 'civilization' to fully comprehend her character's motivations." Convincing or not, "Teresa" represented a new movement in Adams's work toward the depiction of nonurban and non-middle-class lifestyles, a movement that testifies to the sometimes criticized diversity of her work and her humanistic, although rarely overtly political, interest in the plight of the oppressed.

Another interesting tendency is apparent in the critical reception of *To See You Again,* one that most female authors encounter at one point or another in their careers. There is an urge in some of her reviewers to place Adams within, or in direct opposition to, a gendered concept of writing. Typifying the first of these responses, William Buchanan states in *Studies in Short Fiction* (1983): "The blurb on the jacket suggests a comparison with Katherine Mansfield. This comparison seems apt. Both use mainly women protagonists, and their stories show a very feminine concern for the quality of relation-

ships and moods. . . . The blurb goes on to suggest a comparison with Flannery O'Connor. This comparison does *not* seem apt. There is nothing feminine about Ms. O'Connor's stories." Buchanan's characterizations of "feminine" and "masculine" writing obviously reveal far more about his preconceived notion of gender difference than they do about Adams's art, but they nonetheless represent a not uncommon mode of interpreting her stories. Carolyn See, in *The Los Angeles Times* (13 April 1983), parodies this tendency to reduce all artistic output to the gender of the producer, asserting that Adams is similar to O'Connor or Mansfield only in that "she is also a woman and writes short stories. It might be more productive to think of Alice Adams as comparable to Walter Cronkite because you can believe what she says. Or to Albert Michelson, Einstein's predecessor, because of her experiments in motion, time and light, or to evangelist Terry-Cole Whittaker, because Adams insists—philosophically and intellectually—on the possibility of happiness for intelligent people. Or to Norman Mailer because she'd knock him out in the first round." See finds in *To See You Again* a strong and accurate representation of the diversity that marks the life of most women as "neither slave nor feminist, but something in between," rather than a trite encapsulation of "feminine" emotional homogeneity.

The title story of the collection is also its most impressionistic one. Based loosely on Thomas Mann's *Death in Venice* (1912), the narrative details the passionate fixation of a female college instructor with her attractive student Seth. Laura's love is played out purely on an internal level; she never confronts Seth or betrays herself in front of him, and indeed the story opens with his departure from her senior-level English class and also ostensibly from her life. Her anguish at his departure becomes a metaphor for the greater losses within her marriage to Gerald, a once handsome young architect who has become crushed under the weight of recurrent and deadening depression. Her desire for Seth, which is never explicitly sexual in nature, becomes a desire for regeneration in general. Imagining what he will look like when he reaches her age, she muses "at that time, your prime and our old age, Gerald's and mine, Gerald will be completely well, the cycle flat, no more sequences of pain. And maybe thin again. And interested, and content. It's almost worth waiting for." A thin shaft of hope, one of the most recurrent motifs in Adams's fiction, pierces the gloom of a relationship dulled by years of depression.

Source: Christine C. Ferguson, "Alice Adams," in *Dictionary of Literary Biography,* Vol. 234, *American Short-Story Writers Since World War II, Third Series,* edited by Patrick Meanor and Richard E. Lee, Gale Group, 2001, pp. 3–15.

Sources

Adams, Alice, "Greyhound People," in *The Stories of Alice Adams,* Knopf, 2002.

Andersen, Beth E., Review of *The Stories of Alice Adams,* in *Library Journal,* Vol. 127, No. 13, August 2002, p. 147.

Applebome, Peter, "Alice Adams, 72, Writer of Deft Novels," in *New York Times,* May 28, 1999, p. B11.

Fisher, Ann H., Review of *The Last Lovely City,* in *Library Journal,* Vol. 124, No. 3, February 15, 1999, p. 186.

Frank, Michael, "Graceful Collages and Mysterious Pairings: The Stories of Alice Adams," in *Los Angeles Times,* November 17, 2002, p. R5.

Jacobs, Rita D., Review of *The Last Lovely City,* in *World Literature Today,* Vol. 73, No. 4, Autumn 1999, p. 735.

Review of *The Stories of Alice Adams,* in *Publishers Weekly,* Vol. 249, No. 35, September 2, 2002, p. 50.

Further Reading

Burroway, Janet, and Susan Weinberg, *Writing Fiction,* Longman, 2003.

If after reading Adams's work you find yourself interested in attempting fiction writing, this is one of the best books to invest in. This is the book that many writing teachers use to help explain elements of the story such as point of view, setting, plot, and so forth.

Charters, Ann, *The Story and Its Writer: An Introduction to Short Fiction,* Bedford Books, 1999.

There are 124 different short stories from around the world in this collection, offering the reader an excellent sampling of contemporary as well as classic selections. Also included are short biographies of the writers and commentary on their work.

De Angelis, Barbara, *Confidence: Finding It and Keeping It,* Hay House, 1998.

De Angelis seems to have a knack for helping people speak out for themselves. Her books are all bestsellers. So, if one is curious about what it might feel like to lack confidence or is wondering how to overcome it oneself, this book might inspire one to spread one's wings and fly, just as Adams's main character did.

Updike, John, ed., *The Best American Short Stories of the Century,* Houghton Mifflin, 1999.

Three of Adams's short stories are contained in this national bestseller, as are a wide range of excellent authors' works. This popular book has been called one of the richest collections of short stories of the twentieth century.

If You Sing like That for Me

Akhil Sharma

1995

"If You Sing like That for Me," a short story by the young Indian American writer Akhil Sharma, first appeared in *The Atlantic Monthly* in May, 1995, when Sharma was just 24 years old. It was featured in *The Best American Short Stories 1996* and was awarded an O. Henry award that same year, marking Sharma as a young writer to watch.

Told in the first person by Anita, a young Hindu woman living in the suburban areas of New Delhi between 1966 and 1977, during the time when Indira Gandhi was prime minister, it is a story that explores the rather classic theme of the evolution of a character from a naive idealist to a realist. Anita's family arranges for her to marry Rajinder, a young banker from a family of farmers. Anita is secretly opposed to the marriage, but nevertheless, simply because she cannot think of a valid reason not to, she accepts. The story chronicles Anita's initial feeling of panic at being married to a stranger, her feelings of jealousy towards her younger, more ambitious sister, and the conditional love she and her parents reciprocate—a relationship that is characterized by artificiality and resentment, ultimately affecting Anita's fundamental ability to love herself.

As time goes by, Anita's anxiety and terror at the thought of her marriage subsides, and she slowly learns to accept Rajinder, until suddenly, one evening, she awakens to both an oncoming monsoon and an overwhelming feeling of being in love. However, when she attempts to act on this feeling of love she realizes, through Rajinder's pragmatic and

stoic reaction to her, that her idea of love is based on artificiality and idealism and does not reflect the reality of her life.

Author Biography

Akhil Sharma was born in 1972 in New Delhi, India. Subsequently, he moved with his family to Edison, New Jersey, where he grew up. His parents spoke Hindi exclusively while at home, and Sharma visited India every other summer during his childhood and adolescence. His strong ties to India and familiarity with the common culture provides the basis for his authentic portrayals of the details of everyday life in India that characterize his works.

As a child, Sharma enjoyed writing and attempted to emulate the style of the science fiction writers he admired. He attended Princeton University where he received a bachelor of arts degree in public policy, but he did not abandon his love of writing and went on to study creative writing under such luminaries as Toni Morrison, Tony Kushner, Russell Banks, and John McPhee. He spent one year as a Wallace Stegner Fellow in creative writing at Stanford, and worked briefly in Hollywood as a screenplay writer. He went on to graduate from Harvard Law School.

Sharma has developed a reputation as one of the most promising up-and-coming writers in the United States. His first published story, ''If You Sing like That for Me,'' appeared in *The Atlantic Monthly* in May 1995, just as he was entering Harvard Law School. It was subsequently published in *The Best American Short Stories 1996,* and received the prestigious Second Place O. Henry Award in 1996. Since then, he has had several stories published in both *The Atlantic Monthly* and *The New Yorker.*

After law school, Sharma went on to work as an investment banker. In 2000, at the age of 29, Sharma debuted his first novel, *An Obedient Father,* which he wrote between his long work hours. An excerpt of the novel was published in the June, 2000 issue of *The New Yorker;* it generated a fair amount of outcry and controversy for its frank depiction of incest between the main character and his young daughter. Nevertheless, the novel was released to widespread critical acclaim. It was named a *New York Times* Notable Book for 2000. Sharma himself won *The Voice Literary Supplement*'s Year 2000 ''Writers on the Verge'' prize. He also received the

Akhil Sharma

Hemingway/PEN New England Award in 2001 for his novel.

In January 2004, W.W. Norton announced that they would publish Sharma's next novel, tentatively titled *Mother and Son.* This novel is based on his previous New Yorker short story, ''Surrounded by Sleep.''

Plot Summary

The story opens with a scene that will also close the story: Anita, the narrator, awakens from a short sleep to find herself, for the first time and the last time, deeply in love with her husband. The narrative voice, which is placed 30 years after this moment, proceeds to relate the events leading up to this pivotal instance of intense emotion.

The story flashes back to seven months before that moment, two days after Anita and Rajinder are married. They are moving into a small flat in Defense Colony, a community outside of New Delhi. Anita feels terror and anxiety at being married to Rajinder, a small, slightly overweight man whom she barely knows. However, her anxiety is also coupled with the compulsion she feels, as an obedient wife, to be pleasing to him, even though she knows she is not physically attractive. Anita's sharp sense of inadequacy and guiltiness pervades the narrator's tone throughout the story.

As the furniture is moved into the new flat—which Rajinder selected himself—the only thing that gives Anita a sense of happiness or relief is the sight of the mattress because it represents sleep, and with sleep, her dreams. Throughout the story, sleep and dreams will remain the only thing that Anita looks forward to.

Anita and Rajinder are formal with each other, and Anita does not often speak. Over dinner, she gathers the courage to say she admires the prime minister Indira Gandhi, only to have her courage squelched by Rajinder's brother Ashok, who ridicules her opinion.

The story flashes back to three months before the wedding, during the matchmaking session between Anita's family and Rajinder's family at a restaurant. Ashok, Rajinder, and their widowed mother are present; Anita is present with her mother and her father, whom she calls Pitaji. Conversation between the two parties is stilted at best, and Rajinder and Anita do not speak at all. Rajinder's mother reveals that he is a banker and, with a master of arts degree, the most educated member of their family. Anita's mother, with characteristic unthinking cruelty, says that Anita was too lazy to get an education beyond her bachelor of arts degree, but her little sister Asha is obtaining her doctorate. Anita's feelings are hurt, but she indicates that it was normal for her mother to treat her that way.

Anita is not impressed by Rajinder's appearance and does not necessarily have the desire to get married. However, she does not express her feelings, expecting that the match with Rajinder will not go through.

Before leaving, Anita summons the courage to ask Rajinder if he enjoys movies. She asserts herself by saying she likes them "very much."

Two days later, Anita agrees to marry Rajinder even though she does not want to. She still believes that something will happen to sabotage their plans. She persists in this denial until the day of the engagement ceremony which she, as tradition dictates, does not attend. As her sister, Asha, relates the details of the ceremony between Pitaji and Rajinder, Anita, feeling disconnected and shocked, realizes

that she is truly going to marry Rajinder. She grows sadder at the realization that she will stay in India and grow old, while the more ambitious Asha will complete her Ph.D. and go to the United States.

On their wedding night, when the new couple receives blessings from their parents, Pitaji whispers "I love you" to Anita, in English. The use of English sets off a series of sad memories for Anita: she remembers how, when she was young, Pitaji would come home drunk. After receiving a sharp rebuke from his wife, he would hold Anita and cry, telling her in English that she was the only one who loved him. Anita would feel sad and distrustful at the same time, not knowing if his tears were a farce.

Ma would then tell the girls in language that was as theatrical as Pitjai's tears how Pitaji refused to come home while their youngest brother, Baby, was ill; and when Baby died, she did not bother to telegraph him. This flashback for Anita reveals not only the source of hatred between her parents, but the damaged version of love that she was exposed to as a child, characterized by manipulation and deceit.

The narration continues on with the wedding night. Anita repeatedly imagines telling Rajinder that she has made a mistake in marrying him, up until the moment they awkwardly make love. Making love with Rajinder remains a chore to Anita through the coming months. Through the completion of the winter and into the spring months, she slowly becomes used to being married to Rajinder, whom she finds "thoughtful and generous." She would spend her time during the hot, drought-ridden summer attending to household chores, bathing, and escaping to the world of her dreams during her much-anticipated afternoon naps. She would pretend that the monsoon was coming because "the smell of the wet earth and the sound of the rain have always made me feel as if I have been waiting for someone all my life."

Two weeks before the coming of the monsoon, Pitaji suffers a heart attack. As Asha and Anita ride to the hospital together, Asha speaks frankly of her abhorrence of her father, a severely obese, lifelong alcoholic who mistreated their mother. Anita is shocked and awed at her ability to be so frank and feels ashamed of her own sentimental feelings. Anita, Asha, and her mother take turns staying with Pitaji at the hospital over the next two weeks. Pitaji tells Anita stories about his childhood, and Anita began feeling tender towards him, but remained ever distrustful. He sobs to Anita at the thought that his wife cannot forgive him for Baby's death. Still,

Anita does not trust him. "Something about the story was both awkward and polished, which indicated deceit. But Pitaji never lied completely, and the tiring part was not knowing."

When Anita returns to her flat two weeks later she falls asleep, only to be awakened not only by the coming monsoon, but by a sudden, intense feeling of being completely in love with her husband. She prepares for Rajinder to come home and anxiously plans her approach to him.

When Rajinder comes home, although Anita is overcome by the new feeling of being in love, they go about their evening routine of a meal and listening to the radio. However, as the evening wears on and the monsoon begins its entrance to the city, Anita seduces Rajinder amid the downpour.

After making love, Rajinder and Anita lie in bed, talking. Anita's feeling of being in love is still very strong. Rajinder, however, seems to not perceive the change in Anita; he talks about himself and his pending promotion at the bank, and refuses to allow Anita to caress him. Rajinder goes on to talk about how his life is going according to a schedule he had made up when he was in college—a schedule that included obtaining a good job, obtaining promotions, obtaining material goods, and obtaining a wife. When Anita asks if she was part of his plans, he says that she did not fulfill his initial requirements, but he accepted her because he "believe[s] in moderation" and not in the idealized romances portrayed in the movies. "There are so many people in the world that it is hard not to think that there are others you could love more," he says, and, seeing that he has hurt Anita, quickly reassures her that he does love her, but he tries "not to be too emotional about it."

The conversation with Rajinder squelches the idealized, hyper-feeling of romance and love that Anita had cultivated all evening, and she sinks into disappointment.

Characters

Anita

Anita is the narrator of the story. She is approximately 56 years old at the time that she relates the story, which takes place when she is 26 years of age and newly married. The focus of Anita's story is the one moment in her life that she felt completely in

love with her husband, Rajinder. Anita and Rajinder's marriage was arranged. Although Anita was opposed to the marriage from the beginning, Anita, with a lack of action that characterizes her throughout the story, says nothing to derail the marriage. Instead, she expects that something will come up to cancel it. When the marriage does happen, it initially causes her great anxiety and feelings of terror. Anita characterizes herself as timid, unambitious, and as having been slow in school. She is prone to daydreaming and to self-delusion, both of which she uses as tools to escape from the anxiety her marriage causes her. Anita is also plagued by a sense of guilt and inadequacy that is the effect of her parents' manipulation of her, and especially, of her mother's favoritism of her more talented younger sister. Anita's fantasies and idealizations of love are contrasted sharply with the pragmatism of her husband, Rajinder—a pragmatism that ultimately shatters Anita's cherished idealizations.

Asha

Asha is Anita's younger sister. She is her sister's complete opposite: where Anita is timid and fearful of speaking her thoughts truthfully, Asha is forthright. Anita describes her as hard-working, ambitious, and intelligent. Asha eventually obtains a Ph.D. and moves to America, where she ends up in a happy marriage. Anita contrasts herself with her sister constantly and suffers from feelings of jealousy and inadequacy in comparison to her.

Ashok

Rajinder's older brother Ashok is a contrast to Rajinder. Anita describes him as "burly," and she is intimidated by him. He, unlike Rajinder, who went on to obtain a higher education in the city, remained a farmer in Busra like the rest of his family.

Baby

Anita's little brother, known as Baby, has died many years before the setting of the story. His death is the source of the bitterness that characterizes the relationship between Anita's parents.

Pitaji

Anita's father, Pitaji, suffers a heart attack; his recuperation in the hospital, and Anita's time spent taking care of him, comprise a significant portion of the story's plot. Anita has mixed feelings for Pitaji. Since her childhood, Pitaji has used Anita as a pawn against her mother. When he would come home drunk and her mother would treat him with disdain, Pitaji would manipulate Anita with his "impressive" tears and self-pity. Anita regards him as deceitful, as well as weak-willed.

The bitterness between Pitaji and Ratha is rooted in the death of Baby, the youngest in the family. Pitaji refused to come home from working in another city when Baby was sick, and Ratha therefore refused to inform Pitaji of Baby's death. Despite this deep bitterness, Pitaji claims to love his wife, but is unable to realize it.

Rajinder

In contrast to Anita's propensity for delusion, fantasy, and inaction, Rajinder, her husband, is a pure pragmatist and a man of action. He is the first in his family to obtain a college degree, and he is quickly moving up the ranks as a banker in Delhi. He and Anita are married via arrangement between their families. Anita at first regards Rajinder as a small, unattractive man and is privately opposed to marriage to him. However, over the months he proves to be an attentive and thoughtful husband, and she gets used to him. Rajinder shatters the love that Anita begins to feel for him at the conclusion of the story with his pragmatic views of love and his utterly practical description of their arranged marriage as an exchange of commodities.

Rajinder's Mother

Rajinder's mother clearly regards Rajinder as her favorite son. She is proud of him for becoming a banker and breaking away from the family farm. It is under his mother's influence that Rajinder chooses to marry Anita, who did not fulfill his earlier requirements for a wife; while he would have preferred someone with a higher degree, he bowed to his mother's wish for a daughter-in-law who was better suited to the traditional role of housekeeper.

Ratha

Anita describes her mother, Ratha, whom she calls "Ma," as clever and hard-working, much like her sister Asha. Although she loves her daughter Anita, Ratha favors the more ambitious Asha and is prone to making Anita feel inadequate and unworthy of love. Ratha is resentful of her husband for his negligence during the sickness and death of their youngest child. Nevertheless, she claims to love her husband, but is unable to realize it through her bitterness.

Themes

Love

"If You Sing like That for Me" portrays several differing views on love through ways in which different characters relate to the idea of love.

For Anita, having love is something that she dreams about, but is ultimately something she finds unattainable. Throughout her childhood and up until she is married, she feels loneliness, largely as a result of her mother favoring Asha, the more intelligent and ambitious daughter, over Anita. While Anita does not wish to have an arranged marriage, the one good thing she believes a marriage could bring is an end to her loneliness. Now, trapped in an arranged marriage characterized by formality and a lack of passion, she spends her days dreaming of the coming of the monsoon and, with it, an idealized lover who will dispel her loneliness: "I liked to lie on the bed imaging that the monsoon had come . . . the smell of wet earth and the sound of the rain have always made me feel as if I have been waiting for someone all my life and that person has not yet come." Love is in the realm of dreams, romance, and idealization for Anita. But when she finally attempts to project her ideas of love onto Rajinder, her husband, by transferring her idealizations to him, her idealistic approach to love is shattered by the reality that she and her husband Rajinder have a relationship based on commodity, and not on love. Anita's disillusionment is the central moment of the story.

Anita's father, whom she calls Pitaji, often uses love to manipulate his daughters and wife. For example, in order to retaliate against his wife, who has treated him with bitterness since the death of their youngest child, Pitaji would tell the young Anita, "No one loves me. You love me, don't you, my little sun-ripened mango?" When Pitaji tells Anita that he loves her best of all, she thinks he is manipulative and does not believe him, because she has always known Pitaji to use love as a tool of manipulation.

Rajinder, in stark contrast to Anita's romanticized idealizations of love, approaches the idea of love with a complete lack of romance and fantasy and, instead, with utter pragmatism. To Rajinder, the pursuit of love is an impediment to progress and success. Citing his successes in life and career thus far, he says, "I believe in moderation . . . Other people got caught up in love and friendship. I've

Topics for Further Study

- "If You Sing like That for Me" opens with the scene that closes the story: that of Anita awaking to the feeling of being in love with her husband Rajinder. Why do you think Sharma introduces the story this way? How does it affect the way in which the story is written and the story is told?

- How would you characterize the relationship between Anita and her mother? Anita and her father? Between Anita's parents themselves? How do these relationships affect Anita's ability to love Rajinder?

- A "foil" is the literary term for a character

whose attributes contrast sharply with those of the main character. Describe Anita's sister, Asha. How does Sharma use her as a foil to help us see Anita more clearly? What purpose do you think Asha has as a character and as a literary device in the story?

- The marriage of Anita and Rajinder, the main plot device of the story, is an arranged marriage—a common custom in India. Do you think that the story makes a statement about the practice of arranged marriage? What does the story say about this type of relationship and how do you think it is said?

---

always felt that these things only became a big deal because of the movies." And later: "There are so many people in the world that it is hard not to think that there are others you could love more." As well as regarding love as an obstacle in life, rather than a goal, Rajinder makes it clear that his marriage to Anita was based on his life goals and on commodity, rather than on any pursuit of love on his part: "I had wanted at least [a wife with] an M.A. and someone who worked, but Mummy didn't approve of a daughter-in-law who worked. I was willing to change my requirements." To him, obtaining a wife is like obtaining a promotion and obtaining a car. Rajinder's clear articulation of his views on love cause Anita's disillusionment.

Arranged Marriage

Arranged marriage is still the norm in India, and it is the means by which Rajinder and Anita are brought together. Anita is opposed to marrying Rajinder, but she agrees because, as a woman in India, in a culture that looks down on women remaining single and provides little opportunity for financial freedom for women, she has little option but to get married.

Ultimately, "If You Sing like That for Me" can be seen as a subtle indictment of the practice of

arranged marriages as an institution that treats people as little more than commodities and neglects to take human emotion and passion into consideration. Rajinder's words to Anita at the end of the story make it perfectly clear that their relationship is one based on commodity. She was chosen for her ability to make a good housewife and mother; he, it is known, was chosen by Pitaji for his ability to provide a comfortable life for Anita. Rajinder does not see love as an important facet of their relationship. His pragmatic understanding of their marriage as a practical arrangement ultimately denies Anita a relationship based on love for the rest of their marriage.

Sentimentality

In the same way that Pitaji uses love to manipulate his family, so too is he a master of using sentimentality as a tool of manipulation. Sentimentality is, by definition, the opposite of sincerity; the aim of sentimentality is to appeal to the emotions to elicit a desired response. In Pitaji's case, his sentimental words about his wife are designed to make Anita feel sorry for him. He says to her: "At your birthday, when [Ratha] sang, I said, 'If you sing like that for me every day, I will love you forever.'" Anita recognizes that these words are rehearsed; the practiced, staged nature of his expression of sentiment is therefore indicative of manipulation and deceit.

Subsequently, Anita herself indulges in sentimentality towards Rajinder in her sudden, over-the-top, over-romantic feelings towards him. The recurring motif of sentimentality throughout the story serves to question the authenticity of each character's love, especially that of Pitaji for his family and, later, of Anita for her husband.

Sibling Rivalry

Anita suffers throughout the story from a sharp sense of inadequacy. This is a direct result of her mother's constant comparison of her to her younger sister, Asha, whom Anita describes as ambitious, hard-working, and clever. Anita feels betrayed by her mother's public comparison between her daughters; likewise, Asha's own straightforward and confident behavior makes the timid Anita feel even more inadequate. Anita is plagued throughout the story by a feeling of bitterness at her sister's better fortune. This, together with her loneliness, causes Anita to constantly escape into daydreams.

Style

Point of View

"If You Sing like That for Me" is told in the first-person narrative voice from the point of view of the main character, Anita. A significant portion of the story is devoted to Anita's interior life and her very private feelings: she is secretly opposed to her arranged marriage; she experiences a barely controlled anxiety and depression when she is first married; and she indulges in daydreams and fantasies. Most significantly, Anita experiences a life-changing, intense, but temporary feeling of love towards her husband. It is the explanation of this feeling that is the central, driving purpose of the story. This focus would not be possible without the insider perspective that only a first-person voice can give.

Symbolism

The most prevalent symbol in the story is that of the monsoon. Anita directly associates the coming of the monsoon, which brings relief from the

drought of summer, as a symbol of the arrival of an imaginary lover, who, like the monsoon, would bring relief from the drought of her loneliness.

The monsoon becomes a reality as the story progresses, but it still remains a symbol of the arrival of love for Anita, so much so that she comes to believe that, with the coming of the monsoon, she has fallen deeply in love with Rajinder. The monsoon continues to carry its direct association with love as Anita, for the first time, kisses and fondles Rajinder with passion and desire in the rain.

By the end of the story, however, Anita, having been harshly disillusioned from her idealization of Rajinder as being the true love she had been waiting for, no longer sees romance in the rain: "The rain scratched against the windows. . . I was cold and tried to wrap myself in the sheet, but it was not large enough." No longer does the rain symbolize the arrival of relief, but merely the arrival of more disappointment and dissatisfaction.

Character as Foil

A "foil" is a character whose nature contrasts strongly with that of another character, thus highlighting the aspects that differ between them. Anita's sister Asha works as a foil to Anita. Asha is ambitious, clever, and hard-working, and her talents have enabled her to go to America. Her personality, which is also strong, confident, and not afraid of her own opinions, contrasts sharply with Anita, whose approach to life is characterized by inaction and feelings of inadequacy, timidity, and passivity. The sharp contrast between the sisters, particularly the contrast between proactivity and inaction—suggests that Anita could have escaped the fate of an arranged marriage and that her unhappiness is her own doing.

Historical Context

Political and Cultural Orientation of India

Although Akhil Sharma wrote "If You Sing like That for Me" in 1995, he placed it sometime during the prime ministership of Indira Gandhi, which lasted from 1966 to 1977 and again from 1980 to 1984, when she was assassinated by her Sikh bodyguards. Presumably, because the main character Anita speaks in praise of Gandhi, the story takes place before 1975, when Gandhi declared a State of Emergency in order to avoid impeachment, governing India as a regime and imprisoning scores of intellectuals and dissidents, causing the prime minister to fall, for a time, from favor.

Although there are no politics directly involved in the story, small details are included that hint at the political and cultural environment that Anita and Rajinder would have lived under in New Delhi during this time. Most notably Anita complains, "Perhaps love is different in other countries … where the climate is cooler, where a woman can say her husband's name, where the power does not go out every day, where not every clerk demands a bribe." As evidenced in this quote, the India that Sharma portrays with accuracy is characterized by government corruption on every level.

Sharma explained his interest in writing about India in an interview with *Publishers Weekly:*

> I presented India as incurably corrupt because it is. It's a place where individual power is so rampant because there are so few checks and balances. Once at a train station in India I saw this man who was chained to a bench. He had been caught [boarding a train] without a ticket. The stationmaster decided to punish him, and he kept him chained there three or four days. That's the sort of absolute power you see everywhere.

The India of Sharma's work is also characterized by certain contradictions: it is a country in which a woman is the prime minister, but where Anita is subservient to her husband; it is an India of high levels of education among its population, but is also surrounded by squalor; it is an India that is the largest democratic country on earth, but in which government corruption pervades even to the lowest everyday levels of operation.

The Practice of Arranged Marriages

The arrangement of marriages is still the prevalent custom in India, not only among Hindus but across other religious and cultural groups as well. The practice extends to Indian families across the diaspora, especially among first generation immigrants, who often return to India to find spouses for their sons and daughters.

Arranging marriages involves two families taking active roles in procuring spouses for their children. This usually involves determining the suitability of a match based on caste—or class—and the level of education, as well as on the dowry offered by a woman's family to that of the man. For women, there is an emphasis on beauty and suitability as a housekeeper and mother; for men, there is an emphasis on the ability to provide for a family. While in the past it was not uncommon for children to be betrothed at a young age, often to spouses whom they did not know or consent to, the story "If You Sing like That for Me" portrays arranging marriages as a more democratic practice—into which, in modern times, it has largely evolved. Anita, although she does not take advantage of her position, nevertheless has the opportunity to back out of the marriage; and her sister ends up choosing her own husband in America. Arranged marriages, it must be remembered, are the norm in India and are widely accepted, even though it is a foreign concept to Western sensibilities.

But arranged marriages in India have not gone without problems, particularly in light of women's rights. Most notably, in recent years there has been an epidemic of a practice known as "bride burning," in which a family, usually out of spite for receiving an unsatisfactory dowry, would cause a so-called kitchen accident in which the new daughter-in-law would be burned to death. CNN reported on August 18, 1996, that Indian police had received more than 2,500 reports of bride burning per year. Salman Rushdie's story "The Firebird's Nest," published in the June 23, 1997 issue of *The New Yorker,* directly addresses this topic.

Critical Overview

Akhil Sharma is one of a generation of up-and-coming Indian writers across the English-speaking diaspora that have appeared since the later 1990s. "If You Sing like That for Me," his debut work published in *The Atlantic Monthly* in 1995, drew instantaneous critical acclaim for him. It received the Second Place O. Henry Award for that year (beating out such better-known short story writers as Joyce Carol Oates and Jane Smiley) and was listed in *The Best American Short Stories 1996.*

But Sharma did not become a well-known literary name on the national scale until the publication of his first novel, *An Obedient Father,* which received nationwide review, was named a *New York Times* Notable Book, and was the recipient of the

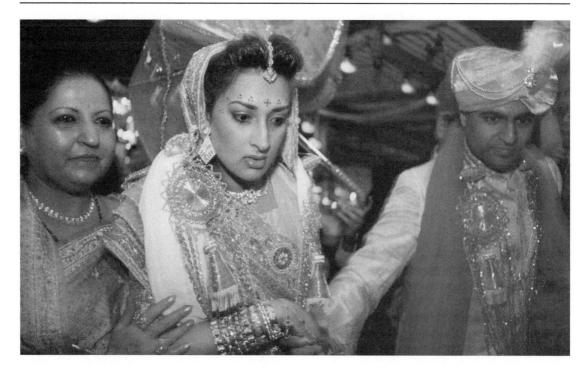

Hindu bride at her wedding, similar to the one described in "If You Sing like That for Me"

prestigious literary award, the Hemingway/PEN New England Award. The novel is set in India, as is much of Sharma's other work including "If You Sing like That for Me." Even though Sharma grew up in New Jersey, much of his work hearkens back to strictly Indian themes, placing him by virtue of not just his ethnicity but his subject matter amid a new generation of interesting, up-and-coming Indian writers working in the English language.

An Obedient Father was published a year after Jhumpa Lahiri, another Indian American writer based in Boston, won the Pulitzer Prize for her collection of short stories, *The Interpreter of Maladies,* and three years after the Indian writer Arundhati Roy received worldwide acclaim for her novel *The God of Small Things*—two big achievements in the literary world that have opened the doors of publishing houses to a new generation of Indian writers.

The sudden interest of publishers in Indian writers working in English was the subject of several newspieces at the turn of the twenty-first century. Mervyn Rothstein wrote in *The New York Times* of these writers:

> They are often called Midnight's Grandchildren in homage to another seminal Indian novel, Salman

Rushdie's *Midnight's Children,* the dark parable of Indian history since independence . . . . Now the new generation of writers have in many ways broken away from the magic realism that characterizes much of Mr. Rushdie's work.

Until the publication of Roy's *The God of Small Things,* Rushdie's most influential works—published in the 1980s—had been regarded as the quintessential English-language literature of India; but the new generation of writers is replacing Rushdie's magical realism and evolving a new voice.

Both Rothstein and *Time* magazine place Sharma amid this new generation of Indian writers. Rothstein calls his style "quintessentially American" and *Time* says his writing "should appeal to anyone with a taste for red-blooded American realism and farce."

Notably, these books, written by Indian writers in English from across the globe, focus on the subject of India and on Indian immigrants. In a market—English-language literature—that is dominated by white writers and white readers, it is remarkable that Indian writers have of late garnered so much attention, bringing a multicultural angle to the American experience, and giving a new voice to the experience of the Indian immigrant that had not previously been heard in the mainstream.

Criticism

Tamara Fernando

Fernando is a freelance writer and editor based in Seattle, Washington. In this essay, Fernando presents how the character of Anita in Sharma's story uses fantasy and idealism in an unsuccessful attempt to escape from reality.

The short story "If You Sing like That for Me," by Akhil Sharma, opens with a scene that is the focus of the story. Anita, the first person narrator, relates:

> ... [S]even months after my wedding, I woke from a short, deep sleep in love with my husband. I did not know then, lying in bed and looking out the window at the line of gray clouds, that my love would last only a few hours and that I would never again care for Rajinder with the same urgency. . . .

This opening scene is the central point around which the entire story is constructed. The story continues to relate the events leading up to this pivotal moment of intense and singular emotion for Anita, and then goes on to relate the events that cause her love to "last only a few hours" and never return. The narrative movement of the story, through its concentration on this pivotal moment in Anita's life, reveals the source of this otherwise inexplicable intense feeling of love: it is born of an idealism and escapism that characterizes Anita's views of life; and its permanent disappearance is brought about by the very reality that Anita continuously tries to escape.

The reality that Anita continuously tries to escape from is that of her marriage and, by extension, her position as a woman in India. As a woman in India, Anita doesn't have much of a choice but to have an arranged marriage to a man who can support her, and to raise his family. Although she does not want to, she is betrothed and wed to Rajinder, a man whom she meets only one time before her engagement, and whom she finds, at best, unremarkable.

Anita is bitter and sad that this is her assigned lot in life; she questions why she must remain in India and get married, while her younger sister, who was blessed with more ambition and cleverness than

she, will get to go to America and enjoy greater freedom there. However, Anita says nothing to anyone about being against marrying Rajinder, and instead faces the impending marriage by not accepting the reality of the situation. She does not believe that the match between her and Rajinder will be made, and she deludes herself into thinking that something will come up—"His family might decide that my B.A. and B.Ed. were not enough, or Rajinder might suddenly announce that he was in love with his typist"—that will save her from being married off. This ability to delude herself from reality is shown again and again in the story, and is crucial to the development of the climactic moment at which she suddenly feels in love with her husband.

The marriage initially causes Anita intense anxiety:

> I would think of myself with [Rajinder's] smallness forever, bearing his children, going where he went, having to open always to his touch, and whatever I was looking at would begin to waver, and I would want to run.

But slowly, she adapts to her life as a married housewife by pretending that it is not her that is leading her life: "I did not feel as if I were the one making love or cooking dinner or going home to see Ma and Pitaji . . . No one guessed that it was not me."

As before, Anita finds herself retreating into self-delusion in self-defense, and eventually, delusion becomes the driving impetus in her life; the most active part of her existence during these early months of marriage, the part of her life that brought her happiness, were her daily naps and the accompanying dreams. Throughout the narrative, Anita often discusses how she looks forward to sleeping with an urgency that eclipses other aspects of her life, even the sickness of her father. While she is caring for him, for example, she wants "desperately for Asha to come, so that I could leave, and bathe, and lie down to dream of a house with a red-tiled roof near the sea." Her obsession with sleep is indicative of a clinical depression; however, her obsession with sleep also reveals that she spends a significant portion of her life indulging in dreams as a method of escapism from that very life. In fact, she has replaced her real life—her dispassionate and formal marriage to Rajinder, her small flat in a stifling city—with a dream that represents her ideal of life.

That house near the sea she mentions is discussed at length earlier in the narrative, when Anita

What Do I Read Next?

- Winner of the 1980 Booker Prize, *Midnight's Children* is by India's most famous English-language writer, Salman Rushdie. Written in his trademark style of magical realism, the epic-like novel takes an angry and satirical aim at the political corruption of India and its post-colonial relationship with Pakistan.

- *The God of Small Things,* a novel by Arundhati Roy, was awarded the Booker Prize in 1997. Roy lives and writes in India. This, her debut novel, takes place in Kerala, India, in the 1960s. Roy tells the story of a young brother and sister who are subject to tragedy involving the death of their English cousin, caste brutality, and the squelching of socialist uprisings that marked the era and location.

- *The Interpreter of Maladies,* a collection of short stories written by Indian American Jhumpa Lahiri, was awarded the Pulitzer Prize in 1999. The collection of stories depicts the experiences of several different Indian characters, both in the United States and in India, and their struggles with their relationships in love and life.

- ''Cosmopolitan,'' a short story by Akhil Sharma, first appeared in *The Atlantic Monthly* in 1997 and received an O. Henry Award in 1998, for which it was published in *Prize Stories 1998: The O. Henry Awards,* edited by Larry Dark. ''Cosmopolitan'' is the story of a man who, after being abandoned by his wife and daughter, leads a lonely and solitary life in a New Jersey suburb until he begins a romance with the woman next door.

- Sharma's debut novel, *An Obedient Father,* received much critical acclaim upon publication in 2000, as well as controversy over its unflinching scenes of incest. The novel takes place in India during the presidency of Rajiv Gandhi. Told in the first person by Ram Karan, a corrupt civil servant with the guilt of past crimes on his shoulders, the corruption and downfall of Ram mirrors the political landscape of India at the time. *An Obedient Father* was long-listed for the Booker Prize, named a New York Times Notable Book, and received the Hemingway/PEN New England award for 2001.

- ''Surrounded by Sleep,'' by Akhil Sharma, a short story published in the *New Yorker,* December 2001, is the story of a young Indian boy whose family deals with the tragic paralysis of his older brother shortly after they move to New York state from India.

- Bharati Mukherjee's novel *Jasmine* (1989, reprint, Grove Press, 1999) is an almost fablesque account of what it means to become an American. Jasmine, widowed in India at a young age, travels as an illegal immigrant to the United States, crossing the country and reinventing her identity time and time again, while accumulating an extended, multi-cultural family for herself.

- Vikram Seth's novel *A Suitable Boy* (1993) is set in India during the presidency of Jawaharlal Nehru. It relates in a saga-like fashion the complex relationships between several families, both Hindu and Muslim, painting a realistic portrait of Indian society at the time.

- *Arranged Marriages: Stories* (1995), by Indian American writer Chitra Banerjee Divakaruni, presents the fictional stories of eleven Indian women, both in the United States and in India, and their different experiences with arranged marriage. As related in Sharma's ''If You Sing like That for Me,'' arranged marriage remains the prevalent means of forming marriages in India today.

- *Mimic Men* (1967), by Nobel Laureate V. S. Naipaul, is the story of a Caribbean-Indian's life as he travels from the Caribbean to Britain. The novel addresses, with satire and irony, issues of displacement that faced members of the diaspora of the post-colonial, Indian community.

describes her daily routine, which of course includes a time especially for sleep:

> Around two, before taking my nap, I would pour a few mugs of water on my head. I liked to lie on the bed imagining that the monsoon had come. Sometimes this made me sad, for the smell of wet earth and the sound of the rain have always made me feel as if I have been waiting for someone all my life and that person has not yet come. I dreamed often of living near the sea, in a house with a sloping red roof and bright-blue window frames, and woke happy, hearing water on sand.

Her dreams are a constructed, fantasy landscape that allow her to escape from her life and provide her with happiness, and to imagine that she is living not in a small flat with an insignificant man, but with a nameless figure who represents her one, ideal, love. Significantly, Anita associates the coming of the monsoon, which signals relief from the stifling heat of summer, with the arrival of the one special person into her life, thus, bringing relief from her loneliness. The coming of the monsoon becomes, then, a symbol for Anita of her version of an "ideal love": that is, one, specific, designated person that is meant for her. It is a feeling and a fantasy that, as indicated in the passage above, she indulges in as a daily ritual.

So disconnected is Anita from the realities of her daily life, that, when the pivotal moment occurs in which Anita suddenly finds herself intensely in love with Rajinder, it comes as a surprise. For although she has come to regard Rajinder, over the first seven months of their marriage, with affability, there is no indication of the development of stronger feelings. Indeed, immediately prior to experiencing this feeling, Anita had spent two weeks completely separated from Rajinder while she tended to her sick father. She specifically indicates that she did not miss Rajinder in the least.

However, looking closely at the passage describing her experience of this sudden feeling of love, certain clues that echo earlier aspects of the story arise to help explain her extreme emotional state. Significantly, the highly-charged motif of the monsoon enters the afternoon that Anita awakens to the feeling of being in love: "The sleep that afternoon was like falling. . . . I woke as suddenly. . . . It was cool, I noticed, unsurprised by the monsoon's approach—for I was in love."

The true arrival of the monsoon recalls the fantasy of the monsoon that Anita plays over and over in her mind and, with it, the arrival of her "ideal love" to dispel her loneliness. Now, Anita

> Rajinder refers to 'his wife' as a commodity, placing her in the same category as his job and a car."

awakens to the arrival of the monsoon and, simultaneously, to the otherwise inexplicable feeling of being in love with Rajinder.

So direct is this association, and so sudden and intense is her feeling, that the reader is led to believe that her feeling is somehow based, not on an authentic love specifically for Rajinder, but on the delusion she has been cultivating over the past months. It is almost as if her feeling is a conditioned response to her very deeply cultivated association between the coming of rain and her dream of experiencing true love. The monsoon—that which she has been dreaming of for months—has finally become a reality. Likewise, it seems that Anita makes the jump from dreaming of an ideal lover to idealizing Rajinder. She dotes on him nervously and idealize his physical appearance, thinking, for the first time, that he looks handsome and suddenly she desires to know him intimately.

At the opening of the story Anita says that her feeling of love, which came upon her only once in 30 years of marriage, lasted but a few hours. Such a sudden and complete ending to so intense an emotion seems as inexplicable then as the sudden appearance of this emotion. However, just as the emotion grew suddenly from her idealism, it was shattered by the sudden clarity of the reality of her marriage, which comes at the end of the story.

That night, after she and Rajinder make love, while her intense idealization of Rajinder persists, they lie together in bed. Rajinder speaks, with satisfaction, at how his life is going according to a self-imposed schedule. He lists all of his accomplishments and desires: "I wanted a car, and we'll have that in a year. I wanted a wife, and I have that." But when Anita asks playfully if he had planned for her specifically, he answers:

> No. I had wanted at least an M.A. and someone who worked, but Mummy didn't approve of a daughter-in-law who worked. I was willing to change my requirements. Because I believe in moderation. . . . Other

people got caught up in love and friendship. I've always felt these things only became a big deal because of the movies. . . .

There are so many people in the world that it is hard not to think that there are others you could love more.

Rajinder's words show Rajinder to be a pragmatist, which is a person whose approach to life is based on practicality and reality—the complete opposite of Anita, whose mind is occupied with ideals and fantasies. Rajinder's words describe the philosophies guiding his life. He does not believe that finding "true love" is a worthy pursuit of one's life, because he believes—as is evident through his mention of movies—that any importance placed on romance is based on fantasy and not on reality. He approaches the idea of love with a mathematic practicality—based on the sheer number of people in the world, the chances are that you can always find someone to love more. Thus, love is not a worthy pursuit for him.

Instead, he describes his marriage to Anita in terms that strip it of any romance, presenting it, with characteristic pragmatism, as what it literally is: an arrangement that was not based on love to begin with, but an exchange of commodities. Rajinder refers to "his wife" as a commodity, placing her in the same category as his job and a car. He recognizes that he was chosen by Anita's father for his proven ability to be a good provider. Anita, it turns out, was chosen for her potential to be a traditional housewife.

Rajinder's pragmatism towards love and marriage is based on reality and, thus, by its very nature, deconstructive of Anita's ideals and fantasies about love. It is the cause of the complete disappearance of her intense love for Rajinder. Her feeling of love is squelched not so much because Rajinder's pragmatism is cruel, but because Rajinder's realistic pragmatism reveals her feelings to be based not in reality, but in the ideals about love that he derides.

The story closes with a line that represents the sudden inadequacy that Anita, stripped of her ideals and fantasies of her husband and her life, now faces: "I was cold and tried to wrap myself in the sheet, but it was not large enough." Stripped of her ideals and fantasies, she is left to the cold reality that all of her escapism has been designed to protect her from—her despair at being, as a woman in India, a commodity to be given in marriage.

Source: Tamara Fernando, Critical Essay on "If You Sing like That for Me," in *Short Stories for Students,* Thomson Gale, 2005.

Joyce Hart

Hart is a freelance writer and author of several books. In the following essay, Hart searches for the source of the protagonist's unrequited love in Sharma's short story.

Anita, the protagonist in Akhil Sharma's story "If You Sing like That for Me" is a tragic figure of sorts. She appears to be in great need of love but cannot figure out how to get it. She does not ask for much out of life, and maybe that, in itself, is a major part of her problem. Does she truly know what she wants? Or does she just take whatever comes her way? Anita also comes from what appears to be an unsupportive emotional environment. But have these circumstances permanently scarred her or does she use her previous experiences as excuses to close herself off, denying herself the small but possibly significant opportunities to feel loved. The end of Sharma's short story has the power to wrench the hearts of even the most detached readers, knowing what they do about Anita by the time the conclusion of this sad story is reached. So are the consequences that befall Anita at the end of the story unearned or did she set herself up for the tragedy?

There are four major characters in Anita's life who are sources of potential love: her mother, her father, her sister, and her husband. None of them appears to understand Anita or know what she needs. For example, Anita believes that her mother loves her. But the comments that her mother shares at the restaurant when Anita is introduced to her future husband, Rajinder, make the reader question the significance of that love. "I wanted Anita to be a doctor," Anita's mother says after having just boasted about Anita's sister and two of Anita's uncles. Then her mother adds: "but she was lazy and did not study." Anita quickly dismisses her mother's criticism. She and her mother loved each other, Anita states, but there were times when something inside her mother "would slip and she would attack me." Now, is this statement an honest analysis of her mother or is Anita rationalizing away an emotional pain?

In an attempt to further explain her mother, Anita adds more information that pretty much sums up Anita's own personality. First, Anita builds her mother up by stating that she is "so clever." And it is this cleverness that stymies Anita. It throws her off guard, leaving her feeling inferior. But Anita does not seem to reflect on this, or at least not at this point in the story. Rather, she deflects it, preferring to believe that it is her love of her mother that makes

Anita feel "helpless." Later in the story, however, Anita states a little more honestly that she believes her mother did not love her as much as she loved Anita's sister. Once Anita admits this to the reader (and therefore to herself), she is also able to confess that knowing this fact has allowed her to rescind some of love she originally expresses for her mother. She takes a step once removed from her emotions and even boldly mocks her mother's tears and her mother's pain at the loss of a baby. "Ma knew how to let her voice falter as if the pain were too much to speak of," Anita says, inferring that her mother's tears were merely a dramatic display, intended to arouse emotions in those who were observing her. But Anita does not fall for her mother's play-acting. In contrast, Anita states that she is "more impressed" with her father's tears. Her comparison is done, but necessarily to demonstrate how much she loves her father. Rather, she seems to do this as if to say that she does not much love her father, but she loves her mother even less. It is difficult to understand where the love exists between daughter and mother. Although Anita believes there is love between them, the story does not portray any moment in which that love is truly exposed. It is also impossible to determine whether it is the mother who has not nourished the daughter or the daughter who has turned away. In other words, has the mother not given love to Anita, or does Anita not know how to receive it?

What is known is that in the absence of a full-hearted mother's love, Anita turns to her father. She does not, however, rush into his arms. She might love her father, but she does so from a great distance. And from the details that are provided in the story, there are many reasons why she has moved far away from him. The first time Anita's father is introduced, he does not make a remarkable impact. He tries "to impress Rajinder [Anita's future husband] with his sophistication," by speaking in English. However, Anita demonstrates to the reader that her father's English is not very good. As soon as Anita shares this information with the reader, the story immediately jumps to a scene in the restaurant where the family is dining. It is a visual image of a swinging door opening to the kitchen, where a cow is standing "near a skillet." It is hard not to associate Anita's father with this cow, since just previous to this image, Anita was talking about her father. Now, since the story takes place in India, the cow is not as misplaced as it would have been had the restaurant been located in New York City, for example. But keep in mind that the intrusion of the

> She seems only to pretend to love her father, imagining some merit in his character, no matter how small it might be. Her heart is closed to him, even though she might wish somewhere deep inside of her, that it was not."

cow into the story was purposeful. So what was intended? Well, at the least, the image is distracting enough to make the reader have an uneasy feeling. And this could be the author's attempt to convey a similar uneasiness that Anita was experiencing as she listened to her father's broken English, especially in knowing that his display was intended to impress her future husband. In other words, through Anita's eyes, her father is as misplaced as the cow.

In another part of the story, Anita recalls a different time that her father used English. It was shortly after her wedding ceremony, when her father whispers that he loves her. These words make her cry but not for the sentiment that could have been shared between them. Rather, Anita cries because she remembers her father coming home drunk so many times in her youth. "No one loves me," her father would often tell her as he held her in his lap, the smell of alcohol saturating his breath. "You love me, don't you, my little sun-ripened mango?" One would think that Anita might have received some emotional nourishment from these outbursts. But she was well aware that her father was drunk when he would say this, and she knew his intentions were not fully directed at her. She was wise enough to realize her father's comments were expressed in an attempt to grab Anita's mother's attention: "He would be watching Ma to make sure she heard." In the morning after his drunken sprees, Anita would care for him, bringing him water so he could take medicine that would make him heave. And it was his vomit, not his love, that Anita associated with the whispered words of English that he offered on her wedding day. And it was these experiences that eventually caused her callous feelings toward her father.

So by the time her father suffered a heart attack, Anita had very little compassion left for him. He was "so fat," she states, that the heart attack did not come as a surprise. "I felt no fear," Anita says, referring to the idea of her father's possible death. Then she adds: "perhaps because I just did not care." Momentarily, however, Anita does feel a resurgence of love. Her father's scare with death shakes a vague apology out of him as he is recovering. Anita is not sure what he is apologizing for, but she is somewhat pleasantly surprised by his words. "I suddenly wanted to love him," she states. But it might have been too little, too late. Their chances of love were scarred by the past they share. Anita could no longer trust him. Instead of accepting her father's apologies and offering forgiveness in exchange, Anita ends up turning cynical. "Why do people always think hurting others is all right, as long as they hurt themselves as well?" In the end, Anita decides that she has had enough. When she hears her father lament one more time about how his wife does not love him, Anita tries to persuade him that he is wrong. But it is not evident that Anita believes her own arguments. If she cannot forgive her father, how could she believe that any one else could? Even though she tries to convince her sister to see some good in their father, one can't help but imagine that it is really Anita trying to convince herself. She seems only to pretend to love her father, imagining some merit in his character, no matter how small it might be. Her heart is closed to him, even though she might wish somewhere deep inside of her, that it was not.

Anita's sister Asha barely appears in the story at all. In comparison to the other characters, Asha seems insignificant. But this is not completely true. Asha could have been a role model for Anita, even though she is younger than Anita. Instead, Asha is a sort of thorn in Anita's side. Anita wishes she had done everything that Asha has done. When their father takes them out of school at a very young age, Asha fights her way back to the classroom, insisting on a good education despite her father's belief that it was a waste of time to educate women. When they go to college, it is Asha who works hard and earns a scholarship to go to the United States, a place that Anita had dreamed of going. And when she marries, it is Asha who finds a partner whom she can love. Anita has done none of these things. But she could have. She lacks ambition and determination. She also lacks self-esteem. But why is this so? Why has one come out a fighter and the other come out a loser? At one point in the story, Anita implies her

own guilt, admitting that one cannot always blame parents for the disappointments of life.

And finally, there is Anita's husband, Rajinder—a man that Anita only passively chose to marry and, admittedly, a man she does not love. As the story opens, Anita is staring out at the sky. It is a summer morning sky but it is "a line of gray clouds" that Anita is focusing on. The clouds will eventually blossom, filling the skies with darkness and finally bursting in rain. These rain clouds are a good metaphor of Anita's life. Although the rain brings a welcomed relief from the heat and drought, if one focuses only on the temporary loss of sunlight, the rain can be depressive. Likewise, it depends on how one looks at life. For instance, Anita seems barely interested in her own life. She allows others to make decisions for her. Then, she attempts to make do with what comes her way. She has no one to blame for her situation but herself. She had no intention of marrying Rajinder. "The neutrality of Rajinder's features, across the restaurant table from me," Anita relates upon the first time she saw him, "reassured me that we would not meet after that dinner." She then adds that she could not "imagine spending my life with someone so anonymous." This conclusion, however, does not stop her from responding in the affirmative, when a couple of days later her father asks her if she would marry the man. For the remainder of the story, Anita attempts to attract her husband's attention. Although she believes herself to be unattractive, she does her best to wrap herself in decorative apparel that might allure him, even to the point of forsaking her own comfort. But nothing seems to work. It is not until she has left Rajinder in order to assist her father during his recuperation from a heart attack, that Anita thinks of Rajinder in terms of love. She comes home hopeful that at last she has found what she has been looking for. Rajinder, however, quickly dismisses her, letting her know that she is but one more detail in his plan to become a successful man. Rajinder, in the end, is incapable of love.

So when one carefully examines the circumstances that are presented, one has to question this short story as a caution or a tragedy, or perhaps both. Yes, it is tragic when people cannot find love. But who in this story is truly to blame for that? Is Anita a tragic figure because she did everything within her means to find love and was turned down at every opportunity? Or is she a pathetic character who did not have enough gumption to fight for what she wanted? These are questions the reader must attend carefully, for the narrative and the plot oscillate between tragic circumstance and passive desire. As a result, unrequited love is exposed in all its complexity as the source of very personal and familial tensions.

Source: Joyce Hart, Critical Essay on "If You Sing like That for Me," in *Short Stories for Students,* Thomson Gale, 2005.

Gale

In the following essay, the author discusses responses to Sharma's first novel titled An Obedient Father.

According to a *Publishers Weekly* reviewer, Akhil Sharma's debut novel, *An Obedient Father,* made him a "supernova in the galaxy of young, talented Indian writers." An Indian-born, American-educated investment banker, Sharma had been published in such periodicals as *Atlantic* and *New Yorker* by the time he was twenty-three, as well as serving as a screenwriter to Steven Spielberg, prior to publishing *An Obedient Father.*

In *An Obedient Father,* Sharma introduces Ram Karan, an aging and second-rate functionary in New Delhi, and tells the story of acts of incest he committed against his daughter when she was a teenager, presenting it against the broader picture of a thoroughly corrupt modern Indian society. As black-humored novels go, said Richard Eder in a *New York Times* review, this book "weaves the national into the personal without a trace of the didactic. What is more astonishing is [Sharma's] success in joining the amiably picaresque aspects of the corruption—India's and Ram's—with the ghastly evil of its underside."

Lowly, slovenly, and unambitious, Ram Karan works as a bagman for the unethical head of a Delhi school district. His chief job is collecting bribes for himself and for his superiors. Compounding his questionable lifestyle is the fact that his now-adult daughter, Anita, a widow, has come to live with him, bringing her eight-year-old daughter. The presence in his house of his daughter and her youngster stir Karan's guilty memories of the incestuous relationship he had with his daughter long ago, but he is powerless to curb his impulses, and finds himself heading toward a similar situation with his granddaughter and a dramatic confrontation with Anita. "It's easy to brand Karan as vile and despicable, but such epithets don't capture the complexity of his personality or the subtlety of Sharma's prose," declared *New York Times* writer Akash Kapur. "Karan—like most of Sharma's characters, who

scheme their way through a fog of self-deception and self-righteousness—is less evil than weak. He possesses little of evil's dark grandeur and all the pathos of a man too frightened to do anything but play by the rules in a world in which corruption, extortion and even murder are the norm."

Nation contributor Amitava Kumar took a similar view. "It is to Sharma's great credit as a novelist that I was as often horrified by Karan's abuses and compulsive degradations as I was held captive by his pellucid dissection of shame that exposes a geography of self-delusion and national wrongdoing." To Shashi Tharoor, writing in the *Washington Post,* the author's American upbringing put him at a disadvantage in describing some of the realities of Indian life. "The inaccuracies are at first mildly irritating, then become intolerable. The making of cheese was never 'illegal' in Delhi; the soft drink was called Lehar Pepsi, not Pepsi Lahar. . . . since many of these details involved pivotal elements in Sharma's plot, they render much of his story implausible to an Indian reader." Inaccuracies aside, however, Tharoor praised Sharma as a novelist who "proves that it is possible to write engagingly about unsympathetic characters."

"Guilt has always been pervasive in my view of the world," Sharma told Sybil Steinberg in a *Publishers Weekly* interview. "I feel guilty because I have a brother who's very sick. I think anything I would write would examine that motivation." As for causing a scandal by painting a negative picture of Indian society, Sharma noted, "I presented India as incurably corrupt because it is. It's a place where individual power is so rampant because there are so few checks and balances." He believed that he would not suffer the same slings and arrows as did author Philip Roth when the latter published the incendiary Jewish comedy-of-manners, *Goodbye, Columbus,* in the 1960s: "There's a saying in India: If you want to keep a secret, put it in a book. I believe that this book will not be read by the Indian community."

Source: Gale, "Akhil Sharma," in *Contemporary Authors Online,* Gale, 2002.

Sources

Rothstein, Mervyn, "India's Post-Rushdie Generation; Young Writers Leave Magic Realism and Look at Reality," in the *New York Times,* July 3, 2000, p. E1.

Rushdie, Salman, ''The Firebird's Nest,'' in the *New Yorker,* June 23, 1997.

Sachs, Andrea, ''The Subcontinentals: Young, Internationally Savvy Indian Writers Are Making Smart, Splashy Literary Debuts,'' in *Time,* Vol. 155, No. 14, April 10, 2000, p. 130.

Sharma, Akhil, ''If You Sing like That for Me,'' in *The Best American Short Stories 1996,* edited by John Edgar Wideman and Katrina Kenison, Houghton Mifflin, 1996, pp. 282–306.

Yasui, Brian, ''Bride-Burning Claims Hundreds in India,'' *CNN.com,* http://www.cnn.com/WORLD/9608/18/bride.burn/, August 18, 1996, (accessed November 19, 2004).

Further Reading

Forbes, Geraldine, *Women in Modern India,* Cambridge University Press, 1996.

A history of women, politically and socially, from the nineteenth century through the end of the twentieth century in India, Forbes's well-researched work includes first-person accounts of women's true experiences of living in India.

Hagedorn, Jessica, ed., *Charlie Chan Is Dead: An Anthology of Contemporary Asian American Fiction,* Penguin Books, 1993.

Hagedorn's anthology was a breakthrough publication when it came out; it is perhaps the best known anthology of writing from across the Asian American spectrum, including writers with origins in East Asia, South Asia, and Southeast Asia. It was published at a time when the study of Asian American literature was just coming into focus in universities, and writers like Amy Tan were just beginning to receive attention from the general American readership.

Mehrotra, Arvind Krishna, *History of Indian Literature in English,* Columbia University Press, 2003.

Two hundred years of Indian literature written in English—up to the publication of *The God of Small Things* by Arundhati Roy—are covered in this collection of historical essays, including well-known poets and novelists as well as scientists and sociologists whose writings have made a significant mark on the development of English-language literature in India.

Rustomji-Kerns, Roshni, ed., *Living in America,* Westview Press, 1995.

Living in America is one of the first anthologies published in the United States featuring fiction and poetry from largely unknown Indian writers in America, reflecting on the Indian American experience.

In the Zoo

Jean Stafford

1953

Jean Stafford was a post–World War II American author whose fiction remained within the realist and symbolist traditions dating back to the nineteenth century. Influential in the high literary society of her time, Stafford was married to the poet Robert Lowell for six years and then married to two other men. She never forgot her rural Western roots and difficult childhood, however, and themes from her younger life continually reappear in her writings. One such story, entitled ''In the Zoo,'' is a psychological portrait of two orphans remembering their traumatic childhood in a small Rocky Mountain town.

Stafford published ''In the Zoo'' in 1953, as the most active years of her career as a fiction writer were drawing to a close. Two years later, the story won the O. Henry Memorial Award for best short story of the year. One reason for the story's success is its rich characterization, through which Stafford creates memorable characters such as Gran, the manipulative and cruel foster mother of the girls, and Mr. Murphy, a jobless, alcoholic Irishman who treats the sisters with kindness and love. The story is also compelling because of its sophisticated use of symbolism—particularly the animals that represent various people and themes from the sisters' childhood—and its striking, moving climax, which occurs when Gran turns the sisters' puppy into an attack dog and lets it kill Mr. Murphy's monkey. Through these techniques, Stafford comments on themes of psychological trauma, confinement, and the nature of love and companionship. ''In the Zoo''

is now available in *The Collected Stories of Jean Stafford* (1969), which won a Pulitzer Prize in 1970.

Author Biography

Born in the rural Californian town of Covina in 1915, Stafford was the youngest child of four. Her father was a fiction writer who lost his fortune in the stock market while living in San Diego in 1920, at which point the family moved to Colorado and struggled to live on the income from the children's jobs, allowances from their family, and the income Stafford's mother collected from taking sorority girls as boarders in their home. Stafford attended the University of Colorado on a scholarship, where her roommates introduced her to drinking and sexual experimentation until one of them committed suicide in her presence, an event which deeply affected Stafford and her writing. After graduating with a degree in English, Stafford traveled to Europe on a fellowship from the German government to study philology at the University of Heidelberg.

At the Boulder Writers' Conference in the summer of 1937, Stafford met the poet Robert Lowell, with whom she was in a car accident that left her with serious and disfiguring injuries. They were married in 1940, but divorced six turbulent years later, after Stafford had begun a career as a novelist and had published the bestseller *Boston Adventure* (1944). In 1947, Stafford published *The Mountain Lion*, which did not sell as well as her previous novel. After her divorce from Lowell, Stafford began to publish short stories in the *New Yorker* magazine. In 1950 she married Oliver Jenson, a staff photographer at *Life* magazine. She divorced him in 1953, after she published her third novel, *The Catherine Wheel* (1952), which is about an aristocratic Bostonian woman and the twelve-year-old boy who is in her charge.

Stafford continued to publish short stories, including "In the Zoo," through the mid-1950s, in magazines and collections. From 1959 until his death in 1963, she was married to the *New Yorker* columnist A. J. Liebling. In 1969, she published *The Collected Stories of Jean Stafford*, which won a Pulitzer Prize. By this time, however, she had stopped writing fiction, concentrating instead on reviews, articles, and essays. Biographers have speculated a variety of reasons for this shift, ranging from Stafford's health problems and heavy drinking to her desire to keep to the realistic style of writing that

was no longer the dominant form in the 1960s. Stafford spent the final fifteen years of her life in relative seclusion at her home in eastern Long Island, dying of complications following a stroke in 1979 and leaving her estate to her housekeeper.

Plot Summary

Sitting in a zoo in Denver, Colorado, two sisters eat popcorn while watching a blind polar bear, a family of grizzlies, a black bear, and a group of monkeys. The narrator's sister Daisy is accustomed to seeing off her sister in Denver every other year, while the narrator is on her way back east. Daisy comments that the polar bear reminds her of someone named Mr. Murphy. This comment sets the sisters to thinking about their childhood in Adams, a small town fifty miles north of Denver. Orphaned at eight and ten, the sisters grew up there with a foster mother unrelated to them called Mrs. Placer, or Gran, who ran a boarding house in which, like her, all of the boarders complained and gossiped about the rest of the town.

Mr. Murphy was a gentle, jobless Irishman who spent his time drinking, playing cards, and enjoying all of his animals, which ranged from a parrot that spoke Parisian French to two small, "sad and sweet" capuchin monkeys. Before they reached adolescence, the girls loved him and his monkeys, thinking of them like "husbands and fathers and brothers." One day Mr. Murphy gives them a present of a half-collie, half-Labrador retriever puppy. At first, Gran would not hear of keeping him, imagining all of the horrible things he would do, but she agrees after she hears that the puppy would make a good watchdog.

The puppy, whom the girls named Laddy, made a great mess at first but learned quickly and soon Laddy became a charming dog, escorting them to school and enjoying himself with hunting weekends in the mountains. Gran became angry after one of these long weekends, however, and decided to train Laddy herself, renaming him "Caesar" and taking him away from the girls. By disciplining him with a chain and occasional cuffs on the ears, Gran changed Caesar into a powerful attack dog. The police demanded that he be muzzled after he began biting and harassing strangers at the house, but Gran largely ignored them.

Upset, the girls did not tell Mr. Murphy what was wrong because they knew, from the time a boy squirted his skunk with a water pistol and Mr. Murphy responded by throwing a rock at the boy's back, that he could become dangerously angry. However, Mr. Murphy heard about the dog's transformation anyway and determined, enraged, to confront Gran. When Mr. Murphy arrived outside of Gran's house with the eldest of his monkeys on his shoulder, Gran released Caesar, who pounced on the monkey and killed it. Mr. Murphy began sobbing; very early the next morning he poisoned Caesar's meat, killing him.

When the sisters saw the dog dying, they ran into the mountains wishing they could flee the town. The police arrested Mr. Murphy while he was giving the monkey a solemn requiem mass, but no one felt sorry for Gran, and he was released. Mr. Murphy withdrew even more from society, giving his monkey a daily requiem, and the sisters could never visit him again. Gran continued to manipulate the girls, undermining the narrator's relationship with a boyfriend and ruining her pleasure from being cast in a play.

At the zoo, the sisters discuss why they never ran away, and while Daisy cites the difficulties of the Great Depression, the sisters agree that the real problem was the guilt that Gran made them feel. The narrator muses about the long-term effects of the years with Gran, and the sisters rush to catch a cab so Daisy can take her adrenaline injection for asthma. They both feel overwhelmed and affected by the experience, but as they board the train they gossip about the porter in a manner similar to that of Gran and the boarders. The narrator writes Daisy a letter from the train about how nothing can be as bad now that Gran is dead, while a Roman Catholic priest waits for the writing table. The narrator then breaks out in an "unholy giggle," picking up a gossip column to disguise the real reason for her laughter, whatever it may be.

Jean Stafford

Characters

Mr. Beaver

One of Gran's boarders, Mr. Beaver leaves for the Y. M. C. A. after Caesar attacks him in the dining room.

Blind Polar Bear

The blind polar bear at the zoo reminds the sisters of Mr. Murphy and inspires their reminiscences. "Patient and despairing," he is an object of scorn, called a "'back number,'" or something out-of-date, by a farmer and the monkeys across from him. Why the polar bear reminds them of Mr. Murphy, aside from the fact that he is scorned by the gossiping society of monkeys, is one of the intriguing aspects of the story.

Caesar

When he is a puppy, before Gran changes his name to Caesar and makes him an attack dog, Laddy is a genial and charming puppy. The sisters received him as a present from Mr. Murphy, and they treat him with love, pampering him and allowing him to go away for long hunting weekends. After Gran takes charge of him, however, chaining him to the house and cuffing him on the ears when he misbehaves, the dog rapidly becomes an "overbearing, military, efficient, loud-voiced Teuton," which is like a description of a German soldier. Gran's philosophy with Caesar is that, "A dog can have morals like a human," but his morals rapidly become nothing but viciousness and ruthlessness.

Clancy

The black bear in the zoo is "a rough-and-tumble, brawling blowhard," whose roaring bravado would make him a man of action were he a human.

Daisy

Two years older than her sister the narrator, Daisy "lives with a happy husband and two happy sons" in a town two hundred miles west of Denver. The girls had moved there to work at a dude camp, or a ranch that city people visit, after Grandma died; Daisy presumably stayed there while her sister went east. Clumsy and awkward as a child, Daisy is asthmatic as an adult and needs to carry around injections of adrenaline. She is extremely close to her sister despite the fact that they see each other very infrequently, and they share the bond of helping each other through the "terror and humiliation" of their childhood. When the time comes to leave her sister at the end of the story, Daisy reveals how much she cares about her sister by clinging to her on the train platform.

Jimmy Gilmore

Jimmy is a boyfriend of the narrator's, but Gran makes the narrator uncomfortable about the relationship, and it ends soon afterwards.

Gran

Gran, which is what Mrs. Placer asks the girls to call her, is the sisters' foster mother, whom the narrator describes as "possessive, unloving, scornful, complacent." A childhood friend of their grandmother, she takes in the orphaned sisters and becomes the beneficiary of their parents' life insurance policy, which the girls have been told is quite meager. Gran is a childless widow who moved to Colorado for the sake of her dying, tubercular husband, and she spends her time gossiping about the people of Adams. An extremely powerful and effective manipulator, Gran surrounds herself with people loyal to her by making them feel that she is a good-hearted and self-sacrificing person. Her main method of keeping the girls under her thumb is to make them feel guilty, convincing them that they owe her for the sacrifice she has made in taking care of them.

The narrator provides a one-sided evaluation of Gran, and neither she nor Daisy acknowledges any gratitude to her for bringing them up. Although a reader might decide that Gran is at least somewhat generous and motherly, the narrator makes a strong case for her foster mother's basic cruelty by providing numerous examples of her slyness and hypocrisy. Gran constantly urges her foster daughters and her boarders to resent others. She gets what she wants by tricking and deceiving those around her. Her only motivation for doing any good deeds is money (although the sisters' parents' life insurance policy is apparently a pittance) and an excuse to feel self-righteous. The most horrific example of Gran's pitiless nature, however, comes at the dramatic moment when she allows Caesar to kill Mr. Murphy's monkey. The fact that none of the townspeople have any sympathy for Gran after Mr. Murphy kills Caesar reveals that they, like the narrator, believe her to have purposefully killed the monkey. This episode serves to illustrate the most damning flaws of her character.

Laddy

See Caesar

Mr. Murphy

A "gentle alcoholic ne'er-do-well," Mr. Murphy is the girls' close friend and a fellow victim of Gran's cruelty. Gran calls him "black Irish," which refers to Irish people with dark hair but has a vague connotation of Spanish roots. She is right that he has very heavy drinking habits, since he is drunk nearly all of his waking hours. He loves his animals very deeply and protectively, but his brand of love is not possessive or demanding, which is why the girls think of him and his monkeys as representing the idealized male figures in their lives. On the other hand, however, Mr. Murphy has the capacity to become quite violent when he is angry, and he is antisocial to the point that he is unable to function.

The sisters have difficulty telling him much or confiding in him, for example, about Gran's transformation of Laddy, because of this unpredictable side, and because they cannot find a way to speak directly or earnestly to him. Their idealization of Mr. Murphy is not solely the result of having no other male figures in their lives, however, and the story reveals a great admiration for his kindness and sweet nature. Whatever his faults and peculiarities, he is a kind and generous man who cares about them. He is the right kind of figure to balance with the part of their lives dominated by Gran, and he is vital to the girls' difficult struggle to grow up healthily and independently.

Narrator

The unnamed narrator of the story is a humorous and affable but socially awkward woman who is still attempting to escape her difficult childhood in rural Colorado. She is similar in character and temperament to her sister Daisy, and they have an extremely strong bond stretching back to their traumatic childhood. However, while Daisy has stayed west of Denver and started a family where the sisters had worked after Gran died, the narrator has moved east where she is a "spinster," or an older unmarried woman.

Pondering why they stayed in Adams so long, the narrator and Daisy decide that it was partly due to the financial hardships of the Great Depression, but chiefly because Gran connived to make them feel guilty and trapped. There is occasionally a sense that the narrator is biased and perhaps somewhat bitter in her recollections of Gran, but this bitterness is grounded in numerous examples of Gran's cruel parenting style. The only provocations the sisters seem to have given her were their lack of social graces and awkwardness, which the narrator and her sister retain to some degree in their middle age, and these traits are due in large part to the guilt and insecurity that Gran made them feel. When she criticizes the train porter and mocks the Roman Catholic priest at the end of the story, the narrator reveals that she has absorbed a number of Gran's personality traits, and that the difficulties of her childhood still haunt her.

Pastor

The pastor of the sisters' church tries to raise their spirits about going to live with Mrs. Placer, candidly stressing her Christian goodness and "sacrifice" in taking care of the girls.

Mrs. Placer

See Gran

Shannon

Shannon is Mr. Murphy's elder capuchin monkey, the one that Caesar kills when Mr. Murphy is about to confront Gran. "Serious and humanized, so small and sad and sweet," the two monkeys are touching and gentle creatures that the sisters consider like the male figures of their childhood.

Themes

Childhood Trauma

Daisy and the narrator's psychological trauma, stemming from their childhood with Gran, is not confined to their flashback, and it does not end with Gran's death. In fact, it continues to trouble them into their middle age, as is clear from the immediate urgency of the sisters' memories when Daisy mentions Mr. Murphy, from the intensity of their emotional farewell, and from the earnest letter that the narrator writes to her sister from the train. The sisters are no longer traumatized and defenseless orphans, but they are still attempting to deal with the "terror and humiliation" of their childhood.

The sisters' close relationship with each other and their abilities to build new lives for themselves suggest some hope in their attempt to move beyond their earlier psychological trauma. However, there are a number of clues at the end of the story to suggest that the narrator and her sister have not emerged from their difficult childhood at all. The sisters' somewhat snide comments about the porter at the end of the story, which sound very much like the reaction that Gran and her boarders might have to the situation, support this reading of the story, as does the narrator's final laugh, if one takes its "unholy giggle" to be similar to Gran's.

Confinement and Control

Confinement and control, including power over those who have been excluded and shunned from society, are common themes in Stafford's short story. Mr. Murphy, his animals, the animals in the zoo, Daisy, and the narrator have all been terrorized with harassment and scorn and confined in various kinds of cages. Their personality types are part of the reason for their separation from those around them. Mr. Murphy is a good example of an outcast with little desire to integrate himself into normal society. However, Stafford emphasizes that it is mainly due to society's manipulative cruelty that confined characters feel too guilty and insecure to escape from their tormentors. Gran and her boarders, like the monkeys in the zoo, represent the subtle and possessive nature of the social structures that confine people into obedience and rob them of their independent joys.

However, the themes of confinement and control in Stafford's story are more complex than a straightforward tale of two orphans struggling against an oppressive society represented by Gran and her gossiping boarders. Characters in the story such as Laddy and the girls tend to internalize their own confinement until they actually believe that it is right and proper. This is why Caesar can gradually become such a vicious dog, and why there is the suggestion that the sisters have internalized some of Gran's habits. For Stafford, the controlling mindset

Topics for Further Study

- Research the economic and social conditions of the Great Depression, focusing on its effects on small towns in the American West. What lifestyle changes were necessary for widows like Gran, or orphans like Daisy and the narrator? How did those unable to find work survive? How desperate were conditions for various types of people in a town like Adams? Discuss the defining elements of this period and the effects that its economic troubles might have had on young women like the sisters of "In the Zoo."

- There is some ambiguity in Stafford's story over whether Daisy and the narrator manage to emerge from the psychological difficulties of their childhood, or whether they continue to be traumatized in their middle age. How do you feel about the sisters' ability to deal with their childhood in later life? Describe how each sister has reacted to growing up with Gran and discuss how this experience continues to shape their later lives. What is Stafford implying about the effects of childhood trauma? How does she address the difficulties of overcoming a childhood characterized by an oppressive and manipulative caretaker?

- Animals are important symbols in Stafford's story, expressing the main themes and bringing their meaning to life. Using a dictionary of "archetypes," or universal symbols, explore the associations of the animals of "In the Zoo." Then, discuss what the various animals represent in Stafford's story and why you think she uses

each animal for that role. How do the archetypical meanings of these animals compare and contrast to their functions in Stafford's story? What other symbols does Stafford use in her story, and how do they relate to universal archetypes?

- Many of Stafford's short stories explore a difficult childhood, often from the standpoint of an adult dealing with traumatic memories. Read several of her other stories, available in *The Collected Stories of Jean Stafford*, such as "The Liberation," "The Tea Time of Stouthearted Ladies," "The Philosophy Lesson," and "The Mountain Day." Discuss these stories in relation to "In the Zoo." How do they compare in style and technique? How are their themes similar; how are they different? How does Stafford treat childhood trauma in each story? How do the female characters differ in their ability to cope with this trauma and move past it?

- Stafford often uses events from her own life directly or indirectly in her fiction. Read about Stafford's life in a source such as David Roberts's *Jean Stafford: A Biography* (1988), and speculate about the ways in which "In the Zoo" may be autobiographical. How do you think Stafford's own childhood affected her treatment of the events of the story? What new insight about the story do you gain from what you read in Stafford's biography? Discuss how the autobiographical elements of "In the Zoo" enhance or detract from the quality of the story.

is like a disease, capable of spreading into the psychology of the animal or person being confined and making it very difficult for them to escape even from themselves.

Love and Companionship

Related to the themes of confinement and control, discussed above, is Stafford's commentary on

love and companionship, of which the most important examples are the girls' relationship to Mr. Murphy, their relationship to Gran, and their relationship with each other. Everyone in the story, but particularly those confined by or excluded from society, needs some kind of love and companionship, but Stafford stresses that there are two very different ways that people and animals can provide this for each other. The first is the possessive form of companionship, which the narrator calls "unloving," represented by Gran. This is a protective, but also stifling and manipulative, type of love that leads to sickening guilt and even, as with Caesar, horrible violence. The second type of companionship is that which Mr. Murphy shares with the girls, and the narrator thinks of this type of love as an idealized way of getting along with "no strings attached."

Stafford uses these various types of companionship to comment on the true nature of love and its different forms. The downsides of the undemanding form of love, which the narrator associates with all of the male figures missing from her life, are its danger of disappearing and its potential for loneliness. Although Mr. Murphy is a kind and loving companion, he is isolated from society and the girls cannot depend on him. Gran's more constant form of love, however, is so self-serving and manipulative as to not really be love at all, although she does take care of the girls throughout their youth. The strongest loving connection in the story is that between Daisy and her sister. Although they see each other quite infrequently and their relationship is undemanding, theirs is a lifelong and dependable connection that seems to have been more vital than anything else in their struggles to be happy and healthy people.

Symbolism

One of the most important techniques through which Stafford is able to develop her themes and bring to life the story of the sisters' childhood is her sophisticated use of symbolism. There are a number of examples of an object or event that suggests or represents something else in the story, including Stafford's use of the animals in the Denver Zoo to symbolize Mr. Murphy and Gran. The characteristics of these symbols allow Stafford to comment on what the symbolic objects represent in the girls' lives and in the themes of the story; it is significant, for example, that the symbols for the figures from their childhood are caged in a zoo, because this suggests that their childhood is somewhat contained and caged in their minds.

Stafford uses animals as symbols throughout the flashback to the sisters' childhood as well. Mr. Murphy's monkey Shannon seems to symbolize some "small and sad and sweet" aspect of the girls' childhood which is murdered by Gran and Caesar, while Laddy's transformation into Caesar symbolizes the manner in which Gran manipulates and changes people. Stafford's symbolism is often quite complex, however, and many of her symbols have multiple meanings. Thus, for example, Gran's training of Laddy could also symbolize, in a more abstract way, the violence that results from inhibiting and controlling a natural personality. One of the benefits of Stafford's sophisticated use of symbolism is its ability to portray the subtlety of such themes.

Style

Realism

With its attention to detail, its logical narrative, and its realistic psychological character portraits, "In the Zoo" can be considered a work of realism, a type of literature that stresses accurate representations corresponding to real life. Many writers were beginning to focus on alternative modes of storytelling when "In the Zoo" was published in 1953, but Stafford remained within a tradition of short fiction dating back to the nineteenth century. The signs of Stafford's realism include her specific description of animals such as the blind polar bear, her descriptive characterizations of unique personalities like those of Mr. Murphy and Gran, and her extended descriptions of the landscape, such as that of the mountainous town of Adams.

Historical Context

America in the 1950s

The cultural environment in the United States during the 1950s, the era of the "baby-boomers," or sons and daughters of World War II veterans, was relatively conservative. War hero Dwight D. Eisenhower was president for most of the decade, and he was very popular due in large part to the economic prosperity of the period. Set against the complacency and consumerism characteristic of the conservative mainstream, however, was an environment of racial tension and a battle for civil rights. Moreover, exciting innovations in the arts, including rock and roll music, bebop jazz, "Beat" literature, and abstract impressionism in the fine arts, took hold among the younger generation and the various groups of people dissatisfied with mainstream culture.

Compare
&
Contrast

- **1930s:** The Great Depression is in full swing and millions of Americans struggle to keep their finances under control.

  1950s: The booming postwar economy of the 1950s is encouraging many middle class families to move to the suburbs, although economic conditions remain difficult for many lower class families.

  Today: The United States is the only economic and military superpower, and a large segment of the population continues to enjoy a prosperous economic environment despite the downturns in the economy following the September 11, 2001, terrorist attacks.

- **1930s:** Racism and racial oppression is widespread and the Ku Klux Klan is actively lynching African Americans.

  1950s: There is a great deal of racism in the United States, but the Civil Rights movement is beginning to win major legal breakthroughs, including the Supreme Court decision in 1954 to integrate all schools.

  Today: All races are equal under the law but there is still economic and social inequity among the races in the United States. Affirmative action legislation encouraging integration in the workplace and schools is one way that politicians and activists are addressing the issue.

- **1930s:** There is considerable anti-Irish and anti-Catholic sentiment in the United States. Large numbers of Irish people had immigrated during the Irish potato famine of 1845 to 1921, and many of these immigrants suffer discrimination, resentment, and unemployment during the Great Depression.

  1950s: Anti-Irish and anti-Catholic sentiment is somewhat less pronounced than it was before World War II, but it will continue to be a major issue when the first Irish Catholic president, John F. Kennedy, is elected in 1960.

  Today: Forty-four million Americans identify themselves as having some Irish heritage, and anti-Irish, anti-Catholic feelings are nowhere near as widespread as they were in the 1930s or 1950s.

Like the country itself, literature enthusiasts were divided between conservative and liberal tendencies. Some American writers and readers became involved in innovative movements occurring in Europe, and some forged the new and uniquely American style known as Beat literature, in which new spiritual philosophies and technical experimentation produced daring poetry and fiction. Allen Ginsberg, a brilliant poet and critic, became known as a spokesperson for the Beat movement, while the Beat novelist Jack Kerouac wrote influential and widely-read novels about a defiant younger generation. While new views of literature were being formed and writers were experimenting with different styles, some preferred to continue the realist tradition stretching back to nineteenth-century authors Gustave Flaubert and Henry James. Stafford was one of these authors, producing realistic short stories and novels in a traditional style.

Small Town America during the late 1920s and the Great Depression

In the United States, the decade following the Allied victory in World War I was characterized by a prosperous economy and an increase in conservatism, although there were also a number of breakthroughs in women's rights. Alcohol was prohibited between 1920 and 1933, which led to a large illegal racketeering network. The nineteenth amendment gave women the right to vote for the first time in 1920. Women's rights, prohibition, and economic prosperity were not as central to life in rural America, however, as they were in big cities. A small town in rural Colorado, like Adams in "In the

Zoo," would have been slower to see the effects of these changes, and it would not have felt the effect of the stock market crash of 1929 as rapidly as big cities full of stockholders.

When the effects of the Great Depression of the 1930s were felt in rural and small town America, however, they were often very severe. Prices, values, and incomes dropped throughout the country, and although a great proportion of working class jobs remained stable, many farmers and low-income workers found themselves out of work and/or extremely poor for many years at a time. Although President Franklin Roosevelt instituted a variety of reforms meant to create new jobs and expand social services, it was not until the United States entered World War II in 1941 that it recovered from the economic downturn. Small town residents would often be forced to make sacrifices and work long, difficult hours to make ends meet. The situation was perhaps worst for ethnic minority groups, particularly African Americans, who encountered widespread oppression and racism.

Critical Overview

Critical reactions to Stafford's writings have been largely favorable, although Stafford's novels have been criticized for their lack of distance from autobiographical material and their tendency to be overwritten. Joyce Carol Oates applies this criticism to Stafford's short stories in her 1979 essay "The Interior Castle: The Art of Jean Stafford's Short Fiction," in which she wrote, "Some of the stories, it must be admitted, are marred by an arch, overwritten self-consciousness, too elaborate, too artificial, to have arisen naturally from the fable at hand." However, Stafford's short stories from the mid-1950s were generally reviewed very positively, and *The Collected Stories of Jean Stafford* won a Pulitzer Prize in 1970. "In the Zoo" won the O. Henry Memorial Award for best short story of the year in 1955, and Oates cites its climax as a brilliant moment from one of Stafford's finest "[s]ubdued and analytical and beautifully-constructed" stories.

Critics consider Stafford a realist writer, and, as Jeanette W. Mann writes in her 1996 *Dictionary of Literary Biography* entry on Stafford: "The critical response to Stafford's fiction has also been within the conventions of the realistic tradition; the standard critical readings of her work are historical and biographical." Criticism that specifically discusses

"In the Zoo" tends to take the position that the sisters have not escaped the traumatic events of their childhood. In her *The Interior Castle: The Art and Life of Jean Stafford* (1992), Ann Hulbert writes that the story centers around "an insidious destruction of spirit that rendered her characters ... anxious souls ill equipped to face the world." Similarly, Mary Ann Wilson argues in *Jean Stafford: A Study of the Short Fiction* (1996):

> As the story moves toward its bitter conclusion, Stafford makes it clear that while the sisters may have separated themselves geographically from their nightmarish childhood, emotionally they are still trapped there—to an extent even they do not realize.

Criticism

Scott Trudell

Trudell is an independent scholar with a bachelor's degree in English literature. In the following essay, Trudell explores the feminist implications of Stafford's short story, arguing that it retains a traditional understanding of gender roles.

"In the Zoo" is a story about confinement and oppression, and a number of characters including Laddy, Mr. Murphy, and the sisters find their spirits constricted and their joys inhibited. Laddy is denied his weekend hunting trips and freedom of movement, Mr. Murphy is robbed of his pet monkey and his sense of justice, and the girls are made to feel guilty about a wide variety of pleasures ranging from maintaining friendships to dating to acting in plays. The elements that are confined and suppressed in the story share a common characteristic, however: they are very often related to masculinity. Stafford dramatizes the control and suppression of elements she associates with men and manliness, a practice that raises questions about her views on gender relations and feminism. A close reading of "In the Zoo" reveals that, although masculine symbols and characters are thoroughly suppressed, Stafford's story is not at all a feminist text, and it actually treats freedom and joy as exclusively masculine ideas.

The clearest example of manliness being suppressed, controlled, and denied comes when Gran takes charge of Laddy. Before his transformation, Laddy is a portrait of masculine virtue; he is "exceptionally handsome" and charming, he escorts

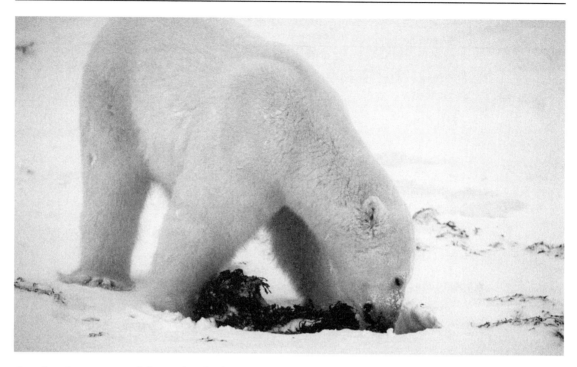

A polar bear, one of the animals featured in the story "In the Zoo"

the sisters to school and protects them, he has no feminine "spherical softness," and he even has an "aristocratically long" nose, which is a symbol signifying a long penis. He has a "bronzy, lustrous black" coat and his swaggering style as a chaperone for the girls makes him sound almost like a man of state, although he is also a strong and slightly wild dog of action able to make friends easily. He finds a hunting companion in the firemen's dog Mess, a red beast as unruly as his name implies, and comes back from his hunting trips "spent and filthy." These excursions, which Stafford calls "randy, manly holidays," enrage Gran enough to change Laddy's name and transform him into a cruel-tempered attack dog.

Laddy's alter ego Caesar, while not virtuous, kind, or charming, is also an embodiment of masculinity in its most vicious and violent sense. He becomes a "military" male, "overbearing . . . efficient, loud-voiced," constantly harassing and attacking other men. Stafford is careful to emphasize Caesar's human qualities, describing him as "dismayingly intelligent and a shade smart-alecky," and citing Gran's declaration, "A dog can have morals like a human," as the motivation behind her training him. Laddy is also "intelligent," however, and Caesar is not particularly more "human" than

Laddy except in the sense that he denies his natural pleasures. Both alter egos are expressions of human masculinity, and both take on men's roles in the girls' lives.

Caesar and Laddy are not the principle men in the girls' lives, however; Mr. Murphy and his two capuchin monkeys are the chief male figures that Daisy and the narrator think of as their "husbands and fathers and brothers." As the narrator points out, before she and Daisy reached puberty, "We loved [Mr. Murphy] and we hoped to marry him when we grew up." Theirs is a hearty and undemanding love, "jocose and forthright, [with] no strings attached," and the girls feel the same romantic way about the monkeys, which fascinate them and draw their deepest affections. Calling them and Mr. Murphy "three little, ugly, dark, secret men," the narrator emphasizes that they are the opposite of Gran since they "minded their own business and let us mind ours." This darkness, ugliness, and secretiveness also seems tied to their masculinity. Like Laddy/Caesar, Mr. Murphy has a dark and violent side that comes out when he encounters cruelty; after Laddy is transformed into Caesar, Mr. Murphy becomes something of a dark masculine "hero" in the sisters' lives when he kills Caesar after Caesar kills the monkey.

What Do I Read Next?

- Generally recognized as Stafford's finest novel, *The Mountain Lion* (1947) is the story of a lonely girl who writes fiction and poetry that no one else understands, following her experiences growing up with her brother in California and Colorado.

- Jack Kerouac's *On the Road* (1957) is a classic of Beat literature that follows the radical Dean Moriarty on his quest for thrilling adventures. It was written only five years after ''In the Zoo,'' but it is vastly different in style, theme, and content.

- ''The Jolly Corner'' (1908), by Henry James, is a classic short story of American realism in which a middle-aged man visits his childhood home in New York City after living abroad for many years, finding himself haunted by his past and by what might have been.

- Jennifer J. Freyd's *Betrayal Trauma: The Logic of Forgetting Childhood Abuse* (1996) is a learned psychological study of the ways that abuse victims are able to access their childhood memories as adults.

- Stafford's short story ''The Liberation'' (1953), available in *The Collected Stories of Jean Stafford* (1969), focuses on Polly Bay, a thirty-year-old unmarried woman who lives with her aunt and uncle in Adams, Colorado, until she moves east in hopes of escaping from her troubled past.

There are a number of reasons why Stafford emphasizes the influence, both symbolic and actual, of masculinity in the girls' lives. Partly it is a technique to make their psychological portrait more accurate and compelling, since they are orphans with no father figure and no constant and supportive male figure in their lives. Mr. Murphy's ''noncommittal'' and undemanding role, as well as the violence and abruptness of the masculine forces in the story, seem appropriate to girls unused to any committed male presence, and Stafford is aware of this as she depicts their personalities. The sisters' view of masculinity as something inconstant also helps to explain why the narrator cannot maintain a long-term sexual relationship, either with her adolescent boyfriend Jimmy Gilmore or, seemingly, with anyone in her middle age.

What is perhaps most interesting about Stafford's treatment of gender in the story, however, is that she consistently uses examples and symbols of masculinity to represent freedom and joy. When she first introduces him, the narrator describes her and Daisy's relationship with Mr. Murphy, the only loving male in their lives, as the ''one thin filament of instinct'' they have left. She goes on to tell the story of how the one present he gave them, their beloved Laddy—a

name that suggests the dog's boyish, ''sanguine'' wildness—is duly transformed by Gran and killed along with their favorite monkey, leaving them deprived of their full-blooded escape to freedom and joy. Like Caesar, they are chained to Gran's boarding house by their feelings of guilt and inadequacy. They see the mountains not as signs of freedom but as imposing, massive cages that confine them, and when they hike up to them after Caesar's death, it becomes clear that their own freedom has died as well; Daisy feels powerless and confined enough to wail: ''If only we were something besides kids! Besides girls!''

It should come as no surprise that Daisy wishes she were a boy here, since Stafford has persistently associated instinct, pleasure, and freedom with masculinity. In fact, the author begins to establish this association in the opening images of the story, before she introduces the narrator and Daisy, with her description of the ''blustery, scoundrelly, half-likable bravado'' of Clancy the black bear. The only zoo animal approaching mightiness and freedom, he releases ''Vesuvian'' roars at ''his audience of children and mothers.'' Stafford writes, ''If he were to be reincarnated in human form, he would be a man of action, possibly a football coach, probably a

> Clancy could never be symbolized as a woman of action in the symbolism of 'In the Zoo' because this kind of active, instinctive freedom is reserved for masculine symbols and male characters."

politician." Clancy could never be symbolized as a woman of action in the symbolism of "In the Zoo" because this kind of active, instinctive freedom is reserved for masculine symbols and male characters.

Since it is related to instinct and viciousness as well as freedom, masculinity is naturally also associated with the greatest displays of power in the story, which is why Caesar is the instrument of the most terrifying moment in the girls' childhood. However, it is only through Gran's elaborate training that Caesar is capable of murdering Shannon the capuchin monkey, and, like Mr. Murphy, Caesar's vicious side only emerges when he is subjected to cruelty. Mr. Murphy, meanwhile, is rather harsh in throwing a rock into a boy's back and poisoning Caesar, but these actions are not displays of power; Mr. Murphy is no match for Gran, and like his monkeys, he is actually extremely vulnerable. Indeed, masculine violence is generally not a source of power in Stafford's story. Manly characters become violent when they are oppressed or confined, but they are mainly locked in a cage, isolated from society, or killed off by the end of the story.

In fact, almost all of the masculine symbols and characters in the story are conquered and confined by the manipulative feminine power represented by Gran. The story's all-knowing, self-martyred matriarch, Gran is like a great mother bird, and her house is like a big nest, except that Gran controls and punishes her nestlings, making them "trod on eggs that a little bird had told them were bad." The problem is that this power is not really power at all, just as Gran's love for the girls is not really love at all. It is an inhibiting and self-defeating need to manipulate others that leads to none of the joy and freedom that is associated with masculine power. The fact that maleness tends to be oppressed and

caged in the story, therefore, does not imply any triumph of feminine power. Instead, it suggests that the female characters in the story have trapped their own freedom and joy, which is why the sisters, too, are animals in the zoo, being watched and ridiculed by the gossiping monkeys.

Few critics would call Stafford a feminist, and in her later years Stafford was actually critical of the women's movement, arguing against the concept of "women's writing." In her fiction, Stafford not only remained within the male-dominated realist and symbolist traditions, but frequently portrayed women as weak, insecure, and powerless. In her 1987 book *Innocence and Estrangement in the Fiction of Jean Stafford,* Maureen Ryan argues that Stafford tends to use women as symbols for the loneliness, alienation, and insecurity throughout her fiction. Therefore, one might expect a short story about two middle aged women revisiting their childhoods to be full of confined and oppressed freedoms and joys. What is surprising about "In the Zoo," however, is that it refuses to envision instinctive, independent joys as attainable or even remotely possible for feminine characters. Like its main characters, the story is trapped inside a convention in which freedom and joy are exclusively associated with men and masculinity.

Source: Scott Trudell, Critical Essay on "In the Zoo," in *Short Stories for Students,* Thomson Gale, 2005.

Mary Anne Wilson

In the following essay excerpt, Wilson provides an overview of "In the Zoo," commenting on Stafford's "relentless detail" and themes of bitterness and no escape.

The most brilliant example of Jean Stafford's Adams stories with older protagonists is the story that received the O. Henry Prize, "In the Zoo" (1955). Charlotte Goodman points out that this story was written during a creative burst of energy in Stafford's career right after her first two volumes of short stories were published in 1953: *Children Are Bored on Sunday* and *The Interior Castle.* Narrated by what Goodman calls an older version of Polly Bay in "The Liberation", "In the Zoo" begins with two elderly sisters sitting in a Denver zoo, where they have met to see each other off, as they do after their periodic visits. The blind polar bear they are watching reminds them of Mr. Murphy, a childhood friend. Thus begins a reminiscence of their lonely childhood as orphans raised by a mean-spirited, unloving foster mother, Mrs. Placer, in Adams, Colorado. They remember listening to Mrs. Placer and her boarders complaining about their miserable lives; they remember the dog Mr. Murphy gave them and how Mrs. Placer took him over and trained him to be mean and spiteful like herself; they remember the dog killing Mr. Murphy's monkey, after which Murphy poisoned the dog. Thereafter, Murphy gets older and sicker, and the girls are forbidden to see him. They grow up, their foster mother dies, and both sisters go their own way—one, Daisy, marries and has two sons; the other, the narrator, never marries, and as the story progresses, her strident, whining tone begins to sound more and more like the embittered Mrs. Placer she can never forget.

This story uses a frame technique, literally beginning and ending "in the zoo," enclosing the past in what appears to be an equally grim present. This frame narrative also begins with the narrator ironically describing the zoo animals in distinctly human terms: she imagines that their little community here in the zoo is riddled with all the cruel social snobberies plaguing their human counterparts. Across from the blind polar bear is a cage of "conceited monkeys" who scornfully note his behavior and that of his neighbors, the "stupid, bourgeois grizzlies." As they remark on the polar bear's resemblance to Mr. Murphy, a flood of memories returns, bringing with it images of the western town that haunts them: "[W]e are seeing, under the white sun at its pitiless meridian, the streets of that ugly town, its parks and trees and bridges, the bandstand in its dreary park, ... its mongrel and multitudinous churches, its high school shaped like a loaf of bread, the campus of its college, an oasis of which we had no experience except to walk through it now and then, eyeing the woodbine on the impressive buildings."

Living in the shadow of this Dickensian stepmother who constantly reminds them of her sacrifices and who delights in finding examples of her "solitary creed" that "life was essentially a matter of being done in, let down, and swindled," Daisy and her sister grow up lonely, isolated, and sensitive to the slightest wrongs done to them. In their childhood desperation the sisters find some escape in a precursor of the zoo where the adult sisters find themselves: Mr. Murphy's menagerie of a fox, a skunk, a parrot, a coyote, and two capuchin monkeys whose soulful glances recall a nearly human

sorrow. But the focus of all their childhood affections is the puppy Mr. Murphy gives them.

In relentless detail Stafford documents how the embittered "Gran," as Mrs. Placer has them call her, transforms this lovable, harmless animal into a growling, suspicious beast: "Laddy" becomes "Caesar," a tyrant and bully of the weak, and an apt symbol of how Gran poisons everything within her grasp. When Caesar kills Mr. Murphy's monkey, Murphy vows revenge, and the very next day poisons the dog. This grotesque scenario forms the climax of the inner narrative—reinforcing, as Daisy's sister narrates from the perspective of maturity, the sisters' utter powerlessness in the face of such unremitting cruelty. With this example of animalistic behavior, it is no surprise that, as the narrator remarks, she and her sister "lived in a mesh of lies and evasions, baffled and mean, like rats in a maze." Dehumanized by their surroundings, thwarted in their efforts to rise above this crippling environment, the sisters often stare at the massive mountains circling the town and covet their aloofness.

As the story moves toward its bitter conclusion, Stafford makes it clear that while the sisters may have separated themselves geographically from their nightmarish childhood, emotionally they are still trapped there—to an extent even they do not realize. As the sisters prepare to leave, the dialogue they exchange with each other replicates in tone and expression Gran's conversations with her boarders. They complain that the train conductors serve widows and spinsters last; Daisy notices a woman "nab the redcap [her sister] had signaled to"; Daisy's sister suspects the porter of having designs on her luggage; and the alfalfa fields she sees from her train she is certain must be full of marijuana. They seem willing to concede that "life [is] essentially a matter of being done in, let down, and swindled." As Ann Hulbert notes, "In the Zoo," unlike the Emily stories, "reversed the Vanderpool plot line of progress toward healthy maturation." Instead, she continues, what Stafford dramatizes is "an insidious destruction of spirit that rendered her characters ... anxious souls ill equipped to face the world."

Source: Mary Anne Wilson, "Part I," in *Jean Stafford: A Study of the Short Fiction,* Twayne Publishers, 1996, pp. 52–54.

Shelley Ratcliffe Rogers

In the following essay excerpt, Rogers explores the use of synecdoche and other symbolism while linking "In the Zoo" and Stafford's essay "Letter from Germany."

In the journalistic piece 'Letter from Germany' Stafford, writing in the first person, plays a role akin to that of Evan Leckie in the short story. She observes and chronicles the state of a defeated and war-torn nation, previously 'the enemy' (but it is also the country by whose ancient 'magic' she has been seduced when living there as a student). She notes the German hatred of the occupying Americans and feels the attendant psychological discomforts of a member of the 'conquering side.' There is a degree of moralizing also. She notes the 'valid' pity but asks that it be tempered in the light of Germany's 'universal self-pity':

> There is the categorical denial on the part of almost everyone that anything was known of the concentration camps, but hand in hand with this, in certain quarters, goes a vicious hatred of the few Jews who, having escaped in the early days of the Third Reich, have now returned . . . The one man in a thousand who admits that he was a member of the National Socialist Party adds the explanation that he joined it because he was bullied by threats to the welfare of his family. It is objectionable to hear a nation spoken of as if it were an intractable and neurotic individual, and yet so widespread is this German fad of wearing blinders that at last one's hackles cease to rise when it is said by the Americans 'They haven't learnt their lesson even now.' It is unfortunately true; it is also unfortunately true that their foreign tutors do not seem thus far to have fired them with the desire to learn.

This essay is not only a piece of detached but first-hand reportage, however. While the gist of the passage quoted above could be debated and discussed, other features of the essay are at work on a more subliminal level which render Stafford's 'position' much less certain. The two approaches, straightforward and surreptitious, are intertwined but render the consciously figurative aspect inconspicuous. If noted, the metaphors or symbols are enigmatic, being both actual and selectively representational. An example of this 'plying' appears early in the essay:

> My eye had been equally appalled in sections of other German cities, where the buildings had been modern, and reinforced-concrete blocks had been ripped apart, so that now, emerging from the wounds, there are snarls of steel, scabby with black rust. In the middle of the zoo in Frankfurt there is such a sight; the exposed entrails of a burst tower rise in a wrathful tangle above the tops of the surrounding linden trees.

This cannot be seen merely as a descriptive and straightforward account of the architectural desolation of war-torn Germany. The paramount image of the twisted tower rising above the zoo compound must evoke and emblematise the horror of the concentration camps. The zoo, so tangentially noted, is the metaphor for the incarceration of humans, herded and confined like animals, vivisected, their humiliation and unnatural condition rendered a spectacle. The tangled tower recalls the chimneys of the gas chambers; it remains, twisted and in remnants, like the persecuted Jewish race, like the humanity and integrity of the German people, like the optimism and liberal humanism of the Western world. Contrasted to the foliage of the trees, it rises phallic and metallic, a testament to war lords in the industrial world. The linden or lime trees represent a pastoral, natural alternative, and more. Lime flowers, with their sweet scent, such a contrast to the stench of incarceration and incineration, have always been used for their healing properties. Stafford may have known that the tree was dedicated to Venus, (not Mars, certainly), or that in the Middle Ages St. Hildegard used linden to help ward off plague. The linden is also powerfully associated with romantic German *lieder* betokening, as in Schubert's *Winterreise,* a pre-Wagnerian innocence. Other words in the passage contribute to the contrast, and conflation, of animate and inanimate, of flesh and metal: concrete blocks have 'wounds' and the tower, 'exposed entrails'; reaction to pain is combined with descriptions of metal, simultaneously evocative of the wounded and of weaponry: 'snarls of steel,' 'scabby with black rust,' 'wrathful tangle.' 'Reinforced concrete blocks' of 'German cities, where the building had been modern' do not attest to the architecture of advanced industrialisation, commerce and culture; the civic centre, the zoo, the gas-chamber share the same facets.

'Letter from Germany' ends with a passage which is as difficult to decipher. Again Stafford refers to the zoo in Frankfurt; this time the atmosphere is one of festivity but the tone is ironic: 'The zoo, in the midst of dreadful destruction, had been a winning sight.' Stafford evokes the noise of animals, delighted children and adults relaxing. Things appear to be 'back to normal'; peace has been restored. But, this is how the 'letter' concludes:

> There was an air of holiday kindliness and humor and warmth. But then I came to the pool where the rhinoceros wallowed and rolled, and I saw a boy trying to put a small monkey, which he had on a leash, into the hideous mouth of the outsize animal. The monkey was terrified and would not step in between those monstrous teeth, upon that nasty tongue. Sometimes, in his battle, he fell into the water, and then the look on his face was one of unutterable defeat and misery. The crowds had never seen a sight so comic, and they could hardly steady their cameras, they were laughing so hard. Suddenly the monkey got away and, trailing his leash behind him, ran like the wind; his

master went after him with a yell of fury through the bright sunlight, between the brilliant flowers, underneath the lovely weeping-willow trees.

The locus is repeated but this time the tower is missing. There is another kind of edifice in its place however, the less easily identifiable edifice of the instruments of persecution, oppression and horror. The small monkey, obviously, is the victim, prey, in this battle, to his young 'master' who commits him to the jaws of 'the outsize animal.' The scene in the zoo becomes an allegory of what has gone before; the devouring rhinoceros standing for institutionalized Nazism, or for any instrument of oppression, the all-consuming machine of grandiose tyrannous states. The youth, fresh-faced and exuberant, represents the ignorance and brutality of 'everyman' so easily appropriated to a cause. The laughing crowds and the cameras evoke the mass rallies of Nazism but they also denote the oblivious ease with which another's pain and degradation can become a spectator sport. Once again, reinforcing the link with the earlier passage, Stafford incorporates imagery of the natural world in contraposition to 'battle,' 'defeat,' 'misery' and 'fury.' The garden imagery of bright sunlight and brilliant flowers is complicated by the elegiac weeping willows. The garden works to show that the veil of normality, order and festivity in sunshine and amidst blooms cannot mask the bestiality of humans which persists.

Stafford leaves us with the image of the terrified monkey, coerced, abused and attempting escape. In the context of this report's historical points of reference the animal is humanized. A terrified and impotent victim, it is evocative of recent human victimization and stands for more than an instance of cruelty to pets. This maltreatment renders the subject, monkey representing man, instinctual and animalistic. The misery he connotes is 'unutterable,' beast-like, but not beastly. The 'corpulent spider' and 'the invader, a rat,' co-residents in Stafford's Nuremburg hotel room in the opening of the letter are also humanized in that fat generals and invading troops are evoked. The personifying aspects suggest humans who are bestial but the signifying process comes full circle: animal-human-animal. The metaphoric or associative chain continues. A spider's predominant feature is not its obesity but its fine, thin legs; rats are usually furtive and to be seen scurrying away rather than invading. At the same time, the body of a spider is spherical and seems parasitically fat; rats are unwelcome and invasive. There are fears and phobias attendant on both the entrapping arachnid and the gnawing ro-

> " Perhaps the conflation of fascism and religion in Mrs. Placer has some relation to Stafford's letter from Heidelberg in which she noted the German people's 'conversion' and the 'new Messiah' in Nazi Germany."

dent. There are no static equivalences or stereotypes. Stafford exploits tropes which reveal oscillation, inversion, or deconstruction of fixed meaning within the primary signification of post-war Germany.

This kind of representation is not merely evasive, ignorant or a-political; it appears to be innocuous and a little cliched. The imagery, however, is carefully delineated in both the journalistic report and the short story, even if it is more evocative than immediately apparent. Stafford should not be seen to be naively non-committal on a complex and horrific situation but as duly representing the complexity. She seems to delight in leading the reader up false trails, making us complicit with stances which she then subverts, or mocking our misreading. She replicates an aspect integral to Nazism itself: the power and duplicity of rhetoric.

Stafford often uses animals as synecdochic for the plight of society's victims. The imprisoned cat, ironically named Mercy, in *Boston Adventure,* the drowned mother cat and her kittens at the close of 'An Influx of Poets,' a story about marital breakdown and the end of one woman's aspirations for a family, and the dog whose entire 'personality' is changed by a new regime and a new name in 'In the Zoo' (1953) are all symbolic of societal horrors and indicate the inhumanity of humans and the dehumanization of their victims. 'In the Zoo' provides a link with the two passages in 'Letter from Germany' referring to Frankfurt Zoo immediately after the war. This short story takes place in Denver, Colorado. Two sisters are propelled into remembering their orphaned childhood during the Depression in a small town fifty miles north of Denver, Stafford's fictionalised Boulder, which she names Adams. The link I am making between the zoos, in post-war Frankfurt and in the Rocky Mountains, provoking memories of the 1930s from a post-war perspective, is not as tenuous as it might at first appear. The language used by Stafford in this story relies on the reverberations of fascism, on our post-holocaust apprehension.

An obvious connection between the two writings is in the rather mannered use of animals to represent human traits and the incorporation of human characters who are described in terms of animals. The story opens with a description of a variety of bears at the zoo. A blind polar bear is described as 'patient and despairing,' 'keening harshly in his senility.' The grizzly bears next to him are 'a conventional family,' two parents and two offspring. The conventions are Western, middle-class, suburban. The two sisters in this tale fall outside that familial paradigm, having been orphaned when eight and ten. The black bear is a down named Clancy, a 'blowhard' who loves his 'audience of children and mothers.' His patriarchal correlation is more explicit:

> If he were to be reincarnated in human form, he would be a man of action, possibly a football coach, probably a politician. One expects to see his black hat hanging from a branch of one of his trees; at any moment he will light a cigar.

Across the grass are the 'conceited monkeys,' primitive but astute: '. . . firmly secure in their rambunctious tribalism and in their appalling insight and contempt.' Conversely, as the sisters remember their childhood in Adams, the churches of the town are described as 'mongrel'; the two sisters remember arriving in Adams 'cringing.' Other memories include descriptions of their stultifying existence to their foster-mother's boarding house:

> We little girls, washing the dishes in the cavernous kitchen, listened to their even, martyred voices, fixed like leeches to their solitary subject and their solitary creed—that life was essentially a matter of being done in, let down, and swindled . . . Steeped in these mists of accusation and hidden plots and double meanings, Daisy and I grew up like worms . . . Daisy and I lived in a mesh of lies and evasions, baffled and mean, like rats in a maze.

'Eight upright bloodhounds' constitute the boarding house clientele.

The repressive regime under which Daisy and the narrator lived as orphans in Mrs. Placer's (Gran's) care had a profoundly debilitating effect. Although Stafford includes elements of a nineteenth-century novel, this regime has distinctly twentieth-century overtones in the attention to indelible psychological effects and to analogies of genocide or holocaust which, though certainly not twentieth-century inventions, seem alien to a nineteenth-century novel tradition.

> These things are engraved forever on our minds with a legibility so insistent that you have only to say the name of the town aloud to us to rip the rinds from our nerves and leave us exposed in terror and humiliation.

The theories of behaviorism and conditioned responses are consciously combined with the animal analogies; the children live like 'rats in a maze.' The crux of reminiscence in this story is the character change which the children's pet dog undergoes when he becomes Mrs. Placer's responsibility. The tale of the re-conditioning of a dog and the description of the girls' ineradicable conditioning evokes the behavioral psychologist I. P. Pavlov and his work with the salivation of dogs (more explicitly, in Stafford's 'The Bleeding Heart' (1948), Rose Fabrizio studies 'books on psychology' and reads about 'Pavlov's submissive dog'). The conclusion of 'In the Zoo' reveals that the sisters' response will never be eradicated; like Pavlov's animals they respond automatically. They will never be able to 'unlearn those years' and once the process of stimulus and memory is instigated, they fall prey to Gran's regime again even though she is dead and the sisters no longer reside in Adams. More alarmingly, the culmination of their conditioning has made them similar to their foster mother. Although the two sisters have moved away in more senses than one, their conversation and thoughts reveal that they are replicating her suspiciousness, bigotry and smug pessimism.

Stafford refers to and parodies recent psychological studies of behaviorism. At one point she has the indignant Mrs. Placer state: 'A dog can have morals too.' Stafford pokes fun at the concept that morality is merely conditioning and at the concept that response in animals can be applied to human behavior. There is irony in the notion that the bigoted Mrs. Placer should be the one to instil morality in any creature. She perceives the dog's immorality after a three day jaunt, led on a debauch by a 'caddish' red hound called Mess. Stafford also uses a network of religious terminology with heavy irony. 'Sacrifice' is the word Mrs. Placer uses to describe her guardianship, a word the children are 'never allowed to forget.' Her daily inventory of 'slights' and 'impudences' amounts to 'daily crucifixion'; she and her like-minded guests are 'martyred,' adhere to their 'creed.'

Laddy's 'conversion,' his attainment of an acceptable morality, is appalling. There is no doubt as to the fascist implications of her methods. Perhaps the conflation of fascism and religion in Mrs. Placer has some relation to Stafford's letter from Heidelberg in which she noted the German people's 'conversion' and the 'new Messiah' in Nazi Germany. Other 'dogmas' are indicated when the contents of Mrs. Placer's bookcases are described:

> . . . it had contained not books but stale old cardboard boxes filled with such things as W. C. T. U. tracts and anti-cigarette literature and newspaper clippings relating to sexual sin in the Christianized islands of the Pacific.

Mrs. Placer, however, represents more than narrow-mindedness. The fascist link is made very clear in the description of how she has transformed Laddy; her political aspirations are first indicated in re-naming the dog Caesar:

> A week or so after he became Caesar, he took up residence in her room . . . She broke him of the habit of taking us to school (temptation to low living was rife along those streets; there was a chow—well, never mind) by the simple expedient of chaining him to a tree as soon as she got up in the morning. This discipline, together with the stamina-building cuffs she gave his sensitive ears from time to time, gradually but certainly remade his character. From a sanguine, affectionate, easygoing Gael (with the fits of melancholy that alternated with the larkiness), he turned into an overbearing, military, efficient, loud-voiced Teuton. His bark, once wide of range, narrowed to one dark, glottal tone.

Such a passage can seem dangerously stereotypic and as reductive as Mrs. Placer's world view. It is surely meant, however, to act metonymically; recent history lends reverberations to this contraposition of creativity and militarism, of plurality and absolutism, democracy and totalitarian oppression. This polarization seems to demand that the opposition of 'feminine' and 'masculine' be included as well; Klaus Theweleit's study of the fascist 'male' fear of 'femaleness' and of the flow and plurality of desire could easily be brought to bear:

> In patriarchy, where the work of domination has consisted in subjugating, damming in and transforming the 'natural energy' in society, that desiring-production of the unconscious has been encoded as the subjugated gender, or femaleness; and it has been affirmed and confirmed, over and over again in the successive forms of female oppression.

Stafford can be seen to gesture towards a critique of patriarchy with her satirical, anthropomorphic descriptions of the bears early in the text. In their trapped existence the two sisters, as children, exclaim: 'If only we were something besides kids! Besides girls!' As grown women, boarding the train which is momentarily an emblem for life in general, one of them sardonically remarks: '"Spinsters and Orphans Last" is the motto of this line.' But Stafford modifies her feminist perspective by problematizing that essentialist opposition which equates masculinity or militarism or tyranny with 'male.' Mrs. Placer is a childless widow, surely one of society's 'orphans and spinsters' but she is described as 'marshalling her reverse march,' 'she rallied and tacked and reconnoitered'; her guests are 'bloodhounds.' Laddy's initial appeal is that he will be a 'watchdog' and in disposition less of a mongrel than an Alsatian, one suspects. Mrs. Placer is the victim who has turned aggressor, the oppressed who perpetuates oppression.

At the heart of the story is the shocking image of the mauled monkey, Mr. Murphy's pet:

> Caesar . . . was on Mr. Murphy in one split second and had his monkey off his shoulder and had broken Shannon's neck in two shakes . . . In one final, apologetic shudder, the life was extinguished from the little fellow. Bloody and covered with slather, Shannon lay with his arms suppliantly stretched over his head, his leather fingers curled into loose, helpless fists. His hind legs and his tail lay limp and helter-skelter on the path . . . We stood aghast in the dark-red sunset, killed by our horror . . .

This mode of description is common in Stafford's work. It is particularly reminiscent of the overdeterminedness of red in *Boston Adventure*. Sophie's cat in *Boston Adventure* is similarly mauled; Caesar's death throes, caused by the poisoned meat left for him in retaliation by Mr. Murphy, are similar to Ivan's epileptic convulsions in *Boston Adventure*. The description of Caesar's death is extended, in this instance, not to an emblematic red sunset, but to 'red rocks':

> He suffered an undreamed-of agony in Gran's flower garden, and Daisy and I, unable to bear the sight of it, hiked up to the red rocks, and shook there, wretchedly ripping to shreds the sand lilies that grew in the cracks.

Like the displacement and condensation of Freudian dream-symbol and like Pansy's colour-correlated memories in 'The Interior Castle,' red becomes the complexly determined 'floating signifier' whose reference to blood, or to a sunset, or rocks, comes to represent all of these but much more. Pain, horror, visual impact and psychic wound become synthesized into a representative colour. However, it is blood that gives the colour red its resonance. The yellow that stands for a particular summer, for instance, can be instigated by a yellow sun, flower, garment and so forth; all of these can determine the symbolic value of Yellow in a screen memory but yellow still remains comparatively innocuous. Red has its determinants such as crimson geraniums, red wine, a birthmark, a sunset and the sight of blood; but the red of even mundane objects cannot be divorced from a correlation with blood. Moreover, the complex symbolic value of blood itself, in ritual, sacrament, in very life and death, complicates any resonance in the colour. In 'In the Zoo' the red rocks or the red sunset are noted after the sight of the bleeding creature mauled to death. The network of redness takes its impact from the horror of split blood and of violent death.

Source: Shelley Ratcliffe Rogers, '"A Heady Refreshment': Secrecy and Horror in the Writing of Jean Stafford," in *Literature & History,* Vol. 3, No. 1, Spring 1994, pp. 31–63.

Carroll Viera

In the following essay, Viera explores symbolic connections between the polar bear in "In the Zoo" and a passage from George Eliot's The Mill on the Floss.

Jean Stafford's "In the Zoo" revolves around an unusual symbol, the polar bear. A possible source of this symbol is a passage from George Eliot's *The Mill on the Floss,* in which a polar bear is endowed with precisely the same symbolic overtones as Stafford's bear.

In Stafford's story the bear functions as a device for setting the plot into motion and as a symbol of the crippling effects that the repressive environment of their aunt's home has on two young orphans. At the outset of the story "the blind polar bear slowly and ceaselessly shakes his head in the stark heat of the July and mountain noon . . . Patient and despairing, he sits on his yellowed haunches on the central rock of his pool, his huge toy paws wearing short boots of mud."

The bear reminds the narrator and her sister of a childhood friend, but he also symbolizes their own psychological condition. Feeling isolated and set apart, they identify themselves with the bear, whose neighbors, the other animals, are "firmly secure . . . in their appalling insight and contempt." Because the bear in his helplessness, despair, and entrapment so accurately reflects their own entrapment into distrust and despair forced upon them by circumstances, he is the central symbol of the story. In his symbolic significance he bears a striking resemblance to an identical symbol from *The Mill on the Floss.*

In the analogous passage from Eliot's novel, Lucy Deane has just entreated Maggie Tulliver to abandon her attitude of sadness. Maggie replies, "It is with me as I used to think it would be with the poor uneasy white bear I saw at the show. I thought he must have got so stupid with the habit of turning backwards and forwards in that narrow space, that he would keep doing it if they set him free. One gets a bad habit of being unhappy." One of the great themes of *The Mill on the Floss* is the influence of an oppressive environment on young lives. Maggie's asceticism, which is in sharp conflict with her inner being, is initially forced upon her by outward circumstances, especially by her father's financial ruin. But, as Maggie admits in comparing herself to the polar bear, her mental condition has ultimately become a matter of habit, a habit that persists long after her father's debts are paid. Environment and character interact to shape the individual.

Stafford also explores this theme. The two sisters, denigrated from girlhood by their aunt, are as entrapped as the bear they observe at the zoo. After reaching adulthood, they remain with the aunt until her death, for she "held us trapped by our sense of guilt." Even the old woman's death fails to free them emotionally: they remain suspicious of strangers in casual encounters, thus inadvertently persisting in attitudes at variance with their essential natures, attitudes which their aunt had deliberately inculcated in them as children. Like Eliot's bear and like Maggie, Stafford's two characters continue to live in a psychological cage after they are physically free. The identical use of the highly unusual symbol of the polar bear to express an analogous theme suggests that the passage in Eliot's novel may have inspired Stafford's story.

Source: Carroll Viera, "'In the Zoo' and *The Mill on the Floss,*" in *American Notes & Queries,* Vol. XX, Nos. 3 and 4, November/December 1981, pp. 53–54.

Sources

Hulbert, Anne, *The Interior Castle: The Art and Life of Jean Stafford,* Alfred A. Knopf, 1992, p. 302.

Mann, Jeanette W., "Jean Stafford," in *Dictionary of Literary Biography,* Vol. 173, *American Novelists Since World War II, Fifth Series,* edited by James R. Giles and Wanda H. Giles, Gale Research, 1996, pp. 260–70.

Oates, Joyce Carol, ''*The Interior Castle:* The Art of Jean Stafford's Short Fiction,'' in *Jean Stafford: A Study of the Short Fiction,* by Mary Ann Wilson, Twayne Publishers, 1996, pp. 136–39; originally published in *Shenandoah,* Vol. 30, Winter 1979, pp. 61–64.

Ryan, Maureen, *Innocence and Estrangement in the Fiction of Jean Stafford,* Louisiana State University Press, 1987, p. 9.

Stafford, Jean, ''In the Zoo,'' in *The Collected Stories of Jean Stafford,* Farrar, Straus and Giroux, 1969, reprint, 1992, pp. 283–303.

Wilson, Mary Ann, *Jean Stafford: A Study of the Short Fiction,* Twayne Publishers, 1996, pp. 52–54.

Further Reading

Avila, Wanda, *Jean Stafford: A Comprehensive Bibliography,* Garland Publishing, 1983.
    This book lists Stafford's complete writings and cites, with annotations, sources of criticism and biography on the author and her works.

Hassan, Ihab H., ''Jean Stafford: The Expense of Style and the Scope of Sensibility,'' in *Western Review,* Vol. 19, Spring 1955, pp. 185–203.
    Hassan's essay discusses Stafford's works with particular attention to the themes of age and childhood.

Jenson, Sid, ''The Noble Wicked West of Jean Stafford,'' in *Western American Literature,* Vol. 7, Winter 1973, pp. 261–70.
    Jenson's article argues that Stafford wishes to civilize the American West with East Coast values.

Roberts, David, *Jean Stafford: A Biography,* Little, Brown, 1988.
    Roberts's book provides a thorough and definitive biography of Stafford.

Walsh, Mary Ellen Williams, ''The Young Girl in the West: Disenchantment in Jean Stafford's Short Fiction,'' in *Women and Western American Literature,* edited by Helen Winter Stauffer and Susan J. Rosowski, Whitston Publishing, 1982, pp. 230–42.
    This article analyzes the Western stories in *The Collected Stories of Jean Stafford* in terms of how they relate to the Western tradition.

The Kugelmass Episode

Woody Allen

1977

"The Kugelmass Episode," first published in the May 2, 1977, issue of *The New Yorker,* is Woody Allen's fantastic tale of a dissatisfied humanities professor who has himself transported into the fictional world of Gustave Flaubert's *Madame Bovary.* Professor Kugelmass, unhappily married to his second wife, wants to have an affair, so he has a magician-entertainer named The Great Persky project him into Flaubert's novel, where he embarks on a passionate affair with the title character, the spoiled and beautiful Emma Bovary. Allen presents a hilarious look at what happens when living out one's fantasy becomes a reality and satirizes contemporary society in the process. The story's humor comes not only from its bizarre situation but from its broadly drawn characters, parody of the entertainment industry, spoof of the male midlife crisis, ironic look at literature and its study, and satirical depiction of Jewish culture and manners. Although the story is a farce and immensely funny from beginning to end, "The Kugelmass Episode" does tackle the serious question of the human condition in modern times. Kugelmass, like Allen's heroes in other stories and films, is a *schlemiel,* or hapless bungler who finds himself the victim of circumstances (often of his own making) in an absurd and confusing world. The story draws on Jewish humor and culture as well as classical and modern literature, using lowbrow humor to spoof high art. "The Kugelmass Episode," which was published the same year Allen won his first Academy Award for the movie *Annie Hall,* won an O. Henry award for

best short story in 1978. The story was included in Allen's collection *Side Effects* in 1978, and has been widely anthologized. It appears in the 2003 collection, *Fierce Pajamas: An Anthology of Humor Writing from The New Yorker.*

Author Biography

Woody Allen was born Allen Stewart Konigsberg in Brooklyn, New York, in 1935. Allen decided when he was just a child that he wanted to write and make movies. At 15 he changed his name to Woody Allen, and at 16 was hired to write jokes for radio and television. In the early 1950s he first attended New York University, where he failed motion picture production and English, and then City College of New York, where he also flunked out. He wrote for television for five years, writing for Sid Caesar and winning an Emmy nomination, but found this career stifling and turned to standup comedy.

In 1965 Allen wrote and starred in his first film, *What's New, Pussycat?* The following year he made his directorial debut with *What's Up, Tiger Lily?* and wrote a Broadway play, *Don't Drink the Water.* Around this time he became a regular contributor of humorous fiction and essays to *The New Yorker* and other publications.

He rose to fame with the 1969 release of *Take the Money and Run,* a spoof of gangster movies that he wrote, starred in, and directed. His reputation as one of America's most gifted comic filmmakers solidified with *Bananas* (1971), *Everything You Always Wanted to Know About Sex (But Were Afraid to Ask)* (1972), *Sleeper* (1973), and *Love and Death* (1975). Two collections of his prose writings, *Getting Even* (1971) and *Without Feathers* (1975) appeared during these years. In 1977, Allen won an Oscar for *Annie Hall,* which was hailed as one of the first truly intelligent and complex American comedies. That same year, ''The Kugelmass Episode'' appeared in the *The New Yorker.* The story won an O. Henry Award the following year and was published in his third and final prose collection, *Side Effects* (1980). Allen's 1978 *Interiors,* his first attempt at serious drama, met with mixed success, but 1979's *Manhattan,* an autobiographical work shot in black-and-white, was admired by critics and audiences. Allen continued to produce hit movies throughout the 1980s.

In 1992, he suffered a much-publicized break-up with his third wife, the actress Mia Farrow, after

Woody Allen

he admitted to an affair with Farrow's adopted daughter, Soon-Yi Previn. Caught in a bitter custody battle, his ex-wife alleging he had molested another of their children, Allen's reputation suffered considerably, but he continued to make movies, and he and Previn married in 1997.

In addition to making films at a rate of about one per year, Allen plays jazz clarinet with the New Orleans Funeral and Ragtime Orchestra. Over his career, he has received fourteen Academy Award nominations and three Oscars, eight British Academy of Film awards, and numerous prizes from the New York and Chicago Film Critics Circles, the Writers Guild of America, the Cesar Awards in France, and the Bodils in Denmark. In 2002, Allen received the *Palme des Palmes,* the Cannes Film Festival's lifetime achievement award. He lives in Brooklyn with his wife and two adopted children.

Plot Summary

''The Kugelmass Episode'' opens with Kugelmass, a middle-aged, unhappily married humanities professor seeking the advice of his analyst, Dr. Mandel. He is bored with his life, and he needs to have an affair. His analyst disagrees, however, telling him "there is no overnight cure" for his troubles, adding that he is "an analyst, not a magician." Kugelmass then seeks out a magician to help him solve his problem.

A few weeks later, he gets a call from The Great Persky, a two-bit magician/entertainer who shows him a "cheap-looking Chinese cabinet, badly lacquered" that can transport the professor into any book, short story, play, or poem to meet the woman character of his choice. When he has had enough, Kugelmass just has to give a yell and he is back in New York. At first Kugelmass thinks it is a scam, then that Persky is crazy, but for $20, he gives it a try. He wants a French lover, so he chooses Emma Bovary. Persky tosses a paperback copy of Flaubert's novel into the cabinet with Kugelmass, taps it three times, and Kugelmass finds himself at the Bovary estate in Yonville in the French countryside.

Emma Bovary welcomes Kugelmass, flirting with him as she admires his modern dress. "It's called a leisure suit,'" he replies romantically, then adds, "It was marked down.'" They drink wine, take a stroll through the countryside, and whisper to each other as they recline under a tree. As they kiss and embrace, Kugelmass remembers that he has a date to meet his wife, Daphne. He tells Emma he will return as soon as possible, calls for Persky, and is transported back to New York. His heart is light, and he thinks he is in love. What he doesn't know is that students across the country are asking their teachers about the strange appearance of a "bald Jew" kissing Madame Bovary on page 100.

The next day, Kugelmass returns to Persky, who transports him to Flaubert's novel to be with Emma. Their affair continues for some months. Kugelmass tells Persky to always get him into the book before page 120, when the character Rodolphe appears. During their time together, Emma complains about her husband, Charles, and her dull rural existence. Kugelmass tells her about life back in New York, with its nightlife, fast cars, and movie and TV stars. Emma wants to go to New York and become an actress. Kugelmass arranges it with Persky that the next liaison with Emma is in New York. He tells Daphne that he will be attending a symposium in Boston, and the next afternoon, Emma comes to New York. They spend a wonderfully romantic weekend together, and Emma has never been as happy. Meanwhile, a Stanford professor, reading Flaubert's book, cannot "get his mind around" the changes that have taken place to the

novel: First a strange character named Kugelmass appears, and then the title character disappears.

When Persky tries to return Emma to the novel, his cabinet malfunctions, and she is forced to stay in New York. Kugelmass finds himself running between Daphne and Emma, paying Emma's enormous hotel bills, and having to put up with his lover's pouting and despondence, and the stress begins to wear him out. He learns too that a colleague who is jealous of him, Fivish Kopkind, has spotted Kugelmass in the book and has threatened to reveal his secret to Daphne. He wants to commit suicide or run away. But the machine is fixed at last, and Kugelmass rushes Emma to Persky's and eventually back to the novel. Kugelmass says he has learned his lesson and will never cheat again.

But Kugelmass is at Persky's door again three weeks later. He is bored and wants another affair. Persky warns him that the machine has not been in use since the earlier "unpleasantness," but Kugelmass says he wants to do it, and asks to enter *Portnoy's Complaint.* But the cabinet explodes, Persky is thrown back and has a fatal heart attack, and his house goes up in flames. Kugelmass is unaware of the catastrophe, but soon finds that the machine has not thrust him into *Portnoy's Complaint* at all but into a remedial Spanish textbook. The story ends with Kugelmass running for his life "over a barren, rocky terrain" as the "large and hairy" irregular verb *tener* ("to have") races after him on its spindly legs.

Characters

Charles Bovary

Emma Bovary's husband Charles is a doctor whom Kugelmass calls a "lacklustre little paramedic" who is "ready to go to sleep by ten" while Emma wants to go out dancing. Emma refers to her husband sarcastically as "Mr. Personality." He falls asleep during dinner as she is talking about the ballet.

Emma Bovary

Emma Bovary is the title character of Gustave Flaubert's novel *Madame Bovary,* into whose world Kugelmass gets transported by The Great Persky. In

Allen's story she speaks in the "same fine translation as the paperback" version of the novel before she suddenly acquires a twentieth-century New York way of speaking. She is much like she is in the Flaubert novel: beautiful and spoiled, interested in material possessions, irresponsible, bored with her bourgeois existence, looking for love and excitement. She detests her marriage and life in the country and is enthralled by Kugelmass's stories of Broadway nightlife, fast cars, Hollywood, and TV. She and Kugelmass begin a torrid affair when he visits her in the pages of the novel, but she soon wants to visit New York and begin an acting career. In New York, she goes out on the town with Kugelmass and buys new clothes to take home, another sign of her shallowness and interest in material possessions. When she finds herself unable to get back to the novel, she complains to Kugelmass that watching TV all day is boring; she wants to take a class or get a job. She then locks herself in the bathroom and refuses to come out. Selfish and vapid, Emma Bovary is a parody of the demanding mistress as well as of the air-headed aspiring actress searching for fame and fortune.

The Great Persky

The Great Persky is the magician who transports Kugelmass into Emma Bovary's world using a badly lacquered, cheap-looking Chinese cabinet. Persky, an unsuccessful entertainer, is described as short, thin, and waxy-looking, and lives in a broken-down apartment house. The fact that he is a magician reinforces the theme of reality versus illusion in the story, and he also is a parody of a two-bit entertainer that used to be a staple on Vaudeville. Persky is also a satire of the quintessential New York Jew; he uses colorful colloquial expressions and has a pessimistic but relaxed outlook on life. When Kugelmass asks Persky if being transported in the cabinet is safe, he says, "Safe. Is anything safe in this crazy world?" When his cabinet malfunctions and Kugelmass is distressed, Persky is not overly worried and tells Kugelmass to relax and to get help for his personal anxiety. He can't help in that area, Persky says, because "I'm a magician, not an analyst."

Professor Fivish Kopkind

The professor is Kugelmass's colleague, a professor of comparative literature at the City College of New York. Kugelmass says Kopkind, who has always been jealous of him, has identified him as

Media Adaptations

- The Audio CD *Fierce Pajamas: Selections from an Anthology of Humor Writing from the New Yorker,* a recording of the collection edited by David Remnick and Henry Finder, includes a reading of "The Kugelmass Episode."

- *The Kugelmass Affair* is Jonathan Karp's stage adaptation of Allen's story.

- The web site http://www.woodyallen.com/ offers comprehensive information on Allen's life, movies, books, plays, and standup comedies. It also includes interviews with the author and links to other useful information.

- Allen's film *The Purple Rose of Cairo* (1985) uses a device similar to that found in "The Kugelmass Episode": a character from a movie steps off the screen, into the theater, and into the life of the moviegoer Cecilia.

the sporadically appearing character in *Madame Bovary* and has threatened to tell everything to Kugelmass's wife.

Kugelmass

A humanities professor at the City College of New York, Kugelmass is bored with his humdrum life and is transported to the pages of Gustave Flaubert's *Madame Bovary,* where he has an affair with the title character. Kugelmass is described as aging and "bald and hairy as a bear," and he thinks, mistakenly, that he has "soul." He is distrustful, pessimistic city man who races around town trying to get what he wants; he is forever in pursuit of something better. He is drawn in the Jewish tradition of the *schlemiel*—a hapless bungler who gets caught up in an awful and absurd situation beyond his control, a powerless man at odds with his environment. But he is also an irresponsible, selfish, shallow man who wants a lot for very little—he wants to escape his humdrum life and unhappy marriage, but not at the expense of his career or marriage. After The Great Persky transports Kugelmass to Yonville, and he begins an affair with Emma Bovary, he can't believe his luck and is happy for a while; he has never been particularly successful (he failed Freshman English). He thinks that he deserves happiness after all his ''suffering,'' and when he begins an affair with Emma thinks he ''has the situation knocked.'' But when things start to go wrong and Persky cannot get Emma back to Yonville, Kugelmass starts to panic. He takes to drink and wants to escape again, this time either by suicide or moving to Europe. After Persky finally returns Emma to the Flaubert novel after her New York interlude, Kugelmass repents and says he has learned his lesson. But three weeks later he is asking Persky again to transport him into another fictional realm. Kugelmass is like many Allen heroes—a nervous, inept New York Jew who hopes for the best but also worries constantly, thinks he has a situation ''knocked,'' then finds himself in trouble that he cannot handle. But he doesn't learn from his mistakes, because the call of flesh is more powerful than that of his head. Kugelmass is also very much like Emma of Flaubert's *Madame Bovary* in that he is dissatisfied, selfish, and irresponsible, and has a ridiculous idealized notion of love and romance.

Daphne Kugelmass

Daphne is Kugelmass's current, and second, wife. Kugelmass considers her an ''oaf'' and a ''troglodyte'' who had promise (and money) but has now grown fat. She is demanding and spends her time doing mundane tasks—looking for bathroom accessories, for example. She suspects that her husband has a ''chippie'' on the side, senses his tension, but never catches on to his affair.

Dr. Mandel

Dr. Mandel is Kugelmass's analyst. Kugelmass confides to Dr. Mandel that he needs to have an affair, but the doctor tells him his problems run much deeper and that what he needs is to express his feelings. He says he has no overnight cure for Kugelmass because ''I'm an analyst, not a magician.''

Rodolphe

Rodolphe is Emma Bovary's lover in the novel *Madame Bovary*. Kugelmass wants to get into the novel before Emma meets Rodolphe because he can't compete with him; he is fashion magazine material. Rodolphe is from the landed gentry, he says, and has nothing better to do than flirt and ride horses.

Themes

Literature and Literary Study

One of the principal targets of Allen's satire in ''The Kugelmass Episode'' is literature and its study. Kugelmass is a humanities professor at the City College of New York in Brooklyn, but, it turns out, he ''failed Freshman English.'' (Allen himself attended CCNY and failed English at New York University.) He doesn't speak like an educated man at all, but uses colloquialisms and a very New York Jewish speech pattern; the only time he deviates from this is to call his wife a ''troglodyte'' (a cave dweller) and to whisper sweet nothings into Emma Bovary's ear. Kugelmass is dissatisfied with his life, and he yearns not for love but for a cheap idealization or glamorization of it that is the stuff of romance novels. He decides he wants to have an affair with Emma Bovary because she is French— ''that sounds to me perfect,'' he says. But what he doesn't even consider is that Flaubert's novel is not about perfect love at all but the ridiculous idealization of it by the title character—which leads to her utter ruin. In fact Kugelmass is very much like Flaubert's Emma: dissatisfied and disillusioned by marriage, searching not for love but for shallow fulfillment that is mistaken for something much grander. But Kugelmass is also like Emma's husband, Charles, who is a bumbling, aging man who is really no good at his job. However, Kugelmass the literature professor does not realize these things at all.

Allen throws in a number of references in his story to classics of literature that reinforce the absurdity of Kugelmass's quest and resound with his general predicament. The Great Persky asks Kugelmass what his pleasure is in terms of female heroines to have an affair with. He suggests the social-climbing title character of Theodore Dreiser's *Sister Carrie* and the mad Ophelia in Shakespeare's *Hamlet,* for example. At the end of the novel, Kugelmass asks to be projected into Philip Roth's *Portnoy's Complaint,* a book about a Jewish man who talks to his analyst about his sexual troubles. Throughout the story, Allen uses lowbrow humor to poke fun at serious, high art by combining it with absurd and farcical situations. The fact that a person can be projected at all into a work of fiction is ridiculously comic, and that it is Flaubert's serious naturalistic novel is even more incongruous.

Literary study is also satirized in the story as students and professors all over the country begin to wonder about what is happening as a ''bald Jew''

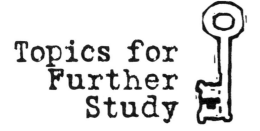

Topics for Further Study

- Research the terms *satire, farce, parody, irony, spoof,* and *send-up.* What are the differences between them? Where are these different elements found and how are they used in "The Kugelmass Episode?"

- Write a short story that satirizes a situation of your choosing. Choose two or three characters that will be familiar to your readers, exaggerate their character traits, and put them into an absurd situation that emphasizes those traits.

- One of the most famous discussions of the nature of reality is Plato's "Allegory of the Cave" in his philosophical treatise *The Republic.* Plato says that humans live in a state of ignorance and mistake the "false" images they see around

them for the true reality of the world. Read the "Allegory" and write a short essay on how the "false images" Plato talks about can be construed as the images seen in art. Do you see any parallels between these "false images" and the images projected on a movie screen? Explain those differences.

- Do a research project on the history of American Jewish humor and humorists, from Vaudeville through radio, television, stage, and screen. How have Jewish comics and comedians contributed to the understanding and appreciation of the American Jewish experience? In what unique ways do you think they have contributed to the understanding of the human condition?

---

enters Flaubert's novel. Rather than thinking that something crazy is happening, the teachers think that their students are on pot or acid. A Stanford professor, unable to simply see the text for what it is, remarks that it shows that the mark of a classic is that "you can reread it a thousand times and always find something new."

Pursuit and Possession

Perhaps Allen's most serious target of satire in "The Kugelmass Episode" is modern humans' pursuit of satisfaction. Kugelmass is dissatisfied and undergoing a midlife crisis, but rather than seek meaning, he looks for romance and glamour to relieve the boredom in his life. When things go wrong and Emma can't get back to the Flaubert novel, he tells Persky that all he is prepared for at this point in his life is "a cautious affair." He is prepared to lie and cheat on his wife but he doesn't want to work too hard or to give up the other things in his life—his job, his comfortable existence—to get what he wants. The irony at the end of the story is that Kugelmass, who has been in the pursuit of things that he thinks he must have, is himself pursued by "having," as the "large, hairy" irregu-

lar verb "tener" chases him over a rocky landscape. Emma is also in pursuit of shallow and meaningless things—idealized romance and fame—that she thinks can make her happy.

Art and Life/Fantasy and Reality

A recurring theme in Allen's fiction and films is the line between art and life, between fantasy and reality. Fantasy in the story is seen on two levels. On the one hand, there are straightforward fantasies, for example Kugelmass's wish have a beautiful woman by his side and Emma Bovary's desire for an acting career and fame. But Allen plays on that idea and Kugelmass's fantasy becomes, literally, a fantastic journey into another dimension.

In the story, Kugelmass is bored and seeks a release from his dull, humdrum existence. He wants to escape from the reality of his oaf-like wife Daphne and have an affair. He doesn't want an ordinary dalliance, a "chippie" on the side as his wife says, but excitement, softness, glamour; he wants to "exchange coy glances over red wine and candlelight." He turns to Persky to help him, and even though it should be apparent that things will probably not work out (the unsuccessful magician lives in a run-down apartment building and uses a cheap-looking Chinese cabinet as his transporter), he willingly suspends his disbelief and hopes for the best. As a sign of his desperation to escape his reality, Kugelmass the distrusting city man accepts that Persky knows what he is doing. His fantasy comes to life when he is thrust into the world of Flaubert's novel and begins his affair with Emma Bovary, but Kugelmass soon finds that living with one's fantasy poses many hazards. Once again, Kugelmass wants to escape—this time his fantasy-turned-reality—either by committing suicide or running away to Europe. He is relieved when Emma is finally transported back to Yonville. Art in the story is an escape from real life, with its fat and dull people and mundane situations. But even though it is a tempting escape, it is still an illusion, and illusions by definition are not all they seem to be.

New York Jewish Culture

"The Kugelmass Episode" is very much a story about a New York Jew, and Allen presents a number of details to emphasize the Jewishness of his principal characters. Kugelmass teaches at City College of New York The word "Kugel" in the title character's name refers to a sweet noodle dish that is served at Passover. In fact all the "real" characters in the story are Jewish—Kugelmass, Daphne, Dr. Mandel, Persky, and even Kugelmass's jealous colleague, Fivish Kopkind. Allen's characters have stereotypical Jewish traits, from Kugelmass's anxiety and concern about money to Persky's pessimism. The story uses elements of Jewish humor, with the main character cast as a *schlemiel,* or bungler, the use of exaggeration for comic effect (Kugelmass notes, for example, that Emma's hotel tab reads "like the defense budget") and its concerns with the anxieties of urban life. But while Allen satirizes Jewish culture, speech, and manners, he never does so harshly, and his characters are crazy but ultimately likeable, and the colloquial speech they use in the face of such serious situations is perhaps the most humorous element in the story.

The Entertainment Industry

"The Kugelmass Episode" pokes fun at the entertainment industry, especially in its satirical portraits of Persky the Great and Emma Bovary. Persky is an unsuccessful entertainer who nonetheless continues at his trade and hustles to earn a living. He built his cabinet for a booking for the Knights of Pythias that "fell through," he tells Kugelmass, and he aims to make money from

Kugelmass from his contraption. Emma, when she comes to New York, becomes a parody of an actress with aspirations to fame. She wants to dine at Elaine's, a landmark restaurant in New York that serves Italian-Jewish comfort food and which is the haunt of many celebrities (she wants to see and be seen). She thinks anyone can act and wants to be coached by the great Strasberg so she can win an Oscar. Both these characters show the most shallow side of the entertainment industry, that focuses not on art but on money and fame.

Style

Farce/Satire

"The Kugelmass Episode" uses humor and comic situations to poke fun at people and situations and to show the absurdity of human desires and pursuits. The humor in the story can be classified as *satire,* which is the ridicule of ideas, institutions, particular individuals, or humanity in general to lower the reader's esteem of them and make them laughable. The story may also be viewed as a *farce,* which is a comedy characterized by broad satire and improbable situations. Satire and farce are used by writers to different effects, sometimes reducing ideas or people to absurdity to proffer a moral criticism against injustice or social wrongs. Allen does not seem to offer heavy moral lessons in his story, but his humor does expose human foibles and critiques modern humanity's particularly crass pursuit of bodily satisfaction, material wealth, and fame. The story is a *parody* of a number of types of people and situations. The characters are broadly drawn and have stereotypical traits. Kugelmass is an ironical portrayal of a middle-aged Jewish man undergoing a sexual crisis; his wife Daphne is a satire of an over-the-hill, unrefined and materialistic Jewish wife; Emma is a spoof of shallow, celebrity-seeking, and untalented would-be actor; and Persky sends up Jewish speech and manners as well as cheap entertainers.

Using these characters, Allen also satirizes literature and high art, material pursuits, Jewish culture, and the entertainment industry. One of Allen's techniques in his satire is to present a serious situation or moment and then undercut its importance with an absurdity. The entire fantastic situation of being transported into a fictional realm is undercut by characterizing it in mundane terms. The cabinet Persky uses for Kugelmass's amazing journeys is cheap and "badly lacquered." When it malfunctions, Persky crawls under it and bangs it with a large wrench; the problem, he reveals, was with its transmission. Allen undercuts serious romantic moments often by using colloquial expressions and incongruities. Emma is dazzled by Kugelmass's modern dress, which he tells her he got on sale. She is enthralled by stories of New York, and he talks about O. J. Simpson's "rushing records." Throughout the story, situations and people are mocked, practically everything they say and do reduced to complete silliness.

Colloquial Language

Much of the humor of "The Kugelmass Episode" comes from his characters' manner of speech, as they use slang and expressions that undercut the seriousness of the situations they are in. The tone of the language emphasizes the New York setting and Jewish characters. Persky in particular uses extremely colorful phrases and one can almost hear a Brooklyn Jewish accent. When Kugelmass is skeptical of his transporting cabinet, he tells Kugelmass "It's the emess," then asks for a "double sawbuck" to transport him to *Madame Bovary*. Kugelmass, a literature professor, uses colloquial language most of the time, and when he an Emma become close begins to call her "sugar" and "cupcake." At first Emma speaks in the "same fine English translation as the paperback," but by the end of the story she is telling Kugelmass that "watching TV all day is the pits." Over and over, weighty and important matters are made absurd by the way the characters talk about them, bringing them into the realm of the ordinary and mundane.

Historical Context

New York City, Comedy, and the Jewish American Experience

The first Jews to settle in North America arrived in New York City, then the Dutch port of New Amsterdam, in 1654. By the end of the century they had established synagogues, and by 1740 Jews were entitled to full citizenship. Jewish families settled all over New York and the community set up hospitals, businesses, and cultural organizations. Immigration to New York by European Jews continued in the nineteenth century, intensifying in the 1880s. Between 1880 and 1920, the Jewish population in New York City swelled from 60,000 to more

than 1.5 million. Between the two world wars, the Jewish community in New York evolved from an immigrant community divided by language, politics, and culture into an English-speaking, upwardly mobile American citizenry. Jews began to play an increasingly significant role in the general cultural life of New York. Many of New York's leading entertainers, writers, artists and art patrons were of Jewish origin, and American intellectualism began to become closely associated with the New York Jewish community.

As Jewish immigrants began to assimilate, their humor began to integrate into mainstream American entertainment. Many Jews became successful Vaudeville acts, and future stars such as The Marx Brothers, Jack Benny, George Burns, Milton Berle, and The Three Stooges began their careers in Vaudeville. By the mid-1920s, a literary form of humor created by Jewish comics came out of Vaudeville: stand-up comedy. When Vaudeville theaters were replaced by nightclubs in the 1930s and 40s, comedy became less physical and began to focus on language and observations about the incongruities and anxieties of life. Jewish comedy began to reflect its intellectual tradition of exhaustive reasoning and questioning. Before the second world war, much Jewish humor relied on self-caricature, but after 1945 Jews ran into less discrimination and new possibilities opened up to them, and they began to get into radio and television. Television signaled a return to physical comedy, and in the early 1950s the Jewish comic Sid Caesar created *Your Show of Shows,* which used a combination of physical comedy, one-liners, and intellectual wit to offer social commentary and satirize highbrow culture. Among Caesar's writers were the Jewish comics Mel Brooks, Neil Simon, Carl Reiner and Allen. *Your Show of Shows* did not directly address Jewish issues, and in fact fearing the anti-Semitic sentiments of its audience pointedly avoided presenting any sense that it was created by Jews. However, it did make numerous Jewish references and used inside jokes, and the Jewish background of the writers helped to produce humor laced heavily with irony and caustic wit.

By the end of the '60s, the presence of Jews in the New York comedy scene had moved from vaudevillian acts to the forefront of radical social change. The brash humor of Lenny Bruce in that decade heralded an age of intelligent, sophisticated comedy that tackled important social issues and also spoke unashamedly and irreverently about the Jewish experience. In 1969, Allen's *Take the Money and Run* presented a Jewish protagonist who was no

Compare & Contrast

- **1970s:** There are approximately 5.5 million Jews living in the United States, of which about 1.2 million live in New York City. Jews make up approximately 15 percent of the population of New York City.

  Today: There are approximately 6 million Jews living in the United States, of which just under 1 million live in New York City. Jews make up 12 percent of the population of New York City.

- **1970s:** While Jews account for less than 2 percent of the United States' population, approxi-

mately 80 percent of the country's comedians are Jewish. Most of them are from New York City.

  Today: Jews make up 2.5 percent of the United States' population, while 70 percent of the country's comedians are of Jewish descent. Most of them are from New York City.

- **1970s:** Lorne Michaels's television comedy program *Saturday Night Live* premieres. Nearly all the writers who work on the show are Jewish.

  Today: *Saturday Night Live* continues its successful run. Only one of the writers on the show is Jewish.

---

longer the Jewish vaudevillian clown of old but a neurotic, analytic, intellectual New York Jew, thoroughly urban and anxiety-ridden. This persona, taken from his standup routine, appropriated some of the techniques and types from the Jewish humorist tradition, for example casting the hero as a *schlemiel,* a bungler and lovable failure who is to be pitied. But it was also much more clever and self-consciously reflective even while being self-deprecating and zany. In the 1970s, as the social climate in the country changed, Jewish comedy writers began more and more to emphasize their Jewishness, and Allen's string of hit movies is a testament to the increasing tolerance of Jewish culture and ideas in the mainstream. Like his story "The Kugelmass Episode," Allen's films poked fun at the Jewish American experience but never in mean-spirited way, offering rather a gentle look at what it means to be Jewish in America and paying tribute to the particularly Jewish ability to find humor in the most unlikely situations.

In 1975, the television comedy variety show *Saturday Night Live,* whose writers were almost all Jewish, was launched in New York and televised nationwide. The program often parodied Jewish manners, people, and culture and encouraged performers to be open about their Jewish identities. Since then, the American comedy scene has em-

braced Jewish comics and Jewish humor. The synthesis of Jewish and mainstream comedy is seen in the work of Billy Crystal, Jerry Seinfeld, and Larry David, for example, whose verbal jabs and neurotic self-observations have popularized the sensibility of Jewish humor. But the work of these contemporary Jewish comics has also in some ways sublimated Jewish comedy's very Jewishness by making it "all-American." Thus, while New York Jewish humor defined comedy in twentieth-century America, in the twenty-first century, Jewish American humor and its particular fusion of intellectual and lowbrow satire has become assimilated to the degree that it is regarded as one of the defining elements of American humor.

Critical Overview

"The Kugelmass Episode" is generally acknowledged to be a classic short story and one of the finest pieces in Allen's relatively small output of prose fiction. It was well received critically when it first appeared in *The New Yorker* in 1977, evidenced by it being short-listed for and then winning the first prize in the following year's O. Henry awards, the annual prizes given to short stories of exceptional merit. However, partly because of Allen's enormous popularity and success as a filmmaker, "The Kugelmass Episode" and his other prose works have received almost no sustained critical or scholarly attention. The short story is routinely cited by critics from all disciplines as a "classic" and a brilliantly funny example of a fantasy in which art and life intersect and frequently appears on college reading lists for modern and supernatural fiction and, ironically, Freshman English. Two short critical pieces on the story appeared in 1988 and 1992 issues of the *Explicator* discussing the work's Jewish references and relationship to reader-response theory and criticism. But otherwise, most critical commentary on Allen's work tends to focus on his films and, to a lesser extent, his plays. Nonetheless, "The Kugelmass Episode" continues to be read, being frequently anthologized in collections of American short stories, humor, and Jewish writing, and in 2003 was included in print and audio versions of an anthology of stories from *The New Yorker.* *Side Effects,* Allen's third prose collection in which the story was published in 1980, also continues to be in print, ensuring that the piece enjoys wide readership.

Criticism

Uma Kukathas

Kukathas is a freelance editor and writer. In this essay, Kukathas discusses how Allen explores the theme of art as an escape from reality in "The Kugelmass Episode" and in his film The Purple Rose of Cairo.

In his 1985 film *The Purple Rose of Cairo,* Allen tells the story of Cecelia, a lonely woman trapped in a bad marriage and dead-end job who escapes the misery of her existence by going to the movies. During one of Cecelia's daily visits to the (fictional) film *The Purple Rose of Cairo* to see her screen idol Gil Shepherd, the character Tom Baxter, played by Shepherd, turns to Cecelia and begins a conversation with her. He confesses he's been watching Cecelia while she has been watching him, and is falling in love with her. Much to the horror of the audience and other characters in the film, he decides to climb out of the movie and run off with her. He flees to the real world, where all he wants to do, he says, is lead a "normal" life, to "be real." Cecelia later enters Baxter's movie world with him, where

she experiences for a time glamour, adventure, love, and hope. But both Baxter and Cecelia soon find that the fantasy worlds they have entered have their pitfalls. More importantly, reality begins to set in, and in the end both are forced to return to their old lives, the only places where, they realize, they can really belong.

Allen's romantic comedy has obvious parallels to his humorous short story "The Kugelmass Episode" in the way it explores the viewer/reader's relationship to art and art's relationship to reality. Indeed, the 1977 story can be viewed as a prototype for the film that appeared eight years later. Both of these works use similar methods to examine the line between fantasy and reality and to show how seductive fantasy can be. The treatment of the theme of art versus reality in "The Kugelmass Episode" is not as developed as it is in Allen's film, and the moral lessons it teaches are far less obvious. But it nevertheless delves into serious problems, forcing readers to think intelligently about the role of art in people's lives as well as their responsibility toward it. By comparing Allen's story with *The Purple Rose of Cairo,* the complexity of these themes becomes more obvious and the existential concerns and moral lessons, veiled in the story in screwball satire, become a little more clear.

In both "The Kugelmass Episode" and *The Purple Rose of Cairo,* Allen presents the allure of art and its power to offer solace and hope. In "The Kugelmass Episode," Allen pokes fun of people's impulse to find refuge in art and also in art's capacity to provide relief from the dreariness of existence. Kugelmass seeks an escape from reality in art for the basest of reasons: he is having a midlife crisis, feels that he is running out of "options," and thinks he'd better have an affair while he still can. He doesn't really turn to art for solace; rather, art happens to present itself as a means for him to satisfy his lust. Kugelmass is a literature professor, but art so far has done little to offer meaning to his weary soul. Only when The Great Persky suggests that he use his transporting cabinet to "meet any of the women created by the world's best writers" does he decide that this is the type of fantasy world he will escape to. He decides to go to the France of *Madame Bovary,* where he begins an affair with the title character. Once there, he is happy because he is "doing it with Madame Bovary" and thinks he has the "situation knocked." Being in the French countryside is a nice touch, but the most important thing for Kugelmass is that he has fulfilled his very particular fantasy—of having an affair with a beau-

Merlin, King Arthur's magician, a famous forerunner to the magician the Great Persky who enables Kugelmass to enter the novel Madame Bovary *in "The Kugelmass Episode"*

tiful, sexy woman. Kugelmass is completely seduced by the world of art, but all that world is for him is a place where he can get what he wants without having to pay very much for it.

"The Kugelmass Episode" satirizes the entire notion of the seductiveness of art as it shows Kugelmass's desire for escape in crass terms. *The Purple Rose of Cairo* develops the idea of art's allure more fully and delicately, showing why humans choose to escape to it. For Cecelia, the world of the movies is a complete world, and she loves everything about it: the glamorous people, the adventure, the romance. She falls in love with Baxter because he is perfect; even after he has a fistfight with her husband, not a single hair is out of place and there is no blood no his face. Art for Cecelia offers an escape because it depicts a perfect world, one where there is no joblessness, no despair, no cruelty, and where there is the possibility of romance, love, and hope. It also offers a perfect morality, where good always triumphs and evil fails. Her real world, in comparison, is disappointing, deceitful, and the good guys never win. Cecelia turns to art to satisfy her desires, and the escape offered by art is magical and wonderful. The world

of art is far superior to her real world, and it is no wonder that day after day Cecelia sits in front of the screen losing herself in its illusions of beauty and its perfect morality.

Allen is not saying that all art depicts a perfect world, but shows how audiences are seduced by it because of the alternative it offers to the complexity of the real world. Art may not portray life as being perfect, but it has a certain integrity and meaning that are missing from real life—or at least people think it has these qualities. The literary critics in "The Kugelmass Episode" don't know what to make of it when the text of *Madame Bovary* changes; the novel has an expected progression, unlike life, and the Stanford professor "cannot get his mind around" the fact that suddenly it does not. A member of the movie audience in the film says she wants "what happened in the movie last week to happen this week. Otherwise what's life all about anyway?" In both the story and the film, Allen shows how audiences' expectations of art are misguided in serious ways. They expect art to deliver certain truths when in fact it cannot. One of the things Allen does in both these works is use the genre of comedy, which is supposed to provide happy endings, and

What Do I Read Next?

- *Madame Bovary* (1857), by Gustave Flaubert, the novel in which Kugelmass gets projected, is the story of a young wife of a country doctor who yearns for excitement in her boring rural existence and engages in several illicit affairs.

- Philip Roth's comic novel *Portnoy's Complaint* (1969), also mentioned in the story, is a continuous monologue as narrated by its eponymous speaker, Alexander Portnoy, to his psychoanalyst about his sexual frustrations and escapades. The novel is also a humorous exploration of the Jewish American experience.

- *The Big Book of Jewish Humor* (1981), edited by William Novack, is a collection of Jewish and Jewish-inspired humor from contributors such as Woody Allen, Max Apple, Gary Epstein,

Lenny Bruce, Joseph Heller, David Levine, Sam Levenson, G. B. Trudeau, Judith Viorst, S. Gross, Jules Feiffer, and others.

- Allen's three collections of humorous prose are brought together in *The Complete Prose of Woody Allen* (1991).

- Jasper Fforde's *The Eyre Affair: A Novel* (2002) is a humorous mystery novel about a criminal who steals characters from English literary works and holds them for ransom.

- "The Secret Life of Walter Mitty" (1939), American humorist James Thurber's best-known story, is about a middle-aged, middle-class man who escapes from the routine drudgery of his suburban life into fantasies of heroic conquest.

---

infuse it with the unexpected, with sadness and absurd tragedy. Cecelia is betrayed by the movies and doomed to return to her horrible life, and Kugelmass, not learning his lesson about the dangers of living an illusion, is projected finally into an absurdist oblivion. Allen departs from the traditions of comedy to bring into focus the shifting boundaries of art and reality and to show how people's expectations of art influence their thinking not only about art but their lives as well.

Both Kugelmass and Cecelia are seduced by what art can offer them, but their mistake is in believing that art can offer a permanent escape. For Kugelmass, things start to go horribly wrong when Persky's transporter malfunctions and Emma Bovary is unable to return to her novel. Kugelmass finds very quickly that his fantasy-turned-reality is a liability, and he chooses to end it as soon as he can. But the allure of it is too strong, and three weeks later he is in Persky's apartment asking to be projected into *Portnoy's Complaint*. There he meets with his hilariously bizarre ending—thrust by mistake into a remedial Spanish textbook and running for his life as he is chased by a large and hairy

irregular verb. The ending to Cecelia's story is more tragic and more poignant. She believes at first that she can have a life with Baxter, leaving her husband for him. The movie studio then sends the actor Shepherd to convince his character to get back into the film, and Shepherd asks Cecelia to choose him over his screen persona, promising them a life together. Baxter goes back to his film, but then Cecelia is betrayed by Shepherd; after he gets Baxter back into the movie, he returns to Hollywood, and Cecelia is back to her dreary existence, her only respite once again the magic of the movies.

Even to the end, Kugelmass believes that art can offer something more than a passing diversion to his life, that it can transform it in some way that will have permanent rewards. This leads to his downfall. Cecelia finally recognizes that perfection isn't a substitute for reality, and she chooses reality instead. But reality is as harsh as it had always been, with its imperfect morality, and she is once again alone and in a state of hopelessness and despair. The lesson that both characters learn, and which we can learn from their stories, is that painful though it is, humans must return to and live with reality, and

---

> Allen departs from the traditions of comedy to bring into focus the shifting boundaries of art and reality and to show how people's expectations of art influence their thinking not only about art but their lives as well."

reality has no happy ending. Art can offer some refuge from the harshness of reality, but we cannot stay there permanently. We might find, as Cecelia does, that the world of reality is amoral and unwelcoming, but it is the only place we have the freedom to choose our own way. The problem with both Kugelmass and Cecelia is that they are too weak to face up to this freedom and to accept responsibility for their own lives. They both look for an easy solution, thinking they can escape the responsibility of making their own lives meaningful. But to escape that responsibility, Allen shows, is to escape to an illusion, and that illusion, no matter how seductive, can never last very long.

Source: Uma Kukathas, Critical Essay on ''The Kugelmass Episode,'' in *Short Stories for Students,* Thomson Gale, 2005.

Laurie Champion

In the following essay, Champion explores how readers and the protagonist ''enter the text'' in ''The Kugelmass Episode,'' reversing the phenomenon of reader-response.

In his short story ''The Kugelmass Episode,'' Woody Allen extends the relationship between reader and text posited by reader-response critics. ''The Kugelmass Episode'' portrays a distinct relationship between reader and text, a connection that represents a reversal of reader-response criticism: the protagonist literally enters the text *Madame Bovary* and metaphorically interprets it. When humanities professor Sidney Kugelmass tells the magician The Great Persky, ''Make sure and always get me into the book before page 120,'' he means it literally. Kugelmass adds to the meaning of *Mad-*

ame Bovary, just as we add to the meaning of ''The Kugelmass Episode.'' We read Allen's story, metaphorically ''entering the text''; likewise, readers of *Madame Bovary* in Allen's ''The Kugelmass Episode'' metaphorically enter Flaubert's novel.

Kugelmass tells his analyst that he wants to have an affair. When Dr. Mandel, the analyst, cautions him, ''You're so unrealistic,'' Kugelmass decides that he needs a magician rather than an analyst. Persky calls him, and Kugelmass says, ''I want romance. I want music. I want love and beauty.'' Persky explains: ''If I throw any novel into this cabinet with you, shut the doors, and tap it three times, you will find yourself projected into that book. . . . You can meet any of the women created by the world's best writers.''

Kugelmass wants a French lover, so he chooses Emma Bovary, who represents the antithesis of his wife. He thinks that Daphne is ''an oaf.'' She is also overweight, and he implies that he only married her for her money. But, he thinks, Emma is ''beautiful. . . . What a contrast with the troglodyte who shared his bed.'' He says, ''I've earned this. . . . I've suffered enough. I've paid enough analysts.''

Persky throws a ''paperback copy of Flaubert's novel'' into the cabinet with Kugelmass. When he meets Emma, Kugelmass says, ''She spoke in the same free English translation as the paperback.'' Kugelmass's illusions turn into reality as he has his affair with Emma Bovary. ''My God, I'm doing it with Madame Bovary! . . . Me, who failed freshman English.'' His escapades with Emma provide him with excitement that his real life lacks.

Professor Kugelmass's ''mythical journey'' is his trip to a fantasy land, a journey into the illusory force of art. One of the most interesting and marvelous techniques of ''The Kugelmass Episode'' is that the protagonist literally enters the text. Critics who use reader-response criticism center their interpretations around examinations of the effects of the text on readers. This critical method entails the notion of readers ''entering the text'' and responding to the text as interpretative techniques. In ''Post Reader-Response: The Deconstructive Critique,'' Pam Gilbert summarizes the fundamental principles of reader-response theories, They focus, she observes,

> on the reader's contribution to the meaning of a text, and in that way they are seen to represent an assault of a sort on the traditional notion of literature as ''expressive realism''—the notion that literature is a reflection of the ''real'' world, that literary texts have single determinate meanings, and that the authority

for their meanings lies with the author, who ''put'' the meaning in the text in the first place. (235)

Reader-response criticism assumes that the reader is the text's interpretative authority.

Allen's story also demonstrates reader-response techniques when ''enter the text'' is interpreted as ''read the text.'' Allen shows the effects that Kugelmass's literal entrance into *Madame Bovary* has on those who read *Madame Bovary* while Kugelmass and Emma are in the novel. The narrator says that students all over the country ask, ''Who is this character on page 100? A bald Jew is kissing Madame Bovary?'' One professor explains his confusion: ''I cannot get my mind around this. . . . First a strange character named Kugelmass, and now she's gone from the book. Well, I guess the mark of a classic is that you can reread it a thousand times and always find something new.''

Throughout his oeuvre, Woody Allen frequently depicts artists who are involved in the creative process, or spectators who, like Kugelmass, are affected by their exposure to art. He often juxtaposes the notion of an ideal life that art portrays against his protagonists' flawed lives. In ''The Kugelmass Episode,'' he broadens this theme: the protagonist's concept of an ideal life and his subsequent illusory views compel him to seek art as a way of confirming his illusions. Attempting to merge his idealized life with his real life, Kugelmass literally enters an artistically created world, the text.

Source: Laurie Champion, ''Allen's 'The Kugelmass Episode,''' in *Explicator,* Vol. 51, No. 1, Fall 1992, pp. 61–63.

John Harty

In the following essay, Harty discusses naming in ''The Kugelmass Episode.''

Woody Allen created two inside jokes when he wrote ''The Kugelmass Episode,'' originally published in *The New Yorker* in 1977. The short story contains cryptic joshing in both the protagonist's name Kugelmass and in that of the magician—The Great Persky. These two names refer to items often made fun of by Allen—the Jewish culture and show business, respectively.

First, a plot review will help in the comprehension of the chosen names. Kugelmass has married an oaf named Daphne. Extreme unhappiness causes Kugelmass to search for a woman to have an affair with, and in distress he decides to seek help from a

Dr. Mandel, an analyst who warns Kugelmass that an affair won't solve his problems and that ''[he's] an analyst, not a magician.''

Curiously Kugelmass gets a phone call from a magician, The Great Persky, who will later tell him that ''[he's] a magician, not an analyst.'' Persky has a magic cabinet in which Kugelmass gets transported to the novel. *Madame Bovary,* where Emma is found to be bored with her spouse and in search of romance, stating to Kugelmass, ''I've always dreamed that some mysterious stranger would appear and rescue me from the monotony of this crass rural existence.'' The two become lovers both within the novel (art) and back in New York (reality). Soon Emma gets bored with life in a New York hotel as the novelty wears off. Initially, Persky has difficulties getting the magic cabinet to work, but finally he is able to send her back to her novel, Kugelmass reverts to his old life but eventually returns to Persky again, this time asking for *Portnoy's Complaint.* Instead, Persky's magic cabinet sends Kugelmass to a remedial Spanish book where he is chased by the verb *tener* while the magician dies of a heart attack and his magic cabinet bursts into flames.

Kugel is a Jewish holiday dish eaten to celebrate Shavuot, a time set aside for the remembrance of the gift of the Ten Commandments, the end of the barley harvest, and the offering of the first fruit at the Temple. During this season dairy dishes (Kugel) are often prepared because of several traditions: (1) during biblical times the Jews did not have time to cook meat after leaving the Sinai; (2) the Torah is often thought of as milk and honey; and (3) during the period from May to early June, the Spring harvest, milk and cheese are plentiful. Kugel is traditionally served on Friday nights or on the Sabbath, and there are several variations of the dish which include cheese, potato, and Lokshen (a sweet noodle pudding).

''Kugel'' in the name Kugelmass therefore emphasizes that the protagonist goes on a holiday, or what might be termed a lark, from his overweight spouse. The dessert of the story consists of the affair with Madame Bovary, whose name itself in English echoes the cow from whom milk comes and then cheese and so forth to be eaten by Kugelmass. The protagonist, as might the errant husband in any culture on a Friday night or weekend away from his wife, searches for a woman or his ''mass of Kugel,'' and he wants her to be French and respectable. Emma fits this role, but after the initial attraction between the two, the magic wears off and she means less and less to Kugelmass who is all but desperate to get Persky to send her back to her novel.

Allen's selection of the name Persky for the magician pays tribute to Lester Persky, a film producer who started out in New York by forming an advertising agency. Persky, the real one, eventually created Persky-Bright Productions, a film company that has been quite successful financing motion pictures that were originally stage productions, possibly an accidental connection with "Kugelmass." Persky's work includes *Hair, Fortune and Men's Eye's,* and *Equus.*

So Woody Allen had a few devices hidden under his narrative sleeve, known only to the select few while the rest of us simply enjoyed his sad story of another schlemiel schlepping along. Kugelmass and "Kugelmass" are archetypally Woody Allen.

Source: John Harty, "Allen's 'The Kugelmass Episode,'" in *Explicator,* Vol. 46, No. 3, Spring 1988, pp. 50–51.

Sources

Champion, Laurie, "Allen's 'The Kugelmass Episode,'" in *Explicator,* Vol. 51, No. 1, Fall 1992, pp. 61–63.

Harty, John, "Allen's 'The Kugelmass Episode,'" in *Explicator,* Vol. 46, No. 3, Spring 1988, pp. 50–51.

Further Reading

Abramovitch, Ilana, and Sean Galvin, eds., *Jews of Brooklyn,* University Press of New England, 2001.
   This is a kaleidoscopic look at the history, culture, and community of Brooklyn's Jews, from the first documented settlement of Jews in the borough in the 1830s to the present day Jewish presence.

Bakalar, Nick, and Stephen Kock, eds., *American Satire: An Anthology of Writings from Colonial Times to the Present,* Plume Books, 1997.
   This collection brings together some of the best American satirical prose and poetry, from the 1800s to the late twentieth century.

Epstein, Lawrence, *The Haunted Smile: The Story of Jewish Comedians in America,* Public Affairs, 2002.
   This history of how Jewish comedians changed the face of American entertainment, from vaudeville to the movies to television, includes anecdotes, personal stories, samples from comedians' stand-up material, immigrant sociology, and details tying the Yiddish language to Jewish American humor.

Lax, Eric, *Woody Allen: A Biography,* Da Capo Press, 2000.
   Allen's friend Lax offers a lighthearted account that includes the filmmaker's own opinions about this life.

No. 44, The Mysterious Stranger

Mark Twain's posthumously published story "No. 44, The Mysterious Stranger"—a bizarre tale of supernatural and dreamlike events that take place at the dawn of the age of modern printing in Europe— is the last major work of fiction by one of the greatest American authors of the nineteenth century.

"No. 44, The Mysterious Stranger" is narrated by August Feldner, a sixteen-year-old printer's apprentice living in a remote Austrian village in the late fifteenth century. The print shop in which he works is located in a run-down old castle, which houses over a dozen people, including the print master, his family, and the various men who work in the shop, as well as a magician. August relates the magical events that occur in the castle after the arrival of a strange boy who says his name is "Number 44, New Series 864,962." Twain's central themes in this story include dreams and the imagination, as well as ideas, knowledge, and thought.

The publishing history of Twain's "No. 44, The Mysterious Stranger," subtitled "Being an Ancient Tale Found in a Jug, and Freely Translated from the Jug," is almost as interesting as the story itself. In 1916, six years after his death, Twain's editors published a story entitled "The Mysterious Stranger," which they attributed to Twain's authorship. However, it was discovered during the 1960s that the story as it was originally published had been significantly altered by the editors in a manner that was clearly not Twain's intent. Thus, the story that passed for "The Mysterious Stranger" for over 50

Mark Twain

1969

years is now considered to be illegitimate. In 1969, the authoritative version of the story, ''No. 44, The Mysterious Stranger,'' based on Twain's original manuscript, was published for the first time. The following entry is based on a reading of the latter version of the story, which will be referred to in shorthand as ''The Mysterious Stranger.''

Author Biography

Mark Twain is the pen name of Samuel Langhorne Clemens, who was born November 30, 1835, in Florida, Missouri, the youngest of six children. The family eventually moved to nearby Hannibal, Missouri, which Twain later described as an ideal place for a boy to grow up. When he was eleven years old, his father died, and Twain was made to find work in order to help support the family. At thirteen, he ended his formal education and became a full time printer's apprentice, an experience that formed the basis of the print shop described in his posthumously published story ''No. 44, The Mysterious Stranger.''

During the early 1850s, Twain worked intermittently for various newspapers founded by his brother Orion, and traveled throughout the United States, contributing humorous travel sketches to popular periodicals. In 1856, Twain met the riverboat pilot Horace Bixby, who inspired him to learn to pilot steamboats traveling up and down the Mississippi River. Twain's experiences as a ''cub'' pilot apprenticed to Bixby, and later as a licensed pilot, are recounted in his autobiographical novel *Life on the Mississippi* (1877). With the advent of the Civil War, however, river trade between North and South was suspended, and Twain was compelled to find work elsewhere.

During the 1860s, Twain traveled extensively throughout the western United States and Europe, building his reputation as the author of humorous travel sketches published in a variety of journals and newspapers. He first published under the pen name Mark Twain in 1863, at the age of 27, based on the phrase ''mark twain'' used by riverboat pilots to designate areas of the river deep enough to ensure safe passage. His first great success came with the publication of the tall tale ''The Celebrated Jumping Frog of Calaveras County'' in 1865, which brought him critical attention and national recognition.

Twain married Olivia Langdon in 1870, and the couple moved to Hartford, Connecticut, where they resided for some 20 years. Many of Twain's most highly regarded works were published during the 1870s and 1880s, including *The Adventures of Tom Sawyer* (1876) and *The Adventures of Huckleberry Finn* (1884), considered to be his masterpiece and a landmark in American fiction.

In his final decades, Twain met with personal tragedy and financial ruin. Despite international success as one of America's preeminent authors, Twain went bankrupt during the early 1890s. He worked diligently giving lecture tours throughout Europe, Africa, and Asia, in order to pay off his debts. During this period, the eldest of his three daughters died of meningitis. In 1904 his wife died, and a few years later another one of his daughters died as a result of an epileptic seizure. Not longer after, his one remaining daughter became mentally ill. Twain died in Connecticut, on April 21, 1910.

Plot Summary

''The Mysterious Stranger'' is narrated by August Feldner, a sixteen-year-old printer's apprentice. The events of the story take place in 1490, in the small village of Eseldorf, Austria.

August lives and works in a run-down old castle where the print shop is located. Heinrich Stein, a man in his mid-50s and the master of the print shop, is referred to throughout the story as ''the master.'' The master lives in the castle with his wife, Frau Stein, and her seventeen-year-old daughter from a previous marriage, Marie Vogel. The master's sister, Frau Regen, and her seventeen-year-old daughter Marget Regen also live there. In addition to August, there are six other men who work in the print shop and live in the castle: Adam Binks, Gustav Fischer, Moses Haas, Hans Katzenyammer, Barty Langbein, and Ernest Wasserman. A magician by the name of Balthasar Hoffman lives in the castle as well.

One day, a boy of about sixteen or seventeen shows up at the castle, dressed in rags and begging for food. When he is asked his name, he tells them it is ''Number 44, New Series 864,962.'' On hearing this unusual name, most of the members of the household protest that he should be turned out. However, Katrina, the old cook, comes to his defense, and insists that he be taken in. The master agrees to allow Number 44 to work in the castle doing chores.

Soon, the master offers Number 44 a position as apprentice in the print shop. Most of the men working in the shop take an immediate disliking to Number 44, and do everything they can to overwork and humiliate him. August feels sympathy for Number 44, but knows that if he says anything in Number 44's defense, he will be ostracized by the others. The inhabitants of the castle begin to believe that Number 44 has magical powers, and they assume that the magician, Balthasar, has given him these powers.

Eventually, August secretly befriends Number 44. Number 44 explains that, although Balthasar did give him some magic power, he already had magical powers before he arrived. Number 44 states that he wishes to promote the idea that his powers come from Balthasar, so as to bolster the magician's reputation. Number 44 teaches August to make himself invisible. August also learns that Number 44 can read his thoughts.

The men who work in the print shop demand that Number 44 be turned out, but the master refuses to do so. Finally, they decide to go on strike until Number 44 is gotten rid of. The print shop is supposed to complete the publication of an order of Bibles, but the work cannot get done as long as the men are on strike. Upset by these events, the master becomes ill and takes to his bed.

In the midst of this crisis, the itinerant printer Doangivadam arrives at the castle. Upon learning of the situation, Doangivadam immediately takes sides with Number 44 against the other print shop workers. One night, they all go up to the shop and find that invisible workers are magically printing the Bibles. By morning, the Bible order is complete and the crisis is over, though the men are still on strike.

The men of the shop determine that Balthasar has given Number 44 the magical powers to complete the Bible printing without them. They threaten to have Balthasar burned as a heretic unless he promises to prevent Number 44 from performing any more magic. Balthasar states that, if Number 44 performs any more magic, he will cast a spell that will reduce the young man to ashes.

One night, the men are all eating together, and suddenly each man finds that his Duplicate has appeared in the room. The Duplicates, who look exactly like their Originals, explain that they are

Mark Twain

willing to work in the print shop, and give their wages over to their Originals, who will be able to get paid without working. Once this is agreed to, the Duplicates and the Originals live together in the castle, the Duplicates doing all the work and the Originals lounging around.

Seeing that Number 44 has performed magic in causing the Duplicates to appear, Balthasar turns him to ashes right before everyone's eyes. They hold a funeral and bury Number 44's remains—but when August returns to his room that night, Number 44 is sitting in a chair, alive and well. No one but August knows that Number 44 is not really dead.

Meanwhile, word has gotten out that Balthasar magically killed Number 44. The local priest, Father Adolf, determines that Balthasar is possessed by the Devil, and orders that he be burned at the stake. However, Balthasar cannot be found anywhere. Father Adolf then determines that the Duplicates are evil spirits, and condemns them to be burned at the stake. But each time he captures one of them, the Duplicate disappears before he is burned, and reappears in the print shop. One day, Number 44 magically disguises himself as Balthasar, and is seen in the town. Father Adolf, believing that he is Balthasar, arranges to have him burned at the stake, but he magically escapes before he is burned.

August realizes that he is in love with Marget, the master's niece. He discovers, however, that she is only in love with him in her dreams, when she is sleeping. August is able to make himself invisible and come to Marget in her dreams, during which her Dream-Self believes that her name is Elisabeth von Arnim and his name is Martin von Giesbach. But when she wakes up, she has no memory of this, and simply ignores August. During her waking hours, when she is her Day-Self or Waking-Self, she is in love with August's Duplicate, who calls himself Emil Schwarz.

One night, August sneaks into Marget's bedroom. When Marget, her maid, and her mother, Frau Regen, see him there, they scream and tell him to leave. The women believe it was his Duplicate, Emil, and not August, who snuck into the room. When the master learns of this, he orders that Emil must now marry Marget. Meanwhile, Marget's maid is about to tell one of the other maids about this incident, and thus spread a rumor that will ruin Marget's reputation.

August tries to come up with a scheme to prevent Marget's marriage to Emil, and calls on Number 44 to help him. They decide to magically transform the maid into a cat, so that she cannot spread any rumors about Marget. Once the maid is turned into a cat, Number 44 gives August the power to understand cat language. The cat then explains to them that she much prefers being a cat to being a maid, because as a maid she was constantly having to work and wait on other people. August and the cat agree that she will be his pet, and he names her Mary Florence Fortescue Baker G. Nightingale.

Emil comes to August's room and, much to August's surprise, says that he doesn't care if he marries Marget or not. He explains that he is a Dream-Being from the Empire of Dreams. He explains further that he is August's Dream-Self, the part of him that travels throughout space and time while August is sleeping. Emil hates being trapped in a physical body, in the form of August's Duplicate, and begs to be released from imprisonment in this body. Number 44 arrives, disguised as Balthasar, and grants Emil's wish, causing his physical form to dissolve into thin air so that he may return to the Dream-World.

Meanwhile, Father Adolf, Katrina, and a small army of men from the village have congregated in the castle, threatening to capture Balthasar and have him burned at the stake. Number 44, still disguised as Balthasar, steps into their midst, then suddenly makes himself disappear in a flash of blinding light, while simultaneously causing an eclipse to occur, which darkens the sky outside.

Back in August's room, Number 44 comes to visit August, and congratulates himself on the trick he played on the others. Number 44 decides to make time go backwards twenty-three hours. Then he arranges an Assembly of the Dead who form a Procession of thousands and thousands of skeletons of deceased people from throughout history, including such famous figures as King Arthur, Cleopatra, and Noah.

Number 44 then tries to explain to August who and what he is. He asserts that time and space, as well as life and death, mean nothing to him, and that he is capable of traveling throughout the universe and throughout history at his whim. Number 44 states that his existence is beyond the bounds of what any human being could conceive of. He explains that "Life itself is only a vision, a dream," and that his existence is "pure Thought," without physical matter. Number 44's parting words to August are:

> It is true, that which I have revealed to you: there is no God, no universe, no human race, no earthly life, no heaven, no hell. It is all a Dream, a grotesque and foolish dream. Nothing exists but You. And you are but a Thought . . . wandering forlorn among the empty eternities!

In the closing line of the story, August states, "He vanished, and left me appalled; for I knew, and realized, that all he had said was true."

Characters

Father Adolf

Father Adolf is the presiding priest in Eseldorf. When he learns of the magician Balthasar's magical powers, Father Adolf determines to have him burned at the stake as a heretic. However, he succeeds only in arresting Number 44, who is magically disguised as Balthasar, and who magically escapes before being burned. Father Adolf then declares that the Duplicates are evil spirits, and condemns them to be burned at the stake. However, every time he arrests one of the Duplicates, the Duplicate magically escapes before being burned, and Father Adolf eventually gives up trying. Father Adolf represents a medieval mentality of superstition, which he uses to justify asserting his power over others.

Adam Binks

Adam Binks is a sixty-year-old proofreader who lives in the castle and works in the print shop.

Doangivadam

Doangivadam is an itinerant printer. When the men in the print shop go on strike, August prays for Doangivadam to come and help with the situation. A few days later, Doangivadam arrives at the castle, and immediately takes the side of Number 44 against the other print shop workers. Doangivadam expresses his approval of August for befriending Number 44.

August Feldner

August Feldner, also known as Martin von Giesbach in Marget Regen's dreams, is a sixteen-year-old printer's apprentice and the narrator of "The Mysterious Stranger." When Number 44 arrives at the castle, August is immediately sympathetic to him. However, he is afraid to show his sympathy, for fear of being ostracized by the other men who work in the print shop. August manages to secretly befriend Number 44, who teaches him how to make himself invisible. August also learns that Number 44 can hear his thoughts. After the magician Balthasar apparently kills Number 44, August is the only one who knows that Number 44 is still alive. August witnesses many strange and fantastical events in the presence of Number 44, who takes him on various adventures traveling throughout the world and backward in time.

August falls in love with Marget, the master's niece, but finds that she only loves him when she is dreaming and he is invisible. During these dreams, Marget believes that her name is Elisabeth von Arnim and that August's name is Martin von Giesbach. August finds that he has a rival for Marget's love in his Duplicate, Emil Schwarz, whom Marget is in love with during her waking hours. After Number 44 magically dissolves Emil into thin air, August no longer has a rival for Marget's love.

In the end, Number 44 tells August that nothing in the universe exists, except for pure Thought, and that life is all a dream and an illusion. August concludes the story by stating, "I knew, and realized, that all he said was true." This ending implies that the whole story of "The Mysterious Stranger," as well as all of the characters in it, is a creation of

Media Adaptations

- "The Mysterious Stranger" was adapted to film and released in 1982. Directed by Peter H. Hunt, this film is a loose adaptation, which portrays Twain's tale as the daydream of a printer's apprentice living in nineteenth-century America.

August's imagination. Thus, Number 44's magical powers symbolize the extensive powers of August's imagination.

Gustav Fischer

Gustav Fischer is a twenty-seven-year-old printer who lives in the castle and works in the print shop.

Moses Haas

Moses Haas is a twenty-eight-year-old printer who lives in the castle and works in the print shop.

Balthasar Hoffman

Balthasar Hoffman is an astrologist and magician who lives in the castle. When Number 44 arrives and seems to display magical powers, everyone assumes it is Balthasar who has bestowed these powers upon him. Later, Balthasar magically reduces Number 44 to ashes. When Father Adolf learns of this event, he declares Balthasar a heretic and condemns him to be burned at the stake. However, no one is able to find Balthasar after this point. Throughout the rest of the story, Number 44 appears magically disguised as Balthasar. Number 44 tells August that he hopes to promote Balthasar's reputation as a magician by arranging things so that the others attribute various magical events to Balthasar's powers.

Katrina

Katrina is a sixty-year-old cook and housekeeper who lives and works in the castle. When

Number 44 first arrives, everyone is ready to throw him out, but Katrina rushes to his defense. Throughout the story, Katrina treats Number 44 as if he were her own son, and does everything she can to prevent others from harming him. When Balthasar reduces Number 44 to ashes, and everyone believes him dead, Katrina is distraught.

Hans Katzenyammer

Hans Katzenyammer is a thirty-six-year-old printer who lives in the castle and works in the print shop.

Barty Langbein

Barty Langbein is a fifteen-year-old assistant who lives in the castle and works in the print shop.

Marget's Maid

Marget's maid is present when August sneaks into Marget's room one night, and the maid believes it was August's Duplicate, Emil Schwarz, who sneaked into the room. The maid intends to inform one of the other maids in the castle about this event, and thus start a rumor that will ruin Marget's reputation. However, Number 44 magically transforms Marget's maid into a cat, so that she cannot tell anyone about what happened. After she is turned into a cat, she tells August in cat language (which Number 44 makes it possible for him to understand) that she actually prefers being a cat to being a maid, because as a maid she always had to wait on people. The cat and August agree that she will be his pet, and he names her Mary Florence Fortescue Baker G. Nightingale.

Mary Florence Fortescue Baker G. Nightingale

See Marget's Maid

The Master

See Heinrich Stein

Number 44

Number 44 gives his full name as ''Number 44, New Series 864,962.'' Everyone is astonished by this unusual name, and many of them assume he

must be an escaped convict, and that it is his prison number. Number 44, a boy of about sixteen, appears at the door of the castle one night, dressed in rags and begging for food. Heinrich Stein, the master of the print shop, agrees to put him to work in exchange for food and lodging. Soon, the master gives Number 44 a job as an apprentice in the print shop. Number 44 works tirelessly, but the other men working at the print shop do everything they can to humiliate him, insult him, and increase his work load.

August secretly befriends Number 44, and Number 44 slowly reveals to August more and more of his magical powers. Number 44 teaches August to make himself invisible and to fly, as well as demonstrating other magical feats. He states that, while he acquired some of his magical powers from Balthasar, he already had magical powers before he arrived at the castle. Number 44 explains that he wants everyone to think his magic comes from Balthasar, so as to promote the magician's reputation. One night, Balthasar magically reduces Number 44 to ashes. However, the next day August finds Number 44 still alive and well. For the remainder of the story, Number 44 usually appears to August and others disguised as Balthasar. When Father Adolf declares Balthasar a heretic and sentences him to be burned at the stake, Number 44 magically disguises himself as Balthasar, and is arrested and prepared to be burned at the stake. However, he magically escapes before being burned.

In the end, Number 44 does his best to explain to August what he is and where he comes from. In the final lines of the story, he tells August that life is all a dream and that nothing in the universe really exists, except for pure Thought. Number 44 thus implies that he himself is nothing more than a dream or illusion, created by August's imagination.

Frau Regen

Frau Regen is the sister of Heinrich Stein, the print shop master, and lives in the castle.

Marget Regen

Marget Regen, the seventeen-year-old daughter of Frau Regen and niece of Heinrich Stein, lives in the castle. Although August is in love with Marget, Marget only loves August when she is sleeping and he appears in her dreams (which he does by making himself invisible). In these dreams,

Marget thinks that her own name is Elisabeth von Arnim, and that August's name is Martin von Giesbach. During her waking hours, Marget is in love with August's Duplicate, who calls himself Emil Schwarz. After Emil proposes to Marget's Waking-Self, and she accepts, August/Martin proposes to Marget's Dream-Self (Elisabeth), and they conduct a marriage ceremony in her dream. Later, after Emil is believed to have entered Marget's bedroom at night, Heinrich Stein commands that he marry Marget. However, Emil is soon afterward dissolved into thin air by Number 44, so August no longer has a rival for Marget's love.

Emil Schwarz

Emil Schwarz is the Duplicate of August Feldner and looks exactly like him. While Marget falls in love with the August who appears in her dreams, during her waking hours she is in love with Emil. August thus regards Emil as his rival for Marget's love. When the master commands that Emil must marry Marget, August hopes to prevent the marriage. However, Emil discusses the situation with August, and admits that he really doesn't care if he marries Marget or not. Emil states that he is August's Dream-Self, and normally roams freely throughout time and space while August is asleep. Emil begs to be released from the physical body of August's Duplicate, in which he is trapped. Number 44 arrives, disguised as Balthasar the magician, and grants Emil's wish by magically dissolving his body into thin air, so that he can return to the Dream-World.

Frau Stein

Frau Stein is the wife of Heinrich Stein, the print shop master. She has a mean disposition.

Heinrich Stein

Heinrich Stein, a man in his mid-50s, is the master of the print shop. He is referred to throughout the story as "the master." The master is described as "a scholar and a dreamer or a thinker," who loves learning and study. He has a kindly disposition, but is not very effective in asserting himself with his family and employees. The master decides to take Number 44 into the castle and employ him as an apprentice in the print shop. Despite the complaints of the other print shop workers, Stein refuses to send Number 44 away.

When the men go on strike just before a large Bible publishing order is due, the master becomes so distraught that he falls ill and takes to his bed. After the Bibles are magically published on time, Stein immediately recovers his health.

Marie Vogel

Marie Vogel is the seventeen-year-old daughter of Frau Stein from a previous marriage, and lives in the castle. Like her mother, she has a mean disposition.

Elisabeth von Arnim

See Marget Regen

Martin von Giesbach

See August Feldner

Ernest Wasserman

Ernest Wasserman is a seventeen-year-old apprentice who lives in the castle and works in the print shop.

Themes

Dreams and the Imagination

In "The Mysterious Stranger," Twain uses magic as an allegory for the realm of dreams and the imagination. In the Dream-World of our imaginations, he suggests, we can do and be anything, as if by magic.

Twain fills his tale with numerous magical occurrences. Some of the magical elements of "The Mysterious Stranger" are directly associated with the realm of dreams. The Duplicates who appear in the castle one night turn out to be the embodiment of the Dream-Selves of the men they resemble. August's Duplicate, who calls himself Emil Schwarz, explains that he is August's Dream-Self, and that he comes from the Dream-World. Emil further explains that the Dream-Self comes alive only when the Waking-Self is asleep. The Dream-Self nor-

Topics for Further Study

- ''No. 44, The Mysterious Stranger'' is based in part on Twain's experiences as a printer's apprentice during his youth. Write a research paper on technological developments in the printing process during the nineteenth century.

- Read another short story by Mark Twain, which can be found in collections such as *The Celebrated Jumping Frog of Calaveras County, and Other Sketches* (1867). Write an essay discussing the ways in which Twain uses humor in this story to comment on American society.

- The setting of ''No. 44, The Mysterious Stranger'' in fifteenth-century Austria is based in part on Twain's experiences traveling in Austria in the late nineteenth and early twentieth centuries, during the reign of the emperor Franz Joseph. Write a research paper on the political and social conditions of Austria during this period.

- ''No. 44, The Mysterious Stranger'' is a fantastical tale in which magical and supernatural events occur. Write your own short story involving fantastic, magical, or supernatural occurrences.

mally has no physical existence, and so is free to roam throughout time and space at will. However, the Dream-Self is dependent on the physical existence of the Waking-Self—it is born with the individual and dies with the individual. Twain thus makes a distinction between the Waking-Self, or Day-Self, which is the physical being who goes to work each day, and the Dream-Self, which emerges when we are sleeping and is free from the constraints of physical existence.

Number 44 performs such magical feats as mind-reading, flying, becoming invisible, time travel, and many other wondrous things. Number 44's extensive magical powers represent the possibilities of the human imagination, the powers of which reach far beyond what humans are capable of in their waking or conscious lives. August is intro-

duced to Number 44's way of perceiving reality, and so his mind is expanded to encompass a greater range of possibilities than he had previously imagined. In the conclusion to the story, Number 44 asserts that everything in the universe is a dream, a creation of the human imagination: ''*Nothing* exists; all is a dream. God—man—the world, —the sun, the moon, the wilderness of stars: a dream, all a dream.''

Thought

Thought is also a central theme of ''The Mysterious Stranger.'' The story takes place in a print shop at the dawn of the age of printing in medieval Europe. Historians regard the dawning of the print age as an extremely important development in the history of modern thought. New developments that made mass-publishing possible meant that books could be made available to a much broader segment of the population than ever before. This increased availability of books meant that the spread of knowledge and ideas throughout Europe increased tremendously.

The print shop where August works is a very small operation located in a remote Austrian village, yet it represents a bastion of enlightenment within a community steeped in superstition and ignorance. As August explains, in 1490 printing was still a new art, and ''almost unknown in Austria.''

> Very few persons in our secluded region had ever seen a printed page, few had any very clear idea about the art of printing, and perhaps still fewer had any curiosity concerning it or felt any interest in it.

August thus stands on the cusp of two different eras in the history of human thought. On the one hand, he was raised in the village and shares the traditional, medieval superstitions and limited viewpoint of the townspeople. On the other hand, working in the print shop, publishing books on a variety of subjects, including math, science, and philosophy, he is exposed to cutting edge advances in knowledge and ideas.

The appearance of Number 44 further expands August's knowledge and understanding of the world. Number 44 frequently makes references to the future, and often offers food to August that comes from time periods and cultures that don't yet exist. Number 44 also takes August back in time, exposing him to a broad-sweeping perspective on human history. August's newly acquired perspective on human civilization helps to expand his mind and further enlighten him to ideas beyond the confines of his remote and backward little village.

Toward the end of the story, Number 44 tells August that he is nothing more than pure Thought, and that Thought is the true essence of human existence.

supernatural occurrences. By setting his story in a remote time and place, and by infusing it with elements of magic and fantasy, Twain is able to explore themes of dreams and the imagination without limiting himself to the requirements of realist fiction. Through the fantastical character of Number 44, Twain ultimately postulates that the realm of dreams, fantasy, and the imagination are more relevant to human experience than are the experiences we associate with concrete, physical reality.

Style

Narrative Point of View

"The Mysterious Stranger" is narrated in the first-person voice by August Feldner, a sixteen-year-old printer's apprentice. Thus, all of the events of the story are related solely from August's point-of-view. This limited first-person narrative point-of-view is central to the story. Toward the end, Number 44 asserts that everything in August's universe is a creation of his own imagination. Because the story is told from August's perspective, it is entirely possible that he has merely imagined these people, places, and events, or even that the entire story is a dream from which he will soon awaken.

Local Color Fiction

"Local color" fiction was a new development in American literature in the post-Civil-War era, when much of Twain's writing was published. Local color fiction is characterized by a focus on small communities existing within a specific region of the United States, and exhibiting habits, customs, and cultural practices specific to that region. Twain's fiction often takes place in the American South, among small communities along the Mississippi River. Although "The Mysterious Stranger" takes place in Austria, it shares some characteristics of local color fiction, in that it is set in a small, remote village community in which the inhabitants share many superstitions and many qualities of regional quaintness. Many critics have noted that Twain based his fictional town of Eseldorf, Austria, on his own experiences growing up in the small town of Hannibal, Missouri.

The Fantastical in Fiction

"The Mysterious Stranger" is a fantastical tale, meaning that it includes elements of magic and

Historical Context

Austria in the Fifteenth and Sixteenth Centuries

For many centuries, Austria was not a nation, but a duchy within the Roman Empire. Beginning in the thirteenth century, the Austrian region was ruled by the hereditary House of Habsburg, which lasted until the early twentieth century. The history of Austria in the fifteenth century, when Twain's story takes place, was dominated by the Habsburg ruler Frederik III. Frederik inherited the position of archduke of the Austrian lands in 1424. In 1440 he was elected king of Germany, and in 1452 he was crowned Roman Emperor. Like the magician in Twain's story, Frederik had a strong interest in studying astrology and magic, as well as alchemy.

Upon his death in 1493, Frederik was succeeded by his son, Maximilian I. Like his father, Maximilian I eventually ruled as emperor of Rome, king of Germany, and archduke of Austria. During the sixteenth century, under Maximilian I, the Habsburg dynasty reached the height of its powers, becoming a major European force. By various means, including marriage, military pressure, and treaties, Maximilian added to the Austrian territories the Netherlands, Hungary, Bohemia, Burgundy, Spain, and the Spanish empire, including colonial holdings in the Americas.

The Dawn of Modern Printing

"No. 44, The Mysterious Stranger" takes place in a printing shop in late fifteenth century Austria, and is based in part on Twain's experiences as

Compare
&
Contrast

- **1490s:** Austria is a duchy within the Roman Empire, ruled by the hereditary Habsburg dynasty. Frederik III is archduke of Austria until his death in 1493, when his son, Maximilian I, succeeds him.

  1900s: Austria is a part of the Austria-Hungary Dual Monarchy, ruled by Franz Joseph, a descendent of the Habsburg dynasty.

  Today: Austria is an independent democratic nation with a parliamentary system of government, based on the constitution of 1920 (revised in 1929).

- **1490s:** The continents now known as the Americas have been inhabited for centuries by many different peoples with many different languages. After Christopher Columbus's venture to the "New World" is completed in 1492, western European cultures begin to establish settlements in the Americas.

  1900s: The United States of America is a democratic nation, based on the Constitution of 1776. All adult males have the right to vote. Due to the aggressive policies of the United States government, Native Americans have become a small minority in America, most of them living on reservations.

  Today: The United States remains a democratic nation. All adults, both men and women, have the right to vote. Most Native Americans still live on reservations, although, since the 1970s, Native Americans have organized to achieve equal civil rights.

- **1490s:** Modern book printing techniques are still new to European culture. Printing methods using movable type, developed by Johannes Gutenberg, represent the most advanced printing technology.

  1900s: Many innovations developed throughout the nineteenth century have resulted in significant advances in the printing process. Among these new technologies are the use of steam engines to mechanize the printing press, advances in the reproduction of multi-color illustrations, the use of cylindrical devices for transferring ink to paper, and the integration of photographic processes. A significant advance made in 1904 is the development of a technique known as "offset" printing. Some aspects of the printing process once performed by individual craftsmen have now been mechanized.

  Today: Advances in computer technology have significantly altered many aspects of book-printing. Many steps in the printing process once performed by individual craftsmen or mechanical machines are now accomplished through computer technology. Books can even be purchased from retailers on the Internet and printed at home by the consumer.

---

a printer's apprentice in mid-nineteenth century America.

The process of modern book printing first developed in Europe over the course of the fifteenth century. Twain thus sets his story at a time when printing was still a relatively new process, and represented a significant advance in the intellectual history of Europe. The development of the printing press made it possible for greater numbers of people to have access to knowledge and ideas through the dissemination of larger quantities of books at lower prices.

The innovation that inaugurated modern printing methods was the invention of moveable type. Moveable type involves individual letters or characters carved or molded out of wood, clay, or metal, which can be arranged to create a text. When ink is applied to these letters, they can be impressed upon a piece of paper in order to reproduce the text. In Asia, various methods of movable type were developed between the 11th and 14th centuries. However, this knowledge did not find its way to Europe, and so European methods of print developed later and along different lines.

The innovations of the German printer Johannes Gutenberg advanced European printing methods by creating a moveable type, inventing a mechanized printing press, and developing an ink compatible with this process. Gutenberg's printing process is dated from the 1450s; his most significant achievement was the publication of the bible now known as the Gutenberg Bible, the first complete book to be printed in Europe using moveable type. Gutenberg's inventions are regarded as a watershed in European intellectual history, ushering in the dawn of the modern printing age. The printing methods he invented remained essentially unchanged until the nineteenth century, when a number of significant improvements were made to the process.

Critical Overview

"The Mysterious Stranger," Twain's last major work of fiction, was not published until after his death. In order to appreciate critical reactions to "The Mysterious Stranger," it is important to understand the problems that have arisen regarding the manuscripts on which published versions of the story have been based. Upon his death, Twain left behind three different unpublished manuscripts of three different stories sharing a number of similarities. These manuscripts were entitled, "The Chronicle of Young Satan," "Schoolhouse Hill," and "No. 44, The Mysterious Stranger."

The first published version of a story entitled "The Mysterious Stranger" became available in 1916. However, during the 1960s, scholars came to the conclusion that this version of the story had been significantly tampered with by editors and was not true to Twain's intentions. The editors of this first version, which is now referred to as the "Paine-Duneka text," were Albert Bigelow Paine and Frederick A. Duneka of Harper & Brothers publishing company. Paine and Duneka created this illegitimate text by grafting the ending of one story ("No. 44, The Mysterious Stranger") onto the body of another story Twain had left unfinished ("The Chronicle of Young Satan"), editing out material which they deemed controversial, deleting about

one quarter of Twain's words, altering and importing a character from one story into another, and adding several paragraphs of their own writing—all of which they combined into a story which they attributed to Twain without informing the public of the radical changes they had made to his original manuscripts.

In 1969, Twain's original manuscript entitled "No. 44, The Mysterious Stranger" was published for the first time as the authoritative text of the story. Scholars have since agreed that the "Paine-Duneka text" should no longer be regarded as a legitimate work, and that this more recent version is the only one which should be presented to readers as "The Mysterious Stranger," by Mark Twain. William M. Gibson, in an "Introduction" to *Mark Twain's Mysterious Stranger Manuscripts* (1969), referred to the Paine-Duneka text as "an editorial fraud," based on a version of the story which was "cut, cobbled-together, partially falsified." Gibson asserted that Paine, "altered the manuscript of the book in a fashion that almost certainly would have enraged Clemens [Twain]." Sholom J. Kahn, in *Mark Twain's Mysterious Stranger: A Study of the Manuscript Texts* (1978), somewhat more charitably remarked, "Paine's arrogant procedure, however sincere, muddied the waters of Mark Twain scholarship for two generations." Because of this long-running confusion over the text of "The Mysterious Stranger," critical responses to the earlier, "Paine-Duneka text" are no longer applicable to Twain's story.

Understandably, much of the critical discussion of "No. 44, The Mysterious Stranger," since the authoritative text came to light in the 1960s, has focused on ongoing issues and questions regarding the various unpublished manuscripts Twain left upon his death. Critical discussion of the story itself has tended to focus on two central questions: Who is Number 44?; and, What is the meaning of the final chapter?

Critics agreed that the identity of the supernatural character Number 44 is ambiguous. Kahn observed, "the mystery of the stranger's identity is one of the chief cruxes of the plot in 'No. 44.'" Derek Parker Royal, in "Terrible Dreams of Creative Power" (1999) observed:

> What is the nature of No. 44? . . . . the figure refuses neat critical categorization and eludes the grasp of even the most careful examination. He is simultaneously an impish prankster, a satanic figure, a benevolent fatalist, a childlike innocent, a philosophical pragmatist, a social determinist, a showman and per-

A sixteenth-century printing shop like the one used for the setting in "No. 44, Mysterious Stranger"

former, dream substance, and, perhaps most important, an artist and creator.

Critics have explored the implications of the final chapter of "The Mysterious Stranger" from several different perspectives. Many have asserted that the story's conclusion is a celebration of the imaginative mind and the process of artistic creation. Others have examined the philosophical implications of the conclusion, suggesting that it resonates with the philosophy of Plato or Descartes.

Kahn summed up Twain's achievement in commenting that "No. 44, The Mysterious Stranger" represents "the fruits of a truly creative imagination exploring many corners of the human condition in a fresh and profound way."

Criticism

Liz Brent

Brent holds a Ph.D. in American culture from the University of Michigan. In this essay, Brent discusses Twain's use of print shop terminology in "No. 44, The Mysterious Stranger."

August Feldner, the narrator of Mark Twain's "No. 44, The Mysterious Stranger," works as an apprentice in a print shop. August often describes events, situations, and characters in terms familiar to the printing trade. Thus, throughout the story, he expresses himself through metaphors drawn from printing terminology.

In comparing the personality of Marie Vogel, the step-daughter of the print master, to that of Marget Regen, the niece of the print master, August makes extensive use of metaphors drawn from the printer's trade. He describes Marie Vogel in the following terms:

> She was a second edition of her mother—just plain galley-proof, neither revised nor corrected, full of turned letters, wrong fonts, outs and doubles, as we say in the printing-shop—in a word *pi*.

In stating that Marie was "a second edition of her mother," August indicates that, just as the second edition of a published book is almost exactly the same as the first edition, so Marie resembles her mother almost exactly. In describing her as "just plain galley-proof, neither revised nor corrected," August is referring to a preliminary stage in the printing of a book before it has been edited, revised, and corrected. He then lists a variety of errors that

What Do I Read Next?

- *The Celebrated Jumping Frog of Calaveras County, and Other Sketches* (1867) is a collection of early short stories by Twain, considered among his best.

- *Life on the Mississippi* (1883) is an autobiographical novel based on Twain's experiences as a river boat pilot when he was a young man.

- *The Adventures of Huckleberry Finn* (1884) is regarded as Twain's masterpiece and as one of the greatest American novels of the nineteenth century. Huck Finn runs away from home along with Jim, an escaped slave, with whom he travels down the Mississippi River on a raft.

- *A Connecticut Yankee in King Arthur's Court* (1889), by Twain, is a fantastical novel in which a nineteenth-century American finds himself transported to the royal court of King Arthur in Medieval England.

- *Luck of Roaring Camp, and Other Sketches* (1870) is a collection of short stories by Bret Harte, a "local color" author and contemporary of Twain. Harte's tales, set in California mining camps, are both humorous and sentimental.

- *The Country of the Pointed Firs* (1896) is a novel by Sarah Orne Jewett, another of Twain's contemporaries and also a "local color" author. Jewett writes of community life in a small maritime village on the coast of Maine.

---

can occur in a print text at this stage in the process: "turned letters" are letters that are upside down; "wrong fonts" are letters in the wrong size or design; "outs" are letters that have been accidentally left out of a text; and "doubles" are words that have been accidentally repeated. August sums up his description of Marie in describing her as "pi," which is a printer's term referring to a hodge-podge of mixed-up type, such as may result from dropping a form filled with individual letters of movable type. In other words, Marie has an extremely flawed personality, similar to the flawed text of a galley-proof, which contains many errors, or a jumble of individual letters of print type, without order or significance.

In contrast to his description of Marie Vogel, whom he doesn't like, August uses print terminology to express his admiration for Marget Regen, whom he is in love with. He states, "She was a second edition of what her mother had been at her age; but struck from the standing forms and needing no revising, as one says in the printing-shop."

Like Marie, Marget is described as a "second edition" of her mother. However, while Marie is compared to a text that is full of flaws and errors,

Marget is compared to a text that is perfect and flawless. Standing forms are trays of type that have already been set and corrected, and can be made available for printing subsequent editions of a book. Thus, in describing Marget as "struck from the standing forms" he implies that, as her mother was also flawless, she in turn inherited her mother's perfect character without alteration. That Marget "needs no revising" means that, like a text that is without errors, she is without flaws and perfect as is.

Later in the story, Doangivadam, an itinerant printer, also uses terminology from the printing trade to express himself metaphorically. When Doangivadam asks Number 44's name, and Number 44 replies, "No. 44, New Series 864,962," Doangivadam asserts: "My—word, but it's a daisy! In the hurry of going to press, let's dock it to Forty-Four and put the rest on the standing-galley and let it go for left-over at half rates."

Doangivadam is responding to the fact that Number 44's full name is rather long, and a mouthful to pronounce. He suggests that "in the hurry of going to press," meaning to save time, they shorten his name to Forty-Four. A standing-galley is a place where units of type are stored for reuse; thus he suggests the extraneous letters and digits in Number 44's name (''New Series, 864,962''), be set aside as extraneous material. Further, he jokingly implies that these extraneous elements of Number 44's name could be sold off at half-price for reuse by someone else.

At another point in the story, August tells the old cook Katrina of his experience of Ernest, a fellow printer, exposing him to ridicule and anger from the other men working in the shop. Ernest had found out that August had secretly become friends with Number 44, and he had announced this fact to the other men. August comments that Katrina, who sides with Number 44, ''was full of pity for me and maledictions for Ernest, and promised him a piece of her mind, with foot-notes and illustrations.''

Here, August uses the book printing concepts of foot-notes and illustrations as a metaphor to indicate that Katrina expressed in graphic terms with detailed explanations her desire to punish Ernest for threatening to harm him.

Through the narration of August, Twain further employs metaphors drawn from printing technology in the introduction of the characters referred to as Duplicates, who are magical copies of the print shop workers, referred to as the Originals. An original in printing refers to an original piece of text, whereas duplicate refers to a printed copy of the original. As in print an original version of a text is regarded as more authentic, so the men referred to as Originals in the story regard themselves as the authentic versions of their bodily forms, while the Duplicates are seen as mere copies.

When, toward the end of the story, Number 44 creates an eclipse to darken the sky, then disappears in a blinding flash of light before the eyes of a crowd of people, August states that the effect of the eclipse made Number 44's dramatic display of magic ''grand and stunning—just letter-perfect, as it seemed to me.'' In printing, a text that is letter-perfect has been type set without a single letter out of place. So August expresses his awe and wonder at the spectacle Number 44 has created, regarding it as a magnificent event that was carried off to perfection.

With the stylistic device of employing terminology from the printing process as a basis for metaphorical descriptions in ''No. 44, The Mysterious Stranger,'' Twain skillfully demonstrates that August's perspective and vocabulary are influenced by his trade, thus creating a narrative voice unique to his story.

Source: Liz Brent, Critical Essay on ''No. 44, The Mysterious Stranger,'' in *Short Stories for Students,* Thomson Gale, 2005.

Derek Parker Royal

In the following essay, Royal examines the enigmatic nature of the character of No. 44, finding him ''neither ominous nor upbeat, but an unstable mixture of both that is representative of many of Twain's later figures.''

In his later fiction Twain most fully explores the dynamics of authority and its relationship to the culture of his time. In *A Connecticut Yankee in King Arthur's Court, Pudd'nhead Wilson,* and the *Mysterious Stranger* manuscripts, he wrestles with larger troubling issues in ways that he had not, or could not, in his earlier works, and invests these ongoing dialogues in three of the most dominating characters in his canon. Whereas most of their predecessors were either two-dimensional or exceedingly forthright representations, Hank Morgan, David Wilson, and No. 44 are all problematic and highly enigmatic figures of authority who resist any sense of critical closure. This Twainian power figure is given full, and often disturbing, expression in his completed works, *A Connecticut Yankee* and *Pudd'nhead Wilson.* Control lies at the heart of Hank Morgan's sojourn at Camelot. He plans from the very beginning to ''boss the whole country inside of three months,'' and fulfills his desire by erecting a technological nightmare of death and destruction. Pudd'nhead Wilson, although less obviously power-hungry than Hank, nevertheless falls into the same mold. His power is of a more subtle and clandestine nature. Through his hobby of fingerprinting, he holds in his hand the identity of Dawson's Landing, and reveals this information to great effect in the dramatic courtroom scene. Much like Tom Sawyer and Hank Morgan, Wilson manipulates the dissemination of knowledge in order to give him the edge-and the reputation-in the community. All of these later characters live by the adage ''knowledge is power.'' However, with Pudd'nhead Wilson there arises an interesting question: what exactly is his game? Although we know his parentage, his birthplace, and his desired trade, he nonetheless remains an enigmatic character aloof from both the town and the reader. There is a dearth of information on the psychology of Wilson. What is to be made of this freethinking young lawyer with a taste for irony, fingerprinting, and palm reading? Just as Hank Morgan is to Camelot, David Wilson is, in his own way, a mysterious stranger to Dawson's Landing.

What further confounds an unambiguous reading of Hank Morgan and David Wilson is an almost equal amount of benevolence that stands alongside their less attractive sides. If, in their more problematic moments—their desire for control, their need for attention, and their propensity (either intentionally or not) for mischievousness—Hank and Wilson embody the spirit of Tom Sawyer, then their compassionate and selfless side would tend to suggest strains of Huck Finn. Although not necessarily diametrically opposed, Tom and Huck are nonetheless two distinct types whose traits intermingle uncomfortably in many of Twain's later protagonists. While Hank Morgan does set out to ''boss'' Camelot through a highly staged and condescending series of manipulations, at the same time he voices his desire for a democratic inclusiveness that will uphold the dignity of even the most disenfranchised individual. Even though David Wilson uses courtroom dramatics to establish his reputation and popularity (and in the process relegitimizes racial delineations), he nonmaliciously does so in the name of justice. Depending on where you are in *A Connecticut Yankee* and *Pudd'nhead Wilson,* Hank and Wilson will read as either a devil or an angel, as either a selfish manipulating showman or an innocent pensive ethicist.

The enigmatic stranger returns with full dramatic force in the guise of Young Satan or No. 44. This character is the literary descendent of Twain's collection of manipulative pranksters and outsiders, embodied previously in the guise of Hank Morgan and David Wilson. All three—Hank, Wilson, and 44—are mysterious outsiders who come into a foreign world and, through a series of manipulative games, profoundly alter the course of events. All are performers—much in the mold of Tom Sawyer—whose feats are a mystery to their audience, but whose secrets are merely commonplace to their authors. All manipulate their audiences by controlling knowledge and information. All are revealers of truths that expose societal shams, individual hypocrisy, and illegitimate sources of power. All three are able to make life-and-death decisions with relatively little moral effort. All possess a fatal and even apocalyptic power that seems to have fascinated their creator. Finally, and perhaps more importantly, all three embody a series of oppositions that constantly vie for dominance, yet none of whose possibilities ever attain a privileged position within the text.

Yet, the question remains, what is No. 44? Much more than was the case with Hank Morgan

> ❝ Indeed, it is Twain's own intentional and grand ambiguity, this mystery that rests at the very heart of 44, that dogged him throughout his project and ultimately rendered it unfinished."

and David Wilson, 44's identity seems purposefully clouded in a dreamlike ambiguity. Indeed, it is Twain's own intentional and grand ambiguity, this mystery that rests at the very heart of 44, that dogged him throughout his project and ultimately rendered it unfinished. From 1897 to 1908, Twain worked on four different versions of his mysterious stranger narrative, each one revealing a different angle, and in some cases a profound twist, on the nature of No. 44. An obvious, but nonetheless highly pertinent, example of this is 44's metaphysical origin. Is he an angel or is he a devil? And if he is an uncertain mixture of the two, is he more devil than angel, or is it the other way around? The answers vacillate both between and within the various texts. In ''The Chronicle of Young Satan,'' he seems to be an amalgamation of both possibilities. As Young Satan reveals relatively early in the narrative, any investigations into the motives behind his actions will offer no answers, for his actions are beyond the human scope of the terms ''good'' and ''evil.'' Those designations, he tells Theodor, are the result of man's degrading ''Moral Sense'' and are therefore alien to the young stranger. ''We cannot do wrong; neither have we any disposition to do it, for we do not know what it is.'' In one significant passage, the creation of his clay people, Young Satan reveals characteristics that suggest both the devil and Christ. Immediately after telling the boys his name, ''Satan'' (Twain italicizes the name for emphasis) then ''held out a chip and caught a little woman on it who was falling from the scaffolding and put her back where she belonged.'' Although he possesses his uncle's name, he nonetheless plays the savior figure by snatching the woman from her death. But the possible significance of this action is undermined in Satan's next statement, when he says "she is an idiot to step backward like that and not notice what she is about," and later when he crushes with his fingers two men for fighting. Reproachment and condemnation have taken the place of forgiveness. Certainly, in a Judeo-Christian sense, Young Satan is an unambiguous expression of neither supreme deity.

Other signs in the text are mixed. Young Satan has taken his uncle's name, but he is nonetheless a self-professed angel. "It is a good family-ours," Satan tells the boys, "there is not a better. [My uncle] is the only member of it that has ever sinned." This last word is significant because it suggests some type of implied morality, an ethical dimension that Satan had previously strongly denied. Satan, in essence, begins to deconstruct himself. He possesses—in human terms—angelic qualities, such as a propensity for music and poetry, yet cryptically states that "it was from [his] uncle that he drew his support." By the end of the fragment, the reader knows no more about Young Satan than he did at the beginning. He is as insubstantial as a blank screen or transparent film, seemingly nothing more than a collection of each reader's projections. This characterization of Young Satan as transparent film is not just metaphorical, as Theodor describes it during one of Satan's more memorable exits:

> He thinned away and thinned away until he was a soap-bubble, except that he kept his shape. You could see the bushes through him as clearly as you see the delicate iridescent colors of the bubble . . . . He sprang—touched the grass—bounded—floated along—touched again—and so on, and presently exploded, —puff! and in his place was vacancy.

The reader, in a critical act of deciphering Young Satan, can indeed empathize with Theodor's experience. Not only is the figure elusive, but his construction is precarious enough to where even the most careful of inquiries will—puff!—leave the critic empty-handed.

In "Schoolhouse Hill," 44's nature is less problematic. He seems, in the fullest sense, to be angelic. "I am not a devil," he tells Oliver Hotchkiss. Yet, although his father is indeed Satan (a familial holdover from "Young Satan"), he states emphatically, "I don't admire him." At his own admission, he was raised "partly in heaven, partly in hell," but this seems nothing more than a playful trope employed to convey his fallen parentage, for, just a few pages later, 44 tells Hotchkiss "I was in heaven; I had always lived in heaven, of course."

In this, a lighter and more humorous version of Twain's mysterious stranger, No. 44 is not so much an enigma as he is a metaphysical Tom Sawyer. He may be impish, but his heart is in the right place. Similarly, the servant devils that No. 44 summons from hell are not imposing demons, but cute "velvety little red fellows." More important, the "Schoolhouse Hill" 44 is an angel with a mission: "The fundamental change wrought in man's nature by my father's conduct must remain—it is permanent; but a part of its burden of evil consequences can be lifted from your race, and I will undertake it. Will you help?" There is little difference in tone between 44 asking Hotchkiss to assist in this Promethean task and Tom Sawyer encouraging Jim and Huck to join in on one of his adventures. Furthermore, in "Schoolhouse Hill," 44 takes on the obvious role of a savior figure—quite a departure from the amoral and shadowy figures of the other two manuscripts.

But if Twain casts a fog around the stranger in the "Young Satan" manuscript, he remains almost silent in the last version, "No. 44, The Mysterious Stranger." Indeed, silence thematically permeates the text. Every time August or his duplicate Emile attempts to raise the question of his origin, No. 44 holds his tongue with "that mysterious check which had so often shut off a question which I wanted to ask." When August asks No. 44 the question that we all want to ask, "what are you?", he replies "Ah . . . now we have arrived at a point where words are useless."

More significantly, No. 44's ghostly effects function in a similar manner. On three notable occasions, each accompanying one of 44's demonstrations, August is stricken by an awful silence. First, when he sees the printing press working by itself, he is shaken by "a soundless emptiness, a ghostly hush":

> all the different kinds of work were racing along like Sam Hill—and all in a sepulchral stillness. The way the press was carrying on, you would think it was making noise enough for an insurrection, but in a minute you would find it was only your fancy, it wasn't producing a sound . . . abundance of movement, you see, plenty of tramping to and fro, yet you couldn't hear a footfall; there wasn't a spoken word, there wasn't a whisper, there wasn't a sigh—oh, the saddest, uncanniest silence that ever was.

In each of the two other cases, the silence anticipates the ghostly performance. Immediately before the one-man minstrel show, August feels the profound silence of his solitude as he awaits No. 44: "It was awfully still and solemn and midnighty, and this made me feel creepy and shivery and afraid of ghosts." Then when he hears the dry, bony noise of the skeleton creeping up on him in the murky moonlit hall, "it shriveled me up like a spider in a candle-flame." Later, immediately prior to the Assembly of the Dead procession, August feels "the thickest and solidest and blackest darkness" surrounding him, with "a silence which was so still it was as if the world was holding its breath."

These scenes are strikingly similar to the ghostly stillness that Huck experiences at the end of chapter one of *Adventures of Huckleberry Finn.* Up in his room, awaiting the arrival of Tom Sawyer to provide some relief from his stifling life at the widow's, Huck notices a series of lonely, mournful sounds that spark his superstitious interests. Along with an owl, a whippoorwill, and crying dog—powerfully forbidding omens to the superstitious—he listens closely as:

> the leaves rustled in the woods ever so mournful . . . and the wind was trying to whisper something to me and I couldn't make out what it was, and so it made the cold shivers run over me . . . Then away out in the woods I heard that kind of a sound that a ghost makes when it wants to tell about something that's on its mind and can't make itself understood . . . Pretty soon a spider went crawling up my shoulder, and I flipped it off and it lit in the candle; and before I could budge it was all shriveled up.

Similar to the dark stillness that August experiences, the sounds that Huck hears outside his window all arouse dread. Significantly, these are noises that produce little sound. The leaves rustle mournfully the wind speaks in a whisper that he cannot comprehend, and, most telling of Huck's spooked disposition, a ghost cannot make itself understood. As is the case with August, the distressful portent of it all is encapsulated in the image of a spider in a flame, an indication for the superstitious that trouble is near at hand.

Forrest Robinson argues that such scenes in *Huckleberry Finn* reveal the fears, death wishes, and superstitious dread of Huck that emerge naturally from the text of the young boy's account; and that, further, these awful feelings spring from two psychological vulnerabilities that plague him throughout the novel: guilt over the safety of Jim and a mortal dread of solitude. Robinson asserts that "Huck Finn is not a very happy person," and that from the superstitious reveries of the first chapter to the false hopes of "the Territory ahead" in the last, Huck's plight is a depressing one:

At no point are we inclined to view Huck's narrative as a humorous riot of naive superstition; the acceleration of his terror is too immediate and authentic for release into comedy. Rather, we come away impressed with the vague but nearly palpable dread which emerges from Huck's solitude. Left to himself, he is at once fearful that his life will continue, and that it will end.

The silences in Huck's world, and all of the terrors that they betray, are similar to those of August's. The only difference between the two is the source from which these silences spring. In Huck's case, the dread arises because of a neutral silence in the world over which no one has any control. The silence is out there in Huck's world regardless of whether he experiences it, and it is only because of the psychological predisposition that he himself nurtures that he falls prey to his feelings of guilt and loneliness. Indeed, were it not for these psychological influences, Huck's life throughout the novel might resemble the Edenic life he experiences with Tom and Joe on Jackson's Island in *The Adventures of Tom Sawyer,* or the two or three idyllic days and nights he shares with Jim prior to the arrival of the King and the Duke. In fact, the language of this section of Huckleberry Finn bears the point. At the beginning of their self-imposed isolation, Jim and Huck waste their days away watching "the lonesomeness of the river," and "listening to the stillness." These moments of "just solid lonesomeness" do not frighten Huck, nor do they trigger any adverse feelings. This is one of the only sections of the book where the predominance of silence and stillness commingle with feelings of happiness.

In contrast to Huck's, August's silences and the mortal dread they produce are not natural to his world, but artificially constructed by the impish No. 44 (and by association, as August learns during No. 44's final revelation, constructed by himself). In each of the three cases cited above—the scenes at the printing press, the one-man minstrel show, and the Assembly of the Dead—August's fears spring from this metaphysical influence. It is important to remember that prior to the arrival of No. 44, August's life resembled the Eden of Jackson's Island. "Austria was far away from the world," as he recalls, and the town of Eseldorf "was a paradise for us boys." Even with the oppressive fear of the Church and Father Adolf looming in the background, August's life apparently holds no major difficulty. It is not until No. 44 comes along and "enlightens" August that he begins to set himself off from the others and feel the effects of his silent world.

This arrival of No. 44 brings about a bittersweet change over August (and Theodor); much like the silence underlying 44's metaphysical origins, his influence is likewise problematic. In the final chapter that Twain intended for *The Mysterious Stranger,* 44 is nothing more than a vision, a dream. ''I am but a dream,'' he tells August, ''your dream, creature of your imagination.'' Therefore, if No. 44 is a dream, the product of thought, then the nature of that dream—August's creative imagination—is of an unsteady power. It can both enlighten and emancipate as well as bind and manipulate. As the textualized embodiment of August's own mind, No. 44 bestows upon the child a magnificent creative ability, yet it is this same ability that reveals to him the darker underside of such powers, that of solitude and destruction. Then, August Feldner joins the ranks of the other powerful figures in Twain's later fiction, Hank Morgan and Pudd'nhead Wilson. The power that August creates—the power that he authors—is as frightening as it is liberating.

Three key passages from the final version of the *Mysterious Stranger* manuscript illustrate this point, and each one focuses on annihilation and August's ever-increasing solitude. Similar to the passages on silence cited above, the references to solitude and lonesomeness all come at significant points in the narrative and signal to the reader the awesome influence this tragic solitude has on him. As with the silences, all feelings of solitude have as their source the power of No. 44. The first instance of this comes soon after 44 and August witness Johann Brinker's elderly mother being burnt at the stake for being a witch. When August pities her for being given a cruel entrance to heaven, 44 shocks him by showing him otherwise. No. 44 produces before him the depths of hell, and ''Before I could beg him to spare me, the red billows were sweeping by, and she was there among the lost. The next moment the crimson sea was gone, with its evoker, and I was alone'' (emphasis added). August's last short and abrupt clause, ''and I was alone,'' demonstrates the sheer force of this phenomenon.

Another such moment comes immediately after the Assembly of the Dead. Witnessing the almost endless procession of historic personages, ''a kind of pathetic spectacle'' as he notes, August is stricken by an emptiness similar to that he experienced at the ghostly printing press: ''For hours and hours the dead passed by in continental masses, and the bone-clacking was so deafening you could hardly hear yourself think. Then, all of a sudden 44 waved his hand and we stood in an empty and soundless world.'' Although August is left standing with 44, as he learns in the next important passage, he is actually the source of 44, and therefore is entirely alone.

In the third significant passage, the most critically discussed section of any among the unfinished manuscripts, August's fears of solitude become a solipsistic dream/nightmare. This is in the last chapter of the book, where No. 44 reveals to him that ''Life itself is only a vision, a dream.'' August calls this revelation ''electrical,'' suggesting that it is as terrifying as it is invigorating: ''Nothing exists; all is a dream. God—man—the world, —the sun, the moon, the wilderness of stars: a dream, all a dream, they have no existence. Nothing exists save empty space—and you!'' August is once again alone, but this time it is for good and is accompanied by words of redemption.

August is definitely delivered at the end, but the question remains, delivered into what? The ''optimistic'' critics describe 44 as a positive figure, and view his final words as some sort of salvific message. But there is a problem with this approach. ''Salvation'' is a problematic word, for No. 44's revelation is as much a nightmare as it is a dream. Even solipsistic hope seems utterly dampened by 44's last words: ''Nothing exists but You. And You are but a Thought—a vagrant Thought, a useless Thought, a homeless Thought, wandering forlorn among the empty eternities!'' Earlier, August discovers just how forlorn this empty eternity actually is when he speaks with his duplicate, Emile Schwarz. Emile talks of an almost aimless wandering that echoes that of Hank Morgan's ''plodding sad pilgrimage, this pathetic drift between the eternities,'' and suggests an endless progression between hope and despair. In an extended passage, Emile describes to August the existence of his disembodied self in terms of ''general space,'' and describes it this way:

> that sea of ether which has no shores, and stretches on, and on, and arrives nowhere; which is a waste of black gloom and thick darkness through which you may rush forever at thought-speed, encountering at weary long intervals spirit-cheering archipelagoes of suns which rise sparkling far in front of you in glories of light, apparently measureless in extent, but you plunge through and in a moment they are far behind, a twinkling archipelago again, and in another moment they are blotted out in darkness.

Here we have a key passage, curiously overlooked by many critics, that sheds much light on the troublesome ending of the novel, and likewise gives us a solid clue into the enigmatic nature of No. 44. Twain's "Conclusion of the book" is neither a condemnation of life—either in the existential or social sense—nor a salvific escape hatch. The ending does lapse into solipsism, but nevertheless portrays this solipsism as a nihilistic prison. The creative imagination, if it is an answer, is much like Emile's mystifying yet tragically solitary out-of-body experiences, a Sisyphean journey through endless darkness to transitory twinkling archipelagos.

This final creative expression emanates from a tragic Mark Twain who is unhappy with the world in which he lives but who is equally depressed by the more hopeful alternatives he might envision. Perhaps it is too simple to view what has become known as Twain's darkening literary vision as a result of the increasing tragedy that plagued his life. Certainly it is reasonable to assume that a part of the pessimistic side of the mysterious stranger could be due to the writer's series of losses during the early twilight of his life: the death of Suzy, the terminal illness and subsequent death of Livy, financial worries, and the ever-present fear that his creative powers had dried up. Yet if this is the case, it nonetheless contributed to an already-present literary predisposition that was there from his early years as a writer. Instead of reading Twain's oeuvre as a linear progression from light-hearted humor to an ever-increasing pessimism, perhaps it would be more fruitful to see in his entire output a constant negotiation between alternate possibilities, and that the seeds for his nihilistic No. 44 were sewn from the very beginning. From his earliest works he had attempted to give voice to the uncomfortable twin feelings of hope and despair. The jocular attitudes in *The Innocents Abroad* often give way to images of destruction and futility. The idyllic boyhood reveries in *Huckleberry Finn* are everywhere undermined by the abuse and helplessness that Huck and Jim encounter. These twin feelings are perhaps most vividly expressed in *Roughing It*, where the narrator Sam seeks to ascend the heights of the Dead Volcano of Haleakala, "which means, translated, 'the house of the sun.'" Inside the crater of the dead volcano, Sam soon becomes enveloped by white clouds:

> a ghostly procession of wanderers from the filmy hosts without had drifted through a chasm in the crater wall and filed round and round, and gathered and sung and blended together till the abyss was stored to the brim with a fleecy fog ... Thus banked, motion ceased, and silence reigned.

In a passage that foreshadows the powerful light and dark imagery of Emile Schwarz's journey between twinkling archipelagos, Sam tells us that while standing within this shrouded crater, "I felt like the Last Man, neglected of the judgment, and left pinnacled in mid-heaven, a forgotten relic of a vanished world." Yet immediately after this dark reverie, he notices the bright rays of the rising sun, "the messengers of the coming resurrection." The power of these two juxtaposed experiences, the dour and the redemptive, strikes Sam as "the sublimest spectacle I ever witnessed, and I think the memory of it will remain with me always." Apparently, the two experiences that so struck Sam the narrator left Mark Twain the writer with a poignant dialectic that he was never able to fuse satisfactorily. No. 44 and the creative power of the imagination presented another in a series of ways out. But even through solipsistic playfulness, he could not escape the double-edged nature of No. 44 and his message, for as Emile tells August, every progression from darkness into dazzling light leads invariably back into the still gloom of darkness. The nature of No. 44, read in this way, is neither ominous nor upbeat, but an unstable mixture of both that is representative of many of Twain's later figures. In this sense, we can read the last words of August as an ambiguous and frustrating admonition of creative realization: "He vanished, and left me appalled; for I knew, and realized, that all he had said was true." Twain, in an attempt to work through his last major narrative, was left standing on the edge of his own dead volcano, awaiting the dawn of an uncertain possibility.

Source: Derek Parker Royal, "Terrible Dreams of Creative Power: The Question of 'No. 44,'" in *Studies in the Novel*, Vol. 31, No. 1, Spring 1999, p. 44.

Sholom J. Kahn

In the following essay excerpt, Kahn uses the ideas of seventeenth-century, French philosopher René Descartes to explicate the meaning of Twain's "The Mysterious Stranger" manuscripts.

What was it, after all, that Mark Twain succeeded in saying in "No. 44"? We must accept the legitimacy of nuanced variety in interpretations, but we must insist also on the primacy of Mark Twain's own text. Though chapter 34 has been much read and analyzed, this has usually been done in misleading contexts. We have noted most of the previous interpretations—nihilism, solipsism, "extreme Platonism," the magic of art, hoax, escape from reality—and we have seen that there is some justification for all of them in words Mark Twain actually wrote. I should like, however, to suggest yet another framework, one basic to the history of modern thought and truer on the whole to the fundamental character of Clemens's mind.

I think of Mark Twain as a sort of archetypal modern American, exquisitely sensitive to many of the currents of religion, philosophy, science, society, and culture that made the nineteenth century so exciting and upsetting. And in "the revolution from the medieval to the modern universe," the combination of radical skepticism with the mathematical-mechanical logic displayed by Descartes was both a climax and a new beginning. Whether or not Clemens read Descartes, and I have found no mention of Descartes in the literature about Clemens, there are advantages in placing him in the large Cartesian contexts: a surprising number of aspects of "No. 44" are lit up by Descartes's *Discourse* and *Meditations*. To paraphrase T. S. Eliot in his "Shakespeare and the Stoicism of Seneca": "I propose a Mark Twain under the influence of Descartes' rationalism. But I do not believe that Mark Twain was under the influence of Descartes directly." Whether he was influenced by the Cartesian tradition, of course, is another matter.

Cartesian Science and Skepticism

Jacques Maritain concluded an important essay, "The Dream of Descartes," by writing about "the idea of what the modern world calls The Science" and "the emotional and reverential compliments evoked by this word," which "plays in the mythology of modern times a role as majestic and as formidable as Progress itself." But Maritain emphasized, from his perspective as a believing Catholic in the twentieth century, that this is "not the true science, science such as it exists and is brought about by scientists, science submissive to things and to extra-mental reality." It is instead a sort of phantom caricature, characteristic of the "sorrowful" many "who have lost the good of the intellect" (Dante's *Inferno,* 3:18), it is "the Mid-Autumnal Night's Dream conjured up by a mischievous genius in a philosopher's brain." Maritain's version of Descartes supplies an ambience for the problems we have found to be at the heart of "No. 44."

I do not mean to exaggerate Clemens's philosophic learning or sophistication when I contend that there are fundamental affinities between the dream of Descartes and what we may call "the dream of Mark Twain." I mean by this phrase not just the actual dreams reported by Clemens, nor

even his use of dream materials in his writings, though these are included. I mean rather, to use his own word, the entire "vision" of life and death that might be taken as summing up his life's work. This aspect of any writer's achievement is at once the most important and the most difficult to state; and it is the final battleground, the area of ultimate controversy, on which generations of critics will struggle to articulate their fullest and truest judgments about, in this case, Mark Twain's oeuvre. Until fairly recently, the tendency has been to make light of his intellectual concerns, even while acclaiming the truth and profundity of his art. But during the last decade, partly as the result of the wider availability of the writings of Mark Twain's last years, increasing numbers of critics have been taking him more seriously as a thinker. They have been thinking of him not as a technical philosopher, but as a "true wit" and a "man of judgment," in S. J. Krause's formulation.

There is no need to rehearse in detail the well-known autobiographical passages in Descartes's *Discourse on Method* (1637), which is usually considered to mark the beginning of a distinctively modern philosophy in Europe. Coming to these after study of Mark Twain, we are struck by many analogies: Clemens's lifelong education through travel is paralleled by Descartes's summary of his youthful observation of the "extravagant and ridiculous" things approved by "great peoples," discovered by "mingling with people of various dispositions and conditions in life, . . . collecting a variety of experiences," and so forth. The Frenchman restricted himself to Europe, whereas the American began by "learning the river" and eventually girdled the entire globe; but the principle was the same. And with reference to the "Stranger" texts: there is an analogy between Descartes's education and "Satan's" plan to study the human race; and the movement in Descartes from the outside social world to "within myself" is like the central pattern we found in "No. 44."

In part 2 of the *Discourse,* Descartes tells of the famous winter day in Germany spent "shut up in a room heated by a stove" holding "converse with my own thoughts," which led to his determination to rely on "the plain reasoning of a man of good sense in regard to the matters which present themselves to him." This historic moment may be paralleled, in a sense, by Mark Twain's Austrian sojourn, during which he decided to retreat into the "self-reliance" of writing his own thoughts, for himself, in fictions "not for publication." Further, the effort of many of Mark Twain's later writings—the elaborate critical examination poured into *What Is Man?*; autobiographical dictations; a wealth of essays; as well as more imaginative, satiric, and fantastic, works—may be thought of as his personal effort to go beyond the "opinions" he had encountered as a youth and those that had been pressed upon him all his life by an all-too-friendly environment.

Finally, consider for example the paragraph in chapter 34 that gives the details ("hysterically insane—like all dreams") of conventional belief: "a God who could make good children as easily as bad, yet preferred to make bad ones," and so forth. This, as well as Forty-four's act of stripping away all external reality ("God—man—the world,—the sun, the moon, the wilderness of stars"), can be readily understood as an act of ultimate doubt, not unlike Descartes's act of imagining the deceptions of an "evil genius":

> I shall suppose, then, not that God, who is very good, and the sovereign source of truth, but that a certain evil genius, no less wily and deceitful than powerful, has employed all his ingenuity to deceive me.... I persuade myself that nothing has ever existed of all that my memory, filled with illusions, has represented to me; I consider that I have no senses; I assume that body, figure, extension, motion, and place are only fictions of my mind. What is there, then which can be held to be true? Perhaps nothing at all, except the statement that there is nothing at all that is true. But how do I know that there is not something different from those things which I have just pronounced uncertain, concerning which there cannot be entertained the least doubt? Is there not some God, or some other power, who puts these thoughts into my mind? That is not necessary, for perhaps I am capable of producing them of myself. Myself, then! at the very least am I not something? . . . But there is I know not what deceiver, very powerful, very crafty, who employs all his cunning continually to delude me. There is still no doubt that I exist if he deceives me; and let him deceive me as he may, he will never bring it about that I shall be nothing, so long as I shall think something exists. Accordingly, having considered it well, and carefully examined everything, I am obliged to conclude and to hold for certain, that this proposition, *I am, I exist,* is necessarily true, every time that I pronounce it or conceive it in my mind. (*Meditations,* 1)

Just as Descartes actually assumed "God, who is very good," so Mark Twain prefixed to Forty-four's statement that "God" has "no existence," an exclamation by August: "*By God* I had had that very thought a thousand times in my musings!" (my italics).

> **"The achievement of 'No. 44' is that Mark Twain managed to weave so much of his dream of life, his vision of man and the universe, so skillfully into this text."**

I am well aware that the parallels or affinities I have been suggesting are literary, not philosophical or logically precise. But they could be multiplied and would add up to a fairly coherent world view. One may conceive of the last dozen years of Mark Twain's writings as constituting an almost separate career—a new start, a distinct "final phase." What his "dreams," loosely considered, share with those of Descartes is a spirit of search for religious truth. A flash of lightning in Descartes's second dream led to "the admirable science"; for the American, a more gradual accession of independence led to a burst of fresh creativity and truth saying.

It needs only a slight shift to put both Descartes and Mark Twain into a psychological perspective. Very easily, we can understand Descartes's God and "evil genius" as analogous, for example, to angels and devils, principles of good and evil, heroes and villains, and we can move thereby into the world of modern literature. So Georges Poulet, concentrating on "human time," wrote an essay of a different sort than Maritain's but also titled "The Dream of Descartes." What emerged as especially important for Poulet were the notes of terror and alienation in Descartes. He showed the connection between the first dream, the "Spiritus malus" (as it appears in the original Latin) of the second *Meditation,* and a movement toward the world of instinct and modern irrationalism:

> The proximity of the body results in the estrangement or enfeeblement of the mind. In the midst of human society, which . . . seems to be so well adapted to the tragic conditions of life, Descartes discovers himself to be "bent and unsteady" and intensely aware of this tragedy. And it is then that he awakens with a feeling of spiritual sorrow and associates with the sorrow the idea of a temptation.

The root causes of this sorrow are "physical exile and material solitude," to which are added "moral exile and solitude''; as Poulet generalized in his introduction, ''the seventeenth century is the epoch in which the individual discovers his isolation.'' And, we may add, the United States is the country in which this general modern tendency toward individualism has been carried to an extreme, idealized, and realized as a way of life and major theme of literature.

We need go no deeper into this historical development to realize that Mark Twain was not being morbid and eccentric when he explored these issues in ''No. 44.'' He has Forty-four say: ''All things that exist were made out of thought—and out of nothing else''—thus blending rationalism with something like the traditional Creation ex nihilo. On this, August comments ironically: ''It seemed to me charitable, also polite, to take him at his word and not require proof, and I said so.'' Thus Clemens was aware of certain implications of Cartesian rationalism and also quizzically skeptical of traditional ''proofs.'' Like Huck Finn, he had ''been there before''; he was content to end this chapter with ''I was alone'' and to end his book with Forty-four saying: ''You have existed, companionless, through all the eternities.''

''Nothing exists but You'': this extreme position, this stern doctrine (which Poulet relates to ''the Calvinist *Credo:* I believe, therefore I am'') can be seen as a remote American echo of the Cartesian *cogito.* And some of the consequences for literature can be traced back to the generation of Rabelais and Montaigne, before Descartes; and to Swift, Voltaire, and others, after him. The mind of man, that ''glory, jest and riddle of the world,'' struggles to maintain a world view independent of merely orthodox or traditional views, sometimes by a radical criticism of, or rebellion against, them: the latest phase of this development is probably represented by that varied group of writers and thinkers loosely labeled *existential.* One of the main difficulties produced by this sort of radical assertion of freedom is a lack of stability and security; as one critic of Kafka has put it, ''the quest ends in the seeker's confrontation with his own image''; and ''the irony that topples'' Kafka's ''lesson down like a house of cards'' is that ''the way that is everywhere is nowhere.'' But that is the subject for yet another book.

A Last "Image of Hannibal"

Getting back to Mark Twain: there was undoubtedly much of the fantastic and dreamlike in his career and writings, which ranged from a tiny village on the banks of the Mississippi to the courts of emperors and the yacht of a Standard Oil tycoon, from America's primitive frontier to its developing ''imperialist'' phase in the twentieth century. A fabulous success story, one would think; and yet, when Mark Twain wrote ''My Boyhood Dreams'' in Sanna, Sweden, during the months when he was trying to get on with ''The Chronicle of Young Satan,'' he began: ''The dreams of my boyhood? No, they have not been realized.'' Later in the same piece he applied this notion, satirically, to the career of John Hay:

> In the pride of his young ambition he had aspired to be a steamboat mate . . . I look back now, from this far distance of seventy years, and note with sorrow the stages of that dream's destruction. Hay's history is but Howells's, with differences of detail. Hay climbed high toward his ideal; when success seemed almost sure, his foot upon the very gangplank, his eye upon the capstan, misfortune came and his fall began. Down—down—down—ever down: Private Secretary to the President; Colonel in the field; Chargé d'Affaires in Paris; Chargé d'Affaires in Vienna; Poet; Editor of the *Tribune*; Biographer of Lincoln; Ambassador to England; and now at last there he lies— Secretary of State, Head of Foreign Affairs. And he has fallen like Lucifer, never to rise again. And his dream—where now is his dream? Gone down in blood and tears with the dream of the auctioneer.

This is a characteristically humorous statement of the truth that experience is gained at the expense of childhood innocence, and power at the expense of freedom and carefree irresponsibility.

We come back, then, to the central fact that Mark Twain was the ''poet'' of America's coming of age. In a variety of modes, he captured much of the public and private realities and tensions of that complex process. It is foolish to rebuke him for dealing so much with experiences of adolescence, because that was his main theme, his prime subject matter; his Odysseus, someone has observed, was Huckleberry Finn. It is therefore highly appropriate, in a sense inevitable, that his last major work should be a novel of growing up, of young love, and of the search for self-knowledge.

But what a sea change there is in his metamorphosis from Hannibal, Missouri, to Eseldorf, Austria! And how beautifully right that he should have gone back, as we have seen, to the earliest facts, the deepest roots, of his knowledge of the world and human nature, to his apprenticeship to the ''art'' of printing, which led eventually to his rise in the ''literary guild.'' The same man who said he gained his fullest knowledge of mankind as a steamboat pilot (''met him on the river!''), was also saying thereby that his truest insights went back to the village of his boyhood and his encounters there with work, men, women, mystery, and miracle.

The achievement of ''No. 44'' is that Mark Twain managed to weave so much of his dream of life, his vision of man and the universe, so skillfully into this text. His last ''image of Hannibal,'' to use Henry Nash Smith's phrase (with additional echoes, especially in the courtship sequence, from his encounters with Elmira, New York, and Hartford, Connecticut), has been enriched and enlivened by a lifetime of experience and practice of the art of fiction. Despite some relatively minor flaws, I think it a work of sophistication and maturity; the frisky journeys and gambols of its ''dream-sprites,'' presided over by Forty-four and spread out in space and time, are the fruits of a truly creative imagination exploring many corners of the human condition in a fresh and profound way.

No single work of fiction pretends to cover all the ground, but the master works illustrate universal truths implicit in the provincial and concrete. And when we get to know him better, I have little doubt that Mark Twain's mysterious stranger will take his place in the gallery of immortals that includes, among others, Pantagruel, Don Quixote, Gulliver, Candide, Ishmael, Huckleberry Finn, Hank Morgan, and David Wilson. Probably not as an equal—he is in some ways a queer specimen—but as a beloved, eccentric cousin, not too far removed.

Source: Sholom J. Kahn, ''Epilogue: The Dream of Mark Twain,'' in *Mark Twain's ''Mysterious Stranger'': A Study of the Manuscript Texts,* University of Missouri Press, 1978, pp. 191–99.

Sources

Gibson, William M., ''Introduction,'' in *Mark Twain's Mysterious Stranger Manuscripts,* edited by William M. Gibson, University of California Press, 1969, pp. 1–34.

Kahn, Sholom, Jr., *Mark Twain's ''Mysterious Stranger'': A Study of the Manuscript Texts,* University of Missouri Press, 1978, pp. 4–25, 199.

Royal, Derek Parker, ''Terrible Dreams of Creative Power: The Question of No. 44,'' in *Studies in the Novel,* Vol. 31, No. 1, Spring 1999, pp. 44–59.

Twain, Mark, *No. 44, The Mysterious Stranger,* University of California Press, 2004.

Further Reading

Dolmetsch, Carl, *''Our Famous Guest'': Mark Twain in Vienna,* University of Georgia Press, 1992.
Dolmetsch provides an account of Mark Twain's travels in Austria, discussed in the social and cultural context of Austrian history.

Eisenstein, Elizabeth L., *The Printing Revolution in Early Modern Europe,* Cambridge University Press, 1993.
Eisenstein discusses the impact of advances in print technology on social, intellectual, and cultural life in early modern Europe.

Emerson, Everett, *Mark Twain: A Literary Life,* University of Pennsylvania Press, 2000.
Emerson offers a critical biography of Twain's life and work.

Fishkin, Shelley Fisher, *Lighting Out for the Territory: Reflections on Mark Twain and American Culture,* Oxford University Press, 1997.
Fishkin provides a collection of essays on the significance of Mark Twain to nineteenth-century American literature, culture, and society.

Hindman, Sandra, ed., *Printing the Written Word: The Social History of Books, circa 1450–1520,* Cornell University Press, 1991.
Hindman discusses the impact of advances in print technology and book publishing on fifteenth- and sixteenth-century European culture and society.

Lause, Mark A., *Some Degree of Power: From Hired Hand to Union Craftsman in the Pre-industrial American Printing Trades, 1778–1815,* University of Arkansas Press, 1991.
Lause discusses developments in the working conditions of print shop employees in eighteenth- and nineteenth-century America.

Steinberg, S. H., *Five Hundred Years of Printing,* Oak Knoll Press, 1996.
Steinberg provides a concise historical overview of the history of printing and book publishing from the fifteenth century through the twentieth century.

Ward, Geoffrey C., and Dayton Duncan, *Mark Twain,* Knopf, 2001.
Ward and Duncan offer a pictorial biography of Twain, based on the documentary film biography directed by Ken Burns.

"Repent, Harlequin!" Said the Ticktockman

Harlan Ellison

1965

Harlan Ellison's short story, "'Repent, Harlequin!' Said the Ticktockman," first appeared in *Galaxy* magazine in December 1965, and earned Ellison both a Hugo and a Nebula award in 1966. The story was first collected in *Paingod and Other Delusions* in 1965, and has been frequently anthologized over the years, appearing in *Nebula Award Stories 1965* (1966) and *The Essential Ellison: A 50-Year Retrospective* (2001) among other anthologies. Indeed, the story has been anthologized more than 160 times since its first publication, and has been translated into many languages. In 1997, Ellison and Rick Berry collaborated on a lavishly illustrated, over-sized edition of the story, published by Underwood Press, with a new introduction by Ellison.

The world of the Harlequin is one run by the Master Timekeeper, generally known as the Ticktockman. In this world, people are on time, or run the risk of having their lives shortened by the minutes of their tardiness. Into this depressingly gray world steps the gaudily dressed Harlequin, throwing jelly beans at workers changing shifts. A comic hero, the Harlequin threatens the existence of the state, and brings the wrath of the Ticktockman down on himself.

Compared by some critics to George Orwell's novel *Nineteen Eighty-Four* (1949) and Aldous Huxley's equally famous novel, *Brave New World* (1932), "'Repent, Harlequin!' Said the Ticktockman" is both dark and humorous, a

twentieth-century cautionary tale of mechanical tyranny.

Author Biography

From his early days, Harlan Ellison has been an individualist and social gadfly. Born in Cleveland on May 27, 1934, he published his first short story in 1947 in the *Cleveland News*. By the age of 17, he demonstrated his interest in science fiction by founding the Cleveland Science Fiction Society.

Ellison was not one to suffer the restrictions of academia. Although he attended Ohio State University for two years, he was asked to leave by University administrators. Subsequently, he went to New York where he continued his writing career. While in New York, he joined a gang in order to research his novel, *Rumble*. Ellison's next job was with the United States Army, serving from 1957 through 1959. In the years after his military service, Ellison started both a magazine, *Rogue,* and a publishing firm, Regency Books. Throughout this period, Ellison wrote many short stories and essays.

After moving to Los Angeles in 1962, Ellison began writing for television in addition to successfully publishing both novels and short stories. His list of credits for television include episodes of such popular shows as *The Outer Limits, Burke's Law,* and *Route 66.* His best-known television screenplay, however, was his script for *Star Trek* in 1967, "The City on the Edge of Forever." For this episode, he won a Hugo Award in 1967, and a Writer's Guild of America Award in 1968.

In 1965, Ellison wrote "'Repent, Harlequin!' Said the Ticktockman," perhaps his most famous and anthologized story. First appearing in *Galaxy* magazine in December 1965, the story received critical acclaim, winning both a Hugo and a Nebula Award. Subsequently, Ellison included the story in his 1965 collection, *Paingod and Other Delusions.* Although the volume takes as its subject agony in many different manifestations, stories such as "'Repent, Harlequin!' Said the Ticktockman" also suggest Ellison's sense of humor.

During these same years, Ellison wrote some of the stories for which he is most famous, collected in books such as *I Have No Mouth and I Must Scream* (1967) and *The Beast That Shouted Love at the Heart of the World* (1969). In 1967, Ellison edited and annotated one of the most important science

Harlan Ellison

fiction anthologies ever published, *Dangerous Visions*. This volume, and the 1972 *Again, Dangerous Visions,* firmly connected Ellison with "New Wave" science fiction, although this is a label that Ellison rejects.

In the 1970s and 1980s, Ellison continued to produce short stories, novels, screenplays, and essays, focusing on critical cultural commentaries. In 1987, a comprehensive collection of Ellison's work, *The Essential Ellison: a 35-Year Retrospective* was edited by Terry Dowling, with Richard Delap and Gil Lamont who updated the collection in 2001 with *The Essential Ellison: a 50-Year Retrospective.*

Although Ellison has been actively writing for more than fifty years, he continues to be involved in a dizzying array of activities. Ellison's long 1992 short story "The Man Who Rowed Christopher Columbus Ashore" appeared in the prestigious *The Best American Short Stories* (1993). In 2000 and 2001, he was a consultant and host for a radio series of 26 one-hour short story dramatizations. The series aired on National Public Radio and included an adaptation of "'Repent, Harlequin!' Said the Ticktockman." In addition, Ellison continues to produce graphic novels, computer games, screenplays, and an assortment of other creative works. Always the voice of resistance, in 2002, Ellison took America Online to court for copyright infringement. Ellison shows no signs of slowing the pace of his work; indeed, new technologies have opened new avenues for his fertile imagination.

Plot Summary

"'Repent, Harlequin!' Said the Ticktockman" is the story of a future world, controlled by a tight schedule and the ticking of a clock. In charge of this world is the Ticktockman, a robot-like figure with the power to shorten or terminate anyone's life as a penalty for running late.

The story begins with a long quote from Henry David Thoreau's essay, "Civil Disobedience." In this passage, Thoreau asserts that most men "serve the state thus, not as men mainly, but as machines, with their bodies." Further, a "very few" men serve the state with their consciences, a service that forces them into resistance of the state. These men, according to Thoreau, are heroes, and often, martyrs.

Ellison then shifts to the story, beginning somewhere in the middle. He sets the story in the future, at a moment when one individual is resisting the enforced schedule of this extremely regimented society. Worse still, this man, called the Harlequin, has become a hero to some of the lower classes. As such, he represents a threat to the state, and has consequently come to the attention of the Master Timekeeper, otherwise known as the Ticktockman.

The Harlequin, so named for his habit of dressing in the medieval fool's garb of motley, is a trickster figure. He disrupts workers as they try to change shifts, thus disrupting the master schedule. In one instance, he drops 150,000 dollars' worth of jelly beans on workers on automatic sidewalks, trying to change shifts, delaying the master schedule by seven minutes. For this crime, the Harlequin is ordered to appear before the Ticktockman.

Ellison then shifts to what he calls "the beginning." In this section, he offers examples of the increasing intrusion of time schedules into people's lives. He writes, "And so it goes. And so it goes. And so it goes goes goes goes goes tick tock tick tock tick tock and one day we no longer let time serve us, we serve time and we are slaves of the schedule. . .bound into a life predicated on restrictions because the system will not function if we don't keep the schedule tight." As a result of this,

all citizens are required to wear "cardioplates" that measure their punctuality, and allow the Ticktockman to turn them off should they literally run out of time.

The story then shifts again into the ending. The Harlequin is at home with his wife or girlfriend, Pretty Alice, who is disgusted with his inability to be on time. Ultimately, she turns his name over to the Ticktockman, which allows his forces to capture the Harlequin.

As it turns out, the Harlequin is not someone very special, just a man named Everett C. Marm "who had no sense of time." Confronted with the demand to repent, Marm tells the Ticktockman to "Get stuffed!" As a result, he is sent to Coventry for brainwashing. To kill him outright would be to martyr him; by brainwashing, the authorities are able to put him on television and broadcast his recantation.

It might appear that the story ends with Marm's demise and failure; however, at the last moment readers discover that the Ticktockman himself is running three minutes late.

Characters

The Harlequin

The Harlequin, whose real name is Everett C. Marm, is a "man who had no sense of time." Dressed in motley fashion, the Harlequin disrupts the daily activities of the society in which he lives through practical jokes (such as showering shift workers with jelly beans) and his general lack of attention to time. Physically, the Harlequin is a small man, "elfin and dimpled and bright-eyed." He becomes a sort of hero to the lower classes, the people who through their daily work allow the entire system to run. Because of this, he comes to the attention of the Ticktockman who sends out his minions to find out who the Harlequin really is.

As a man, Everett C. Marm is not "much to begin with," but as the Harlequin, he is a danger to a society that depends on punctuality and smooth running of its machinery. His general nonconformity and his anarchistic actions threaten the culture. Indeed, he incites crowds of people to "saunter a while," to "enjoy the sunshine." When he tells the crowd, "down with the Ticktockman," he is essentially committing treason. Consequently, the Harlequin is captured, apparently brainwashed, and made to appear on television to recant.

Because "'Repent, Harlequin!' Said the Ticktockman" is a kind of allegory, none of the characters are developed or rounded, nor are they intended to be. Although the Harlequin is the main character, he represents a type of character rather than a realistic individual. His reply to the Ticktockman, "Get stuffed!" is indicative of his status as the trickster/rebel, the character who refuses to cooperate with authority in spite of the danger to himself.

Everett C. Marm
See The Harlequin

Pretty Alice
Pretty Alice is Everett C. Marm's girlfriend or wife. She is someone who "wants to belong," someone who finds living in the conformity and regularity of the society both comfortable and desirable. She is disgusted with Marm's role as the Harlequin, and she is out of patience with Marm's habitual lateness. Ultimately, she betrays the Harlequin to the Ticktockman by revealing his real name.

The Ticktockman
The Ticktockman is the Master Timekeeper of the society. As such, his role is to make sure that everything runs smoothly and on time. He also has the capability of monitoring each citizen's punctuality and deducting the total number of late minutes from the life span of each individual. Thus if a person arrives five minutes late for work, the Ticktockman deducts those five minutes from the person's life. Ultimately, the Ticktockman turns off anyone whose tardiness becomes chronic or who accumulates too many late minutes.

The character of the Ticktockman represents the fusion of the totalitarian dictator with the all-powerful machine; he has both the will and the means to keep the System operating through the cardioplate technology that allows him access to an individual's every movement and biological processes. As such, this character is a villain.

Because the Ticktockman wears a mask, it is difficult for the reader to determine if he is a human or not. It is just as likely that he is a robot as a human being. Certainly, the noise he makes, "mrmee,

Media Adaptations

- "'Repent, Harlequin!' Said the Ticktockman" was adapted as a graphic novel in 1997 by Ellison and illustrator Rick Berry. The book was published by Underwood Books.

- A collection of Ellison short stories is available as an electronic book, released by Fictionwise.com in 2003, and available for download through Microsoft Reader. Volume 1 includes the story, "'Repent, Harlequin!' Said the Ticktockman."

- A recording of Ellison's adaptation of "'Repent, Harlequin!' Said the Ticktockman" for the radio series *2000x,* released in 2000, is provided by Hollywood Theatre for the Ear and is available through Audible.Com. Ellison narrates the story, and Robin Williams plays the Harlequin.

mrmee, mrmee" at the end of the story, when he himself is running three minutes late, suggests that he is mechanical rather than human.

Themes

Conformity and Individualism
In "'Repent, Harlequin!' Said the Ticktockman," Ellison clearly sets his hero, the Harlequin, in opposition to both the totalitarian regime of the Ticktockman and the master schedule and to the masses of people who choose to conform to the strictures of the society. His opening quotation from Thoreau makes this clear. Thoreau argues that most people serve the state without thinking and without moral reflection. Consequently, for Thoreau, these people have no more worth than "horses and dogs." Real heroes, then, are those who "serve the state with their consciences." Ellison draws on Thoreau's image of "wooden men" who "can perhaps be manufactured" in his description

Topics for Further Study

- Read Thoreau's 1849 essay, ''Civil Disobedience.'' What are the circumstances in which Thoreau wrote this essay? What are the main points that he makes? Why do you think that Ellison chose to use the quote that he did to start ''''Repent, Harlequin!' Said the Ticktockman?''

- Examine the adaptation of ''''Repent, Harlequin!' Said the Ticktockman'' by Ellison and Rick Berry as a graphic novel, looking particularly at the illustrations. How do the illustrations change or affect your reading of the story? What techniques does illustrator Berry bring to Ellison's short story? Pick some of the drawings that you would have done differently, redraw them according to how you think they should appear, and share with your class why you think your adjustments help convey the story better.

- Read Ellison's classic collections of essays on television, *The Glass Teat* (1970) and *The Other Glass Teat* (1975). What does Ellison have to say about the influence of television on American culture? Consider the ways television has changed since the 1970s. Write an essay about what you imagine Ellison might say about the television of the present day.

- John W. Campbell, writer and editor of *Astounding Science Fiction* and *Analog*, is considered the father of modern science fiction. Research Campbell's life and identify those writers on whom Campbell had the most influence. Write an essay that explores what you see as Campbell's legacy to the field.

---

of shift workers heading for their jobs: ''With practiced motion and an absolute conservation of movement, they sidestepped up onto the slow-strip and (in a chorus line reminiscent of a Busby Berkeley film of the antediluvian 1930s) advanced across the strips ostrich-walking till they were lined up on the expresstrip.''

The futuristic society of the story is one that values conformity and discourages individual differences. Indeed, the Harlequin's idiosyncrasies are considered ''a strain of disease long-defunct, now, suddenly, reborn in a system where immunity had been forgotten, had lapsed.'' Personality itself had been ''filtered out of the system many decades before.'' In a culture that depends on workers arriving on time at factories to do line work, conformity ensures the utmost efficiency in the production of uniform manufactured products. Individualism, then, is dangerous to ''The Ones Who Kept The Machine Functioning.''

It is in his description of Pretty Alice and the Harlequin, however, where Ellison most clearly demonstrates the contrast between conformity and

individualism. Pretty Alice criticizes the Harlequin for speaking with ''a great deal of inflection.'' In addition, she is irritated that he dresses differently from other people. But most of all, Pretty Alice is angry that the Harlequin is always late, in spite of his promises not to be. This anger eventually leads the conformist Alice to turn in the non-conformist Harlequin to the Ticktockman, who tells the Harlequin that Alice ''wants to belong; she wants to conform.'' Even love, then, does not seem to have the power to conquer the suffocating sameness of the culture. Ironically, Alice's betrayal makes the Harlequin even more of an individualist; his loss of Pretty Alice means that he stands alone against the inquisition of the Ticktockman.

Science and Technology

Like many writers of speculative fiction, Ellison seems to have mixed feelings about the ways science and technology affect the lives of citizens of industrialized nations. On one hand, the society in ''''Repent, Harlequin!' Said the Ticktockman'' appears to be prosperous; everyone seems to have a job, and even the Harlequin, who is late for everything, has access to an airboat and manages to secure the money to buy 150,000 dollars' worth of jelly beans. Technology and attention to the clock has made the culture and its people efficient to the maximum degree. Indeed, the entire culture of "'Repent, Harlequin!' Said the Ticktockman" serves technology. Like worker bees in a hive, the people report to work at exactly the same time each day, each to do his or her specific task designed to make the entire machine of the society run smoothly. This efficiency results in an orderly and safe climate for the citizens, "a society where the single driving force was order and unity and equality and promptness and clocklike precision."

It is science and technology, however, that also enable the government to monitor the individual lives of its citizens for promptness. Time cards and cardioplates are the means through which this happens. The cardioplate appears to be a device that each person wears that both monitors and regulates the flow of blood through the heart to the brain. When a cardioplate is turned off, the person dies. Ellison writes, "What they had done, was devise a method of curtailing the amount of life a person could have. If he was ten minutes late, he lost ten minutes of his life.... And so, by this simple scientific expedient (utilizing a scientific process held dearly secret by the Ticktockman's office) the System was maintained."

Style

Allusions

Literary allusions are references to familiar characters, real people, events, or concepts used to make an idea more easily understood. Moreover, allusions serve as a sort of intellectual shorthand; by inserting an allusion in a story, the writer succinctly inserts an additional text, or history, or philosophical system into his or her story, in just a word or two. For example, Ellison's opening passage from Thoreau's "Civil Disobedience" not only provides the image of the hero into the story, it also embeds the whole notion of civil disobedience, Thoreau's metaphor of marching to the beat of a different drummer, and the incident of Thoreau's night in jail for his refusal to pay income tax, among other ideas and events. Likewise, by choosing to use Bolivar, Napo-

leon, Robin Hood, Dick Bong, Jesus, and Jomo Kenyatta as descriptors of how the lower classes thought of the Harlequin, Ellison is able in just a few words to insert the stories and historical events associated with each of these figures into his story.

One of the most important allusions in the story comes in the final page. "So they sent him to Coventry.... it was just like what they did to Winston Smith in NINETEEN EIGHTY-FOUR, which was a book none of them knew about, but the techniques are really quite ancient, and so they did it to Everett C. Marm...." *1984* is a book by George Orwell, written in 1949. The main character, Winston Smith, is a quiet bureaucrat who works in the ironically named Ministry of Truth. Smith secretly rebels against the government, and begins an illicit affair with Julia. Although they love each other, she betrays him during her torture and brainwashing. The novel, with its warning about the dangers of totalitarian society, hit a responsive chord in England and the United States; the world of *1984* seemed very close to the so-called "Iron Curtain" of the Soviet Bloc nations. Ellison's use of Orwell's title inserts the entire novel into the short story. Readers familiar with Orwell's work will recognize that the Harlequin is both brainwashed and destroyed as a result of his nonconformity. They will also recognize that Ellison has a larger purpose in this story, to warn his readers of the dangers inherent in contemporary industrial society.

Utopias and Dystopias

A utopia is an ideal place that does not exist in reality. Utopian literature creates an ideal world. Generally, utopian novels are novels of ideas where people have developed systems or technologies that allow them to focus on what is truly important in life. The word "Utopian" comes from the name of book written by Thomas More in 1516 about a perfect, imaginary place called "Utopia." Other famous utopian books include Plato's *The Republic* and H. G. Wells's *A Modern Utopia*.

Although "'Repent, Harlequin!' Said the Ticktockman" takes place in a futuristic world filled with technological conveniences, it belongs to a uniquely twentieth and twenty-first century variation of the utopia called a "dystopia." Rather than a description of an ideal place, a dystopian novel describes an oppressive and horrific world of the future where some of the most troubling aspects of contemporary society have expanded and defined the world of the future. Examples of this genre include George Orwell's *1984,* as well as Margaret Atwood's *The Handmaid's Tale* (1985) and *Oryx and Crake* (2003).

Dystopias generally serve as cautionary tales, warning readers of what will come if present conditions are not corrected. In '''Repent, Harlequin!' Said the Ticktockman,'' Ellison warns against the homogeneity of modern life, and of the way that time and schedules are kept at the expense of individual human creativity.

Historical Context

McCarthyism and the Cold War

In the two decades before the writing of '''Repent, Harlequin!' Said the Ticktockman,'' a series of events occurred in the United States that marked the culture for years to come. In 1945, the Second World War ended. The Potsdam Conference effectively divided up Eastern Europe into spheres of influence. Consequently, the Soviet Union gained control over large sections of the area and quickly closed down access and communication to and from those countries. Winston Churchill in a famous speech referred to this part of the globe as the ''Iron Curtain,'' and this metaphor persisted until the breakup of the Soviet Union many years later.

Thus, the ''hot'' Second World War degenerated into a cold war, a time when Western nations vied with the Soviet Union for power and control. Because both sides were developing considerable nuclear arsenals, the cold war was in deadly earnest; during the 1950s and 1960s, Americans lived with the very real fear of nuclear annihilation.

The fear of the Soviet Union and the fear of communism led to what has been described as ''The Red Scare'' in the United States. In 1950, Senator Joseph McCarthy began widespread accusations and investigations of suspected communist activities in the United States. He and his followers managed to elicit great support. Not only were government workers required to take loyalty oaths to keep their jobs, ordinary citizens were called upon to testify against their neighbors, coworkers, and friends. Many businesses and firms refused to hire anyone who had been accused of being a

communist, even if they had not been found guilty of any wrongdoing. This led to what has been called a ''blacklist.'' Many writers, actors, artists, and directors found themselves on this list and out of work for many years.

At the height of McCarthyism, the hearings were televised and viewed by Americans all over the country. Many people cooperated with the investigations and accusations as a way of keeping themselves safe from suspicion. Those who chose not to testify and who spoke out against McCarthy's group were often punished through the loss of jobs and income. Like the conformists of '''Repent, Harlequin!' Said the Ticktockman,'' many American citizens strove not to be noticed, rather than to stand up for what was right. Ellison came of age during the McCarthy era; his steadfast support of the individual's duty to resist oppressors of any persuasion reveals the deep impression this period had on him.

The Vietnam War

In 1954, the French defeat at the battle Dien Bien Phu ultimately led to American involvement in Vietnam. In response to a vacuum of power quickly filled by communist nationalists led by Ho Chi Minh, American presidents Eisenhower, Kennedy, and Johnson, fearful of the spread of communism in Southeast Asia, sent first advisors and later troops to prop up a faltering and corrupt government in South Vietnam in their fight against the communist nationalists. In 1965, American public opinion, while still largely in support of the Vietnam policies of the American government was beginning to turn. As more men were drafted for service in Vietnam, and as the casualty lists grew larger, Americans began to question American involvement.

In many ways, '''Repent, Harlequin!' Said the Ticktockman'' reflects the growing unrest with the Vietnam War. Ellison's use of Thoreau initially recalls Thoreau's own stance against the Mexican War. His refusal to pay income taxes used to support what he considered an unjust war landed him in jail. Likewise, Ellison reminds his readers that unthinking conformity and support of repugnant government decisions leads to a society where the government controls all. The Harlequin in many ways resembles the anti-war protestors of the 1960s in his essentially peaceful yet naive confrontation with the raw power of the state. The fictional Harlequin's jelly bean drop foreshadows real flowers in the

Compare & Contrast

- **1960s:** The use of technology grows dramatically during the decade. Supercomputers are linked together to increase their power, and there is both widespread optimism about technology as well as unease with how technology will be used in the future.

  Today: Computers are in nearly every home, and most computers are linked to the Internet. This linkage offers ready access to a great deal of information, but many computer uses have concern that the linkages can also divulge private information to a large audience.

- **1960s:** The Soviet Union reaches superpower strength, and the United States engages in a cold war with that nation. Americans fear the Soviet way of life, seeing in communism a denial of individuality.

  Today: The Soviet Union no longer exists, and communism is no longer a world force, except in China where the emphasis is still on the community rather than on the individual.

- **1960s:** Clocks and watches have hands and faces, which are significantly human descriptions of their working parts. Most importantly, clocks and watches are analog; that is, the second hands, minute hands, and hour hands move at a continuous, continual, and consistent rate. Measuring time, for most people, is somewhat approximate.

  Today: Clocks and watches increasingly have digital displays that render seconds, minutes, and hours in discrete units. As a consequence, timekeeping for most people has become more precise.

gun barrels of National Guard troops, as does the Harlequin's arrest and imprisonment foreshadow the violence of the 1968 Democratic National Convention.

In the end, it is unlikely that Ellison would support either the government position on Vietnam, or the crowd mentality of many of the war protests. Rather, Ellison demonstrates through this story the importance of the individual of conscience resisting both.

Critical Overview

While Ellison's audience has largely been a popular one, academic writers also find much to say about Ellison and his work. George Edgar Slusser, for example, in an early study of Ellison's work, *Harlan Ellison: Unrepentant Harlequin,* connects Ellison to the tradition established by Poe, Hawthorne, Melville and Twain, that of the "mythical allegory."

D. R. Eastwood, on the other hand, examines "'Repent, Harlequin!' Said the Ticktockman" through the lens of Aristotelian rhetoric, suggesting that the story is a form of "Deliberative Rhetoric," as is Orwell's *1984.* That is, these stories "caution citizens that their governments are encroaching upon their freedom and thereby diminishing their lives." He specifically identifies "'Repent, Harlequin!' Said the Ticktockman" as a parable.

Thomas Dillingham, in an article for *Dictionary of Literary Biography,* identifies the Harlequin as one of Ellison's most famous creations, and connects him to other famous literary characters such as Winston Smith from *1984* (1949) and the hero of Ken Kesey's *One Flew over the Cuckoo's Nest* (1962). He concludes that with this story, "Ellison thus adds his entry to the special subgenre of twentieth-century works that explore violation of the mind as the ultimate form of slavery."

Other critics praise Ellison for his development as a writer, as evidenced by the story. Joseph Patrouch, for example, cites "'Repent, Harlequin!'

Picture of a harlequin from the Cezanne Exhibition in Paris, 1995

Said the Ticktockman'' as Ellison's ''breakthrough'' story, the story that shows ''Ellison growing out of the formula.''

Nonetheless, while most critics applaud ''"Repent, Harlequin!' Said the Ticktockman'' for its daring experimentation and message, one who finds what he considers a fatal flaw in the story is Michael D. White. His concern is that Ellison does not pay attention to historical processes in the story, and thus, although this is a story concerned with time, it is nonetheless a static story. He writes that Ellison's ''weakness stems from his inability to place this mechanistic, efficiency-oriented, and profit-geared system in the proper light of its historical origins and development. The system's past is absorbed in its present-future.''

Ellen Weil and Gary Wolfe, in their 2002 study *Harlan Ellison: The Edge of Forever,* however, refute White's interpretation, arguing that it is not Ellison who portrays time as static; rather, it is the society the Harlequin wishes to undermine that destroys history. They argue, ''One of the subtler ironies of the story is that it reveals how a society that ostensibly worships time in fact destroys or negates it. . . .'' For Weil and Wolfe, ''"Repent,

Harlequin!' Said the Ticktockman'' is the ''central story'' in *Paingod and Other Delusions.*

Other critics variously see ''"Repent, Harlequin!' Said the Ticktockman'' as an apocalyptic story (Oscar de Los Santos); as a mock epic (Stephen Adams); or as a representation of Mardi Gras madness (Earle V. Bryant). The centrality of ''"Repent, Harlequin!' Said the Ticktockman'' to the canon of Ellison's work suggests that there will be continuing readings of the story in the coming years.

Criticism

Diane Andrews Henningfeld

Henningfeld is a professor of English literature at Adrian College who writes widely on literary topics for academic and educational publications. In this essay, Henningfeld identifies the ways that Ellison exploits the archetype of the Trickster through the character of the Harlequin, through the narrator of the story, and through his own role as writer of the tale.

''"Repent, Harlequin!' Said the Ticktockman'' is a deceptively simple tale. It is clearly a parable, a short illustrative story intended to teach a moral lesson. Set in a surreal future world where workers ride to work on moving sidewalks and everyone dresses alike, the characters of the story are more types than personalities.

Ellison draws on an established tradition to create his main characters: the Italian commedia dell'arte, a theatrical form that flourished throughout Europe from the late Middle Ages through the 18th century. In the commedia dell'arte, actors wear masks to identify the stock characters they are playing, and the plots are highly stylized and conventional. A Harlequin is a principal stock character in the commedia dell'arte, and is often witty, capricious, and wily. Dressed in a tight costume covered with colored diamond shapes, the Harlequin also carries a slapstick with which he hits other characters. Anyone watching a production will recognize the mask of the Harlequin immediately; indeed, in the commedia dell'arte, the mask is more important than the player.

In creating his character of the Harlequin, Ellison not only utilizes the conventions of the commedia

What Do I Read Next?

- Beginning in the 1940s, Isaac Asimov wrote a series of short stories and novels concerning the interaction between robots and humans. Most famously, Asimov developed the Three Laws of Robotics in these works. Examples of this work are Asimov's *I, Robot* (1952); *Robots and Empire* (1985); and *The Complete Robot* (1983).

- George Orwell's novel *1984* (1949) is an important book for any student interested in speculative fiction, dystopian novels, or grim visions of a mechanized future. Written at the beginning of the cold war, and depicting the near future, *1984*

is a classic novel and necessary background for students of Ellison's *"'Repent Harlequin!'"*

- Aldous Huxley's *Brave New World* (1932) is another classic of dystopian literature.

- *Science and Literature: Bridging the Two Cultures* (2001), by David Wilson and Zack Bowen, while a sometimes difficult book, offers a compelling interdisciplinary examination of the ways science and the humanities interact with each other. The final chapter, which discusses Huxley's *Brave New World,* is particularly useful for students of the dystopian novel.

dell'arte to provide a quick understanding of the role of this character, he also reaches deep into an almost universal archetype, the trickster. Trickster figures function in oral tradition and literature across cultures; tricksters play important roles in North American Indian legends as well as in stories from such widely diverse areas as Japan, Africa, and South America. These figures are paradoxical; on the one hand, they are often represented as immature pranksters. On the other, they are also often cultural heroes. Tricksters both destroy and recreate systems, undermining power and authority structures.

Everett C. Marm, in his guise as the Harlequin, is clearly a trickster figure. Small, impish, with an "elfin" grin, he fits the physical description of the trickster archetype. Further, Tricksters tend to be young and rebellious, jokesters who undermine the established order through their own refusal to go along with the rest of the crowd. Ellen Weil and Gary K. Wolfe write that "'Repent, Harlequin!' equates anarchic, immature behavior with the creative force in an otherwise mechanized society."

Earle V. Bryant also identifies the Harlequin as a type of trickster. In his article suggesting that the Harlequin bears close resemblance to a Mardi Gras float rider, Bryant introduces yet another incarnation of the trickster figure, the Lord of Misrule, who,

for a day, turns the world upside down. He calls the Harlequin a "rebel who uses merriment, not only as a curative to revitalize a populace that has forgotten how to laugh, but also as a weapon to topple a tyrannical regime . . . . "

The Harlequin, however, is not the only trickster in "'Repent, Harlequin!' Said the Ticktockman." The narrator of this story serves a similar function but in a slightly different arena, that of literature. The narrative voice in this story is ironic and parodic, and breaks many of the conventions of storytelling. As Ellen Weil notes, "the relationship between author, storyteller, and narrator is . . . complex." In the first place, the narrator uses a series of allusions as he describes the Harlequin. "[H]e was considered a Bolivar; a Napoleon; a Robin Hood; a Dick Bong (Ace of Aces); a Jesus; a Jomo Kenyatta." These allusions, while descriptive, are also jarring. How do Jesus and Dick Bong end up on the same list? How does a rebel independence fighter like Bolivar or Jomo Kenyatta compare to men dedicated to world domination like Napoleon? The narrator uses these allusions to both inflate and deflate the description of the Harlequin.

The narrator also chooses to wreak havoc with the chronology of the story. He refuses to tell his listeners the story in chronological order. Rather, as

''"Repent, Harlequin!" Said the Ticktockman' is shot through with irony: where readers expect the elevated language of epic as in Milton, they get an informal, futuristic slang more reminiscent of Vonnegut; where they expect a hero like Christ or Jomo Kenyatta, they get Everett C. Marm; and where readers expect a grand gesture, they get jelly beans.''

he tells the reader, ''Now begin in the middle, and later learn the beginning; the end will take care of itself.'' By so ordering the story, the narrator undermines conventional audience expectations of how stories should be told. Instead, he chooses how to structure the story, thus both destroying and recreating the time sequence. Thus, both the Harlequin and the narrator serve as temporal anarchists: The Harlequin refuses to obey the laws of time in his society, and the narrator ignores the ''laws'' of sequential storytelling.

Finally, the narrator breaks the ''third wall,'' that empty space that separates actors from audience. He chooses to speak directly to the reader in very informal prose, thus creating himself as a character in the story. He uses second person, addressing the reader as ''you,'' bringing the reader directly into the story.

In these three ways, the narrator acts as a literary trickster, a character in his own story who refuses to use the structured and conventionalized formats of storytelling. Like the Harlequin, he mixes up reader response as readers attempt to reassemble the story into something they are familiar with. This narrator, clearly an individualist, deviously resists the ''formula'' science fiction story; he is a rebel against the fossilized genre in which he finds himself.

It is possible to move out from the story one more level, to find the master trickster behind ''"Repent, Harlequin!' Said the Ticktockman.'' This trickster is Harlan Ellison himself, the writer with the name so curiously close to his hero's pseudonym. The similarity extends beyond the name to physical characteristics. At five feet four inches, Ellison resembles the hero he creates. The similarities are so obvious that writer George Slusser titled his 1977 study of Ellison and his work *Harlan Ellison: Unrepentant Harlequin.*

Ellison clearly understands himself to be a trickster, an individual who, through his refusal to go along with the conventions of the science fiction genre as it was at the beginning of the 1960s, creates a new and sometimes grittier kind of writing. Even Ellison's reluctance to be identified as a ''New Wave'' science fiction writer speaks to his trickster qualities. The quintessential literary anarchist, Ellison refuses to be boxed into any genre or convention.

In the social arena, Ellison also plays the trickster, a kind of David to cultural Goliaths. In the 1970s, the behemoth he attacked was television; more recently, Ellison has taken on media giant AOL Time Warner. Again, the irony is evident. Ellison made his mark (or at least part of his mark) as a television scriptwriter, and has exploited the new computer/Internet technology with web sites, CD–ROM games, and digital recordings. In so doing, he once again displays his understanding of himself as trickster, the individual who both uses and undermines the cultural conventions and technologies of his day.

Identifying with the Harlequin is not a new strategy for Ellison, who writes himself into many of his stories. As Michael Moorcock argues, ''Almost all the characters in these stories are, of course, Harlan Ellison. Harlequin the gadfly is an idealized Ellison, justifying his penchant for practical jokes, giving it a social function (one can almost see him as a 'good' version of Batman's adversary, the Joker.)''

Stephen Adams demonstrates another way that Ellison plays the trickster with his own writing by using devices and conventions associated with the epic tradition. In addition to beginning in medias res, or in the middle, Ellison also uses ''catalogs, elaborate similes, an arming scene, launching of a ship, a dangerous woman, battles, single combat. . . .'' Yet Ellison does not use the conventions in a traditional way. According to Adams, he ''introduces epic conventions in order to parody them, twist them, turn them upside down." What he creates is not epic at all, but rather mock-epic.

Finally, Ellison plays the trickster with many of his stories by ongoing revisions and changes in later editions so a reader may find differences from collection to collection. In addition, Ellison adds introductions and annotations to his stories that often alter audience reception. Nowhere is this more evident than in "'Repent, Harlequin!' Said the Ticktockman." Ellison's story is a parable, an instructive story with a moral message. The introductory quotation from Thoreau makes his purpose evident, as does the commentary from his narrator. He also connects the story to George Orwell's *1984*, suggesting that he has a strong message he wants to send readers about heroic individuality. And yet, when "'Repent, Harlequin!' Said the Ticktockman" appears in Moorcock's 1979 collection of Ellison's works, *The Fantasies of Harlan Ellison,* it is with an introduction by Ellison saying that he wrote the story to explain his own unremitting failure to arrive anywhere on time: "I am always late. . . . I've decided that unlike most other folk with highly developed senses of the fluidity of time, the permanence of humanity in the chronostream, et al, I got no ticktock going up there on top. So I had to explain it to the world, to cop out, as it were, in advance. I wrote the following story as my plea for understanding. . . ." These comments, appearing as a headnote before the story itself, utterly undermine the apparent high moral message of the story and render it nearly trivial. Thus, while critics such as Thomas Dillingham argue that Ellison's story is about a "gesture of defiance" and that that gesture, "no matter how self-defeating, may be the only self-authenticating effort an individual can make," Ellison says that the story is about his own lack of punctuality. Ever the trickster, Ellison subverts critical commentary—like his Harlequin—by metaphorically "inserting thumbs in large ears," "[sticking] out his tongue, [rolling] his eyes and [going] wugga-wugga-wugga."

This is surely a trickster's tale. "'Repent, Harlequin!' Said the Ticktockman" is shot through with irony: where readers expect the elevated language of epic as in Milton, they get an informal, futuristic slang more reminiscent of Vonnegut; where they expect a hero like Christ or Jomo Kenyatta, they get Everett C. Marm; and where readers expect a grand gesture, they get jelly beans. Nevertheless, in the gap between reader expectation and Ellison's

story, there is still room for the moral lesson, a lesson that nearly disappears in the Harlequin's defeat and subsequent television appearance, a lesson that Ellison himself subverts with his later explanations. The moral of the story is that any individual, even someone with a name like Everett C. Marm, can and must stand up to the totalitarian hegemony of schedule and power. No matter how small the gesture, Ellison argues in this story, no matter how small the David and how huge the Goliath, it is the making of the gesture that is important. Thus, what appears as defeat for the Harlequin opens a tiny window in the "mrmee, mrmee, mrmee" of the Ticktockman.

Source: Diane Andrews Henningfeld, Critical Essay on "'Repent, Harlequin!' Said the Ticktockman," in *Short Stories for Students,* Thomson Gale, 2005.

Carol Ullmann

Ullmann is a freelance writer and editor. In the following essay, Ullmann discusses how time is tenuous in Ellison's story and how the Harlequin is able to exploit that weakness to further his cause of civil disobedience.

Ellison's short story "'Repent, Harlequin!' Said the Ticktockman" features a futuristic dystopia—the opposite of a utopia—where humanity is so enslaved to time that even the very vitality of one's heart is controlled by "The Ones Who Kept The Machine Functioning Smoothly." People move from task to task with machine-like regularity; those who are late are punished by having proportional time shaved from the end of their lives, until the end catches up with the present and those people are turned off. Ellison here represents tardiness as a crime fit for the ultimate punishment: the death penalty:

> . . . and one day we no longer let time serve us, we serve time and we are slaves of the schedule, worshippers of the sun's passing, bound into a life predicated on restrictions because the system will not function if we don't keep the schedule tight.

> Until it becomes more than a minor inconvenience to be late. It becomes a sin. Then a crime. Then a crime punishable by . . .

The reader enters the story in the middle of its action where the conflict is created by one man's rebellion against the System and its strict order of

> The Harlequin's success at undermining the Ticktockman's sense of time foreshadows the eventual downfall of this society."

time. The Harlequin acts out in ridiculous ways: ruffling shoppers with zany behavior; dropping jellybeans on workers as they change shifts; shouting blasphemous things from rooftops. The extremity of his conduct mirrors the severe actions the Master Timekeeper (known behind his back as the Ticktockman) ''and his legal machinery'' must take to maintain order and timeliness. The society that the Ticktockman serves is ruled by time. Through his public outbursts, the Harlequin shows the System and the Ticktockman that time is tenuous, thus undermining the Ticktockman's power and, eventually, the order of society. Ellison's story is meant to provoke thought, primarily on civil disobedience, but also on the meaning of time and its usefulness as a tool of control.

Modern Western sense of time is not fixed, but always slowly changing along with societal values. Currently most people keep a day planner or personal calendar to track activities, meetings, and important dates. Many people begin the day being awaked by an alarm clock. Clocks are found in most public areas. And while it is generally considered rude to be late, most people expect there to be some flexibility for unexpected contingencies. The order that time brings to modern life is perceived as a characteristic of civilized life. Thus it is good to pay heed to the time, to have meetings, to schedule events. The organizing strength of time—its consistency, its steady beat—is portrayed in Ellison's story by the machine-efficient flow of society: supply and demand, work and rest.

In contrast to the orderliness that time brings to people's lives, time is also perceived as a prison or a cage. People may now and then feel burdened by their packed schedules and never-ending parade of commitments. Yet they feel obligated to continue— or perhaps schedule a vacation. These days sponta-

neity is not always an option because it is too random, too uncontrolled. In '''Repent, Harlequin!' Said the Ticktockman,'' the Harlequin relishes spontaneity. He brings relief to his predictable society, dropping sweet, brightly-colored jelly beans into people's lives as they come and go from work, creating a holiday, a reprieve from the workday.

The Harlequin also brings chaos, as the supply and demand of the economy suffers from unexpected delays in the schedule. This is what is meant by time being tenuous. Timeliness has become so important in this society that it is, in fact, a weakness because it is *too* important. Time has become such a crucial feature to how this future society is organized that a small ripple causes big waves. The Harlequin exploits this weakness to make his point that this rigid world is awful and needs to change and have more flexibility.

In this story, time is represented by the human heart (known colloquially as a ''ticker'') which is controlled with a cardioplate. The heart is like a living clock, which this society oppresses in the name of order and civilization. Time is thus a tool of life and death that is wielded by totalitarian leaders. Although they control the passage of a person's life, it is not against the passage of time that the Harlequin rebels. He fights the control of time, seeks to return choice of how time passes to the individual.

The Harlequin gambles with his life but he is beyond caring for life in this world. ''After all, his name was Everett C. Marm, and he wasn't much to begin with, except a man who had no sense of time.'' The Harlequin probably knows he will die sooner rather than later and the only way for that to not happen—and for this to be a tolerable world in which to live—is for society's values to change. And for that to change takes tremendous effort. He uses his limited time to work toward that change.

The Harlequin shows how time is tenuous with his pranks. Schedules are easily thrown off by minor, unexpected disturbances, sometimes by minutes, sometimes by hours. Eventually, as a wanted man, just his presence disrupts the schedule, throwing off a carefully maintained balance of supply and demand. The products listed are so silly-sounding (wegglers, popli, Smash-O, swizzleskid) as to make the reader question even how important the supply-demand cycle is when it's delivering only junk and not the necessities of shelter, food, and warmth.

While the everyday citizen may see only a tremor, the effect the Harlequin has on society is, from the point of view of those at the top, that of an earthquake and just as potentially devastating.

> ... in a society where the single driving force was order and unity and equality and promptness and clocklike precision and attention to the clock, reverence of the gods of the passage of time, it was a disaster of major importance.

Though the Harlequin tries to reach everyone with his public outbursts—ladies of fashion, workers changing shifts, Thursday shoppers, physicians—he ultimately does not convince society as a whole that time is tenuous and living one's life is more meaningful than living a schedule. Some people are happy in the moment of his disruptions but none make a change or a choice like the Harlequin's. In fact, at the end of the story they all accept the brainwashed Harlequin's broadcast apology as proof that society's order is right: ''and if that's the way the system is run, then let's do it that way, because it doesn't pay to fight city hall, or in this case, the Ticktockman.''

While time can bring a sense of control and orderliness, along with it comes a burden of responsibility to maintain that incessant pace. The Harlequin's power is in his abilities to move beyond the expected, embrace spontaneity, and have no fear as to the repercussions of his actions (as seen in the scene with Pretty Alice showing him the Wanted poster). His power is also his guilelessness: the Harlequin is what he is, without reservation or disguise. Despite his nickname, he hides behind no masks, literal or figurative. He stands in polar opposition to society's desire for order, and especially in opposition to the Ticktockman.

Even the physical characteristics of the two main characters are diametrically opposed. Where the Ticktockman is tall, the Harlequin is elfin, or small. One is soft-spoken and controlled; the other is loud and wild. The Ticktockman keeps the machine of society running smoothly while the Harlequin seeks to undermine its regularity. The Harlequin, in fact, equates timeliness itself with death: '''Don't be slaves of time, it's a helluva way to die, slowly, by degrees . . . down with the Ticktockman!'''

The Harlequin is unsuccessful at convincing the masses to behave differently, to have less regard for time. His pranks are no more than minor disrup-

tions in individual lives; however, the Ticktockman appears to be intrigued by this troublemaker. The Ticktockman first threatens to turn off the Harlequin's cardioplate and then immediately says that he's not going to do that. Although he is known as a man of few words, the Ticktockman wants to speak with the Harlequin—he claims to want to know *who* he is, not just *what* he is. What is most telling of the Harlequin's success with the Ticktockman is that at the end of the story, the Ticktockman is three minutes late, doesn't care that he's late, and is muttering *''mrmee, mrmee, mrmee, mrmee''*—which is onomatopoeia for Marm, the Harlequin's real last name. The Ticktockman seems to have become insane, as if, perhaps, he were the one who went through reprogramming. Or even, as if, the Harlequin and the Ticktockman changed identities. The Ticktockman is masked, therefore, who would know? The author leaves these questions unanswered at the end.

The Harlequin's success at undermining the Ticktockman's sense of time foreshadows the eventual downfall of this society. As the Master Timekeeper, if the Ticktockman has lost his regard for the schedule then it is only a matter of *time* before society suffers many more of the same delays and disruptions that were originally caused by the Harlequin's pranks. Although punished with death, the Harlequin's cause thus will live on. And if the Ticktockman does not change things himself, another Harlequin, another trickster will rise. As acknowledged in the beginning of the story, the Harlequin spirit is inexplicable and irrepressible. Kill it, breed it out, vaccinate against it and this personality will always reappear—just as Everett C. Marm, a man with no sense of time, was born and lived in a world where time was sacred, above human life.

Ellison begins his story by quoting from Henry David Thoreau's seminal work of nonfiction *Civil Disobedience*. This long essay was inspired by a night Thoreau spent in jail after refusing to pay taxes, which was his opposition to the U.S.-Mexican War. Thoreau's other famous feat was the two years of solitude that he spent living in a cottage at Walden Pond in Massachusetts. Although the Harlequin is a poster-child for civil disobedience, he never chooses to remove himself from society. Unlike Marshall Delahanty, he does not run, he does not seek the solitude of nature, and he does not place himself outside the reach and influence of society. The Harlequin's mission, like any trickster, is to cause chaos and change and to do this he must be in the thick of things.

The ultimate proof of time's tenuousness is the brevity of individual human life as compared to the rest of history. The Harlequin, giving up this own life without repentance, seems to know this. Unfortunately, the brevity of individual human life means that it's that much easier for humanity to be doomed to repeat history's mistakes. "'Repent, Harlequin!' Said the Ticktockman'" is a story that stands as a modern fable, exposing some faults and weaknesses of today's society in hopes that by exposing them, humanity never spirals down that path.

Source: Carol Ullmann, Critical Essay on "'Repent, Harlequin!' Said the Ticktockman," in *Short Stories for Students*, Thomson Gale, 2005.

Earle V. Bryant

In the following essay, Bryant calls Marm "one of the most memorable characters in modern short fiction" and draws connections between his actions and that of a float rider in a Mardi Gras or Carnival parade.

At one point in Harlan Ellison's futuristic short story "'Repent, Harlequin!' Said the Ticktockman," Everette Marm, the tale's rebel protagonist, swoops down in his airboat on a group of factory workers about to begin the five p.m. shift and bombards them with a multitude of jelly beans. "One hundred and fifty thousand dollars worth of jelly beans cascaded down on the expresstrip. Jelly beans! Millions and billions of [them . . .] coming down in a steady rain, a solid wash, a torrent of color and sweetness out of the sky from above." Marm's reason for unleashing this "attack" on the plant workers is to disrupt the smooth flow of his time-conscious society, a flow that he sees as stultifying and ultimately fatal. As Ellison makes clear in the tale, Marm lives in a world—a "poisonously gray society," as Michael White so aptly describes it—in which punctuality and conformity are the law and tardiness and individualism are felonies punishable by death. Like George Orwell's Oceania in *1984* or Ray Bradbury's world of the future in *Fahrenheit 451*, it is a totalitarian society "where the single driving force [is] order and unity and promptness and clocklike precision and attention to the clock."

It is against this "terrible world" that Marm rebels. The weapons that he uses in his rebellion,

however, are not bullets and bombs; they are pranks and high jinks, outrageous stunts designed to arouse his fellow citizens from the unthinking conformity and blind adherence to "sanity and metronomic order" in which they are enmeshed. Accordingly, when Marm swoops down in his airboat on the workers entering the roller-bearing plant and showers them with jellybeans, he is attempting to show them that life can and should be a joyous affair and not the government-mandated robotic existence they are leading. In this scene, as well as throughout the story, Ellison wants us to see Marm as a comic rebel-hero. There is, however, another image that Ellison wants to project in this scene: that of a doubloon-dispensing float rider in one of New Orleans' annual Carnival parades.

One indication that this is Ellison's intention is the jellybeans that Marm unleashes on the factory workers. Although Ellison explicitly states that there are "[m]illions and billions" of jellybeans and that they are of various colors, he is careful to specify only three of the colors: purple, yellow, and green, the traditional colors of New Orleans' Mardi Gras. Marm's dispensing of the jellybeans creates an unabashedly festive atmosphere among the factory workers—indeed as Ellison describes it, "a holiday." That holiday, Ellison is suggesting, is the granddaddy of all holidays, Mardi Gras. Ellison's hero, Mardi Gras Marm, tries to infuse his quasi-robotic society with the "quite-mad coocoo newness" of laughter and frivolity signified by his one-man Carnival parade.

But to recognize Ellison's connection more clearly, it is necessary to call to mind exactly what a typical float rider (to the extent that there is one) in a New Orleans Carnival parade looks like and does. Arrayed in colorful costumes and perched on floats that tower as high as eighteen feet in the air, Mardi Gras float riders toss doubloons, strings of colorful plastic beads, cups, small rubber toys, and various other trinkets (or "throws," as they are called) down to the thousands of people lining the parade route. Most of the time the throws land on the ground and parade-goers scramble after them. Much the same thing happens in Ellison's story. From his airboat/float, Marm hurls his Carnival throws—that is, his jellybeans—to the crowd below. Like a Mardi Gras float rider, Marm is wearing a costume—his signature "clown suit." Once Marm has showered the factory workers with his jellybeans, they make a mad dash for them: "The shift workers howled and

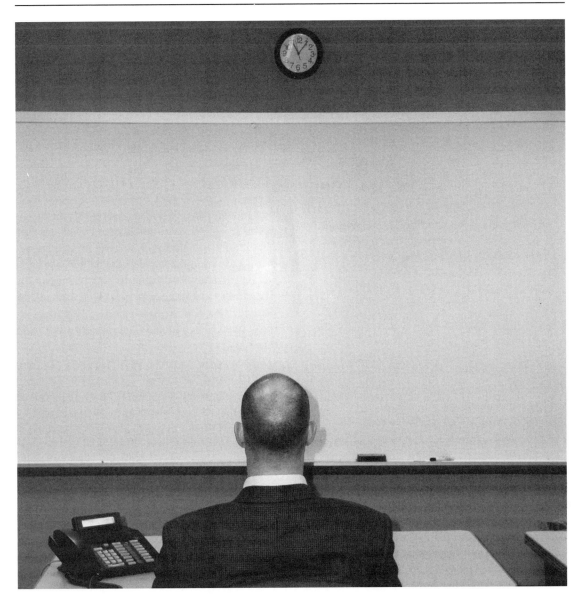

Businessman looking at a clock, illustrating the force of time in the workplace

laughed and were pelted, and broke ranks[. . .] and everyone [scrambled] thisawayandthataway in a jackstraw tumble, still laughing."

Once we recognize that Ellison is forging a link between Marm's unleashing his "torrent of color and sweetness [. . .] from above" and the practice of Carnival float riders' unleashing their torrent of *throws,* it is not difficult to see why he connects the one with the other. Viewing Marm as a doubloon-tossing Mardi Gras float rider greatly reinforces the image of him as a rebel who uses merriment, not only as a curative to revitalize a populace that has forgotten how to laugh, but also as a weapon to

topple a tyrannical regime that lords it over a world in which, as White remarks, "Homo sapiens [has] become Homo automatus." That is not to say that because Marm tosses jellybeans instead of Molotov cocktails he should not be taken seriously as a freedom fighter. In his unorthodox approach to revolution, Mardi Gras Marm emerges not only as one of Harlan Ellison's most original and successful creations, but also as one of the most memorable characters in modern short fiction.

Source: Earle V. Bryant, "Ellison's "'Repent Harlequin!'" Said the Ticktockman,'" in *Explicator,* Vol. 59, No. 3, Spring 2001, pp. 163–65.

Oscar De Los Santos

In the following essay excerpt, De Los Santos examines the traits of Ellison's "underdog" or "trickster" characters, including Marm in "'Repent Harlequin.'"

There is only one end to creation. What is created is destroyed, and thus full circle is achieved.

Ellison, "The Region Between"

. . . the search for your soul in a soulless world requires special maps.

Ellison, *Deathbird Stories*

As the decade draws to a close and we approach the end of the twentieth century, virtually every mode of artistic expression is projecting its own version of apocalypse via works that contemplate the end of humankind. For many authors, however, this is not a new investigation. Such is true of Harlan Ellison, who focused on apocalyptic themes in his first sold short story ("Glowworm," 1956) and who has frequently returned to this theme throughout his career. In much of his fiction, Ellison struggles to project warnings about humanity's demise even as he celebrates our past accomplishments and potential.

Whether writing one of his many essays, television or motion picture scripts, or short stories (a body of material comprised of over 1,200 separate works thus far), Ellison most frequently channels his energies into works of science fiction, fantasy, and horror. When he does turn to speculative fiction, one of his most frequent principal characters—a character who appears in many guises but who embodies the same qualities from story to story—is the trickster: the angry, feisty, marginalized underdog; the little guy who won't go down without a fight, who wishes to clog up the works of (in)human conformity and make a race rise above mediocrity. This character will fight apathy and submissive attitudes in others even when he believes that he himself no longer wishes to live. Ellison has said that an author must cannibalize his existence in order to find the material about which to write. We can also take this to mean, as is fundamentally the case, that an author is all of his/her characters. Certainly this is very true of Ellison and his underdogs. When we examine the great body of work that Ellison has produced in an effort to effect changes in the attitudes of readers, fellow writers, and humanity in general, we find that Ellison is himself a marginalized fighter—for just as his fictional constructs often fight to stave off global or cosmic apocalypse, Ellison himself engages in less fantastic but no less daunting battles: to kick humanity out of its apathetic complacency and to elevate his chosen profession—writing, especially that produced in the field of speculative fiction—to new levels of quality. Indeed, the goals of many of Ellison's principal characters and Ellison himself are very similar: to prevent different forms of apocalypse. In his fiction, Ellison's underdogs struggle to prevent the death of (in)human life; in his life, Ellison fights to prevent the death of good writing.

Anyone who reads a book or two of Ellison's—fiction or non-fiction—quickly realizes that he seldom shirks from brutal, scathing critical assessments of his subject matter. Maybe that is why he has been called "probably the most controversial writer ever to hit science fiction" by fellow science fiction writer and critic Lester Del Rey and why most science fiction fans have heard of Ellison, whether they read him or not. Most people have very strong positive or negative feelings about Ellison the writer, but even stronger feelings about Ellison's fiction: they either love his work or they hate it. Those who love it admire Ellison for shoving a textual mirror in society's face and exposing its hypocrisy, neuroses, and shortcomings with stark objectivity; those who hate it often do so for the same reason and for its abrasive tone and negativity. While it is true that a great deal of "doom and gloom" may be found in the Ellison canon, it is also true that Ellison frequently undercuts his often dystopic settings and his cynical characters with the actions taken by those characters. If it is true that actions speak louder than words, as the old cliche tells us, then it is valuable to analyze a few of Ellison's principal characters, assess their actions, and see if what they *do* contradicts what they *say,* or what they seem to think about themselves and their respective environments. Doing so yields a better understanding of the tension that is inherent in so many Ellison tales and that resides in the author himself. Ellison's characters may rant and rave; they may purport to be on the brink of giving up on themselves and/or their fellow humans—but they seldom do so. Time and again, we see characters and author fighting the good fight: helping out their species (human or alien) and committing themselves to take some form of positive, life-affirming action rather than simply giving up. For Ellison's characters, such actions are diversified, but many involve great struggle against virtually impossible odds; indeed, the stakes are often of apocalyptic proportions.

In an essay called "True Love: Groping for the Holy Grail," Ellison confesses, "I find that the only thing worth the time and energy is the company of others; people are my business and I cannot conceive of ever having discovered all there is to discover about the human heart in conflict with itself (as Faulkner put it). I would much rather sit and talk to someone than alienate myself by watching a ballgame" (363). However, time and again readers find Ellison at odds with humanity: "I swear to God," he has said, "just one day I'd like to get up and not be angry . . . at the world." If we use his fiction as a gauge, we find that Ellison's anger is largely derived from humanity's willingness to settle for mediocrity rather than strive to reach its fullest potential in all facets of its existence. In its desire to settle for the easy solution, humankind sets up traps for itself by relinquishing control of its destiny to debilitating constructs or power-abusing governing systems. And yet, even as he warns us that we are on the brink of destroying ourselves either by doing nothing or by doing the wrong things, Ellison points the way to right actions via his characters. A close examination of several of his marginalized creations provides further evidence of the internal struggle between optimism and pessimism that fuels so much of Ellison's fiction.

One of the best examples of the Ellison underdog is the impish trickster at the heart of "'Repent, Harlequin!' Said the Ticktockman." "'Repent, Harlequin!'" explores a future in which humanity has literally imperiled its own existence as a result of an ever-increasing obsession with punctuality and time. Ellison shows that in our efforts to manage our time with greater efficiency and to better our lives, we have become enslaved by time. Thus, the existential angst resulting from the knowledge that we are responsible for what we do or fail to do as the minutes go by, is replaced by a new worry in a perceptive few: that we have doomed ourselves to living aesthetically dead, stagnating lives by placing our destinies in the hands of powers that measure success and value solely on an individual's ability to keep strict schedules and meet deadlines.

The Harlequin (or Everett C. Marm, his real name) is the only character brave enough to stand up to the Ticktockman, the only one willing to tell this dictatorial megalomaniac to "Get stuffed." Everyone else seems to have forgotten that humanity created the Ticktockman—the precise schedule runner and Master Time Keeper. Everyone else now lives in fear of the power they have allowed the Master Time Keeper to possess: he can shut off any

> When we examine the great body of work that Ellison has produced in an effort to effect changes in the attitudes of readers, fellow writers, and humanity in general, we find that Ellison is himself a marginalized fighter. . . ."

individual's internal biological timepiece permanently with the flick of a switch, a radical punishment induced for repeated tardiness and general ineptitude when it comes to punctuality. Everyone lives with this fear except the Harlequin, who realizes that a society that relinquishes control of its existence to one entity or one small governing body—mechanical or otherwise—is in grave danger of becoming extinct. This is especially true of a society that forgets how to stand up for itself and work to correct its mistakes, or is too frightened or too lazy to do so. Ellison reminds us of our "straw man" shortcomings when he quotes Thoreau's *Civil Disobedience* at the beginning of his tale: "The mass of men serve the state thus, not as men mainly, but as machines, with their bodies. . . . In most cases there is no free exercise whatever of the judgment or of the moral sense; but they put themselves on a level with wood and earth and stones; and wooden men can perhaps be manufactured that will serve the purpose as well" (*Essential Ellison* 877). The role reversal is striking as one reads more of the short story: in Ellison's world, a machinelike government now governs human beings, and most individuals accept the situation. Ellison describes the governing body, the culture and its leader mechanistically: "The Ones Who Kept The Machine Functioning Smoothly, the ones who poured the very best butter over the cams and mainsprings of the culture . . . the Ticktockman and his legal machinery" (878). The author's descriptions emphasize the automated nature of the future world. It may be alive, but it is a vacuous, artificial life. Except perhaps, for Everett C. Marm, the Harlequin, who goes out of his way to discombobulate the efficiency of his world in the most absurd fashion possible, swooping over individuals on a mechanical flying device and creating mayhem with one of the most innocuous of products: jelly beans, a hundred and fifty thousand dollars' worth, to be precise, dropped onto a crowd and throwing off all activities for seven minutes: ''The System had been seven minutes' worth of disrupted. It was a tiny matter, one hardly worthy of note, but in a society where the single driving force was order and unity and equality and promptness and clocklike precision and attention to the clock, reverence of the gods of the passage of time, it was a disaster of major importance'' (880).

The Harlequin is caught in the end, turned in by a woman he knew, someone who didn't like her punctuality and be-told-what-to-do-and-when-to-do-it world disrupted by an upstart, even if the upstart was her boyfriend. And though Marm never buckles under the Ticktockman's interrogation, he is eventually ''worked . . . over'' [brainwashed] and made to appear on the ''communications web'' and admit that he was wrong about trying to fight the system. But in the end, he may have made a difference after all, because the Master Time Keeper is three minutes late to work one day and throws the society's entire system slightly off schedule. Thus, Ellison's trickster succeeds in changing a seemingly unchangeable system, and even though the change is minor, as Ellison's narrator observes, ''if you make only a little change, then it seems to be worthwhile'' (886).

Source: Oscar De Los Santos, ''Clogging Up the (In)Human Works: Harlan Ellison's Apocalyptic Postmodern Visions,'' in *Extrapolation,* Vol. 40, No. 1, 1999, pp. 5–20.

Harlan Ellison

The short essay ''One Small Daring Footnote: Circa 2005'' was especially written by Harlan Ellison to introduce this reprinting of his essay ''A Time for Daring,'' in which he takes issue with the popular complacence of many science fiction writers toward science fiction writing through the latter 1960s, declaring that many of the underestimated, overlooked science fiction authors are those who actually elevate science fiction to ''a level with all great art.''

ONE SMALL DARING FOOTNOTE: CIRCA 2005

At the beginning of the seventh paragraph in the essay that follows, you will read as follows: ''Ten years ago the first Milford Science Fiction Writers Conference was held. . .''

That would've been 1957.

I wrote those words in 1967.

As I write *these* words, today, just for you, it is still the first week in January, the new millennium, year 2005. The hereafter-following essay is nearly forty years old. I was a brash, pugnacious, 33-year-old in 1967. I was a smartass, just like you. The guy writing these words today, January 2005, is looking at age 71 come this May.

I'm still a smartass. The only difference is summed succinctly in this quotation from the great novelist Isaac Bashevis Singer: ''When I was a little boy, they called me a liar, but now that I'm grown up, they call me a writer.''

I started to update the piece when I was asked to allow it to be reprinted here. I gave up on page 2. Doctors are lucky: they get to *bury* their mistakes.

Which is not to say the thoughts and braggadocio and advice and hubris and epiphanies and contumely running amuck in these pages is anything I repudiate. I said them, I'll pay the price. (One of the hardest lessons for an artist to learn is that television talk show hosts and politicians need to be liked, need to be admired, need to be loved—as the social critic Quentin Crisp once observed, ''Artists in any medium are nothing more than a bunch of hooligans who cannot live within their income of admiration''—but that mad need to be well-liked can be murder on a writer. Dostoyevski was a ratbastard, by all accounts, but I'd accept that rap, and consider it a fair cop, if I could write *The Idiot* or *The Brothers Karamazov*.) I said these things, and someone dug them up for presentation here, now almost forty years after they were current, and I have to stand by them because they were true and accurate from the mouth of a 33-year-old me; and though I'm a lot older, I'm no less a smartass, no less devoted to what I write, and if I'm not loveable (hell, my *wife* thinks I'm just fine, thank you), well, at least I'm consistent.

I run my own life. I have *always* run my own life. Good or bad, profitable or riding in boxcars, writing as well as I'm able or missing a spark plug or two, humble or puffed up like a banjo player who had a big breakfast, I have run my own life.

Pasteur said, ''Chance favors the prepared mind.''

That's the banner under which I stand. I'm responsible, as you must be, for what you become, and for how the world judges you. If you can be ethical and courageous and daring, well, you might have a shot at Posterity. Be a *mensch*.

(Look it up. It's Yiddish.)

So. I do not refute thee, o words of my smartass youth. All I ask is that you remember it was written nearly forty years ago, and this: I'm still here, still working, still learning.

Which is better than a poke in the eye with a flaming stick.

* * *

A TIME FOR DARING

I've reached a point now where I don't mind people who've known me for ten or twelve years who come up and hit me with a shot: I don't mind that at all because I know where they're at. They're consistent. But people I've met for the first time, who think they have the right, the audacity to come up and—bam! bam!—give me a real zinger, and I'm supposed to stand there and say, ''ha ha, you're right, I'm an imbecile! . .'' As I told Lee Hoffman, I've just about had it. I resent it and they don't really know who I am, or where I'm at, or what I do. All they know is that thirteen years ago I was a snot-nosed kid, and I'm not snot-nosed any more and they resent it. And Lee said, ''They're never going to forgive you for starting where they started, going further, then rubbing their noses in it.'' That set me to remembering; it set me to extrapolating; and to drawing some conclusions. The conclusions that I've drawn are all inextricably involved with the work I've been doing, work I hope some of you *like*.

Many of you may remember stories that I wrote seven, ten, twenty years ago, stories I may have written just to eat, just for money; and wrote because, as I said elsewhere, and Ted Sturgeon has said very kindly, one has to keep working. I have to keep my muscles limbered, and if that means writing garbage from time to time, okay, I'll write whatever I have to write to keep working.

But the conclusions that I've drawn, I am sure are going to offend you. And the offense is going to be greater for those of you who have known me for a long time, who've known me for years. It's certainly going to infuriate Ted White and Al Lewis, not to mention that staunch coterie who still contend that Doc Smith, God rest his wonderful soul, is the

> One half of the room despised it; it was awful.... and the other side of the room loved me.... That story, '"Repent, Harlequin!" Said the Ticktockman,' ... was picked by Terry Carr and Don Wollheim for the World's Best Science Fiction: 1966...."

highest pinnacle of excellence any science fiction writer can attain. I knew Doc Smith and admired him vastly and would be a snot-nose again if I denigrated him. His work is something else.

So, I have to build a solid groundwork for these insults, and that requires telling a couple of stories.

Now, I suppose that generically, these are Harlan Ellison stories, because they're about me, but in a sense they're apocryphal. First a footnote:

A year or so ago, I did a television show that I liked a lot, and when I knew it was coming on I sent out some post cards to people saying, Please watch this thing. Everybody interpreted it as log rolling for a Hugo nomination. They were saying, You dirty huckster you, you swine you! As if it were terrible that I'd said, ''I did a nice thing, would you like to look at it?'' They all said, That's not right; you're not supposed to mention these things. So I suppose this part of my talk will be considered log rolling again for a Hugo and if so, Vote, kids. It's stiff competition.

Ten years ago the first Milford Science Fiction Writers Conference was held by Damon Knight up in Milford, Pike County, Pa., a nice idyllic spot. I wrangled myself an invitation. I think I had about eight or ten stories published, and I was living in the same building with Bob Silverberg, and writing furiously ten thousand words a night. Most of it was not really worth reading. (I had written at this point the story that James Blish called the worst single story he ever read in his life . . . He's *right*! It's awful!) I went up there, for the conference, and I had some very firm ideas about what I believed a science fiction writer should do. I had not at that point realized that I was not a science fiction writer, I was a writer, and one is not the other.

So, there I was, this little guy who had not published very much, and I was surrounded by Sturgeon and Algis Budrys, and Charlie De Vet, and Cyril Kornbluth, for God sakes, and Fred Pohl, and Damon Knight. I stood around and God, it was like being at Mount Rushmore.

And they came down on me, man, like Rutley Quantrell's army. They wiped up the floor with me. If I opened my mouth and said, ''Uh,'' they said, ''What do you mean, 'Uh'?'' Everybody's a critic. '''Uh'? What is that?'' I had brought along my typewriter. I bring along my typewriter everywhere. I had it up in the room up there and I would go up and I would peck out a few paragraphs, a few lines, and they were saying, That smart-ass—what is he doing with a typewriter, trying to show us up? What is he, a wise guy?

I could do nothing right. They made me feel like two and a half pounds of dog meat.

I never went back to the Milford Conference. I couldn't hack it. It really took something out of me. I went back to New York and brooded like crazy. I didn't know if I was any good. All I knew was that I knew how to put down words on paper and people bought them. But at that time, I thought maybe that was the end. It isn't, and I learned that shortly thereafter.

Last year, I went back to Milford.

They have this Writer's Workshop and through the seven days of the conference everybody lays out a story on a big table and then everybody discusses it. But only those who've laid out a story, who put it on the line, can talk, can make a comment. No wives are allowed, no girlfriends, no chicken flickers, nothing; just the workers.

This workshop table is filled with stories, and they change them every day; they have a list of who is going to be talked about on that day. There were bits and pieces of stories that hadn't sold, short stories that were rejected maybe ten, twelve times and they couldn't figure out why, maybe a portion of a novel in work and they wanted some comment on it, things like that. Well I don't have any of those. I sell what I write, everything I write. So I went up to

the Tom Quick Inn, which is where I was staying, and I sat down and wrote a short story, which I had been thinking about for some time, and I put it on this table, and the procedure is that you sit here and they go around the room from the left of you. Everybody comments once, what they thought of the story. They've all read it the night before and they lay it on you, you know; they really come on. There was a pretty sizable bunch of people there, like Keith Laumer and Norman Spinrad and Larry Niven; Damon Knight was there and his wife, Kate Wilhelm; Tom Disch—a bunch of professionals— Sonya Dorman, who's a marvelous writer; she writes under the name of S. Dorman. (Please look for her stories; they're excellent. There is one in the new *Orbit* collection that Damon Knight published.)

I laid this story out with a couple or three carbons, so everybody could get a chance at it the night before.

Point: When I sat down to write this story, I said, I am going to write a story that is going to knock them on their ass. I'm going to write a story so good that they can't ignore it. I'm going to write a story to get even for ten years ago—that's how good that story's going to be, and it's going to be a prize winning story.

So, anyhow, they started talking about it and there's a coterie up there composed of Damon Knight, his wife Kate Wilhelm, their current fair haired boy, Tom Disch, who couldn't write his way out of a pay toilet if he had to, a few other people; they're all on one side of the room. Keith Laumer and Norman Spinrad and Larry Niven are on the other side of the room and there's a bunch of other nice people sitting around. It started off with Damon.

Now, Damon was putting together the first *Orbit* collection, and he was looking for stories, so I said, ''I'd like to submit this to you, Damon, if you like it.'' So he read it the night before, and it was Damon who set the tone. He said, ''This is . . . I don't know what you're doing here, Harlan, I really don't. I don't understand this story, I don't know what it means, I don't know what you're going for.'' And I don't say anything. I'm sitting there, quiet. I'm cool.

Next, it's Kate Wilhelm. ''You know I was reading this last night and I'm forced to concur with Damon's opinion. I find this story derivative and unappealing, and stupid and dumb and badly typed and everything, you know . . .'' Man, I type the cleanest first draft in the *world,* baby.

So, we worked our way through the Friends of Damon Knight Society and we got around the other side of the room. Keith Laumer said, "This is one of the most brilliant stories I've ever read. It's fantastic; I love it. I think it's great." Then we hit Walter Moudy and he said, "I think it's a classic. I've never read anything quite like this. It's new, it's fresh, it's different."

One half of the room *despised* it; it was awful. Damon, needless to say, rejected it from *Orbit,* and the other side of the room loved me. So Fred Pohl was coming up for the last day, and before Damon could get to him, I hit him with this story and asked, Do you like it? He read it on the spot, and he said, Yeah, I'll give you a top rate in *Galaxy* for it. I said, Thanks a lot, and he bought it. That story, "'Repent, Harlequin!' Said the Ticktockman," was in Fred Pohl's *Galaxy,* it was picked by Terry Carr and Don Wollheim for the *World's Best Science Fiction: 1966,* and it won the Science Fiction Writers of America Nebula, which Damon had to give me.

And as if that weren't insult, we added the injury because Doubleday is publishing the SFWA Nebula Award anthology, and it's right in there, and Damon's got to edit it and say something cool about it. And now it's up for the Hugo and it's gonna lose to Zelazny naturally, but I don't mind, because I've proved my point.

I'm going back to Milford *this* year and I'm going to give them another chance.

It seems incredible that a field as small as ours could support as handsomely and with as much room as it does, three warring coteries of writers. I'm not sure many of us are even aware of it, because we take what is given to us in science fiction magazines and since we have a limited number of editors we get pretty much what they like. But we're in the middle of a vast upheaval in the science fiction field. And I would like to try and really go into it at great length and bore the *ass* off you.

The three coteries, to begin with. First of all, there's Damon Knight's group, which I like to refer to as Damon Knight's group, and which will hereinafter be referred to as Damon Knight's group. These are the people who accept only that which they like and they have positions of a certain amount of authority—Damon's an editor at Berkley Books, and his wife Kate Wilhelm is a writer and Damon edits *Orbit.* They get people like Tom Disch published, and since Judy Merrill is also in that in-

group, she writes a laudatory review of *The Genocides* in *F&SF.* The book is not a very good book, to be nice about it, and from her review we'd have thought we had a new Nathanael West in our midst.

Then on the other side, we've got Al Lewis's group. Now Al Lewis believes that stories of science fiction . . . I realize I'm putting words in your mouth, and you'll be able to shoot me down later, but since this is my group, baby, you'll have to sit there and put up with it. Al's feeling—and I'm sure that this is not exactly precise—his idea of the man of the future is standing on this slidewalk going through future time and he looks around and says, "look at this fantastic world that we live in, isn't it incredible, I say to you, Alice of the future 20432209, isn't this a grand world in which the buildings rise up a full screaming two hundred feet into the air, isn't this a marvelous slidewalk that's going at 25 miles an hour, and we have one over there that goes at 35 miles an hour, and another one right next to it at 45 miles an hour, to which we can leap, if we want to . . ."

Al believes that technology is the single motivating force in our culture and Al is wrong, but I'm not about to argue with him on that point. I think this field is big enough to support all kinds of dumb things. That isn't important. We sitting here are the last of the fastest guns in the west. We may find it a little difficult to understand.

For, I don't know how many years I've been kicking around, about thirteen or fourteen, something like that, but Christ, Forry Ackerman, you've been what—thirty five years in the field?

VOICE: Forty.

Forty. That's even more frightening. All right, for forty years science fiction fans have been saying, *we're not Buck Rogers.* You know, like we've got some substantiality, we've got things we can teach you. We're going to the moon. "You're going where?" "We're going to the moon." I've got a copy of an article that was written in the *Cleveland News* back in '52, when I was in the Cleveland Science Fiction Society, and they sent this reporter down to laugh at us, and he came down and he did a whole nice big thing, and you know, "the room tilted at full momentum as these people decided that we were going to the moon." I mentioned to him about Heinlein's sliding roadways. You know, we could use them for conveying freight and things like that and you know he did this whole article with just this kind of tongue in cheek kind of crap that you've seen a million times after a science fiction convention or some magazine will write thinking they're very cute and clever and not realizing that they are forty years out of date.

But we've always said, *respect us,* look at us, we've got something, for Christ's sake, we're over here, you know. Ignore the western, ignore the detective story, and forget Salinger for a minute, we're over here. Right? Well, baby, I hate to shake up your nervous system, but that's been happening for about ten years. We are no longer way out there in the back eddy. The big boys are coming to us and they're looking at what we're doing. A couple of days before we came here, Theodore Sturgeon and I—we're both working doing scripts for the ''Bob Hope Chrysler Theatre''—Ted had gone up there to see Gordon Hessler, one of the producers, and met Gordon and sat and talked to him for a while. I went up a couple of days later, and I walked in and Gordon came out from behind his desk. He's a lovely charming man and he said, ''Hi, Harlan; I want you to meet John O'Swarz, who is from France,'' and this little guy, this little intense dark, electric cat leaped out of his chair and came over and grabbed my hand with both of his and pumped it like crazy and said, ''Monsieur Ellison, I'm overwhelmed, I do not know what to say, to meet you, to find out that you are alive, that you exist, you are . . . In one week to meet Theodore Sturgeon, and Harlan Ellison in one room is fantastic.'' He said, ''We know your work over there, every story of yours. We know you more than Salinger, more than Hemingway, more than Steinbeck, we know you and Sturgeon.'' We're underground heroes over there. And it scares the crap out of you when someone comes from way over there . . . and it also annoyed me because I haven't gotten one dime from reprint money over there.

We are accepted. We're *there.* Stop pushing. (That's a good line from me. I'll have to remember that.)

The man sitting here: Digby Diehl from *Los Angeles Magazine.* He's doing an article on us. He doesn't say anything, he just comes and sits, and he does. Stanley Kubrick is doing a picture with Arthur C. Clarke. He called for Arthur C. Clarke, and he said, ''Look, I want to do this science fiction picture in Cinerama and I want you to do a book and I'll do the screenplay and we'll exchange bylines, me on your book and you on my movie, and we'll do a whole thing.'' Yeah, that's cool.

Isaac Asimov gets *Fantastic Voyage* in the *Saturday Evening Post.* He doesn't get a dime for it. That's another story. That's power politics.

The ABC Project '67 series: They go and get Robert Sheckley, and Robert Sheckley does a show for them. An hour original.

Gene Roddenberry of ''Star Trek'': When he started the project he had his staff compile a book of the top 1000 science fiction stories, which he sent out to all the writers who might possibly work on the series, with this admonition: ''These are the best; we want *better,* we want *different.* Don't try to cop these ideas, because we know where they're at, right?'' That's Roddenberry, he goes and he hires top TV writers like Adrian Spees, and John D. F. Black, who just won the Writers Guild Award, and Barry Trivers, who won it a couple of years ago. But in addition he hired Sturgeon and he had Phil Farmer working for him and he had A. E. van Vogt writing for him, and I'm writing for him and Robert Bloch is writing for him and Jerry Sohl and Robert Sheckley . . . anybody he can get hold of who knows anything at all about writing for the visual medium, who is a science fiction person. He wants to do it right. No more giant ants, or plant aphids that eat Cleveland, none of that. This is the real scan.

Every month you go in your bookstore and there are new books—in paperbacks, in hardcovers. What do you think all this is? Chopped liver? I mean, they *know* who we are. But we don't know who *they* are. We're still fighting the Civil War, friends. We're still back there screaming help, help, we're not dumb, we're not dumb. They know we're not dumb. And the more we argue about it, the more they cease to hear us, because we've now reached a noise level where no one's paying attention.

What I'm trying to say is that the mainstream has accepted us, but we haven't accepted the mainstream. We're still back here playing power politics. All us little fans are still doing our little convention thing and having our little internecine warfare and we're afraid. We're petrified to go out there and stand up and maybe get a belt in the belly.

Now this fear and terror by fandom of being assimilated is the same thing that every ethnic group has in its ghetto: ''You're gonna marry him?! He's a goy! What is that?'' Right? Or ''I don't wanna see our race mongrelized.'' That's exactly what it is. We're afraid to get into the big stream. Somebody like a Herman Wouk will come along and do *The Lomokome Papers*—you all remember that awful book—and we'll say, Well, see: that's what's going to happen to us. But we ignore *Cat's Cradle* and we ignore *White Lotus* and we ignore *Clockwork Orange* and we ignore *Only Lovers Left Alive* and all of these pure science fiction books, which are done by people outside the field, who have taken the ideas that we've put forth, who have used all of these tremendous concepts that we spent thirty-five years developing and they're using them; it's a matter of course for them. They say, ''Sure these guys have proved it already; we don't have to. We can go ahead from there.''

Now, what I'm trying to say is that we've become important to the mainstream. Truly important. This is steam engine time for science fiction. *It's science fiction time.* Science is passing us by. We're on the moon and we're doing the freezing the bodies thing, and ''Time Tunnel'' comes on TV this Fall (it's a piece of crap, but it comes on, and people will know what it's all about, going back in time; they'll be able to understand that). So it's our time now, friends.

Now is when we catch the gravy.

Now is when everything pays off for us.

Now is when a man like Sturgeon is going to collect what he's been due for all these many years. You know: like writing penny a word and two-cent a word stories for the pulps; now all of a sudden he's going to get three, four, five, six, $10,000 for a television script, for a book. This is what we deserve. We paid our dues . . . it's time for us now.

But we're being held back . . . we're being fettered in many respects and torn apart by the conservatives. Now, no offense. We're being hamstrung in the magazines and in the books and by the entrenched power structures—you know, the Damon Knight gang—and by the people among us who are short-sighted, who continue to contend that they are the far seekers, that they are the future-seers. They're the ones that still want the stories that were written 25 years ago, for Christ's sake. And every time somebody tries to do something new, they say, ''Whew, where is this cat at . . . what is he doing?'' It's like in the jazz idiom: a man like Ornette Coleman, five to eight years ago started blowing new sounds and a few people picked up on it and said, ''this guy has got it . . . this man is saying something.'' And everybody else said, ''Huh?'' They're scared 'cause they don't know where it's at and they're afraid. They're afraid they're going to get left out in the cold. They're afraid they're not

going to be au courant. They're not going to be with it, and so they put it down. And that's what is happening to an awful lot of important science fiction.

A man like David Bunch has been writing for ten years. The only place he could get his stuff published until recently was in Ron Smith's *Inside Magazine*—you know, a fanzine—or a few other places, literary magazines, little places, where he could sneak it in and they didn't know it was science fiction. He would say that this was a parable of the future. *Now* Bunch is published in most of the bigger magazines, and his work is understood and seen, because *we* have caught up with *him*. You know, we thought *Demolished Man* was a big step forward . . . that was a nice story with a lot of interesting typography. The guys who were really writing it—the guys who were really saying it—are the guys we have *shamefully* ignored for years.

It's a time for daring. Now is the time for brilliance and invention. And no one is suggesting that the roots of science fiction be ignored or forgotten or cast aside. Solid plotting, extrapolation, trends and cultures, technology—all of these things are staples that are necessary to keep the genre electric and alive because that's what we are. That's what makes us not *Peyton Place*. Okay: granted. But why should we who know and love this medium see it expand its frontiers in the hands of William Burroughs and John Hersey and Anthony Burgess and Thomas Pynchon while we stare back in wide-eyed wonder, because we never considered writing *A Clockwork Orange* or *White Lotus* or *The Crying of Lot 49* or *Nova Express*?

Take a look at Burroughs' *Nova Express,* friends. Now, that's science fiction and it's fresh and it's daring and it's different. And it will beat out any bloody thing that James Blish or Damon Knight have written in the last five years.

Now I don't mean to pick on any single person expressly. There are dozens of writers I could point to. Writers whom you respect and if they were standing up here you would come up and say, ''Can I have your autograph?'' And you should, because they paid their dues. Mr. van Vogt was here and I don't know if he still is here—I would hate to pin him when he isn't here—but van Vogt's stuff, in many ways was very daring . . . twenty-five years ago. But his stuff isn't there any more. There are new guys who are doing it.

Why should we have to stand back and wince in pain as the Herman Wouks, the Ayn Rands, the Rosser Reeds demean our literary form? Why should we have to sit there and say, ''These guys are doing it because we didn't have the guts to do it''? And have to put up with their bad writing? We're lucky we've gained a few good writers—writers like Burgess. But we've got an awful lot of schleps, too. And it's a pain that we have to sit here and put up with it.

The tragedy of what we are *now* is the tragedy of what we've been doing for thirty years. We've been leaching the vitality out of our best writers—our Sturgeon, our Farmer, our Philip Dick, our Kurt Vonnegut. We've sent them off to other fields because they couldn't make a living with us. They had to write for the ''in-group.'' They had to write for us and please us and pleasure us because God-forbid they should come to a convention and have someone say, ''What do you mean—what is *Inside-Outside* actually about, Mr. Farmer—what are you trying to say? What are you doing? Ha?'' We've sent them off to the other field. Vonnegut to the mainstream comedy novel; Sturgeon to Westerns, movie adaptations, TV writing; Farmer to white-collar jobs, too many paperback commitments; Phil Dick to the edge of lunacy. This is what we've done to our good writers, because we've been too busy reading the hacks. And why have we been reading the hacks? Because we can understand them; they will give us a nice technological thing that we can play with and toy with . . . and we like that a lot. But when they really demand something of us, when they write something really new and fresh and different and inventive, we don't know where they are. We look at them and we say, ''You missed that time, but you'll make it the next time; maybe you'll write *Slan* next time, baby.'' We complain that our best men have left us. That they have gone on. That they deserted the ship. And it's precisely the opposite: the ship has deserted them. They have outgrown us. They've gone away because they're bigger than us; they need more, they have to have more. And they find it selling mainstream stories which you laugh at; you say, ''Well, you know, if I want to read that crap, I'll read the mainstream.'' I'm not talking about book-of-the-month-club selections, friends; I'm talking about stories that demand inventiveness and demand a bigness, a fullness from the writer that you can't get most of the time out of science fiction.

Because we have literally bound ourselves into a bag that we can't get out of.

For too long we have allowed those of us who formed our idiom to tell us what is good and what is bad. We've allowed them to say, ''Well this is a good story, because it's in *Analog* and this has gotta be a bad story because it's in *Amazing*. Well, now if it's in *Amazing,* probably it's because they're reprinting . . .''

These writers have grown too big and too important and too dedicated to their art and that's the operable phrase. Before they are science fiction writers, they are *writers,* and you can read them in any other idiom, any other genre, and they will be just as sharp; they don't demean themselves. Somebody said yesterday, ''He was lost in Hollywood writing for television.'' Well, I got so lost last year, friends, writing science fiction for television that I won the top award of the Screen Writers Guild. I beat out a Purex Special, a Chrysler Theatre, and the pilot for ''Run for Your Life''—on a show that had a budget like $1.98. And it was pure science fiction—it wasn't anything else.

You don't get lost if you're a writer—if you really work. These people have left us for the very simple reason that they're too big and too talented to be constrained by our often vicious, often ungrateful little backwater eddy. They burst into the mainstream and the mainstream has taken notice of them. Sturgeon comes to Hollywood and Hollywood knows it. His name is in the trade papers, and the producers want to see him. Alan Arbor used to be the producer on ''The Fugitive''; he's now doing the new one, ''The Invaders.'' He calls for Sturgeon. Gene Roddenberry wired ahead to New York—''Have Sturgeon there; I must talk to him. I want him to work for me.'' You walk on the set and actors who don't know much of anything except what their own faces look like, say ''Theodore Sturgeon?'' And they know him. This man isn't unknown; no one who is *good* is unknown. And yet at the same time, here we sit and you have the audacity to make me a ''Guest of Honor'' and I'm nothing—and Vonnegut has *never* been a Guest of Honor; he's never been *asked* to be a Guest of Honor. Here's a man that has written a novel that has been one of the seminal influences in our field. Something that almost any writer can look at and say, ''Yeah, it's so simple to write like that—that you can't do it.'' Great art looks simple, but it isn't. It's like watching Fred Astaire dance—try it and you'll fall on your ass. Vonnegut is big—he's important—and we gave the Hugo to a minor effort by Clifford Simak for a novel that any one of us who write science fiction could have written, chiefly because he's ''one of our own.''

It's a crime.

It's a shame.

And we've been doing it for too long. I stand before you as nothing more, really, than an emissary of the open mind. If you're going to continue to call yourselves science fiction fans—the chosen people—we see the future—the golden ones—all of that crap we've been swilling down for twenty-five, thirty years, you damn well better be able to see what's in your midst. Because you are losing men that you should have working for you. You are losing men that you are ignoring and laughing at and you're losing men who are going to change your form and put it where it's supposed to be: on a level with all great art.

Source: Harlan Ellison®, "A Time for Daring," in *The Book of Ellison,* edited by Andrew Porter, ALGOL Press, 1978, pp. 101–16; Copyright © 1967 by Harlan Ellison. Renewed, 1995 by The Kilimanjaro Corporation. "One Small Daring Footnote: Circa 2005" by Harlan Ellison. Copyright © 2005 by The Kilimanjaro Corporation. Reprinted by arrangement with the Author. All rights reserved. Harlan Ellison is a registered trademark of The Kilimanjaro Corporation.

Sources

Adams, Stephen, "The Heroic and the Mock-Heroic in Harlan Ellison's 'Harlequin,'" in *Extrapolation,* Vol. 26, No. 4, Winter 1985, pp. 285–89.

Bryant, Earle V., "Ellison's "'Repent, Harlequin!'' Said the Ticktockman,'" in the *Explicator,* Vol. 59, No. 3, Spring 2001, pp. 163–65.

De Los Santos, Oscar, "Clogging Up the (In)Human Works: Harlan Ellison's Apocalyptic Postmodern Visions," in *Extrapolation,* Vol. 40, No. 1, 1999, pp. 5–20.

Dillingham, Thomas F., "Harlan Ellison," in *Dictionary of Literary Biography,* Vol. 8, *American Science Fiction Writers,* edited by David Cowart and Thomas L. Wyner, Gale Research, 1981, pp. 161–69.

Eastwood, D. R., "Three by One: Harlan Ellison's 1966, 1968, 1969 Hugo-Winning Short Speculative Fiction," in *Hypothesis: Neo-Aristotelian Analysis,* Vol. 20, Winter 1977, pp. 16–21.

Ellison, Harlan, "'Repent, Harlequin!' Said the Ticktockman," in *The Essential Ellison: A 35-year Retrospective,* edited and introduced by Terry Dowling, with Richard Delap and Gil Lamont, Nemo Press, 1987, pp. 877–86.

Moorcock, Michael, "Foreword," in *The Fantasies of Harlan Ellison,* Gregg Press, 1979, pp. x–xi.

Patrouch, Joseph, Jr., "Harlan Ellison and the Formula Story," in *The Book of Ellison,* edited by Andrew Porter, ALGOL Press, 1978, pp. 45–64.

Slusser, George Edgar, *Harlan Ellison: Unrepentant Harlequin,* Borgo Press, 1977, pp. 3–4.

Weil, Ellen, "The Ellison Personae: Author, Storyteller, Narrator," in *Journal of the Fantastic in the Arts,* Vol. 1, No. 3, 1988, pp. 27–36.

Weil, Ellen, and Gary K. Wolfe, *Harlan Ellison: The Edge of Forever,* Ohio State University Press, 2002, pp. 137–41.

White, Michael D., "Ellison's Harlequin: Irrational Action in Static Time," in *Science-Fiction Studies,* Vol. 4, 1977, pp. 161–65.

Further Reading

Ellison, Harlan, "Ellison on Ellison," in *Locus,* Vol. 47, No. 1, July 2001, pp. 6–10.

In this article, Ellison reviews his long career, noting changes in his art and in his beliefs, providing an excellent background for the study of his fiction.

Erlich, Richard D., and Thomas P. Dunn, eds., *Clockwork Worlds: Mechanized Environments in SF,* Greenwood Press, 1983.

In addition to including a chapter on Harlan Ellison, this collection of essays considers the larger subject of mechanical environments and science fiction responses to technology.

James, Edward, and Farah Mendlesohn, eds., *The Cambridge Companion to Science Fiction,* Cambridge University Press, 2003.

This is an excellent collection of essays concerning such topics as gender, politics, and race in science fiction as well as illustrating a variety of critical approaches to the genre.

Porter, Andrew, ed. *The Book of Ellison,* ALGOL Press, 1978.

Porter has assembled an introduction by famed science-fiction writer Isaac Asimov, six critical articles, ten essays by Ellison himself, and a nonfiction checklist in this useful book. Although written over two decades ago, it still has merit for the student who wants to know more about Ellison.

Rikki-Tikki-Tavi

Rudyard Kipling

1895

Rudyard Kipling's endearing ''Rikki-Tikki-Tavi'' initially appeared in 1895 as part of the second volume of *The Jungle Book,* a collection of children's stories set in colonial India that Kipling wrote while living in Brattleboro, Vermont. Telling the tale of Rikki-tikki-tavi, a brave and heroic mongoose, and his battle against the evil king cobras, Nag and Nagaina, ''Rikki-Tikki-Tavi'' is a war story that depicts in the simplest of terms the triumph of good over bad. Emulating the contemporary trend in children's literature to create imaginary worlds to appeal to a child's imagination, ''Rikki-Tikki-Tavi'' takes place entirely in a small garden populated by anthropomorphized birds, snakes, muskrats, and frogs.

By imparting values particularly characteristic of Kipling's Victorian society, including loyalty, productivity, hard work, and courage, the story serves an educational purpose. ''Rikki-Tikki-Tavi'' also implicitly affirms the Victorian assumption of British superiority and its faith in the inherent goodness of empire-building.

In its use of suspense and pacing, ''Rikki-Tikki-Tavi'' is a wonderful example of Kipling's expertise in storytelling and a testament to why his stories remained popular into the early 2000s. ''Rikki-Tikki-Tavi,'' both as part of *The Jungle Book* and as an independent story, appeared in numerous incarnations throughout the twentieth century. As of 2004, numerous versions of *The Jungle Book* volumes were in print, including a paperback version

by Penguin that included a critical introduction by Daniel Karlin.

Author Biography

Poet, novelist, and short story writer Rudyard Kipling, the first English writer to receive the Nobel Prize in Literature, was the most popular literary figure in the late nineteenth century. He was born December 30, 1865, in Bombay, India, to John Lockwood Kipling and Alice MacDonald Kipling. Both of his grandfathers had been Methodist ministers and, though Kipling did not practice Christianity as an adult, the symbolism and values of the religion heavily influenced his work. He had one younger sister, Alice, who was known as Trix.

As was the custom of the time, at the age of six Rudyard was sent to boarding school in England, where he was subjected to severe strictness, bullying, and abuse. In 1878 he was sent to a military training school, where he also encountered bullying, but where he was able to form the values preached in "Rikki-Tikki-Tavi": courage, loyalty, and an ethic of hard work.

His poor eyesight kept Kipling from advancing into a military career, so at the age of sixteen he returned to his parents in Lahore, India, and began his career as a journalist, first at *The Civil and Military Gazette,* from 1882 to 1887, and then as a worldwide correspondent for the *Pioneer,* from 1887 to 1889. He became quite popular for his work, especially for his satirical and humorous verse. When he returned to England in 1889 at the age of twenty-four, he was already regarded as a national literary hero.

In 1892 Kipling married Caroline Balestier and moved to Vermont, near Caroline's family. Their two daughters, Josephine—who was to die at the age of six of pneumonia—and Elsie, were born there. Fatherhood inspired Kipling to write the children's stories which remained his most enduring works. Both volumes of *The Jungle Book* were published during Kipling's time in Vermont. The Kiplings returned to England in 1896 after a bitter quarrel with Caroline's family; their only son John was born later that year. They remained based in England and traveled regularly around the world.

Kipling was a prolific writer, and his skill at storytelling, his immensely readable and song-like verse, his refusal to mince words, and the strong

Rudyard Kipling

sense of British patriotism that characterized his work made him immensely popular with a wide audience. However, his receipt of the Nobel Prize in 1907 was met with disapproval from some literary critics and writers, who considered him vulgar and lacking in craftsmanship.

The death of his son John during World War I, combined with his own failing health, affected Kipling's writing deeply. His output decreased dramatically after this period. Kipling died on January 18, 1936 and is buried in the Poets' Corner in Westminster Abbey.

Among Kipling's most well-known and enduring works are *Captains Courageous* (1897), *Kim* (1901), the first and second volumes of *The Jungle Book,* and the poems "If," "White Man's Burden," and "Recessional."

Plot Summary

A song-like poem serves as prologue to "Rikki-Tikki-Tavi," prefiguring the battle between the mongoose Rikki-tikki-tavi and Nag, the king cobra. The struggle between the mongoose and snake is the central focus of the story and the poem, which foreshadows the conflict but only hints at its resolution and creates a sense of suspense and expectation before the story even begins.

In the first paragraph the setting and the main characters are introduced: Rikki-tikki-tavi, who is established as the hero, with the help of Darzee the tailor-bird, fights a battle in the garden of a bungalow in colonial India. Rikki's curious and energetic personality is also established.

Rikki-tikki-tavi, washed by a flood from his parents' home into the garden of a bungalow, lies unconscious in the garden path. Teddy, the boy who lives in the bungalow, happens upon him with his parents. They take him into the house and revive him. Rikki-tikki-tavi regains his energy and endears himself to the family with his energetic, curious, and friendly nature.

That night he sleeps with Teddy, much to the consternation of Teddy's mother. Teddy's father reassures his wife that Teddy is safe with a mongoose because, as the natural predator of snakes, he would be able to protect Teddy if one were to enter the house: the expression of fear and the realistic threat of poisonous snakes foreshadows Rikki's future conflict with the local king cobras.

The next morning, Rikki explores the garden. He meets the tailor-birds Darzee and his wife, who are mourning because Nag, the garden's resident king cobra, ate one of their babies. As Rikki is conversing with the birds, Nag, who knows that Rikki the mongoose poses a mortal danger to him and his family, emerges to confront Rikki. He is described as ''evil'' and ''horrid,'' as well as foreboding in size and strength. Nag introduces himself as being marked by Brahm himself, the greatest god in the Hindu pantheon, creating a reference to the sacred status of snakes in Hinduism, the predominant religion of India.

As Nag faces off with Rikki-tikki, Nag's wife, Nagaina, makes a surprise attack on Rikki from behind. However, Rikki escapes unscathed because Darzee warns him in time. The snakes, defeated, retreat into the grass.

Rikki, who has not fought snakes before, returns to the bungalow, feeling confident about his quickness against the snakes and gaining confidence in his skill. Teddy runs up the path to pet Rikki, only to be confronted by Karait, the ''dusty brown snakeling''—a fatally poisonous snake who hides in the dirt. For the first time in the story

Rikki's eyes glow red—the sign that a mongoose is about to attack. He manages to leap onto Karait and kills him with a swift and strong bite. Teddy's parents run out from the bungalow just in time to find Rikki killing the snake. They are very grateful to him for protecting Teddy.

Later that night, after the family has gone to bed, Rikki patrols the house. He runs into Chuchundra, the cowardly muskrat, who hints that Nag may have a wicked plan in store that night. Soon after talking with Chuchundra, Rikki overhears Nag and Nagaina plotting outside the bathroom's water sluice. They plot to kill the human family in order to get rid of Rikki-tikki-tavi. Rikki also learns that they have a nest of unhatched eggs.

Nag sneaks into the bathroom to lie in wait for the humans, and Nagaina leaves. Rikki is afraid, but he is driven by loyalty to the family and by his honor as a mongoose to attack the snake. When Nag finally falls asleep, Rikki leaps onto Nag and grabs hold of his neck. He bites and hangs on while Nag thrashes about, until the snake is dead. The big man, hearing the commotion, runs into the bathroom with his shotgun and shoots Nag, but the snake has already been killed by Rikki.

The next morning, Rikki, who knows he now has to face Nagaina, enlists the help of Darzee and his wife in destroying the snake and her eggs. Darzee is busy singing a triumphant song about Rikki's defeat of Nag, much to Rikki's annoyance. Darzee informs Rikki that Nagaina's eggs are hidden in the melon patch, but he does not understand why Rikki wants to harm them. Darzee's wife, however, does understand that ''cobra's eggs meant young cobras later on''; she distracts Nagaina by pretending her wing is broken, buying Rikki time to destroy the eggs.

While Rikki is destroying the cobra's eggs, Nagaina, who is angry with the big man because she thinks he killed Nag, heads up to the house to attack the human family. Rikki, with a warning from Darzee's wife, runs up to the veranda and finds Teddy and his parents sitting within Nagaina's striking distance.

Rikki shows her the last of her eggs to distract her from the human family, and he tells her that it was he who killed Nag, not the big man. Rikki draws Nagaina to fight, but rather than engage Rikki she manages to rescue the last of her eggs, and she rushes towards her lair. Rikki, in hot pursuit, follows her down into her cave. Darzee, who witnesses

Rikki's descent, begins to sing about Rikki's imminent death.

After a highly suspenseful period, however, Rikki emerges dusty and exhausted from the lair and announces that Nagaina is dead. The Coppersmith bird, the garden crier, announces Nagaina's death to the whole garden. The birds and frogs rejoice, and Rikki-tikki-tavi is rewarded for his efforts both by being considered a hero by the denizens of the garden and by being given a permanent place in the human family's home, where he remains as their protector for the rest of his life.

The story closes with a reproduction of Darzee's unfinished song of triumph, "Darzee's Chaunt," which he composed after the death of Nag. The style of the song, which calls on the birds of the garden to praise Rikki for delivering them from the evil Nag and Nagaina, is reminiscent of Christian hymns of praise, and like the heroes of ancient, classic epics, Rikki is immortalized in these songs of praise.

Media Adaptations

- "Rikki-Tikki-Tavi" was adapted as an animated film in 1975. It was directed by Chuck Jones, narrated by Orson Welles, and is available on VHS from Family Home Entertainment (reissued 2001).

- A downloadable audio recording of stories from *The Jungle Books,* including "Rikki-Tikki-Tavi," is available at http://www.audible.com and is narrated by Flo Gibson.

Characters

Alice
See Teddy's Mother

The Big Man
The big man is an Englishman who has just moved, with his son Teddy and wife Alice, into the Indian bungalow where the main action of the story takes place. The big man owns a "bang-stick"—a shotgun—and when he shoots Nag into two pieces during Rikki's battle with him in the bathroom, Nagaina wrongfully blames him for the death. As an Englishman in India during the late nineteenth century, the big man represents imperial England's presence in India and thus gives a historical and cultural context to the story. He and his family take Rikki-tikki-tavi into their home and thereby earn his loyalty and protection. The big man and his family's gratitude to Rikki for saving their lives earns him a lasting place in their home.

Chuchundra
A muskrat who lives in the bungalow, Chuchundra is portrayed as a cowardly creature who weeps and whines when he speaks. He tips Rikki off to Nag and Nagaina's planned attack on the big man and his family. Chuchundra's cowardliness serves as a foil to Rikki-tikki-tavi's courage.

The Coppersmith
When Rikki-tikki-tavi successfully kills Nagaina and emerges from her lair unhurt, the Coppersmith, a bird who serves as the garden crier, announces Rikki's triumph and the demise of Nag and Nagaina to the denizens of the garden.

Darzee
A tailor-bird who, together with his wife, keeps a nest in the bungalow's garden, Darzee is described as "a feather-brained fellow" because he fails on more than one occasion to competently assist Rikki-tikki-tavi against their common enemies, Nag and Nagaina. Darzee, unlike Rikki, is severely lacking in foresight. He begins to sing a song of triumph after the death of Nag but before Nagaina and her eggs are destroyed, for which Rikki scolds him. His lack of foresight serves as a foil to Rikki's own impetus for action. Darzee also plays the role of a bard. He composes songs about Rikki-tikki-tavi's showdowns against Nag and Nagaina, which are used to highlight Rikki's heroic aspects.

Darzee's wife
Darzee's wife plays a pivotal role in assisting Rikki against the snakes—and is therefore called "sensible"—by serving as a decoy to distract

Nagaina and allow Rikki time to destroy the cobras' unhatched eggs.

Karait

Karait, a small, quick, poisonous snake who lives in the dust, is confronted by Rikki-tikki-tavi when he threatens to fatally bite Teddy. Karait is the first snake that Rikki kills, and his success gives Rikki the confidence to battle against the more dangerous cobras.

Nag

One of two king cobras who reside in the garden of the bungalow, Nag, along with his wife Nagaina, are Rikki-tikki-tavi's archenemies. Nag and his wife are depicted as evil. His enormous size—''five feet long from tongue to tail''—and strength make him a formidable and, therefore, worthy opponent for Rikki, the hero of the story. Prior to Rikki's arrival in the garden, Nag and Nagaina held free rein over the garden. Nag is killed by Rikki-tikki-tavi inside the bungalow when he, at Nagaina's bidding, enters it to kill the human family. Nag's name is derived from the Hindi word for snake.

Nagaina

Like her husband Nag, Nagaina is characterized as evil. While Nag is foreboding in his size and strength, Nagaina is said to be intelligent. It is she who formulates the plan—which Rikki thwarts—to kill the human family in order to rid the bungalow of the mongoose, who is her natural enemy. She is killed by Rikki in her lair, to which she flees to protect the last of her eggs.

Rikki-Tikki-Tavi

Rikki-tikki-tavi, whose name is derived from his characteristic chattering noise, is a young mongoose who, at the beginning of the story, has little experience but, by the end, has become a mongoose of legendary strength and fighting ability. He is rescued by a human family and taken into their home after he is swept away from his parents' nest during a flood. As a mongoose, Rikki is the natural enemy of snakes, and his presence in the garden threatens the resident king cobra couple, Nag and Nagaina, who become Rikki's archenemies. Rikki is emblematic of the archetypal hero: he exhibits the qualities of courage, strength, and loyalty, and he uses his virtues to fight evil. Prior to arriving in the garden, Rikki had never fought a snake, and his ultimate triumph over the cobras not only protects the lives of the birds and the humans he befriends, but it also serves as his coming of age.

Teddy

Teddy is the little boy who lives in the bungalow with his parents. He, of all the human characters, is most fond of Rikki-tikki-tavi. His innocence and vulnerability as a small child make him an easy target for the poisonous snakes of the garden and the most in need of Rikki-tikki-tavi's protection.

Teddy's Mother

Teddy's mother, Alice, lives in the bungalow with her son and her husband, the big man. She initially has misgivings about keeping a wild animal as a pet, but Rikki later earns her trust and affection by protecting her and her family from the cobras.

Themes

Courage

''Rikki-Tikki-Tavi,'' as a children's story, is designed both to entertain and to disseminate the values of virtuous behavior. Courage, one of the characteristics exhibited by the hero, Rikki-tikki-tavi, is one such virtue. Rikki, knowing that he has to kill Nag in order to protect the human family, is fearful of the cobra's size and strength, but his fear is trumped by his own courage, and he succeeds in killing the snake. He is rewarded for his courage by being deemed a hero and given a permanent place in the home of the humans. The virtue of courage is further emphasized by the story's portrayal of shameful cowardliness; Chuchundra, the fearful muskrat who ''never had spirit enough to run out into the middle of the room'' is unable to overcome his fear and, therefore, elicits disdain from Rikki and the other garden creatures.

Loyalty and Duty

Kipling was deeply influenced by the codes of honor and duty evangelized at the military prep school he attended in his late childhood. Loyalty especially figures as a theme in ''Rikki-Tikki-Tavi.'' Rikki is loyal to the human family that takes him in, and his loyalty drives him to protect them from the

Topics for Further Study

- The characters of Nag and Nagaina are portrayed as villains in ''Rikki-Tikki-Tavi.'' The use of snakes as a symbol of evil is common in Western civilization. Can you think of other stories, myths, or folk tales that use this motif? Research the folktales and mythologies of another, non-Western culture, such as the Chinese culture or the Hindu culture. Are snakes used as symbols in these cultures and, if so, what do they represent?

- The Hindu god Brahm, or Brahma, is mentioned in the story ''Rikki-Tikki-Tavi,'' but nothing about the god's significance in Hinduism is revealed. Research the following about the Hindu religion. Who is Brahm? What is his significance in Hinduism? What role does he play?

- The British maintained a strong presence in India until 1947, when India finally was granted independence and became the independent nations of India and Pakistan. What events led up to India's independence? Why did Britain feel compelled to let go of such a large and vital part of its empire?

- Kipling was largely derided in the early 2000s for promoting British imperialism, which embodied a sense of the superiority of British civilization and culture. Do you think that ''Rikki-Tikki-Tavi'' reflects this attitude? Do you think that it is fair or accurate for Kipling to be judged by twenty-first century political and cultural standards? Look at another of his works, the controversial poem ''White Man's Burden.'' Assess whether this poem promotes imperialist ideologies.

---

cobras, even to the point of risking death. Rikki also risks death out of a sense of duty regarding his heritage as a mongoose: when he attacks Nag he ''was battered to and fro. . . . he made sure he would be banged to death, and, for the honour of his family, he preferred to be found with his teeth locked.''

British Imperialism

Kipling is well known for promoting British imperialism in his writing; Victorian-era imperialism was not just the practice of colonization, but it reflected an attitude and philosophy of assumed British superiority, and even the children's story ''Rikki-Tikki-Tavi'' reflects this racial prejudice. The story makes clear that the family living in the bungalow in India is an English family, and it is intimated that Rikki is a very lucky mongoose for having been rescued by humans who are white: ''every well-brought-up mongoose always hopes to be a house-mongoose . . . and Rikki-tikki's mother . . . had carefully told Rikki what to do if ever he came across white men.'' The white family's home and way of life—which dramatizes the British presence in India—is idealized and, in the specific use of the term ''white men,'' portrayed as superior to the indigenous cultures of India. The culture of the Indian people and their Hindu religion is further symbolically denigrated in the story when Nag, the villain, is directly associated with the Hindu god Brahm.

Survival

Survival is the motivating factor behind the actions of all of the characters, and it seems to be the only law that governs the fantasy world of the garden: the act of killing, for example, is not against the laws of the garden but is consistently portrayed as a means towards the more important goal of survival for both the heroic and villainous characters.

This preoccupation with survival reflects the values of social Darwinism that were prevalent during the late nineteenth century. Social Darwinism applied the biological theories of natural selection, put forth by Charles Darwin, to human behavior. Encapsulated in the catchphrase ''survival of the fittest,'' certain modes of social Darwinism argued that some groups of people—those of a certain race or nation, for example—were more "fit" for survival than other groups and should, therefore, for the good of humanity, be given a superior role of power. In "Rikki-Tikki-Tavi" the human family succeeds in surviving and the snakes are eliminated; when their roles are viewed as representations of the British and Indian struggle for control of the Indian subcontinent, the survival of the British family implies both British superiority and British domination.

Progress and Work

In Victorian England, during which the Industrial Revolution took place and the British Empire expanded greatly, progress and hard work were idealized. Kipling emphasizes the virtue of hard work by contrasting Rikki-tikki-tavi's heroic behavior with the "unsensible" behavior of Darzee. When Darzee, the "feather-brained" tailor-bird begins to sing a song of triumph after the death of Nag, Rikki-tikki-tavi grows angry with him because he knows that Nagaina is still alive and, therefore, his work is only half done: "Oh you stupid tuft of feathers! . . . Is this the time to sing?" "You don't know when to do the right thing at the right time." Darzee further impedes Rikki-tikki-tavi's progress against the snakes by not helping him distract Nagaina from her eggs. Darzee's wife flies off to help Rikki-tikki against Nagaina, leaving Darzee to "continue his song." He is portrayed as foolish in his preference for sitting in the nest and singing rather than accomplishing hard work.

Style

Setting: The Fantasy World

"Rikki-Tikki-Tavi" illustrates a trend in children's literature especially characteristic of late nineteenth century and early twentieth century: like the works of Lewis Carroll, L. Frank Baum, Beatrix Potter, Kenneth Grahame, and J. M. Barrie, "Rikki-Tikki-Tavi" is set in a fantasy world: a garden populated by animals who can talk and who have distinctive personalities. Setting stories in imaginary places was seen as especially appealing to and appropriate for the active imagination of children. Prior to this period, stories were not specifically written with a child's point of view in mind, and literature for children was largely adapted from

works for adults, such as Shakespeare, the Bible, and classical literature.

Anthropomorphism

Anthropomorphism is the attribution of human characteristics to non-humans, such as animals, plants, and objects. The animal characters in "Rikki-Tikki-Tavi" all are characterized by distinct, human-like personalities. Anthropomorphism is commonly found in children's literature and serves to create a fantasy world that is compatible with the active imaginations of children. Anthropomorphism is the key characteristic of fables, simple moral tales, like Aesop's fables, which use animals that can talk to teach lessons about human behavior and morality.

Epithet

An epithet is an adjectival phrase attributed as a title to a character, focusing on a specific characteristic: for example, in Greek mythology the goddess Athena is often referred to as "Grey-Eyed Athena." In Homer's epics epithets are used to label the heroes, for example "Nestor, Breaker of Horses." In direct imitation, Rikki-tikki-tavi is called "Red-Eye," and Darzee also refers to him as "Killer of the terrible Nag" and "Rikki-tikki with the white teeth." Kipling uses this classical device in order to heighten the act of Rikki-tikki-tavi's story and make clear his status as a legendary hero.

Imitation of the Christian Hymn

"Darzee's Chaunt," the song of praise Darzee sings to celebrate Nag's death, is reproduced at the end of the story. The song, which praises Rikki-tikki-tavi for ridding the garden of Nag, is reminiscent of Christian hymns of praise to Christ: in Christian belief, Christ is the savior of humanity because, by dying and then rising from the dead, he conquered death and opened heaven to humanity. A common pattern of the Christian hymn is praising Christ as savior by exhorting others to praise Christ. "Darzee's Chaunt" imitates this hymnal device in his praise of Rikki-tikki-tavi as he exhorts the other birds to praise him:

> Sing to your fledglings again,
> Mother, oh lift up your head!
> Evil that plagued us is slain,
> Death in the garden lies dead.

Just as Christ is praised in Christian hymns for saving humanity from death, so the song praises Rikki for saving the garden from Nag, who represents Death for the garden. The use of this hymn device draws parallels between Rikki and Christ and between Nag and Satan.

Historical Context

British Imperialism in the Late Nineteenth Century

When "Rikki-Tikki-Tavi" was first published as part of the second volume of Kipling's *Jungle Book* in 1895, Great Britain commanded the most powerful empire the world had ever seen. The Indian subcontinent was one important part of the empire, which thousands of "Anglo-Indians," like Kipling himself, called home. The form of imperialism during Kipling's time was characterized by forceful imposition of British government and British culture upon the natives of a region. But imperialism was not just the practice of the British Empire's acts of colonization of other lands and people; as historian Lerner writes in *Western Civilizations:* "To combat slave-trading, famine, filth, and illiteracy seemed to many a legitimate reason for invading the jungles of Africa and Asia." British imperialism was a philosophy that assumed the superiority of British civilization and, therefore, the moral responsibility of bringing their enlightened ways to the so-called "uncivilized" people of the world. This attitude was taken especially towards non-white, non-Christian cultures in India, Asia, Australia, and Africa. This philosophy of moral responsibility served to rationalize the economic exploitations of other peoples and their lands by the British Empire, and its subsequent amassing of wealth and power. It was nevertheless, during Kipling's time, largely embraced and unquestioned by the British population, and Kipling, being no exception, expressed ideas of cultural superiority and patriotism in much of his writing. In the early 2000s his reputation was negatively affected by his racist support of British imperialism.

British imperialist assumptions were so ingrained in the late Victorian era, that they surfaced in children's literature as well—literature that is, by its nature, meant to impart the values and morals of the adults' society to its young readers. "Rikki-Tikki-Tavi" is a prime example. The narrative specifically establishes that Rikki-tikki is very lucky to be a "house-mongoose" in the home of a British family, specifically noting that his mother taught him to aspire to the homes of "white men." That his mother had taught him to aspire to living in a white-

man's home implies both an idealization of British culture and a perceived inferiority of the non-white, Indian civilization that it dominated.

Social Darwinism

The late nineteenth century was marked by a dramatic shift in theories of philosophy, religion, and science following the mid-century publication of *On the Origin of the Species,* in which Darwin put forth the groundbreaking theory of natural selection. Natural selection is the process by which organisms who have characteristics suited to their environment have a better chance of survival and thus are able to mature, reproduce, and thus pass on their characteristics to their offspring; while those less suited to the environment do not tend to reach maturity and have offspring. The theories put forth by Darwin revolutionized the biological sciences, affected religious beliefs, and revised certain conclusions currently held in the physical and social sciences.

In the mid-nineteenth century, Herbert Spencer, widely regarded as the first social Darwinist, wrote *Social Statics,* in which he applied the biological theories of evolution to the study of human society. Spencer coined the subsequently familiar phrase "survival of the fittest" which describes the result of competition between different social groups of human beings. Social Darwinism was typically used by individuals who believed in the superiority of one group of people over another—groups based on nationality or race, for example—to justify the practice of unfair balances of power, institutionalized practices of exploitation, and philosophies of superiority such as imperialism.

The story "Rikki-Tikki-Tavi," written at the height of the British imperialism forty-five years after Spencer, reflects an implicit acceptance of the "survival of the fittest" theory of social Darwinism. The entire premise of the story is a battle for survival between a mongoose and its human family, on one side, and a family of snakes on the other. That the British family is not eliminated and, instead, remains to rule over the garden, can be viewed as suggesting the strength, superiority, and invulnerability of the British who rule in India.

Critical Overview

"Rikki-Tikki-Tavi" enjoyed unwavering success as a children's story well into the early 2000s, by

Compare & Contrast

- **1890s:** English readers are fascinated by portrayals of "exotic" British colonies like India, written primarily by British writers such as Rudyard Kipling and E. M. Forster, who offer depictions of India from the perspective of the British colonizer.

  Today: Ethnic Indian writers and novelists writing in English, such as Salman Rushdie and Arundhati Roy, offer the early twenty-first-century, English-language readership award-winning work portraying the life and culture of India from an Indian perspective.

- **1890s:** England commands the largest worldwide empire, spanning the globe, and India is one of its largest and most important components.

  Today: India, Pakistan, and Bangladesh, formerly the Indian Empire of Great Britain, are each independent, self-governing nations. Strong influences of British rule remain, however, including forms of government and the adoption of English as an official national language.

- **1890s:** The practice of British imperialism reflects a racist belief of white British superiority over the non-white nations of the world, rationalizing their government-sanctioned conquest and rule of other races.

  Today: While attitudes of racism still exist, human rights movements in the United States and Europe in the twentieth and early twenty-first centuries provide a strong cultural and political opposition to government-sanctioned racist policies in Western countries.

---

which time it was considered a classic and appeared in numerous editions and anthologies.

Kipling himself was the subject of criticism since he began publishing in his early twenties. His receipt of the Nobel Prize in 1907 was met with wide approval from the general readership with which he was immensely popular and dismay by the literary world. He was perceived by the literary establishment as a writer of verse, rather than of prose; the simple style of much of his prose was considered little more than entertaining; over the decades many found his blunt, straightforward politicizing both unrefined and offensive.

The English poet T. S. Eliot, however, years after Kipling's death, found value enough in his verse to publish a newly edited collection in 1941; in his introductory essay he defended Kipling's abilities as a poet. However, by 1941, Britain had faced one world war, was embroiled in another, and its once-powerful empire was crumbling; the unquestioned optimism and belief in the superiority and the romance of imperialism that was so much a part of Victorian-era philosophy was replaced by cynicism and pessimism that characterized the post-war, post-empire era. Kipling's work was markedly characterized by what became his dated promotion of British imperialism—a theme that appeared even in the children's story "Rikki-Tikki-Tavi"—and by this time the greatest defense Kipling needed was not for his questionable talent, but for the incorrectness of his political views. Eliot attempted a defense by writing: "Poetry is condemned as 'political' when we disagree with the politics; and the majority of readers do not want either imperialism or socialism in verse. But the question is not what is ephemeral, but what is permanent . . . we have therefore to try to find the permanent in Kipling's verse."

Eliot's defense of Kipling was famously rebutted in 1945 by George Orwell, who called Kipling a "prophet of British Imperialism" and wrote, "Kipling *is* a jingo imperialist, he *is* morally insensitive and aesthetically disgusting."

Throughout the years Kipling himself suffered for expressing the imperialist superiority that marked the mindset of Britain during his time, as did most of

Mongoose fighting a snake

his poetry and prose. But there was evidence in the early 2000s of an effort to take a fresh look at Kipling and his work. Geoffrey Wheatcroft writes in *Harper's Magazine* that, having the benefit of an objectivity possible after a century of removal from Kipling's Victorian England, it may be possible "to start taking [Kipling] seriously as a political writer without embarrassment." He further defends Kipling's inherent talent: "Kipling is a truly great writer, whose gross and glaring faults are overwhelmed by his elemental power. . . . Whether or not one likes 'Kipling and his views,' he was astoundingly perceptive."

Criticism

Tamara Fernando

Fernando is a freelance writer and editor based in Seattle, Washington. In this essay, Fernando explores Kipling's use of snake symbolism to promote British imperialism.

"Rikki-Tikki-Tavi," Rudyard Kipling's famous children's story about the battle between a mongoose and two cobras, seems to be a straightforward tale in which the hero and villains are clearly defined and good triumphs over evil. However, like most stories that deal with such themes, the methods by which good and evil are defined and represented can serve to make a greater ideological point. Kipling, who wrote during the height of British imperial power, was a well-known proponent of British imperialism, and his ideologies were not absent from his children's stories. In the case of "Rikki-Tikki-Tavi," Kipling uses the cobras, Nag and Nagaina, as a symbol of evil in order to demonize the Hindu culture and thereby promote the British agenda of rule over India.

When Nag is first introduced, he is described in simple adjectives that serve to clearly attribute an evil nature to him:

> . . . from the thick grass at the foot of the bush there came a low hiss—a horrid cold sound that made Rikki-tikki jump back two clear feet. Then inch by inch out of the grass rose up the head and spread hood of Nag, the big black cobra. . . . and he looked at Rikki-tikki with the wicked snake's eyes that never change their expression. . . .

Both objective and subjective adjectives are used to describe him: while an adjective like "black" reflects an objective observation, other adjectives, such as "horrid" "cold," and "wicked" that do

What Do I Read Next?

- *The Jungle Books,* published in two volumes in 1894 and 1895, Kipling's most famous and endearing work, is a collection of stories for children set in the jungles of India and featuring animals as their main characters. The most famous are the stories featuring the character of Mowgli, a boy raised by wolves in the jungle. ''Rikki-Tikki-Tavi'' appears in the second volume.

- *Puck of Pook's Hill* (1906) is one of Kipling's lesser-known children's novels. Like the *Jungle Books* it features a fantasy world in which Puck the fairy of Shakespeare's *A Midsummer Night's Dream* appears to children who are performing the play and leads them on adventures.

- *Just-So Stories* (1902) is another collection of children's stories by Rudyard Kipling. This series of stories draws on the folklore of India to explain in a fanciful manner the origins of different animals. Some stories include ''How the Leopard Got Its Spots'' and ''The Cat That Walked by Himself.''

- *Captains Courageous* (1897) is a coming-of-age novel by Kipling that relates the adventures of a rich, spoiled boy who is rescued from a shipwreck by a fishing boat. This novel is typically classified as appropriate for young readers.

- *Kim* (1901) is often said to be Kipling's most mature novel. The main character Kim, also known as Kimball O'Hara, is the orphaned son of an Irish soldier who lives on the streets of India. In a search for his destiny, he embarks on travels that bring him across such figures as the Tibetan Dalai Lama. Although the novel does contain several racial stereotypes, it has also been praised in modern times for its ability to rise above the racism that characterized other contemporary works.

- *The Wind in the Willows,* by the Scottish writer Kenneth Grahame, is a collection of children's stories published in 1924, about the same time that Kipling wrote. Like many of Kipling's children's works, it, too, features an imaginary world populated by distinctively characterized animals, emulating a popular trend in children's writing.

- *A Passage to India,* a novel by English writer E. M. Forster, was first published in 1924 when India was still a part of the British Empire. The novel, although incorporating some distinctly British, colonialist points of view, explores the controversies surrounding relationships between the different races and offers the hope of reconciliation and mutual respect.

- *Orientalism* (1978), a work of criticism by the post-colonial theorist Edward Said, is a seminal criticism of British imperialism and its aftermath. In particular, Said concentrates on the use of literature by Victorian Britain to promote colonization and the exploitation and oppression of other races.

---

the most to cast Nag as evil, are descriptions based not on fact but on the narrator's subjective bias.

Aside from these subjective descriptions, however, there is little else to indicate why Nag—and by extension, his wife Nagaina—merit the attribution of evil.

The concept of evil itself is, of course, also subjective. It is commonly applied to that which falls outside of the bounds of the laws and morals that govern a particular society. It might be construed that the snakes are evil because they kill—but killing, in the world of the bungalow garden, is not an act that deviates from its laws. The only governing law is the law of survival, by which all the characters, snakes included, are primarily motivated.

The big man who lives in the bungalow does not hesitate to keep a mongoose to kill snakes or to use his shotgun against the snakes as well (as he does twice in the story) in order to protect himself and his family from death. At the same time, Nag and Nagaina would not hesitate to kill the humans in order to preserve their lives and the lives of their children: That survival is their sole motivation in attacking the humans and Rikki-tikki-tavi is evident when Nagaina explains the rationale of their ambush to Nag: "When the house is emptied of people . . . [Rikki-tikki-tavi] will have to go away, and then the garden will be our own again. . . . So long as the bungalow is empty, we are king and queen of the garden; and remember that as soon as our eggs in the melon-bed hatch . . . our children will need room and quiet."

Not only is killing for survival regarded as acceptable behavior, it is exalted as heroic. Rikki-tikki-tavi is deemed a hero for bringing about the death of Nag and Nagaina. He even resorts to what would otherwise be considered less-than-scrupulous means to achieve his triumph when he fatally attacks a sleeping Nag. In fact, the only character who expresses any reluctance at killing—Darzee the tailorbird, who refuses to help Rikki destroy the cobras' eggs—is called "a feather-brained little fellow" for not understanding that the act of taking life is vital to his own self-preservation.

The narrator's choice of adjectives in describing the snakes, then, is not justified by any evidence of deviant behavior. The perception of the snakes as evil, therefore, is based solely on the snakes' adversarial relationship to Rikki-tikki-tavi and especially to the human family.

Indeed, the narrative voice's bias towards the human family's point of view not only casts the snakes as evil, but it idealizes and, therefore, depicts as good the human family. Rikki-tikki considers himself to be a lucky mongoose for having been taken in by a human family because "every well-brought-up mongoose always hopes to be a house mongoose." The narrative goes further than simply idealizing all of humanity, however, in specifying that "Rikki-tikki's mother . . . had carefully told Rikki what to do if ever he came across white men." The use of the very specific term "white men" creates an exclusivity that leaves out any non-white cultures and races from its representation of what is ideal. Specifically, as this white family is a British family stationed in an army facility in colonial India, it leaves out the non-white and non-Christian, indigenous Hindu culture, and idealizes the British.

> " . . . it is not such a big leap in the mind of the Victorian reader from the association of Nag with evil to the association of the god Brahma and therefore all of Hinduism and Indian culture with Satan."

That the colonial British family is put on a pedestal reveals that the narrator espouses a worldview characteristic of the British during the time in which the story was written. Great Britain, in the late nineteenth century—the time during which "Rikki-Tikki-Tavi" was published— commanded a worldwide empire larger than the world had ever seen before, of which India was the most important piece. Victorian-era imperialism was characterized by the practice of appropriating others' land for colonization and financial self-interest; it also reflected a paternalistic, self-righteous attitude that assumed British superiority and the moral obligation of British to spread their culture as they conquered other countries.

It would not have been difficult for Kipling's contemporary, Victorian, British, Christian readers—who shared his and the narrator's worldview—to view the cobras as evil to begin with; like Teddy's mother, who "wouldn't think of anything so awful" as snakes crawling through her house, the average British reader already would have associated Nag and Nagaina with evil, not only because snakes are truly potentially lethal to humans, but because in Judeo-Christian tradition the snake is a traditional symbol of evil. This symbol appears in the serpent of in the Garden of Eden in Genesis, which Jews and Christians interpret as the representation of Satan, and it appears in the dragon mentioned in Chapter 12 of Revelations, also taken to be a symbol of Satan.

The symbolic use of the snake continued throughout later Christian and European folklore: St. Patrick was supposed to have driven all the snakes from Ireland, and in the legend of St. George, a community converts to Christianity in his honor after he rescues them from an evil dragon. In these myths, the serpent/dragon figures are allegorical representations of non-Christian religions dispelled by dominating Christianity, and this recurring motif consistently demonizes non-Judeo-Christian gods by associating them with the symbolic representation of Satan.

The vilification of the snake is a particularly Western, Judeo-Christian pattern. In many other cultures the snake plays just the opposite role. In Hinduism specifically, the main religion of India, snakes, particularly king cobras, are held in reverence and awe. In certain parts of India, an actual cult of snake worship exists: the ancient, annual Nag-Panchami festival is held in honor of snakes, during which time they are welcomed into the home and given offerings of milk (the word "Nag" in Hindi means snake). Snakes also play an important part in the religious symbolism of Hinduism. Shiva, one of the most important gods in the Hindu pantheon, is often portrayed with a snake around his shoulders. The snake, because it continually sheds and grows its skin, is used as a symbol of eternity. In stories of creation, the god Vishnu, another important god in Hinduism, is said to have reclined on the back of a thousand-headed cobra during the destruction and recreation of the universe.

Kipling, although not a practicing Christian as an adult, had a childhood influenced by Christianity, and much of his writing reflects themes that draw Christian motifs. He would have been well aware of the association that his Western readers would draw with the image of the snake in the story. At the same time, Kipling, who spent his early childhood in India and later, as an adult, traveled the subcontinent as a journalist, was well versed in the mythology and religious practices of Hindus, and, while he makes use of Christian mythology in depicting Nag and Nagaina as villains, he also makes use of Hindu snake mythology. When Nag first makes his introduction in the story, he invokes his sacred status in Hinduism: "*I* am Nag. The great god Brahm put his mark upon all our people when the first cobra spread his hood to keep the sun off Brahm as he slept."

However, with Nag's next line, the association made between him and the god Brahm is used to inspire not reverence but fear: "Look, and be afraid!"

The god Brahm, or Brahma, in Hinduism is, in simple terms, roughly comparable to the Christian God. He is the god associated with the creation of the universe. In Hinduism, a religion that does not necessarily subscribe to mutually exclusive notions of good and evil to begin with, Brahma especially contains no connotation of unequivocal evil. But here, the evocation of his name and his symbol are used to inspire a sinister fear, in association with the already-described evil nature of the snake.

This evocation of the Hindu deity causes a direct association between the snake characters and the Hindu religion in India, just as there is a direct association between the human characters and the British Empire. Casting Nag and Nagaina as evil and associating them with the Hindu culture, however, presents them and what they represent from a biased Western viewpoint and not from the point of view of Hinduism: it is not such a big leap in the mind of the Victorian reader from the association of Nag with evil to the association of the god Brahma and therefore all of Hinduism and Indian culture with Satan.

The conflict between Nag and Nagaina—symbols of the Hindu culture which has now effectively been demonized—and the human family—a representation of the British presence in India—then takes on a larger meaning for the Victorian, imperialist readership, much like the stories found in the old European dragonslayer myths: the defeat of the demonic Hindu snake, and the survival of the British family to rule over the garden instead, becomes a rationalization of the British colonization of India, the imperialist ideologies of British superiority, and the moral obligation the British felt to bring "enlightened" ways to India.

In both portraying Nag as evil, reflecting the symbolism of Western Judeo-Christian tradition, and drawing an association between Nag and the Hindu god Brahm, Kipling appropriates the symbolism of the Hindu religion and, stripping it of its original meaning, interprets it based solely from the perspectives and philosophies of the West. This act of appropriation does not just misrepresent and demonize Hinduism; it symbolically annihilates it and replaces it with a Western point of view. In so doing, Kipling effectively performs a literary and cultural colonization of India.

Source: Tamara Fernando, Critical Essay on "Rikki-Tikki-Tavi," in *Short Stories for Students,* Thomson Gale, 2005.

Sources

Eliot, T. S., *A Choice of Kipling's Verse,* Faber & Faber, 1941, pp. 5–36.

Kipling, Rudyard, "Rikki-Tikki-Tavi," in *The Jungle Books,* Golden Press, 1963, pp. 123–33.

Lerner, Robert E., Standish Meacham, and Edward McNall Burns, *Western Civilization: Their History and Their Culture,* Norton, 1993, pp. 811–39.

Orwell, George, "Rudyard Kipling," in *Collected Essays,* Secker & Warburg, 1961, pp. 179–94.

Wheatcroft, Geoffrey, "A White Man's Burden: Rudyard Kipling's Pathos and Prescience," in *Harper's Magazine,* September 2002, pp. 81–84.

Further Reading

Cain, Peter, and Tony Hopkins, *British Imperialism, 1688–2000,* 2d ed., Longman, 2001.

When this comprehensive history of the British Empire was first published, it was received with critical acclaim. It was later updated to relate imperialism to modern-day international politics.

Ferguson, Niall, *Empire: The Rise and Demise of the British World Order and the Lessons for Global Power,* Basic Books, 2003.

Ferguson offers a history of British imperialism of the nineteenth and twentieth centuries and applies it to the international policies of the twenty-first century.

Gilmour, David, *The Long Recessional: The Imperial Life of Rudyard Kipling,* Farrar, Straus and Giroux, 2002.

Kipling's legacy endured a long history of vilification, but this biography offers a fresh, early twenty-first-century perspective on his life and ideologies.

Mallett, Phillip, *Rudyard Kipling: A Literary Life,* Palgrave Macmillan, 2003.

Mallett concentrates especially on Kipling's writing life and family life.

Think of England

Peter Ho Davies

2000

"Think of England" (2000) began as a short story, which was later included in the anthology *Best American Short Stories 2001*. However, after intermittent periods of revision, it became part of a historical novel that Peter Ho Davies has been working on for the past few years. The story is essentially the beginning of *The Bad Shepherd* (Houghton Mifflin, 2005), a novel which centers on a Welsh barmaid's relationship with a German prisoner of war who works on her family's farm and lives on the grounds of what was once a summer camp. In bringing his characters to life, however, Davies is careful to navigate the line between history and fiction, saying. "One of the things I enjoy about fiction is its slyness. The ability to slip things in. Working with historical material, where there's already some factual basis, accentuates that slyness for me. It spurs my imagination." Rather than focus on historical moments that could potentially burden the narrative with their familiarity, Davies directs his attention instead to composing stories that embody ". . . small bubbles, pockets of history— chapters that aren't well known, or, if they are known, ones that have an overlay of popular myth." "Think of England" is one such story.

"Think of England," which is set on the evening of June 6, 1944, D-Day, tells the story of sixteen-year-old Sarah, a Welsh barmaid who conducts a clandestine affair with Colin, one of the British "sappers," or military engineers, who have come to build a mysterious base on the site of an

abandoned summer camp near her village in North Wales. Nationalism runs high as the war effort galvanizes the Welsh and English who gather in The Quarryman's Arms to have a pint and to listen to Churchill's radio broadcast, a situation that increases Sarah's risk of being ostracized from her community if she is discovered conducting a romance with an Englishmen, especially one in the British armed forces. ''Think of England'' is at once a coming-of-age tale and a tale of redemption, albeit one in which redemption occurs quite unexpectedly.

Author Biography

Peter Ho Davies was born in Coventry, England, on August 30, 1966, to a Chinese mother, Sook Ying Ho, and a Welsh father, Thomas Enion Davies. Peter Ho Davies received a bachelor of science degree in physics from the University of Manchester in 1987, and a bachelor of arts degree in English from Cambridge University in 1989. After this he moved to the United States to attend Boston University, where he received a master's degree in Creative Writing in 1993. For a brief period Davies worked in publishing in Britain, Singapore, and Malaysia, having been at one time the UK business manager for *Varsity* magazine.

Davies' stories have been published in a wide variety of magazines and literary journals, including *Harpers, Gettysburg Review, The Atlantic, Story,* and *The Paris Review.* His work has been widely anthologized in such annual publications as *Prize Stories: The O. Henry Awards* (1998) and *Best American Stories* (1995, 1996, 2001). His debut story collection, *The Ugliest House in the World* (Houghton Mifflin, 1998), received the PEN/Macmillan Silver Pen Fiction Award and the *Mail on Sunday*/John Llewellyn Rhys Prize. Davies' second collection, *Equal Love* (Houghton Mifflin, 2000), was a finalist for the *Los Angeles Times* Book Prize. In 2003, Davies was named one of twenty ''Best of Young British Novelists'' by *Granta* magazine.

A recipient of fellowships from the National Endowment for the Arts and the Fine Arts Work Center in Provincetown, in addition to being named a Guggenheim fellow for 2004, Davies has taught creative writing at the University of Oregon, Emory University, and the University of Michigan, where he has directed the master of fine arts program in Creative Writing. His novel *The Bad Shepherd*,

Peter Ho Davies

from which ''Think of England'' is excerpted, is scheduled for publication by Houghton Mifflin in 2005.

Plot Summary

The story opens on the evening of the D–Day invasion, with The Quarryman's Arms filled with patrons who have come to hear Winston Churchill's radio broadcast. Sarah, the story's protagonist, pulls pints behind the lounge bar while Jack Jones, the pub's owner, tends the public bar. The pub has the tallest aerial for miles around, and for this reason it enjoys a large clientele. At Jack's urging, Sarah steps onto a crate to warm up the wireless.

The crowd in the lounge bar consists mainly of English soldiers. A regular, Harry Hitch, asks for his ''usual.'' Most of the soldiers are ''sappers,'' military men on a work detail. One in particular, Colin, has caught Sarah's eye. Unbeknownst to friends and family, much less the patrons in the bar, Sarah and Colin have been ''sweethearts'' for the past week. They have agreed to meet when Sarah gets off from work. As Sarah hears Churchill's speech, she thinks of the men doing battle on

Omaha Beach, and she feels proud to be of service to the men in uniform who have come to the pub.

Once Churchill's speech ends, Sarah turns the radio to a broadcast featuring dance music from the Savoy in London, and she sees that the patrons are clapping one another on the back and smiling at the soldiers, including the locals. The men have been transformed into heroes through the actions of their countrymen far away. Colin seems even more handsome—"like the lobby card of a film star"—now that Sarah views him in this new light.

As Sarah pours pint after pint for her customers in the lounge bar, she notices that the patrons in the public bar have begun to file out. She sees her father, Arthur, among the men, and she wonders if they are leaving because they must rise early and tend to their work on their farms or if they are leaving because they feel out of place in the midst of the British soldiers' celebration. She would like to buy her father a pint, but she knows that he is much too proud for that. Their relationship has changed since her mother's death three years ago, for Sarah is now in charge of keeping the farm's books, a responsibility her father entrusted to her once she obtained a job at the pub. Sarah is sad to see the men go, but she knows that their absence decreases her chances of being seen with Colin when they rendezvous after hours.

The pub is filled with soldiers and diehards now, and Sarah observes that for once the talk isn't about politics. The village is nationalistic in its views toward the British, and Sarah thinks it is "like so much tosh" that disputes are still being fought with as much fervor as they were when they first arose more than forty years ago. The majority view in the village is that the war is an English war and, therefore, one that does not concern the Welsh. The Welsh still consider the English to be "occupiers," but Churchill's rousing broadcast has temporarily put an end to such divisiveness, yet a palpable tension between English and Welsh patrons still exists within the pub.

On this night when the air is charged with patriotism, Sarah, though she is proud to be Welsh, wishes she could be British. Her father, a "staunch nationalist," would never entertain such a thought, for he has never forgiven Churchill for the riots that occurred at Tonypandy. Sarah knows that nationalism and provincialism go hand in hand, yet she suspects that at the heart of every nationalistic argument is the desire "[t]o be important, to be the center of attention, not isolated." She feels excited

because the soldiers and the broadcast crew from the BBC Light Program are coming to her, thus eliminating her own sense of isolation.

The sappers are building a mysterious base located on the site of an old holiday camp. Boys from the village spy on the camp, descending from the trees at dusk to explore the buildings while pretending to be commandos. Speculation about who will occupy the base runs rife throughout the village, but Jack hopes that the Yanks will come because they spend the most money. The villagers hope to see film stars like James Stewart or Tyrone Power pass through on their way to East Anglia, but, as is so often the case, they must settle for "gangly, freckle-faced farm boys" instead. One such boy, a tail-gunner from "Kentuck," presents Sarah with a gift of a torn parachute which contains enough silk for a petticoat and two slips. When Sarah tries to politely return the gift, the tail-gunner insists that she keep it, saying, "Why, you're what we're fighting for!"

As Sarah watches Colin talking to one of his fellow soldiers, she wonders if Colin will give her a gift to remember him by. She thinks that she could get him to tell her about who the camp is for, but she reconsiders, realizing that it would be "unpatriotic" and "disloyal to Britain." More important, such an act would be disloyal to Wales. She wouldn't want to give the British an excuse to call the Welsh unpatriotic. "Only the Welsh, it occurs to her, are allowed to declare themselves that." Sarah continues to speculate about the new camp, especially since Colin told her that the work is almost completed. She realizes that there will be nothing to keep Colin in the village once the work is done.

Harry Hitch interrupts Sarah's reverie with a request for another scotch. Harry, who is a star with the BBC Light Program, tells jokes that Sarah can't quite understand even though her "good school-room English" got her the job at the lounge bar where so many English patrons gather. Harry tells offensive jokes that make fun of the Welsh language and temperament. Harry continues his monologue as each joke is met with cheers and applause. Sarah glances at Mary Munro, a radio actress, for support. Mary tries to persuade Harry to stop, but he refuses.

Harry begins to make fun of Sarah's youth and naïveté by telling jokes that question a girl's innocence and sexual experience. Sarah, offended by Harry's insinuation, throws his drink in his face. From across the room, Colin asks Sarah if she's all right. Harry feigns remorse for his comment, but then starts another round of jokes when Sarah accepts his hand offered in reconciliation. Sarah tries to prevent Colin from making a scene, but he challenges Harry, taking a swing at him. Harry takes a pratfall to make Colin look foolish. Jack prevents Colin from taking another swing by grabbing him around the chest, forcing the breath out of him. Mary and Tony, the sound engineer, help a drunken Harry out of the bar.

Sarah recalls something Mary said to her once about Harry's past, that his wife had been killed in the Blitz. "You wouldn't think to look at him, but it was true love," Mary told her. Sarah begins cleaning up the bar as a call for last orders is made in both English and Welsh. She catches herself swaying gently to the music on the radio when Jack turns it off. He says the dishes can wait and lets her go home early. Sarah suspects that Jack knows of her rendezvous with Colin, so she must be especially careful not to be seen with him. Sarah's romantic feelings reach a higher pitch when she recalls her promise of going somewhere "more private" with her new sweetheart.

Colin waits for her around the corner from the pub. He calls to her, and as she goes to meet him, Sarah anticipates what the night will bring. She considers herself to be rather worldly for a girl of sixteen, having kissed most of the local boys, even David, the village's evacuee from London. She thinks that she has "acquitted herself well" with Colin, and that she has maybe even surprised him on occasion with her knowledge about physical intimacy.

Sarah rides on the handlebars of Colin's bike, feeling slightly self-conscious about the way Colin stares at her bum. Colin pedals through the night, the bike gathering speed as they coast downhill, Sarah's skirt billowing to reveal her legs. When she moves to adjust her skirt, Colin places his hand over hers, saying, "Hold still, love. I've got you."

They arrive at Camp Sunshine, and Sarah remembers viewing the camp from the hillside during the hot summer months when she was young and tended her father's sheep. She recalls seeing the pool below her and imagining its coolness. Such retreats were not for the locals who could barely afford the occasional day trip to the sea. With this memory firmly in mind, Sarah asks Colin to take her to the pool. He had thought that one of the cottages would be a more comfortable place for them to tryst, but he pedals toward the pool and the nearby playground, where they stop to play on the swings.

Sarah is eager to see the pool once again, and she mistakes the tarpaulin that covers the pool for the surface of the water itself. Colin explains that the tarpaulin is there to keep out leaves and other debris, and he disappears underneath the cover to demonstrate that the pool has been drained. At first Sarah doesn't know where he has gone, but then she sees him mimic the dorsal fin of a shark as his language takes on a flavor of sexual innuendo. Colin takes Sarah by the hand and leads her into the deep end of the pool, imitating various other sea creatures along the way in an attempt to physically possess her.

Sarah and Colin begin kissing, and she feels herself turning in his arms as his grip upon her tightens. Soon she finds herself pressed against the pool's tile wall that "smells sharply of dank, chlorine, and rotten leaves." Colin, in an attempt to manipulate Sarah's affection for him, tells her that he will be leaving soon. He wonders if she will miss him when he's gone. He tries to weaken her resolve by telling her that he could be at the front by this time next month, and that he wished he had something to remember her by, something to help him keep up his "fighting spirits." Sarah, enamored of her sweetheart and eager for experience, acquiesces, allowing Colin to slide his hand against her thigh, pushing the silk slip out of the way.

When Sarah realizes Colin's true intent, she tells him, "*Nargois!*" but he doesn't understand Welsh and so continues his assault. Sarah feels pressure and pain, and she thinks twice about screaming for help for fear of getting caught. Finally, she lifts her head and catches Colin under the chin, forcing him to step back. He curses at her with a word she doesn't understand, and she curses at him in Welsh in retaliation. Hearing a language he doesn't comprehend makes Colin even more angry now that his sexual overtures have been rebuffed. "Why don't you just give it up and speak English, like the rest of us?" he says. He changes his attitude, however, and tries one last time to resume his "lovemaking," but Sarah, afraid of what additional harm may come to her, is already straightening her clothes and looking for an exit. Colin's realizes that Sarah is no longer susceptible to his charms, and he begins cursing at her again.

Just when Sarah fears another attack from Colin, she hears shouts coming from above as flashlights dart across the landscape. She is relieved that help has arrived, but with that help comes the chance of being discovered with an English soldier. Before she can ask Colin what they should do, he disappears by scrambling up a ladder and out into the night.

Weak and shaking from the attack, Sarah manages to climb out of the pool. She hears shouts coming from across the camp, and she thinks that the local boys are up to their mischief again. She hurries over to the playground where the bicycle has been left. As Sarah mounts the bike, she notices that her slip has been torn, and she feels like weeping for having lost her innocence in such a violent fashion.

Sarah's body hurts as she pedals home. She knows that she is stealing Colin's bike, yet she could care less about the consequences. She knows that he won't ask about it, but if he does, "she'll pretend that she's forgotten her English."

Characters

Arthur

Arthur is Sarah's father and a widower who entrusts the family finances to his daughter now that she has a paying job. He is a sheep farmer who visits The Quarryman's Arms occasionally. He prefers to remain at the public bar with his Welsh-speaking friends rather than enter the lounge where Sarah serves the English-speaking patrons. He wears a "frayed dark suit" that was his "Sunday best" before Sarah was born.

Colin

Colin is one of the "sappers"—men who mend roads, dig ditches, or lay bricks—who is working on the new military base near the holiday resort. He is a corporal in the British military. He's known Sarah for a week, but she considers him to be her "sweetheart." The only physical description given of him is that he has a mustache. He lures Sarah to the abandoned campsite and assaults her sexually.

David

David is the only boy whom Sarah has kissed lately—nothing more than "goodnight kisses," but she once kissed him longer "to make him blush on his birthday." An evacuee from England, David is

younger than Sarah. He is described as being "a bit moony."

Harry Hitch

Harry Hitch is the "star" of a BBC radio comedy show that airs on the Light Program. Harry has a voice that belies his physical presence. Harry is a regular at The Quarryman's Arms, and he frequently makes fun of the Welsh, whom he refers to as "Taffs." He cracks jokes filled with innuendo and double entendre, but becomes insulting when he's had too much to drink. Harry starts to attack Sarah verbally, but his colleagues from the BBC and Jack, the pub's proprietor, stop him before he causes too much trouble. Mary Munro suggests that the reason why Harry drinks so much is because he lost his wife in the Blitz. "You wouldn't think to look at him, but it was true love," she tells Sarah.

Jack Jones

Jack Jones is the proprietor of the Quarryman's Arms. He protects Sarah, intervening on her behalf when Harry Hitch insults her with a joke about Welsh girls. Jack lets Sarah leave early on the evening of D-Day. Sarah suspects that Jack, a Welshman, knows she's seeing a British soldier, so she must be discreet when keeping her rendezvous with Colin.

Mary Munro

Mary Munro is an actress who is known for the many voices and accents she performs for BBC radio. She intervenes when her colleague, Harry Hitch, has too much to drink and becomes verbally abusive toward Sarah. Mary also gives Sarah the following advice: "All you need to know about Englishmen, Welshmen, or Germans, for that matter, is that they're all men. And you know what they say about men: one thing on their minds . . . and one hand on their things."

Sarah

Sarah, a sixteen-year-old Welsh barmaid, is the story's protagonist. She yearns for attention and experience, yet she risks being ostracized by her father and her village, which is a very nationalistic community, if her romance with Colin, a member of the British military, is discovered. Sarah works in the lounge side of the pub because she speaks "good schoolroom English." Even though she's only sixteen, she's been working at the pub for nearly a year. Sarah longs to receive the attention of a film star, and this need allows Colin to take advantage of her. At the summer camp, she tries to fight him off, but not until he's taken her virginity.

Tail-Gunner from Kentuck

The tail-gunner from Kentuck is an American airman who passed through north Wales on his way to East Anglia and stopped in at the pub for a drink. He gave Sarah a bundle wrapped in brown parcel paper that contained a torn parachute, which provided enough silk for her to make a petticoat and two slips. At first she tried to give the bundle back, but the soldier insisted that she keep it because, he said, "You . . . . Why, you're what we're fighting for!"

Tony

Tony is a second engineer for the BBC. He works with Harry Hitch on a radio comedy show for the BBC's Light Program. He helps Mary Munro escort Harry Hitch out of the pub when he becomes drunk and obnoxious.

Themes

Nationalism

Nationalism, and the abiding undercurrent of patriotism that often accompanies it, remains a galvanizing force within The Quarryman's Arms. The pub is divided into two separate sections to accommodate its Welsh- and English-speaking patrons; Sarah, with her "good schoolroom English," has been hired to tend bar in the lounge while the pub's owner, Jack, serves the Welsh patrons at the public bar, where they talk constantly about politics. Old wounds, such as those inflicted by the British during the Great Strike and the Tonypandy Riots, are not forgotten by the Welsh, and they continue to demonstrate a deep-seated mistrust of the British as a result. Drawing upon their memory of the historical incidents mentioned above, the Welsh regard the war as England's war, for the British are regarded as "occupiers" who persist in the "imperialistic, capitalistic" ways they first demonstrated during the Great War. By comparison, the Welsh view themselves as more moderate and agrarian.

Media Adaptations

- Audio Editions offers *The Best American Short Stories 2001* on four cassettes or five compact discs, each story read by its author. The set, which is available at http://www.audioeditions. com (accessed November 29, 2004), contains abridged versions of prize-winning stories such as "Think of England" and features, in addition to Peter Ho Davies, such noted authors as Ha Jin, Alice Munro, Rick Moody, and Dorothy West.

Sarah realizes that these nationalistic attitudes persist in part because of provincialism and isolation, and that everyone, regardless of where they may come from, wants to be the center of attention rather than isolated. Nationalism is a form of defense, a way of protecting that which is valuable, like the museum treasures that are kept in the old stone quarry. "And nationalism is a way of putting it back in the center, of saying that what's here is important enough," she concludes. "It's a redrawing of the boundaries of what's worthwhile."

Nationalism is also expressed through the language and culture of the story's characters. Harry Hitch, a broadcaster with the BBC, makes fun of the Welsh language and temperament, using the one word of Welsh he knows ("ta" or "thanks") to order more drinks. He denigrates the Welsh language because he, being British, expects English to be the main language spoken throughout the United Kingdom, forgetting that its territories and peoples are anything but homogenous. There is also the implication that he, as a paying customer, should be served in the language to which he is accustomed. Colin, another Englishman, also demonstrates this attitude of nationalistic superiority when he insists that Sarah speak English whenever they are together. (She had tried to give him Welsh lessons, but he quickly abandoned them.) This attitude contributes to the story's climactic scene, and thus reveals the cultural perspectives of both characters, when Sarah tells him, "*Nargois!*" as he forces himself

Topics for Further Study

- How does Davies' use of a historical event—D-Day—set the story's tone and atmosphere? How does a sense of place influence the characters' actions? Think of a story that you would like to write, about whatever topic you choose. Write the story, but place the setting during a major historical event. Did the elements of the historical event have any effect on your narrative choices or your characters' lives? How did the historical context have an effect on the way you envisioned your story, especially once you began to write?

- Research the Blitz. On which cities did German army focus its attacks? How many people were displaced, and where did they go once the attacks had begun? What type of support did the refugees receive, and where did it come from? Assemble this information into a visual presentation that you can share with your class, explaining the various results of your research.

- The word *blitz* is the abbreviated form of what German noun? Discuss the word's derivation and meaning. What other foreign words have passed into the English language as a result of World War II?

- Research the history of stone quarrying. What types of methods are used to extract the stone? Is northern Wales known for one particular type of stone, or is a variety of stone quarried in that region? For what purpose is the stone used? Does stone quarrying remain a viable industry in North Wales today?

- Listen to a recording of the Welsh language being spoken. To which language group does it belong? Investigate the language's historical development. How does its pronunciation and orthography differ from English? Is Welsh spoken by a majority of the people living in Wales?

- Trace the construction of Edward I's six major castles in North Wales. What similarities and differences do the castles possess? How did the design of each castle enhance its function as a fortress? Design a three-dimensional castle for an actual historical area in North Wales and describe for the class why you built the castle the way you did. This will require researching the area of North Wales in which you would have had your castle, keeping in mind elements like climate, population of people, and the proximity of enemies and what weapons they used, that may have affected the way you designed your structure in the past.

---

upon her. Her defiant stance is emblematic of the long history between Wales and England.

Film Stars

Davies refers to film stars in the story to underscore an atmosphere of provincialism and the sense of isolation that many of the villagers, especially Sarah, experience. For example, whenever American airmen pass through North Wales on their way to bases in East Anglia, members of the village search their faces with the hope of glimpsing one of the famous enlisted men like James Stewart or Tyrone Power, but instead they usually encounter one of the "gangly, freckle-faced farm boys" like the tail-gunner from Kentuck. Consequently, the villagers' expectations are deflated and their sense of isolation remains firmly in place. Sarah, on the other hand, feels as though the world is coming to her when Churchill's broadcast concludes and so many British soldiers and workers for the BBC celebrate the D–Day invasion.

Though Sarah has only seen swimming pools at the movies, she identifies with Esther Williams, the swimming champion turned film star, whom she considers to be "the most beautiful woman in the world." Sarah longs for a glamorous life like that of her movie idol, and this need for attention, based as it is upon a naïve perception of the outside world, subsequently contributes to her misjudging Colin's true character.

Style

Imagery

Though "Think of England" does not abound with imagery, Davies chooses images that loom powerfully in the reader's imagination. Furthermore, these images enhance the story's characterization as they visually render a character's psychological state. For example, when the tail-gunner from Kentuck first presents a torn parachute to Sarah, she declines his gift for fear he will get into trouble, though she immediately calculates that the parachute contains enough silk for "a petticoat and two slips." Even though the tail-gunner insists that she accept her gift, Sarah's fears manifest themselves once more, this time in a dream in which the tail-gunner parachutes after having bailed out from his downed plane, his silhouetted form "hanging in the night sky, sliding silently toward the earth, under a canopy of petticoats." She has difficulty reconciling the tail-gunner's gift of a parachute with its intended purpose, especially since silk undergarments constitute a luxury during wartime. Later, the image of the torn slip symbolizes Sarah's loss of innocence as she pedals homeward, vowing to mend the tear with needle and thread. The tears she sheds suggest that her broken heart and psyche will take much longer to repair.

Sarah's longing to live a more glamorous life manifests itself in the image of a swimming pool. Sarah considers the film star Esther Williams, who was once a swimming champion, to be beautiful and, therefore, someone to be admired and emulated. Sarah remembers seeing the camp's swimming pool from high above a hillside when she was young and tended sheep with her father, and the image of the pool suggested a life that would forever remain separate from her. Because her family was poor and could not afford a camp membership, Sarah was forced to swim in the sea. This memory is revived when Colin takes her by the camp at night: the first place Sarah wants to see is the pool. However, the pool has been drained and covered with a tarpaulin, which Sarah mistakes for the water's surface until Colin demonstrates that the pool is indeed empty. Thus, Sarah's hope of fulfilling her fantasy of sitting poolside and running her hand through the water like a movie star ends in disappointment as she's greeted by the smell of dank, rotting leaves and chlorine.

Another image associated with Sarah's coming of age is that of her well polished shoes, which she snaps together quickly to prevent Colin from looking up her skirt. As she rides atop the handlebars of Colin's bicycle, the shoes remain polished and without a mark, like Sarah's reputation. Shortly thereafter, when Colin leads Sarah into the emptied pool, she scuffs her shoes on the tiles, and she immediately thinks, "*I just polished them,*" knowing, perhaps, that the scuffed shoes are a sign that she is no longer innocent. Davies, through the use of figurative speech, reverses this image to comment on Colin's cowardly lack of responsibility when Sarah realizes his true character: "A clean pair of heels, she thinks, the English phrase so suddenly vivid she feels blinded by it." Through the use of a single image, Davies delves into the psychological state of one character as he comments upon another.

Figurative Speech and Gesture

Throughout the story there is an abundance of puns, jokes, and gestures that propel the narrative forward. Davies uses figurative speech to state indirectly opinions and beliefs that would be too awkward for his characters to state in a forthright manner. For example, Harry infers that the Welsh are afraid to do battle against the Germans when he tells the joke about the "Taffy" who, because he could not comprehend English spelling, enlisted in the RAF, the Royal Air Force, instead of the NAAFI, which is an organization committed to providing military servicemen with recreational and leisure services. This, Harry suggests, is the only way that the Welshman would enlist in the military—by accident. Although Harry's jokes are laced with sexual innuendo and border on the obnoxious, he would risk a better chance of causing a brawl if he did not conceal his sentiments—namely, that Welsh girls are poor, inexperienced lovers—under the cloak of humor. Finally, Sarah throws a drink in his face out of disgust, but this does not prevent Harry from making more jokes at her expense.

Colin also uses gestures and figurative speech to suggest his physical desire for Sarah. If he had made a crude overture to possess her physically, then he most certainly would have been rebuffed. Colin wastes no time communicating his desire, for when they arrive at the pool, he disappears under the tarpaulin, pushing his hand up from below so that it mimics a shark's dorsal fin cutting through the waves. "What's that?" asks Sarah. "Me manhood," Colin responds, the taut fabric acquiring yet another association. He continues to mimic other sea creatures in an attempt to get close to Sarah physically, finally wrapping his arms around her in the guise of an "octopus." His childish play succeeds, however, for soon he and Sarah kiss.

Historical Setting

Davies sets "Think of England" against the backdrop of a historical event like the D–Day invasion to establish an atmosphere that the reader can immediately identify, which in this story is one of fervid nationalism. Specifically, Davies uses this historical context to examine nationalistic beliefs that exist within a context of wary tolerance. These are not the nationalistic beliefs expressed by the competing forces of the Axis and Allied nations, however, but those of two nationalities—the English and the Welsh—who are fighting on the same side. This setting, which remains unburdened by an excess of historical fact and detail, allows for the story to develop a more complex and resonant tone, one that is enhanced by the realistic style of writing and the divided loyalties of the characters themselves. Furthermore, a historical setting like the one found in "Think of England" offers the reader a fictional glimpse into an aspect of history that might not otherwise be explored.

Historical Context

Eagle Tower

The castle constructed by Edward I at Caernarvon is a "conscious imitation" of the fortress at Constantinople, the city that had been the seat of the Roman Empire for nearly a thousand years. The castle's architect, Master James of St. George, no doubt was familiar with the discovery of bones at Caernarvon that were believed to be the remains of Magnus Maximus, the father of Constantine, the first Christian emperor of the Roman Empire. The castle, which is constructed of light-colored stone and features octagonal towers, emphasizes an impressive display, a symbol of domination and strength. Furthermore, the castle's design imparts an "especial dignity," though the castle's appearance in no way discounts its function as an instrument of war.

The Eagle Tower at Caernarvon Castle features vaulted wall-chambers of both octagonal and hex-agonal design, with large central apartments, a kitchen, and two chapels. The tower was probably designed for one of Edward I's loyal friends, Otto de Grandson, a Savoyard who became the first justiciar of Wales. According to legend, Otto de Grandson saved Edward's life by sucking out the poison from a wound Edward had received after being attacked by an assassin in Syria. The Eagle Tower, with its triple turrets, stands, therefore, as a testament to an enduring friendship.

The Great Strike of 1903

The Penrhyn quarry in Wales was the site of a labor struggle that began in November 1900 and ended in November 1903. According to John Davies, author of *A History of Wales,* "The dispute arose from the special nature of the quarryman's craft, from the particular ethos of the quarrying communities and from the way in which the second Baron Penrhyn (1836–1907) interpreted his rights as an employer." The differences in the two parties couldn't be more dramatic, with Baron Penrhyn occupying his castle and the quarrymen and their families living in villages. He was Anglican, Tory, and "arrogantly English," whereas the quarrymen, who spoke only Welsh, were Calvinist church-goers who challenged the current political climate. Baron Penrhyn and his family provided schools and hospitals for the quarrymen's families, but in exchange for these basic services they expected absolute obedience.

Because the quality of the rock varied greatly, the quarrymen would usually reach an agreement, known as a "bargain," with the management that allowed the quarrymen to negotiate their wage based on the amount of work that needed to be done. Thus, the quarrymen regarded themselves more as contractors rather than employees. Management, however, eliminated the quarrymen's autonomy by abolishing the bargain completely. The quarrymen realized that they must organize themselves into a union if they wished to retain the bargain and a higher pay rate. When the Great Strike began in November of 1900, it divided Great Britain, arousing the attention of the Free Labour movement, who opposed trade unions, and those who provided support to the strikers by contributing money. There were approximately 2,800 men working at the Penrhyn quarry when the strike began, but by the spring of 1902, 700 had returned to work while 1,300 sought work in the coalfields of South Wales. Soldiers had to be brought in to protect the strikebreakers, who were called "scabs" and, in Welsh, *"cynffonwyr,"* or "blacklegs." The slate industry in Wales never quite recovered from the strike.

Tonypandy Riots of 1910

The riots at Tonypandy, a mining town in Wales, were the culmination of a period in British labor relations known as the "Great Unrest." Miners sought to prevent a wage system that the colliery owners wanted to introduce, whereby miners would be paid according to the amount of coal produced. However, some types of coal were easier to mine than others, and the owners accounted for this difference by paying an allowance, which they eventually refused to pay for fear of having to pay high wages. In October of 1910, workers at the Cambrian Combine refused to accept a lower wage offer. In November, more than 800 men were locked out, and 12,000 miners went on strike. Scuffles soon broke out between the striking miners and police as the rioting spread to the streets of Tonypandy, where many shop windows were broken.

Once the riots had ended, the current Home Secretary, Winston Churchill, sent troops to keep the peace. The miners believed that Churchill had sided with the colliery owners, and that this show of force constituted a "conspiracy against the working class." The occupation lasted for months, and the miners, forced by poverty to accept the colliery owners' terms and conditions of employment, returned to work nearly a year later. The residents of Tonypandy, and, indeed, most of Wales, never forgave Churchill for robbing the miners of what had been a hard-won, albeit temporary, victory.

London Blitz

The Blitz, an abbreviated form of the German word *Blitzkrieg,* or "lightning war," was the Luftwaffe's sustained bombing campaign of major British cities, particularly London, during World War II. The Blitz began on September 7, 1940, and extended through May 1941. The Luftwaffe challenged the Royal Air Force (RAF) in an attempt to establish control of the skies above Britain, with the first air raids occurring over the docklands in London's East End. The attacks eventually encompassed the ninety-five boroughs and districts that comprise the greater London area, leaving one in six Londoners homeless. Those residents who did not remain in London sought refuge in the English countryside or in countries within the United Kingdom. Fires, floods, and food shortages were com-

mon. The raids originally took place during both the day and night, but the Germans switched to nightly raids to protect their aircraft, though the British were able to detect the German planes using radar.

In November of 1940, the Germans began attacking industrial cities such as Birmingham, Coventry, Manchester, and Sheffield. The Germans sought to cripple British manufacturing, as well as spread fear and diminish morale throughout the countryside. Ironically, the Blitz strengthened British resolve to defeat the Nazis. In spite of the violence and devastation wrought by the Germans on a nightly basis, British citizens remained defiant, seeking shelter in tube stations at night and going about their business during the day fortified by an "extraordinary blossoming . . . of comradeship and good will."

D–Day

D–Day is a military term used to indicate the day on which an attack or operation will begin, though the most famous D–Day in history is the one which occurred on June 6, 1944, the day the Allied Forces landed on the beaches of Normandy by the light of a full moon. The amphibious attack was originally planned to take place one day earlier, but bad weather delayed the assault against the German stronghold on Omaha Beach, which was marked by steep cliffs and, therefore, offered the greatest protection against attack. The risk of casualties was high, as it was on the other landing points of Utah Beach, Juno Beach, Sword Beach, and Gold Beach, which were not actual beaches but code names used for purposes of secrecy.

The Battle of Normandy (code-named *Operation Overlord*) inaugurated the Allied Forces' campaign to liberate Europe from Nazi control. In addition to the amphibious assault staged at each of the five landing points, paratroopers from two U.S. airborne divisions were dropped on both the advance and rear flanks to secure the landings. Rather than confront German forces in a head-on assault, as was done in World War I at the expense of a great many lives, U.S. President Franklin D. Roosevelt and British Prime Minister Winston Churchill suggested to the Allied commander Dwight D. Eisenhower that the Allied Forces attack the periphery of western Europe and allow insurgency movements (such as the French Resistance) within the Nazi-controlled territory to break through enemy lines and usher troops in. This plan was achieved brilliantly once the Battle of Normandy was won and the Allied Forces were able to force German troops into a position of retreat.

Critical Overview

Unfortunately, there is little criticism available for "Think of England," in part because Davies has yet to publish his novel *The Bad Shepherd*, from which the latest version of the story is excerpted. Although "Think of England" is included in the anthology *Best American Short Stories 2001*, reviews of that book generally refer to the composition of the volume as a whole, offering plot summaries of a few selected stories rather than focusing on the individual achievements of their authors.

Contemporary Authors Online quotes Jay A. Fernandez's review of Davies' short story collection *The Ugliest House in the World* for *Washington Post Book World*, which observes that Davies writes with "equal authenticity" about disparate historical periods and locales, "evoking time and place with what appears to be an impressive acuity." Also quoted in *Contemporary Authors Online*, a writer for *Kirkus Reviews* notes that the stories in Davies' debut collection exhibit an "unblinking, persuasive view of human nature, as well as a deft hand at plotting." According to *Contemporary Authors Online*, Davies' second collection, *Equal Love*, garnered praise from *Publishers Weekly* for the author's diverse perspectives on the theme of love and the obligations that exist between people, stories which remain unified by Davies' "compassionate voice, sure craftsmanship, and complex vision." Similarly, Jacqueline Carey, in a review for *The New York Times*, noted that Davies' stories are not "dominated by a single, overweening voice: he emphasizes the most basic bonds between people rather than their individual opinions, their quirks of personality."

Criticism

David Remy

Remy is a freelance writer in Warrington, Florida. In the following essay, Remy considers the way

nationalistic beliefs shape the story's characterization and dramatic development.

In Peter Ho Davies' short story "Think of England," the men who frequent The Quarryman's Arms are divided by more than socioeconomic class or their respective languages and cultures; they are divided by an intense nationalism that allows old enmities to persist and flourish, especially during a time of war when everyone must account for his actions and decide if the present course is indeed correct. Once again, the Welsh and the English find their fortunes married to each other, and, once again, they cooperate, however grudgingly. Neither one can fully accept the other's differences. Rather than challenge one another outright, they do so indirectly through furtive glances, jokes, and insinuations. This undercurrent of nationalism is not lost upon Davies' protagonist, for Sarah comprehends both the Welsh- and English-speaking worlds as they occupy their respective places in the pub, though her understanding of nationalistic tendencies is more often than not a projection of her own need to belong to a world outside the borders of her village. Thus, Davies uses nationalistic ideas and beliefs to shape dramatic tension and characterization within the story.

A sense of history pervades the story, one that the Welsh patrons at the public bar are loathe to forget, for The Quarryman's Arms was once a refuge for striking quarrymen; their tankards hang from the ceiling as a testament to the village's undying loyalty even though quarrying has been replaced by sheep farming as a way of life. Still, men like Sarah's father, Arthur, can remember how English troops moved in to quell the Great Strike and the riots at Tonypandy, forever depriving laborers of the opportunity to earn a decent wage. The strikers' rebellious spirit gave rise to nationalistic fervor in the twenties and thirties, and the village would not have survived without it, for British domination at that time was almost too much to bear. Hearing Churchill's voice on the wireless evokes these memories of oppression for the Welsh, as though old hostilities had been renewed against them and not the Axis Powers.

The Welsh patrons' long memories make them cautious, if not suspicious, of the English when they are in their company. Davies uses this sense of history to create a dramatic tension within the story as the Welsh, keeping to the public bar, "nurse their

Sappers from the Royal Engineers at work constructing the Bailey Bridge across the Thames in 1950

beer, suck their pipes, and steal glances down the passage to where Sarah is serving.'' The Welsh sit quietly assessing the English, so many of them dressed in military uniforms made of Welsh wool, as they celebrate the D-Day invasion. The current military actions recall those of the past when the Welsh referred to the British as ''occupiers.'' Indeed, that is the name the Welsh give to the ''sappers,'' or military construction crew, that is building a base on the outskirts of the village. The past is the present, and the two nationalities remain divided. Davies uses these separatist views to underscore the effects that history can have on a place and its people, especially when these people are forced by necessity to coexist.

Even the younger generations, as embodied by sixteen-year-old Sarah, are aware that nationalism can exact a high price. Because so many of the people in her village distrust the British, her affair with Colin must be kept secret. If she is seen with him outside the pub, she risks being ostracized from her father, a ''staunch nationalist.'' Sarah must also keep an eye on Jack, whom she believes is aware of her rendezvous after work, and this suspicion gives even greater weight to her actions. In other words, the village's nationalistic view of the British

draws her toward, rather than shelters her from, the type of love she has always imagined—one filled with glamour, romance, adventure, and even a bit of danger, which, unfortunately, she finds in large supply.

As the story's protagonist, Sarah is keenly aware of her surroundings, though she remains largely unaware of people's private motivations. This incongruity between her interior state of mind and her view of the outside world creates tension within the story that arouses the reader's compassion. Sarah knows that her ''good schoolroom English'' has earned her a job at the lounge bar so that she may act as a buffer between the pub's Welsh proprietor and his English patrons. Like so many of his compatriots, Jack, a veteran of the Great War, blames English imperialism and capitalism for the struggles the Welsh have had to endure. Though the Welsh temporarily set aside their circumspection to celebrate the landings at Normandy, they believe that the outcome of this second world war will be no different than the first as far as they are concerned. Sarah is wise enough to comprehend that provincialism and isolation have contributed to her countrymen's nationalistic views; however, she rather simply believes that their nationalism stems from a

What Do I Read Next?

- Peter Ho Davies' forthcoming novel *The Bad Shepherd* will be published in 2005 by Houghton Mifflin. The novel, of which "Think of England" comprises the first chapter, tells the story of Sarah (whose name has been changed to Esther during the course of the novel's composition) and a German prisoner of war who comes to work on her farm while a mysterious base is being constructed near the village. Other excerpts from the novel have been published as short stories in such publications as *Granta, The Paris Review,* and *The Virginia Quarterly Review.*

- Thus far Davies has published two short story collections: *The Ugliest House in the World* (1997) and *Equal Love* (2000). One story from the first collection, "A Union," contrasts personal beliefs with ideology as quarrymen confront their principals to take a political stance. Davies' stories are renowned for their mystery, humor, and a "bittersweet melancholia," but most of all they are marked by an abiding sense of humanity that establishes an intimate bond between author and reader.

- Andrea Barrett's collection *Ship Fever and Other Stories,* which won the 1996 National Book Award for Fiction, features characters who often use science as a means of establishing relationships and finding love, though, as so many of these characters discover, the ways of the heart are not so easily measured. Writing with deft economy and resonant detail, Barrett combines historical characters with fictional ones to create worlds in which entire lifetimes are encompassed within the span of a mere few pages.

- Published to commemorate the fiftieth anniversary of the D–Day invasion, Stephen Ambrose's book *D–Day, June 6, 1944: The Climactic Battle of World War II* (1994) provides a comprehensive history of the invasion that broke Germany's hold on Europe, comprised as it is of more than 1,400 interviews with sailors, infantrymen, paratroopers, and civilians who witnessed the landings at Normandy first-hand. The author describes in panoramic detail the personalities, political conflicts, and unexpected events that shaped this decisive moment in world history. Ambrose incorporates battlefield accounts to portray the unyielding commitment and initiative that transformed many a dog soldier into a hero.

---

desire "[t]o be important, to be the center of attention, not isolated," a desire she knows all too well and which contributes significantly to the story's denouement.

Consequently, the spirit of the celebration makes Sarah yearn "to be British tonight of all nights." She is a young woman who would rather live in the present moment than talk of "past glories." Sarah is proud to be Welsh, but she feels "a long way from the center of life, from London or Liverpool or . . . America." The soldiers and the crew from the BBC Light Program who have come to the pub to listen to the D-Day radio broadcast have brought the world to her instead. Caught up in the evening's festivities and the renewed hope that has been sown as a result

of the Allied invasion, Sarah views nationalism as part of provincialism, that isolating force in her life, but she also views nationalism as "a way of putting it [North Wales] back in the center, of saying that what's here is important enough. It's a redrawing of the boundaries of what's worthwhile."

Despite a need to belong to something greater and more encompassing than the life she leads presently, Sarah does not forget her Welsh roots. Though she remains curious about the mysterious base under construction at the camp grounds, Sarah refrains from asking Colin about it for fear of betraying the war effort and seeming unpatriotic, for "It [i]t wouldn't do to give the English an excuse to call the Welsh unpatriotic. Only the Welsh, it occurs to her, are allowed to declare themselves that.'' In this regard, Sarah's view of Welsh identity is no different from her father's or that of the other farmers in The Quarryman's Arms. When Sarah's mettle is put to the test, as it is during her encounter with Colin at the pool, she falls back on the language and mores which she has known throughout her life and which have preserved her sense of personal and cultural identity. In a scene that is symbolic of historic relations between the English and Welsh, Sarah expresses herself defiantly in her native language rather than that of her oppressor— ''*Nargois!*'' By uttering a single word, she asserts her indomitable Welsh spirit.

Davies' use of nationalism in ''Think of England'' offers the reader a complex view of life in North Wales, a life that is shaped as much by history and nationalistic pride as it is by current events. The nationalistic perspectives of both the English and the Welsh in The Quarryman's Arms affect Sarah equally, bringing her character to life in a way that is a true coming-of-age story, though in the end it is her ''Welshness'' that renders by far the deepest impression.

Source: David Remy, Critical Essay on ''Think of England,'' in *Short Stories for Students,* Thomson Gale, 2005.

Bryan Aubrey

Aubrey holds a Ph.D. in English and has published many articles on contemporary literature. In this essay, Aubrey discusses ''Think of England'' in the context of the historical relations between the English and the Welsh, and the role of Welsh nationalism in the twentieth century.

In ''Think of England,'' Davies returns to the same setting he chose for his story ''A Union,'' which appeared in his first short story collection, *The Ugliest House in the World.* ''A Union'' takes place in 1899, during a bitter strike at a slate quarry in North Wales. The strike drags on for months as the ruthless employers refuse to give any ground. Hated English soldiers are called in to keep order in the town. Eventually, the union runs out of money and the men straggle back to work. This unnamed town, forty-five years later, is the setting for ''Think of England.'' The village is still scarred by the memory of the strike. Even sixteen-year-old Sarah knows all about how for a generation families of the strikers refused to talk to families of the ''scabs''— men who broke the strike by going back to work. Old resentments continue to be felt in the village, even though Sarah thinks such things are silly,

> When Sarah's mettle is put to the test, as it is during her encounter with Colin at the pool, she falls back on the language and mores which she has known throughout her life and which have preserved her sense of personal and cultural identity."

especially since the quarry has been in decline for years and now employs only one in five of the men in the village. Sarah has learned that only the rise of Welsh nationalism in the 1920s and 1930s kept the town from dying, by reminding the quarreling people of their common enemy, the English. This background sets the stage for the theme of the story, which is the uneasy relations between the Welsh and the English, and the continuing strong national identity of a culturally threatened people.

Davies neatly links nationalistic tensions with sexual aggression, both overt and covert. The title of the story is an ironic allusion to Queen Victoria's oft-quoted advice to those of her female subjects who were horrified at the prospect of meeting the sexual demands of their husbands: ''Close your eyes and think of England.'' Whether knowingly or not, the young English soldier Colin alludes to the famous advice when he says to Sarah, as his sexual pursuit of her heats up, ''Who says you Welsh girls don't know your duty. Proper patriot you are. Thinking of England.'' Patronizing, crass, unfeeling and insulting, the remark well illustrates the dominant metaphor of the story. The sexual aggression of the English men—first the drunken, seedy Harry with his stream of offensive, sexist jokes, and then Colin, who knows what he wants from this young Welsh girl and becomes abusive when he is thwarted—is a metaphor for the relations between the colonizing English and the exploited Welsh. That, at least, is how it might be described from the point of view of the Welsh nationalists.

The subject of Welsh nationalism has never grabbed the world's headlines. When people think

> **" But for the Welsh, as for many minority ethnic groups around the world, the preservation of their language is one of the keys to the survival of their distinct cultural identity."**

of conflict within the United Kingdom over the last thirty-five years, they think not of Wales but of Northern Ireland, where civil unrest has led to thousands of deaths. Nonetheless, Welsh nationalism has at times in the twentieth century been a potent force that the British government, based in London, England, has had to deal with.

Modern Welsh nationalism began in 1925, with the formation of the political party Plaid Cymru (literally, the Party of Wales), the goal of which was to educate the Welsh about their national history and culture. In the late 1960s and 1970s, Plaid Cymru became a powerful electoral force in Wales, winning several seats in the British parliament. During this period there were also hundreds of violent incidents organized by groups such as the Free Wales Army, which placed bombs in public buildings and water pipelines, and the Movement for the Defense of Wales. In 1980, Welsh nationalists set fire to many holiday homes owned by the English in Wales. These homes were unoccupied for most of the year and had an adverse effect on Welsh community life. Davies touched on this issue in his short story, "The Ugliest House in the World," in which a man who has lived for forty years in England retires to a village in North Wales only to have Welsh nationalist slogans daubed on his house.

Relations between the English and the Welsh have a long and complicated history. In 1485, the two kingdoms were united when the Welshman Henry Tudor, leading a mostly Welsh-speaking army, defeated Richard III at the battle of Bosworth to become Henry VII. As John Osmond points out in his "Introduction" to *The National Question Again: Welsh Political Identity in the 1980s,* following Henry Tudor's victory, the Welsh gentry moved to London and began to identify themselves as

British rather than Welsh. Within a short period, Wales was legally incorporated into England by the Act of Union of 1536. Even the phrase "British Empire" was coined (in 1580) by a Welshman, Dr. John Dee, who was scientific advisor to Elizabeth I. Since those early days, Welshmen have often played important roles in British politics. One of the most powerful British prime ministers was the Welshman David Lloyd George, who led the nation during World War I, a war in which two-thirds of Welsh males between the ages of 20 and 40 participated (and which the Welsh nationalists in "Think of England" regard as a war of English imperialism). According to Osmond, Lloyd George "retains an immense psychological influence in Welsh politics because of the way he fused Welsh and British aspirations."

This quotation touches on the vital question: do the Welsh identify with being Welsh or with being British, or somehow with both? Osmond writes of an "ambivalence of identity that runs like a fault line through Welsh society." In surveys conducted between the 1960s and the 1980s, the majority of the Welsh population reported that they identified themselves as Welsh rather than British, although the figures fluctuated considerably. According to Osmond, most Welsh "think of themselves as both Welsh and British, in differing proportions according to the circumstances and the subject under discussion."

This kind of dual identity hovers just beneath the surface in "Think of England." Traditionally, North Wales is more thoroughgoing Welsh than the Anglicized south, and the village in the story is strongly nationalist. The native Welsh and the visiting English, who are mostly soldiers building a new military base nearby, gravitate to different rooms in the pub. They speak different languages and interpret history differently. The Welsh nationalists regard World War II, as they did World War I, as a capitalist, imperialist war fought by England. However, after Winston Churchill, the British prime minister and "voice of England," makes his announcement about D-day on the radio, such anti-English talk in the public bar, where the Welsh assemble, is for a moment stilled. Even if the staunchly Welsh locals do not confess to feeling British at that moment—a proud moment in British history—they are at least not as militantly Welsh as usual. And young Sarah, who comes from a different Welsh generation, wonders shrewdly whether "the locals are as filled with excitement as she is, just too proud to admit it." For herself, she "yearns to be British tonight of all nights.'' Although Sarah, in a ''half-conscious way,'' is proud of being Welsh, she is impatient with Welsh nationalism, which she regards as just a way the locals have of making themselves feel important, of overcoming their sense of isolation. She is quite ready to engage in a flirtation with an English soldier, even though she is aware that this might be considered a ''national betrayal,'' and she certainly does not want to have to admit to her nationalist father that she is going out of the pub with a young Englishman.

And yet in the climax of the story, Sarah, who wants at least for one night to be British rather than Welsh, is forced back into her Welsh identity by the arrogance and aggressiveness of the English Colin. The sudden conflict that flares up between them highlights their national differences through their use of language. Although Sarah speaks English fluently, Welsh is her first language; her ''schoolroom English'' has been learned from textbooks. When she feels frightened by Colin's sexual advances, she lapses back into her native tongue, yelling at him in Welsh, which he does not understand. Then when she accidentally catches him on the chin as she lifts her head, he insults her by yelling an obscene English word that is unknown to her. She in turn curses him in Welsh, which prompts him to tell her, in exasperation, to speak English. At that moment Sarah recalls an incident that occurred between them the previous week. He asked her to teach him some Welsh, but then when she mocked his pronunciation, he sneered, ''Ah, what's the point? Why don't you just give it up and speak English, like the rest of us?'' Sarah responded with a little lecture in which she repeated the nationalist arguments she had heard about the importance of preserving the Welsh language.

This exchange shows in a nutshell a typical interaction between a dominant culture dealing with a cultural and linguistic minority. The dominant culture often fails to take the claims of the other seriously, arrogantly assuming that if the smaller group would just see reason and assimilate into the majority culture, there would be no problem. Interesting in this context is the fact that in the story, one of Harry Hitch's many anti-Welsh jokes pokes malicious fun at the Welsh language, which to unaccustomed English ears sounds strange (since it has less in common with English than either French or German) and also looks daunting on the printed page. But for the Welsh, as for many minority ethnic groups around the world, the preservation of their language is one of the keys to the survival of their

distinct cultural identity. This is why twentieth century Welsh nationalists placed so much emphasis on the survival and promotion of the language. They had some notable successes, such as the Welsh Courts Act of 1942, which allowed Welsh speakers to give evidence in Welsh in court, and the Welsh Language Act of 1967, which established equal validity for Welsh with English in Wales. In spite of these efforts, however, the percentage of Welsh speakers in the population of Wales has steadily declined throughout the twentieth century. In recent decades, economic changes have led to a drift from rural communities, where Welsh was more common, to urban areas that are more thoroughly penetrated by English language and culture. There has also been a movement of English speakers into communities that were formerly mostly Welsh-speaking. Recent surveys suggest that just under 20 percent of Welsh people are able to speak Welsh, although almost all of them are bi-lingual and may speak English far more often than they speak Welsh. Villages such as the one in ''Think of England,'' where most people are Welsh-speakers, are becoming increasingly uncommon. Although Sarah, wanting to evade questions from Colin about the whereabouts of his bicycle, decides ''she'll pretend she's forgotten her English,'' the reality of the twenty-first century is likely to be that more and more people will forget their Welsh.

Source: Bryan Aubrey, Critical Essay on ''Think of England,'' in *Short Stories for Students,* Thomson Gale, 2005.

Peter Ho Davies and Jeremiah Chamberlain

In the following interview, Davies discusses the short story craft and how his novel extracts, such as ''Think of England,'' differ.

Peter Ho Davies, the son of Welsh and Chinese parents, grew up in Britain before moving to the United States in 1992 to pursue his M.A. in creative writing from Boston University. His first published story in the U.S. was anthologized in *Best American Short Stories 1995* and later became the title story for his first collection, *The Ugliest House in the World* (1998). This book received the Oregon Book Award, the MacMillan Silver PEN Award, and the prestigious John Llewellen Prize. His second collection, *Equal Love* (2000), was a finalist for the *L.A. Times* Book Prize and named a *New York Times* Notable Book of the Year. His short fiction has been published in such places as *Harper's Magazine,* the *Atlantic, Paris Review, Ploughshares, Story,* and

Granta. In addition to having been anthologized in *Best American Short Stories* three times, his short fiction has also been selected for *Prize Stories: The O. Henry Awards.* He's received fellowships from the NEA and the Fine Arts Work Center in Provincetown. And this spring he was the recipient of a Guggenheim Award to complete work on his novel-in-progress, *The Bad Shepherd.* Davies lives and teaches in Ann Arbor, where he is the director of the MFA program in creative writing at the University of Michigan. He is about to be a new father. This interview with Jeremiah Chamberlin took place in Ann Arbor in May 2004.

[*Interviewer*]: *You have a wonderful range as a short-fiction writer. Not only are your stories told from myriad points of view in different periods of history, but the topical material stretches from bark robbing to Chinese funeral rituals to Welsh labor strikes to siblings dying of AIDS. Are you purposeful in your range? That is to say, do you push yourself to write beyond your own boundaries and experience?*

[*Davies*]: Yeah. I guess there are two reasons for that. One is a good aesthetic reason and the other is a slightly more embarrassing, pragmatic reason. Because I've been a short story writer for the majority of my career, I feel that one of the advantages, one of the pleasures of the form, is to be able to write a different story every time you sit down to work on a new piece of fiction. And one of the attractions of the form of a collection is that you can range rather wildly story by story across its length. You are not limited in voice, in time, in place, in style, in effect, or tone. So there's an aesthetic pleasure. In *Flaubert's Parrot,* Barnes talks about his character's admiration for Flaubert and the fact that Flaubert was a writer who never wrote the same book twice. I like that. Who has the time to write the same story twice? I'm not taking a long career for granted necessarily. So once you've done the best you can with something, why would you replicate it? That, I suppose, takes me from the aesthetic pleasure in variation to the very practical one. When you publish your first story, it becomes a touchstone, a place of confidence, something you go back to in grim moments and you think, ''At least I could do *that.*'' But then everything you write afterwards, for a little while, you compare to that thing. The first draft of the new story *always* sucks compared to the last draft of the old story. That sense of competing with yourself can be kind of crushing, even overwhelming. I published my first story when I was twenty-one and I didn't publish my next story until I

was twenty-six. This was for a variety of reasons, but one of them at least was that I was trying to write the same story again. Yet every effort to that end would seem to fall short. What I eventually learned was to stop trying to do the same thing. It helped me deal with that sense of competition with myself. So if the last story was very serious, why shouldn't the next one be comic? By changing the framework, changing the terms of comparison, the stories become incommensurable. You can thereby freeze that internal critic, that internal voice of judgment. This method helped me through various writing blocks as well. So that's the pragmatic reason for pushing stories in different directions.

With such diverse topical and structural material, though, how do you then craft a collection to feel whole? How do you order the stories so that the book has a shape?

My two collections represent what I think of as two broad but also divergent approaches to how you put together a collection of stories. *The Ugliest House in the World* is the naïve approach: [*Laughs*] ''Here's all the good stuff I happen to have at the moment, with the longest one in the middle.'' The general advice I'd always heard was that you start with the best story, you have a pretty good one second, and then you end with a really good one. Because, unfortunately, many reviewers might only read the first and last story. I suppose there are certain linkages within some of those stories; there's a little strain of the Welsh historical story. But really those were the best stories I had knocking around. Though I learned it can be dangerous if you don't have an overarching sense of how a collection is coming together. The true (and I hope comic) story I always tell is that when *Ugliest House* was reviewed in Britain, one of the reviews was titled: ''Linked by Flatulence.'' Farting is obviously an important element in the story ''Relief,'' but I hadn't realized that apparently there are also several others where mention is made of flatulence. I thought, ''Oh, my God! This is horrendous.'' Worse, the author photo they used from *Ugliest House,* which has me standing there smiling, had the caption: ''Peter Ho Davies: What's He Smiling About?'' [*Laughs*] When I was working on my second collection, *Equal Love,* I was interested in writing something that was differently structured, had more thematic linkage. Though I stumbled across that to some degree by accident. I had written about half of those stories before I began to think of them as a collection. My wife, Lynne, was reading E. M. Forster's *Where Angels Fear to Tread* at the time, a book I'd read much earlier. We were talking about familial relationships with some friends, and she pointed out the quote that would later become the epigraph for the book. It resonated both with the stories I already had in hand and it also resonated interestingly with the three or four stories I had in mind to write. It was a moment where all those things came together. I could see it as a book in some sense, and as a book that wasn't that far from completion. In terms of putting the collection together, a few things went on in *Equal Love* as I was writing the rest of the stories and conscious of exploring this parent-child dynamic. I didn't want it to be just fathers and sons, but mothers and daughters as well. And I wanted to make sure that the stories reflected on the relationship both from the children's point of view and the parents' point of view as well as at different phases of their respective lives. To some degree I was also interested in that title term, what "equal love" could mean in terms of equality, race, and sexuality, so that the whole case reflects on the equality of love in different ways.

Theme plays an important role in your work, both in individual stories and in your collections as a whole, yet it never feels obtrusive. Some writers overdo theme. The component parts of a story fit together so neatly that they end up feeling fake or forced. Is theme something that you're particularly conscious of when you're writing? And if so, how do you utilize this element of craft?

The process of writing a story is often a process of unpacking the thematic contents. You know you're done with a story when you finally understand why you wrote it in the first place. This, for me, is often a thematic question in certain ways. But the truth is that it's not always the case that you're absolutely done with a piece at that stage. What I tend to find as I'm working through a piece is that thematic echoes or resonances will suggest themselves. One of the ways I feel my way toward what the story is about in the early stages of the revision process is by punching up that thematic stuff. This means that there are probably drafts that overly play out thematic issues or put them overtly on the page. But in later revisions, having internalized the theme to some degree, I can then turn it down. The real question we're talking about here is one of subtlety. I guess one of the reasons I'm willing to trust readers of a short story to find thematic resonances or thematic contents without feeling as though I need to make it too overt is because I have a great deal of faith that people will read a story more than once. That may be naïve, and I'm certainly not

> *Part of the revision work I'm doing right now is to combine scenes that may have been written from two or three different points of view in the past into one definitive scene."*

saying that people should always read *my* stories multiple times, but as a story reader myself, part of the way I think about apprehending a story is through multiple readings. Maybe that allows me to be a little more relaxed about how much I want someone to get on the first reading. I want to offer a certain pleasure, I don't want them to be puzzled or confused by the piece, but there's a layering effect, and I have some faith that people will go back.

You've published a number of excerpts from your novel-in-progress, The Bad Shepherd, *in places such as* Granta *and* Ploughshares *over the last few years. One piece, "Think of England," was even anthologized in* Best American Short Stories—

Much to my embarrassment, since it's a novel extract. At the time I thought it was going to be just a story!

Well, the one thing that seems noticeable to me about the novel extracts as compared to your short stories is their pacing. The extracts, as one might expect, are much slower. They take their time in a different way than the stories do. And the descriptive language seems richer and more evocative than in much of your shorter work. Were these stylistic elements you consciously employed during your writing process, or do you find this type of shift merely indicative of working a novel?

That's a great observation. Initially, it wasn't a conscious strategy. But I think the impulse comes from a couple of different things. Certainly one of them is the feeling of the expansive space of a novel. At the moment, probably more bloody expansive than I need it to be! [*Laughs*] It's partly a result of being a historical piece that's set in north Wales, which is not a very well-known area, so it feels to me as though there's a good deal of period and geographical details that need to be evoked. It's also the desire to give people that sense of immersion that a novel can provide in a time and a place and in the lives of the characters. I was certainly conscious of the fact that I had more room to breathe. You can take deeper breaths, I suppose, because it feels like you're there for a marathon rather than a sprint. As a short story writer, there may also be the feeling that you have to steel yourself to write a novel. You've got to flex those muscles; you've got to bulk up. Another thing I'm thinking about—because this is a very interesting observation—is that because the pages of the novel have been worked over so many times, they have a greater density than some of my other work. Part of the revision work I'm doing right now is to combine scenes that may have been written from two or three different points of view in the past into one definitive scene. And so that's bringing to bear a lot of different information from a lot of different approaches to the work, which is certainly adding a lot to the work in terms of detail and layering.

Some of the stories you set in Wales have a noticeably thicker "accent" than others. The slang that the characters use, as well as certain tonal qualities of the piece, are markedly more Welsh at times. Is that shift based solely on the particular voices of characters, or were you hoping to convey something else as well?

Yeah. It's largely dictated by the voice of the character. Some are just more into colloquial language than others. To some degree it can be a class thing or a period thing; other times it's purely informational. In the British stories, for example, you'll find I try to slip in a contextual detail just to locate people in the locale rather swiftly. This is more an aside than an answer to your question, but when I was working on *Equal Love* and I sent it to my British publisher, one of the things that my editor expressed was a mild disappointment with the fact that there were fewer British-based stories than in *Ugliest House*. This was something I had been very conscious of. I'd wanted *Equal Love* to be a book I'd written (or attempted to write) set largely in the U.S. because I felt it was an important thing to do if I was going to stay in the States and continue to teach here. Though I did worry a bit about losing my British accent. In the first three or four years of being here, I could go back to Britain, go to a pub with some friends, and throw the switch. Immediately I'd shift from saying "soccer" to "football." I knew the pop culture references. But somewhere around that third or fourth year, I couldn't access it

as quickly. Partly that's just becoming embedded in a more American idiom. But also I just wasn't in touch with it anymore. So I decided with *Equal Love* that I would try to translate one of the stories in the American version of the book into a British setting and idiom. I chose the story that's now titled "Everything You Can Remember in 30 Seconds Is Yours to Keep" partly because I really liked the reference to that old game show that I'd watched growing up as a child in Britain. Also, it felt like a bit of a stretch to have an American character caught up in that show and I thought I could do more with the piece in a British setting. As I worked my way through the new revision, I kept asking myself what changes would be necessary. I'd done a little translation work before, so I thought of the process in translation terms. What would be the parallels? What would be the language, the appropriate reference points? And as I wrote about the British characters, I got slightly closer to them because I knew them in a slightly different way. I could share their histories. Oddly, I was then able to take back that little extra knowledge to my American characters. So now there exists in the U.S. edition the U.S.-set version of the story. And in the British edition of the book there is a British-set version of that story.

Did you keep the same title in both collections?

Yes. Though what's even more confusing is that the story was originally published in *Granta* magazine under the title "Fit Mother." They preferred the American version of the story. I have a lovely letter from the editor, Ian Jack, who's involved with their book publication division as well, who seemed worried that I was planning on translating the whole collection! The note related an anecdote about James Joyce and his encounter with one of the great American editors of the period, someone who had seen *Dubliners* in manuscript. Joyce and the editor sat down, and the man said to Joyce: "I love these stories, Mr. Joyce. They're wonderful. I have only one tiny, small suggestion. I'd like you to call the book *New Yorkers.*" [*Laughs*] I think Ian was suggesting that I should be careful not to think about doing this. Of course I had no intention of doing it with the whole book, but I thought it was a very interesting exercise. I like both versions, and I think both versions benefit from the existence of the other. Though I've never done it since. The one comment Ian did make when he saw the British version of the story—and I subsequently revised it because I think he was right—was that I'd overcompensated. I always joke that I know when I go back to Britain and sit in a pub that I sound much more British than I do when I'm teaching a class or attending a faculty meeting here. And I'm always worried that I'll start to sound like the artful dodger: "Gor' blimey, guv'ner! Stone the crows! Lor' luv a duck!" But my worst fear is that it will show up on the page. And Ian's response to the story was that it felt, in regards to the Britishisms, a bit "over-egged." It's a great phrase. Like a flan, I guess. And he was right. So I turned it down a bit. It was over-voiced and it was over-accented because of a kind of anxiety and lack of confidence on my part. We're often tempted as writers to write these very "voicey" pieces. There's a certain strand of work that's very voicey, that lives and dies by its voice. But many of them, I feel, live *only* by their voice. Now I look at those pieces and say, "Ah, yes. That's a bit over-egged." [*Laughs*] I think it's an interesting critical term for a certain kind of work.

Two of your most recent pieces of short fiction, "The Criminal Mastermind," which was published recently in Harper's, and a forthcoming story of similar style and subject matter entitled "The Name of the Great Detective," are both quite abstract compared to much of your other work and seem rather pointed in their politics. Is this new work indicative of needing a break from the novel, a political response to the current cultural climate, or simply another example of pushing yourself stylistically as a writer?

The stories do represent a certain response to writing a novel. Or, more accurately, given that I wrote both of them in the winter semester last year, they're both probably reactions to *not* working on the novel. I have a lot of difficulty writing when I'm teaching and directing the program. I describe them, particularly given their content, as "jail breaks" from the novel, from the stylistic and voice envelope of the novel. Some of the thematic ideas of entrapment, imprisonment, escape, crime, and justice—because the novel deals, in part, with Nazi war criminals like Hess and Göring in Nuremberg— were no doubt floating around in my mind. They just found another outlet in these stories. At the time I was also teaching a history of the short story class in which part of the thesis, an idea that is not unique to me by any means, is the concept that the short story has these two very broad, fairly distinct streams. One is the more realistic stream that you find in writers like Chekhov and later Carver. The other is a more fantastical stream that runs most obviously through Kafka and Borges and Barthelme. And you can argue that both of those can be represented in the birth of the modern short story in the work of

Gogol. "The Overcoat," even though it has fantastical elements, feels in the portrayal of the little man like a realistic story, albeit slightly heightened. And "The Nose," of course, feels like it runs in that completely fantastical vein. However, I think both of these approaches represented responses to the same issue, which is the brevity of the story. Because a story is so brief, you don't have a lot of room to explain things. One attitude, then, is to just tell a story about the world you recognize because that way you don't have to explain that world. The other attitude is to say, "Well, I'm just going to tell you this fantastic tale and I'm not going to bother to explain this fantastic world." So stories represent a limited amount of space to explain and contextualize. And I realized, talking about this with my students, that I'd worked almost exclusively on one side of that divide. I suppose that my argument was that those two streams weren't as distant as one might argue, and I just thought it would be curious to work in that other vein. I'd already been knocking around some of the logical progressions in the story "The Great Detective" and had thought about them from various angles and even written about the ideas a couple of different drafts. But I'd always struggled voicing some of those ideas of what a perfect crime would be in a realistic story. And I just thought that that could be a very interesting way of approaching the material in a different vein.

So you wrote "The Great Detective" prior to "The Criminal Mastermind"?

It's almost as though I had to write "The Great Detective" before I could write "The Criminal Mastermind." The material suggested its partner. Having written about a detective, it seemed logical to write about a criminal. The way I think of both of these stories to a certain extent are as thought experiments. They feel like logical progressions. *If* this premise, *then* this progressive series of corollaries follows from that premise. The narrative energy is driven by logic, even if the premise you begin from is kooky. So you see those ramifications played out with a kind of inevitability that I think can approach the tragic, but also the tragi-comic. With regards to the political elements, I have to admit that I was not deeply focused on that aspect of the stories as I wrote them. Though as I revised the stories, I was very conscious of the possibility of tilting them in ways that would be very much caught up in the politics of the moment. When "The Criminal Mastermind" came out in *Harper's,* people would say to me: "Who were you thinking of as the criminal? Were you thinking of, say, Saddam

Hussein, for instance?'' No. That wasn't in my mind remotely as I wrote it. I don't think he'd even been captured yet. If I was thinking of anyone, I might have been thinking about the German war criminals because of the novel I've been working on for the last five years. But it wasn't a conscious thought. Still, the legal environment is so charged at the moment that I think a lot written about this period would feel imbued with political significance. It just feels that we live in heightened political times.

Speaking of history and politics, I was interested by your choice to have such a well-known historical figure as Rudolph Hess be a character in your novel. You could have very easily chosen to hide behind the veil of fiction and written a character who resembled Hess in all ways but name, a character that your reader would easily recognize as Hess, yet despite the risk of criticism and scrutiny you decided to take him on directly. Was it challenging to give life to this man because of the weight of historical record?

Hess, oddly for me as a writer, is not as hard a historical figure to give life to than perhaps some others might be. Where the historical record is concerned, Hess remains an enigma: we don't really know why he flew to Britain, or if his amnesia was real. If it was real, then what was it in response to? What psychological trauma made him so forgetful? There are lots of theories. Was he on a peace mission to Britain to allow Germany to concentrate on the eastern front? Had he essentially been expelled from Hitler's inner circle and was fleeing in fear for his life? Or was he just simply mad? He's the Hamlet of the Third Reich in a certain sense. And I've been attracted over time to these little bubbles of history where we just don't know what went on in that space. And *that's* the space, where the historical record has a blank surface to it, into which we can interpose fiction very easily. That's a vacuum that fiction goes into. People ask me: ''Were your parents great storytellers?'' And the answer is, no. Much less so now that I've started to publish work. [*Laughs*] As a kid, my mother told me little snippets of some stories, or some parts of her life in Malaysia when she was a kid. But they wouldn't be linked up. They wouldn't have any narrative movement to them. My father would do the same; there'd be a little bit here, a little bit there. But in your mind, you make stories of those things. You put together these unconnected pieces. And they may not resemble the truth exactly, but there's a way you've made sense of them by linking them up. Hess has a gap

like that. And fiction goes into that space. Also, there's a thrill to finding unexpected or surprising truths, factual truths, buried in fiction. When I was researching the book, I knew that Hess had been held in a Welsh safe house for a time. But what I did not know was that Hess's father's first wife—not Hess's mother but the woman his father had married before his mother—was a Welsh woman. When I discovered that Hess's father had worked in Britain and had married a Welsh woman and that this woman had died and had been buried in a Welsh cemetery, then it had to be Hess. Because it's such a bizarre coincidence. I've been to that graveyard and I've seen the grave. If it was fiction you couldn't make it up!

So what responsibility do you have to history as a fiction writer? Can you only write about those pockets where there's little or no record? Or can you overlay fiction over the top of history?

The instinct to lay fiction over the top of history, if you like, is simply the instinct to understand *why* certain things happened. I've talked about Hess as a character, as a mysterious figure in the Second World War. In the same way, how Göring gets the cyanide pill in prison that he kills himself with is a minor mystery of the end of the Second World War. History, I think, to some degree, after various investigations, has to stand back out of factual responsibility and say: ''We just don't know. We don't have the answers to that. We can't ascertain the truth. Maybe it'll come out in research, but we just don't know.'' And yet, as human beings, we want to know! So I suppose there's a desire—and I think it's a responsible desire—to understand the world, to posit possibilities and hypotheses. Given my scientific background, I think that's how we apprehend the world: we posit our hypothesis, we put it out there, we test it through the writing and we test it through the fiction, test it arguably through the publishing and the reading, to see whether it rings true to people. Whether it's the truth or not, it has the possibility to provide an explanation. One of the consolations of fiction is that it provides explanations for things we don't understand in life, in our own lives, and in the world around us.

Your short fiction seems so conscious of structure and form. There's a wonderful elegance to your work, structurally. Do you think that there are a limitless number or forms? Or, as writers, do we tend to recycle structures?

I certainty don't feel myself to be inventing structures when I'm writing stories. Very often you're given the gift of a great idea. It just comes from somewhere. Then the struggle is to find a form, a voice, a style that best serves that idea. My sense is that there are enough structures out there already to serve most of the stories I want to tell. There's an argument that says if you have something very original you want to say, then you should generate a very original voice or form or style with which to tell it. I think that's true, but I also think that storytelling has been around a long time. It's about communication. I don't want to invent a new language to communicate with you. I want to use the language that we know. Issues of form are part of that language.

So do form and structure operate best when they're invisible?

For me that's true. As a reader, when I see form and structure fronted in the course of the story, I become very conscious of the writer. In some instances I think it's very useful to be aware of who's telling you the story because it can lend itself to very interesting effects. But I don't want it to be there in most of the stories I come across—it feels as though it's an indication of some "slippage" on the part of the author. I want to pay attention to the world that's being created, not to the writer who's created that world. Because form is a language, a means of communication, when you alter it radically, you may very well have created a new and original form, but you run the risk that no one will be able to understand the "grammar." Like with language, we don't create new words so much as combine the existing ones in fresh, hopefully exciting new ways. So I think it's possible to approach form in that fashion. It doesn't have to be a straightjacket. There's a bit of wiggle room with the way in which we combine certain ideas or forms or structures. And I think that that can provide some amount of novelty, but also some comprehensible and recognizable novelty.

Stories often come to bear, in a certain sense, on a singular image. When writing a novel, do you find ourself looking for that crystallizing moment in the arc of a chapter?

I absolutely do. That's one of those storytelling instincts or touchstones or places of trust where you feel the writing is going well. When I come across them, I'm very excited. The anxiety for me is whether a novel can bear moments like that in every single chapter. In a collection, for example, when you come to that crystallizing moment in a particular story, that climax, I want that experience to be so

satisfying that you can't read on. Not simply because there's so much to think about, but also that there's a charged emotional state that makes you want to stay in that place. The story collection as a whole is something that story-by-story should stop you in your tracks, whereas the novel is all about keeping you going forward. My story-writing instinct is to try and end each chapter the way I'd end a story. But does that serve the novel? I'm not sure. As a reader of novels, there are plenty of books I like where I can stop at the end of a chapter and say, "Yeah. I'm going to read just a chapter today. I'm going to get a lot out of this chapter and then read another one tomorrow."

Since we're on the topic of reading what are some influential books that have come through your life? It's stock question, but was there a particular book that made you want to be a writer? Or books and writers you feel have influenced your style?

My standard caveat to this question is that we're lousy judges of our own influences. Though I tend to think that the most influential books we read are the ones we read in our teens. Because that's often the period when we first encounter real books. That is to say, adult literature. So, in my early teens, the only thing I ever read and the only thing I wanted to write was science fiction. I read and wrote a lot of bad science fiction. But probably the single most influential book in my life was called *Who Writes Science Fiction?* It was a book of interviews with science fiction writers. I hadn't read half the authors in the collection, but it made me think that people with scientific backgrounds—my father was an engineer, I was going to go to college and study science—could also be writers. So the very idea of being able to put myself in the shoes of these scientists and engineers, which I *could* do, and then think of them as writers, made it possible for me to imagine myself becoming a writer. And I was struck, in the ways that you would be struck as a teenage boy, by Ray Bradbury saying, "I became a writer because I wanted complete strangers to fall in love with me." For a teenage boy, that sounded pretty damn good! [*Laughs*] The book also had an interview with Kurt Vonnegut, which led me to Vonnegut's science fiction. Then Vonnegut became my gateway drug to literary fiction. Because once you read *Slaughterhouse Five,* it's a very small step to reading *Catch 22.* And when you read *Catch 22,* it's not that big a step to reading *The Naked and the Dead.* With Mailer, you're in the complete literary mainstream of modern American fiction. And once you've gone into Mailer, it's very easy to go into

Hemingway. I loved Hemingway and I read everything by him I could lay my hands on. I think of both Vonnegut and Hemingway as early writing teachers. From Vonnegut, I learned that paragraphs mattered; each paragraph is like a self-contained joke. Each paragraph did *work*. It gets you from a premise to a punch line. And it just made me think a little bit more about structure beyond the level of sentences. Hemingway taught an obvious lesson: you don't need to have two adjectives for every noun. Which, of course, as a fourteen-year-old, is what your teachers are praising you for. ''Oh, what a big vocabulary you've got in every freaking sentence you wrote!'' Those writers were enough to keep me going through much of my teens.

A friend of mine, Mike Hinken, a writer whose own work I admire, has a theory that writers who were formerly scientists have an inherent interest in systems and patterns, in identifying and classifying, and that those impulses might go a long way toward the way in which they utilize structure and form. Would you agree with this assessment?

I think that might be true. To look at the most recent stories of mine, those logical progressions aren't very far from certain things I enjoyed about science: you follow the progressions and they make sense, they fit together in certain ways. So I'm certain that those kinds of impulses played through.

But unlike someone such as Andrea Barrett or your colleague here at the University of Michigan, Eileen Pollack, both of whom also have very strong science backgrounds, and in whose writing scientific elements often show up either in the lives of their characters or as story components, you rarely write about science in your work.

I guess that's because I was a bad science student. Frankly, I don't think I'd ever write about science well or with much authority. But also, while I was studying science in Britain, I was a double major. The degree was called ''Physics and the Analysis of Science and Technology.'' I studied the history and philosophy of science as much as the physics itself. I remember being particularly struck by Thomas Kuhn's ideas of the scientific revolutions and the notion that scientists are engaged, most of the time, with what is known as ''normal science.'' You work with an accepted theory and an accepted hypothesis without questioning them. But the more scientists work within a theory, eventually someone will bump up against the limit of it and find a flaw in it, a question mark, something that's not quite working ultimately. Others will continue

to work within the theory productively and usefully. Maybe even the person who discovers this anomaly won't pursue it immediately, but will just set it aside. But sooner or later, somebody will come back to that anomaly, and it will be the spark that destroys the current theory, forcing it to be replaced by something larger and bigger. We go in, we reevaluate the whole thing, and we create a new theorem. That's how science progresses by these leaps forward, these revolutions. The logical structure is a vision of evolution, in a way, but it's an evolution of ideas. That's great to me. Working through a story is the extrapolation of possibilities.

So do you see yourself ''solving'' rather than ''creating'' stories?

I think of it as a problem-solving activity, but one that's more complicated than, say, a physics problem because *I'm* creating the problem. Part of my task is to clarify what the problem is. In the early draft of a story, the workshop question is not ''How do we fix this problem?'' but ''What exactly is the problem?'' You have to spend a lot of time figuring out what is exactly problematic in the story. Of course, describing the problem is ultimately perhaps the end of the story. It's such a Chekhovian idea: we don't have to provide the answer; we just have to express the questions as clearly as we can.

You received a Guggenheim this year. So for the first time in a number of years, you won't be teaching this fall. What are your thoughts on the writer in academia? Does time in the classroom inspire you, or does academic life stifle a writer? How do you strike a balance between teaching and writing?

The issue of balance is like the Holy Grail for writers in academia. When I first started teaching, I kept beating myself up about it. I felt like I was failing because I couldn't figure out how to balance the job and the writing. But I've found out now after talking to enough older colleagues that not everybody gets that balance. And, in fact, the people who don't get that balance are probably the people I respect most. Because in the way they are ''unbalanced,'' so to speak, they are unbalanced in favor of their teaching. They put something else and somebody else before themselves. In some cases, it probably cost them a book. Or, at least, delayed the publication of a book by three or four years. Because writers are generally selfish creatures, that selflessness is impressive to me. It also made me feel like I didn't have to feel like a fool for working hard as a teacher. For me, though, teaching has often spurred my writing. It's certainly clarified my ideas about writing. It's also true that I'm not the kind of writer who can sit at my desk for eight hours a day. It's just not the way I'm wired. So I've got to do something with the rest of the time! [*Laughs*] And I like the social interaction. Teaching also feels to me—and I'm not saying I'm Albert Schweitzer here—like a less selfish activity. It feels like an engagement with other people, an opportunity to give something to other people. Which is not to say that I don't get a lot back from my students as well, I do, but it makes me feel very whole as a person. Now, in a perfect world, would I want to have a full teaching load *and* write? No. In a perfect world, I'd love to have just one class per semester. But teaching itself—partly because I've done it for a while now—is mostly pleasurable. Particularly teaching workshop. The academic life is a little more complicated than just the teaching and the writing, though, because there's also the administrative side, which is harder. Luckily I'm fairly good at this and I can get through bureaucratic tasks quickly. But once I'm done, it's like I've been drinking caffeine for five hours. My brain is just spinning. And that ain't no way to write. Because writing isn't about doing a task in five minutes, it's about doing a task in five hours. Still, I'm lucky because I get to teach graduate students, and I get to teach writing students. As a writing teacher I'm spoiled because almost every student in the class wants to be there. Not necessarily to be with me, but to be in a writing class in general. It isn't an economics class. The part of teaching that's serving students, engaging with students, is easy.

The last question I'd like to ask is one that my friend Dan Wickett, the founder of The Emerging Writer's Network, always poses to his interviewees. Since we've already been talking about Bradbury, this feels particularly apt. The question is: If you were a character in Fahrenheit 451, *what book would you memorize for posterity?*

The one that comes to mind—and I'm mentioning this because we haven't talked about it and yet I do think it's a book that had an influence—is *Zen and the Art of Motorcycle Maintenance.* I must have read it five or six times when I was in college. I haven't read it in a long time. But in ways that I couldn't put my finger on now exactly, I think it was an important text for me. I think it was a book that shaped some of the ways I thought. I remember seeing on the jacket of that book when I bought it for class: "This book will change your life." You read that and you instantly think: "Bullshit. Not going to happen. My life ain't changed yet." But it might be

the truest blurb I ever read. There's an intellectual fervor to that book; thought and feelings seem inextricably linked. There are elements of melodrama, but it's got power to it. I value a lot of things in that book. It was a pop-cultural phenomenon, but it's a book that feels like it's got legs to me. So if I were to be a mouthpiece for a text, if I wanted to embody a piece of writing, I guess I'd be happy to embody that one.

Source: Peter Ho Davies and Jeremiah Chamberlain, "Interview with Peter Ho Davies," in *Virginia Quarterly Review,* Vol. 80, No. 3, Summer 2004, pp. 1–11 (see also http://www. virginia.edu/vqr/viewmedia.php/prmMID/8945).

Sources

Ambrose, Stephen E., *D–Day June 6, 1944: The Climactic Battle of World War II,* Simon & Schuster, 1994, p. 501.

Bolick, Katie, "On the Sly," in *Atlantic Unbound,* December 16, 1998, http://www.theatlantic.com/unbound/factfict/ff9812.htm (accessed September 16, 2004).

Carey, Jacqueline, "Ties That Grind," in the *New York Times,* March 19, 2000, p. 11.

Chamberlin, Jeremiah, "Interview with Peter Ho Davies," in the *Virginia Quarterly Review,* June 23, 2004, http://www.virginia.edu/vqr/viewmedia.php/prmMID/8945 (accessed November 29, 2004).

Contemporary Authors Online, "Peter Ho Davies," in *Contemporary Authors Online,* Gale, 2003.

D'Este, Carlo, *Decision in Normandy,* E. P. Dutton, 1983, pp. 65, 107–19.

Davies, John, *A History of Wales,* Penguin, 1993, pp. 169–74, 485–93.

Davies, Peter Ho, "The Bad Shepherd," in *Ploughshares,* Vol. 29, Issue 2–3, Fall 2003, pp. 12–21.

———, "Contributors' Notes," in *The Best American Short Stories 2001,* edited by Barbara Kingsolver, series edited by Katrina Kenison, Houghton Mifflin, 2001, p. 347.

———, "The Ends," in the *Paris Review,* Vol. 162, Summer 2002, pp. 10–14.

———, "Leading Men," in *Granta,* No. 81, Spring 2003, pp. 194–222.

———, "The New Corporal," in the *Virginia Quarterly Review,* Vol. 80, No. 3, Summer 2004, pp. 90–107.

———, "Think of England," in *The Best American Short Stories 2001,* edited by Barbara Kingsolver, series edited by Katrina Kenison, Houghton Mifflin, 2001, pp. 62–77.

de Groot, Jerome, "Interview with Peter Ho Davies," in *Bookmunch,* http://www.bookmunch.co.uk/view.php?id=1213 (accessed November 29, 2004).

FitzGibbon, Constantine, *The Winter of the Bombs: The Story of the Blitz of London,* W. W. Norton, 1957, pp. xii–xv.

Keegan, John, *Six Armies in Normandy: From D–Day to the Liberation of Paris, June 6th–August 25th, 1944,* Viking Press, 1982, pp. 69–71.

Keen, Richard, and Ian Burgum, *Wales,* Cassell Paperbacks, 2001, p. 17.

Manchester, William, *The Last Lion: Winston Spencer Churchill, Visions of Glory, 1874–1932,* Little, Brown, 1983, pp. 417–18, 796–99.

Morgan, Kenneth O., *Wales in British Politics, 1868–1922,* 3d ed., 1980, reprint, University of Wales Press, 1991, p. 250.

Morgan, Ted, *Churchill: Young Man in a Hurry, 1874–1915,* Simon and Schuster, 1982, pp. 284–87.

Morris, Jan, *The Matter of Wales: Epic Views of a Small Country,* with photographs by Paul Wakefield, Oxford University Press, 1984, pp. 54, 66, 69–70, 165.

Osmond, John, ''Introduction,'' in *The National Question Again: Welsh Political Identity in the 1980s,* edited by John Osmond, Gomer Press, 1985, pp. xix–xlvi.

Platt, Colin, *The Castle in Medieval England and Wales,* Barnes & Noble Books, 1996, pp. 63–75.

Rodger, George, *The Blitz: The Photography of George Rodger,* with an introduction by Tom Hopkinson, Penguin, 1990, pp. 8–11.

Ziegler, Philip, *London at War, 1939–1945,* Alfred A. Knopf, 1995, pp. 150–61.

Further Reading

Morgan, Kenneth O., *Wales in British Politics, 1868–1922,* 3d ed., 1980, reprint, University of Wales Press, 1991.
   Morgan, an author of more than twenty-five books on British history, explores the indifferent, if not contemptuous, attitude mid-Victorian Britain had toward the Welsh. Eventually, this attitude evolved into an intelligent, though at times slightly patronizing, understanding of Welsh nationalism, which Morgan addresses thoroughly from a political and sociological point of view.

Nixon, Barbara M., *Raiders Overhead: A Diary of the London Blitz,* rev. and enl. ed., Scolar Press, 1980.
   Nixon's personal account of her duty as an air raid warden describes in detail the role she and other wardens performed in service of their fellow Britons during the Blitz. Nixon offers a view from the ground, as it were, as London prepared for the Germans' nightly attacks. What makes the book even more remarkable as a historical record is that Nixon was one of the few female wardens working in a male-dominated field.

Reynolds, Quentin, *A London Diary,* Random House, 1941.
   Reynolds, a former journalist and broadcaster, offers a glimpse into the ways Londoners carried on with their everyday lives during the Blitz. Filled with amusing, enlightening anecdotes, Reynolds's diary demonstrates why so many citizens were regarded as heroes by their fellow countrymen.

Rodger, George, *The Blitz: The Photography of George Rodger,* with an introduction by Tom Hopkinson, Penguin, 1990.
   Rodger, a photojournalist and founding member of Magnum Photos, captures the humanity and integrity of those who endured the onslaught of the German attacks on London. Rodger's photographs exhibit a consummate skill with the camera that never imposes distance between the photographer and his subject, thus creating scenes which appear to occur naturally because they lack artifice.

Stanier, Peter, *Quarries of England and Wales: An Historic Photographic Record,* Twelveheads Press, 1995.
   Illustrated with a selection of photographs taken by the British Geographic Survey, this book documents the methods and machinery used in stone quarries during the period from 1904 to 1935. Quarrying stone is one of the oldest industries known, and Stanier's history captures the timeless quality of this endeavor whose legacy endures in architectural monuments and civic engineering projects throughout Great Britain.

Glossary of Literary Terms

A

Aestheticism: A literary and artistic movement of the nineteenth century. Followers of the movement believed that art should not be mixed with social, political, or moral teaching. The statement "art for art's sake" is a good summary of aestheticism. The movement had its roots in France, but it gained widespread importance in England in the last half of the nineteenth century, where it helped change the Victorian practice of including moral lessons in literature. Edgar Allan Poe is one of the best-known American "aesthetes."

Allegory: A narrative technique in which characters representing things or abstract ideas are used to convey a message or teach a lesson. Allegory is typically used to teach moral, ethical, or religious lessons but is sometimes used for satiric or political purposes. Many fairy tales are allegories.

Allusion: A reference to a familiar literary or historical person or event, used to make an idea more easily understood. Joyce Carol Oates's story "Where Are You Going, Where Have You Been?" exhibits several allusions to popular music.

Analogy: A comparison of two things made to explain something unfamiliar through its similarities to something familiar, or to prove one point based on the acceptance of another. Similes and metaphors are types of analogies.

Antagonist: The major character in a narrative or drama who works against the hero or protagonist. The Misfit in Flannery O'Connor's story "A Good Man Is Hard to Find" serves as the antagonist for the Grandmother.

Anthology: A collection of similar works of literature, art, or music. Zora Neale Hurston's "The Eatonville Anthology" is a collection of stories that take place in the same town.

Anthropomorphism: The presentation of animals or objects in human shape or with human characteristics. The term is derived from the Greek word for "human form." The fur necklet in Katherine Mansfield's story "Miss Brill" has anthropomorphic characteristics.

Anti-hero: A central character in a work of literature who lacks traditional heroic qualities such as courage, physical prowess, and fortitude. Anti-heroes typically distrust conventional values and are unable to commit themselves to any ideals. They generally feel helpless in a world over which they have no control. Anti-heroes usually accept, and often celebrate, their positions as social outcasts. A well-known anti-hero is Walter Mitty in James Thurber's story "The Secret Life of Walter Mitty."

Archetype: The word archetype is commonly used to describe an original pattern or model from which all other things of the same kind are made. Archetypes are the literary images that grow out of the "collective unconscious," a theory proposed by psychologist Carl Jung. They appear in literature as incidents and plots that repeat basic patterns of life. They may also appear as stereotyped characters. The "schlemiel" of Yiddish literature is an archetype.

Autobiography: A narrative in which an individual tells his or her life story. Examples include Benjamin Franklin's *Autobiography* and Amy Hempel's story "In the Cemetery Where Al Jolson Is Buried," which has autobiographical characteristics even though it is a work of fiction.

Avant-garde: A literary term that describes new writing that rejects traditional approaches to literature in favor of innovations in style or content. Twentieth-century examples of the literary *avant-garde* include the modernists and the minimalists.

B

Belles-lettres: A French term meaning "fine letters" or "beautiful writing." It is often used as a synonym for literature, typically referring to imaginative and artistic rather than scientific or expository writing. Current usage sometimes restricts the meaning to light or humorous writing and appreciative essays about literature. Lewis Carroll's *Alice in Wonderland* epitomizes the realm of belles-lettres.

Bildungsroman: A German word meaning "novel of development." The *bildungsroman* is a study of the maturation of a youthful character, typically brought about through a series of social or sexual encounters that lead to self-awareness. J. D. Salinger's *Catcher in the Rye* is a *bildungsroman*, and Doris Lessing's story "Through the Tunnel" exhibits characteristics of a *bildungsroman* as well.

Black Aesthetic Movement: A period of artistic and literary development among African Americans in the 1960s and early 1970s. This was the first major African-American artistic movement since the Harlem Renaissance and was closely paralleled by the civil rights and black power movements. The black aesthetic writers attempted to produce works of art that would be meaningful to the black masses. Key figures in black aesthetics included one of its founders, poet and playwright Amiri Baraka, formerly known as LeRoi Jones; poet and essayist Haki R. Madhubuti, formerly Don L. Lee; poet and playwright Sonia Sanchez; and dramatist Ed Bullins. Works representative of the Black Aesthetic Movement include Amiri Baraka's play *Dutchman,* a 1964 Obie award-winner.

Black Humor: Writing that places grotesque elements side by side with humorous ones in an attempt to shock the reader, forcing him or her to laugh at the horrifying reality of a disordered world. "Lamb to the Slaughter," by Roald Dahl, in which a placid housewife murders her husband and serves the murder weapon to the investigating policemen, is an example of black humor.

C

Catharsis: The release or purging of unwanted emotions—specifically fear and pity—brought about by exposure to art. The term was first used by the Greek philosopher Aristotle in his *Poetics* to refer to the desired effect of tragedy on spectators.

Character: Broadly speaking, a person in a literary work. The actions of characters are what constitute the plot of a story, novel, or poem. There are numerous types of characters, ranging from simple, stereotypical figures to intricate, multifaceted ones. "Characterization" is the process by which an author creates vivid, believable characters in a work of art. This may be done in a variety of ways, including (1) direct description of the character by the narrator; (2) the direct presentation of the speech, thoughts, or actions of the character; and (3) the responses of other characters to the character. The term "character" also refers to a form originated by the ancient Greek writer Theophrastus that later became popular in the seventeenth and eighteenth centuries. It is a short essay or sketch of a person who prominently displays a specific attribute or quality, such as miserliness or ambition. "Miss Brill," a story by Katherine Mansfield, is an example of a character sketch.

Classical: In its strictest definition in literary criticism, classicism refers to works of ancient Greek or Roman literature. The term may also be used to describe a literary work of recognized importance (a "classic") from any time period or literature that exhibits the traits of classicism. Examples of later works and authors now described as classical include French literature of the seventeenth century, Western novels of the nineteenth century, and American fiction of the mid-nineteenth century such as that written by James Fenimore Cooper and Mark Twain.

Climax: The turning point in a narrative, the moment when the conflict is at its most intense. Typically, the structure of stories, novels, and plays is one of rising action, in which tension builds to the climax, followed by falling action, in which tension lessens as the story moves to its conclusion.

Comedy: One of two major types of drama, the other being tragedy. Its aim is to amuse, and it typically ends happily. Comedy assumes many forms, such as farce and burlesque, and uses a variety of techniques, from parody to satire. In a restricted sense the term comedy refers only to dramatic presentations, but in general usage it is commonly applied to nondramatic works as well.

Comic Relief: The use of humor to lighten the mood of a serious or tragic story, especially in plays. The technique is very common in Elizabethan works, and can be an integral part of the plot or simply a brief event designed to break the tension of the scene.

Conflict: The conflict in a work of fiction is the issue to be resolved in the story. It usually occurs between two characters, the protagonist and the antagonist, or between the protagonist and society or the protagonist and himself or herself. The conflict in Washington Irving's story "The Devil and Tom Walker" is that the Devil wants Tom Walker's soul but Tom does not want to go to hell.

Criticism: The systematic study and evaluation of literary works, usually based on a specific method or set of principles. An important part of literary studies since ancient times, the practice of criticism has given rise to numerous theories, methods, and "schools," sometimes producing conflicting, even contradictory, interpretations of literature in general as well as of individual works. Even such basic issues as what constitutes a poem or a novel have been the subject of much criticism over the centuries. Seminal texts of literary criticism include Plato's *Republic,* Aristotle's *Poetics,* Sir Philip Sidney's *The Defence of Poesie,* and John Dryden's *Of Dramatic Poesie.* Contemporary schools of criticism include deconstruction, feminist, psychoanalytic, poststructuralist, new historicist, postcolonialist, and reader-response.

D

Deconstruction: A method of literary criticism characterized by multiple conflicting interpretations of a given work. Deconstructionists consider the impact of the language of a work and suggest that the true meaning of the work is not necessarily the meaning that the author intended.

Deduction: The process of reaching a conclusion through reasoning from general premises to a specific premise. Arthur Conan Doyle's character Sherlock Holmes often used deductive reasoning to solve mysteries.

Denotation: The definition of a word, apart from the impressions or feelings it creates in the reader. The word "apartheid" denotes a political and economic policy of segregation by race, but its connotations—oppression, slavery, inequality—are numerous.

Denouement: A French word meaning "the unknotting." In literature, it denotes the resolution of conflict in fiction or drama. The *denouement* follows the climax and provides an outcome to the primary plot situation as well as an explanation of secondary plot complications. A well-known example of *denouement* is the last scene of the play *As You Like It* by William Shakespeare, in which couples are married, an evildoer repents, the identities of two disguised characters are revealed, and a ruler is restored to power. Also known as "falling action."

Detective Story: A narrative about the solution of a mystery or the identification of a criminal. The conventions of the detective story include the detective's scrupulous use of logic in solving the mystery; incompetent or ineffectual police; a suspect who appears guilty at first but is later proved innocent; and the detective's friend or confidant—often the narrator—whose slowness in interpreting clues emphasizes by contrast the detective's brilliance. Edgar Allan Poe's "Murders in the Rue Morgue" is commonly regarded as the earliest example of this type of story. Other practitioners are Arthur Conan Doyle, Dashiell Hammett, and Agatha Christie.

Dialogue: Dialogue is conversation between people in a literary work. In its most restricted sense, it refers specifically to the speech of characters in a drama. As a specific literary genre, a "dialogue" is a composition in which characters debate an issue or idea.

Didactic: A term used to describe works of literature that aim to teach a moral, religious, political, or practical lesson. Although didactic elements are often found in artistically pleasing works, the term "didactic" usually refers to literature in which the message is more important than the form. The term may also be used to criticize a work that the critic finds "overly didactic," that is, heavy-handed in its delivery of a lesson. An example of didactic literature is John Bunyan's *Pilgrim's Progress.*

Dramatic Irony: Occurs when the reader of a work of literature knows something that a character in the work itself does not know. The irony is in the contrast between the intended meaning of the statements or actions of a character and the additional information understood by the audience.

Dystopia: An imaginary place in a work of fiction where the characters lead dehumanized, fearful lives. George Orwell's *Nineteen Eighty-four,* and Margaret Atwood's *Handmaid's Tale* portray versions of dystopia.

E

Edwardian: Describes cultural conventions identified with the period of the reign of Edward VII of England (1901–1910). Writers of the Edwardian Age typically displayed a strong reaction against the propriety and conservatism of the Victorian Age. Their work often exhibits distrust of authority in religion, politics, and art and expresses strong doubts about the soundness of conventional values. Writers of this era include E. M. Forster, H. G. Wells, and Joseph Conrad.

Empathy: A sense of shared experience, including emotional and physical feelings, with someone or something other than oneself. Empathy is often used to describe the response of a reader to a literary character.

Epilogue: A concluding statement or section of a literary work. In dramas, particularly those of the seventeenth and eighteenth centuries, the epilogue is a closing speech, often in verse, delivered by an actor at the end of a play and spoken directly to the audience.

Epiphany: A sudden revelation of truth inspired by a seemingly trivial incident. The term was widely used by James Joyce in his critical writings, and the stories in Joyce's *Dubliners* are commonly called ''epiphanies.''

Epistolary Novel: A novel in the form of letters. The form was particularly popular in the eighteenth century. The form can also be applied to short stories, as in Edwidge Danticat's ''Children of the Sea.''

Epithet: A word or phrase, often disparaging or abusive, that expresses a character trait of someone or something. ''The Napoleon of crime'' is an

epithet applied to Professor Moriarty, arch-rival of Sherlock Holmes in Arthur Conan Doyle's series of detective stories.

Existentialism: A predominantly twentieth-century philosophy concerned with the nature and perception of human existence. There are two major strains of existentialist thought: atheistic and Christian. Followers of atheistic existentialism believe that the individual is alone in a godless universe and that the basic human condition is one of suffering and loneliness. Nevertheless, because there are no fixed values, individuals can create their own characters—indeed, they can shape themselves—through the exercise of free will. The atheistic strain culminates in and is popularly associated with the works of Jean-Paul Sartre. The Christian existentialists, on the other hand, believe that only in God may people find freedom from life's anguish. The two strains hold certain beliefs in common: that existence cannot be fully understood or described through empirical effort; that anguish is a universal element of life; that individuals must bear responsibility for their actions; and that there is no common standard of behavior or perception for religious and ethical matters. Existentialist thought figures prominently in the works of such authors as Franz Kafka, Fyodor Dostoyevsky, and Albert Camus.

Expatriatism: The practice of leaving one's country to live for an extended period in another country. Literary expatriates include Irish author James Joyce who moved to Italy and France, American writers James Baldwin, Ernest Hemingway, Gertrude Stein, and F. Scott Fitzgerald who lived and wrote in Paris, and Polish novelist Joseph Conrad in England.

Exposition: Writing intended to explain the nature of an idea, thing, or theme. Expository writing is often combined with description, narration, or argument.

Expressionism: An indistinct literary term, originally used to describe an early twentieth-century school of German painting. The term applies to almost any mode of unconventional, highly subjective writing that distorts reality in some way. Advocates of Expressionism include Federico Garcia Lorca, Eugene O'Neill, Franz Kafka, and James Joyce.

F

Fable: A prose or verse narrative intended to convey a moral. Animals or inanimate objects with human characteristics often serve as characters in fables. A famous fable is Aesop's "The Tortoise and the Hare."

Fantasy: A literary form related to mythology and folklore. Fantasy literature is typically set in non-existent realms and features supernatural beings. Notable examples of literature with elements of fantasy are Gabriel Garcia Marquez's story "The Handsomest Drowned Man in the World" and Ursula K. LeGuin's "The Ones Who Walk Away from Omelas."

Farce: A type of comedy characterized by broad humor, outlandish incidents, and often vulgar subject matter. Much of the comedy in film and television could more accurately be described as farce.

Fiction: Any story that is the product of imagination rather than a documentation of fact. Characters and events in such narratives may be based in real life but their ultimate form and configuration is a creation of the author.

Figurative Language: A technique in which an author uses figures of speech such as hyperbole, irony, metaphor, or simile for a particular effect. Figurative language is the opposite of literal language, in which every word is truthful, accurate, and free of exaggeration or embellishment.

Flashback: A device used in literature to present action that occurred before the beginning of the story. Flashbacks are often introduced as the dreams or recollections of one or more characters.

Foil: A character in a work of literature whose physical or psychological qualities contrast strongly with, and therefore highlight, the corresponding qualities of another character. In his Sherlock Holmes stories, Arthur Conan Doyle portrayed Dr. Watson as a man of normal habits and intelligence, making him a foil for the eccentric and unusually perceptive Sherlock Holmes.

Folklore: Traditions and myths preserved in a culture or group of people. Typically, these are passed on by word of mouth in various forms—such as legends, songs, and proverbs—or preserved in customs and ceremonies. Washington Irving, in "The Devil and Tom Walker" and many of his other stories, incorporates many elements of the folklore of New England and Germany.

Folktale: A story originating in oral tradition. Folktales fall into a variety of categories, including legends, ghost stories, fairy tales, fables, and anecdotes based on historical figures and events.

Foreshadowing: A device used in literature to create expectation or to set up an explanation of later developments. Edgar Allan Poe uses foreshadowing to create suspense in "The Fall of the House of Usher" when the narrator comments on the crumbling state of disrepair in which he finds the house.

G

Genre: A category of literary work. Genre may refer to both the content of a given work—tragedy, comedy, horror, science fiction—and to its form, such as poetry, novel, or drama.

Gilded Age: A period in American history during the 1870s and after characterized by political corruption and materialism. A number of important novels of social and political criticism were written during this time. Henry James and Kate Chopin are two writers who were prominent during the Gilded Age.

Gothicism: In literature, works characterized by a taste for medieval or morbid characters and situations. A gothic novel prominently features elements of horror, the supernatural, gloom, and violence: clanking chains, terror, ghosts, medieval castles, and unexplained phenomena. The term "gothic novel" is also applied to novels that lack elements of the traditional Gothic setting but that create a similar atmosphere of terror or dread. The term can also be applied to stories, plays, and poems. Mary Shelley's *Frankenstein* and Joyce Carol Oates's *Bellefleur* are both gothic novels.

Grotesque: In literature, a work that is characterized by exaggeration, deformity, freakishness, and disorder. The grotesque often includes an element of comic absurdity. Examples of the grotesque can be found in the works of Edgar Allan Poe, Flannery O'Connor, Joseph Heller, and Shirley Jackson.

H

Harlem Renaissance: The Harlem Renaissance of the 1920s is generally considered the first significant movement of black writers and artists in the United States. During this period, new and established black writers, many of whom lived in the region of New York City known as Harlem, published more fiction and poetry than ever before, the first influential black literary journals were established, and black authors and artists received their first widespread recognition and serious critical appraisal. Among the major writers associated with this period are Countee Cullen, Langston Hughes, Arna Bontemps, and Zora Neale Hurston.

Hero/Heroine: The principal sympathetic character in a literary work. Heroes and heroines typically exhibit admirable traits: idealism, courage, and integrity, for example. Famous heroes and heroines of literature include Charles Dickens's Oliver Twist, Margaret Mitchell's Scarlett O'Hara, and the anonymous narrator in Ralph Ellison's *Invisible Man*.

Hyperbole: Deliberate exaggeration used to achieve an effect. In William Shakespeare's *Macbeth,* Lady Macbeth hyperbolizes when she says, ''All the perfumes of Arabia could not sweeten this little hand.''

I

Image: A concrete representation of an object or sensory experience. Typically, such a representation helps evoke the feelings associated with the object or experience itself. Images are either ''literal'' or ''figurative.'' Literal images are especially concrete and involve little or no extension of the obvious meaning of the words used to express them. Figurative images do not follow the literal meaning of the words exactly. Images in literature are usually visual, but the term ''image'' can also refer to the representation of any sensory experience.

Imagery: The array of images in a literary work. Also used to convey the author's overall use of figurative language in a work.

In medias res: A Latin term meaning ''in the middle of things.'' It refers to the technique of beginning a story at its midpoint and then using various flashback devices to reveal previous action. This technique originated in such epics as Virgil's *Aeneid.*

Interior Monologue: A narrative technique in which characters' thoughts are revealed in a way that appears to be uncontrolled by the author. The interior monologue typically aims to reveal the inner self of a character. It portrays emotional experiences as they occur at both a conscious and unconscious level. One of the best-known interior monologues in English is the Molly Bloom section at the close of James Joyce's *Ulysses.* Katherine Anne Porter's ''The Jilting of Granny Weatherall'' is also told in the form of an interior monologue.

Irony: In literary criticism, the effect of language in which the intended meaning is the opposite of what is stated. The title of Jonathan Swift's ''A Modest Proposal'' is ironic because what Swift proposes in this essay is cannibalism—hardly ''modest.''

J

Jargon: Language that is used or understood only by a select group of people. Jargon may refer to terminology used in a certain profession, such as computer jargon, or it may refer to any nonsensical language that is not understood by most people. Anthony Burgess's *A Clockwork Orange* and James Thurber's ''The Secret Life of Walter Mitty'' both use jargon.

K

Knickerbocker Group: An indistinct group of New York writers of the first half of the nineteenth century. Members of the group were linked only by location and a common theme: New York life. Two famous members of the Knickerbocker Group were Washington Irving and William Cullen Bryant. The group's name derives from Irving's *Knickerbocker's History of New York.*

L

Literal Language: An author uses literal language when he or she writes without exaggerating or embellishing the subject matter and without any tools of figurative language. To say ''He ran very quickly down the street'' is to use literal language, whereas to say ''He ran like a hare down the street'' would be using figurative language.

Literature: Literature is broadly defined as any written or spoken material, but the term most often refers to creative works. Literature includes poetry, drama, fiction, and many kinds of nonfiction writing, as well as oral, dramatic, and broadcast compositions not necessarily preserved in a written format, such as films and television programs.

Lost Generation: A term first used by Gertrude Stein to describe the post-World War I generation of American writers: men and women haunted by a sense of betrayal and emptiness brought about by the destructiveness of the war. The term is commonly applied to Hart Crane, Ernest Hemingway, F. Scott Fitzgerald, and others.

M

Magic Realism: A form of literature that incorporates fantasy elements or supernatural occurrences into the narrative and accepts them as truth. Gabriel Garcia Marquez and Laura Esquivel are two writers known for their works of magic realism.

Metaphor: A figure of speech that expresses an idea through the image of another object. Metaphors suggest the essence of the first object by identifying it with certain qualities of the second object. An example is "But soft, what light through yonder window breaks?/ It is the east, and Juliet is the sun" in William Shakespeare's *Romeo and Juliet.* Here, Juliet, the first object, is identified with qualities of the second object, the sun.

Minimalism: A literary style characterized by spare, simple prose with few elaborations. In minimalism, the main theme of the work is often never discussed directly. Amy Hempel and Ernest Hemingway are two writers known for their works of minimalism.

Modernism: Modern literary practices. Also, the principles of a literary school that lasted from roughly the beginning of the twentieth century until the end of World War II. Modernism is defined by its rejection of the literary conventions of the nineteenth century and by its opposition to conventional morality, taste, traditions, and economic values. Many writers are associated with the concepts of modernism, including Albert Camus, D. H. Lawrence, Ernest Hemingway, William Faulkner, Eugene O'Neill, and James Joyce.

Monologue: A composition, written or oral, by a single individual. More specifically, a speech given by a single individual in a drama or other public entertainment. It has no set length, although it is usually several or more lines long. "I Stand Here Ironing" by Tillie Olsen is an example of a story written in the form of a monologue.

Mood: The prevailing emotions of a work or of the author in his or her creation of the work. The mood of a work is not always what might be expected based on its subject matter.

Motif: A theme, character type, image, metaphor, or other verbal element that recurs throughout a single work of literature or occurs in a number of different works over a period of time. For example, the color white in Herman Melville's *Moby Dick* is a "specific" *motif,* while the trials of star-crossed lovers is a "conventional" *motif* from the literature of all periods.

N

Narration: The telling of a series of events, real or invented. A narration may be either a simple narrative, in which the events are recounted chronologically, or a narrative with a plot, in which the account is given in a style reflecting the author's artistic concept of the story. Narration is sometimes used as a synonym for "storyline."

Narrative: A verse or prose accounting of an event or sequence of events, real or invented. The term is also used as an adjective in the sense "method of narration." For example, in literary criticism, the expression "narrative technique" usually refers to the way the author structures and presents his or her story. Different narrative forms include diaries, travelogues, novels, ballads, epics, short stories, and other fictional forms.

Narrator: The teller of a story. The narrator may be the author or a character in the story through whom the author speaks. Huckleberry Finn is the narrator of Mark Twain's *The Adventures of Huckleberry Finn.*

Novella: An Italian term meaning "story." This term has been especially used to describe fourteenth-century Italian tales, but it also refers to modern short novels. Modern novellas include Leo Tolstoy's *The Death of Ivan Ilich,* Fyodor Dostoyevsky's *Notes from the Underground,* and Joseph Conrad's *Heart of Darkness.*

O

Oedipus Complex: A son's romantic obsession with his mother. The phrase is derived from the story of the ancient Theban hero Oedipus, who unknowingly killed his father and married his mother, and was popularized by Sigmund Freud's theory of psychoanalysis. Literary occurrences of the Oedipus complex include Sophocles' *Oedipus Rex* and D. H. Lawrence's "The Rocking-Horse Winner."

Onomatopoeia: The use of words whose sounds express or suggest their meaning. In its simplest sense, onomatopoeia may be represented by words that mimic the sounds they denote such as "hiss" or "meow." At a more subtle level, the pattern and rhythm of sounds and rhymes of a line or poem may be onomatopoeic.

Oral Tradition: A process by which songs, ballads, folklore, and other material are transmitted by word of mouth. The tradition of oral transmission predates the written record systems of literate society.

Oral transmission preserves material sometimes over generations, although often with variations. Memory plays a large part in the recitation and preservation of orally transmitted material. Native American myths and legends, and African folktales told by plantation slaves are examples of orally transmitted literature.

P

Parable: A story intended to teach a moral lesson or answer an ethical question. Examples of parables are the stories told by Jesus Christ in the New Testament, notably "The Prodigal Son," but parables also are used in Sufism, rabbinic literature, Hasidism, and Zen Buddhism. Isaac Bashevis Singer's story "Gimpel the Fool" exhibits characteristics of a parable.

Paradox: A statement that appears illogical or contradictory at first, but may actually point to an underlying truth. A literary example of a paradox is George Orwell's statement "All animals are equal, but some animals are more equal than others" in *Animal Farm*.

Parody: In literature, this term refers to an imitation of a serious literary work or the signature style of a particular author in a ridiculous manner. A typical parody adopts the style of the original and applies it to an inappropriate subject for humorous effect. Parody is a form of satire and could be considered the literary equivalent of a caricature or cartoon. Henry Fielding's *Shamela* is a parody of Samuel Richardson's *Pamela*.

Persona: A Latin term meaning "mask." Personae are the characters in a fictional work of literature. The persona generally functions as a mask through which the author tells a story in a voice other than his or her own. A persona is usually either a character in a story who acts as a narrator or an "implied author," a voice created by the author to act as the narrator for himself or herself. The persona in Charlotte Perkins Gilman's story "The Yellow Wallpaper" is the unnamed young mother experiencing a mental breakdown.

Personification: A figure of speech that gives human qualities to abstract ideas, animals, and inanimate objects. To say that "the sun is smiling" is to personify the sun.

Plot: The pattern of events in a narrative or drama. In its simplest sense, the plot guides the author in composing the work and helps the reader follow the work. Typically, plots exhibit causality and unity and have a beginning, a middle, and an end. Sometimes, however, a plot may consist of a series of disconnected events, in which case it is known as an "episodic plot."

Poetic Justice: An outcome in a literary work, not necessarily a poem, in which the good are rewarded and the evil are punished, especially in ways that particularly fit their virtues or crimes. For example, a murderer may himself be murdered, or a thief will find himself penniless.

Poetic License: Distortions of fact and literary convention made by a writer—not always a poet—for the sake of the effect gained. Poetic license is closely related to the concept of "artistic freedom." An author exercises poetic license by saying that a pile of money "reaches as high as a mountain" when the pile is actually only a foot or two high.

Point of View: The narrative perspective from which a literary work is presented to the reader. There are four traditional points of view. The "third person omniscient" gives the reader a "godlike" perspective, unrestricted by time or place, from which to see actions and look into the minds of characters. This allows the author to comment openly on characters and events in the work. The "third person" point of view presents the events of the story from outside of any single character's perception, much like the omniscient point of view, but the reader must understand the action as it takes place and without any special insight into characters' minds or motivations. The "first person" or "personal" point of view relates events as they are perceived by a single character. The main character "tells" the story and may offer opinions about the action and characters which differ from those of the author. Much less common than omniscient, third person, and first person is the "second person" point of view, wherein the author tells the story as if it is happening to the reader. James Thurber employs the omniscient point of view in his short story "The Secret Life of Walter Mitty." Ernest Hemingway's "A Clean, Well-Lighted Place" is a short story told from the third person point of view. Mark Twain's novel *Huckleberry Finn* is presented from the first person viewpoint. Jay McInerney's *Bright Lights, Big City* is an example of a novel which uses the second person point of view.

Pornography: Writing intended to provoke feelings of lust in the reader. Such works are often condemned by critics and teachers, but those which can be shown to have literary value are viewed less harshly. Literary works that have been described as pornographic include D. H. Lawrence's *Lady Chatterley's Lover* and James Joyce's *Ulysses.*

Post-Aesthetic Movement: An artistic response made by African Americans to the black aesthetic movement of the 1960s and early 1970s. Writers since that time have adopted a somewhat different tone in their work, with less emphasis placed on the disparity between black and white in the United States. In the words of post-aesthetic authors such as Toni Morrison, John Edgar Wideman, and Kristin Hunter, African Americans are portrayed as looking inward for answers to their own questions, rather than always looking to the outside world. Two well-known examples of works produced as part of the post-aesthetic movement are the Pulitzer Prize-winning novels *The Color Purple* by Alice Walker and *Beloved* by Toni Morrison.

Postmodernism: Writing from the 1960s forward characterized by experimentation and application of modernist elements, which include existentialism and alienation. Postmodernists have gone a step further in the rejection of tradition begun with the modernists by also rejecting traditional forms, preferring the anti-novel over the novel and the anti-hero over the hero. Postmodern writers include Thomas Pynchon, Margaret Drabble, and Gabriel Garcia Marquez.

Prologue: An introductory section of a literary work. It often contains information establishing the situation of the characters or presents information about the setting, time period, or action. In drama, the prologue is spoken by a chorus or by one of the principal characters.

Prose: A literary medium that attempts to mirror the language of everyday speech. It is distinguished from poetry by its use of unmetered, unrhymed language consisting of logically related sentences. Prose is usually grouped into paragraphs that form a cohesive whole such as an essay or a novel. The term is sometimes used to mean an author's general writing.

Protagonist: The central character of a story who serves as a focus for its themes and incidents and as the principal rationale for its development. The protagonist is sometimes referred to in discussions of modern literature as the hero or anti-hero. Well-known protagonists are Hamlet in William Shakespeare's *Hamlet* and Jay Gatsby in F. Scott Fitzgerald's *The Great Gatsby.*

R

Realism: A nineteenth-century European literary movement that sought to portray familiar characters, situations, and settings in a realistic manner. This was done primarily by using an objective narrative point of view and through the buildup of accurate detail. The standard for success of any realistic work depends on how faithfully it transfers common experience into fictional forms. The realistic method may be altered or extended, as in stream of consciousness writing, to record highly subjective experience. Contemporary authors who often write in a realistic way include Nadine Gordimer and Grace Paley.

Resolution: The portion of a story following the climax, in which the conflict is resolved. The resolution of Jane Austen's *Northanger Abbey* is neatly summed up in the following sentence: "Henry and Catherine were married, the bells rang and everybody smiled."

Rising Action: The part of a drama where the plot becomes increasingly complicated. Rising action leads up to the climax, or turning point, of a drama. The final "chase scene" of an action film is generally the rising action which culminates in the film's climax.

Roman a clef: A French phrase meaning "novel with a key." It refers to a narrative in which real persons are portrayed under fictitious names. Jack Kerouac, for example, portrayed various friends under fictitious names in the novel *On the Road.* D. H. Lawrence based "The Rocking-Horse Winner" on a family he knew.

Romanticism: This term has two widely accepted meanings. In historical criticism, it refers to a European intellectual and artistic movement of the late eighteenth and early nineteenth centuries that sought greater freedom of personal expression than that allowed by the strict rules of literary form and logic of the eighteenth-century neoclassicists. The Romantics preferred emotional and imaginative expression to rational analysis. They considered the individual to be at the center of all experience and so placed him or her at the center of their art. The Romantics believed that the creative imagination reveals nobler truths—unique feelings and attitudes—than those that could be discovered by logic or by scientific examination. "Romanticism" is also used as a general term to refer to a type of sensibility found in all periods of literary history and usually considered to be in opposition to the principles of classicism. In this sense, Romanticism signifies any work or philosophy in which the exotic or dreamlike figure strongly, or that is devoted to individualistic expression, self-analysis, or a pursuit of a higher realm of knowledge than can be discovered by human reason. Prominent Romantics include Jean-Jacques Rousseau, William Wordsworth, John Keats, Lord Byron, and Johann Wolfgang von Goethe.

S

Satire: A work that uses ridicule, humor, and wit to criticize and provoke change in human nature and institutions. Voltaire's novella *Candide* and Jonathan Swift's essay "A Modest Proposal" are both satires. Flannery O'Connor's portrayal of the family in "A Good Man Is Hard to Find" is a satire of a modern, Southern, American family.

Science Fiction: A type of narrative based upon real or imagined scientific theories and technology. Science fiction is often peopled with alien creatures and set on other planets or in different dimensions. Popular writers of science fiction are Isaac Asimov, Karel Capek, Ray Bradbury, and Ursula K. Le Guin.

Setting: The time, place, and culture in which the action of a narrative takes place. The elements of setting may include geographic location, characters's physical and mental environments, prevailing cultural attitudes, or the historical time in which the action takes place.

Short Story: A fictional prose narrative shorter and more focused than a novella. The short story usually deals with a single episode and often a single character. The "tone," the author's attitude toward his or her subject and audience, is uniform throughout. The short story frequently also lacks *denouement*, ending instead at its climax.

Signifying Monkey: A popular trickster figure in black folklore, with hundreds of tales about this character documented since the 19th century. Henry Louis Gates Jr. examines the history of the signifying monkey in *The Signifying Monkey: Towards a Theory of Afro-American Literary Criticism,* published in 1988.

Simile: A comparison, usually using "like" or "as," of two essentially dissimilar things, as in "coffee as cold as ice" or "He sounded like a broken record." The title of Ernest Hemingway's "Hills Like White Elephants" contains a simile.

Social Realism: The Socialist Realism school of literary theory was proposed by Maxim Gorky and established as a dogma by the first Soviet Congress of Writers. It demanded adherence to a communist worldview in works of literature. Its doctrines required an objective viewpoint comprehensible to the working classes and themes of social struggle featuring strong proletarian heroes. Gabriel Garcia Marquez's stories exhibit some characteristics of Socialist Realism.

Stereotype: A stereotype was originally the name for a duplication made during the printing process; this led to its modern definition as a person or thing that is (or is assumed to be) the same as all others of its type. Common stereotypical characters include the absent-minded professor, the nagging wife, the troublemaking teenager, and the kind-hearted grandmother.

Stream of Consciousness: A narrative technique for rendering the inward experience of a character. This technique is designed to give the impression of an ever-changing series of thoughts, emotions, images, and memories in the spontaneous and seemingly illogical order that they occur in life. The textbook example of stream of consciousness is the last section of James Joyce's *Ulysses.*

Structure: The form taken by a piece of literature. The structure may be made obvious for ease of understanding, as in nonfiction works, or may obscured for artistic purposes, as in some poetry or seemingly "unstructured" prose.

Style: A writer's distinctive manner of arranging words to suit his or her ideas and purpose in writing. The unique imprint of the author's personality upon his or her writing, style is the product of an author's way of arranging ideas and his or her use of diction, different sentence structures, rhythm, figures of speech, rhetorical principles, and other elements of composition.

Suspense: A literary device in which the author maintains the audience's attention through the buildup of events, the outcome of which will soon be revealed. Suspense in William Shakespeare's *Hamlet* is sustained throughout by the question of whether or not the Prince will achieve what he has been instructed to do and of what he intends to do.

Symbol: Something that suggests or stands for something else without losing its original identity. In literature, symbols combine their literal meaning with the suggestion of an abstract concept. Literary symbols are of two types: those that carry complex associations of meaning no matter what their contexts, and those that derive their suggestive meaning from their functions in specific literary works. Examples of symbols are sunshine suggesting happiness, rain suggesting sorrow, and storm clouds suggesting despair.

T

Tale: A story told by a narrator with a simple plot and little character development. Tales are usually relatively short and often carry a simple message. Examples of tales can be found in the works of Saki, Anton Chekhov, Guy de Maupassant, and O. Henry.

Tall Tale: A humorous tale told in a straightforward, credible tone but relating absolutely impossible events or feats of the characters. Such tales were commonly told of frontier adventures during the settlement of the west in the United States. Literary use of tall tales can be found in Washington Irving's *History of New York,* Mark Twain's *Life on the Mississippi,* and in the German R. F. Raspe's *Baron Munchausen's Narratives of His Marvellous Travels and Campaigns in Russia.*

Theme: The main point of a work of literature. The term is used interchangeably with thesis. Many works have multiple themes. One of the themes of Nathaniel Hawthorne's "Young Goodman Brown" is loss of faith.

Tone: The author's attitude toward his or her audience may be deduced from the tone of the work. A formal tone may create distance or convey politeness, while an informal tone may encourage a friendly, intimate, or intrusive feeling in the reader. The author's attitude toward his or her subject matter may also be deduced from the tone of the words he or she uses in discussing it. The tone of John F. Kennedy's speech which included the appeal to "ask not what your country can do for you" was intended to instill feelings of camaraderie and national pride in listeners.

Tragedy: A drama in prose or poetry about a noble, courageous hero of excellent character who, be-

cause of some tragic character flaw, brings ruin upon him- or herself. Tragedy treats its subjects in a dignified and serious manner, using poetic language to help evoke pity and fear and bring about catharsis, a purging of these emotions. The tragic form was practiced extensively by the ancient Greeks. The classical form of tragedy was revived in the sixteenth century; it flourished especially on the Elizabethan stage. In modern times, dramatists have attempted to adapt the form to the needs of modern society by drawing their heroes from the ranks of ordinary men and women and defining the nobility of these heroes in terms of spirit rather than exalted social standing. Some contemporary works that are thought of as tragedies include *The Great Gatsby* by F. Scott Fitzgerald, and *The Sound and the Fury* by William Faulkner.

Tragic Flaw: In a tragedy, the quality within the hero or heroine which leads to his or her downfall. Examples of the tragic flaw include Othello's jealousy and Hamlet's indecisiveness, although most great tragedies defy such simple interpretation.

U

Utopia: A fictional perfect place, such as "paradise" or "heaven." An early literary utopia was described in Plato's *Republic,* and in modern literature, Ursula K. Le Guin depicts a utopia in "The Ones Who Walk Away from Omelas."

V

Victorian: Refers broadly to the reign of Queen Victoria of England (1837–1901) and to anything with qualities typical of that era. For example, the qualities of smug narrow-mindedness, bourgeois materialism, faith in social progress, and priggish morality are often considered Victorian. In literature, the Victorian Period was the great age of the English novel, and the latter part of the era saw the rise of movements such as decadence and symbolism.

Cumulative Author/Title Index

Henry, O.
　The Gift of the Magi: V2
　Mammon and the Archer: V18
Hills Like White Elephants
　(Hemingway): V6
The Hitchhiking Game
　(Kundera): V10
Høeg, Peter
　Journey into a Dark Heart: V18
A Horse and Two Goats
　(Narayan): V5
Houston, Pam
　The Best Girlfriend You
　　Never Had: V17
How I Contemplated the World
　from the Detroit House of
　Correction and Began My Life
　Over Again (Oates): V8
How to Tell a True War Story
　(O'Brien): V15
Hughes, Langston
　The Blues I'm Playing: V7
　Slave on the Block: V4
A Hunger Artist (Kafka): V7
Hurston, Zora Neale
　Conscience of the Court: V21
　The Eatonville Anthology: V1
　The Gilded Six-Bits: V11
　Spunk: V6
　Sweat: V19

I

I Have No Mouth, and I Must
　Scream (Ellison): V15
I Stand Here Ironing (Olsen): V1
"If I Forget Thee, O Earth . . ."
　(Clarke): V18
If You Sing like That for Me
　(Sharma): V21
Imagined Scenes (Beattie): V20
Immigration Blues (Santos): V19
In Another Country
　(Hemingway): V8
In the Cemetery Where Al Jolson Is
　Buried (Hempel): V2
In the Garden of the North American
　Martyrs (Wolff): V4
In the Kindergarten (Jin): V17
In the Penal Colony (Kafka): V3
In the Shadow of War (Okri): V20
In the Zoo (Stafford): V21
The Indian Uprising
　(Barthelme): V17
The Interlopers (Saki): V15
The Invalid's Story (Twain): V16
The Invisible Man or Battle Royal
　(Ellison): V11
Irving, Washington
　The Devil and Tom Walker: V1
　The Legend of Sleepy Hollow: V8
　Rip Van Winkle: V16

J

Jackson, Shirley
　The Lottery: V1
Jacobs, W. W.
　The Monkey's Paw: V2
James, Henry
　The Beast in the Jungle: V6
　The Jolly Corner: V9
Janus (Beattie): V9
The Japanese Quince
　(Galsworthy): V3
Jeeves Takes Charge
　(Wodehouse): V10
Jeffty Is Five (Ellison): V13
Jewett, Sarah Orne
　A White Heron: V4
The Jilting of Granny Weatherall
　(Porter): V1
Jin, Ha
　In the Kindergarten: V17
Johnson, Charles
　Menagerie, a Child's Fable: V16
The Jolly Corner (James): V9
Journey into a Dark Heart
　(Høeg): V18
Joyce, James
　Araby: V1
　The Dead: V6
　Eveline: V19
A Jury of Her Peers (Glaspell): V3

K

Kafka, Franz
　A Hunger Artist: V7
　In the Penal Colony: V3
　The Metamorphosis: V12
Kew Gardens (Woolf): V12
The Killers (Hemingway): V17
Kincaid, Jamaica
　Girl: V7
　What I Have Been Doing
　　Lately: V5
King of the Bingo Game
　(Ellison): V1
Kingston, Maxine Hong
　On Discovery: V3
Kipling, Rudyard
　Mrs. Bathurst: V8
　Rikki-Tikki-Tavi: V21
Kitchen (Yoshimoto): V16
Kohler, Sheila
　Africans: V18
The Kugelmass Episode (Allen): V21
Kundera, Milan
　The Hitchhiking Game: V10

L

La Grande Bretèche (de
　Balzac): V10

The Lady with the Pet Dog
　(Chekhov): V5
The Lady, or the Tiger?
　(Stockton): V3
Lagerlöf, Selma
　The Legend of the Christmas
　　Rose: V18
Lahiri, Jhumpa
　A Temporary Matter: V19
Lamb to the Slaughter (Dahl): V4
The Last Lovely City (Adams): V14
Lawrence, D. H.
　Odour of Chrysanthemums: V6
　The Rocking-Horse Winner: V2
Le Guin, Ursula K.
　The Ones Who Walk Away from
　　Omelas: V2
Leaving the Yellow House
　(Bellow): V12
The Legend of Sleepy Hollow
　(Irving): V8
The Legend of the Christmas Rose
　(Lagerlöf): V18
Lessing, Doris
　Debbie and Julie: V12
　Through the Tunnel: V1
　To Room Nineteen: V20
The Lesson (Bambara): V12
The Life You Save May Be Your Own
　(O'Connor): V7
Life (Head): V13
The Lifted Veil (Eliot): V8
Little Miracles, Kept Promises
　(Cisneros): V13
London, Jack
　To Build a Fire: V7
Long Distance (Smiley): V19
The Long-Distance Runner
　(Paley): V20
Lost in the Funhouse (Barth): V6
The Lottery (Jackson): V1
Lullaby (Silko): V10

M

The Magic Barrel (Malamud): V8
Mahfouz, Naguib
　Half a Day: V9
Malamud, Bernard
　Black Is My Favorite Color: V16
　The First Seven Years: V13
　The Magic Barrel: V8
Mammon and the Archer
　(Henry): V18
The Man That Corrupted Hadleyburg
　(Twain): V7
The Man to Send Rain Clouds
　(Silko): V8
The Man Who Lived Underground
　(Wright): V3
The Man Who Was Almost a Man
　(Wright): V9

Nationality/Ethnicity Index

Subject/Theme Index

In the Zoo: 179–181
Mood
  Boule de Suif: 50–51
Morals and Morality
  Boule de Suif: 22, 27–29, 31–40
  Conscience of the Court: 56, 59,
    62–63, 65, 69–71
  *No. 44, The Mysterious Stran-
    ger:* 221–222
  Rikki-Tikki-Tavi: 256,
    260–263, 266–268
Music
  Crazy Sunday: 73–74, 78
  Rikki-Tikki-Tavi: 257–259, 262
Mystery and Intrigue
  No. 44, The Mysterious Stranger:
    220–222, 225
Myths and Legends
  The Arabian Nights: 16–17
  Eyes of a Blue Dog:
    100, 105–107
  Rikki-Tikki-Tavi: 267–268

N

Narration
  The Arabian Nights: 9
  Boule de Suif: 34–37, 41–42
  Conscience of the Court: 57, 59
  Crazy Sunday: 77–78, 81–82, 86,
    88–89, 97–98
  Eyes of a Blue Dog: 100–112
  Gorilla, My Love: 116–117, 122,
    124, 128–135
  Greyhound People: 138–144,
    147–152, 154
  If You Sing like That for Me:
    157–158, 162, 165
  In the Zoo: 174–175, 177, 179,
    182–183, 185
  No. 44, The Mysterious Stranger:
    218, 220–221, 223–225
  Rikki-Tikki-Tavi: 266–267
  *''Repent, Harlequin!'' Said the
    Ticktockman:* 239–241
Nationalism and Patriotism
  Think of England: 271–272, 275,
    278, 280–285
Nationalism
  Think of England: 275
Naturalism
  Boule de Suif: 27
Naturalism
  Boule de Suif: 22, 27–28
Nature
  Boule de Suif: 48–51
  *If You Sing like That for
    Me:* 161–162
  In the Zoo: 173, 177, 179, 186
  *No. 44, The Mysterious Stran-
    ger:* 220–225
  Rikki-Tikki-Tavi: 258,
    263, 265, 268

Think of England: 278, 280
*''Repent, Harlequin!'' Said the
  Ticktockman:* 249
New York Jewish Culture
  The Kugelmass Episode: 198
1970s
  Gorilla, My Love: 116,
    122, 124–125
1930s
  Crazy Sunday: 78–79
North America
  Greyhound People: 145–146
  In the Zoo: 179–181
  *The Kugelmass
    Episode:* 199–200
  *No. 44, The Mysterious Stran-
    ger:* 215–216
  *''Repent, Harlequin!'' Said the
    Ticktockman:* 235–237

P

Painting
  Boule de Suif: 48–50
Parody
  The Kugelmass Episode:
    192, 198, 200
Perception
  Eyes of a Blue Dog:
    100, 105–107
Permanence
  Greyhound People: 145–146
  *The Kugelmass
    Episode:* 203–204
  Rikki-Tikki-Tavi: 259–260, 264
Persecution
  In the Zoo: 186–187, 189
Personification
  *No. 44, The Mysterious Stran-
    ger:* 221, 224
Philosophical Ideas
  Boule de Suif: 31–32, 34
  *If You Sing like That
    for Me:* 168
  No. 44, The Mysterious Stranger:
    221–224, 226–227
  Think of England: 292
  *''Repent, Harlequin!'' Said the
    Ticktockman:* 235
Plants
  In the Zoo: 186–188
Pleasure
  Boule de Suif: 38–40
Plot
  Boule de Suif: 38–39, 41
  Crazy Sunday: 93–94, 96–98
Poetry
  Rikki-Tikki-Tavi: 257, 264–265
Point of View
  Gorilla, My Love: 120, 122, 125
  Greyhound People: 143, 147
  Rikki-Tikki-Tavi: 267–268
  Think of England: 287–288

Politicians
  If You Sing like That for Me:
    156, 158, 162–163
Politics
  The Arabian Nights: 11
  Boule de Suif: 24, 28–30, 37–43
  Eyes of a Blue Dog: 106–107
  Gorilla, My Love: 116,
    118, 123–124
  Greyhound People:
    139, 144–145
  *If You Sing like That
    for Me:* 163
  In the Zoo: 187–189
  Rikki-Tikki-Tavi: 263–265
  Think of England: 272, 275,
    278–279, 284
  *''Repent, Harlequin!'' Said the
    Ticktockman:* 235–237
Postmodernism
  Eyes of a Blue Dog: 106
Pragmatism
  *If You Sing like That
    for Me:* 168
Pride
  Boule de Suif: 39–41, 44–47
  Think of England: 284–285
Progress and Work
  Rikki-Tikki-Tavi: 262
Promiscuity and Moral Confusion
  Boule de Suif: 29
Prostitution
  Boule de Suif: 24,
    27–29, 31, 33–46
Psychology and the Human Mind
  Crazy Sunday: 86, 91
  Eyes of a Blue Dog: 100,
    104–107, 109–111
  In the Zoo: 186, 188–189
  The Kugelmass Episode:
    193–194, 196
Punishment
  *''Repent, Harlequin!'' Said the
    Ticktockman:* 241, 243
Pursuit and Possession
  The Kugelmass Episode: 197

R

Race
  The Arabian Nights: 1, 10–11
  *Conscience of the
    Court:* 52, 57–71
  Gorilla, My Love: 116, 122–124
  In the Zoo: 179–181
  Rikki-Tikki-Tavi: 261–264
Recreation
  The Kugelmass Episode: 192,
    194, 198–199
Regionalism
  *No. 44, The Mysterious
    Stranger:* 215